The Guardian
of the Amulets

The Guardian of the Amulets

Jessica S. Andersen

Five Star • Waterville, Maine

1 3978440

First Edition
First Printing: February 2003

Set in 11 pt. Plantin by Christina S. Huff.

Printed in the United States on permanent paper.

Library of Congress Cataloging-in-Publication Data

Andersen, Jessica S., 1973–
    The guardian of the amulets / Jessica S. Andersen.
        p.   cm.—(Five Star first edition expressions series)
        ISBN 0-7862-4704-5 (hc : alk. paper)
        1. New Hampshire—Fiction.   I. Title.   II. Series.
    PS3601.N43 G8 2003
        813'.6—dc21   2002035942

Dedication

To my Mom, for always packing the cooler.

Prologue

The Atlantic Ocean clawed its way to the boardwalk, and the wind beat a fierce tattoo upon the door, but within the two-room shop the woman hunched over the steaming cauldron paid no heed to the rising storm.

She sniffed the bubbling mixture, tucked curly brown hair behind one ear, and frowned. It wasn't quite right yet.

The wax bubbled sluggishly in the double boiler, and she glanced at the mold near her elbow. What was missing? The heavy jewels were tied to each wick so they'd be hidden within the wax. The scrap of parchment they'd been wrapped in was hidden in the cave. So what had she forgotten?

She snapped her fingers, and the saucer-pawed lion cub curled by the radiator raised his reddish head and looked at her with a glint of amusement in his golden eyes.

"I forgot to scent them."

Thor yawned, exposing two rows of jagged teeth and a long pink tongue, and she imagined his voice in her head saying, *So do it now and then come rub my tummy.*

The door rattled wildly as the wind slammed inland from the Atlantic. She resisted looking over her shoulder, finally beginning to believe that it was just a hurricane outside the candle shop and not a pair of blocky men with scarred faces and wicked knives. She thought that maybe, just maybe, she'd lost them this time.

Maybe this time she'd be safe.

She ran absent fingers over her swollen belly and pressed both hands to her aching back. She *had* to be safe, because she wasn't alone anymore. There were two of them now, three if she counted Thor.

I certainly hope you would count me! What kind of gratitude is that after I saved your life in Miami? Humph.

She ignored the imagined words and split the molding paraffin into three parts. She colored each to suit the gemstone it would contain: a deep ruby red, a vivid sapphire blue, and a verdant emerald green. Her fingers danced over the row of oils, and it was as if an unseen force directed her hand as she mixed. She thought she caught a blood-red glimmer out of the corner of her eye; but when she looked, the gems in their heavily worked gold settings were lying where she had left them, quiescent and dim in the candle-light.

Maybe she'd imagined their power.

You're not imagining anything, but they're not going to hurt you, silly. However, if you're so set on hiding them, get on with it and let's go home—I'm hungry.

She ignored the voice, irritated that she was unable to block out the words and not a little worried that she might be losing her mind. She'd only heard voices like this on one other occasion—

On Santa Caribe Island.

But the Santa Caribbean lions never left that one little island, where they coexisted with the native warriors and lurked about the hotel . . .

The hotel. Christine shuddered and gave the heavy ruby necklace a wary glance before mixing three scented oils into the wax. She wouldn't think about the island now. Wouldn't think about the hotel. She'd think about casting candles.

With its blend of geranium, lime, and jasmine, the

crimson candle would smell of action, of courage, and of sexual power.

"Three qualities that I am completely lacking at the moment," she muttered.

Thor rumbled from his place near the fire, and she forced herself to continue pouring the candles. There was no sense in dwelling on the past or on her foolish trust in a man she should've known could never walk the straight and narrow. She could only go on from here. She needed to hide the amulets and disappear—for her own safety and that of the child she carried.

She cast the blue candle, knowing that its combination of basil, peppermint, and myrrh would carry the scents of wisdom and decisions well made.

"We can only hope," she said, and young Thor yawned a sleepy agreement. If she couldn't claim wisdom, she could at least hope that her decisions were the right ones. They certainly hadn't been the easy ones.

She mixed oils for the final candle, wearing a smile that had once been her usual expression but now felt strange and stiff on her face. The green candle would smell of tea-tree, vetiver, and patchouli—the scents of healing and fertility.

"We've got that covered, don't we?" Again she stroked the hard globe of her stomach and this time was rewarded by a vigorous kick. Her child, conceived on the first and last night of her marriage, would grow up in this little Cape Cod town and never know its father.

Trying not to remember the feel of her husband's gentle, scarred hands on her flesh, forcing herself not to dwell on his cruel deception, she poured scented wax into the three prewarmed molds and tilted them to prevent bubbles from forming on the surface.

She thought the amulets glowed slightly before becoming

imprisoned within pillars of pure color, but she told herself that it was a trick of the light, an illusion spawned by the flicker of the beeswax candles she'd lit when the lights went out at dusk.

She refused to believe it was a glimmer of power beyond the scope of Cape Electric Co.

"I hate you," she whispered once the gems were out of sight. "You destroyed my life." She felt a little better having said it, but even without the calm voice in her head telling her so, she knew it was not the amulets that were at fault—it was the men who would kill to possess them.

After placing the molds in a tepid water bath, she let herself out the rattling back door and closed it firmly, lest rainwater blow onto the tender candles.

Being a cat—albeit a very large one—Thor elected to stay inside the shop, which comforted her. She had learned over the weeks they'd been together that he wouldn't allow her out of his sight if there was danger.

She didn't bother with her raincoat because she welcomed the stinging pellets that cut through her loose shirt and drawstring pants and soaked her to the skin. Tilting her head to the sky, she wallowed in the feel of the rain on her face and the brush of wet cotton against her breasts and belly.

Never had she felt so alone.

She walked far from town, down to the end of the last jetty. She could see no light but that of the storm itself, an unearthly radiance of churned surf and pregnant clouds. Electricity crackled as she stood with her toes on the last stone, at the end of the Earth. She lifted her face and felt the fury of the hurricane pour through her, felt the beat of her baby's heart, felt the purr of her lion companion from his place next to the hearth, felt the dormant power of the hidden amulets, and above all felt the jagged, gaping hole in her chest where her heart had once been.

There must be something there still, some lump of flesh that resolutely pumped blood through her body even when she wished it wouldn't, but that was all. She had left the rest of her heart on that foul, evil island.

Left it with her husband.

She fumbled with chilled fingers to strip the gold band from her left hand and held the small, hard circle to numb lips. She kissed the inscription she had once believed, then stood to fling her wedding ring into the uncaring surf.

But she couldn't do it.

She could no more sever that last link than she could stop the storm with a thought. Some traitorous part of her, some remnant of that lost heart still refused to believe in his betrayal. Sinking to the slimy, barnacle-roughened boulder, she huddled with her face pressed hard against her cold knees and wept hot, bitter tears—for herself, for her baby, for the wild boy next door who had grown into a man.

She never saw the seventh wave as it raced toward shore with storm-wrought fury and reached to pluck her from the land and into the sea. She heard Thor's roar of anguish in her head. The cold water closed over her, buffeted her.

She sank down.

Left the storm behind.

And fell into blackness.

Chapter One

Eight years later

Michael Finch thought it ironic that the search for his wife ended in Farewell. Ironic and oddly appropriate.

He stood on a barnacle-covered rock at the end of the last jetty, far beyond the outskirts of the little Cape Cod town, and stared again at the paper that had brought him to the place with the oddly prophetic name. Although the clipping was almost a decade old, he'd found it just a few days before.

He'd already memorized the text.

Unidentified Woman Drowns on Cape Cod, cried the headline before the article went on to describe her. Dark hair. Brown eyes. No identification save for a gold wedding band inscribed with the words *I promise.*

His heart twisted as he remembered how love had shone in Chrissy's innocent eyes when she read those words on their wedding day.

As he remembered how badly he had failed in his promise.

Twenty-four hours after the minister pronounced them man and wife, she had been gone. Vanished.

Michael barely felt the breeze flirt through his short brown hair and paid little heed when the seventh wave crested over the rock beneath his feet. A small part of him was happy to know where she was after all these years, even if it was Heaven—for his Chrissy would have gone to no other place.

It was meager consolation that she couldn't have returned to him if she'd wanted to. She had died in Farewell, drowned anonymously in the storm surf of Hurricane Cleo. In a way, her death was easier to bear than learning she'd walked out of their honeymoon suite without a word in order to set up cozy housekeeping somewhere else. With someone else.

But that still left six months when she'd tacked across the country using false names and cheap disguises, with the investigators Michael's best friend had paid for just a short step behind. She'd been running. Hiding.

From her husband?

Michael fought the urge to crumple the newspaper into a rude ball and fire it into the Atlantic, as if destroying the printed words would make the events unhappen. Instead he folded the page along well-worn creases and tucked it inside his wallet next to a faded photograph of a dark-haired bride.

"So, Christine. This is where it ends?" It seemed anti-climactic.

He looked back across the rippling waters of Pirate's Cove and tried to say good-bye to his wife. Though his friends—Jonas in particular—had been at him for years to give up the search, to bury Chrissy and move on with his life, Michael had yet to do so. He hadn't been able to let go while he still had hope that she was alive. Now that hope was gone.

And with it his heart.

He closed his eyes and tipped his face to the thin sunlight. A gull cried out, lonely in the empty sky.

There was no more for him to do; no more prayers to whisper into the echoing darkness, no more hope that she'd show up one day and fling herself into his arms with tearful apologies, explaining that she'd loved him always but had been held captive on Santa Caribe Island by the native warriors and their strange feline familiars.

It was over, but still Michael couldn't grieve for his wife, or even for himself. The driving force that had propelled him for so long was too suddenly quelled. The place in his heart reserved for her was still too full of life.

"How could I not know that you died?" His voice, harsh with eight years' worth of unshed tears, fell softly upon the purple periwinkles and the striped bass whose shadows undulated in the lee of the jetty. "I should've felt something. How could I not feel something?"

There was no answer in the salt spray or the call of the solitary gull, but the place in Michael's heart that the bright, sparkling girl next door had filled for twenty-two of his thirty-five years began to empty and grow cold.

So very cold.

"Hey, Mister. Are you lost?"

Michael started and looked around in confusion. He was sitting on a park bench in what appeared to be the Farewell town common. His feet were wet with salt water, but he didn't remember walking in the ocean. For that matter, he wasn't sure how he came to be on the bench. Or what time it was. What day.

"Are you okay?"

He looked over at the little girl and nodded, summoning a grin. He'd always been a sucker for kids, though he'd not been around many in the last few years, given the sort of work he'd been doing. "I think so."

She was cute—all blonde braids and huge eyes staring at him like a pair of blue question marks. "My name is Thor. I'm pleased to meet you."

Michael was surprised that such a deep, purring voice had come out of the slight body. "Thor? That's a strange name for a little girl."

The child giggled, high and sweet. "I'm not Thor, silly. I'm Kayla!" Now her voice sounded like a child's. The other must've been his imagination. "This is Thor."

A nightmarish beast stepped out from behind the girl at her gesture, and Michael had to stop himself from shrinking back at the sight. Or snatching up the child and running for his life.

How had he missed seeing the creature right away?

The enormous cat's pelt was a rusty chestnut, lighter at the tips of his sparse mane. A bold splash of white ran down between his eyes in a startling blaze that reminded Michael of . . . something. The thing's shoulder was level with the nearest picnic table, and its head was bigger than Michael's own. A fierce, almost intelligent light burned in the cat's golden eyes, and it glared at Michael as if daring him to make a wrong move.

No wonder the kid didn't think twice about talking to strangers. She had a mutant mountain lion for a bodyguard.

Michael nodded but didn't offer a hand to be sniffed. He liked both of his hands just where they were—on his wrists. He said, "Nice cat."

She dimpled and nodded. "Thanks. He likes you too. Are you renting one of the beach cottages with your family?"

He didn't bother to mention that the lion didn't look particularly taken with him. There probably weren't too many people who'd contradict this kid when that thing was drooling over her shoulder.

"No." He pictured himself in one of the little shingled houses with a wife and a few kids and a dog or two. Is that what his life would be like if he hadn't screwed up? "I have no family."

Well, technically he had a couple of cousins and a few friends back in New Hampshire. He spoke to them occasionally by phone but couldn't go home without Christine; she was too much a part of everything there. Without even trying he could picture her in every corner of the town, under every tree, on every doorstep.

He couldn't even work without her. He glanced down at his hands, at the fine tracery of white lines that laced his palms and fingers. They were the marks of a craft he'd once known, the artist he'd been when the muse danced in his head and made his fingers see the beauty locked in a simple piece of wood.

He'd been that artist once, when the little girl next door had made him want to better himself and a gnarled old man had shown him how to take wild energy and direct it toward beauty rather than lawlessness.

Gone now, all gone. His art had gone as completely as she had, and with as little warning. Just as he had returned to their bridal suite to find nothing but a note, he had woken one day not long after to find that the beauty in his head had died. Or maybe the magic had just up and left him.

Why not? His wife had.

"I'm sorry." Kayla looked at him with a wisdom beyond her years. "I made you sad."

"It's okay, kid. It doesn't take much these days." Michael smiled wryly and stood up, feeling the soggy material of his pants stick to his legs. "I've got to go take care of something. See you around." Or not.

He waved at the child and the enormous cat and walked back to Pirate's Cove. As he passed the last of the boardwalk shops, a voice whispered in the back of his head, one that purred at the edges and hadn't come from a little girl's mouth:

She's not in the cove. But you're getting closer.

An hour later, as he walked back into the little town where Christine must've spent her final days, Michael scrubbed a hand across his face, heard old calluses rasp against stubble, and wished he knew what to do next. He'd meant to leave Farewell, just as he'd meant to chuck his useless wedding ring into the ocean, but in the end he had done neither. At the last moment, something stopped him and he found himself returning the ring to its place on his left hand and walking back to town.

Wondering.

What had she been doing on Cape Cod? For that matter, why had she left Santa Caribe with just the clothes on her back? It was so unlike the girl he'd known that, eight years later, he still had trouble believing that she took off just because they'd had a little fight in the hotel restaurant.

Had she lost her memory? That was his favorite scenario—that she had been annoyed enough to take a boat back to the mainland, had fallen overboard, hit her head, and developed a soap-opera case of amnesia.

Jonas had always maintained that she had run away with the hotel's day manager, who'd also disappeared that night. Michael didn't think so, but he didn't really care as long as he found his wife. He had almost caught up to her when she'd used her credit card to call his workshop from a bus stop in Miami, but she'd left no message and was gone by the time he got there, leaving her purse behind.

It wasn't until last week, when he'd discovered the obituary in one of the PI's files, that he ceased believing she would awaken one day with her memory miraculously restored, find him, and fly into his arms full of tears and happy promises.

He didn't know why the team investigating her disappearance hadn't shown him the obituary right away, but perhaps it had been overlooked. There were probably hundreds of Jane Does reported each day, and the investigators wouldn't have been able to track down every single one.

He'd ask about it when he next spoke to Jonas, who'd paid for the investigation out of his vast resources. Michael knew his friend was on the island, negotiating yet another settlement with the native population of the rainforest paradise he all but owned. In fact, maybe Michael could be of use on Santa Caribe.

He hadn't been back to the island since his aborted honeymoon. In fact, he hadn't seen Jonas face to face in almost as long. Their relationship had degenerated to the occasional e-mail and secretary's message.

Somehow, though he'd been the troubleshooter on scene for many of Jonas's large projects over the years, it had been easier to let the friendship lapse.

Less painful.

Maybe, Michael thought, going to Santa Caribe would be a good step. He could see Jonas. Spend some time on his friend's island paradise and perhaps help out with the staffing problems the hotel had been having of late.

Michael glanced around.

He should leave.

He should go back to work.

Get on with his life.

But he couldn't. He couldn't leave without knowing why Christine had abandoned their honeymoon suite. Why she'd left him.

Michael stood in the center of the town common, deserted of children and lions now, and looked around for a likely source of eight-year-old gossip as he made his plan. He would reconstruct Christine's last days. Perhaps he could find a local she had spoken with. Maybe someone would know why she'd run. Once he understood that, he would lay his wife to rest and move on with his life.

And do what?

He couldn't go back to being a carver—that door had been

closed to him since Christine's disappearance. As much as he appreciated the job, he didn't want to work for Jonas indefinitely. And . . .

Well, he'd figure that out later.

Heaving a sigh, Michael forced himself to focus on the task at hand—locating someone who had been in Farewell eight years ago and might have spoken with a runaway bride. He glanced around the postcard-pretty little town.

The library? The graceful brick edifice was the kind of place his wife might've gone into to find peace, but it looked closed, as did the Town Hall beside it. They would wait until another day.

Mary Jean's diner was a possibility, but the restaurant probably saw hundreds of tourists each year, and the servers were unlikely to remember a lone woman, even one as lovely as Christine Finch . . . had been.

He scanned the boardwalk for other options. The Farewell Inn? A good option, but it looked deserted. The animal shelter? Probably not a place she would go, nor was the yoga center next door, or the candle shop—

Prrrrrrrr.

Michael spun around, expecting to see the mutant cat springing on him from behind. But it wasn't there.

He stood for a moment, waiting for his heart rate to slow. No lion. Must've been his imagination. Now, where was he? Oh yeah, trying to decide which of the shopkeepers might remember a single dark-haired woman from almost a decade ago.

The door to Dewdrop's Candle Shop was slightly open, swinging a bit with the hint of a sea breeze that had sneaked its way over the dunes and across the commons. That was all the invitation Michael needed.

She liked candles.

Michael nodded at the thought, which wasn't quite his

own. He had to start somewhere. Why not speak with the candle maker?

The shop smelled of wax and vanilla and cinnamon. It reminded him of his twentieth birthday, when fourteen-year-old Chrissy had given him a pair of vanilla-scented candles she had dipped with her grandmother's help.

He had loved her even then, feeling a helpless sort of emotion all tangled up with hormones and guilt and the knowledge that he, with his drunken father and juvenile record, would never measure up to her standards.

Now, almost without direction, his feet had stepped into the small store and carried him past a wax replica of downtown Farewell, complete with dogs and children. The scent of chocolate floated above the other smells, and he noticed an empty muffin basket on the glass counter, which was covered with candles and crumbs.

His eyes were drawn to four wax pillars locked securely in the display area of the counter. Three of the candles seemed to fill his vision and pulse with lurid color, with the promise of power. The promise of fulfillment. Of control and riches untold. He felt his flesh tighten, though whether from fear or excitement, he couldn't tell.

Red. Green. Blue.

He reached a hand toward the red candle. Could have sworn his fingertips grew warm.

The colors bled together, then separated and twined together again, seemingly shot through with ancient gold. He stared at them, mesmerized.

"Horst? Is that you?" The question startled him and he jumped. Stared around guiltily, suddenly beset with the feeling that he shouldn't have reached for the red candle.

That it was dangerous.

"Horst?"

Her voice was tense, breathless, and came from behind a swinging door at the rear of the store. Something about the timbre of her voice made the fine hairs on Michael's neck stand up. A massive shudder crawled down his back, and he wondered again whether he was afraid or excited—and why he should be either.

There was a crash and a quick oath. "Are Big Jim and his boys with you? I need help getting the candles out of the display case. The lock's jammed and I have to get out of here. Fast."

A woman hustled through the door with a large box in her arms, and Michael felt a warm rush of interest. Snug blue jeans cupped her pert derriere and fondled femininely curved legs before ending raggedly at her bare ankles. As she struggled with the load, her baggy sweatshirt slid off one creamy white, softly muscled shoulder, and Michael had the sudden urge to press his lips right where her shoulder joined her neck.

Even as he had the thought, a curl of red touched the edge of his mind. Heat. Madness.

The woman's curly hair, a rich chocolate two shades darker than Chrissy's had been, flirted with her bare shoulder, and the sight of that lush brown fluttering over pale cream made Michael's heart stutter even as he cursed himself for the feeling.

She was built like his wife had been, only more so. Everywhere that Chrissy had been bones and angles, this woman was round and inviting.

Chrissy. A sharp pang reminded him that he shouldn't be looking at another woman when he'd just learned of his wife's demise. But it had been eight years since he'd seen his wife.

Eight very long, lonely years.

The curvy woman continued, still with her back to him as she packed the box with quick, nervous motions. "I need to

21

hide the candles in the cave. If the man Kayla said she talked to is Garibaldi, if he's found me . . ." Then, apparently realizing that Horst hadn't responded, she straightened from the display case. Her shoulders tensed as if she expected a blow from behind.

"Horst?" She turned slowly, fearfully.

"No, I'm . . ."

Michael Finch, he started to say. But then his brain shut down. His tongue glued itself to the roof of his mouth. And his mind was filled with the undeniable, horrible, wonderful, staggering realization—

His wife was alive.

Chapter Two

He's here, thought the woman who now called herself Dewdrop. *It's over.*

After all these years, she didn't feel the terror she had expected. Instead, a sort of weary relief washed its way through her. It was finally ended, though not by the man she'd expected.

When Kayla had described the strange man in the park—a big man with a dark suit, shiny shoes, and short brown hair, Christine's first thought had been *Garibaldi.* He'd finally found her. She'd known he would eventually. He wasn't the kind who gave up easily. Or ever.

But it wasn't Garibaldi. It was Michael. Her husband.

Her betrayer.

And in a way, she'd rather Garibaldi had found her first. His method of torture was direct—fists, knives, hot whispered promises, and cruel finger.

But Michael?

He could destroy her without touching her. He already had.

And he could destroy her doubly now. On the heels of that thought came the terror she had expected. Kayla! She had to protect her daughter. Had to hide her.

As every rational neuron she possessed screamed for her to run, to escape, Dewdrop reached a trembling hand to touch him and prove that he was just another illusion, one of those dreams that came to her in the night and made her cry with terror and ache with longing. One of those dreams that woke her up drenched with perspiration and throbbing with need.

Michael.

His image, his beloved face had come to her many times in the past when she was weak and needy and ready to believe in fairy tales. But it had always taken the shape of the boy she had kissed down by the lake or the young man who had laughingly grappled with her in the woods by her house.

She didn't know this ghost, this stranger who looked like Mikey but more so. This man's face was older, tireder, sadder, infinitely more handsome—

And stunned.

"Christine?" he whispered, the word seeming to come straight from his soul, but that was a lie. He had no soul. No heart. No honor.

His hand rose to touch hers, fingertip to fingertip, and the old magic flared between them at the press of flesh on flesh, causing an answering warmth low in her belly.

Michael.

His touch was more painful to her than three cracked ribs and a broken collarbone had been. And the single word was devastating.

Christine. It was the name of a girl who had died eight years ago on Santa Caribe Island. She panicked.

With the echo of gunshots and harsh voices ringing in her ears, Dewdrop jerked her hand away from the stranger who wore the face of her husband, her betrayer. She spun away from the three big candles and the power they contained—

And ran for her life.

Michael stood there in the candle shop for a dazed moment, his brain refusing to accept what his eyes and his heart, his tingling fingertips and his throbbing, yearning body told him. Desire spiraled through his chest, an elemental reaction that carried on its heels the twin emotions of hope and wonder.

She was here.

Here.

Alive.

Just as it had taken him several days to grasp Christine's death, it took him precious seconds to comprehend her survival.

Seconds that she was using to flee him again.

She was alive, so she hadn't been kept from his arms by death. And she had recognized him right off, so his fantasy that she'd suffered from amnesia and would one day return to her senses and look him up was just that—a fantasy.

Oh yeah, she'd recognized him all right. His quick flash of relieved pleasure was replaced by confusion. He had never pictured their reunion this way. Where were the tears? The violins? The babbling confessions that would wipe away the past eight years in a few sentences?

Was she sorry her past had come back to haunt her? Maybe a husband back in New Hampshire didn't fit in with her life now. Did she have a man here? His stomach clenched. Did she have children, a family? All of the things they had planned to have together?

I promise. The inscription on his ring was mocked by the empty echo of her feet in the next room. Confusion curdled to anger as the questions played fool to eight years of dedicated, faithful searching.

The sharp slam of a door slapped him back to reality. He had to catch his wife. He hadn't come all this way to lose her again before she explained how they'd gone from lovers to enemies in a night.

How he'd gone from lover to loner.

"Christine, wait!" he shouted, and sprinted in pursuit, fearing his wife had left him—again.

As he bulled through the swinging door into the space where she obviously created her wares, he caught a flicker of movement in the workroom's single window. Ignoring the fanciful candles and the heavy scent of flowers and spice, he slammed through the rear door, again yelling her name with equal parts anger and entreaty. "Christine!"

"Hold it! Stop right there!"

Michael skidded on the boardwalk, suddenly confronted by a wall of angry muscle.

The command had been issued in a deep, resonant voice that sounded as if the man were speaking from inside a whiskey barrel. It wasn't a bad analogy, since he was built like a whiskey barrel on legs.

A seven-foot-tall whiskey barrel on legs.

With friends. Big ones.

Seeing that all fifteen hundred or so pounds of human flesh dressed in well-used fishing apparel appeared very, very angry, Michael held out his hands in the age-old gesture of *hey, no weapons, I'm your friend.*

"Easy, guys. I'm not here to start trouble." The wall of muscle didn't move, nor did any of its members return Michael's feeble attempt at a smile. "I'm just looking for my wife."

He could hear her footfalls fade with distance and knew that she was gone.

The grizzled hulk standing beside Whiskey Barrel looked like everyone's image of a career longshoreman. Apparently their leader, he stepped ahead of the others and snarled, "Clear out, bub. We don't want your kind in Farewell."

Michael nodded. "Okay." He paused. "What kind is that, exactly?"

He could hear voices whisper from the depths of memory, saying, *He'll never amount to anything. Just look at his father. Of course he runs with Jonas Harding—they're birds of a feather, those two. They'll probably end up sharing a cell someday—that kind always does.*

There was an ugly rumble from the group. "He doesn't even know what he did wrong," muttered a hulking youth whose wrists and ankles sprouted from his clothing in a way that suggested a recent growth spurt.

"He knows," claimed the longshoreman. "Else he wouldn't be chasing after her looking to do murder." The man started forward, followed by Whiskey Barrel and the others.

All of them radiated anger and simmering violence.

Michael backed away and held his hands out again. "I don't suppose you'd consider letting me by, would you? You don't really want to get in the middle of this. It's between my wife and me."

"This is Farewell, buddy. We take care of our own, and we don't think much of a man who uses his fists on a lady." The longshoreman made a fist and slammed it into the palm of his other hand with a sound like that made by a breaching humpback whale.

"What?" Incredulity made Michael's voice crack on the word. Even at his worst, he'd never lay a hand on a woman, particularly after having seen what Old Harding's fists had done to Jonas when the three of them—Michael, Jonas, and Christine—had all been children.

"You heard us. Did you think she'd be too afraid to tell us what happened? How do you think she explained the shape she was in? What was that story she tried to pass off at first? Oh yeah. She fell down some steps, right? Did you tell her to say that?"

Whiskey Barrel loomed beside the longshoreman, and the others distributed themselves in a loose semicircle that backed Michael up against the rough clapboards of the candle shop. Whiskey Barrel stepped forward and jammed his finger in Michael's chest. "You don't hit women in Farewell and get away with it."

Something finally clicked. "Wait! You've got it all wrong." He held up his hands and shook his head in negation. "I didn't hit Christine. I would never hurt her. I—"

Love her.

That's what he tried to say, but it wasn't easy to get the words past a mouthful of knuckles.

Besides, as the ground rushed up at him and the world faded to black, Michael wasn't even sure if it was the truth anymore.

He'd looked for Christine too long, too hard.

And been too badly hurt by her.

"Hey Mikey! Come on in! The water's great!"

The girl stood half out of the pond to wave an invitation; and Mike, as he preferred to be called, now that he was a mature twenty-one-year-old, wished she hadn't done that. Little Chrissy had been easier to ignore before he had gone off to art school on a full scholarship, when she'd been eleven to his seventeen.

Never mind that she had nagged him into applying in the first place, claiming he was wasting himself on his job at the sawmill. He knew she meant wasting himself hanging out with Jonas, boosting cars and filching cigs, but back then she'd been awfully hard to argue with.

Four years later she was still way too young for him to think what he was thinking, but there was far more of her to try to ignore. He tried valiantly to keep his eyes on hers, rather than on the wet shirt plastered to her torso, and reminded himself that she was way too good for him. Way too young for him. And still awfully hard to argue with. "From where I'm standing it looks a bit cold, sweetheart."

She shook her head innocently. "Not at all. Please, Mikey. I've barely seen you since you came back for the summer. Now you'll be off again when you've practically just arrived. Come on," she coaxed. "Just a little swim. What can it hurt?"

More than she knew, Mike thought wryly. Still and all, the water was cold enough to dampen his enthusiasm, and Chrissy was right—he'd been avoiding her.

"I guess I've got a moment." He tried for a totally cool tone even as his heart thumped at the thought of stripping down to his shorts in front of her. But that was dumb; they'd skinny-dipped together plenty of times in the past. Nothing had changed, had it?

Yeah, right.

The sparkling New Hampshire lake was beyond cold when he finally slid in, and Chrissy gave a glad cry and paddled over to wind herself around him in play. She tugged on his ear in mock anger. "You've been avoiding me, haven't you, Mikey?"

If it had been anyone else, he would've told them his name was "Mike" now. But it was little Chrissy. She could call him whatever she wanted.

He shrugged, the motion sliding her arms closer around his neck and nestling her a little tighter against his chest, much to his body's evident joy. He shifted away, lest that joy become evident to her as well. "I've been busy, Chris. You know how it is. I was going to stop by before I left, honest."

She replaced her tugging fingers with her teeth and gave a nip at his earlobe that shot a spear of sizzling warmth directly through his core. He fought to hold still as his feet sank into the ooze at the bottom of the lake. The girl cuddled closer and his body proved in grand style that the cold-water thing was a myth.

"Sure you were." She shrugged. "The thing is, Mikey, I've missed you. We used to be friends. What happened? Why don't you come around anymore? Did I do something wrong?"

He looked away. "You didn't do a thing, little one. It's just that we're both growing up, and things can't just go on like they used to. I'm twenty-one. You're fifteen. It doesn't work like it did when we were kids. Understand?"

Her lower lip poked out stubbornly, deliciously, and a droplet of water beaded on it and begged him to touch it with his tongue. "No. Who cares what other people say? I don't."

"It's not other people, Chris. It's me." With what remained of his brain, he thought of telling her that she didn't interest him anymore, that she needed friends her own age. She'd hate him for a while, but maybe in the end it would be for the best. Age aside, she deserved better.

But he couldn't lie to Chrissy. He just couldn't. It would be like lying to the other half of himself.

He looked down into her trusting eyes and tried to ignore the press of her young breasts against his chest as he searched for the right words.

His silence was too long and she looked away. "Never mind. I didn't mean to be a pest." She breathed deeply, causing her hard, round nipples to press more firmly against Michael's chest. He quivered and searched for control. "But since you're leaving tomorrow, can I ask you a favor before you go?"

He took a deep breath. A favor between friends. He could do that. Better that he grant her boon and leave town again before he went crazy and asked her to marry him next month on her sixteenth birthday, when she'd be of legal age to wed.

Legal, but not moral, he reminded himself. She needed to grow up first. Grow up and marry a nice boy. He ground his teeth until he thought he felt a molar crack, and asked, "What favor?"

"Kiss me."

Mike's brain stuttered, then splintered into a thousand fragments of glowing color as all of the blood drained out of his head for good.

"Excuse me?" His voice attained several octaves simultaneously.

Chrissy raised one eyebrow, a talent he'd always admired. "From the look of horror on your face, I'd say you heard me." She pushed away from him and frog kicked to the other end of the pond, where her clothing lay in a neatly folded pile. "Never mind. Forget it," she called over her shoulder.

It took him a moment to recover enough to pursue. "Hang on! Chrissy, wait!" He caught up to her on land and yanked the dry T-shirt out of her hands before she could put it on.

That was probably a bad idea. She looked even better than he had imagined in the wet shirt and tiny swimsuit, and her slick, cool thighs pressed fleetingly against his when he took her arms to keep her from running.

"Let go of me." She looked away, trying to hide the tears he could hear in her words. He gentled his touch and held her close while the water on their skin chilled in the rising breeze.

He asked simply, "Why me?"

They had never spoken of love. They didn't have to talk about the dreams they shared, or the moments when each could speak the other's thoughts. They didn't need the words, because the connection simply *was*.

She shrugged jerkily, still not looking at him. "I told you to forget it. It was just that I always figured you'd be the first boy that kissed me, and I don't know when I'm going to see you again, so I thought it was now or never. Don't worry, though. It's not important."

But he could tell from the tension in her body and the lingering tears in her eyes that it was a big deal indeed. So instead of doing the right thing, the safe thing, and staying far away from her, Mike used one pond-chilled finger to tip her chin up so she would look at him.

"I think it's very important, Chris. I'm flattered." And he lowered his lips to hers and tasted . . .

Fur?

Michael spluttered and flailed wildly, sitting half up before the spearing agony in his head and the crushing weight on his chest forced him back down again. An irritated-sounding growl came from somewhere above his face, lasting so long he felt his chest vibrate with the rumble.

Huh?

There hadn't been an animal growling at the pond where he'd first kissed Chrissy. For that matter, her young girl's kiss had tasted of innocence and sunshine, not hair and old blood.

Ergo . . . he'd been dreaming about kissing Chrissy.

He still did that often, but over time the dream had become a pleasant memory, more than an immediate experience that made his heart pound and his palms sweat like they were now.

And oh lord, did his head hurt. And he couldn't breathe very well. That had to be because of . . . Michael searched his throbbing brain for information.

He remembered something about a whiskey barrel. Was he drunk? Hung over? No . . .

Memory came crashing back in an avalanche of bittersweet emotion, and he wished for a moment for the return of sweet, dreaming unconsciousness. Christine was here. Here! In Farewell, where she hadn't drowned after all.

So who the hell had died wearing her wedding ring?

The warm weight on his chest shifted a bit, fur tickled his cheek, and suddenly Michael was suffocating. He thrashed and opened his eyes, squinting against the bright light to bring into focus—

Another pair of eyes.

Yellow cat eyes.

Big ones.

The little girl's lion was sitting on his chest, squeezing the breath out of him. Michael froze and tried to decide whether or not screaming was a good idea, and the creature began to growl again. Its paws, each bigger than two of Michael's palms together, prodded at him in an alternating, kneading motion.

It was tenderizing him before it ate him. How civilized.

The weight shifted slightly off Michael's chest, and for one hopeful moment he thought that the lion was going to give him room to escape. Then it started to lick him, growling all the while.

Only it wasn't growling, he realized. The darn thing was purring.

The kid, Kayla, had said the lion liked him. Maybe she knew something he didn't.

Tentatively, he reached up and scratched, very gently, behind the lion's ear. It responded by tilting its jaw to allow him better access. Unfortunately, it also increased the pressure of its kneading, which was now threatening to crack a rib or two.

"Could I persuade you to let me up, Thor? It's Thor, right?"

Right.

Michael looked quickly around as the cat stood aside. There was that strange, deep voice again.

But he and Thor were alone in what looked like the back room of Dewdrop's Candle Shop. So he asked the big cat, "What happened?"

Thor didn't know, or if he did, the cat had his tongue. But that was silly, Michael thought. Cats didn't talk, even really big ones.

As the room stopped spinning, Michael took stock. It was late afternoon from the looks of the shadows, so he hadn't been out for too long. But how had he gotten into the shop? Had he crawled in here and onto the cot?

"Why'd they let me go if they thought I'd hurt Christine? And why'd they think that in the first place?"

Thor remained mute on those subjects as well. The cat picked up one saucer-sized paw and began delicately licking between harpoonlike claws with a tongue the size of a ham steak.

Michael might have been concussed, but he wasn't stupid. As his thoughts began to clear, he tried to piece together what had happened. Christine must have been injured when she arrived in town. Beaten. A sick ball of revulsion formed in his stomach and low, leaden anger began to pulse, clearing away some of the confusion that webbed his brain.

Someone had hurt his Chrissy.

A man had taken his fists to her. What was that name she had mentioned with fear in her eyes and a scream on her lips? Garibaldi? Had he hurt Christine?

He'd kill the bastard.

No matter that the incident was years past, hot rage poured through Michael, spiked with a nasty dose of guilt. She'd been hurt and he hadn't protected her. What if she hadn't left of her own free will after all? What if the Santa Caribbean police had been wrong in passing the incident off as spousal abandonment? What if she'd been kidnapped?

Lurid pictures of little Chrissy trussed up in the bottom of a powerboat leapt into his mind. He saw her beaten, raped, tossed aside like a sack of laundry.

But if that was the case, why hadn't she contacted him, and why had she run from him just now?

Was she ashamed of what had happened? Did she blame him for her injuries, blame the silly fight they'd had that night for her leaving? Condemn him for not finding her sooner?

She must. And why not? He blamed himself.

"Where is she, Thor? I have to talk to her. What the hell went wrong with us?" There were too many questions to ask, too many answers to find.

The words echoed back at him, mixed with the smell of wax and scented oils, and the cat bent to lick its tail with typical feline disregard for the importance of things while the voice in his head said, *Find her. Ask her.*

Michael shook himself. Now he was hearing things. He needed help.

Sluggish with pain and heartache, Michael poked through his pockets in the hope that the shockproof guarantee on his cell phone wasn't just a sales tool. His pants and shoes had been a mess even before he bled on them, and now his shirt was torn and stained. He had no change of clothing because he hadn't packed an overnight bag when he'd learned that Christine was dead. He'd just gotten in the car and pointed it toward Cape Cod.

He was relieved to find his phone functional, although the casing was cracked. So much for shockproof. He dialed a number from memory while his tongue ventured around his mouth checking for teeth loosened by Whiskey Barrel's fist.

He smiled through split lips when a faintly mechanical

voice on the other end invited him to leave a message.

"Jonas? It's Mike. I know you're busy dealing with problems on the island, but I need your help. I'm in Farewell." Michael faltered slightly at putting the news into words.

"I found Christine. She's . . . alive."

He breathed into the phone until he heard the double beep indicating that his message had been forwarded to a remote hand unit. He smiled.

Jonas would get the good news soon.

Chapter Three

"You can't just leave."

Dewdrop didn't even pause in her packing. "Watch me."

She was in full flight mode and didn't have time for social niceties, even with Horst, her first and best friend here in Farewell. Socks, books, and Kayla's favorite blanket went into a suitcase while the small man watched with those old-soul eyes. "I'm doing what's best for my daughter. That's all I can think about right now, okay?"

She couldn't, wouldn't think about Michael. Not about how her heart had leapt at his voice, or about how his eyes had flared bright with desperate hope in that first instant he'd seen her.

Unfortunately, it was probably hope that she had the amulets and the cash she had taken from the dead man on Santa Caribe. Well, the cash was long spent. And the jewels? They were safely hidden, as was the damning parchment.

Horst sat loosely, his limbs folded in a yogic position that she couldn't have reproduced if she tried. "You aren't even going to talk to him? You're just going to run?"

Dewdrop sighed. "Don't push me, Horst. He lied to me. When I gave him a second chance, he sold me out. So yes, I'm leaving with my daughter. End of story."

She remembered the tiny boat lurching through the waves as she ducked under the searchlights and closed her ears to the shouts, the roars, and the barking of the attack dogs.

"But what if he's innocent? Your evidence against him is largely circumstantial. You loved him once. Doesn't he deserve a chance? Doesn't Kayla?"

Dewdrop shook her head. "No more chances. I stopped thinking he might be innocent after I called him for help and Garibaldi grabbed me. Three broken ribs and a shattered collarbone was enough to convince me that I can't trust Michael." She needn't voice the secret doubts that skittered through her mind when it was in that vulnerable place between sleeping and waking.

But Horst knew. He changed the pattern his legs made as they crossed over and under each other and looked at her solemnly. "If you were that sure of it, you'd already be gone. You're still here, so at least part of you thinks he didn't have a damn thing to do with the murder."

Her hands stilled on the zipper of her daughter's knapsack.

Horst prodded gently. "Talk to me, Christine."

She winced. "Don't call me that. I'm Dewdrop now, and in a few hours I'll be someone else entirely. Because I can't trust Michael with this. He promised, and it only took him a day to break his word." She closed the lid of Kayla's vinyl suitcase with a snap and tested its heft. She said, "I'll miss you, Horst."

He had been the one to pluck her from the hurricane-tossed sea that night, had been the one to help her kill Christine Finch and become Dewdrop.

"Are you sure this is what you want?"

Of course it wasn't. What she really wanted to do was go back in time eight years or more and change everything that had happened since. Everything but Kayla.

"It's what I have to do. I'll miss you," she repeated and turned to leave.

"Aren't you forgetting something?"

She thought quickly. She'd packed their essentials, had told Kayla to wait for her down by the playground, had arranged for Thor's keeping. For a moment she wished she could still imagine the lion's voice in her head as she'd done when he was a cub. She had a feeling he'd know what to do. "I don't think so . . ."

"What about the candles?"

The candles.

"Oh God!" What if she'd forgotten about them? What if she'd left town without hiding them in the cave?

She'd be dead. Kayla would be dead and probably Thor as well, because the amulets represented the sum total of her bargaining power.

Horst shrugged. "Go get 'em now. They're safe in the shop, and Big Jim said he popped the latch. No big deal, right?"

Dewdrop snatched Kayla's suitcase off the floor and slung her own light duffel and the knapsack over one shoulder. "You're right." She kissed Horst lightly on the cheek. "I'll write." She was most of the way to the door before she turned back to look at her friend. "I love you, Horst. I truly will miss you."

The yogi remained sitting in lotus position and smiled enigmatically as she swung out the door.

"I'd miss you too, sweetheart, but I have a feeling you're not going anywhere." Horst paused and smiled at the empty room. "Oh—I'm sorry. I must've forgotten to tell you that I left your husband in the candle shop."

She'd figure that one out pretty soon on her own. If the quiet, purring voice in Horst's head was right, this could very well be the luckiest day in Dewdrop's life.

He tried not to consider the other option. Because if Thor

was wrong, she and Kayla could very well end up dead.

"Come on, Finch," Horst urged the emptiness, "We've got a good feeling about you. Don't you dare let us down."

Dewdrop trudged across the dunes with the weight of her decisions pressing her down into the sand of Pirate's Beach. Since the night she had gone from bride to fugitive, she had made it a point not to look back. Second-guessing was a luxury she could ill afford, but a litany of questions pursued her as she hit the boardwalk and turned toward her store.

Should she have gone to Michael that night? What if the men in their hotel room had meant something else by calling the murder "a wedding present"? What if Michael had been an innocent bystander, unaware of what his luggage contained?

He still wouldn't have believed her. He'd proven the day of their wedding that his friendship with Jonas was more important to him than a promise made to his wife.

Lost in dismal memories, she turned the knob of her shop door with sharp regret. She'd miss this place, this town. In Farewell she'd become a woman she liked—a person who was part Christine Finch and part Dewdrop, a mother who was fanciful enough to dream of faerie castles but practical enough to raise a child and run a business.

In a way, she liked the person she was now better than the green girl who believed the universe centered on Michael Finch. That girl had been sweet and naïve, and Dewdrop sometimes thought it was a wonder she had survived the escape from Santa Caribe.

As she pushed the shop door open, she wondered fleetingly where Michael had gone. Hopefully she had lost him well enough that she would be safe coming back to the shop, but she didn't really have a choice.

She couldn't leave the candles behind.

A familiar growl greeted her when she stepped into the workroom. "Hey, Thor."

She rubbed behind the big cat's ears and tried not to cry. She had loved Thor from the moment the half-grown kitten, already the size of a Labrador, had leapt on Garibaldi and bitten him viciously, buying enough time for them to escape from the white van and flee into the steamy Miami night carrying those three awful, powerful amulets.

Woman and cat had run through the back alleys together, a heartbeat ahead of pursuit, and had leapt aboard an idling furniture truck moments before it left town. Christine had suffered a moment of worry at keeping close quarters with what must be an escaped zoo creature, but Thor had been as cold and lonely as she, and the two of them had crouched together on an ugly sofa for the thirty-four hours it took to reach their destination.

Farewell.

"You're going to live with Horst for a bit, Little Kitty. I'll miss you, but you'll be okay. We'll be okay." She wasn't sure whether she was reassuring the cat or herself, but she didn't think either of them believed it. "I'll come back for you if I can."

"You'd come back for a damn cat but not for your husband, Christine? Or should I call you 'Dewdrop'?" The words were shocking, the tone as familiar to her as her own face.

Her blood chilled, then heated at the rough-honey voice. The suitcase slid from her fingers with a thud. The voice brought back memories of innocence and sunlight, of swimming in the pond and necking in the woodshop. Memories of a boy who could change from badass to artist in the blink of an eye.

She breathed his name, "Mikey."

"Did you really think you had to fake your own death to get rid of me?" A muscle pulsed in his jaw, and the stubble on his cheek and throat rippled when he swallowed convulsively. He looked battered. Bruised. Wonderful. "A simple 'I want a divorce' would've given me the hint, although after only being married two days, you probably could've swung an annulment."

"I . . ." Her throat locked on the words when she saw the anguish in gray eyes she'd once known better than her own. Saw the anger in them.

Wait a minute. She was the injured party here, wasn't she? *He* had lied to *her*, not the other way around. In fact, if she were smart she'd poke him in his beautiful, sad eyes, grab the candles, and run for it before he could call in reinforcements.

But his anger seemed genuine, the hurt that lay behind it unforced. She had the most overwhelming urge to smooth the deep grooves that formed between his eyebrows and kiss away his thunderous frown.

As she watched, that frown melted on its own and took on a wistful quality. Suddenly he looked like the man she remembered, the one she had planned a lifetime with. The boy she had loved.

"Christine?" he asked as if waiting for her to deny it, then, "Chrissy?" His voice hitched on the word and made her wonder if he'd thought of her over the years as much as she'd thought of him.

He crossed the room, his shoes making hollow sounds on the wood floor. His passage swirled the candle-scented air, and little eddies of jasmine and vanilla and peppermint brushed against her face like a touch.

And then it was *his* touch on her face after all these years.

Thor growled deep in his throat when Michael brushed his

fingers across Christine's cheek, but she barely heard. Her body arched into the touch and the past and present blended together in a kaleidoscope of memories and dreams as he pressed his face to her temple.

She remembered being eight years old, sitting by a broken tree swing with Michael's arms around her and his lips in her hair as she cried for her daddy to come home and for her mommy to do something other than stand by the picture window and iron her father's shirts, over and over again until the house smelled of scorched cotton.

Unbidden, her hand drifted upward to touch his rough jaw as he dragged his mouth across her cheek.

She remembered being twelve and escaping to sit down by the lake alone until he found her there, shrugged out of the black leather jacket that was his trademark, and invited her to dance to the music of the setting sun.

He hadn't kissed her then, but he did now. "Chrissy," he whispered before taking her mouth with his. Her eyelids fluttered shut.

She remembered being fifteen and blue with cold from swimming in the lake every afternoon for two weeks, hoping Mikey would happen by. She remembered being sixteen, eighteen, twenty, and sneaking off every minute she could to be with him, praying that her love would be enough to save him from Jonas and the road to hell.

He might have said her name again before his tongue slid between her lips, but she could barely hear over the roaring in her ears. She wrapped her arms around his neck and held on for dear life as he kissed her deeply and she answered in kind, pressing her body against his, trying to make up for eight years in one embrace.

She remembered being twenty-three and a bride. He had been so gentle when he had finally taken her into his bare arms and she had taken him into her body for the first time. She remembered flesh sliding against flesh, breath mingling, cries spiraling together.

He crushed her to his chest and she burrowed close, inhaling his half-forgotten, achingly familiar scent and trying to block out the rest.

She remembered angry words, a napkin thrown on a half-eaten plate of food, then back in their room—

Men fighting over flaming gemstones.

A gunshot.

Blood.

Whimpering, twisting, she fought to escape, not his arms but images born of nightmare. Through the roaring of blood pounding in her ears she heard Thor's snarl escalate to a scream.

She remembered running, hiding, cowering by day and counting the miles by night, then a cry for help. A few words over a muffled phone line, "Michael? I'm in Miami. I need you. Please come."

"No!" she cried, and felt Michael's body lurch sideways as a reddish blur knocked him aside and followed him down to the floor.

"No," she yelled again, this time to stop her guardian's attack. "Thor, stop!"

The lion stood aside, leaving Michael lying on the floor of the candle shop breathing heavily. His shirt was badly torn where Thor's claws had snagged the cloth.

"Bad cat," she admonished halfheartedly. She should be thanking Thor for his impeccable timing. What had she been thinking? She might have loved Michael once, but he'd betrayed her. How could she possibly enjoy kissing him after that?

Blame it on temporary insanity. Blame it on nightmares.

Blame it on loneliness, a weak moment, the sight of him in her doorway looking like the boy she'd lost.

Blame it on hormones, she thought honestly. Chemistry and poor judgment. The memory of what she thought they once had.

And what she would never have again.

"I've got to go," she blurted out as Michael climbed gingerly to his feet, keeping a wary eye on Thor.

"Think again." He stood in front of the main door with his hands on his hips and his legs spread as if he expected her to make a run for it. Smart man. "I've chased you halfway across the globe, searched for you eight damn years. I think that entitles me to an explanation, don't you?"

His shirt gaped open across his chest and a single streak of blood crossed under his right nipple. She watched sweat bead. Saw his skin tighten.

And felt it deep within her own body.

"What happened to you?" she asked inanely, breathlessly, still not running. His mouth was cut and swollen. She could taste his blood on her lips.

He twitched one shoulder. "You tell me. The guys that did it said they were looking out for you."

Looking out for her? No. Looking *for* her. Icy fear sluiced through her.

Garibaldi.

He and his men had arrived.

He would kill her this time. Of that she had no doubt.

Then he would go looking for the amulets. And Kayla. She had to get the candles and go. Right now. But even as she opened the case and picked up a heavy blue candle, she paused.

"Why did they hit you?"

"I guess I didn't have enough information."

As she jammed the other two candles in her daughter's knapsack, Dewdrop wondered. Was Michael out of Garibaldi's loop?

Or he'd never been in it in the first place. He wasn't on their side. He hadn't known about the smuggling or the murder. He hadn't led the men to her hiding spot in Miami.

He'd lied to her about Jonas, but he hadn't betrayed her.

Dear God. Could it be true? Please God, let it be true. Her heart lightened even as he scowled.

"You weren't even going to bother trying to find me before you left, were you? You were leaving without even a crummy note this time."

Note? What note? She hadn't left a note.

He slumped against the wall, rubbing a hand over his face. "Who's going with you? A lover? That Horst fellow you were talking to earlier? Who is he? That's too much luggage for just one person."

She snorted at the thought of Horst as her lover, even as she wondered why Michael didn't notice that one of the suitcases was shaped like Snoopy.

Wait. A lover? She looked into Michael's eyes and saw the anger and reluctant belief.

He thought she'd left him for another man. How could he think such a thing? After she had waited fifteen years to marry him, he thought she would leave him for another *on the day after their wedding?*

Even as she snarled at the injustice, some of that final disagreement came back to her—how he was forever telling her what to do, how he seemed to think that eight years' difference in their ages made him vastly more capable of functioning than she. How he had refused to believe that she was serious about holding him to his promise.

"What lover? Why do you think there was a man?" There

46

had been a man, but not the way Michael meant. Christine shuddered at the feel of the cold, dead fingers under hers.

Michael swore. "The night manager saw you leave in a boat with him. He said you hugged him and kissed him and then you both laughed. Were you laughing at me?"

She pictured the kindly old man who had taken her to the mainland in his boat. She'd told him a story about a husband who beat her. He'd taken one look at her torn clothing and bruised face and loaded her right in his bark. He had a daughter her age, he'd said. A lover? Never. Someone was lying, but she wasn't sure who. Had they lied to Michael to cover her disappearance? The likeliest source of that lie would be Jonas, and she would happily believe him the only culprit, if it hadn't been for her emergency call to the workshop. Michael had taken that call, had sent thugs to Miami for her. Or was Michael lying now, trying to stall her until the others arrived?

Who could she trust besides herself?

"Who hit you?" The strong column of his throat worked as he swallowed. Clenched a fist. "Was it that Garibaldi?"

Her heart stuttered and she clutched the knapsack to her chest. "How did you know about him?"

If he knew about her being hurt, then he must've known the rest. Her quick hope that he had been blameless died a messy death. He had known of her beating and hadn't stopped it. Hadn't rescued her.

Hadn't loved her.

Forsaking the suitcases, she edged toward the back door. If he knew about Garibaldi, then he knew about the stolen jewels. It wouldn't be long before he guessed that they were in the candles. Michael wasn't a stupid man. He'd figure it out very soon.

She had to get to her daughter.

"Did he hit you?" Michael demanded again, grabbing the strap of Kayla's knapsack when Christine tried to pass him.

Refusing to play tug-of-war with her own life, she fought back with words, hoping to make him flinch. "Yes, Michael. He hit me. He broke three of my ribs and my collarbone. Is that what you wanted to know?"

Phantom pain flared in her chest and shoulders, and she lifted her free hand to the scar on her cheek. "I almost lost the baby." It wasn't until Michael let go the knapsack and stepped back that she realized she had said the last words aloud.

"He got you pregnant?" He swore viciously and back-handed the display nearest him, sending a waxen replica of Farewell's lighthouse sailing across the room to land among the seven dwarfs.

Christine opened her mouth to correct him, then found herself staring into the eyes of the candle she had cast in the likeness of Dopey. It seemed oddly appropriate when she considered how stupid she had been, how stupid this man could make her be.

"Yes, he got me pregnant," she whispered.

"Christ, Christine—"

He was interrupted by the crash of the back door and the slap of little feet in the workroom.

"Mom? Hey Mom! I waited for you forever and you didn't come, so Uncle Horst said I should meet you at the shop." Kayla looked sideways at her mother, apparently sensing some of the tension in the room. "That's okay, right? I know I'm supposed to go to one of the hidey places if you don't come for me, but Uncle Horst said to come here."

Christine reached down and nudged Kayla away from Michael, who had gone still as a statue. All the color had drained from his face, leaving it a pasty collection of bruises, scrapes, and hollow eyes.

She knelt down to her daughter's level and brushed a lock of sweet blonde hair from her face. "I may kill your Uncle Horst later, but I'm not mad at you, sweetie."

Momentarily forgetting what was in the knapsack, Christine gave it to her daughter. "Take your bag, baby, and go wait for me outside. I'll be there in just a sec."

The girl had her eye on Michael. "Oh, good! That's the man Thor wanted you to meet, Mommy. He looked better when I saw him in the park, though. Do you like him?"

Christine almost laughed at the question. Did she like him?

She nodded slowly while her daughter waited for an answer.

"He reminds me of someone I knew a long time ago." She paused. "Someone I liked very much."

Chapter Four

Michael supposed that in a way that was true. Once he and Christine had known each other better than they had known themselves. They had laughed at the same things, loved the same things, shared the same dreams and goals. But that was eight years ago.

Eight long years.

And one child.

He looked at Kayla. How could he not have noticed the resemblance at the park? Then again, he hadn't exactly been looking for his supposedly dead wife's features in a child who was, what, seven years old?

Or perhaps seven years, three months.

The smell of wax and the clashing scents of aromatherapy candles were making him dizzy, and he rubbed a hand over his tired face and through his hair, wincing as he touched the lump above his ear.

"How old are you, Kayla?"

Instead of leaving the shop as her mother obviously wanted her to do, the child stood near him and smiled, shifting her knapsack to hold out seven proud fingers. "I'm—"

"Not yours," Christine interrupted, her words punctuated by a growl from Thor.

Michael stared at her hard, remembering that she'd never been able to lie worth a damn. But her expression gave away nothing. Apparently she had learned a few things about poker in the last few years.

His? That Garibaldi's? Someone else's?

"I'm sorry," he said, knowing it wouldn't be enough.

If he hadn't fought with her in the restaurant, hadn't said a few things that would have been better left unsaid, then she might not have gone away that night. If she hadn't left, she wouldn't have been vulnerable to whatever bastard had picked her up. Gotten her pregnant. Raped her? Beaten her, for sure.

His fault.

"I'm sorry," he repeated, mindful of the child standing between them. "It was all my fault. I didn't mean for you to get hurt."

She winced and color flooded her face, leaving the thin scar on her cheek to stand out in pale relief.

Another souvenir from Kayla's father?

"I'm sorry," he said again, impotently. He reached to touch the scar, and Christine avoided his touch with a glare.

"Sorry you lied, sorry I got hurt, or sorry I found out about your little side business? Kayla, out," she snapped, pointing at the door. She raked Michael with her eyes. "Don't bother calling Garibaldi. We'll be gone before he gets here."

The girl lagged behind. "Can he come with us?"

Michael said, "What side business?"

Christine looked ready to scream or cry or both. "No, he cannot come with us," she snapped at her daughter. "Let's go, we're leaving." She tried to herd Kayla out of the shop, followed faithfully by the shaggy red lion. "No, Thor. You're staying here."

That announcement provoked a snarl from the cat and a piteous wail from Kayla. Thor spun around and planted himself in front of Christine. Kayla worked her way up into a full-scale crying jag—and boy, she was loud—and Michael took advantage of the resulting confusion. He grabbed the knapsack.

Christine picked her daughter up and started for the door, ready to leave him again. Michael's heart twisted at the sight of the little blonde head tucked trustingly against dark curls and pale skin.

His?

For the thousandth time, he thought that he would give anything to go back in time and replay that night, to undo whatever had been done. But that was impossible—they could only go forward.

"Christine." He deliberately kept his voice mild. She stopped and turned just inside the shop, clearly past ready to be on the first bus out of town.

"Yes?"

He didn't answer, just dangled the blue knapsack in front of her. "Missing something?"

Oh God. Christine's grip went lax. Kayla slid to the ground, wrapped her arms around Thor, and glared mutinously at her mother.

Christine barely noticed. Michael had figured out where she'd hidden the amulets. It was over.

She thought of the night she had been swamped by a huge wave and tumbled off the jetty into the sea. When she had struggled up from the turmoil beneath the surface to catch a breath of air, fierce pellets of ice had stung her face and flailing hands until it had been easier to let the weight of her child drag them both beneath again.

It felt like that now, like she had been battling to keep her head above the water and her time was almost at an end. But just as Horst's hand had clamped her wrist with wiry strength and dragged her to shore that night long ago, another hand might hold her salvation, if only she was brave enough to take it.

Michael Finch. Betrayer or husband? Fiend or father? Neither or both?

She shook her dark hair out of her eyes and summoned the strength to glare. "What do you want?"

He shouldered the knapsack and grinned a ghost of his old, cocky grin. "A night with my wife."

"Been a while?" She slapped at him with words while the heat flared low in her body, reminding her that it had been a while for her as well. Eight years, to be exact.

He snorted. "Don't flatter yourself, Dewdrop." He drew the name out like a curse. "I don't want your body. I want information." He glanced at Kayla. "An explanation."

On the walk to Horst's little bungalow, Michael noticed that Christine kept the hungry cat between them. It amused and annoyed him that she was going to such lengths to keep him from the child. And it made him wonder just what she was trying to hide.

He assumed that Horst was one of the enormous men who had accosted him outside the candle shop earlier that day. But when the door opened to Christine's soft knock, Michael found himself staring into empty space. He looked down a foot or so and didn't recognize the man grinning up at him.

"Down here, buddy. When the Creator handed out height, I was absent. I'm Horst." The man was clad in bike shorts and a fuchsia sweatshirt advertising Farewell Gay Pride Day.

Michael shook his hand and was surprised at the strength of Horst's grip. Then he remembered the sign next to the candle shop: Horst's Yoga Palace. No wonder the guy was fit. He tied himself in knots for a living.

"Michael Finch."

Horst nodded. "We met earlier, but I'm not sure you were conscious enough for introductions to stick."

Michael vaguely remembered wiry arms lifting him, dragging him onto the cot in the back room. "That was you? Thanks. How'd you get those thugs to let me go?"

"Aw, Big Jim was just protecting Doodles. You scared the heck out of him when you hit your head on the railing and knocked yourself out. He was afraid you were dead."

Christine had returned from settling Kayla in time to hear Horst's words. "Big Jim hit you? I thought you said it was—"

She looked to Horst, who shook his head. "Big Jim and his boys. They were on their way to help you with that display case. When they saw this big guy chasing you yelling someone else's name, they took matters into their own hands, so to speak."

"But I thought . . ."

"It wasn't Garibaldi. There's not even any reason to think he's in town. You jumped to the wrong conclusion, Doodles. Haven't I warned you about that before?"

Christine stared at Horst for a moment, and Michael was sure that they weren't talking about the incident outside the shop anymore. Then she shrugged. "It doesn't matter." She stalked out, saying, "I'm going to say goodnight to Kayla now. She'll sleep here and we'll walk to my cottage."

Horst gestured Michael to a chair at the kitchen table, then took one himself. "Quite a shock you had today," he observed mildly, steepling his fingers in front of his face. "Finding your wife alive and all."

Deciding that Horst probably knew many of the answers he sought, Michael nodded and answered honestly. "That's an understatement. I only found out she was dead two days ago. For some reason, the investigators overlooked the newspaper clipping."

"Truly?" Horst looked surprised. "That's odd. They showed up back in—" He interrupted himself. "Never mind. What are you going to do now?"

Michael frowned, the motion pulling at the bruises on his face and the split in his lip. "Are you asking what my intentions are? Beats me. I came to Farewell to bury my wife. I hadn't planned beyond that. Which reminds me—"

He stood, taking the knapsack with him as he walked to the long row of kitchen cabinets. Horst watched in silence as Michael opened several cupboards before finding what he wanted.

"I took these as a sort of blackmail. They're obviously important to her, though I have no idea why. I have a feeling you do."

Michael took several cans of soup and baked beans out of the cabinet and replaced them with the three candles he took from the knapsack. He didn't miss the way Horst's eyes widened at the sight of them.

"I thought so." He stuffed the cans into the knapsack so the substitution wouldn't be obvious right away.

"Why are you leaving them here?" Horst's eyes were wary as they looked at the closed cupboard door. "They give me the creeps."

Michael shrugged. "They're important to her. I'd like you to keep the candles in case I leave and don't come back."

A sweet voice rose from the other room. Christine was bidding her daughter good night.

"She says Kayla isn't mine." It wasn't really a question, but Michael knew from the look in Horst's eye that there was an answer. Unfortunately, it wasn't the one he wanted.

"It is incredibly, totally not my place to tell you." Horst glanced at the kitchen cabinet. "But if you listen to your heart—and your head—I think you already know the answer."

She's yours, whispered that voice in the back of Michael's mind, the purring one that wasn't really there.

Horst's lips curved, and Michael got the feeling that the little man had heard the voice too.

Michael followed Christine's footprints along the beach and caught up to her on the porch of a tiny cottage near the far arm of Pirate's Cove. They didn't speak as she opened the unlocked door and waved him inside.

It was a homey little place, familiar yet not. The décor was a blend of things he would've expected Christine to choose, like the soft afghan on the threadbare sofa, and things such as the boldly slashed abstract painting over the fireplace that he never would've expected her to like.

As he watched her set a teapot to boil, he was forced to accept that his quick fantasy that they could go right back to where they had been was completely asinine. She wasn't the same woman he had married. She was stronger now, but it was a brittle strength, a bright-eyed defiance that he thought would crumble eventually, leaving—what?

Christine or Dewdrop? Both or neither? He missed the Chrissy he had known, the shy, fragile girl who had loved him utterly. But the woman making tea with quick, nervous hands drew him in unexpected ways.

When she pressed shaking fingers to her temples, he hesitated to go to her.

He didn't know everything about this woman. He couldn't predict her every thought or word as he could have Chrissy's. He knew how she tasted, and the memory sent a quick thrill through his loins. But he didn't know how the curve of her hip would feel beneath his hand, or how her body would feel arched against his as he plunged into her without the daunting barrier of her virginity between them.

The picture had his body leaping to attention, and he coughed against the sudden tightness in his throat. The noise must have startled Christine, for she dropped one of the full mugs of tea. It fell to the floor and broke.

She cursed shakily and dropped to her knees in the puddle of tea and started to gather ceramic shards with jerky motions. She yelped when one of the sharp edges gashed her hand, and Michael hauled her up from the floor and held her palm to the light.

He could feel her trembling under his hand, and when he looked into her eyes and found them unfocused and nearly crossed with pain, he cursed himself for not having noticed sooner.

"You're getting a migraine. Damn it, Christine, why didn't you say something?" Suddenly her unusual gracelessness made sense.

"I'm fine. I don't have time to be sick. Besides, I outgrew my headaches." She pulled away from him and pressed a dishtowel to the cut on her hand. "You said you wanted to talk. So talk." She swayed ever so slightly on her feet.

Michael ignored her snappishness and began to rummage through her kitchen cabinets. "Do you still keep your meds in the kitchen?" He found the pills on a top shelf, far above Kayla's reach. The prescription was a month old. "Outgrew them, you say?" He arched an eyebrow at Christine, but she had closed her eyes and was leaning against the wall.

He popped the top and shook out two capsules. He took a clean cup from the drainer near the sink and half-filled it from a bottle of spring water he found in the fridge exactly where he expected it to be.

"Take these."

"No. They'll knock me out, and you wanted to talk. Let's talk." She turned a delicate shade of green and screwed her eyes shut.

"Don't be stupid," he suggested mildly. "Take the pills and we'll talk in the morning."

"I can't—"

"Trust me."

She shook her head. "You have no idea how much that isn't going to happen." But she took the pills and swallowed the water he held out to her. He knew what she was trying to say. She couldn't be weak in front of him.

He might be a deliberate man, but he wasn't a stupid one. Sometime in the last hour or so, his half-formed belief that she had gone off with a lover had faded, as had some of his anger.

Something had happened to her. Something awful, something he couldn't begin to understand without her help. Something that had taken her away and caused her to doubt him.

Caused her to fear him.

She protested feebly when he lifted her into his arms, and he hushed her with his lips at her temple, kissing the pain away. "It's okay. You're safe with me. I'll protect you, I swear. I'm not sure what happened, but I'll fix it."

He found the bedroom easily and laid her on the narrow mattress where she curled into a hard knot of pain that excluded him. He doused the lights and went back into the kitchen in search of his cell phone.

The battery light was blinking balefully, and he was pretty sure the charger was back in his office at the Harding

58

Building. So he used the phone in the kitchen to place his call.

He got Jonas's answering machine again, only this time there was a weird clicking noise in the background.

"Jo? It's Mike again. I hope you got my other message that Chrissy is alive. I'm here with her now. When you get a chance, can you send the investigators out here? There's something weird going on."

Michael stared out the kitchen window toward the night-black ocean and the silver circle of the moon that splashed blue light down on the waves.

"And Jo? She has a kid. A beautiful little girl." He stared out into the night again and felt a small smile curve his split lip. "I think I'm a daddy."

He stood motionless, letting the hope work its way through him. Jonas's answering machine beeped as the recording ended.

The phone disconnected itself helpfully after some minutes—

After the trace had been completed.

Chapter Five

Christine twisted in her bed. The headache crushed her brain, and the drugs worked their insidious way into her dreams. The sheets tangled around her like arms.

Hot, sweaty arms.

"Christ, she's a pretty one, isn't she?" The voice, rough and urgent, came from behind her ear. She could see out through the tinted windows of the dingy white van, but nobody could see in. Nobody could see him hold the knife to her throat and rub himself against her backside.

The bored man with the switchblade glanced over at her. "Yeah, sure, Garibaldi. She's okay." He returned to his entertainment, which consisted of flicking the knife open and shut. Open and shut. Open and shut.

"Do you think the boss would mind much if we played with her a bit before he gets here?" the man behind her asked.

Christine strained against the coarse ropes binding her wrists and ankles and made mewling sounds around the dirty T-shirt they had jammed in her mouth. At first she'd sagged against the bonds, sure that her life was over. She'd been well and truly betrayed by the one man she trusted. Death seemed a relief.

But that numb defeat hadn't lasted long, not once the men had begun to talk about her as if she were an interesting toy.

Switchblade shrugged. "I don't think so. He just said she called from Miami and we should go pick her up and hold her until he could come question her about the stuff."

"Do you think he'd give us a bonus if we got her to tell us where the stones are?" The man that Switchblade had called Garibaldi chuckled in her ear, and his other hand crept to her stomach, where she carried a tiny seed of life. She had to live. For her child. *Their* child. Bile rose at Garibaldi's slimy touch, but she willed it away and breathed as deeply as she could around the rag, looking for an opportunity to escape.

She could scream later.

"What did you have in mind?" Flicking his knife open and shut, open and shut, Switchblade looked slightly interested. "Can I cut her?"

Christine could feel Garibaldi shrug. "Sure, mark her face up a little, but don't kill her, just in case." He stroked his hand across one of her breasts, heavy and sensitive with pregnancy, and squeezed her nipple until she moaned, which excited him even more. "Then we'll have ourselves a little party while we wait."

His hand moved lower, and Christine realized she had been wrong.

It was time to scream *now*.

"Jesus!" Michael jerked out of the chair where he'd been snoozing and was almost to the bedroom before he even realized where he was. The wailing continued unabated.

"No-ooo!" Christine was thrashing on her bed with her hands held in front of her and the scar on her cheek standing out like a slash of chalk against the fevered flush of her face.

When he reached down to take her in his arms, she reacted like a cornered animal, scratching at him and fighting, screaming and wailing all the while. As he caught an elbow in the teeth, Michael thought fleetingly that it was a good thing that the nearest cottage was out of earshot, otherwise he'd have Horst barging in with a shotgun any moment now.

"Chrissy! It's okay. You're having a dream." A real fun one from the sounds of it. "A nightmare. You're okay. I'm here. You're okay." He held her down until she stopped trying to gouge his eyes out and went limp, sobbing heart-broken cries with her eyes still shut in sleep.

Jesus, she'd nearly taken another eight years off his life, Michael thought as his heart began to slow back to normal. Needing to be comforted as much as he needed to comfort, he kicked off his salty shoes and ruined pants and stripped out of his ragged shirt. Clad in boxers and an undershirt, he crawled into bed beside her.

"You're okay. You're safe." He repeated the words in a mindless litany, stroking her back until she quieted and sank deeper into blessed, drugged unconsciousness.

"It's okay," he said one last time to himself. "You're safe."

He cuddled Christine's warm, curvy body against his and sank his nose into her soft, fragrant curls. As he slid toward sleep, Michael heard a rough-voiced whisper in his head and knew that he had spoken falsely, unknowingly.

You're not safe at all. They're coming.

The next morning, a soft noise woke Michael. His muscles tensed into a battle readiness he hadn't even known he possessed. He scanned the tiny, sunlit room and saw no danger in the plain oak dresser, the cheerful cream trim, the fluttering blue curtains—or the questioning eyes that peered around the half-shut door.

Kayla.

He heard the front door close quietly and guessed that Horst had brought her over and, seeing that Michael was in bed with Christine, assumed that they had discussed matters and resolved them happily.

Or not.

Michael wondered, not for the first time, whose side Horst was on. He seemed awfully ready to push Christine at a man she claimed not to trust. Remembering the odd, almost otherworldly aura that surrounded the yogi, Michael grinned. He didn't know why the man liked him, but he wasn't about to look a gift Horst in the mouth.

Christine sighed and murmured resentfully when he eased away from her and climbed out of bed. He grimaced with the need, but donned his ruined shirt and pants. He didn't think it was time yet to parade around the house in his underwear. Holding a quieting finger to his lips, Michael tucked the covers around Chrissy and left the room, shutting the door firmly behind him and Kayla.

He knew that Chris needed to sleep after a migraine. That much wouldn't have changed in eight years. He found himself wondering what else would be the same.

"I want to show you something." Kayla tugged on Michael's hand and led him to her little bedroom, where Thor lay draped across a tiny child's bed amid a profusion of stuffed toys.

She grabbed an irregular chunk of rough wood off a pint-size desk and held it out to him. "This is my favorite thing of all. When Mommy says I'm old enough to carve wood, instead of just soap and candles, I'm going to carve this. Isn't it pretty?"

It just looked like an irregular chunk of oak to Michael. He felt the breath back up in his throat. "What do you see inside it?"

"A kitten," she said as if it should be obvious. She pushed the knot of wood into his hands and pointed to swirls of grain with one small finger. "See? There's its tail and here's its nose and its ears. It's all curled up like Thor does in winter, only way smaller."

Michael stared numbly at the piece of wood. He remembered when he could touch a rough block of hardwood, close his eyes, and feel how the tree had grown. Once upon a time he could look at a fallen oak and see all the magic that waited inside it. He could touch a burl such as this and feel it vibrate with the desire to be carved. He had taken all of the wild energy that had made him follow Jonas to hell and back and had poured it into the art, the magic, so that he would be worthy of a princess.

Now he stroked the raw wood and felt only bark. He looked at the intertwined grains and found only a pretty pattern. He saw no furry paw or hint of whisker.

But his daughter did.

Christine awoke alone in her bed, having slept as well as she could remember for a long time. There was still a dull ache behind her eyes, but aspirin would take care of that and she'd be ready to face the day.

And Michael.

A deeply feminine part of her knew that he had held her in the night and chased the demons away. That same part of her knew that migraine or no, she wouldn't have let her guard down that far if she had really, truly believed that he would hurt her.

But although her heart claimed him innocent, her angry, distrustful head insisted that he was not entirely blameless. Not entirely trustworthy.

Not entirely safe.

Gingerly, she dressed in jeans, a soft pink jersey, and moccasins. It wasn't until she caught herself posing in front of the floor-length mirror on the back of the door and smoothing the shirt over her breasts that she realized what she was doing.

She was primping.

"Gah!" Thoroughly annoyed with herself, Christine yanked open the door. As she left the bedroom, she gave herself a quick splash of scent—just because she noticed the bottle sitting on her dresser, she assured herself, not because it had been Michael's favorite.

She found Kayla in her room, sitting on the bed with Thor at her side. They were both staring at a piece of wood Kayla kept insisting she was going to carve into a cat.

The little girl looked up. "Is Michael my Daddy?"

Christine thought her heart stopped at the question. Simply stopped. But it couldn't have because a second later it was slamming in her eardrums like the Farewell Pep Band's kettledrum. "Why do you ask that, Kayla?"

In answer, the child reached into her desk drawer and pulled out a faded and creased page torn from a magazine. Christine recognized it even before her daughter smoothed it open.

She remembered Michael's giddy joy when he was featured in a national artisan's magazine. They had made such plans for the extra income the exposure would bring to his carved-furniture business. They had even talked of setting up a studio where he could display his work and add to his growing reputation.

After they married. After he promised her that he would have no more contact with Jonas Harding and that he would never again break the law.

"Where did you get this?"

Kayla ducked her head and looked guilty. "I took it from your drawer. I saw you looking at it one night and crying, so I took it. It's my Dad, isn't it? He could see the things in the wood, right?"

Christine sighed and looked at the picture. He was so young then. His hair was long, his face was unlined, and the grin he had flashed the camera held just a bit of the devil.

Oh God. How she had loved him.

She looked at her daughter, at the rows of carved candles peering down from a shelf, and sighed again for the man who'd lost the magic that had kept him sane. Alive. "Yes, Kayla. That's your father. He could see things in wood like you can."

"Why can't he now?"

Through the gingham curtains, Christine could see where the sand between the dunes had been gouged with deep, angry footprints. She sighed and her heart broke a little for the boy who'd become a man. "I don't know, Kayla. You stay here with Thor, okay? I think I'd better go talk to Michael."

She found him standing at the water's edge, staring off across Pirate's Cove with his hands jammed in the pockets of his wrinkled pants and his tattered shirt flapping in the sea breeze.

"Michael?" She laid a tentative hand on his shoulder, and he stiffened and shrugged her off.

"Are you happy now?" His voice was low and rough.

"Happy?"

"Is that what you wanted? To know how much you hurt me? To know that not only did you keep my daughter away from me, you also took my art when you left? Well, you did. The first time, I thought that maybe it was too soon after you left, that my mind wasn't settled enough to carve. But it didn't get better."

He held his hands up in front of his face. Stared at the

fading scars. "I lost the magic, Christine. When you left, you took my soul with you." He dropped his hands to his sides and whipped around to glare at her. "Are you happy?"

"I—"

"Because whatever you think I've done to you, however angry you are at me for whatever you've been through, believe me, you've caused me plenty of pain too, babe. And Kayla. Jesus, Christine!"

He stalked away from her, then turned and stomped back to where she stood rooted in the sand. She shook her head, not sure how to defend her actions. "Michael, I didn't—"

"A daughter," he repeated, grabbing Christine by the shoulders and shaking her. "I have a daughter."

He moved suddenly, almost violently, and Christine was sure that the time had come. He was going to yank out an ugly snub-nosed revolver, pistol-whip her with it, and drag her carcass to where Garibaldi awaited her.

Instead he clamped his arms around her and held her so hard her ribs twanged where they'd knit long ago. "I have a daughter," he muttered into her hair, and she realized that he was shaking all over.

"I have a daughter," he repeated, and she felt his lips move against her temple as he murmured, "Christine, we have a daughter."

As naturally as breathing, she answered him by turning her lips to his. "Yes. A beautiful daughter," she whispered against his mouth, and when they kissed it was not in anger or punishment or even simple need.

Their kiss was a reminder of the ties that bound them one to another even when they'd been so long apart. It was a celebration of the child they had made between them on a single night of what she had believed to be pure, sustaining love.

But although it began as a symbolic meeting of lips, their contact soon flared bright, and flames licked like a thousand candles along Christine's body where it touched his.

She said his name, or maybe he said hers, it was all the same, and they sank together to the sand of Farewell, and she felt the good solid weight of his body press hers into the lee of the dune.

Their legs tangled and rubbed one against the other, and she moaned when he took his lips from hers and moved them to kiss the hollow behind her ear that only he knew of, and his hand began a leisurely cruise from the nape of her neck to the curve of her hip.

She tried to tangle her fingers in his thick hair, but the short, spiky strands slid from her grasp, so instead she clutched at the shreds of his shirt where they barely covered his slick chest and hard abdomen.

It felt the same, like satin over old mahogany, and she trailed her fingertips up and down his taut belly where the wiry hair narrowed to a point until he grabbed her wrist to hold her hand still while he rolled her underneath him once again.

He took her under with just his lips and his hands and the feel of his body above and around hers, and she thought fiercely, *If this is another dream, then I'm never waking up!*

But it wasn't a dream, she was sure of it. It couldn't be a dream when the rough stubble on his jaw abraded the smooth skin of her throat and the feel of his breath on her scarred cheek brought tears to her eyes.

"Michael," she whispered, just to test the name, and he reared up over her and leaned on one elbow so he could touch the side of her face gently and stroke the scar she had earned in Miami.

"Christine, I—"

There was a popping sound, and surprise appeared on Michael's face as his arm gave way beneath him.

That was when Christine realized she was dreaming after all.

And the nightmare had begun again.

Chapter Six

Michael felt the sting on his upper arm, a quick burning that reminded him of a hot wood chip embedding itself under his skin when his old table saw spat back at him.

Then he smelled the blood. His blood.

Christine gasped as the second popping noise was followed by a puff of sand near his outstretched hand. "Michael!"

Someone was shooting at them. With silenced weapons.

"Christ!" Reacting, he rolled them both over the top of the dune, thinking only to get the mound of grassy sand between his wife and the gun.

His mind went into overdrive, a preternatural sort of clarity that must come with extreme terror, and he saw events unfolding as if in slow motion. He and Christine slid together down the steep dune where it sloped to the sea, and he heard the men above curse.

"They were right here a minute ago. What'd they do, fly away?" The voice was coarse and slow and thankfully coming from behind the wrong dune.

"We better not lose her again or the boss'll have our heads. Remember what happened last time?" There was a general murmur of agreement and Michael wondered what exactly had happened the last time. Wondered who the boss was—and what he had to do with Christine's disappearance eight years earlier.

Get up, run! They're coming! The inner voice sounded faint, far away, and Michael wondered if it had tried to warn him of the men. Wondered if he'd ignored it to kiss his wife.

Michael scrambled to his feet and hauled Christie up after him. She tugged him toward the deserted end of the beach.

"No, this way." He gestured with his chin toward the town. "There's nothing that way except sand, water, and saw grass. We'll get more help in town."

There was a shout from above. "Hey! There's blood over here and marks in the sand." A blonde head popped over the crest of the dune. "There they are! Come on, she's not gone. We'll get our bonus yet."

"No," Christine said with quiet intensity. "Not toward the town. I won't lead them into Farewell." When she saw that he didn't get it, she added, "When Kayla heard the shots she would've run to Horst's house—that's our plan. She's in town, Michael. We have to lead them away and give Horst time to hide her."

Without further argument, spurred by the sight of three men sliding down the dune toward them, Michael clutched his injured arm to his side and ran down the beach in a drunken zigzag, dragging Christine beside him.

The erratic path would foil the aim of their attackers. At least he hoped it would. It always worked in the movies.

"The jetty." She jerked away and sprinted across the shifting sand toward the jetty on which he had stood not quite a day ago, believing her dead.

"What the—?"

She ran to a stone that thrust up from the beach to tower high above the other rocks. "Come on! This way." She waved at him to hurry up and started up the sheer rock face, jamming her hands and feet against the surface and shimmying up like a spider across its web.

She was at the top in a moment, even before Michael reached the base of the stone. "Christine, this is crazy! We'll be trapped!"

Pop! A chip of rock detached from the sheer face and embedded itself stingingly in his cheek. The men were shooting again, and their aim wasn't bad.

Christine looked down at him and beckoned him to climb. "Hurry, Michael. They're getting closer. Just climb! Trust me." Then she disappeared and he heard her footsteps crunch on dried seaweed.

"There he is, get him! Don't shoot him again, you idiots. We'll bring him in, maybe get a double bonus this time." Michael could hear movement at his flank, and the thought of being worth a bonus to anyone was enough to propel him up the rock face.

"Michael! Hurry, they're coming." Christine waved frantically from two rocks away; and sure enough, Michael could hear the sounds of pursuit over the ringing in his ears and the singing pain in his bleeding arm. She had already made it a third of the way out toward the blue water by jumping from rock to rock and seemed appalled that he was so far behind. "They're catching up!" She started to go back for him, but a look at the others changed her mind. "Hurry!"

Michael was about to ask why when there was a brisk clapping noise and the broken lobster pot next to his left foot exploded in a puff of fishy wood.

That weapon hadn't been silenced, and it sounded mean. Apparently they'd decided he wasn't worth a bonus after all.

He looked behind. They were ugly. They were armed. And they were getting closer. A trio of splashes in the foamy water reinforced the second of those observations, and Michael bolted across another few rocks until he reached Christine at the end of the jetty.

He slid to a halt at the last rock and almost fell into the black, roiling water that churned bare inches from the tips of his shoes.

Now what?

Trapped. He spun to face the uglies and shoved Christine behind him, almost pushing her off the jetty. "I hope you have a plan," he hissed, praying there was a reason, other than sheer blind panic that she'd run down the jetty.

"Jump," she hissed back. "Jump in and dive deep. Follow me."

She thought they were going to outswim bullets? He spun around and stared at her in horror, turning his back on the uglies for a second.

"That's your plan? What kind of a plan is that?" He shook his head and turned back to meet his fate, muttering as he did so, " 'Trust me,' she says. 'Trust me.' Well, I did. Now look where it's gotten me."

Christine called him a nasty name behind his back and poked him deliberately on his bloody arm. He ignored her and tried to think. He was a smart man. There had to be a better plan. There had to be some way at least one of them could escape to protect Kayla, he thought, and suddenly realized that Christine might have had to make a similar decision. There must have come a time when she'd chosen to hide herself to protect her child.

He'd have to think about that later.

If there was to be a "later."

Holding his hands out in the same friendly gesture that had gotten him punched by Dewdrop's friends the previous afternoon—God, it seemed like a lifetime ago—he said, "Gentlemen, I'm sure there's been some sort of misunderstanding that we can work out." Either by logic, threats, or payment.

He heard a small splash behind him and figured the idiots were shooting into the water again. He hoped like hell that they'd stick with the idea of capturing Christine rather than killing her.

"Give us the jewelry." Ugly Two of the three spoke first, the words slurred by a scar that ran across his face and bisected his lower lip.

Michael took a quick inventory. Swiss Army watch, ten years old. The silver and turquoise money clip Chrissy had given him for his high school graduation. His wedding band. "I'm not sure what jewelry you mean."

Stall. He had to stall them. That little splash had been Chrissy jumping into the water, he was sure of it. He needed to stall them long enough for her to swim back to shore and run to town. Maybe she could persuade the fisherman and his buddies to help. What they might lack in firepower, they made up for in attitude.

Ugly One waved a baseball bat in the air. Apparently he didn't rate a gun. "You know what jewelry we're talking about. Where'd she hide it? Hey—where'd she go?"

"Into the water, moron. She jumped in and didn't come back up. Must've drowned, so we'll have to get the info out of this one here." Ugly Two stepped forward and leveled the gun at Michael. "Tell us where she hid the amulets."

"I. Don't. Know. What. You're. Talking. About." Michael spaced the words out and enunciated them clearly, hoping that at least one-third of the uglies would get the message.

Ugly Two spat a curse and waved the gun alarmingly. "Tell me! If we don't come back with it . . ."

When Michael made no move to speak, the heretofore silent Ugly Three, a tall man with short brown hair and a wicked slashing scar across his throat, shrugged as if it made no matter, pulled a much larger, fittingly unattractive automatic weapon from beneath his cheerful red windbreaker, and pointed its business end at Michael's left eye.

"He doesn't know a damn thing. Let's just do him and go back to the cottage. If the woman survived in the water, she'll go there for the kid."

Kayla. They were going to kill him first, then hurt Kayla and Christine. Well, thought Michael, if he was going to die, he was taking at least one of them with him. Hopefully he could buy enough time doing so that his wife and child could escape.

With his daughter's name on his lips and an image of Christine in his mind, Michael crouched, ready to leap on his attackers.

Go after her! Dive. Swim down! I've got them.

The roar in his head absolutely wasn't his imagination this time. As Michael turned and leapt into the water, he saw a reddish blur leap up behind the three men. Heard panicked shouts. Gunfire.

And a feline roar of pain.

Then he heard nothing but the thunder of surf on submerged rocks and the awful, inexorable sucking of the riptide that grabbed him and wouldn't let go.

Wouldn't let him breathe.

He was pulled into the darkness, away from light and warmth and men with guns. Away from his daughter and the valiant lion that had spoken in his mind. The water pressed on him as though a thousand fishermen's fists were pummeling him from every direction. Then there was a tunnel, black as night.

Wasn't there supposed to be light at the end of the tunnel?

But there wasn't. There was only the cold and the water and the unbreakable grip of the riptide.

And then it was gone. His head broke the surface and he

could breathe. But he still couldn't see in the pitch black.

"Christ!" He sucked in a lungful of stale air and coughed it back out, sinking with the motion and swallowing another mouthful of brine. His voice bounced back at him from all sides, and the rippling echoes of the water let him know there was no way out. "Where the hell am I?"

And where was his wife?

"Chrissy? Christine!"

He cast around wildly, flailing at the brackish ice water until his hand brushed against cool flesh.

For a moment he had the horrible thought that maybe he'd grabbed hold of some giant eel that lurked in whatever cave they'd come to. But then he touched cloth and fingers and knew that he held his wife's hand.

"Chrissy!" When she didn't answer, didn't move, he shook her in sudden panic. "Chrissy, are you okay?"

Now that was about the dumbest question he'd ever asked. Of course she wasn't okay. He wasn't sure they'd ever be okay again. But he shook her again anyway and was relieved to feel her shiver.

"U-up. On th-th ledge. L-l-lamp." She pointed in the darkness and the water and the echoes. He towed her in that direction and found the ledge by running into it face-first.

"Ow! Urgh . . ." He would've cursed but his mouth was too full of salty water to make it worth the effort. He grabbed the ledge with one hand and boosted Christine out of the water with the other before scrambling up beside her.

"Where's the lamp?" He was sure at least some of the salt in his mouth came from splitting his lip . . . again.

"Over-r by th-th-th wall. Hook. M-matches." She was shaking so hard beside him Michael wondered that she could speak at all. He wondered how much of it was from the freezing cold salt water and how much of it was from worry.

Kayla was out there. Was she okay?

Michael half-expected an answer from within his head, but the purring voice was silent.

Maybe he'd imagined it after all.

He felt carefully for the wall this time. It took his shaking hands half a dozen matches to light the propane lantern, and then he almost doused the flame with the water raining down from his clothes and hair. But the wick caught and held and sent a soft radiance spilling over his scarred hands and across Christine's face. Her eyes were closed, and for an instant the gentle light smoothed away the lines of time and stress and she looked like the eight-year-old girl he had come across in the woods, crying that she'd be good if her daddy came home. He felt a surge of tenderness for that child, and for the woman the child had become.

Shaken, Michael shifted the lantern to light the way, wincing when the bullet wound on his arm pulled. It didn't really hurt yet. He wasn't sure if that was a good sign.

They were in a tiny cave, all right. The sphere of light reflected off rocky walls all around them except where the sandy floor became black, cold water.

Christine was shaking so hard she could barely breathe, but she managed to point at a stack of oilcloth bundles on a ledge a few feet above the water. He ripped open the first and breathed a sigh of relief.

"Thank God." He yanked out several blankets and advanced upon Christine. "Here, get out of those wet clothes and wrap yourself in these."

She stared glassy-eyed at the lantern with her arms folded around her torso and rocked back and forth as she shivered. Seeing that she was in no state to help him, Michael knelt and fumbled with her soggy shirt. His fingers shook with more than the cold when he pushed the material aside and encountered the delicate lace half-shells of her bra.

The woman he married had worn plain, serviceable underthings well suited to a schoolteacher and wife of a backwoods carver, not this frothy, frivolous sort of confection. Then again, that girl hadn't had nearly the body of the woman he was touching now. He traced a slow finger down the lace, feeling warmer by the minute.

Christine's rocking slowed and her eyes began to focus on his finger as it traveled across her breast. Slow blood surged through Michael when the nipple half-hidden by satin pebbled under his touch and her shivering changed to a quiver of awareness.

The cave seemed warmer now, dark and intimate. It seemed a place out of reality. A haven. A space where all could be forgiven.

"Michael." Her voice was barely a whisper but he responded to it, reaching to gather her in his arms.

Ripe pain sliced through his body at the action, and the cold, salty wound on his arm started to throb in earnest. Christine's face suddenly swayed alarmingly back and forth, and the floor bucked wildly. Then he saw the rock and sand rushing up to meet him and he welcomed the black oblivion.

"Michael!" Warmed out of her chilled lethargy by his brief touch, Christine lunged for Michael as he slumped to the ground and rolled toward the water. "Don't you dare," she ordered as she wedged an arm under him. "If you fall in there I'm not going back in after you."

Her words echoed back at her strangely, just as the shadows cast by her little lantern danced and gibbered at her fears. Her body echoed, too, an odd combination of hypothermia and almost painful longing.

Echoes. So many half-forgotten memories. Always before, when she'd swum to Pirate's Cave either to stash provisions or to make sure that the tunnel was still open, she'd found the tiny fissure a welcoming place. A safe place. Sure, there were echoes of its previous occupants in the broken manacles bolted to the wall just above the waterline, and the worn tracks in the rock where she guessed heavy loads had passed on their way to wherever. But the cave itself was a snug bolthole where she'd kept important things. She had always intended to bring the candles here and hide them away.

Now it was too late.

Christine sighed and rolled Michael away from the water's edge. She propped him against the wall as best she could with her chilled, failing strength. His arm was still bleeding sluggishly. She was cold and getting colder by the moment. It wouldn't help them if she passed out too. She needed to get warm.

Then she needed to get out of the cave and keep Kayla away from the men.

Trying to block the memory of Michael's finger on her breast, she yanked her shirt the rest of the way off and pulled a bulky sweater out of an oilskin bag and over her head. Her jeans seemed permanently bonded to her legs, but they soon joined her soggy shirt on the sandy floor, and she replaced them with a similar pair taken from her dry supplies on the ledge.

She'd neglected to provide herself with a fluffy towel or a hairbrush, so she used one of the scratchy wool blankets to dry her hair before piling that blanket on top of the three she'd already layered on Michael's body.

"First aid kit," she muttered to herself as she sorted through the bags she had packed when Kayla was just a baby.

She pushed a waterproof packet aside when it seemed to leap into her hand.

Michael groaned and shifted away from her when she tore what was left of his shirt away from the bullet crease on his upper arm. It was long but shallow, big enough that it must hurt like the very devil, but superficial enough to have Christine drawing a relieved breath.

She swiped at the cut with a couple of alcohol-moistened towelettes she'd taken from the Hyannis Lobster Shack and bound the arm tightly with gauze and tape. If her fingertips traced the quiet line of muscle across his shoulder and upper arm, if her lips touched the skin above her makeshift bandage, if she pressed her face to his chest and listened to the steady thump of his heart and felt the returning warmth of his body—he would never know.

It wasn't like she'd forgiven him or anything.

Satisfied, she rocked back on her heels and surveyed her handiwork. The wound probably needed stitches, but she didn't have needle, thread, or the skill to sew him up. He'd have to live with her version of doctoring for now, until they could get him back to Farewell. He'd probably have a new scar to add to the collection that ranged his body from years of woodworking.

If they lived that long, that is.

The tide had continued to rise, and now the water lapped at Michael's toes. Somehow she would have to get him up onto the higher ledge before they both got wet again, but as she raised the lantern to peer past her supplies, she realized they wouldn't both fit up there.

She had planned for her and Kayla to hide there in an emergency, but never in her wildest fantasies had she imagined sharing the cave with Michael Finch.

"Some of this stuff'll have to go." She pulled a few waterproof sacks down off the ledge and piled the less important items at the back of the cave, farthest from the water.

Michael was showing no signs of returning to consciousness, and she began to worry that he was hurt worse than she had thought. Maybe the knock on the head he'd gotten from Big Jim had shaken something loose.

Did she have one of those instant cold packs in her stuff? She couldn't remember. Muttering to herself again, she started to rifle through one of the remaining waterproof bags, upending it on the ledge and pawing through the contents distractedly.

"Where was that . . ." She pushed aside a bundle of emergency cash and found a flat, plastic-wrapped package. Thinking that it might be the crushable cold pack, she unwrapped it close to the lantern.

A photograph stared up at her. A bride. A groom.

A promise.

The grainy Polaroid had been one of the last things she had grabbed from the honeymoon suite on her way out, and after Miami she had been determined to destroy it and the false happiness it represented. But just as she had kept her wedding ring and hidden it well, she'd kept the picture.

It had been taken at the reception by a bubbly third-grade teacher from the school where Christine had worked with the younger kids. Her name was . . . Janice or something. Christine could barely remember her; it was as if that wedding reception had happened to someone else, someone she once knew.

"Come on, you guys! I want a picture of the two of you." Janice—or whatever her name was—had shooed Michael and Christine close together and snapped a shot that captured the devil in Michael's eye, the adoration in hers.

She touched trembling fingers to his face in the photograph—a young, unlined face that she had trusted with all her heart and soul. Then she looked in the lantern light to find his face in the cave—an older, tiderer face with new lines of strength and character.

His eyes were open and clear, although tinted with pain. He looked from her to the photograph and back again and smiled a wry grin that hovered somewhere between tears and self-deprecating laughter.

"It seems like about a hundred years ago, doesn't it?" he asked in a voice rough with salt water and strain.

He shifted against the bare rock and looked down to where the chilly sea lapped around his feet, then at the makeshift bandage on his arm that was already soaked through with blood. He touched a finger to a stuffed toy that had fallen from the oilskin bag containing Kayla's things and looked back at Christine.

"I think we need to talk."

Chapter Seven

He remembered another time they had "needed to talk."

At twenty-nine, he had been a husband for just a day, but already he knew those words were a very bad sign for the romantic dinner he'd planned.

The wine was expensive, the music live, and the fragrance of some flower or another was carried across the open dining area right to their table. A pair of candles danced their pinpricks of light and gave off a soft scent that he knew she would appreciate, being that candle making was a little hobby of hers. He had chosen the menu ahead of time, selecting a few of their favorites along with a couple of native dishes that he hoped would make her feel adventurous.

But now they "needed to talk." And he had a feeling he knew what the subject would be. Jonas.

With a sharp pang of regret, Michael remembered the floaty yellow thing she had taken into the bathroom with her when she dressed. It wasn't in evidence now, so he had a hunch it was underneath her soft blue dress.

He realized, with the wisdom of a newly married man who has known his bride since the age of eight, that he would have to speak very carefully if he ever wanted to see that tiny piece of yellow lace.

Because they had "needed to talk"—just as they did now in a little cave as far away from their honeymoon as it was possible to get.

★ ★ ★ ★ ★

She shook her head, the shadows reflecting crazy lantern light off rock walls. "Not now—"

"Yes, now," he interrupted. "You need to tell me what in God's name is going on here, and then we need to get out of here and find Kayla." His teeth began to chatter as the damp coolness of the submerged cave worked its way through the layers of wool blanket.

"Don't tell me what we need to do," she flared. He was reminded again that although this woman bore a superficial resemblance to the girl he married, she was much, much more. More stubborn. More bullheaded. More loyal. More beautiful. "Trust me, if I could get out of here I'd already be gone."

The cave suddenly felt colder than it had moments before. "We can't get out? We're trapped in here?" He knew it came out like an accusation, but he didn't really see the value in escaping guns only to freeze to death in a rocky tomb.

"Of course not. I'm not an idiot. We can get out as soon as the tide turns. Right now the tunnel's too long and the currents are too unpredictable to risk it. We barely made it here in the first place."

He remembered being sucked through the tunnel, felt new bruises blooming on his legs and ribs where the riptide had bounced him around. "Where is 'here'?"

It was a cave, obviously, and just as obviously she came here often enough to have a substantial hoard of supplies waiting for her. He realized the implications and squinted at her through the dim light.

"You were planning this. That's why you ran out on the jetty. We're in the jetty." Another thought struck him, belatedly. "You saved my life."

Seeming calmer than he'd seen her since she miraculously

had come back to life the previous afternoon, Christine shrugged. "To take those questions in order, we're in Pirate's Cave. What's a Pirate's Cove without a cave to hide the booty in? I'm pretty sure from the length of the tunnel that we're actually on the land side of the jetty, probably under or inside that first big rock. The tunnel starts out at the end of the jetty under the waterline, and yes, that was my plan."

She shrugged and glanced again at the photograph she still held. "I have lots of plans, very few of which are relevant now. And yes, I probably did save your life. That is, assuming you're not on Garibaldi's team."

Refusing to rise to the bait, he said mildly, "They'd hardly have shot at me if I was part of their gang, nor would they have discussed bringing me in alive for a bonus." He touched his fingers to the bandage that covered the throbbing wound on his arm.

The very idea of swimming back out through the tunnel with his arm on fire from the salt water made him cringe. That cringe turned to a shiver when a wavelet lunged over his feet and added a colder layer to the wet stickiness of his tattered clothing.

"The tide's still rising. You should come up here." Christine jammed the photo back into a drawstring bag and shoved several bundles to the back of the rocky ledge. "I've made room for you so we can both stay dry. I don't think we should risk a fire—the smoke filters out through the rocks, and they'll see it if they're still in the area."

She patted the ledge next to her in invitation, and Michael stood up, conking his head solidly on the ceiling of the cave. He swore halfheartedly at that and again at the shivers that crawled through him at the feel of his cold, soggy pants on his legs.

Divining the source of his discomfort, Christine shook her

head. "I've got stuff for me and Kayla, nothing that would fit you. You could . . . er . . . take them off."

He couldn't be sure, but he had the strong suspicion she was blushing in the lamplight. Some things, it seemed, hadn't changed.

Michael half-expected her to turn away and fiddle with her bags of supplies while he struggled out of his ruined trousers and shredded shirt, but instead he could feel the burn of her gaze on his body as he stripped.

He was reminded of that day at the lake when he had undressed awkwardly in front of her. This time he didn't leave his shorts on, and when he was naked except for the blood-stained bandage on his arm, he tossed the damp blankets to Christine and crawled up onto the ledge.

There was barely room for the two of them, even after they pushed two more bags over the edge, and finally Michael grew tired of Christine's squirming to make herself comfortable while straining to hold herself as far away from him as she could get in the small space.

"Enough," he commanded and grabbed her with his good arm. He resisted the urge to curse when she stiffened against him. "It's okay. I won't hurt you. It's going to be okay."

He drew her toward him until her sweatered back was pressed against his bare chest. "I seem to remember that this used to work."

Sure enough, her curvy bottom nestled snugly against his groin, and her head fit in the hollow between his shoulder and jaw. When he pulled the blankets over them and cuddled her close, he could almost close his eyes and believe that this was real and the rest of his life was the bad dream.

But if this was real, then so were the tears that fell on his arm like warm little raindrops.

"Christine." She cried harder at his voice, deep, shuddering sobs of hopelessness and tiredness and loss.

He could only dim the lantern and hold on to her in the darkness and wish with all his heart that he could turn the clock back.

"Hush." He pressed his lips to her hot face and stroked a hand down her body in comfort. "Shush, baby. It'll be okay. We'll figure everything out together this time. I'll keep you safe. I promise."

They lay nestled together as her breathing slowed and Michael's grew ragged.

The little cave was getting warmer by the minute, and Michael had a feeling that pretty soon he'd need a quick dip in the freezing pool of water. Anguished as she might be, the feel of Christine's rounded little body under his hand was almost more than he could take.

It had been too long since he'd been close to another human being. Way too long. And his body remembered all too well how much he'd loved the girl who had become his wife.

He eased away from her, hoping to put some distance and damp air between them, but she murmured a protest and caught his hand to pull him near again.

When he was snuggled close, she kept hold of his hand and slid it under her sweater where he found nothing except skin and curves. With dreamlike slowness, she guided his touch until his fingertips found one hard, round nipple.

The scent from her hair spilled over them both, leaving him awash in the smell of sea salt, vanilla, and woman. He wallowed in the smell and the feel of her, even as a part of him recognized that this couldn't possibly be happening.

"Christine," he said warningly even as his hand traced the outline of her ripe breast.

Only a day ago he had believed her dead. Just a few hours

ago she had believed him to be—what? A murderer, it seemed. Less than an hour ago he had learned that she had hidden his own daughter from him for eight long years. Bare minutes ago, they had been chased off the end of the continent by men and bullets.

Yet here they lay, in dark, womblike warmth on a rocky ledge in a tiny hollow called Pirate's Cave.

"Hush," she whispered. "We were supposed to have last night together. Let's make up for it now while we wait for the tide."

She murmured in pleasure when his hand closed firmly on her breast, and she arched in acceptance when he stroked a scarred thumb across her sensitive nipple. His body vibrated with a tumultuous need he'd all but forgotten over the years, and blood surged hard in his veins and roared in his head like the surf.

"Chris," he tried with a thick and heavy voice, the words seeming to come from very far away. "We should talk."

She rolled to face him and placed a quieting finger on his lips, rubbing them moist. "Not now. We have time before the tide turns, and then who knows what will happen? We might have only this one time, like we did before. Do you remember?"

Her lips replaced her finger and she kissed him deep, and he remembered, oh yes, he remembered their one night together.

If, at any time during the last eight years, the devil himself had arisen on a puff of fire and brimstone and offered Michael Finch one more night with his wife, he would have cheerfully dispensed with his soul for the chance to touch her again.

So when she placed a palm on his scruffy cheek to hold his face close to hers another moment and whispered, "Love me,

Michael. Love me again like you did before, just once more," he was lost.

He kissed her tear-wet cheek and the curve of her neck where it met her ear. He kissed the soft, ticklish spot beneath her fragrant hair, and then they both pulled her sweater over her head so he could touch his lips to her soft, round shoulder, just as he'd imagined doing when he first walked into her shop.

She shuddered against him, and he ran his hand over her as he might have one of his favorite carvings—an artist's hand appreciating beauty of form and heart.

Sensing that they both needed comfort as much as heat, he took his time, exploring the new soft spots and unfamiliar curves, as well as returning to well-known places that elicited a soft cry or a sound of pleasure.

When he brushed his fingertips across the slight swelling of her belly, she moaned and writhed against him until he had to grit his teeth to prevent himself from tearing her jeans away and pumping eight years of frustration and anger and soul-killing loneliness into her soft, round body.

Instead he trailed his fingers back to her throat and tipped her head until her lips met his in another kiss, full of ripe flavor and the smell of the sea. While their mouths met in that age-old dance of love, his hand traveled back down to unzip her jeans and slide inside to find her bare beneath.

Bare and wet and ready.

Restraint a ragged cloak around him, Michael slid a finger inside her and felt her shock when she contracted around him and cried out into his mouth, and her climax dampened his hand and snapped what was left of his control.

Even as the aftershocks shuddered through her, he was driving her up again with his lips and teeth and hands while he fought to free her from her jeans. When at last she was as naked as he and was teetering on the brink of another glorious fall, he joined her there, sliding into her in a long, smooth thrust that connected them as surely as the past held them apart.

She tipped over that precious edge again, keening and wrapping her arms and legs around him in a joyous celebration of life, while he concentrated on the pain in his abused arm to keep from following her right away. He felt her contract around him, pulsing with the beat of his heart, and he began to move.

She was crying again, tears sparkling like starlight on her cheeks in the faint light of the dim lantern, and she moved with him in perfect, beautiful rhythm, carrying him with her to the edge of the fall, to the end of the Earth.

This time when she tightened around him, she cried his name, the name she had known him by as a young girl, "Mikey!"

With that he was lost, and he fell with her into that whirling, swirling maelstrom of sensation. As he fell weightlessly to the bottom, he knew that once again he had given her not only his seed but his heart and his dreams and his future.

And that they hadn't been enough for her before.

Christine lay bonelessly across Michael's bare chest and tried to find the energy to regret what she had just done.

Nope. Impossible. She permitted herself a small grin into the feeble light of the lantern.

It might not have solved any of their immediate problems, it certainly hadn't explained Miami or minimized their current danger, but it had felt right.

Very right.

Very, very right.

She sighed, and Michael's chest hair tickled her sensitive

upper lip. He sighed as well, and when he spoke, his words rumbled beneath her cheek.

"I suppose it's time to talk now." He sounded resigned, as if he'd rather not talk at all. Ever.

She could sympathize.

"I guess." She pressed her face closer to his chest, unaccountably reluctant to look him in the eye after what they had just done.

That was silly. She was a woman and a mother and had no reason to feel uncomfortable about her body or what she and her husband did together. But that was the crux of the matter—although they had been married eight years, this was only their second time together. Her second time ever. She supposed it was only natural for it to feel a little strange.

But that thought brought another close on its heels, and she jerked her head up and stared into his eyes before she could remember to be ashamed.

"You didn't divorce me, did you?" She realized that the question had come out belligerently and hastened to backtrack. "Not that you didn't have a right to, what with me disappearing and all. And it's not like you had any reason . . ."

He silenced her as she had done him, with a finger to her lips where she hovered above him. "I never divorced you, Christine."

He winced when he lifted his left hand so the gold band reflected in the weak light. "I never gave up hope that I'd find you and you'd want to come back." When she just stared at him, he shrugged with a little embarrassment. "Yeah, foolish of me, but I've always been foolish where you're concerned."

His words were flip but she could see the pain behind them. "I wish—" She faltered and looked at his left hand where it lay across his chest so the wedding band glinted. "I wish I could go back and do it differently."

"Well, we can't." She liked how he said "we" instead of "you," as if they were a team again.

Maybe, just maybe, they could be.

He continued, "We can only go forward from here and deal with what's out there. And to do that, I need to know what happened eight years ago and what's happening now." Michael levered himself up and fumbled to hand her the sweater he had rid her of before. "I've gone over and over that night in my head, trying to figure out what happened, how much of it was my fault, and I've got to admit that I'm stumped, Christine."

He turned the lantern back up to full power and shone it down at the black water. "Still rising, so we've got some time." He sat up and dangled his feet over the edge, wrapping one of the blankets around his shoulders and lap for warmth and modesty.

Christine sat up as well and wriggled into her jeans, needing that fragile protection if she was going to relive the night her life had ended. She too dangled her feet toward the oily water and stared into the moving shadows until they began to take on shape and life.

In the darkness she saw bright yellow sunlight, and in the lantern-lit shadows she saw palm trees and red-plumed parrots.

"Do you remember that night?" Michael's voice seemed far away.

"Of course." She saw blood splash across the flagstones, drip from the palm fronds. Shuddered. "Of course I do."

She drew a deep breath and let herself slide into the memories. She heard harsh voices, remembered two young people who knew each other well enough to wound with words. "We fought."

"I'm sorry," he said simply. "I've regretted the things I

said that night every day for the last eight years."

She glanced over. "You want to hear this or not?" He nodded for her to continue.

"I was mad that you'd brought us to Jonas's island for our honeymoon after you promised you'd give Jonas up and stay on the right side of the law. You were mad that I didn't like your friend, so . . . we fought."

Michael nodded. "You stomped out of the restaurant to sulk."

She glared at him through the dim lantern light. "No, I left so you'd follow me and we could make up in private. In bed." She shook her head as if men were the stupidest creatures on Earth, which they might just be. Michael hadn't thought to follow her. He'd gone to the bar instead.

"I was going back to change into that white filmy thing you liked so much and wait for you." Michael winced. He remembered the white thing very well. "But when I got to our room, there was someone there . . ."

Chapter Eight

The door was ajar, and even though the concierge had assured them that crime on Santa Caribe was minimal, Chrissy paused and put her ear to the crack just in case. She heard voices—low and male.

She frowned, then smiled. Mikey had probably ordered champagne sent up again, maybe with flowers to coax her out of her mad. She pushed open the door to the honeymoon suite and floated into the room in her sexiest fashion, just in case her husband had gotten there ahead of her.

The voices were coming from their bedroom, and Christine tiptoed to the door, hoping to surprise Mikey in the midst of his plans. But it wasn't her husband.

It was a stranger, a small man with piggy eyes and a lop-sided frown. He and another man were pawing through her suitcase, the one Jonas had given her as a wedding present and Michael had insisted she use.

"It's got to be here somewhere. The boss said he put it right in the lining." The other man, an ugly hulk with half his right ear missing, grumbled and reached for Michael's luggage.

Christine shrank back against the wall outside the room where she and Mikey had spent their wedding night. Her mind raced.

What was happening? Who were these men?

And what would they do if they realized she had seen them?

Fear spiked through Christine's chest. Fear and a terrible, terrible foreboding.

She could run, but where? She could hardly go back to the restaurant and tell Michael. He'd never believe it, and even if he did, the two men would probably be gone by the time she cajoled her husband up to the room, and then she'd look like a jealous hag making up stories to prove her point.

He'd accused her of just that in the restaurant.

The hulk grunted in satisfaction and pulled a flat package out of the lining of Michael's suitcase. "Got it." He started to unwrap the thing, then paused. "Should we go somewhere else? I'd rather not be here when the bride returns."

Piggy man shrugged. "The boss said he'd keep her busy at dinner so we'd have enough time to finish up here."

Christine shook her head in confusion. "The boss" was going to keep her occupied? They couldn't mean Michael. He wouldn't have anything to do with these people. Not her Michael. He'd promised.

"We're almost done anyway," Piggy fingered the edge of his jacket, casually twitching buttons aside.

Half-ear missed the motion. "Not much to finish up." He started to unwrap the package. "We'll divide it up and go. Baubles for you, cash for me."

"Well, the boss wanted to alter our agreement a little bit." Pig-boy took Half-ear by the elbow and steered him onto the small balcony that faced the rain forest.

Then they were speaking too low for Christine to hear, and she wanted to yell, "Speak up! Tell me who the boss is. It's not my husband, right?" If it wasn't Michael they were speaking of, she could prove to him that Jonas was not a nice guy.

If it was Michael . . .

She wouldn't think of that now. He'd promised.

With uncommon daring, she crept into the bedroom,

thinking to grab the package and bolt with her proof in hand, but the package wasn't there. When the voices on the balcony grew louder, she froze with one hand on her husband's suitcase.

Christine could hear Half-ear's deep voice carry loudly over Piggy's thinner tenor as the men argued viciously. There was the sound of a scuffle, and she instinctively crouched down beside the bed when a pair of bodies twisted into the room and crashed to the floor.

Pop! The scuffling noises slowed. Ceased.

Christine pressed her face against soft cloth and had a sudden vivid memory of Michael placing her reverently upon that very bedspread the evening before. She heard one of the men stand up. She could see his stubby shadow on the wall behind the bed.

"Well, that's one way to renegotiate a contract, isn't it? The boss'll be happy to have the amulets and the cash as a wedding present."

Wedding present? Michael. Somehow Michael was involved with this. He was in danger. She felt her world tilt beneath her feet.

She was in danger. She had to get out of here.

Her quick, shallow breathing echoed in the room. How could he not hear it? Her heart was pounding harder than the drums of the native band at the bar, and the air whistled in and out of her lungs loud enough to drown out the sounds of Piggy dragging Half-ear across the balcony.

Her gaze darted to the open door. Could she make it out of the room before he noticed? Where could she go?

Not to Michael. Not until she knew what the hell was going on.

Not to the hotel staff—Jonas owned the hotel.

Not to the police—Jonas owned the police too.

She heard a roar in the rain forest. Not there either. If the lions didn't get her, the natives would. She'd heard the stories.

A sound from the balcony startled her, and she saw that in her hesitation she had lost her opportunity to escape. She ducked down again and heard a grunt of effort, the crash of palm fronds and the thud of a heavy object hitting the soft ground three stories below.

Piggy cursed, so close to her he might have been sitting on the bed. "What a mess. I don't suppose I can get house-keeping . . ." He trailed off and Christine could see his shadow prowl into the sitting room, cutting off her route to the hall.

"What the—?" Piggy swore again, bitterly, and yanked the hall door open. Christine's wrap dangled from his left hand. It must've fallen from her shoulders when she had sauntered into the room hoping to impress Michael.

"Mrs. Finch? Christine?" She knew he'd be back any moment. Could she make it to the hallway?

Footsteps returned, and Christine decided she'd rather be on the balcony than cowering behind her marriage bed. Head down, she ran across the bedroom and heard him shout.

She leapt onto the balcony, thinking that she might lower herself from the railing. Her feet skidded on the bloody flag-stones, and she hit the wrought iron with her hip. Half-turned by the impact, she saw Piggy coming at her with his lips pulled back over snaggly teeth and his eyes glazed with a feral sort of pleasure.

Whatever happened next, she was sure he would enjoy it.

She was just as sure that she would not.

Going with instinct, Christine held tight to her purse, the only tangible reminder she had of normalcy—

And jumped.

Once when she was ten years old, she and Mikey had been

playing on the rope swing near their pond, and the rope had snapped when she was swinging over the land. She'd spun in the air for what seemed like forever and had seen the brown earth revolving below her. Had seen the look of horror on her best friend's face.

When she had finally landed, he was there to help her get her wind back and jolly her out of her tears.

That was the Mikey she'd known best. The one she'd loved.

She fell much more quickly this time, her older, heavier body crashing through palm fronds already tainted with blood. This time there was nobody waiting below to make sure she landed safely.

She lay on the ground next to the dead man and gasped painfully as Piggy leaned far out from the balcony above her and looked down.

His worried voice floated out onto the tropical night. "Mrs. Finch? Are you there? Are you okay?" He looked around again to make sure none of the other guests were within range before he hissed, "If you can hear me, you should be wishing you died when you jumped, because I can assure you that what the boss will have in mind for you won't be at all pleasant." He added, as if he relished the thought, "Especially for a new bride."

Her fingers clawed at the rich island soil as if she could bury herself right there, could hide from the events of the night by pulling a thin layer of loam over her bruised body. Her hands bumped against a flat, rectangular object. The package. The dead man must have had it when he fell.

When she touched it, lions roared in the distance and her heart beat thick and fast in her ears. The packet was warm. A trickle of light worked its way up her fingertips, a swirl of red, blue, and green.

Christine heard footsteps approaching and dragged herself into a thick clump of bird-of-paradise and fern, almost unconsciously tucking the package securely inside the negligee she'd worn with Michael in mind. Over the noise of approaching men, she could just hear the words of their leader, the man she would come to know as Garibaldi.

"If you find her, kill her."

He paused, and she imagined the man looking out into the darkness when he spoke again.

"Bring me the jewels. And her heart."

Michael was silent for a long, long time. Christine watched the black water, willing it to sink so she could swim back to land and collect her daughter from the hidey-hole behind Horst's closet.

She'll be okay, Christine told herself. *Garibaldi doesn't know about her*. He has no reason to look for a child.

Or did he?

Michael's words were startling in the silence. "I can't believe that happened to you." Silence. "I can't believe I let them talk me into leaving the island without you. I should've looked harder." More silence, then the words she'd been both dreading and hoping for. "Why didn't you come to me? And not the bull about being mad for what happened in the restaurant. I know you better than that. At least I thought I did."

"Because I—" Christine faltered. Took a breath. She'd never told anyone the real reason. Not even Horst.

"Because you were punishing me? Because you thought I treated you like a child? Because I didn't want you to work after we were married? Didn't give you enough credit?" Michael named some of the things they'd fought about that night, and to Christine they seemed so unimportant in the grand scheme.

Once, they'd seemed worth dying for—before she understood what dying really meant.

"Why, Chrissy?"

Stung by the nickname, she snapped, "Because I thought you were involved, okay? I didn't want to get you in trouble. You'd already made it clear that you cared more about your word to Jonas than your promise to me, and you and he'd pulled enough shady deals in the past . . ."

Michael cursed in the darkness. "A few harmless joyrides hardly equate to murder, Chrissy. Don't you know me better than that?"

She shook her head sadly and slid away from him on the rocky ledge. Her hand bumped against a flat, waterproof packet, and it seemed to lean into her hand. It was warm to the touch, and when she picked it up and pressed it between her palms, she felt calmer. Soothed. "I thought I did, but then you brought me to the island for our honeymoon, and I realized I didn't know you at all."

"I wanted you and Jo to get to know each other better. I'm sure you would've liked him if only you'd given him a chance."

Christine snorted. Yeah, right.

Michael frowned. "You never gave him a chance, even when we were kids. Sure, he was a little wild back then—we both were—but he's rich now, and a good businessman. He's my friend. He gave me a job when I couldn't work wood anymore. He's been there for me." The words *when you haven't been* hung unspoken between them. "He even hired a team of detectives to look for you. I'll bet he was thrilled to get my message about finding you and Kayla."

Her heart stopped, just stopped in her chest. "You told him about Kayla?" She jerked, casting around for a weapon. Something. Anything. Her daughter was in danger. "How could you do that?" she practically screamed.

Kayla.

The package blazed hot in her hands and she jammed it inside her shirt, stood up and tested the water level with a frantic foot. She had to get to her daughter.

"What are you doing? The water's still too high for us to get out—you said so yourself. Come here." He patted the rock condescendingly. "Let's talk about this."

She shook her head. "No. You've talked enough for both of us." She glared at him and saw the beloved face with its worried gray eyes. "Haven't you figured it out yet? It's Jonas. Everything is about Jonas—he wants the stones and he'll do anything to get them. Now you've given him the best leverage possible. You've given him our daughter."

She wanted to strike at Michael, to punish him for coming back into her life and giving her hope. Taking it away.

She wanted to hate him, but she didn't. She just shook her head instead.

And jumped into the oily black water. Felt the riptide snatch her up and send her spinning through the tunnel.

And felt her husband close behind.

Chapter Nine

The first thing they saw when they dragged themselves ashore beside the jetty was a soggy lump of fur at the water's edge.

A very, very large, soggy lump of reddish fur.

"Thor!" Christine knelt beside the big cat and touched his shoulder. Her hand came away stained with blood.

Michael crouched down. "Is he—"

Not quite.

The voice was weak but most definitely not Michael's imagination. He nodded, not bothering to question the fact that the lion was talking to him in his mind. "Glad to hear it. Do you think you can make it to the house?"

Christine looked at him oddly, but he ignored the look to concentrate on the cat, which replied, *Leave me and get the child. The child and the amulets are all that matter. That and the parchment.*

"What amulets? What parchment?"

"You can hear him?"

Michael glanced at Chrissy. She was staring at him.

Then again, he wouldn't have believed it himself a day ago. He shrugged. "Well, since I arrived in town yesterday, I've been hearing *something*, all right. It wasn't until the voice told me to jump off the jetty just as Thor showed up that I figured out whose voice it had to be." He scrubbed a hand across his face. "I'm not even going to think about how weird this is right now. He's been shot at least once. We need to get him to Horst's place, and we need to find Kayla. Then you can tell me about the rest of it."

But it wasn't so simple. When they arrived at the yogi's house, struggling to support the sling they'd rigged beneath the big cat's ribs, they found Horst in the kitchen.

Bound and gagged.

"Kayla?" Christine propped Thor against the refrigerator and bolted for the back of the house, calling her daughter's name with increasing panic. "Kayla!"

She's gone, thought the lion, though Michael hadn't needed the confirmation. He knelt down, untied the other man, and helped him to a chair. "You hurt?"

Horst shook his head. "No, damn it. They surprised me. Kayla came running in, crying about someone hurting Thor. I was getting ready to put her in one of the safe places when three ugly guys burst in, grabbed her, and tied me up." He looked up at Michael with hollow eyes. "They took the candles, too. It was like they knew right where to look."

Christine flew back into the kitchen. "She's gone!" She turned on Michael. "This is all your fault! You told him about Kayla, and now she's gone. I wish you'd never found me."

She might as well have said *I wish you were dead,* because that's how it felt to Michael. "Jonas. You think Jonas is behind all this."

"Of course he's behind all this!" she yelled. "This is all about Jonas, you fool! Why else do you think I've got a Santa Caribbean lion guarding me? I've got something he wants, and when he gets it he'll control the whole damn island for good."

She dropped her head into her hands. "And now he's got my daughter and it's all your fault." She stopped. Took a breath. "I have to get her back. I'll trade her for the candles.

They're back at the cottage in her knap . . ." She trailed off, noticing that the men were shaking their heads. "What?"

"They're gone. Finch left the candles here last night, and the goons grabbed them on the way out. Either they're working with a lion of their own, or somebody on their side has some pretty creepy hunches. They knew right where to look."

Christine glanced from one to the other. "But the knapsack had—"

"Soup," Michael supplied. "Cans of it, for the weight. I thought the candles would be safer here than with us." So far his bright ideas seemed to be scoring zero. "What the hell is the deal with them, anyway?"

But he was talking to thin air. Christine had fled out the kitchen door. Michael figured she'd come back when she realized the knapsack really did have soup in it. So he asked Horst, "First aid kit?" and the men set about doctoring the big cat.

He couldn't think of anything better to do.

"I should've figured you out sooner," Michael said to the lion, feeling only a little foolish. "But I wasn't on Santa Caribe Island for long enough to really get to know the lions."

Neither was I. I was to protect the stones. And the child. I have failed. The golden eyes closed, the great chestnut body sagged.

"Don't give me that!" Horst poked the shaggy lion in its ribs, and the yellow eyes popped back open in surprise. "We're not done yet. We've still got something they need."

Yogi and lion nodded at each other, and Michael was only vaguely surprised to hear both their voices in his head.

The parchment.

"What parchment?" he snapped, finally losing patience.

"What amulets? I'm a step behind here, guys. I think it's time someone explained what the hell's going on."

Thor closed his eyes again. *I hurt. You explain.* And the lion gracefully lost consciousness on the kitchen floor.

"He needs a vet," Horst said worriedly. "One shot went clean through the muscle, but I'm pretty sure another bullet's still in there. Here, hold this." He placed Michael's hand on the pressure bandage that covered the lion's shoulder.

Horst checked the list of emergency numbers on the fridge and used one to place a call. "Marty? Thor's in trouble. Can you come right over? Bring the pony van. We'll probably need to get him to the clinic." He disconnected, grinned crookedly. "Local vet. He'll fix Thor." Then he slid down to sit cross-legged on the floor. "Guess you'd like me to tell you a story while we wait."

Michael nodded, listening for Chrissy to return across the dunes. "Nothing would make me happier. She told me about the men in the room." He cursed quietly. "About her going out the window. Start there."

Horst nodded. Took a breath. Began: "She found the package in the bushes next to the dead guy. She grabbed it and ran, thinking that whatever was in it might be her only insurance policy in the long run. I think she still meant to run to you then, but the hotel was in an uproar, and she heard Jonas's security patrols talking about what was going to happen when they found her. She bribed one of the hotel workers to take her to the mainland by boat, and as they left, she could hear lions roaring and the shouts of the men tracking her."

"She must've been terrified." And he'd been in the hotel bar sulking. How very heroic.

Horst nodded. "If it makes you feel any better, she decided not to go to anyone here in the States because she wanted to protect you. She was on a bus the next day, headed for wherever, when she opened the package. Inside was almost a hundred thousand in cash and three necklaces—one ruby, one sapphire, one emerald."

Michael raised his head in surprise. Hadn't he heard rumors that the recent troubles on the island revolved around a trio of missing amulets? And the natives. And the lions.

The smaller man scrubbed a hand over his face. "Jesus, Finch. You should see these things. They've got to be from some tribal ritual or a royal family or something. Just touch them and you can tell they're really powerful. Spiritual." He paused. "They scare the living spit out of me."

Michael pressed harder on the bandage, and the drowsy lion growled. He eased up. "That's why Jonas has helped me track her all these years. He wanted the amulets. It's been Jonas all along, hasn't it?"

Ever since they'd grown up dirt-poor together—the son of the town drunk and the son of the town whore—Michael and Jonas had been friends. The only thing that had stood between them was Michael's unlikely friendship with little Chrissy, and Michael had been deeply grateful that Jonas had put aside his dislike for her to help Michael find her when she'd disappeared.

But it appeared that he'd really been looking for something else entirely.

Michael shook his head. Felt like punching something.

He had been married forty-eight hours when his wife left him, but at least he'd still had his best friend to lean on, and he could pretend in the darkest corner of the night that somewhere, somehow, Christine still loved him.

But now, in the space of a different forty-eight hours, he'd not only lost his wife again—

He'd also lost his best friend.

He had nothing.

Not so, Thor whispered deep inside his mind, and Michael wondered that the cat could still telepath when he appeared to be out cold. *Your daughter needs you.* And he realized that Thor was right. His wife had mistrusted him over and over. His best friend had ruined his life. But his daughter needed him.

He pictured her trusting blue eyes, the way her fine-boned fingers had stroked the oak burl and the way her mouth had curved when she described the kitten she would carve. His chest tightened. They had to get her back.

If the amulets weren't the way, what was left? Then he remembered. "Thor mentioned a parchment."

Horst nodded. "The amulets were wrapped in it when Chrissy took them. I've never seen the thing. She's kept it separate from the amulets. I think she's scared of it."

"Scared of what?" Neither man had noticed her return. She looked beaten. She glanced down at the motionless lion, who looked smaller that he did when he was awake and bristling with intelligent power. "Did you call Marty?"

Horst answered both questions. "He's on his way, and you're afraid of the parchment. Or, if not afraid, then very, very wary."

She nodded, and when Michael passed the pressure-bandage duties off to Horst and stood, she looked up at him as though feeling wary of her husband too.

As well she should be.

"Why didn't you come to me, Christine? If not that night, why not later, once you were back in the States?"

She looked away, couldn't meet his eyes when she said, "I didn't know who to trust. It sounded like they were talking about you. And the package was in your suitcase."

Michael swore. "So I was tried and convicted without being offered the chance to defend myself. Are you sure you weren't punishing me for not being perfect?"

Christine squared off in his face. "I did give you a chance! I called you from Miami." She touched her side. "I got Garibaldi instead. Three broken ribs, a broken collarbone, and I almost lost Kayla." She touched the scar on her cheek that pulsed red with anger. "Once I knew for certain I was pregnant, my first and only concern was to protect Kayla. I could risk my own life to contact you, but not hers."

Hands gently touching the belly that had held their daughter, she looked at him, her eyes pleading for him to understand. "I had to protect our daughter, Michael. I'm sorry if you think that was wrong."

The phone rang then, interrupting further discussion. Christine answered it and her face blanched.

She identified the caller with equal parts fear and loathing in her voice. "Garibaldi."

Michael felt a chill skitter up his spine and reached for the phone, wanting to keep the man as far away from her as possible.

She waved him aside. Squared her shoulders and said, "I believe I have something you want. The amulets aren't much use without the parchment, are they?" Her voice hardened. Grew cold. "I'll trade it for my daughter."

She listened a moment, and Michael fought the insane urge to reach through the phone and snatch his daughter back from the tall man with the scarred throat and big hands. Then he fantasized briefly about killing Garibaldi. He'd hurt Christine. He'd better not hurt Kayla.

"Fine," Christine finally said. "It's a deal. I'll meet you in the candle shop in twenty minutes."

She hung up the phone and Michael said, "Do you trust him?"

Christine snorted. "Not even as far as I could heave him off a balcony. Remember—I've seen the way he renegotiates deals." She was trying to be brave, but Michael saw her hand shake as she stroked the phone cord. Saw the glimmer of tears in her eyes.

He stepped over to her and tipped her chin up with one finger. Touched his lips to hers. And smiled through the pain.

"That's true. But remember, there's two of us this time."

Chapter Ten

As he crept to the back door of Dewdrop's Candle Shop, which was thankfully cloaked in darkness, Michael felt sillier than he ever had.

In retrospect, he should've stuck with his ripped, bloody, waterlogged shirt and pants, but borrowing clothes from Horst hadn't seemed like such a bad idea. That was, until he faced the prospect of bargaining for his daughter's life wearing a pair of spandex bike shorts two sizes too small and a hot pink sweatshirt that proclaimed "Farewell Gay Pride Day" in three-inch-high letters.

It was like Jonas always said, "There's nothing like going into a negotiation knowing you have the upper hand." Yeah, right.

He could feel Christine's breath hot on the back of his neck, and it gave him the shivers. He wanted to tell her to back off but couldn't risk the noise. Besides, he had already tried to leave her with Horst, and that sure hadn't gotten him very far.

They passed through the back door, and Michael stepped gingerly over the cracked place in the cement stairs where he'd landed after he hit the wrought-iron railing. The very thought gave him a headache.

"Gotcha!" A hand the size of a baseball mitt came out of nowhere and grabbed Michael by his hot pink sweatshirt, and he felt the undeniably sobering imprint of a gun barrel near his left kidney. He froze, and out of the corner of his eye he saw Christine do the same.

They'd talked about marching bravely through the front door and had decided to get the drop on Kayla's captors by sneaking in the back.

Another one of Michael's bright ideas that hadn't quite panned out.

Uglies One and Two marched their captives into the front room of the candle shop, and when they came into the light, Michael was gratified to see that all three of the thugs looked the worse for wear. Thor had not gone down easily.

"Mrs. Finch! How nice to see you again after all this time." Ugly Three, the man that Christine called Garibaldi, lounged in the corner of the shop, ironically sitting on top of the display case that had contained the three precious candles the day before. Now there was just a single blue candle sitting there.

He glanced at Michael and smirked. "Nice shirt, Finch."

"Garibaldi." Christine's voice was level, though Michael knew it was costing her. "How's the throat?"

Ugly Three touched the scar. "Fine. Thank you for asking, Mrs. Finch. Or may I call you Christine? The other seems too formal, considering that you and I share a past . . . association, shall we say?" He leered, and Michael made a silent vow to kill this one himself—with his bare hands if possible.

From woodworker to murderer's assistant to murderer. Was the slide to hell really so easy? Obviously so, when loved ones were involved.

"Where is my daughter?" Christine's voice shook only slightly, and she seemed not to notice the gun that jabbed into her side when she reached into her shirt. Removed a flat package that looked like the one she'd taken from the Pirate's Cave.

Held it up.

"The parchment, Garibaldi. The amulets are just pretty baubles without it, aren't they? Now, we have a deal. My daughter for the parchment."

Garibaldi merely smirked. "Sweetheart, if you've learned anything from this, it's that deals can be renegotiated." He snagged the parchment from Christine's fingers and tucked it into his shirt. Nodded at Uglies One and Two. "Kill them, then the child."

"No!" Christine screamed and tried to wrench herself from her captor's arms. She didn't break free, but Ugly One lost his grip on his gun. That's probably why he'd had a baseball bat on the jetty, Michael thought irrelevantly, not a gun.

Then he thought of nothing more than escaping his own Ugly and saving his wife. He kicked back hard, twisted sharply away from the gun, and was almost deafened when it went off next to his head. Jamming his elbow into Ugly Two's soft ribs, Michael fought to free himself.

Any minute now, Garibaldi was going to start shooting. He was sure of it.

Christine screamed again, and the sound was echoed by another scream. This one sounded rougher, wilder, almost animal, a primal battle cry that made the hairs on the back of Michael's neck rise and shiver.

Behind you!

At Thor's warning, Michael spun and struck out. His fist caught Garibaldi in the throat, just below the twisted scar. The man gagged and retched, stumbled backward. Michael would have chased him, but a bullet from Ugly Two's gun slammed into the display case. It exploded like a dropped light bulb and Michael ducked, lest more bullets follow.

He lunged at Ugly Two, and they both went down in a writhing, punching heap.

Christine yelled. Thor screamed.

And then Ugly One screamed. And was silent.

Michael heard boots pounding on the boardwalk. He glanced around. Garibaldi was gone. Kayla was nowhere in sight. And it sounded as if an army was on its way.

Ugly reinforcements.

With a final, desperate blow, Michael knocked Ugly Two into another dimension. He grabbed the man's gun and placed himself between Christine and the door. Felt Thor step up beside him.

Heard the lion's growl.

The door to the candle shop slammed open, and a rush of men poured into the shop.

Waving oars and fishing gaffs.

"You leave Dewdrop alone, you—Jesus!"

Whiskey Barrel jammed on the brakes, the longshoreman slammed into his back, and the others piled up behind. They took one look at Michael's face. One look at the gun.

And reached for the sky.

The sheriff arrived soon after and took charge of the two prisoners. Garibaldi was gone. So was Kayla.

Christine sat behind the broken display case and whittled away at the stub of a candle with a blunt knife. She heard Michael's voice rise and fall as he spoke with the people gathered in her little shop and she tried not to weep with sheer, helpless frustration.

Her daughter was gone, and Michael wasn't speaking to her. She couldn't blame him, really. She hadn't trusted him back then, and she hadn't trusted him to make the exchange this time. She'd screwed up the negotiation, and now it was over.

She was done. She had played for the highest stakes possible and had lost. How had she been so arrogant as to think she could beat Garibaldi at his own game? Now she had lost everything: the amulets, the parchment, her daughter, and Michael's trust.

But had she ever really had his trust? When they'd been children, he'd always been the leader, the planner. He'd always expected her to follow his lead, which is partly why he assumed she would come to accept his friendship with Jonas. He'd never trusted her to lead.

But then again, she hadn't trusted him to save her that night or now. Because over the years she'd blamed him for all of it.

He could've found her if he'd tried hard enough.

He could've believed her about Jonas in the first place.

He never should have taken her to that island.

In a way, it was all his fault.

He had cost Christine her life and her daughter. She pressed her forehead against the cash register as she realized that she'd been punishing him all this time without even recognizing it.

A boy's voice pulled her from that nasty little discovery.

"Man, you should've seen Thor standing over those two with blood on his whiskers and claws and his ears flat back on his head. It was creepy. He even had blood on that white stripe between his eyes and on the bandage across his ribs." Jim's nephew Scott shuddered in gleeful horror at the memory and ran an impressed hand over Thor's head. The big cat swayed unsteadily.

Horst had related how Thor had been coming out of anesthesia when he'd suddenly lurched to his feet, roared, and galloped to the candle shop. Horst had called Big Jim and his boys, and they'd all converged on the shop quickly.

But not in time to stop Garibaldi from escaping with Kayla.

"I'm sorry the other one got away. We should've chased him, but we wanted to make sure everyone was okay in the shop first." Link Shale's voice was deep with regret, and Christine knew he was thinking of Kayla.

"Thanks for the clothes, Link." Michael strode into the room wearing jeans, cowboy boots, and a white oxford shirt that almost fit across his shoulders. He was carrying the two suitcases that Christine had packed the day before and a small canvas bag with Link's initials on it. "Not that I minded Horst's duds, but they were a little snug and would stand out where we're going."

"Are you sure you shouldn't go to the police? Kidnapping is a federal offense." Horst glanced worriedly at Christine.

Michael shook his head. "If I thought she was still in the country, sure. But she's not, and where we're going, the police belong to the bad guys. I'll drop a word to one of the men in the FBI I met while looking for Chrissy, but I don't know how much good that'll do or how quickly they could help us."

He had barely looked at Christine since Uglies One and Two had been dragged off by the sheriff. Now he glanced down at her, his gray eyes unreadable. "Ready?" He gestured toward the door.

"For what? It's over. He's won. He has Kayla, all three amulets, and the parchment. It's hopeless." She felt as tired as she had right after Miami, as if she had been beaten mentally as well as physically.

"Not necessarily." Michael pulled a flat, waterproof package out of his borrowed jacket.

"What?" She looked at him. Looked at the packet. Felt the warmth of it from where she sat. "What did you do?"

He shrugged. "Performed a minor substitution."

She grabbed the packet, hope and despair battling for dominance in her chest. Hope that he'd saved the parchment, despair because she feared what Garibaldi would do when he figured it out. She unwrapped the bundle. Carefully unfolded the stiff, coarse vegetable fibers.

Stared at the squiggly lines drawn in faded red ink. It was gibberish. She frowned. "I could read this the last time I looked at it. I swear I could."

She'd read the strange words out loud only weeks before Kayla's birth, and she'd been stunned and terrified by the quick sweep of power that had blasted through her. The candles had glowed from within and she'd slammed the parchment down, folded it quickly, and hidden it in the cave, as far away from her as she could get it without destroying it utterly.

She hadn't been able to hear Thor since that day.

Michael glanced over her shoulder, and she felt his nearness like an ache. "I can read it."

He rattled off a string of syllables in a rolling, liquid tongue.

Stopped when he realized the whole room was staring at him. "What?"

"That wasn't English, Finch." Horst nodded at the parchment. "And it was damned weird." He turned to Chrissy. "You used to be able to read this, but now you can't?"

She nodded. "And I can't remember what it said, either. Why do you think that is?" Frustration bubbled, the need to do something other than sit around and talk moved her to anger. She hated that Michael had any sort of role in this. It was her problem. Her mistake. She'd fix it. She snapped, "What does it matter? Read the rest of it and tell us what it says."

Michael glanced at Horst, who shrugged and nodded. He began to read and heard an echo of the words and their translation in his mind in a purring voice that was not his own.

"*. . . and so it came to pass that the Elder forged the stones into*

116

three great powers: the strongest of the three was the red amulet of action and war—the warrior's amulet, then the blue amulet of wisdom and peace, and the green amulet of fertility and health. And he said to his children, "Take these and share them with one another and keep them together yet separate, for he who controls the Three controls the island."

Michael paused. "There's a break and a few lines, then some untranslatable phrases." He read a string of words that had no obvious meaning, even in the language he shouldn't know.

A sizzle of heat and blue light ripped through him.

Christine gasped. "Look! In the case!"

Trying to clear his mind of the whirlwind that had just passed through him, Michael looked to the display case that had once contained the three amulets in their cloaking candles. The blue candle that remained in the case looked soft, gluey. It was sagging to one side.

It beckoned Michael closer. Expanded to fill his vision until all he could see was the listing blue candle. It pulsed.

"Read those words again," Horst hissed, and Michael complied.

Even though he was braced for the whip of power, it staggered him. Scared him. Filled him with terrible joy. He felt tendrils of light and energy reaching out from him and connecting him to the injured lion, to Christine.

And to the candle, which glowed cool blue as the wax flowed away like water and left in its wake a beautiful sapphire gem bound up in a tangle of metalwork and candle wick.

"Christ," Big Jim breathed. Then he crossed himself as Michael read the words for a third time, drinking the power like wine. He lifted his hands to command the blue gem, and it glowed like a starburst at his voice.

And suddenly, he knew things. He understood why the

stars and the moons took the paths they did. He knew why the blood beat through his veins, and why the old dog he'd had as a child had gone into the forest to die.

He understood everything. And nothing.

He spread his hands wide and prepared to call on the blue gem again.

"Michael, stop it!"

He didn't even turn at the voice. It sounded so far away. So inconsequential. But when the parchment was knocked from his hands and the power was interrupted by a rude shove, Michael snarled and turned on the puny intruder. He raised a hand to swat the irritant away—

And saw Christine.

The power drained quickly, sickly, and he realized what he'd almost done.

That, said the voice in his head, *is why she closed herself off from me. If you cannot hear the Guardian, you cannot use the gem. Cannot be used by the power of the amulets.*

Though Michael knew she hadn't heard the lion's words, Christine turned away from him and brushed broken glass away from the melted candle. She lifted the amulet of wisdom and held it at eye level so the sun shone through the facets. She didn't look at him.

"There were two blue candles in the case. I must've taken the wrong one last night."

Michael didn't ask how that had happened. It made as much sense as anything he'd seen so far. Perhaps the amulet hadn't wanted to be taken then.

Perhaps it had been waiting for him. Michael liked the idea. The power flirted with his fingertips again, and he smiled, but the smile turned grim when he remembered what he'd almost done. He'd almost struck his wife, led by the power of the blue stone.

"Or you took the right one," Horst observed. "At least we've still got one of them, and Garibaldi's got a fake candle. Was there anything in the other blue candle?"

She nodded. "Yes, that's why it was in the case—so it wouldn't be sold accidentally." She glanced at Michael and away. That one has my wedding ring in it."

Michael closed his eyes.

She'd kept it.

For all the doubts she'd had about him. For all that she'd thought him capable of murder. For all that she'd run away from him and hidden well. Michael held on to that one thought.

She'd kept his ring.

There might be hope for them yet.

The words whispered in his head—*I promise.*

He held out a hand. "Let's go get our daughter."

Chapter Eleven

They were going back to Santa Caribe Island. To Michael it seemed unbelievable. And inevitable.

She was silent during the long drive to Logan Airport and didn't speak to him as they waited for their flight except to thank him for the soda he brought her and to ask whether he needed money for the tickets.

She was with him, yet not with him. Present in body but not in spirit. It was as if in her mind she had already flown to Santa Caribe to be with her daughter.

Michael, on the other hand, was edgy, twitchy, looking over his shoulder every few minutes. He knew it was foolish, but he felt the crawling sensation of eyes on the back of his neck as they sat in the waiting area for the flight that would take them first to Puerto Rico, then across the ocean to Santa Caribe.

Jonas's island.

He had tried not to think of it, but the knowledge festered at the edges of his mind, and every time he shut his eyes there it was, waiting for him.

He twitched again, stared at the short, balding man sitting across from him. The man reminded him of Cheevers, Jonas's accountant, and Michael tensed, ready to spring on the guy if he so much as made a move in their direction.

"Henry! Here we are, Henry!" A beribboned woman wearing an outrageously floppy hat waved from the gate, and the man who was not Cheevers got to his feet and embraced her and the two travel-weary children beside her.

Michael relaxed, and Christine spoke to him for the first time since they had left Horst's kitchen.

"It gets to you, doesn't it?" She stared as the reunited family wandered off toward the baggage-claim area. "The wondering, the watching. You look at every face in the crowd and wonder, 'Are you the one? Are you looking for me?' "

She scanned the seating area. "After a while you get good at reading people. That guy over there," she pointed at a twenty-something with shaggy hair and a five-hundred-dollar leather jacket, "he's waiting for his girlfriend. He doesn't want to be here, thinks it's a waste of time, but he knows that if he doesn't meet her, he won't get any for weeks, so here he is."

She scanned again while Michael looked at the youth, who was glaring at his watch for the fifth time in three minutes.

"That woman is hiding something. She's nervous, looking around like you just were. But she's looking for the cops. Every time one comes by, she freezes and tries her damnedest to look innocent. Probably has something illegal on her. She's way too uptight to be a pro—I'll bet she's doing it as a favor for a friend. Maybe a boyfriend."

Michael watched her watch the crowd. In her eyes he could see a hundred such crowds, a thousand people she had watched and dismissed, a few people she had identified in time to run.

He hated that she'd been forced to live that way. *My fault,* he thought. His fault that she'd been hunted. His fault for not listening to her. His fault for thinking that she was just jealous of Jonas, just immature, that there was nothing deep or evil in the man he called friend.

What had she seen that he hadn't?

And as he watched her he realized that she was talking because she couldn't bear to be silent anymore, but also that she was not speaking to *him*. She was avoiding him, had been since they'd left their little cave. She scanned the crowd again, and he trapped her chin gently in his hand and turned her face until she was looking, really looking, into his eyes.

"And here? What do you see here?" He held her when she would have looked away. "Tell me, Christine. You used to know me better than I knew myself sometimes. Tell me what you see."

She looked at him, finally focusing her eyes on his face. "Why, Michael? What do you want me to see—that you're scared for your daughter, or that you're angry with me for how I handled everything? I know both without looking for them."

She turned away from him, pulled a pair of dark glasses from her purse, and put them on, even though it was night outside. "The rest of it is all just history."

They were seated separately on the plane, and Michael was almost grateful for that until he strapped himself in next to a buxom woman with red nails and fake eyelashes.

"You going all the way to Santa Caribe, Sugar?" She batted those eyelashes, and Michael thought they looked like a pair of big, hairy spiders trying to do step aerobics.

He grunted in the affirmative, hoping she'd get the hint. Christine was three rows back and on the other side, so he could neither see her nor signal her for help if the woman insisted on talking.

"Me, too! Have you ever been there before? I have and it's just to *die* for. There's this big hotel with all sorts of fun stuff to do, and the beaches are beyond beautiful. If you get tired of lying around tanning, you can take a tour with a native guide of all these creepy tombs and ruins. And the lions! They prowl around everywhere, skulking behind the stones and disappearing into the jungle like they were your imagination." She shuddered artfully, causing her enormous breasts to quiver with jellolike dread.

"I've been there," Michael said shortly. He folded his arms across his chest and closed his eyes in self-defense.

"Hey, Mikey, where're you going?" The voice came out of the trees by the side of the road, and he stopped pedaling his bike and let it coast to a stop in the fallen leaves by the guard-rail.

"Nowhere, why?" Actually, he had been on his way to hang out with little Chrissy, but what self-respecting teen-age boy would admit that? Besides, he knew Jonas would just give him grief about it. He didn't understand Michael's friendship with the little girl.

Michael barely understood it himself.

"Come over here. Viktor and I have something to show you."

Jonas had named his pet after his father, Viktor Harding, since they were both rats. As Jonas liked to say, the only real difference between them was the tail.

Michael didn't like it when Jonas talked that way, but he usually only did it when his father was having a bad spell and his mother was being clumsy and falling down all the time. It seemed to Mike that those times were getting more and more frequent lately; but since it upset his friend to talk about it, they didn't.

"What?" He pushed his way through the stiff branches to where Jonas crouched in a small depression a hundred feet or so from the road.

"Here." Jonas was hunched over a metal contraption, and Michael crouched beside him after giving the area a once-over for poison ivy.

It was a leghold trap, a set of cruel teeth designed to spring shut on an unwary animal and hold it trapped and alive until it was killed or freed. The trap was sprung, and its jaws held both hind legs of a young wild rabbit.

The bunny's eyes were glazed with terror, and Michael could see the fur beneath its throat tremble with its heart-beat. "Aw, the poor little guy. Why do people use these things?"

Viktor sat beside the trap, industriously cleaning his whiskers and looking to Jonas now and again for instruction. Jonas was watching Mikey with hooded eyes.

Mike pried the trap open and swore at the rabbit's crushed hind legs. He also noticed that the skin around the bunny's eyes was broken and looked almost . . . chewed up. With regret, he wrung the rabbit's neck quickly and with as little pain as possible.

"You want to take it?" He offered the carcass to Jonas, knowing that the Hardings couldn't afford to waste food.

"Nah, throw it away or bury it or whatever." Jonas spat in the leaves beside the trap, and Mikey had the feeling he'd let his friend down. "I don't care."

Jonas climbed to his feet and lifted the rat to his shoulder. "Come on, Viktor. Fun's over."

Not quite sure what was meant by that, Michael dug a small hole for the rabbit, but when he went to lay the cooling body into the earth, it turned its head on its broken neck and looked at him with big blue eyes.

"Help me, Daddy," the rabbit said in Kayla's voice. "He says he's going to let the rats eat me if you and Mommy don't come."

★ ★ ★ ★ ★

"Rats!" Michael jolted awake with the image of his daughter tied up in a dark, dank cellar filled with thousands of Viktor's brethren. "He's going to put her in with rats."

"You okay, Sugar?" His seatmate regarded him with interest. "That seemed like one heck of a dream. Were you dreaming about rats? That's awful." She shivered again, and her boobs bounced gleefully.

He ignored that sally, unstrapped himself and struggled to his feet.

"Sir?" A flight attendant appeared at his elbow when he swayed. "Sir, I'm sorry but we're getting ready to land in Atlanta. I'm going to have to ask you to take your seat and fasten your belt."

"I'm gonna be sick." He pushed his way past the woman, feeling greasy sweat break out all over his body as he staggered to the lavatory.

He passed Christine on his way and saw her give him a worried look. He thought she said his name and held out a hand to stop him, but he ignored her. When he reached the tiny bathroom and shut the door, he surprised himself by not being sick. He ran a thin stream of water in the stainless steel bowl and scrubbed handful after handful of it over his face.

Finally he lifted his head and stared at himself in the small mirror. Above the sign that advised him, in several languages, that smoking in the lavatory was prohibited, his face was a waxy green and his eyes were the palest gray.

He wondered, if he looked at himself long enough, would the skin around his eyes start to show rat bites?

"She was right all along not to trust you," he said to his reflection. "You were too damn dumb to see what was in front of your eyes all along, but she saw it."

He took a scratchy brown paper towel from the dispenser and scrubbed it across his face hard enough to make his lip sting and the bruises throb.

"She saw what he was, and you were too stupid to listen to her, weren't you?" He had a fleeting urge to put his fist through the mirror, but the thought of another seven years of bad luck was enough to dissuade him. "It wasn't her fault, moron. She left because you wouldn't believe her when she told you your best friend was a monster."

He pictured rats. A small child crying for her mother.

"She stayed away to protect her daughter from the monster, and what do you do?"

In the mirror his reflection was hollow-eyed and gaunt. Haunted. Despairing. Guilt-ridden.

"You give her right to him."

Michael was silent as they went through the motions of getting their passports stamped by a bored customs official, and Christine thought his face looked green under the rainbow of bruises.

"Mr. and Mrs. Finch?"

Christine started. She almost spun around to see if Michael's mother was behind her. It was the first time she'd thought of Vera Finch in a long, long time, and the memory was bittersweet.

The handsome olive-skinned man in the hotel's red-and-black livery seemed not to notice her reaction as he waited for an answer. Michael remained mute and unapproachable, so she answered, "Yes? I'm . . . Mrs. Finch. Is there a problem with our luggage?"

"No, Ma'am. I'm here to take you to the hotel. Your reservations are all set, and your luggage is already in the limousine, as requested." He gestured for Christine and Michael to precede him out to the street, where a gleaming white car stood ready to receive them.

"Requested by whom?"

The man grinned at her, teeth glowing white against his bronze skin. "By Mr. Harding, of course."

He handed her into the limo and gestured Michael in after.

"So much for sneaking onto Santa Caribe without Jonas knowing about it," she noted, hoping to goad him into breaking the uneasy silence he had claimed since landing. "I told you he'd have our names tagged at the airport."

"We couldn't very well travel under assumed names when we're using our own passports."

It had hurt him to see Christine's eight-year-old passport with its single stamp from their honeymoon. She'd kept it and had gotten one for Kayla. Just in case.

Michael scowled at the bottle of champagne chilling in the silver ice bucket. It was the same that had been served at their wedding.

"True, but I still think we should have chartered a boat from the mainland and come ashore in the dark." Christine looked at her fingernails. Horst had done them just a few days earlier, but they were rough now from nervous chewing. "It worked for me once before."

Michael stared out of the tinted window at the passing palm trees. "Leave it, Chrissy. What's done is done, for better or worse."

She didn't think he was talking about their transportation now. "What do you mean by that?"

"Only that you've made the decisions you've made and I've done the same, and it seems to me that they've put us far beyond the point of no return. You were right about Jonas, I'll admit it, but you still should have come to me. I would've protected you."

Christine was grateful that the man from the hotel had chosen to sit in the front of the limo with the driver and that the privacy screen was up. "Do you blame me?" She tried to remain calm. She had known the time of reckoning was coming ever since their little tryst in the cave. Obviously the old chemistry was still there, but now it was tainted with mistrust and doubt, and so much time between them. "I tried to go to you for help. I told you what happened in Miami. Can you really expect that after all that I would be stupid enough to call you again?"

"You never called me in the first place. I never spoke to you." He continued to stare out the window. For a moment she thought she saw guilt in the reflection, and she wondered what had happened that sent him to the lavatory with terror in his eye and a green tinge to his skin.

"I realize that now. It must've been Jonas, but how was I supposed to know that he'd be in your shop? He never came to the shop, remember? There was too much dust there and it irritated his allergies. The connection was bad and he said all the right things—of course I thought it was you."

And she had cried about it for days and weeks, because until that day in Miami, she had held out hope that Michael was innocent. But he had been innocent anyway. She had been duped. She reached for him, needed to touch him, to feel the real, solid flesh beneath his borrowed shirt, but she was afraid that he'd shrug her off. Her hand hovered barely an inch above his sleeve.

She wanted to tell him that she was sorry, that she never really believed he was guilty of anything other than bad taste in friends, but that would have been a lie.

Of course she had believed it. She had run from him and hid not only herself, but their daughter as well. Her actions then spoke louder than any words now possibly could. They would be too little, too late.

She had not trusted him. She had believed him a murderer. She had believed her Mikey, the one who taught her to ride a bike and fish and dance, was capable of hiring a man like Garibaldi and giving him permission to hurt her.

Somewhere between *love* and *obey* in the marriage vows lay the word *honor*. Perhaps Michael had not honored his wife by taking her to that damned island for their honeymoon, but that was by far outweighed by her own dishonor in believing her husband capable of murder.

She was so ashamed. Her hand fell back and she turned away from him to look at the trees that danced past the speeding car.

She wished Thor had been well enough to travel. Wished she could still hear him in her head. He'd have known what she should do.

Michael glanced over at his silent wife. Christine didn't trust him, and he couldn't really blame her. What kind of man was he to be so blinded by a childhood friendship that he never realized what Jonas had become? What he must have been all along?

Michael didn't blame her for the last eight years or for what was happening now to their daughter. He blamed himself. That was the nasty little epiphany his dream on the plane had brought about. Everything that had happened before and whatever came next could be placed squarely on his head. If only he had recognized the signs. Looking back now, he could name any dozen incidents over the years that should have told him that Jonas was troubled.

Power-hungry.

Mad.

There were only two things that Michael couldn't regret of the last eight years—the existence of his daughter, and those few precious hours he'd spent in the Pirate's Cave with his wife.

He knew now that there would be no going back for him and Christine. They had grown too far apart, had learned to live without each other too well. The green girl who had followed in his shadows for so many years was gone, and in her place was a woman with opinions and depths he could barely begin to understand. Wasn't sure he wanted to.

He might hunger after that new, curvy, fascinating woman, yearn to share her breath and touch her skin, but the unyielding wall of the past would forever come between them, because his mistake, his blindness, might very well cost the life of their daughter.

Christine would never forget that, which was fine with him, since he would never forgive himself.

Michael turned from the window and glanced over at Christine. Her shoulders were slumped in defeat, and he thought he saw the glimmer of tears reflected in the tinted window. She must be thinking about Kayla, worrying what Jonas and his men would do to the child. He thought of his dream, about the rats, and suppressed a crawling shudder.

He wanted to hold his wife, to stroke her face and back and tell her that everything would be okay. He wanted to cuddle her against his chest and wipe her tears away. He wanted to kiss her lips and her eyes and that soft place on the back of her neck, and he wanted her to hold him in return and tell him that they were in this together.

But none of these things would happen. He had lost the right to touch her, and she had lost the faith to believe that what he said was true.

So he turned back to the window with a sigh and noted without interest that they were nearing the Hotel Santa Caribe. They passed a billboard that bore a discreet picture of Jonas welcoming them to his island.

Michael wanted to spit.

Chapter Twelve

"Is there something wrong, ma'am?" The bellhop stood expectantly at the door, waiting for her to enter and approve of the suite that had been reserved for them. He obviously hadn't expected her to balk at the threshold. Then his expression cleared. "Of course, you might wish your groom to carry you across."

The bellhop shot Michael a look, presumably to remind him that one traditionally carried one's companion into the honeymoon suite at the Hotel Santa Caribe.

"No, no. That's quite all right." Christine practically leapt into the room at the thought. It would be too horrible to have him carry her across the threshold again, too much an ugly parody of the perfect honeymoon she had once looked forward to.

Michael followed her into the suite and yanked a bill out of his wallet for the bellhop. A piece of paper fluttered down to land on the cream-colored rug.

Christine grabbed the paper while Michael ushered the bellhop out of the room and shut the door. She remembered that the rug had been the same light color before and wondered fleetingly whether they had replaced the bloodstained part or just cleaned it.

The paper was thin and folded. It was covered with newsprint and she recognized it instantly.

Unidentified Woman Found Drowned in Pirate's Cove.

She stared at it for a moment and thought of how Michael must have felt at seeing the words. He would have felt sorrow at her death and perhaps a sort of relief at finally knowing where she had gone.

"Do you wish I hadn't come?"

Michael's words were soft, the first he had spoken directly to her since their exchange in the limo, and as he used to do when they were children, he gave voice to the thoughts that rattled in her head.

She looked at him and was surprised to find him so close. His gray eyes studied her, measuring her reaction, and she resented the fact that although he could still read her mind, she could not hear his thoughts in return.

Did she wish he hadn't come to Farewell? Hadn't barged into the candle shop looking for information and found her instead? She wasn't sure.

It would have been easy for her to go on as she had been for so long, living with Kayla in their little cottage out on the beach. She had enjoyed watching her daughter grow, had loved the shop and her friends in the town. And if she looked over her shoulder during the day and screamed with terror in her sleep, that was a small price to pay for her child's safety.

And if she cried in the night, remembering the part of her that had once belonged to a man with a crooked smile and carver's hands, then she'd accepted that as well.

I think so, she was going to say, but the words wouldn't come.

If he hadn't come, she would be spending her evenings with Horst, planning the picnic for Farewell Day and fending off the occasional friend's attempt to set her up with this eligible bachelor or that.

And she would be so alone.

She would have missed seeing the light in Michael's eye

when he first saw her, would have missed the tingling aliveness that swam through her every time they were together. She would have missed that first kiss they had shared, would have missed the stunned, disbelieving, pained joy when he realized that Kayla was his. That she had the magic of the wood grain in her fingertips.

And the cave. Would she trade their hour in the cave for a lifetime of cold, predictable, loneliness? No. Never. Not in a million, trillion years.

But when she opened her mouth to tell him that, Michael had turned away. He had read his answer in her silence.

"Yeah, I thought so." His shoulders slumped in weariness, or maybe in defeat. He walked into the bathroom and shut the door.

Christine pressed her eyelids shut and rubbed the heels of her hands across them. She felt a killer headache brewing and tried to push it back with sheer force of will. She did not have time for a migraine.

She spared one look out toward the balcony and shivered. Night fell early on the island, and the first reddish streaks of sunset were spreading tendrils of color across the horizon. In the dusky light, the palm fronds seemed tainted with blood.

Well and truly chilled now, she opened her bag to find the sweater she remembered frantically packing for her and Kayla's flight from Farewell. She smiled a little at the terrible irony. They had gotten out of Farewell all right—all the way to Santa Caribe. That hadn't quite been the plan.

Her bag was empty.

Frowning, she checked the Snoopy suitcase. It was full of little-girl clothes. Michael's bag was packed with the jeans and shirts he had borrowed back in Farewell.

Just in case her clothes were hiding, she looked in her suitcase again. She rifled through the other bags.

Then she stilled as a horrible thought came to her. No. He wouldn't have. He couldn't have.

She walked into the bedroom. Opened the left-hand closet door. She always used the left side of closets—it had been her habit since childhood. Her father had used the right, and she wanted him to have a place to put his stuff when he came home.

Her clothes were there. Not the rumpled flannels, sturdy denim, and expensive underwear she had packed in Farewell, but the clothes she had left in Santa Caribe eight years earlier.

Michael swore softly behind her as her fingers traced across the row of patterned sundresses and skimpy halter-tops. She could have turned to him and cried for the lost years, could have raged at him with her fear for Kayla's safety, could have held him and shared the sorrow she knew he, too, felt.

But she did none of those things. In leaving him so long ago, she had forsaken the right to his comfort, the right to comfort him.

So instead she took a deep breath and searched the closet and the nearby dresser for a light sweater. The clothes she found were familiar, yet not, like clothes that might have belonged to the sister she didn't have. She vaguely remembered buying some of the items in preparation for her wedding trip, but now they seemed sad, outdated, irrelevant to the woman called Dewdrop.

In the back of one of the drawers she found a soft cotton sweater. She pulled the navy-blue bundle out and held it to her face for a moment, not caring that Michael was still behind her, unmoving, unspeaking.

She had knitted him the sweater in a burst of domestic creativity similar to the one that had led her to learn candle making. It still smelled of Mikey—not the man who stood in the room, but the young man she married. It smelled of clean sawdust and the New Hampshire woods in fall, a combination of moist earth, dying leaves, and slumbering life.

Pulling the sweater over her head, she willed the tears back and was relieved to hear her husband leave the room. She wasn't sure she could face him just then. She was fluffing her hair free of the collar when he returned, his eyes serious.

"We're locked in."

"I'm not surprised." She shook her head, thinking he was still trying to fight the truth. "He can't afford to have us running around loose, and he's probably enjoying the thought of us stuck together here. In fact," she glanced around and didn't see a camera eye, "he's probably got some sort of surveillance on us right now."

Michael looked over her shoulder, into the failing light. "But we've got to do something. We can't just sit here. How about . . . ?"

She followed his eyes to the balcony. "Oh no. No. I'm not going over that thing again."

A discreet knock forestalled further discussion, and they moved into the sitting room, toward the door. Reading each other as they once had, Christine glanced through the peephole while Michael positioned himself next to the door. In his hand he held the gun he'd taken from Ugly Two back at the candle shop.

"How did you get that thing through customs?" she hissed under her breath.

Michael cocked a brow. "I took a page out of our friend's book and hid it in the lining of Kayla's suitcase. Who'd have thought Snoopy was armed?" He grinned at her, and the lightning flash of teeth lit his whole face.

She felt her heart skip a beat. She had spent too much time running and hiding. Now it was time for action.

135

And after action would come the time for good-byes.

Trying to ignore the leaden ball that formed in her stomach at that thought, Christine looked through the spy hole again to make sure their caller was alone.

"Bellhop," she whispered to Michael. "Not the same one as before. There's a big guy behind him, armed."

She cracked the door open. "Yes?"

The native boy offered a silver tray bearing a slim, cream-colored envelope. "Message for you, Mrs. Finch."

Christine accepted the envelope, cool and faintly slimy with the knowledge of its sender. She closed the door quickly lest Michael get some idea about jumping the thug and breaking for freedom.

When footsteps in the hall indicated that the men had gone, Michael engaged the safety and stuck the gun in his waistband at the small of his back with an ease that made Christine wonder exactly what sort of work he'd been doing since she left. Had he, with her disappearance, fallen right back into his old ways? Had she, in her leaving, damned him beyond salvation when his only crime was poor judgment?

"What does it say?" He leaned close and she forced herself not to move away when his new scent clouded her senses—a dangerous, compelling mix of sea salt, clean sweat, and wood dust? How could he still smell of wood dust after all this time?

She inhaled again and he plucked the envelope from her numb fingers.

Yes. He still smelled of wood dust. And in that moment the Mikey she had married and the Michael who stood next to her shifted and became one in her mind. Where before she had separated the two in her thoughts, now there was only one man—the one who scowled over the note card and swore sharply under his breath.

One complex, loyal, flawed man. A man with the daring

good looks of an adventurer. A man who had helped her through a fatherless childhood, had kissed her down by their lake, had married her under a bower of colored leaves. The man who kept looking until he found her and the hidden daughter they had created.

If she was honest with herself, she might admit that it was the very wildness that she condemned in him, the lawlessness that she distrusted, that had excited her. Though it had driven them apart, it was an integral part of him, a crucial part of his art. A part of him that she had longed to harness, a part of him that made him the man she had fallen in love with twenty-some years earlier.

And as she looked at him in the dim light of the honeymoon suite, she had the sinking, sneaking suspicion that it would take very little to push her back over that terrifying cliff again.

If she hadn't already fallen.

"Damn him." Michael crumpled the note in one scarred hand, then stopped himself and offered the wadded ball to Christine. "Sorry. Go ahead and read it."

She didn't take the paper. She didn't want to feel the slimy crawl again. "What does it say?"

"That Mr. Garibaldi thanks us for joining him so promptly, that he hopes we like our room as much as we did the last time we were here, and that he'll meet us for breakfast tomorrow and we can negotiate." He swore again and looked for something to punch.

"Nothing about Kayla?" Christine felt that low, leaden ball drop another notch in her stomach. "Nothing at all?"

"No. I would have told you if there was. Go ahead and read it if you don't trust me."

Christine flinched but didn't move. "That was unnecessary."

He stilled, then ran a frustrated hand through his hair. "Yeah. You're right. I'm sorry, I'm just so . . . jumpy, I guess. I don't like being out of control. I don't understand what's happening. Jonas has never done anything like this before."

"At least, not that you're aware of," she corrected.

He acquiesced with a nod. "Sure, there have been times he's been tough. There was even that time he broke a guy's arm in a meeting, but he swore that was an accident and I believed him." He turned back toward the door and jiggled the knob in case the men had left it unlocked.

They hadn't.

"We've got to get to Kayla, hon." It was the first time since they'd been reunited that he'd called her by any of the old endearments, and the sound of it warmed her. "I have a bad feeling about this. I had a dream. We've got to get out of here and find her before something bad happens." If it hadn't already. He knocked a fist against the door, assessing its strength. Shaking his head he said, "Solid oak with a brass bolt. No way I'm breaking through it." He turned toward her with worry in his gray eyes. "I'm sorry, Chris. It's going to have to be the balcony."

She nodded, knowing that there was no other way. They couldn't leave Kayla in Jonas's clutches for another night. There was no telling what he had already done to her. As one, they turned and walked back through the sitting room into the master bedroom where she'd lost her virginity to him on a moon-drenched night eight long years ago.

A low growl, familiar yet not, greeted them, and Michael stopped dead.

Christine peered around his frozen form and stared. "Thor?"

Chapter Thirteen

It wasn't Thor, and the big red lion with the white blaze hadn't bothered to introduce itself. It had just herded them off the balcony and into the night.

"Can you still see the cat?" Christine hung on grimly to the back of Michael's shirt lest she lose him in the thick darkness of the Santa Caribbean jungle. She was puffing with the effort of keeping on her feet as they forged through the thick growth in the wake of the lion that was not Thor.

"I think so. I just hope I'm following the right pair of glowing eyes. I can't believe we're doing this. Remind me why we're doing this again?" He was breathing heavily too, and his words came out in a rush between gasps.

"It's a feeling. Trust me," Christine panted. "At least he got us out of that room. If I'd had to stay there any longer I think it would've driven me mad. Though it would've been nice if he'd let us sneak back into the hotel and look for Kayla after we made it to the ground." She wasn't sure she wanted to remember the precarious descent they'd made from the highest branches of a stout palm tree, with the cat waiting impatiently a few branches beneath.

She swore to herself that if they got out of this mess she was going to spend the rest of her life on the ground floor of any building she happened to enter.

They dodged around a fallen tree that the lion must've jumped right over, and Christine flinched as something the size of a hovercraft buzzed past her ear and into the darkness.

In the hotel room, it had been obvious that the big cat wanted Christine and Michael to follow it, and its growls made clear the fact that disobedience would not be taken lightly. Since they had wanted to get out of the room anyway and they couldn't ignore the animal's uncanny resemblance to Thor, Michael had handed Christine over the balcony rail, and they had jumped into the night together.

"Tell me how you and Thor met again." Michael's breath had leveled off, now that they were back on relatively flat ground and the moonlight that filtered through the high trees gave them some inkling of the terrain.

Christine had just been thinking of Thor and the furniture truck. It felt good to have Michael's mind back working in parallel with hers.

"I told you that I called you from Miami and arranged to meet you."

"Arranged to meet Jonas."

"Yeah, well I thought it was you at the time, okay? Let's not go there right now. Garibaldi grabbed me at the café where I'd arranged to meet—Jonas." She tripped and almost fell flat on her face, but Michael's fingers bit into her arm and held her up until she was back on her feet.

When she was steady, he let go of her arm, and the absence of his touch ached like a wound.

"How bad was it?"

For an instant, she was back in the van with Garibaldi rubbing himself against her backside and the other man flicking his switchblade in and out, in and out. The pleasant dampness of the rain forest suddenly seemed sour and cold, and she shivered in the navy sweater that she wore like a talisman.

She remembered the sick feeling of the switchblade cutting into her cheek and the rough touch of Garibaldi's hands on her tender breasts and soft belly.

"Bad enough."

Michael grunted and helped her over another fallen log. She could just make out the silhouette of their guide up ahead, dark against the silver-hued plants, its eyes an eerie glow in the night when it glanced back to check on the humans' progress.

"Go on."

"Before I went to the meeting I hid the amulets, just in case." She hurried on lest he wonder why she'd hidden the jewels if she trusted him. "I wrapped them in a condom and—swallowed them. When things got bad in the van, I started screaming through the gag and screaming even louder in my head. Then the strangest thing happened. My stomach got warm. Really, really warm. Hot, almost."

"Heartburn?" he asked, and she couldn't tell if he was being sarcastic or not. Heartache had been more like it.

"Weirder than that, lower. It was like the amulets were glowing inside me." She didn't mention that she'd seen them light up since—the night she'd poured the candle wax around them. "Anyway, right about then there was a horrible noise in the front of the van, like we'd hit something head-on, except we'd been sitting still. It was Thor."

"Thor? You're kidding."

Now it seemed that the lion was leading them back the way they had come, or maybe that was a trick of the island. Christine only hoped they would get wherever they were going soon. Her feet hurt and her back hurt, and her stomach was growling like the cats they could hear in the middle distance.

She tried to take her mind off the discomfort by continuing the story, "I'm not kidding. It was Thor, only he was a lot smaller than he is today. Still big enough, though. He broke right through that shatterproof windshield and attacked the guy with the switchblade. The guy dropped his knife, and I grabbed it and stuck it in Garibaldi's throat while he was trying to get the hell away from the half-grown lion that had suddenly appeared in the middle of his nasty little *ménage à trois*."

"You got away before . . ." He trailed off.

She nodded and panted. "Yep. Thor and I hitched a ride on a furniture truck bound out of Miami and slept on an ugly sofa—the one in my living room, I bought it as a sort of good luck charm—all the way to Farewell. He's been with me every day since, until we got on that plane to come here."

There was a low whistle from the branches above them, one that sounded more human than animal, and an answering whistle ahead of the lion, which suddenly sped up as if it knew their journey was at an end. There was an orange glow flickering between the trees.

Christine, who had been propelling herself with the irrational hope that the lion was leading them to Kayla, pulled up in dismay when they reached a clearing and were met, not by her daughter, but by a loose semicircle of fierce-looking men with war paint on their cheeks and wickedly barbed spears in their hands.

Natives. Suddenly all the safety brochures and in-hotel warnings flashed before her eyes. She'd all but convinced herself that the carefully couched threats of violence should guests wander beyond the manicured grounds were nothing more than Jonas's way of controlling things.

Now she wasn't so sure.

One man stepped ahead of the others as Michael and Christine stood frozen in shock. He seemed taller than the others, but only because of the elaborate headdress he wore.

Seeing something familiar in the way he walked, Christine

looked past the parrot feathers and the paint and thought she recognized the handsome olive-skinned man who had met them at the airport.

He worked at the hotel? Fear shivered through her stomach. Was he one of Jonas's men? Was it over already?

He held out a hand, palm up, and for a crazed instant Christine thought he was asking for another tip. "The blue stone, ma'am. Please." He didn't move, but the others shifted, spears and all, until they had completely surrounded Michael and Christine. The lion melted back into the shadows from whence it had come, and she felt the jewel heavy and warm between her breasts, where she had worn it the entire trip, claiming it as costume jewelry at customs.

It seemed to pulse with warmth, and she could swear that a faint blue light came from beneath her shirt. But that couldn't be, because she couldn't hear the lions. She couldn't use the stones.

But that didn't mean she was giving up her remaining leverage. She was going to get her daughter back or die trying.

"No," she said quite clearly to the men with the spears. "You can't have it."

Michael cast about quickly for a route of escape and felt the press of Ugly Two's gun at the small of his back. Damn it, he knew they shouldn't have followed that lion. He knew it had been a stupid idea, but the thing had appeared out of nowhere and led them into the forest just like the white hind in so many fairy tales. Why not follow it? He looked around at the men who encircled them and scowled. This was why.

His back itched and he frantically tried to remember how many shots were left in the gun. His knowledge of weapons was sketchy at best, but he thought it had a half-full clip. Would that be enough to take out an entire native village? He looked into the eyes of the men and remembered Jonas's stories of recent uprisings and atrocities committed just outside the hotel boundaries. He saw in their brown gaze a mixture of distrust, fear, and outright hatred, and he saw at the edges of the firelight the swish of red, black, and tan tails and the twitch of furry ears.

Great. Even if they managed to escape the circle of spear-chuckers, the whole place was swarming with lions.

Just great.

He was opening his mouth to tell Christine to give them the amulet when she squared her shoulders, glared at the head dude, and said, "I will not give you the amulet. My daughter has been kidnapped and I intend to exchange the jewel and the parchment for her. End of story."

They were dead. That's all Michael could think when the spears surged forward, and he tried to shove Chrissy behind him, which was difficult when danger was coming at them from all sides.

A sharp bark from the guy in the big hat had the warriors stopping, then retreating.

"Is this the truth?"

Michael nodded. "Yes. He has taken our daughter to exchange for the blue amulet."

The headman considered this, and Michael was relieved to see a glow of compassion in his eye. Maybe the guy had a daughter.

"And the green and red stones?"

"They were taken from us by a man called Garibaldi. We believe they have been brought here along with our daughter."

The man nodded. "Yes. The Guardians have told us that the stones of power and fertility are in the hotel." He motioned to Christine's chest. "You have the stone of wisdom."

She glared back at him. "I don't care if it's the stone of eternal halitosis, you can't have it. I need it to save my daughter."

The headman looked at her for a moment, then at Michael, then at the two of them together. He nodded as if reaching a decision, then clapped his hands and issued a loud volley of words in a liquid, euphonic language that Michael had never heard before—

Except when it had come out of his own mouth back in Farewell.

Instantly, the spears lowered, and Michael and Christine were propelled into a low building made of branches and leaves lashed together with vines and secured with duct tape. Michael had to grin at that.

"We'll have to suggest that for the next edition of '101 Things to do with Duct Tape'."

"I think one of the elders already e-mailed it to the author." The headman's dry voice came from behind Michael, startling him with its nearness as much as with the suddenly more casual speech pattern.

"Huh?"

The headman grinned and offered Michael his hand, "You can call me Pete." The three exchanged names and handshakes, and Pete set his headdress aside and sat down on a woven mat, gesturing the others to do so as well.

"E-mail?" Christine glared. "What's going on here? And what's with the lions? Are you going to keep us prisoner here? We need to rescue my daughter."

Pete held up a hand to stem the tide. "Of course, Mrs. Finch. I'm not sure I can answer all your questions in the time we have, but I assure you that you will not be prevented from fetching your daughter, if that is what you wish."

"Of course it is what I wish—"

"Please." His calmness settled her, for which Michael was grateful. He had been examining the rude shelter with a craftsman's eye and had seen the signs of haste and impermanence. He wanted to hear what Pete had to say.

"You have other homes, don't you? This is just a traveling camp, right?"

Pete nodded. "You are observant. Yes, this is a Spirit Camp, set up for certain rites only. In this case, set up to facilitate the recovery of our sacred amulets. We have homes and jobs and televisions and computers elsewhere." He sobered. "At least most of us do. The recent troubles have left many of my people homeless."

"Trouble?" Michael was afraid he knew what kind of trouble. Jonas's kind of trouble.

"The men who run the hotel and the resort are trying to gain control of our tribes and the gold mines that have belonged to my people since the time of my great-great-grandmother's mother and before. They wish to own the mines and the workers, and when we resist we are killed, our houses burned, our water poisoned."

Michael felt nausea boil in his gut. Here was another crime of which he had been blissfully unaware. When Jonas had e-mailed him about staffing problems on the island—always inquiring about Michael's progress in looking for his wife at the same time—he had always believed his friend had been talking about a housekeeping strike.

"And the amulets?" Christine's voice was low, strained, and she stared at her hands in the flickering light of the bonfire that shone through the door of the shelter.

"That will be best explained later, if you'll join us for dinner. We can talk afterward." Pete stood, but remained stooped within the low hut. "You are free to roam about the camp, but I wouldn't recommend going into the forest. The

Guardians will not hurt you because you wear the amulet of wisdom, but there are other, darker creatures on the island who are not so kind."

Michael and Christine stared dumbly at each other in the silence that settled within the shelter. The little room was warm and dry, the ceremonial fire crackled softly outside, and Michael suddenly wanted nothing more than to lie down and sleep. If they'd eaten or drunk anything on the island, he might have thought he'd been drugged.

But they hadn't. He was quite simply exhausted.

As if reading his thoughts, Christine cracked a huge yawn and he was obliged to do the same, and for a moment they were in perfect accord, grinning at each other like loons.

Then, as one they sobered. She spoke first, voicing their mutual concern. "Do you think they know we're gone?"

Unspoken lay the question, *Do you think they've hurt Kayla because we escaped?*

Michael considered it as his eyelids grew heavy and three days with too much excitement and not enough sleep crowded him. "Probably, but they still have what we want and vice versa. We're going to make that meeting tomorrow morning and trade the amulet and the parchment for Kayla and get the hell out of here."

He tried to speak positively, but they both knew it wouldn't be quite that easy. Michael had known Jonas for years, as had Christine, and they both knew that he hated to lose at anything.

"Do you think Pete and his buddies will let us make the meeting?"

Michael hadn't thought that far ahead, but he said positively, "Of course they will. I feel bad that the amulets were stolen from them, but that's not our problem. Let them work that out with Jonas after we're gone."

Fatigue won over worry and he started to slide sideways onto a pile of fur and cloth. "Besides," he murmured on the way down, "what're they going to do to stop us?"

What the natives were going to do, Christine discovered an hour or so later, was dance.

Pete tapped discreetly on the frame of the small shelter, and she woke up, at first not realizing that she had been asleep. She seemed to have curled up against Michael while they both slept, and he wouldn't let go of her right away.

So there she was, trapped against his broad chest by his heavy arm, trying to get free when he cuddled her close and started kissing her.

Very, very thoroughly.

Pete coughed delicately and said, "We'll eat in a few minutes. Please join us when you are ready." He withdrew as discreetly as he had come, leaving Christine with no choice whatsoever.

She kissed her husband back.

He was all warm and soft and frowsy, with his eyes half-open and his lips curved up in a sweet smile. She couldn't help herself. She kissed him slowly, sleepily, and as his elegant carver's hands traveled in devastating sweeps up and down her back, she felt the hard knot of tension she had carried for eight long years dissolve in a warm rush.

This was Michael. He wasn't quite the boy she remembered, nor was he the unknown man who had stood in her candle shop and brought the wrath of fate down upon her. He was both of these men and neither. He was a man formed from the troubled boy she had known, tempered by the fires of hell that she herself had been into and beyond.

With a groan, he rolled atop her and buried his face in her hair, kissing her helplessly, hopelessly.

She poured her heart and soul into the moment, trying to tell him without words that she was sorry for having ever doubted him, for having left him, for having kept his daughter away for so long.

The moment he began to wake up fully, she could feel the change, feel him draw back into the protective shell he had donned after their fight in the Pirate's Cave.

He pushed her back gently, firmly, and levered himself off her and onto his knees in one motion.

She could let him go. She probably should, and the girl that she had once been definitely would have accepted his withdrawal. That girl would have said, "We have to talk" or some other nonsense, and the moment would have been lost. But with her lips still swollen from his kisses, the woman she had become was not about to let that happen. She wanted her man, and she wanted him now and damn the consequences. Damn the questions and the doubts. To hell with the fears.

They were born for each other and had been apart through the worst that life had to offer. Now they deserved to be together.

She slid sinuously to her knees, faced him where he breathed hard and fought to master the demands of his own body. She swayed toward him just enough to nip at his lip, drawing blood where it had already been split and making him hiss with the jolt of pain.

Her blood pounded with the sound, and she drifted toward him again, intending to see how well his borrowed shirt was made. Then she felt him stiffen, saw him cock his head toward the doorway. She realized at that moment that the pounding noise in her head was not entirely that of her rapidly beating heart.

It was the drums.

Jesus, that was close, thought Michael. All those heroic promises he had made on the flight to Santa Caribe had almost gone up in smoke when he had awoken with Christine in his arms. Gone was his intent, after he won their daughter back, to send his wife and child back to live without him in their little seaside paradise. Gone was the knowledge that he didn't deserve Christine, that he had failed her so many times, that she was better off without him.

Gone was his determination to set her free.

Almost. *Almost, but not quite.* He scrubbed a trembling hand across his sore face and tried to hear the drums over the pounding of his heart.

"Dinnertime already?" He kept his tone light, willed her to do the same. "We shouldn't keep our hosts waiting then." He rose to a crouch and offered her a hand. "I can't believe we fell asleep."

She ignored his hand and preceded him out of the shelter, and the sight of her curvy little denim-covered backside poking out from beneath his old sweater almost brought him to his knees.

Almost. That seemed to be the word of the day. They almost had Kayla back. Jonas had almost driven Christine out of her mind with that diabolically prepared honeymoon suite. They had almost figured out the connection between the lions, the natives, and the amulets. And Michael had almost groveled on the floor of that little hut and begged Christine for forgiveness. Begged her to take him back and let him spend the rest of his life trying to make up for past mistakes.

Almost.

The food was filling, if not overly exciting, although Christine found that it improved substantially each time the wineskin was passed around. That wineskin, which appeared to be formed of some sort of animal stomach—she decided after the second sip not to look at it too closely—was filled with a sickly sweet concoction that tasted like a cross between alcoholic bug juice and mesquite-flavored barbecue sauce.

It was oddly delicious, especially after the first few swallows.

Though her heart screamed for her to jump up and run far, far away from the native encampment, wanted her to demand her daughter back from the madman who held her, Christine was aware that they were in the forest at the pleasure of the natives—human and lion alike. And she had the strong feeling that she and Michael needed to know the full story of the amulets before they could rescue their daughter.

Besides, after a few circuits of the wineskin, she was in no position to run anywhere.

Michael sat at her elbow, and every time he leaned forward to accept another dish his arm or thigh rubbed up against her until she wasn't sure whether the spinning in her head was from the stuff she was drinking, the dancers that whirled around the bonfire, or his touch.

The drums began anew and the dancers settled, bobbing their lavish headdresses at the two outsiders.

"We want to show you the story of the amulets, that you might understand what has been taken away from us." Christine hadn't realized that Pete was sitting on her other side, but there he was, gesturing for the dancers, men and women of all ages, to begin their tale.

They twirled and spun to the music of drums and an eerie pipelike instrument that sounded to Christine like something from a sci-fi movie, and the stamping feet and nodding headdresses began to spin faster and faster until she wanted to scream for them to stop, to slow down, to let her catch up.

Just when she thought she couldn't stand it any longer, a harsh cry of the pipe caused the dancers to freeze in mid-motion.

There was a sound from the pitch-black forest, a look of terror on the faces of the static dancers, a horrible growl from the night beyond the light of the fire.

That was when the lions joined in the dance, and Christine began to understand what it was that she had been hiding from all these years.

And she was afraid.

Chapter Fourteen

"So let me get this straight." Michael felt the blood throb behind his eyeballs and wished he'd let pass at least half of the wineskin's trips around the fire. "Your people mined the stones in those amulets? And the gold? I didn't think there were any natural resources to speak of on Santa Caribe besides the rain forests. Why don't the maps note your workings?"

Christine shot him a pointed look as if to say *Of course they don't. Jonas doesn't want anyone to know about them.*

"Because we don't want outsiders to be aware of the mines," Pete said, paralleling Michael's own thoughts. "They're for religious purposes only, not enrichment. That's what the dance symbolizes—how the gods gave us the stones and the metal as a way to honor them."

The headman gestured at the amulet that Christine still wore beneath her shirt, and Michael's gaze was drawn to the jut of a full breast on either side of the hidden jewel.

He was having a hard time steering his thoughts away from their torrid embrace in the little hut. In fact, the more of that fruit drink he had consumed, the harder it had become to remember why he had stopped her.

"What I don't understand," said Christine, "is how the amulets came to be in Michael's suitcase." She puckered her forehead endearingly, and he remembered why he hadn't followed up on her offer. He didn't deserve her.

She continued, "I mean, if these things have been hugely significant to your people for hundreds of years, how come they weren't on the island?"

Pete nodded. "A valid question. They were taken from us by foul treachery." He looked into the fire, which was dying now, and the dancers gathered closer to hear the familiar story. Michael found himself leaning in as well, but he was distracted from the beginning of Pete's story by the smell of Christine's hair when it tickled his nose.

He leaned back and tried to pay attention.

"A man from your country came to our island when I was young and befriended my father, who never suspected that the American might not be what he seemed. My father invited him to the ritual dances, took him to the mines, told him the ancient stories. He even adopted the American into his own hearth and gave him a tribal name, one handed down from our forefathers."

Chrissy asked, "When was this?"

Pete stared into the fire, calculating the calendar years. "Perhaps thirteen or fourteen years ago."

Fourteen years ago Christine had been a teenager, and Michael had been just twenty-one. He tried to remember what he had been doing at twenty-one. Probably starting his apprenticeship with one of the world's best woodcarvers, Paul Blankenshemp. Chrissy had been in high school, and Jonas had been . . .

A shiver crawled up Michael's spine and he straightened, unconsciously removing his arm from Christine's shoulders.

Jonas had left New Hampshire after his mother was killed in the one and only burglary in the memory of their little town. Michael had ignored the rumors that questioned the burglar's existence, but he did suddenly wonder where Jonas had gone for the nine months or so following her death.

Michael himself hadn't been in town for Jonas's triumphant return but had heard tales of his friend showing up downtown in a spiffy new car with snazzy new clothes and money to burn. Jonas had begun investing soon thereafter and over time had amassed a fortune that now clocked in at well over the billion mark—on paper at least.

The townspeople had always assumed that Jonas's seed money had come from his parents' estate, but his family had been as poor as Michael's own—he knew that for a fact.

Where had Jonas gotten the money? From Santa Caribe?

Pete continued, "On the night of the harvest festival, when all the wives and mothers are served the best of food and drink by their men—"

"My kind of festival," Christine murmured.

"—the American came to my father and said that there was a problem down in the oldest mine. When morning came and everyone woke with heads thick from drink and dancing, a great cry arose. My father was dead. Six guardians lay by him, shot and killed." Pete bowed his head. "And the amulets were missing. It is the shame of my family that this happened."

"But that's not the last you saw of the amulets, is it?" Suddenly, several highly sensitive memos that Michael had once seen began to make horrible sense.

Pete nodded. "We did not actually see the amulets, but the Guardians told us, eight years ago, that they were on the island. Before we could act, though, they were gone again and Harding's men were scouring the island for a woman who had stolen from him."

Christine nodded. "I had the amulets, but I didn't know what they were or what to do with them. And even when I thought I could hear Thor, he didn't have the answers either."

155

Michael felt a soundless rush of air pass by him and fought not to jerk back when two lions suddenly appeared at Pete's side. One was as black as coal and had eerie emerald eyes. The other was the big reddish cat that had led them into the forest.

There was a butterfly's wing of pressure against his mind, and Michael thought that the lions were speaking. He wondered why he couldn't hear them. Maybe he'd blocked himself off from their voices, just as Christine had.

Michael felt a quiver of fear.

He'd been profoundly disturbed when he had come back to himself after reading the words on the parchment. The power had been so pure, so tempting, that if it hadn't been for Christine's interruption, he might have continued building the blue flame until it consumed everything. It was that seductive.

And when she'd stepped in front of him and taken the parchment, for a moment he'd considered swatting her aside like a fly.

The soft touch feathered against his consciousness again, and he felt it bump up against a solid wall.

Pete's next words confirmed what he'd begun to suspect. "You're both blocked. The Guardians wish to know of this Thor. So do the rest of us."

Christine nodded, looked into the flames. "I found him, or maybe he found me, in Miami."

"When?"

All the dancers had leaned forward as one to hear her answer.

"Eight years ago. He wasn't fully grown then, but he looked as if he'd been through a lot. He helped me escape from two of the men who are up at the hotel now with my daughter. We sort of stuck together after that."

"The amulets called him." When Michael cocked his head, Peter continued, "This is a part of the story that I left out. Just before Harding brought the amulets back to the island eight years ago, a young Guardian was taken from us. We feared him killed, but the others did not cry the death song for him, so that could not be so. We later discovered that he had been bartered for the amulets."

Pete stroked one of the cats under the chin, and it squeezed its eyes shut in aloof acknowledgment. "Guardians are a rare breed, found only on Santa Caribe. There are usually only a hundred or so in existence at any one time. Collectors have offered my people incredible amounts of money for even an untried kitten, though they are not ours to sell."

It all began to make a terrible horrible kind of sense, but Michael knew there had to be another level of meaning. There had to be a reason for Jonas's going to so much trouble to get the amulets back.

Once again, Christine read his mind. "What will the three amulets do if Jonas is able to wield them? And how can he if he can't read the parchment? Thor told Michael that the parchment cannot be read without the help of a lion."

"Since losing the amulets, my people have suffered one catastrophe after another. The gods are angered with our carelessness and have punished us with poor growing seasons, an increase in fatal childhood diseases, poor performance of our stock portfolios, and several hideous disasters in the mines."

Michael wasn't sure about the stock-portfolio connection, but then again, he'd seen the blue amulet in action. He wasn't ready to discount anything out of hand.

"And to answer your second question," Pete continued, "it is to the everlasting shame of my family that my father not only adopted this man, he also taught him to read and speak the ancient language. He does not need the help of a

Guardian." He leaned forward earnestly. "Those amulets are required for our prosperity. Their loss is a stain on my family name. We must get them back."

By *we,* Michael had a feeling Pete didn't just mean the natives. He thought it was time for a reality check. "Not to offend you, particularly when you're sitting between a pair of lions, but my first priority is our daughter. We have to rescue her, and if we have to exchange one of the amulets to do it, then we will."

One of the Guardians shifted and bared his teeth at Michael, but Pete simply laid a calming hand on the creature's head and nodded. "I understand your concern. Be assured that your daughter's safety is of importance to us as well." He nodded again, and the dancers melted among the other huts that surrounded the dying bonfire. "But our priority has to be the amulets. You must understand that from your association with your Guardian." He paused and looked into the shadows as if seeking something. "Speaking of which, why is young Thor not with you?"

"He was injured trying to protect our daughter from the kidnappers," Michael said.

One of the other men nodded. "Your daughter had the amulets?"

"No." Christine shook her head. "Thor has always been partial to Kayla. He follows her wherever she goes, and they get into and out of trouble together. I'd say he's more her Guardian than the amulets'."

The headman frowned and shook his head. "That can't be right. His priority must be the gems."

"He once told me he was Guardian to both the jewels and the child," Michael argued. "Surely he can protect both."

There was a restless shifting among the natives. The black Guardian with the green eyes pulled her lips back in a grimace, and Michael felt that mental feather-touch again. He wondered whether he could pull those subconscious shields down. There was a whole conversation going on that he couldn't hear.

"No. Impossible." Pete shook his head at the red lion. "That's just a fairy tale."

Christine snorted, and Michael felt an answering chuckle working its way through his chest. "This whole damn thing seems like a fairy tale to me, guys. So let us in on it—what's the story?"

The black lion looked at Michael and Christine, and when Pete spoke, it was as though he was translating the lion's words for them. "You have read the parchment? Then you know that the three must not be wielded together. If the three are used by one, then that one will control everything on the island—the people, the Guardians, the other animals. Even the plants will rise up at his command, and that is not what the Elder intended. Worse, the power will begin to control its user, and in the end the island will be destroyed. So it is written."

"But what does this have to do with my daughter?" Christine asked.

"There is a story as old as the gems," answered the black lion through the headman's lips, "that in a time of great need a child will be conceived who holds the power of the gems in her heart. She will be able to command all three gems for good rather than evil, and when the threat is gone, she will be able to put the power away."

He shrugged, and his voice returned to speaking as a man rather than as the mouthpiece of a Guardian. "But I disagree with the Guardians. Your daughter can't be the Spoken One. She wasn't conceived here, and the amulets weren't—" He broke off. Michael and Christine were shaking their heads. "She was conceived here?"

"On our wedding night at the hotel. Don't ask," Michael cautioned. "It's a long story."

"Where were the amulets at the time?" It felt as though every warrior—male and female—and every one of the lions in the shadows held their collective breath, waiting for the answer.

"Five feet away from the bed, hidden in the lining of my suitcase."

The breath was expelled. The fire crackled.

Nobody spoke.

Then finally, the black lion growled softly in the back of her throat and butted Christine's cheek with her enormous head. Then, with a whisper of sound and motion, all of the lions disappeared into the forest. Into the night.

"Where are they going?"

Pete looked from Christine to Michael and back again. "They have gone to watch the hotel. In the morning we will go get your daughter."

The words should have been a relief, but Michael had to ask: "Why didn't the lions know about Kayla? Thor sensed it. Why didn't the others? Too far away?"

The headman looked uncomfortable. "The distance is not much of a factor. I can only assume she's been asleep."

"Or drugged," Michael added.

Nobody said the words they were all thinking.

Or dead.

"Come. Rest now and let the ceremonial wine ease your tensions. In the morning we will plan." Pete rose and gestured Christine and Michael to their grass hut. "And then we will go get your daughter."

Chapter Fifteen

"Do you really think they're going to help us get Kayla?" Christine knotted and unknotted her fingers, a motion he could see by the bloody light of the dying fire that filtered through the chinks in their little shelter.

Michael had learned much about business in the eight years he had been working for Jonas Harding, albeit on the semi-legitimate fringes of what now appeared to be a monstrously evil conglomeration. He was sure that Pete and his men would keep their word and assist in Kayla's rescue, but he also worried that their motives might not be the same as his and Chrissy's. They were obviously hoping that Kayla was this "Spoken One"—whatever that meant—and that she'd save their bacon once she was free.

Michael didn't want to bet on it. Nor did he want to bet his daughter's life on it.

He started to reassure Chrissy, but he saw from her expression that she, too, had learned some hard lessons in recent years. So he told her the truth. "I don't think they mean her ill or that they would hurt her on purpose. But I'm not sure our agenda and theirs are going to coincide exactly. We just want to get her and get the hell out of here."

Christine nodded. "I think you're right. What are we going to do about it?"

And it was that *we* that struck him. In all the times they had been together before, he and Christine had each had their roles. He was the man; she was the woman. He split wood and built things; she cooked, cleaned, and planned to raise their children. She didn't need to work. He would.

Perhaps that had been an immature, stultifying way of looking at the future, but they were doing as their parents had done before them, and their grandparents before that.

And she had rebelled against the thought.

Now Christine sat across from him, her features glowing in the light from the bonfire as she asked him how the two of them together would save a child. And in a flash like the shock of a bucket of ice-cold water dumped over his head, Michael finally understood what she had tried to tell him eight years ago.

Throughout their childhood he'd been the leader, the older one, the strong one. He picked the games, made the rules, and yes, tried to choose her friends. Somewhere along the line, he'd forgotten to let her grow up.

"I'm . . . I'm sorry," he said into the darkness.

"For what? Getting us into this whole ugly mess? I've already forgiven you for that."

He felt her narrow hand on his forearm but didn't really hear her words. He was too busy trying to assemble the words of his apology.

"I'm sorry for what happened at the hotel that night. I'm sorry for bringing you to this island and telling you that you had to like Jonas because I said so, and I'm sorry about the things I said in the restaurant. I guess I just wasn't expecting you to have an opinion."

He knew he had gone too far when she removed her hand and leaned away from him.

"A what?" Her voice cracked in outrage. "You didn't expect me to have an opinion, did you say? What, you thought I was just going to blindly follow whatever you said because you were my *husband?*" She crossed her arms and spat, "Neanderthal."

Ignoring the fact that he'd just been calling himself the same thing in his own mind, Michael bristled. "Well, excuse me. I don't suppose it had anything to do with that little act you pulled the whole time we were courting." He fluttered his eyelashes, even though she couldn't see them, and pushed his voice to a cloying, irritating falsetto.

"Ooh, Michael, you're so big and strong and handsome. So commanding and masculine. I don't care where we go to dinner; I'll like whatever you want. You pick the movie, the wine, our house." He dropped his voice back to its normal tones. "How the hell was I supposed to know you didn't want to be ordered around? You'd done a pretty good impression of humble obedience over the years, trying to be the good girl so your daddy would come back."

"You bastard," she hissed. She shot to her feet and banged her head on the springy branches of the roof. "I loved you."

Michael sprang up as well, not caring that he almost poked a hole in the top of their shelter. His heart was pounding, his blood thundering, and he wanted nothing more than to yank Christine into his arms and kiss her until neither of them could think anymore.

She had loved him, yes. And he had loved her, as one loved a loyal and predictable friend. But the Christine he had married had never defied him like this, never stood up to him and called him names or looked at him as if she would cheerfully have killed him then and there.

He had seen an inkling of this woman that night at the restaurant, when she had laid into him for going back on his word and not only dragging her to Jonas's island, but agreeing to one last business deal with his old friend.

At the time, Michael had been horrified by the passionate,

violently upset woman who faced him over half-eaten breadsticks. Horrified and terribly, terribly turned on.

Now he was just turned on.

She glared up at him, hands on her hips, a scowl on her face. Her chest heaved from the exertion of fighting him, and as he watched by the light of the sputtering fire, she licked her lips once and he was lost.

She didn't know what had happened. One minute they were fighting, and the next minute she was up against the shaky, leafy wall and he was kissing her, oh, kissing her as she had always dreamed he could.

As the power surged through her, she exulted. This, yes, this was what she had wanted eight years ago. This flash and burn and scrape of teeth and tongue. This grind of bodies and clutching flame of fingers on flesh.

This was what she had wanted then and needed now.

So she met him as his equal, bad boy to wild woman, met him tooth for tooth and hand to hand until they sagged together against the center pole of their shelter and the whole thing shook with their passion, raining leaves around them as they fell to the furs. The sounds from without—a soft chuckle and an answering rumble from one of the Guardians—were lost to them as they fought a battle as ancient as humankind.

Warriors each, made such by the tests of time and evil, they came together with vengeance and anger and love all mixed together until she could no longer tell where the rage ended and the tenderness began. It was all one huge, all-consuming emotion, and she was powerless before it.

But for the first time, when she bowed before the power of a greater force, she was not alone. She was not alone in her anger, not solitary in her fear for her daughter, not singular in her cry of fulfillment.

Michael was there with her, sharing her, completing her, and when it was done and they lay beside each other with sweat cooling on their bodies and their clothes half on and half off, Christine knew that for the first time in forever, she was not alone. She lay with her head on his chest and listened to the slowing rhythm of his heart and tried to block out the past, the present, and the future.

To no avail.

"What are we going to do?" she asked again, knowing that as much as each of them needed the release they had found in the other, their problems were far from solved. He still resented her lack of trust eight years ago, still blamed her for keeping their daughter a secret, and probably hated her for making him face the truth about his friend.

White-hot, mind-numbing, incredibly Earth-shaking sex hadn't changed that one bit.

For her part, she loved him. It was as simple as that, yet not simple at all. She had loved him then, too, but had been too immature to deal with him fairly and make him see how important that promise had been to her. In all honesty, he'd had a point when he'd accused her of hiding behind a façade of submissiveness while they were dating.

She had been too grateful for his love, too overwhelmed by his looks and his talent, to risk the relationship by disagreeing with him. Her fault. So it was no wonder he had been shocked by her harpyish behavior that night—she hadn't given him much warning beyond refusing to marry him until he agreed to forsake his friend.

She sighed heavily, and her sigh was echoed by Michael.

"I'm not sure what to do," he said, and she noticed his omission of the word *we*. Hadn't he realized by now that they were a team in this? Or was he planning some sort of Lone Ranger stunt that would protect her and endanger him?

165

The camp had quieted with the passing of midnight, and the only noise from without was the occasional hiss of a breaking ember and the swish of the jungle beyond.

"I don't think we should wait until morning. I think we should sneak in now, find Kayla, and get out before Pete brings his people in." Christine touched the twisted metal that lay coolly between her breasts.

"One person could probably get in easier than a mob," Michael agreed cautiously.

"Two people," she corrected. "And I think so, too. Pete mentioned surveillance cameras in all the rooms, so by now Jonas knows we're gone. He'll be waiting for us to come back, and he's not likely to be too happy with us for wasting his time and money." She snapped her fingers next to Michael's ear as a thought occurred to her, "He's probably got a camera wherever they're keeping Kayla. We've just got to find the security center where the cameras all feed, and from there we'll know where to go."

Christine thought it sounded pretty simple when she put it that way.

Michael eased out from under her and started straightening his borrowed clothing. He wouldn't meet her eye in the reflected light from the embers when he said, "I think it would be better if we split up."

The pit of her stomach dropped at those words, and she reminded herself sternly that he didn't mean it in that context. He just meant that they should enter Jonas's hotel separately. "Okay. Once we get there, I'll go in the front like a regular customer and ask at the desk where the security monitors are and see how far I get. Do you want to climb back up one of those trees and do some looking around?"

Michael shook his head. She could feel the motion more

166

than she could see it in the darkness. "That wasn't quite what I was thinking, Chrissy."

His use of her childhood nickname, whether accidental or on purpose, gave her a clue as to what was coming next. She didn't like it one bit.

"I was more thinking that you should stay here with Pete and his people. That way, if anything goes wrong in the compound, you'll be here with the amulet and the parchment. You can go in with these guys in the morning and pull me out if I get in trouble."

She was right; he was trying to shut her out again, trying to pat her on the head and say, "Nice wifey, sit here until I get back." Well, he was in for a surprise—that tactic hadn't worked well eight years ago, and it wasn't likely to work much better now, whether or not her body was still purring along in the aftermath of some pretty incredible lovemaking.

Even so, she didn't feel any need to get in his face about it. She thought she could try some nice, rational discussion. So she said, "No way."

"What? Why not? It's a good plan." He sounded defensive and a little belligerent, which was his usual tone when he knew he was wrong.

"Maybe so, but I'm not staying behind. I have the amulet, and she's my daughter. I'm going with you." Christine, too, started to rearrange her clothing, catching the occasional whiff of his scent on her skin and hair.

The smell made her nostalgic, even though only minutes earlier they had been tearing at each other voraciously. Something told her it would be a long time before she again felt that jellylike looseness in her limbs and smelled the musk of sex on her body.

"Like hell you are." Michael's voice rose, and she fought the urge to shush him. He stood and she rose with him, trying not to remember that they had been in this position only minutes earlier—yelling at each other nose to nose within the little hut.

"Try again. I'm going to the hotel now, and you can try to stop me but I wouldn't advise it." Christine heard motion outside the tent and felt the amulet grow warm between her breasts. She hoped that what she was planning would work, as her plans had back when she could still hear Thor in her head. Back when the glow of the three amulets had warmed her body and summoned her Guardian.

"Christine." He held his hands out pleadingly. "Please. Do this for me. I love you. I'll worry if you're with me. You didn't trust me once before—please trust me now. I'll get your daughter back for you. I swear it. Just please stay behind."

She wanted to. She wished she could. The words *I love you* shimmered through her heart and stayed there, where she could take them out and think about them later.

But once again fear was stronger than trust or even love. She stepped out of the little shelter, into the cloaking darkness, and faced him in the doorway. "I'm sorry, Michael. I can't."

Michael moved toward her but was driven back by a sudden, fierce snarl. Two Guardians moved up behind her, and with a flick of her wrist she sent one toward him. "Stay here," she ordered.

She wasn't quite sure if she was talking to the big cat or to the man, but the big cat nodded. Her mind was too confused to hear the creature's thoughts, but the lion understood anyway. There was a butterfly's whisper across her mind, a breath of good luck.

The blue stone pulsed beneath her shirt, in time with her heartbeat, and she gestured to the other Guardian to lead the way. "Find Kayla." She closed her eyes and pictured her child, thought the image hard, and aimed it at the cat.

The reddish creature disappeared into the inky black forest, and she repressed a shudder before following it.

The last thing she heard was Michael's voice cursing over the growl of a lion: "Christine! Come back. Let me go with you! Don't do this to us! Don't do this alone!"

He might have said more, but she tuned him out as her heart sank within her and she knew that she had lost him for good this time because she hadn't trusted him enough. He hadn't trusted her enough.

It was the same story, different decade.

She followed the Guardian by wan moonlight and fixed a picture of her daughter in her mind to guide her like a beacon as she tramped through the jungle of Santa Caribe Island.

Alone.

Chapter Sixteen

The Guardian led her back through the jungle, and her heart broke at the thought of leaving Michael behind. Again. Then she jammed the heartbreak deep down and prepared to fight for her daughter's life.

The jungle was humid, rank. The leaves slid over her skin like chilly fingers, and she shuddered and hurried to keep the lion's lean flanks in sight. The journey back to the hotel seemed both shorter and longer than the trip she and Michael had made the day before, and when they passed into the manicured grounds of the Santa Caribe Hotel, Christine was aware of the sinewy bodies that lurked in the shadows and patrolled the edges of the forest. The lions were waiting.

She hoped they wouldn't have to wait long.

The marble lobby was close to deserted. The island's tourism had fallen to a trickle because of the civil unrest between natives and Jonas's people, and there was only one man behind the front desk.

"Can I help you?"

"Tell Mr. Harding that Christine Finch wishes to speak with him. Tell him I have something he wants and I'm willing to negotiate a trade now, not in the morning. I will meet him in his security hub."

The desk clerk either knew exactly what was going on, or he was used to strange messages. His expression didn't change when he lifted the phone and repeated the message.

But his eyes flickered to a section of wainscoting, and Christine knew that she was being watched.

She resisted the urge to give Jonas the finger.

As the elevator rose toward her meeting, Christine marveled at how easy it had been to gain access to the security room. Almost too easy. That didn't make it very secure, did it? She almost giggled, giddy with the thought of seeing her daughter and having this finally be over, after all these years. She sobered when she remembered the look on Michael's face when she had left him in Pete's camp, but there really hadn't been any other way. He'd been determined to do things all his way—again—and she had been just as determined to have her say.

Surely, once Kayla was freed and they had a chance to sit down and talk about it, he would agree that she had been right to leave him behind.

Yeah, she thought, and Kayla really was a magical child who had the power to command an entire island.

The concierge paused in front of an unmarked door and knocked twice before turning the handle. "This way, please, ma'am." He ushered her through the doorway and left.

A big desk took up the center of the room. It faced row upon row of black-and-white monitors, and Christine was about to leap toward them in search of her daughter when she heard movement behind her.

Garibaldi had been standing behind the door. He pushed it closed. She heard the click of a lock.

"Miss me, sweetheart?"

As Garibaldi stepped past, he trailed his fingertips over her hip and across her abdomen in greeting. "I think you have something I want." He nodded to a monitor on the far left and tapped a few keys on the console. The view on the main monitor shifted to show a little blonde girl curled up in the center of a big bed. "And I have something of yours."

"Kayla!" Christine surged toward the monitor, reaching to touch her child's image.

Garibaldi snatched her back and spun her toward a chair. Shoved her into it. "Not so fast." He moved in close, smiled when she leaned away. "I think we have a little business to conduct."

He reached out and fingered a few strands of her hair. "Got it cut, did you, babe? I like it. Your hair kept getting caught in my teeth when we were together in the van." He dropped his hand, let it casually slide across her breast. "Remember how hot it got in that van, babe?"

It wasn't time to scream yet, though she wanted to. It was the voice of her nightmares. The hand of the devil.

But she couldn't. She'd passed the point of no return, and her only goal now had to be saving Kayla. But she'd been wrong, so very wrong to think she could do this without Michael and the others. She tried to call the lions, but her plea bounced up against a mental wall of fear and loathing for the man who held her.

So she breathed deep and made her tone even. "I remember the van very well. How's the scar?"

He snarled and grabbed her by the throat. Pressed hard against her windpipe. "Think that's funny, do you? Just for that I'm going to leave you alive while I do the kid, so you can watch."

"Garibaldi." The mechanized voice came out of everywhere and nowhere, and Christine jerked in response. The voice sounded barely human—if it was human at all.

The awful pressure on her neck eased, and Christine drew a grateful trickle of oxygen into her lungs. Garibaldi said, "Yeah, Boss?"

"Let her go. She's come here to negotiate, and she can't very well do that if you've broken her neck." The metallic voice slithered around the edges of the room, and Christine wished suddenly that she hadn't come. Wished she were back in the grass hut right now in Michael's arms.

Then she caught sight of the motionless child on the video screen. Kayla. She had to get Kayla.

"Take me to my daughter." She meant her words to sound forceful, but Garibaldi must have injured her throat. The words came out huskier than her usual tones. Sexier. "You and your *boss*," she spat the word, knowing that Jonas was watching everything and wondering why his voice sounded so wrong, "can have the amulet once my daughter is safe."

Garibaldi snorted. "Touching. But I suppose threatening her will do me more good than threatening you." He grabbed Christine by the arm and hustled her toward the door.

"Garibaldi."

He stopped. "Sir?"

"Bring the other amulets with you. Once you have the blue stone and the parchment, I want you to bring them directly to me. Do you understand? I need them."

The menace underlying the metallic voice was unmistakable, and Christine shivered in the warm, moist air. Jonas was on the island, then. But where? And why was he remaining invisible?

Dragging Christine with him, Garibaldi slapped at a hidden panel behind one of the monitors. It might have been a wet bar in a previous life. Now it hid three half-melted candles.

Garibaldi plucked the red and green amulets from their waxy prisons. He ignored the smaller blue candle and the golden circle it contained.

Christine felt a warm pulse between her breasts and knew the gem was quickening. She felt a cool blue pressure at the edge of her mind. And she had an idea.

When Garibaldi turned away she pretended to stumble and knocked against the hidden case. The blue candle fell to the floor and rolled half under the desk. The ring bounced free and skittered across the floor.

"Clumsy bitch!" Garibaldi backhanded her across the face and the metallic voice chuckled. "Stop stalling. You're the one who wanted to go see your daughter."

She struggled to her feet and let Garibaldi drag her out into the hall. Very carefully, she avoided looking at the ring that lay just inside the door. She didn't need to look. She knew what was engraved inside.

I promise.

The lights of the Hotel Santa Caribe failed to pierce the gloom of the vegetation that surrounded it. The gloom of the forest rose up on all sides and threatened the gaily lit resort. Michael thought it looked as though a cruise ship had been plonked down in the middle of a rain forest. No matter how hard he tried and how much money he'd poured into the project, Jonas had yet to tame the island.

Michael was beginning to understand why.

"Are your men in place?" he hissed to Pete, who spoke into a headset and nodded.

The headman had been surprised to find Christine gone when Michael's shouts and the Guardian's growls had roused the camp. But Michael had been no less surprised when Pete had barked a few commands and assembled his men—sans face paint and headdresses, dressed in combat fatigues.

"Explain to me again why your mainland government is

involved in this?" Michael whispered while he held a pair of night-vision goggles to his eyes and tried to count the massive bellboys who had pushed the same luggage back and forth in front of the hotel every seven and a half minutes for the past hour.

"Your Mr. Harding is of great interest to both our governments. He stole our amulets, sold them to a drug dealer in Miami, and later traded a young Guardian for their return. Neither the amulets nor the Guardian should have left the island."

The same ugly maid with the prominent Adam's apple paused by the front desk and exchanged a few words with the desk clerk. The clerk nodded and picked up the phone.

"Shift change," whispered one of Pete's lieutenants, and the headman nodded. He murmured, "Five minutes," into his headset, then said to Michael, "The drug dealer was killed a few months later, and the young Guardian escaped. We think this was about the same time your Christine was grabbed in Miami."

His Christine. The words were a knife. She didn't trust him and he didn't deserve her. There wasn't much happy middle ground there.

"Why her? Why my luggage in the first place?"

Pete shrugged. "It was probably all an accident. Harding gave you the luggage as a wedding present—the amulets were already hidden in the lining—and called you to the island. Everything after that was just an unfortunate set of coincidences."

Michael snorted. His life was one big unfortunate coincidence these days.

There was the sound of a warbling birdcall. A low growl. Shadows slid out of shadows and began to advance on the hotel. Some had two legs, some four.

Michael peered through the night-vision lenses and watched a bellhop disappear beneath a black blur. A tail tip twitched where the man had just been. There had been no sound.

"Jesus, those cats are scary," he muttered as he panned the glasses higher, searching for some sign of Christine.

Pete chuckled. "Makes you glad they're on our side, eh?"

Two more guards went down silently, and Michael slid his sights higher.

He saw Christine.

Garibaldi was dragging her down a corridor by the throat. "Jesus!" Michael jolted to his feet and resisted when Pete tried to pull him back down. He had to get to his wife. She needed him and he wouldn't fail her again.

"Finch! Get down!"

The ugly transvestite maid spun around on his way to patrol the pool side of the complex. "Hey! Who's out there?" He caught sight of Michael standing at the edge of the forest, struggling to free himself from Pete's restraining hands. "Hey! Sound the alarm! There's someone out there!"

And all hell broke loose.

When Garibaldi opened the door to the little room, Christine pushed away from him and ran to the bed. Kayla lay in the center of the queen-size mattress, her little body curled up so tightly she barely made a lump under the covers.

"Kayla? Kayla, honey, it's Mommy," Christine said, praying to see some movement.

Praying that not even Garibaldi was so heartless as to hurt an innocent little girl.

She touched her daughter's shoulder, and there it was. A flicker of life, a slight lessening of the tension in the narrow body. Then the girl uncurled like a flower blooming into the light, and she turned to Christine, her tear-streaked face alight with joy.

"Mommy? Mommy! You came!" She held her hands out and Christine swooped down to grab her and pick her up and cuddle her close, inhaling the scent of fear and travel and, underneath it all, the pure shampoo-and-chocolate scent of her daughter.

Kayla started to cry, and she burrowed tightly into her mother's borrowed sweater and clung hard. "I'm sorry. I know I'm not supposed to go anywhere with strangers, but they said they'd hurt Uncle Horst if I didn't, and then I got real sleepy, and when I woke up I was here." She started to wail, working up several octaves at once, and Christine tried to hush her quickly.

"Shut that brat up. I can't stand sniveling."

Kayla stiffened and Christine spun on her captor. "Don't speak to my daughter that way or you'll get nothing, understand? Now," she took a deep breath, "if I give you the amulet and the parchment, do I have the word of both you and your boss," she glanced up at the cameras in all four corners of the room, "that my daughter and I are free to go?"

"Show me the amulet."

She shook her head at Garibaldi. "I don't have it with me. Do you think I'm stupid? You give me your assurances, and I'll tell you where it is."

The blue gem pulsed hotly between her breasts, against her skin, and Christine wondered whether it would have burned Garibaldi if he'd touched it.

A gun appeared in his hand. He leveled it at Kayla's dirty, sweaty face. "How about I shoot your daughter? Mr. Harding is impatient, Christine. He should have had those jewels eight years ago, but you got in the way, didn't you? He planned on having the whole island—and the mines—under his control by now. Instead he's wheelchair-bound, annoyed, and out of patience. I wouldn't recommend that you play games with him now." His voice grew deadly. The gun didn't waver. "Now. Where is the amulet?"

And all hell broke loose. Shouts came from outside the barred window. From the open lobby atrium. From the hallway.

A volley of shots. The roar of lions.

Whoop, whoop, whoop!

Red lights flashed up near the ceiling and claxons sounded. More shots. The sound of running feet.

Garibaldi swore and grabbed Christine, who still held her daughter. "Sir? Mr. Harding, what's happening?"

There was a metallic curse. A squeal of feedback over the intercom. "I don't know. It looks like those damned natives again, only this time they've got the cats with them." There was the sound of movement over the intercom. "Get the amulets and bring them up to the helipad. I'll meet you there."

Garibaldi glanced wildly from side to side. Christine heard running in the halls and screams and roars from outside. She bent and whispered the plan in Kayla's ear.

She looked down at her daughter's eyes. Michael's eyes in a little girl's face, sparkling with fear and reluctant interest. Christine nodded.

"I'm not going to make the 'pad, Boss. I'll take the boat and meet up with you later, okay?"

"Just see that you have the amulets." The intercom clicked off, and Garibaldi pulled Christine toward the room's oversized window.

They were on the seventh floor.

"Too far up to jump this time, are we, Christine?" Garibaldi asked, paralleling her thoughts. She staggered against him deliberately, throwing him off balance and clutching at his shirt to keep herself upright.

Her hand dipped into his pocket.

"Get off me! Jesus, don't be clumsy now. Get the kid and let's go." He gestured with the gun.

"You don't need her, Garibaldi. She'll just slow you down." Christine pressed the amulets she'd lifted from Garibaldi into her daughter's hand and curled the little fingers tightly over them. "I'll make a better hostage."

It was their only hope.

"No." Garibaldi shook his head. "Nice try, though." The running feet and the roaring lions seemed to be getting closer. "Now, out!"

Christine squeezed Kayla hard, and after a surprised moment the little girl went limp, slid through her mother's grasp, and began to howl at the top of her lungs.

"I want my Daddy!" she yelled with more volume than Christine had ever heard come out of her daughter. "I hate you, I wish you were dead! Leave my mommy alone, waaah!"

"Get up!" Garibaldi glanced nervously out toward the hall, then back at the window. "Shut up and stand up!" He nudged Kayla with his toe, and she howled louder and sagged down to grab the bed frame.

Even though she'd told her daughter to throw the tantrum, Christine was starting to cringe a little from the volume.

"Leave her!" yelled Garibaldi over the wails. He grabbed Christine's arm and dragged her to the door. "You're coming with me, and when we meet back up with Mr. Harding, you'd better hope you've got that amulet for him."

Christine felt the blue gem pulse against her chest.

And grow cool as he dragged her through the hotel and into a tunnel.

Away from the other two gems.

Away from her daughter.

And Michael.

Chapter Seventeen

Michael charged up one hallway and down the next, cursing. Afraid. He'd followed his daughter's screams up to the seventh floor. And his heart had all but stopped when they were choked off in mid-wail.

Now they were silent.

"Kayla? Kayla, where are you?" Michael skidded to a stop at an elevator lobby. Hadn't he just been here?

A tawny Guardian loped past him, intent upon its mission. Michael grabbed the enormous cat by its scruff and yanked. "Wait!"

The beast snarled and spun. There was blood in its eye and on its whiskers.

It recognized Michael. Relaxed. He felt a touch at his mind and wished like hell he could bring the barrier down.

He shook his head. "I'm sorry, I can't hear you. But I'm looking for my daughter. Can you sense her? Is she here somewhere?"

The Guardian cocked its head for a moment as if listening, and new fear clenched at Michael. If the cat couldn't find her and she wasn't making any noise . . .

The animal spun and loped off.

"Wait!" Michael charged after it, skidding around a corner in an attempt to keep the thing's tufted tail in sight.

"Hurry up, bitch." Garibaldi swore again when Christine's ankle turned on a small rock and she fell to her elbows and knees. "Get up, come on. Don't think you're going to stall me long enough for your so-called husband to find you. We'll be long gone before he and those native wackos even figure out you're not in the hotel."

Despair tugged at her, and her body cried out for rest, but Christine fought back to her feet and stumbled in Garibaldi's wake, tugged along by the curtain cord he had used to bind her hands and form a crude leash when he'd dragged her out of the hotel.

At least she'd managed to convince Garibaldi that she'd make a better hostage than a screaming seven-year-old.

They hadn't been walking for so long, really; but trying to keep her balance on the slick, sloped surface of the secret tunnel had exhausted her beyond reason. She stumbled again, more from fatigue and a numb, dizzy fear than from any real attempt to slow him down. He snarled and yanked cruelly on the rope, and she ran a few paces to create some slack in the tether.

Her feet weren't even attached to her body anymore; they were under somebody else's command as they trudged one in front of the other on the way to Garibaldi's hidden launch. Her mind flew free of her tired, aching body, and her heart tugged in pain when she pictured Michael's face.

She imagined him smiling at her, loving her, cradling her face in his gentle, scarred hands as he bent to kiss her, and the face she saw was not that of the young man she had married. It was Michael's face, the one he wore now, and she found it infinitely more precious than any memory had ever been.

Let Michael live, she prayed fervently, *and let him know that I didn't leave him this time. Let him know that wherever I am, whatever happens to me, I am still with him and that I love him.*

But she didn't think that the prayer made it past the fear in her mind. Past the blocked place she wished she'd torn down a long time ago.

Panting, Michael glanced through the open door and sagged against the frame. His daughter was sitting on the floor with both arms wrapped around the tawny lion's neck. It was purring and licking her face.

The Guardian had found Kayla.

Wincing at the thought of where that tongue had been recently—as attested by the blood on the creature's whiskers—Michael stepped into the room. "Kayla?"

She looked up and her little face brightened.

"Daddy!"

Michael breathed a prayer of thanks. She was alive.

And she had called him Daddy.

Daddy. What a great word, one that carried with it a whole load of responsibilities and complications and needs—and love and family and home. The things he had always wanted. The things he had been searching for since the day Christine walked out of the restaurant without a backward glance.

"Kayla!" He barely had time to get his arms up before she flung herself away from the Guardian and into his embrace. He ignored the pull of the wound on his shoulder, the throb of the lump on the back of his head from when Big Jim had hit him a lifetime ago. He ignored the arrival of Pete and his men and the enormous cat that watched with wise eyes. He ignored it all and pressed his cheek to the springy curls on the top of his daughter's head.

And closed his eyes.

And thanked God.

She was crying against him, her little body shaking with fear and loneliness and sobs. He knew just how she felt. He was close to tears himself with the thought that Christine had rescued their daughter single-handedly.

She had to be the bravest, stupidest, most wonderful woman in the world. And somehow he was going to find a way to keep her. He turned to find his wife, to gather her in for a family hug.

She wasn't there.

Michael glanced quickly around. Lion. Native agents arriving in camo pants. Small child.

No Christine.

"Where's your mommy?" he asked, fighting for calm when he was on the edge of panic. He must not have succeeded, for Pete's head snapped up and he walked over to father and daughter.

"What's wrong?"

"Where's Christine? She should be here. With Kayla." The child's quivering increased until Michael thought her little bones might shake apart. "Kayla? Where's your mommy?"

"She went with the man."

The words were thin, almost a whisper, but they were enough to congeal Michael's blood in his veins. He didn't need to ask, "What man?" He knew. Garibaldi. He met Pete's eyes over the top of Kayla's head and they both nodded.

With careful hands, Michael detached his daughter from her stranglehold on his neck. "Kayla, honey? Do you know where they went? Did the man say where they were going?"

She shook her head, dashing tears this way and that like a dog shaking off a coat full of water. "The metal man told them to meet him on the heely . . . helly-something, but the bad man said he wouldn't make it. He took Mommy and they left."

"Helipad," Pete guessed, and gestured at two of his men, who nodded and jogged out of the room.

"Metal man?" Michael puzzled.

"Harding." At Michael's puzzled frown, Pete said, "Over the last few years, his health has been declining. He's had throat cancer, several unrelated operations, and is now mostly wheelchair-bound. How can you not know this if you've been working for him all this time?"

"We mostly exchange e-mails and messages via voice mail and secretaries. Look," Michael gestured impatiently, "that's not important now. I have to get to Christine." He glanced down at Kayla. "Do you know where he was taking her, Kayla?"

She shook her head. "No. But Vidar does." She gestured at the tawny lion. "He'll take you."

"But I can't hear what he's saying, and we'll be too late if I follow him." Michael turned to Pete. "Can you ask him to describe where they are?"

"I won't get anything but trees and water, which describes half the damn island."

"No, Daddy. Vidar said he'd *take* you," Kayla insisted, and pointed at the cat again. It turned, presented its back to Michael, and crouched down.

Michael stared dubiously at the lithe, slippery spine. "You're kidding, right?"

"Take this." Kayla held out her hands, which were full of amulets. He reached for the green one, which seemed to wink in the low room lighting. She pushed his hand away and gave him the red one. "No, this one's yours."

There was a murmur from the men. "The warrior's stone."

Michael stared at it, transfixed. The red stone pulsed. Beckoned to him.

Scared the life out of him.

"Sir?" One of Pete's men stood in the doorway. "There was no sign of Harding, but we found this in the security room." He held up a small object.

I promise.

"Give me that." Michael snatched the ring and jammed it onto his pinky finger, next to his own wedding band. And before he could doubt himself or the big cat, he turned to Pete. "That comm device you gave me have a homing chip in it?"

The agent nodded. "I have helicopters and water-patrol cutters standing by. Good luck." He held out a hand, and Michael shook it before passing Kayla to the agent.

"Keep her safe. If anything happens, get her to a guy named Horst in Farewell, Massachusetts. That's on Cape Cod." He paused. "You might also find your missing Guardian there."

And with a quick kiss for Kayla and a quick prayer for himself, Michael Finch climbed onto the back of a lion and went to fetch his wife.

Chapter Eighteen

As soon as he touched the cat's narrow back, the beast leapt to its feet and surged forward. Michael swore and grabbed a double-handful of shaggy mane as he slid to one side.

He centered himself, hung on tight with his legs, and realized where they were.

On the balcony.

"You've got to be kidding me! There's an elevator back in the hall. I'll meet you downstairs." Michael looked at the sheer drop and started to dismount. "Don't even think of—Aaaah!"

The cat leapt into dark air with Michael barely clinging to its side. They hurtled down three stories through a swarm of mosquitoes to land in the topmost branches of a spindly tree.

Michael was too terrified to scream or even close his eyes. He clung like a burr to the cat's furry shoulders as the creature delicately picked its way from branch to branch, tree to tree, in a carefully balanced race against gravity. They landed with a thump amid a group of startled soldiers and set off for the forest at a lurching, ground-covering lope.

And Michael remembered to breathe.

Although he had ridden horseback before, even bareback on one brief occasion, Michael had never experienced anything quite like riding on Vidar's narrow spine as they skimmed down narrow game trails and leapt over fallen trees and piled rocks. In fact, the closest he could come to the feeling was the memory of riding his cousin's Harley on an empty, straight desert highway.

He lay along the cat's back with his face pressed into the warm, heaving shoulder and his feet hooked on Vidar's protruding hipbones. He could feel the slip and slide of heavy muscles beneath his stomach and could hear the clatter and squawk of parrots disturbed by their mad dash.

His right hand began to sting. He looked down and realized he was clutching the red amulet so tight the metalwork had cut his hand. The gem pulsed thickly, a lurid, bloody light coming from within.

Something pressed at the edges of his mind and Michael didn't think it was the lion.

Part of him wished he could break down the barriers and let the warrior's amulet in. Part of him was glad he could not.

Thwack, thwack, thwack.

A light stabbed down into the forest as Pete's men paced them from above, following the tiny beacon in Michael's headset.

At least he hoped it was the good guys. If it was Jonas's helicopter, he was in serious trouble.

The metal man. What had happened to Jonas? And how had Michael missed it?

Vidar lurched over a fallen branch and Michael felt himself slip. He grabbed tight and his sweaty fingers slipped on the coarse fur. They were running downhill now, descending from atop the cliff on which Jonas had built his hotel, dropping down to the rocky beaches of the windward side of the island, far away from the perfectly groomed semicircles of sand near the compound. Michael could feel the big cat tiring beneath him, could feel the great ribs heave with labored breath and the huge paws slam into the earth as fatigue robbed them of spring.

But he sensed that they were nearing their destination.

He squinted into the predawn gloom and thought he caught a glimpse of moon-silvered foam up ahead. They turned down a narrow, rocky path that cut between sandstone outcroppings and wound around scattered boulders. At the apex of one switchback, Michael thought he saw a glimmer of light up ahead. He wanted to call Christine's name but restrained himself.

It was unlikely he could sneak up on Garibaldi while riding a lion the size of a pony, but it probably wouldn't do them any good to advertise their arrival, either. Particularly if Garibaldi still had a weapon.

Michael glanced down at his hand. The red gem glowed more brightly. The pressure against his mind increased. The low throb built until it verged on pain. He could almost hear the gem chanting, *Let me in, let me in. Use me!*

But Michael knew that, as frightening as the power of the blue gem had been when it overtook him in Dewdrop's Candle Shop, the power of the warrior's amulet would be ten times worse.

He'd almost hurt Christine the last time. He couldn't risk it again.

Vidar slowed slightly as he navigated the final turn that brought them down onto the beach, and Michael saw his wife.

She was standing near the surf, looking ragged and worn, as if she'd been dragged face-first all the way from the hotel. Garibaldi had an arm across her throat and a gun at her temple.

Michael felt the rage build. Felt the pressure build. Felt the gem burn hot in his hand.

"Hey, Finch. I've got your woman again." Garibaldi's taunting words carried well, borne along by the nearby waves. "And this time I think I'm going to keep her."

Michael slid from Vidar's sleek back. The exhausted cat sank to the cool sand and panted like a dog.

"Jonas is gone, Garibaldi." Michael had heard the report over his comm. The speedy chopper had lifted off just minutes ago and had quickly outdistanced Pete's men, who'd returned to the island.

Jonas had escaped.

This time.

Michael walked slowly toward the man who held Christine with an easy forearm across her throat and a gun pointed at her temple. Her eyes pleaded with Michael to do something. Anything.

"Who cares?" Garibaldi sneered. "I was leaving him anyway; me and Chrissy here are going to the mainland and have ourselves a high old time, aren't we, sweetie?" With his eyes on Michael, Garibaldi slowly, suggestively, licked Christine's ear. She shuddered, and the big, ugly brute smiled at Michael.

"It'll never happen, Garibaldi. Let her go. You don't even have the amulets anymore." Michael held the red gem up, and in the dead light of dawn, the glow from the amulet looked lurid and somehow *wrong*.

Fingernails scraped at the back of Michael's mind. He could just hear the whisper of an ancient force. *Let me in! I can beat him! Let me in and I will give you the power.*

"Who cares about the damned amulets? They're a fairy tale, nothing more. Harding tried to use all three of them once, and now he blames them for making him sick. He wants them back because he's convinced they'll cure him. You ask me, he's out of his mind." Garibaldi avoided looking at the quick heartbeat of the red gem. "I'll be glad to be rid of him and them." A thundering noise made him look up. With a roar of torque and a grind of overworked rotors, the federal helicopter swung over the ridge and down toward the beach, its spotlight flashing and several dark figures hanging from the side with weapons trained on Garibaldi and his prisoner. "It's over, Garibaldi. Let the woman go and you will not be harmed." The amplified voice rang tinnily from the chopper's loudspeaker.

Garibaldi laughed and pressed the gun tighter to Christine's temple until her eyes rolled with pain and a muffled noise escaped her. "I don't think so. Call them off or I shoot."

"I can't do that," Michael yelled over the noise of the helicopter and the chug of the naval cutter that had appeared in the bay, painting the beach with more light. "They don't work for me."

"Tell them," Garibaldi screamed. Michael saw his finger tighten on the trigger.

"Okay, you win." Michael waved the chopper off and was grateful when the bird dipped back down below the ridgeline. His arm extended the wave to sweep Ugly Two's gun out of his waistband, just in case. "What do you want? What can I give you to let her go? You don't want her—she's nothing to you."

"Nothing? She's nothing?" Garibaldi's face shone red in the light of dawn and the glint of searchlights. "She marked me, Finch. Nearly killed me. Her and her cat." He spat near Michael's feet and touched the scar on his neck with the barrel of the gun.

And at that break in his concentration, Christine acted.

That was all she had been waiting for, that moment when the gun was away from her temple and Garibaldi was focused on something else. Drawing from the self-defense moves she'd badgered Horst into teaching her, Christine sagged down against her captor, throwing him off-balance, then stood up hard and cracked the top of her head under his chin.

"Christine, down!" Michael yelled, and she dropped to the sand as he leveled Ugly Two's gun at Garibaldi and pulled the trigger.

No shot. A click. An empty chamber.

There was a frozen, disbelieving moment when nobody moved. Then Garibaldi smiled. Raised his gun.

And pointed it to Christine's right. She spun and saw a black Guardian emerging from the forest. Saw the blonde child on its back.

Garibaldi chuckled. "Say good-bye to your daughter, babe."

And fired.

Michael saw the black Guardian rear up and place her body between the bullet and the child that clung to her ebony back. He heard the roar of pain. Saw the great black body fall back to the ground. Saw the child disappear beneath.

Kayla!

And he broke.

With one furious, crazy mental swipe, he exploded the barrier he'd built between himself and the power of the stones. Rage, red and hot, slammed into him and then out of him, centering itself in the heart of the red stone.

The madness rose to claim him.

Christine heard the cat's cry of pain as much in her head as in her ears. She saw her daughter's body disappear under an avalanche of lifeless black fur.

And her hand rose to the neckline of the ruined blue sweater that had once belonged to a boy named Mikey. She drew forth the glowing blue amulet. And stalled.

She couldn't do it. She hated the feel of the power, hated

how much she liked it. And feared that once she began to use it, she would never be able to stop.

There was a howling noise, like a thousand Guardians screaming as one, and she saw Michael lift the red amulet. The power punched out of him like flame, and his face contorted with pain and rage and a terrible, terrible glee as Garibaldi was lifted off his feet and sent spinning, broken into the waves.

"Mommy?"

Christine looked down. Her daughter stood there, battered and dirty but whole. The green amulet was looped around her neck. It was glowing a violent, virulent emerald.

The tawny Guardian that Michael had ridden down to the beach sat on its haunches beside her. The black Guardian that had borne Kayla lay in a heap where the forest met the sand.

"Mommy, Vidar says we need to help Daddy now. But it won't work if you don't hear the lion. You have to try to hear him right now. Vidar says I can't bring him back by myself."

The little girl wrapped one hand around the pulsing green amulet and placed the other on the tawny lion's head.

Christine felt a touch on her mind. It dug in with lion's claws and she flinched.

There was an explosion, and she looked back to see the flames shooting higher, the sea boiling where Michael pounded power upon power into the spot where Garibaldi had been. Steam hissed, and the helicopter landed. Men poured from it, and Pete approached the man—who didn't even look like Mikey anymore—and yelled, "Pull it back, Finch. Pull back now!"

With a curl of his lip, the man who didn't look like her husband sent a bolt of flame into the sand beneath the headman's feet. The concussion was deafening. Pete flew backward into the others.

"Now, Mommy! You have to try!"

But she couldn't. She was too afraid of the power. Too afraid of the madman on the beach who sent a curl of flame licking toward the helicopter, sent it spinning into the sky with a flick of his hand.

That was when she saw the glint. A ring. No, two rings on his left hand. One on his ring finger, one on his pinky.

I promise.

I promise. He had promised and failed. But hadn't she failed, too? They had failed each other. And now, after so long, he was wearing her ring.

He had said he loved her back in the grass hut.

And lord, how she loved him.

The knowledge poured through Christine, cool and blue with the power of the amulet of wisdom. The barrier in her mind dissolved like ice in a warm rush of current. She placed her hand on the tawny cat's head beside her daughter's and felt the swirling green slide into her beneath the blue.

She wasn't sure that her daughter was the Spoken One, wasn't even sure she believed in such a thing, but Christine felt something different about the power of the amulet now. Something kinder. Safer.

The green power healed her heart and her body, leaving peace and strength behind. Blue and green twirled around in her mind, unlocking the secret doors that had been barricaded for so many years and giving her such a sweet rush of memories that she thought she'd weep from them.

How she'd loved Mikey back then. And how she loved him now.

Not afraid anymore, Christine left her daughter with the Guardian and walked to the thing that had taken over her husband.

"Stay back!" it hissed, and she saw Michael's fear for her

in a flash of the red-tinged eyes. "Don't make me hurt you."

Flames rose higher, encircled her until she and Michael were alone in a circle of hell.

But she wasn't afraid. She reached out and took his left hand in hers. Laced their fingers together where the matched rings glimmered in the false red light. Looked up into his eyes.

Smiled and said, "You won't hurt me, Mikey. I love you."

The thing that wasn't quite her husband snarled down at her but didn't try to free its hand. Michael's eyes looked out from a red mask of rage. "No you don't! I betrayed you. You don't trust me." The voice thundered with the power of the warrior's amulet, and Christine felt her own blue powers falter beneath the red onslaught.

"Yes, I do. I love you." She paused. Gathered her courage. "And what's more, I trust you."

And she stood up on tiptoe and kissed him full on his red, angry mouth.

Chapter Nineteen

The rage burned clean and pure within him. There was rage at Jonas for having used him to smuggle gems to the island, then watching him mourn Christine for eight years without ever telling him the truth. Rage at himself for not having seen the truth for himself. Rage at Christine for having not trusted him to see it.

Then she was there, in front of him, holding the blue amulet in one fist and his hand with her other. Kissing him.

"I love you." Had she really said that, or was it just an echo of the past that had poured through him when he opened the floodgates of his mind?

"I trust you."

Blue light slid into his mind, and the red fury rose up to push it aside.

Who needed love? He had hate.

He lifted a hand to swat aside Christine and her false declarations of love but realized something was tugging on his hand. Something small and green-feeling. He looked down.

"I love you, Daddy."

He couldn't have remembered those words, could he?

Green energy seeped into him, healing him and pushing the red anger back behind the civilizing doors in his mind. Blue light worked its way into his soul, loving him. And the last of the barriers—not the ones in his mind, but the ones he'd built around his heart—slid down without a noise.

Christine was with him. Within him. Kayla was there. Blue and green and red mingled. Mixed. Separated.

Leveled.

The rage drained slowly, leaving Michael both weak and strong, as a new, cleaner power rose within him.

It was white.

As the sun broke over the horizon and a new day began on Santa Caribe Island, Michael could feel the white light encompass him. His wife. His child. And he could feel the power flow from the little family and the three gems until it covered the entire island.

He could feel the fields quicken with the life being poured into them by the green gem. He could feel the soldiers on the beach, the workers in the mines, and the families in the villages draw breath with new blue knowledge and the belief that it was over.

And just beginning.

With a vicious red shout, the very foundations of the cursed hotel high atop the cliff began to shake. Mortar trembled and cracked. Vines slithered from the nearby forest to claim the courtyard. The pools. The lobby.

Guardians roared in triumph as the Hotel Santa Caribe collapsed in on itself and was gone.

The white light built, glowing from every surface, every person or animal. Except one. The black Guardian lay still and dull on the beach.

Michael looked down at his wife through the shimmering white radiance.

He pulled the tiny ring from his finger and slid it onto hers. He whispered, "I love you. I'll never fail you again. I promise."

He kissed her.

The white light surrounding them blazed higher.
The black Guardian stirred.
And began to purr.

Epilogue

The Atlantic Ocean nudged gently at the beach below the boardwalk, and the gentle sea breeze worked its way between the lace curtains. Christine smiled when she heard a squeal and a mock-ferocious growl from the town common.

Thor must be cheating at hide-and-seek again. The children of Farewell were learning to think really hard about one place while hiding in another, but somehow he always found them.

That's what made it so much fun.

Christine sniffed the bubbling wax, tucked her curly brown hair behind one ear, and frowned. It wasn't quite right yet.

She'd carved the molds as carefully as she could, wanting the replicas to be perfect for the grand opening of Pete's pride and joy, the New Santa Caribe Hotel.

They'd never found Jonas but had claimed the land by eminent domain after all three amulets and the parchment were returned. Pete was certain they'd seen the last of Jonas Harding.

Christine wasn't so sure. Nor was she totally comfortable with the fact that the natives and the Guardians all believed that her daughter was some sort of savior, the Spoken One, whom they could call on the next time the island was threatened.

But then again, what were the odds of that happening?

The wax burped and Christine glanced at the molds again, her attention recalled to the work at hand. What was she missing? She snapped her fingers, and the black lion draped across an enormous basket in the corner lifted her ebony head. The green eyes flashed with curiosity.

"I forgot to scent them."

Sif yawned, exposing two rows of jagged teeth and a long pink tongue, and said, *So much fuss over a few pretty pieces of wax.* She licked a fuzzy yellow head and tucked a questing red nose underneath her, where the spaniel-size kitten rooted eagerly for food. *But I won't mind seeing the island again.*

Surprisingly enough, neither would Christine.

She ran her fingers over her swollen belly and pressed both hands to her aching back.

"Junior acting up?" The voice, low and intimate at her ear, made Christine smile. She leaned back into Michael's warmth.

She hadn't heard him slip through the door that connected his carving studio to the candle shop.

"Junior never acts up. She's perfect." Her husband's hands came up to cup Chrissy's round stomach, and the yellow Cape Cod sun glinted off their matching rings when she covered his fingers with her own.

And she felt the lingering power. It was white. The color of love.

Then he took her hand and pulled her toward the door. "Turn off the wax for a while and walk with me?"

She grinned at the naughtiness of it and nodded.

They walked far from town, down to the end of the last jetty, where they couldn't see even Horst's cheerful yellow cottage. Christine lifted her husband's hand to her lips and kissed a bandaged spot where he'd nicked himself just that morning as he put the finishing touches on the huge carving of the Guardians that would grace the lobby of the new hotel.

When they reached the last rock and her toes curled over the edge of the world, she lifted her face and felt the warmth of the sun, felt the beat of her baby's heart, felt the purr of her lion companions, the laughter of her daughter, and above all felt the full, glowing white place in her chest where she kept all the love she felt for her husband. Her family.

She let go his hand and reached to pull the loose shirt over her head.

"What in God's name are you doing?" But Michael's eyes were interested as she stripped and left her clothing lying scattered on Pirate's Jetty.

"I was thinking of going for a swim." She cut him a coy glance. "Rumor has it there's a cave down there with a few blankets and a scented candle."

And as she jumped into the water and felt the cool blue close over her head, she heard her husband's whoop of joy.

About the Author

After trying on a few careers for size— from sea lion trainer to genetic engineer to patent law to professional equestrian— Jessica Andersen realized that she wasn't searching for her niche . . . she was researching novels! She now shares a small farm in rural Connecticut with her own personal romantic hero, Brian and an assortment of cats, corgis and horses, while writing full time (in between chores!). Jessica hopes you enjoy *The Guardian of the Amulets*, a personal favorite that proves once and for all that cats are people too.

The Harvard Sampler

The Harvard Sampler

Liberal Education for the Twenty-First Century

Edited by
Jennifer M. Shephard
Stephen M. Kosslyn
Evelynn M. Hammonds

Harvard University Press
Cambridge, Massachusetts
London, England
2011

Book design by Dean Bornstein

Library of Congress Cataloging-in-Publication Data
The Harvard sampler : liberal education for the twenty-first century / edited by
Jennifer M. Shephard, Stephen M. Kosslyn, Evelynn M. Hammonds.
    p. cm.
    Includes bibliographical references.
    ISBN 978-0-674-05902-3 (alk. paper)
    1. Education, Humanistic. 2. Harvard University—Faculty.
 I. Shephard, Jennifer M.   II. Kosslyn, Stephen Michael, 1948–
III. Hammonds, Evelynn Maxine.
LC1011.H368   2011
370.11'2—dc22   2011012314

Contents

Contributors

Ali S. Asani
*Professor of Indo-Muslim and Islamic Religion and Cultures,
Faculty of Arts and Sciences*

Lawrence Buell
*Powell M. Cabot Professor of American Literature, Faculty of Arts
and Sciences*

Harry R. Lewis
*Gordon McKay Professor of Computer Science, Faculty of Arts
and Sciences*

Jonathan B. Losos
*Monique and Philip Lehner Professor for the Study of Latin
America and Curator in Herpetology, Faculty of Arts and Sciences*

Charles S. Maier
*Leverett Saltonstall Professor of History, Faculty of Arts
and Sciences*

Karin B. Michels
*Associate Professor of Obstetrics, Gynecology, and Reproductive
Biology, Medical School, and Associate Professor in the Department
of Epidemiology, School of Public Health*

Steven Pinker
*Johnstone Family Professor of Psychology, Faculty of Arts
and Sciences*

Mathias Risse
*Professor of Philosophy and Public Policy, Kennedy School
of Government*

T. M. Scanlon
*Alford Professor of Natural Religion, Moral Philosophy, and Civil
Polity, Faculty of Arts and Sciences*

John H. Shaw
> *Harry C. Dudley Professor of Structural and Economic Geology, Faculty of Arts and Sciences*

Werner Sollors
> *Henry B. and Anne M. Cabot Professor of English Literature and Professor of African and African American Studies, Faculty of Arts and Sciences*

Laurel Thatcher Ulrich
> *300th Anniversary University Professor*

Preface

Once in every generation we have a chance to renew, after our own fashion and in our own time, the ancient mandate to "advance learning and perpetuate it to posterity."

Peter Gomes, 2004

In 2004 the Faculty of Arts and Sciences at Harvard University began a major review of its undergraduate curriculum. Such reassessments of Harvard's mission for undergraduate education are conducted a few times a century; the outcome of one of the most famous such reviews was *General Education in a Free Society* ([1945] 1950), which became widely known as the "Red Book." Written in the aftermath of World War II, it proudly proclaimed its purpose to "cultivate in the largest possible number of our future citizens an appreciation of both the responsibilities and the benefits which come to them because they are Americans and are free." Many have characterized this as a focus on "heritage and change" (e.g., Kirby 2004). The curriculum was revisited during the 1970s, and this review resulted in the institution of a new program, called the Core, described in a less widely read text, the *Report on the Core Curriculum* (1978). The move to the Core marked a shift to a curriculum that sought to "introduce students to the major approaches to knowledge." Although both curricula can be thought "successful" in that faculty produced many outstanding courses, by the early twenty-first century many felt that the Core was no longer quite the generator of new ideas in pedagogy or content that the current generation of Harvard students needed.

New trends in technology, changes in methodologies, and a profoundly different student population, along with some dissent among the faculty about the focus of the Core, led to the launch of a new General Education curriculum in 2009. This new curriculum seeks to "connect in an explicit way what students learn in Harvard classrooms to life outside the ivied walls and beyond the college years." According to the *Report of the Task Force on General Education* (2007), the curriculum should prepare students for civic life in a rapidly changing world (which is increasingly shaped by scientific discoveries), lead them to acknowledge that they are products of their culture as much as participants, and develop their ethical sensibilities.

Although these programs have been influential in their day within Harvard and American higher education more generally, none of our reports nor the curricula they reflect have had the popular appeal of the *Harvard Classics*, colloquially known as "Dr. Eliot's Five Foot Shelf." This fifty-one-volume set of classic works in the Western canon was compiled and edited principally by Harvard University president Charles W. Eliot and first published in 1910. Eliot saw this project as a way for a rising middle-class American to obtain the elements of a liberal education simply by reading "15 minutes a day" from his collection. Adam Kirsch (2001) points out, in an entertaining review for *Harvard Magazine*, that the *Harvard Classics* was wildly successful— selling some 350,000 sets within twenty years of the series' initial publication.

It is worth noting that Harvard itself adopted a mission of public, as well as private, education around the same time. In 1910 Charles Eliot's successor, A. Lawrence Lowell, founded the Commission on Extension Courses "as an experiment in 'popular education' that served those in the community who had the ability and desire to attend college, but also had other obligations that kept them from traditional schools." (In addition to evening and summer courses in the classroom, the Harvard Extension School now offers more than 150 courses online, some of them free.)

Given the widespread interest that every change in the Harvard curriculum has sparked, Harvard's long-standing tradition of public education, and the century that has passed since Eliot undertook his massive work, we thought the time was right to introduce what we hope will become a new series. *The Harvard Sampler* cannot replicate

Eliot's goal of being a compendium of all of what an educated person should know. Indeed, the time for such compilations is long past; the world is far too complicated now. Instead, what we have collected here are original essays by Harvard faculty, experts who can digest the key works in a field and present a synthesis that offers an entry point into a domain of knowledge. Critical to their offerings are the annotated bibliographies, guiding the interested reader to further sources of information; in many cases the essays are accompanied by commentary from the faculty about what they try to accomplish in the courses that serve as inspiration for their chapters.

Any curriculum is an evolutionary project, and hence these essays provide just one small window into this early instantiation of Harvard's new General Education curriculum. Our goal was not to be comprehensive but rather to provide a representative sample of what is emerging at Harvard in the new curriculum. So why pick up this volume right now? Why not wait until we have a "mature" curriculum with courses that have been given to lots of students who would have provided a great deal of feedback? The answer is that many of the courses that have inspired the essays collected here have survived the test of time; these essays reflect the culmination of the authors' thoughts on a set of ideas that have been taught for many years while remaining relevant today. There will never be a fully "mature" curriculum. A curriculum, like a developing mind, is never a finished work; rather, a curriculum must be under constant review and revision to realize its architects' aspirations.

Rather than compiling contributions organized around a single theme, for this volume we deliberately sampled across the spectrum of General Education topics, soliciting essays from faculty representing a variety of disciplines across the arts, humanities, and sciences. These essays cover a wide range of themes, including, among others, the environment, morality, race, religion, globalization, and human rights; these themes are evident in topics as diverse as the human mind, the Internet, evolution, public health, and legacies of the American

Revolution, and these topics come from at least nine different fields, from applied science to literature. These familiar subjects occupy syllabi throughout the academy and are debated in the media every day—their relevance is unquestioned. If there is a common thread, a "conversation" across the chapters, it might be one of choice: How do we make decisions, individually and as a society, and why? What do we need to know and understand—about each other, about ourselves, our history, and our world—in order to make good choices about the way we live? We hope this volume will be the first in a series, and that the conversation will continue in future volumes, where some of the themes we visit here will be amplified even as new ones are added.

These essays provide erudite and thoughtful commentary on some of the major issues of our times that should be of interest to readers who want perspectives on these topics from some of the leading thinkers in their fields.

At the heart of Harvard's new curriculum lie competing but also compelling visions about liberal arts education in the twenty-first century. What topics matter? How should we teach them? How do we move students to think about and analyze problems from many disciplinary perspectives? How does what we teach enable students to function as leaders of the "local, national and global communities in which they will be expected to play important roles" (Thomas 2004)? Each writer speaks to these questions in his or her own way.

We want to thank the faculty who contributed essays to the volume for their thoughtfulness, dedication, and patience, and our editors at Harvard University Press for their enthusiasm and support. And we want to thank you, the reader, for your curiosity and interest.

Further Reading

Gomes, Peter. 2004. "Modesty, Ambition, and Imagination: An Essay on Curricular Reform in Harvard College." In *Essays on General Education in Harvard College.* Cambridge, MA: President and Fellows of Harvard

College. http://isites.harvard.edu/icb/icb.do?keyword=k37826&pageid=icb .page331351.

Kirby, William C. 2004. "Preface." In *Essays on General Education in Harvard College.* Cambridge, MA: President and Fellows of Harvard College. http://isites.harvard.edu/icb/icb.do?keyword=k37826&pageid=icb .page331351.

Kirsch, Adam. 2001. "The 'Five-Foot Shelf' Reconsidered." *Harvard Magazine,* November–December. http://harvardmagazine.com/2001/11/the-five-foot -shelf-reco.html.

President and Fellows of Harvard College. (1945) 1950. *General Education in a Free Society: Report of the Harvard Committee.* Cambridge, MA: Harvard University Press. http://www.archive.org/details/generaleduca tion03244ombp.

Report of the Task Force on General Education. 2007. Cambridge, MA: President and Fellows of Harvard College. http://www.generaleducation.fas .harvard.edu/icb/icb.do?keyword=k37826&tabgroupid=icb.tabgroup116510.

Thomas, Richard F. 2004. "General Education and the Fostering of Free Citizens." In *Essays on General Education in Harvard College.* Cambridge, MA: President and Fellows of Harvard College. http://isites.harvard.edu/icb /icb.do?keyword=k37826&pageid=icb.page331351.

⁓ The Harvard Sampler

Enhancing Religious Literacy in a Liberal Arts Education through the Study of Islam and Muslim Societies

Ali S. Asani

Over the two decades that I have been teaching at Harvard I have been asked many questions about Islam, but I was ill prepared when, a couple of years ago, a student asked me over dinner at a restaurant in Harvard Square: "How can anyone who is rational and intelligent believe in and practice a religion that promotes violence, terror, [and] suicide bombings and is blatantly against fundamental human rights and freedom?" Frequently, what characterizes the majority of the questions I am asked about Islam is not just a profound ignorance about a religion practiced by over a billion people around the world, but a deep-seated prejudice and implicit fear of Muslims. "I am afraid of Muslims," a minister of a church in Boston confessed even as he invited me to participate in an outreach event to promote a better understanding of Islam.

Exacerbating the lack of knowledge about Islam and Muslim cultures in the United States is a widespread illiteracy about the nature of religion in general. Religious illiteracy can be defined as the inability to conceive of religion as a cultural phenomenon intricately embedded in complex cultural matrixes. As a result of this illiteracy, a person is unable to appreciate the significant role that factors such as poverty, social status, gender, and political ideologies can play in shaping what are overtly perceived as purely religious expressions. Religious illiteracy is a direct consequence of a failure of educational systems to provide students with opportunities to engage critically in the academic study of religion. Employing social scientific and humanistic methods, the study of religion seeks to go beyond the faith-centered or devotional approach that is often employed to teach religion in parochial and Sunday schools, *madrasas*, *yeshivas*, and other similar institutions. It posits that religion is a dynamic and powerful force central to the human experience and that understanding it is critical for the study of a broad range of subjects, a fact recognized by the U.S. Supreme Court when it ruled on the importance of providing instruction about religion as a cultural phenomenon in schools: "It might well be said that one's education is not complete without a study of comparative religion or the history of religion and its relationship to the advancement of civilization" (*Abington School Dist v. Schempp* 1963).

At every level of education, from grade school to high school and college, students encounter religion as they study history, literature, art, music, social studies, world civilizations, geography, and so on. Yet neither do the curricula of our schools equip students to think critically about religion as a cultural phenomenon, nor are teachers who teach humanities and social science subjects professionally trained to teach about religion. In this chapter, I discuss the nature of illiteracy about religion and culture that prevails not only in the United States but in many other nations as well, its grave consequences for the ability of students to interpret the multicultural and multireligious world in which they live, and my own attempts to foster literacy through two courses I offer at Harvard in the General Education program. Although employing different perspectives, the courses are designed to help students understand that the manner in which the world's Muslims interpret their religion is significantly influenced by the diverse contexts in which they live. Students come to appreciate that conceptions of Islam are varied and dynamic—as circumstances and situations change, so do understandings of the religion. The courses have two principal goals: first, to foster among students literacy about the nature of religion by using the Islamic tradition as a case study; and second, to combat, through responsible education, one of the most dangerous phenomena of our times—Islamophobia—which is prejudice and fear of Islam leading to the dehumanization of the world's 1.5 billion Muslims.

The Problem: Religious and Cultural Illiteracy

The *Report of the Task Force on General Education* (2007) at Harvard observes that we are faced with the challenge of educating students about a world that is interconnected to a degree almost inconceivable thirty or forty years ago. At the same time, the report points out, it is a world that is deeply divided, unstable, and uncertain. It is one of the great paradoxes of our times that while peoples from different religious, cultural, racial, and ethnic backgrounds are in closer contact with each other than ever before, still this closeness has not resulted in better understanding and appreciation for differences. Rather, our world is marked with greater misunderstandings and misconceptions resulting in ever-escalating levels of tension between cultures and nations. His Highness the Aga Khan (2006), a Muslim leader, has aptly described the nature of these conflicts with the phrase "the clash of ignorances," a clash that perpetuates fear and hatred of peoples different from oneself.

A key factor that is responsible for the clash of ignorances is widespread illiteracy about religion and culture. Lacking the intellectual tools to understand and engage with religious and cultural differences, people tend to paint those who are different from themselves with one color, with a single brushstroke, representing them through simplistic caricatures that can sometimes result in unjust forms of humiliation. In her study on the prevalence of religious illiteracy in American educational systems, Diane Moore (2007), director of Harvard's Program in Religious Studies and Education, identifies some of its consequences: the curtailment of historical and cultural understanding, the fueling of culture wars, and the promotion of religious and racial bigotry.

Our lack of understanding about the ways that religion itself is an integral dimension of social/political/historical experience coupled with our ignorance about the specific tenets of the world's religious traditions significantly hinder our capacity to function as engaged, informed and responsible citizens of our democracy. In these ways, religious illiteracy has helped foster a climate that is both dangerous and intellectually debilitating. (pp. 3–4)

Professor Moore also points out that religious literacy is particularly important for the United States, which, despite being the most religiously diverse country in the world, has a population that is "woefully ignorant about religion" (p. 3). The devastating impact of ignorance on democracy, which is fundamentally premised on the existence of an educated and well-informed citizenry, was best summarized by Thomas Jefferson, one of the Founding Fathers of the United States, when he wrote, "If a nation expects it can be ignorant and free, in a state of civilization, it expects what never was and never will be." Certainly, democracy cannot function when ignorance breeds fear of our fellow citizens who happen to be in some way or another different from ourselves.

One of religious illiteracy's common symptoms is the tendency to associate a religion solely with its devotional practices, such as rites, rituals, and religious festivals. Another is the propensity to attribute the actions of individuals, communities, and nations exclusively to religion. With regard to Islam, it results in the perception that the faith is chiefly responsible for all the actions of anyone who is a Muslim. It also leads to the assumption that everything that happens in a predominantly Muslim country can be attributed to religion. Thus many people commonly assume that Islam is the principal cause of a variety of ills that plague some Muslim majority countries, such as the lack of democracy, economic underdevelopment, unjust treatment, and marginalization of women. To many Muslims, such explanations are as absurd as the claim that Christianity is responsible for the United States, a predominantly Christian nation, having one of the highest crime rates in the world. Illiteracy about religion and culture hinders the ability to look for complex and more plausible explanations rooted in political, economic, and sociological conditions. It also hampers people from realizing that, while religion may be invoked as a legitimizer for certain human actions, the primary motivating forces are often rooted elsewhere. Religious literacy helps students to recognize that all interpretations of religion are essentially human enterprises; the faithful may consider certain religious truths to be divinely revealed, but the meanings they construct from these truths are heavily dependent on their worldly circumstances and realities.

Ultimately, if unchecked, religious and cultural illiteracy strips peoples and nations of their history, their culture, their politics, their economics—in short, their humanity. History is full of examples of conflicts and tragedies that result from a group of people from one religious, racial, or ethnic background failing to accept and to respect the humanity of others. During times of heightened political and military conflicts, religious and cultural illiteracy strongly influences how peoples of different nations, cultures, and religions perceive each other. Frequently, these conflicts are depicted within frameworks and language characterized by hyperbole and absolute opposition: between the civilized and the barbaric, good and evil, "us" and "them." These polarizations have been particularly prevalent in contemporary discussions about differences between Western and Islamic civilizations. Such characterizations, while appealing to many, are troublesome and problematic from a number of perspectives. It is historically inaccurate to talk about Western and Islamic civilizations entirely in oppositional and antagonistic terms when both share common roots in religious ideas and concepts derived from Abrahamic traditions as well as Greco-Roman culture. Moreover, such polarizations are particularly problematic since they are based on stereotypes and humiliating caricatures of "the other."

Historically, stereotypical perceptions have been common between peoples of the Middle East (Arabs, Persians, and Turks) and Europe and the United States. They result from centuries of hostile and confrontational relationships based on the need for political power and control of economic resources, particularly oil in recent years. They are couched in the language of conquest and reconquest, jihad and crusade, colonialism and nationalism, occupation and liberation. In the context of war and armed conflict, such stereotypes serve to dehumanize the other, often leading to tragic consequences. Evident in the events of 9/11 was the dehumanization of Americans by some Saudi terrorists, just as the abuse and torture of prisoners at the infamous Abu Ghraib prison revealed the dehumanization of Iraqis in the eyes of their American captors.

How Do You Know What You Know about Islam?

Let me return to the dinner question that instigated these thoughts. I responded to the student's question with a question of my own: How do you know what you know about Islam? My intent was to engage the student in a dialogue on the construction of knowledge and the importance of examining critically our sources of information. In the ensuing conversation, we discussed the powerful and historically unprecedented role of the media, controlled by corporate conglomerates and sometimes nation-states, in shaping our knowledge about the world in which we live and, in particular, influencing our images of Islam and Muslims. Our conversation reminded me of a well-known story told with slight variations by several different authors, including the famous thirteenth-century Muslim Persian mystic Jalal ad-Din Rumi (d. 1273). The story, which probably originated in India, tells of some blind men who attempted to describe an elephant. Since none of them had the all-embracing vision necessary to see the complete creature, they failed to appreciate it in its entirety. Each man's perception of the elephant was limited to the specific part he touched. It is the same with those who attempt to describe Islam, I explained to the student. A person's description of Islam, whether he or she is Muslim or not, is based on sources of information—what he or she has subjectively experienced, perceived, read, or been taught. Consequently, people hold strikingly contradictory conceptions of Islam depending on their point of view and sources of information: for some Islam is a religion of peace, while for others it is a religion that promotes violence; for some it is a religion that oppresses women and for others it is a religion that liberates women; for some, its teachings are compatible with democracy and fundamental human rights, while others associate them with dictatorship and tyranny.

Clearly, descriptions and characterizations of Islam, its beliefs and doctrines, are sharply contested. This has been particularly the case in the United States and in Europe where, in the aftermath of 9/11 and the 7/7 bombings in London, there have been innumerable public and private debates on the "true" nature of Islam and its alleged role in promoting terrorism. Perceptions of Islam as an anti-American ideology have even prompted two members of the Washington State legislature to walk out of prayers at the beginning of state legislative sessions because they were led by a Muslim imam: they considered their participation in such prayers to be un-American and unpatriotic. Reverend Rod Parsley, an evangelical preacher of the World Harvest Church, goes so far as to claim that America was founded in part to destroy Islam, with 9/11 being a call to arms against this faith that cannot be ignored (Corn 2008).

Anxieties about Islam's being a "fanatical" religion and Muslims being "hate-filled extremists" have fueled the growth of anti-Islamic sentiment and even a deeper kind of Islamophobia. This deep-seated fear and dread of everything associated with Islam has led to violent physical attacks on Muslims or even persons mistakenly assumed to be Muslim. For instance, in the United States, male members of the Sikh community became targets of violence after 9/11 because their ill-informed attackers misperceived their turbans and beards as indicators that they were Muslims. "What we have here is a climate where Islamophobia is not only considered mainstream, it's considered patriotic by some, and that's something that makes these kinds of attacks even more despicable," says Brian Levin, director of the Center for the

Study of Hate and Extremism at the University of California at San Bernadino (Marks 2007). During a United Nations seminar on Islamophobia, Kofi Annan (2004), former secretary general of the United Nations, declared it "at once a deeply personal issue for Muslims, a matter of great importance to anyone concerned about upholding universal values, and a question with implications for international harmony and peace."

Approaches to Studying and Understanding Islam and Religion More Generally

How can we move beyond combative and ill-informed characterizations of Islam? Is it possible to describe Islam, or any religion, objectively, in a manner that is not colored by the subjectivity of perception? Although there exist several ways in which we can approach the study of a religious tradition, here I wish to highlight three distinct approaches: a devotional approach, a textual approach, and a contextual approach.

First, the *devotional approach* is perhaps the most easily grasped since it is the perspective that most people commonly associate with the idea of religion. It understands a religious tradition primarily in terms of its doctrines, rituals, and practices. Representing the perspective of a believer or practitioner, it is traditionally the approach adopted in institutions, such as Sunday schools and madrasas, that impart faith-based education pertaining to the practice of a particular religion. In addition, this approach is also common in many textbooks, at both the high school and college level. It presents the world's religions in monolithic terms, rarely acknowledging the existence of a diversity of interpretations and practices within a tradition as a result of different interpretive contexts. For instance, in such texts, wearing the *hijab* is often represented as religiously mandated for all Muslim women, whereas in reality there are vigorous debates among Muslims about the theological basis of this practice and whether it is in fact Islamic in origin. This approach is often, though not always, exclusivist and sectarian in character, privileging the truth claims of a specific denomination.

Second, the *textual approach* regards the sacred writings and texts as the authoritative embodiment of a religious tradition. According to this approach, a religion is best understood through its scriptures, which are perceived as containing its "true" ethos, or essence. For example, after 9/11, as many non-Muslims sought to understand the possible influence of Islamic teachings on the heinous actions of the terrorists, there was a massive upsurge in sales of Qur'an translations. The underlying assumption was that, in order to acquire a proper understanding of Islam, it was sufficient for a person to read the Qur'an from cover to cover. By adopting this approach, several American and European politicians and public personalities asserted that on the basis of their reading of the Qur'an, Islam was a dangerous religion. Citing certain verses from the Islamic scripture, they claimed that the values Islam espoused were incompatible with the values of Western societies, while others went as far as to compare the Qur'an to Adolf Hitler's *Mein Kampf* and declared that reading it while the country was engaged in a war against terror was an act of treason. For example, in the United States, the television talk show host Bill O'Reilly of Fox News made this comparison in 2002 after the University of North Carolina, Chapel Hill, assigned Professor Sells's book *Approaching the Qur'an* to incoming first-year students as part of their orientation. Why, he asked, should students study what he called "the enemy's religion"? In Europe, Dutch politician Geert Wilders has also made this analogy several times, including in an op-ed piece he wrote in the newspaper *Volkskrant* on August 8, 2007. In their view, Muslim minorities living in Europe and the United States are "Trojan horses," dangerous to the interests of national security. They therefore need to be expelled.

There are several problems with this way of characterizing Islam through the citation of randomly selected verses from the Qur'an. Most obvious is the fact that none of these self-proclaimed experts on

Islam knew Arabic. They had, therefore, relied on translations of the Muslim scripture that, in reality, are more accurately characterized as interpretations of the original Arabic text. In this sense, the so-called translations reflect the ideological biases of the translators. Anyone who compares even a couple of English translations of the Qur'an will become aware that translator bias is responsible for remarkable disparities between different texts, resulting sometimes in contradictory readings. Indeed, we will see below how translator bias can impact the translation and significance of even key terms such as "Islam" and "Muslim" in the Qur'an. It is for this reason that Muslims themselves have insisted on using the Arabic text during prayer and other forms of worship, since they regard it to be the "original" or "real" text.

The more serious problem with this approach is that it attempts to restrict the understanding of religion to what poses as a decontextualized reading but is really the projection of one narrow reading, which, in many cases, is compounded by ill-informed and unrecognized assumptions. If we were to use this approach to study Christianity, for example, we could also declare, by citing certain words attributed to Jesus in the Gospels, that it is an intolerant religion that espouses violence and terror. For example, see Matthew 10:34–35, "Do not suppose that I am come to send peace on the earth; I came not to send peace but a sword." (See also Luke 12:49–53.) By granting absolute sovereignty to the text, this approach ignores a crucial fact: religious texts do not have meaning in and of themselves; they are only given meaning by believers who revere, venerate, and consider them authoritative. Without these communities of believers, scriptures are inconsequential and of little significance. In their interpretations, believers are, however, influenced by the various contexts in which they live. Since these contexts are constantly in flux, the interpretations of scriptural texts are always changing. To illustrate the significant role that the context of the interpreter plays in shaping the reading of scripture, we may consider a paradoxical situation in early twentieth-century America: while members of the Ku Klux Klan read the Bible as a text justifying white racial supremacy, African Americans, struggling for their civil rights as they emerged from a legacy of slavery, saw in the Christian scripture a message of hope and salvation. Each group's interpretation of scripture was strongly influenced by its specific historical, political, economic, and cultural situation.

The recognition of the importance of relating expressions and interpretations of religion to a complex web of many nontheological factors is the central organizing principle of the *contextual approach*. Through this third approach, which emphasizes the need to pay close attention to the contexts of interpretation, we can better understand how a religious tradition can be depicted and practiced in contradictory ways, or how religious texts, such as the Qur'an or the Bible, can be interpreted by believers to justify a wide range of contradictory goals—tolerance and intolerance, liberation and oppression, democracy and theocracy.

The contextual approach provides an effective framework for students to develop skills that will help them to think critically about religion. In contrast to the devotional and textual approaches, it emphasizes that the study of religion must be primarily concerned with human beings who actually practice and interpret it and whose daily lives it influences. On the basis of the cultural studies model described in Diane Moore's *Overcoming Religious Illiteracy*, I contend that religion is a phenomenon that is embedded in every dimension of human experience. Its study, therefore, "requires multiple lenses through which to understand its multivalent social/cultural influences" (Moore 2007, 79). This approach challenges "the assumption that human experience can be studied accurately through discrete disciplinary lenses (e.g., political, economic, cultural, social, etc.) and instead posits an approach that recognizes how these lenses are fundamentally entwined" (p. 79). Such a focus is not meant to discredit the study of the doctrines, rituals, and texts that have come to be identified with various religious traditions, but rather to orient their study primarily to the multiplicities of their human context.

Key to fostering religious literacy through a contextual approach is the realization that even the way we think about and use the term "religion" today is itself a cultural construction. The late Wilfred Cantwell Smith, one of the twentieth century's most influential scholars of religion and for many years Professor of Comparative Religion at Harvard, contends in his book *The Meaning and End of Religion* (1964) that the manner in which we commonly conceive of religions as homogeneous, well-defined, and systemized ideologies, each with a distinctive set of beliefs and practices, is a product of the European Enlightenment. This conception, which is almost universal today, was disseminated globally when European powers colonized large parts of the world, particularly Africa and Asia, from the nineteenth century onward. In the process of colonizing other lands, Europeans categorized their subjects there, on the basis of their practices and doctrines, into "religions" following European Christian paradigms. They then proceeded to label these "religions" as Mohammedanism (the common European term for Islam in the late nineteenth and early twentieth centuries), Hinduism, Buddhism, Confucianism, and so on, forcing their colonial subjects, through various bureaucratic means, to identify themselves primarily in terms of the new categories they created (Smith 1964). In this regard, Professor Smith argues that, from a historical perspective, our notions of religion today are radically different from those of personalities such as the Buddha, Moses, Jesus, and Muhammad, whom we commonly identify as the founders of the world's major religions. In other words, these luminaries would not recognize the religions the world associates with them today. He consequently devotes much of his book to tracing the complex processes by which fluid conceptions of personal faith, experience, and practice attributed to these "founding" personalities were gradually abstracted and systematized as "religion." He uses the term "reification" to refer to these processes that result in the crystallization of narrowly defined and distinctive religious identities.

Fostering Literacy about Islam

The two courses I offer about Islam and contemporary Muslim societies at Harvard are designed to remedy the cultural myopia that af-
flicts prevalent views of Islamic civilizations and Muslim societies by
empowering students with the appropriate content, vocabulary, and
frameworks of analysis. Adopting a contextual approach to the study
of Islam should lead the student to recognize that the experiences and
expressions of the faith are far from homogeneous or monolithic. In the
course of its history, the Islamic tradition has come to be interpreted in
diverse ways around the world, depending on each region's history and
cultural traditions, its social, economic, and political structures, and its
geography and physical location in the world. Recognizing this reality, Abdol Karim Soroush, a contemporary Iranian intellectual, states:

> In reality the history of Islam, like the history of other religions
> such as Christianity, is fundamentally a history of interpretations.
> Throughout the development of Islam there have been different
> schools of thought and ideas, different approaches and interpreta-
> tions of what Islam is and what it means.
>
> There is no such thing as a "pure" Islam or an a-historical Islam
> that is outside the process of historical development. The actual
> lived experience of Islam has always been culturally and histori-
> cally specific, and bound by the immediate circumstances of its lo-
> cation in time and space. If we were to take a snapshot of Islam as it
> is lived today, it would reveal a diversity of lived experiences which
> are all different, yet existing simultaneously. (Noor 2002, 15–16)

The story of Islam is, therefore, not one story but many stories involving peoples of many different races, ethnicities, and cultures, pro-
fessing a myriad of conflicting interpretations. To acquire a correctly
nuanced understanding of Islam and its role in Muslim societies, crucial questions you should ask include: Which Islam? Whose Islam? In
which context? Many Muslims, whose understanding of their religion

is restricted to a particular sectarian version (Sunni, Shi'i, etc.), are often surprised when they encounter the many different ways in which their fellow Muslims practice and interpret their faith. Some are threatened by this plurality and vehemently claim that there is only one true Islam—the version that they believe in. Others, while recognizing diversity, feel the need to emphasize that all Muslims are united by certain fundamental beliefs, such as those expressed in the *shahadah,* the Islamic creed of faith—"there is only one God and Muhammad is His Messenger"—or by common ritual practices such as ritual prayer, pilgrimage to Mecca, and fasting. Yet others willingly embrace this pluralism of belief as a sign of communal strength and God's mercy.

Who Is a Muslim and What Is Islam?

One way we can appreciate the significant role that contexts play in shaping understandings of Islam is by examining the diverse ways in which Muslims have defined key religious concepts. For instance, even fundamental terms such as "islam" and "muslim" may be understood in entirely different ways depending on the specific circumstances of the interpreter. Although today most Muslims generally employ the words "islam" and "muslim" to refer respectively to a religion and a person who adheres to it, they have significantly different meanings in the Qur'an. In this scripture, which Muslims believe to be divinely revealed to Muhammad, "islam" refers not to a systemized religion or belief system but to a private act of faith—the act of submission to God's will. This interpretation is based on the literal meaning of the word "islam," which is derived from the Arabic verb *aslama* (to submit, to surrender). From a linguistic perspective, "islam" is therefore a verbal noun signifying the act of submission, while "muslim" is the agent noun, referring to one who submits—a submitter.* In a theologi-

---

* Arabic is a Semitic language. Most words in Semitic languages, including Hebrew, are derived from roots usually consisting of three consonants. The verb *aslama* originates in the trilateral consonantal root s, l, m. From this root also stems the Arabic noun *salaam* (cognate with Hebrew *shalom*), meaning "peace," popu-

cal context "islam," therefore, signifies submission to God, while "muslim" denotes anyone who has submitted his will to God. Historically speaking, this was the primary sense in which these terms were first understood by the Prophet Muhammad and his early followers in seventh-century Arabia.

A survey of Quranic verses in which these terms occur indicates that not only is it perfectly acceptable to read "islam" as signifying submission and "muslim" as signifying submitter, but that, in the majority of instances, these are clearly the only meanings intended. For instance, the Prophet Abraham (Ibrahim in Arabic), the great patriarch of the three monotheistic faiths—Judaism, Christianity, and Islam—is declared to be a "muslim" in the Qur'an:

> Abraham was not a Jew or Christian but an upright man who had submitted [*musliman*]. (3:67; translations are the author's)

According to verses 131–132 of the Qur'an's second chapter:

> When [Abraham's] Lord said to him, "Submit [*aslim*]" he said "I have submitted [*aslamtu*] to the Lord of the Worlds." And he [Abraham] enjoined his sons as did Jacob: "O my sons, God has chosen the religion for you; do not die except as muslims/submitters [*muslimuna*]."

Submission to the Almighty is an act not limited to humans. As Qur'an chapter 22:18 declares, everything in creation submits to God by prostrating before him:

> Have you not seen how to God bow down all who are in the heavens and the earth, the sun and the moon, the stars and the mountains, the trees and the beasts, and the many of mankind?

In the Quranic worldview, the primordial path of submission to God was preached by a series of prophets (124,000 according to popular Muslim tradition) who were sent by the one God to every people

---

larly used in the Arabic greeting *salaam alaikum*, "peace be upon you." On account of this linguistic association many Muslims also associate Islam with peace.

and every nation. Although these prophets have, over time, come to be associated with communities who appear to follow different paths or religions, they are represented in Quranic discourse as having preached the identical message of submission. Hence, the Qur'an (3:84) commands Muhammad and his followers:

> Say: We believe in God and in what has been sent down to us and to Abraham, Ishmael, Isaac, Jacob and the tribes. We believe in what was given to Moses, Jesus and the prophets from their Lord. We do not make a distinction between any of them. It is to Him that we submit. [Literally, "before Him we are submitters."]

Since submission to God was a central precept in each prophet's teaching, a Jew, Christian, or a follower of any religion who submits to the one God may be called a "muslim." Indeed, the Qur'an portrays the various prophets of God as exemplary "muslims," often illustrating their "muslimness" by narrating anecdotes from their lives. For example, the twelfth chapter of the Qur'an tells the story of the prophet Joseph (Yusuf in Arabic) as a parable for a life of faith. Key events in Joseph's life are recounted with the purpose of upholding him as one who maintained his faith and trust in God in the face of many trials and tribulations. Similarly, Mary, the mother of Jesus, who, incidentally, is mentioned more times in the Qur'an than she is in the Christian Bible, is also portrayed as an exemplary "muslim" woman.

If the Qur'an, the scripture considered to be the foundation of Islamic theology, defines "islam" and "muslim" in such a broad manner, what circumstances gave rise to the narrower understandings of the terms with which we are more familiar today? In other words, why and how did "islam" (submission to God) become Islam, the name of a religion, and "muslim" (anyone who submits to God) become Muslim, a person who is an adherent of the Islamic faith? Professor Cantwell Smith argues that these transformations are the product of reification, the process by which fluid conceptions of personal faith, experience, and practice gradually became abstracted, generalized, and systematized as "religion." This process can be observed in the history of many religious communities. Consider, for instance, the gradual processes by which the disciples of Jesus developed a distinctive identity as Christians as they began to progressively differentiate themselves from Jews. In the Islamic case, reification was similarly associated with the need for Muhammad's followers to differentiate themselves socially and politically as a community (Wensinck [1932] 2007). Their identity evolved from a kind of megatribe, bound together by their shared allegiance to Muhammad's leadership, into a distinctive religious community, whose members referred to themselves as "muslims." The process of reification resulted in the emergence of distinctive rituals, such as the *salat* (ritual prayer) and the *hajj* (pilgrimage to Mecca) as markers of communal identity distinguishing the followers of Muhammad (as Muslims) from other monotheists (Christians and Jews) and later, Sunni from Shia. That decrees of rulers and governors as well as communal practices played a significant role in these developments emphasizes how intricately the complex process of reification was embedded with the promotion of specific political goals. Professor Fred Donner of the University of Chicago dates the beginnings of the process of reification to the eighth century when he claims that the followers of Muhammad first began calling themselves Muslims in the narrower sense of the term (Donner 2009).

To throw further light on the emergence of the term "Islam" as the name of an organized religion, Professor Smith examined the titles of some 25,000 Arabic works written by Muslims over twelve centuries. His research revealed that it is only since the latter part of the nineteenth century that Muslims have increasingly come to think about their religion predominantly in the institutionalized sense as "al-Islam" ("the Islam"). As the notion of "al-Islam" as a religious and sociopolitical ideology gained popularity, concepts such as *iman* (faith in God) and *mu'min* (believer), which were prominently employed by earlier generations of Muslims, dramatically declined in usage in titles. This decline is rather ironic, for it indicates that as Muslims increasingly conceived of "Islam" in ideological terms, the focus on God and faith receded. In explaining this gradual shift, Professor Smith (1964, 105) suggests that the conception of Islam as an ideal religious system, and later a civilization, is the result of Muslims attempting to defend and articulate their faith and their beliefs within European colonial contexts, involving Western conceptions of religion and the idea of secularism:

> On scrutiny it appears that the almost universal Muslim use of the term *islam* in a reified sense in modern times is a direct consequence of apologetics. . . . The impulse to defend what is attacked would seem a powerful force towards reifying. This process has clearly been at work in the Islamic case.

In support of Professor Smith's assertions, Carl Ernst, a professor of Islamic studies at the University of North Carolina, Chapel Hill, observes that the use of the term "Islam" as the name of a religion was first introduced into European languages in the early nineteenth century by Orientalists such as Sir Edward Lane, as an alternate to "Mohammedan religion" or "Mohammedanism," both European terms that Muslims today find offensive. As employed by Europeans, "Islam" was meant to be analogous to the modern Christian conception of religion. Professor Ernst (2003, 11) further asserts:

> The use of the term "Islam" by non-Muslim scholars coincides with its increasing frequency in the religious discourse of those who are now called Muslims. That is, the term "Islam" became more prominent in [Muslim] reformist and protofundamentalist circles at approximately the same time, or shortly after, it was popularized by European Orientalists. So in a sense, the concept of Islam in opposition to the West is just as much a product of European colonialism as it is a Muslim response to that European expansionism.

These observations concerning the importance of the colonial context on the ideological use of "islam" by Muslims are hardly surprising to those familiar with the historical evolution of reified religious identities among other non-European faith communities. In this regard, "Mohammedanism," and later "Islam," were invented European terms just as much as the terms "Hinduism," "Jainism," and "Buddhism," which emerged only in nineteenth-century India as broad labels to group together various philosophical and devotional traditions in South Asia.

Our brief discussion reveals that there are two different ways of thinking about the terms "islam" and "muslim," each with its own contexts: one broader and more universal in meaning, the other reified and narrower. Upon these are premised two fundamentally different worldviews: one inclusive, the other exclusive. Interpreting "islam" as a personal act of submission and "muslim" as submitter forms the basis of a universalist, or at least pluralist, worldview, acknowledging that there are many ways to submit to God, many ways to be "muslim." Such a perspective is more tolerant and respectful of difference, for it affirms that salvation is open to peoples of all faith traditions. On the other hand, interpreting "islam" to refer to a specific religion or ideology creates the potential for fostering a sense of exclusivity and superiority. This is evident in the claims that some Muslims make that since Islam was the last revealed religion, it superseded all predecessor religions, including Judaism and Christianity. In this sense, they consider it is the best of religions and only those who faithfully adhere to its tenets will be granted salvation.

From a historical perspective, the two different interpretations represent, in fact, two conflicting strands within the Islamic tradition that have interacted with each other over the centuries as represented in the thoughts and works of many theologians, poets, and statesmen. They have profoundly influenced how Muslims view and engage with religious diversity. For instance, the Qur'an affirms and confirms what was revealed to prophets prior to Muhammad, specifically designating Jews and Christians as "People of the Book" because they follow scriptures that originate from the same divine source. It states that they are among those who have submitted to the one God and who will be granted salvation. Inclusive and pluralist understandings of "islam" have contributed to tolerant policies toward Jews and Christians in territories under Muslim rule dating as far back as the lifetime of the Prophet Muhammad. We have evidence that in the late seventh century, followers of other religions regarded Islam as an open-minded and tolerant movement. A Nestorian Christian patriarch writing to a bishop in 647 CE confirms that not only did his new Muslim rulers "not fight Christianity, they even commend our religion, show honor to the priests and monasteries and saints of Our Lord, and make gifts to the monasteries and churches." An Armenian bishop records around 660 CE that the first governor of Muslim Jerusalem was Jewish (Donner 2009). Such tolerance is later reflected in the policies of the Arab dynasties of Spain, the Fatimids in North Africa, and the Turkish Ottomans in the Middle East, granting maximum individual and group autonomy to those adhering to a religious tradition other than Islam. We can also cite the example of the Mughal Emperor Akbar (d. 1605) in India, who, much to the dismay of the religious right wing of his time, promoted tolerance among the various traditions that compose the Indian religious landscape, drawing on local Muslim traditions that had extended the category of "People of the Book" to Hindus and Buddhists. This pluralist ethos is still very much alive today, providing a strong countervailing voice to temper exclusivist tendencies within particular Muslim communities.

On the other hand, exclusivist perspectives have provided, in certain circumstances, the bases for the development of a theology promoting the idea of Islam as a religion of empire in order to legitimize claims of several dynasties to political hegemony in various regions of the Middle East, South Asia, and sub-Saharan Africa. Such perspectives also led to the conception of "islam" as an abstract object revealed to the Prophet Muhammad by God in the form of an ideal and perfect system of beliefs and practices, outside the process of normal historical development. Such a view perpetuates what historian Ahmet Karamustafa has termed "the cocoon theory of Islamic civilization," since it refuses to accept the significant ways in which the variegated cultures of the Near East, Asia, and Africa have been incorporated into many aspects of Muslim life and thought, including its theology:

> Islam, it is often observed, came into this world fully grown, and, to boot, in full daylight: a holy book, a prophet, a divine law—all introduced into this world from another world, like a potent drug injected into the body. Exceptionally, however, this drug—which is "true Islam"—does not interact with the body and is only efficacious when it is preserved intact in its pure and pristine state. (Karamustafa 2003, 104)

It is this utopist Islam, unpolluted by human context or any foreign influences, which some contemporary Muslim groups, including the so-called fundamentalists, invoke today in their quest to re-create an ideal and imagined golden-age Islamic state as they respond to the failure of economic and political policies in many Muslim nations to deliver social justice.

Several years ago, "Elizabeth" (not her real name), a student of mine at the Harvard Divinity School, discovered the importance of distinguishing the two different ways in which Muslims employ the terms "muslim" and "islam." During a peace conference on the Middle East, Elizabeth, an ordained minister, found herself engaged in an extensive conversation with a Muslim woman on what it meant to be a Muslim. The conversation ended with "Fatima" (a pseudonym) joyfully proclaiming to Elizabeth, "so you, too, are a muslim." Elizabeth was shocked by this statement and deeply offended to have someone impose a "foreign" religious identity on her. Not only was Islam not her religion but she was terribly ignorant of it, even as she condemned the post-9/11 intolerance of Islam and Muslims. The depth of her own negative reaction surprised her, but it was only later, when she had read more about Islam, that it dawned on her that her peacemaking companion had based her understanding of the term "muslim" on different criteria than those that had shaped her own. Fatima regarded her as a fellow submitter to a common God, fully embracing her as a spiritual companion, notwithstanding her Christian background. As Elizabeth reflected on her experience in retrospect, she wondered that if she, a tolerant person, found her friend's comment to be so jarring, how would it be received by one who blatantly associated the entire Islamic tradition with violence and human rights abuses? Reflecting on this incident, Elizabeth wrote in the journal entry she submitted for my course: "When we understand with our rational minds what is happening within a religious tradition across time and space, we can also challenge ourselves and others to confront the gut-level prejudices that are often masked by intellectual tolerance."

On the basis of the brief example above, the reader will appreciate how the contextual approach and its premise that all constructions of religion need to be situated within specific cultural matrixes can help better inform our understandings of Islamic concepts. Through this approach, we realize that religious concepts can have several contradictory connotations depending on the perspective of the interpreter. This perspective is shaped by the lived reality of a person's day-to-day experience. Therefore, if we want to understand why some Muslims are more inclusive in their worldviews and others less so, we should seek to understand what factors, specific to their individual contexts, have fostered the difference in outlook.

Interdisciplinary Approaches to the Study of Islam

A fundamental premise of the contextual/cultural studies approach is the notion that the study of religion is an interdisciplinary enterprise necessitating the use of several perspectives as a means to appreciate the complexities of religious expression. Studies of Islam and Muslim societies cannot be limited to simply an examination of religious doctrines and concepts. For instance, it is crucial to consider the hegemonic role played by colonial and postcolonial nation-states in shaping the ways an individual Muslim interprets, practices, and experiences his or her faith today. A sociopolitical perspective considers the interplay between historical contexts and ideologies, such as colonialism and nationalism, in shaping contemporary expressions of Islam. To give just a sampling of the diversity of experiences grouped under the label Islam: a Muslim woman living in Taliban-controlled regions of Afghanistan, where pre-Islamic Pushtun tribal codes prevalent in the region mandate that women cover themselves completely from head to toe, experiences her religion very differently from a Muslim woman in Turkey, where secularists vehemently discourage her from wearing a simple head scarf since it is seen as a symbol of religious fundamentalism and a betrayal of cherished Turkish national ideas of secularism. In Senegal, Muslim fraternities espousing a mystical, or Sufi, interpretation of Islam exercise significant political and economic influence, whereas in Saudi Arabia such mysticism is banned, for it is considered a heresy and contrary to the state's official Wahhabi religious ideology. Similarly, being a Muslim in China, a state that is officially atheist and considers its Muslim populations to be ethnic rather than religious minorities, differs from being Muslim in Pakistan, a Muslim majority state in which the invocation of Islam as the ideology for the state and the politicization of religion have led to violent sectarian conflict. In Western contexts, we can look at the experiences of Muslims of Turkish origin in Germany or North Africans in France who have been marginalized in their adopted countries on account of their race and religion and compare and contrast them with those of African Americans, many of whom turned to Islam as an alternative ideology to Christianity in their struggle against institutionalized racism in the United States. The overall point I am making is that the political and social contexts in which a Muslim practices his or her faith are just as important or, some would argue, even more important than doctrines and rituals in determining how contemporary Muslims experience and interpret their faith.

Another framework that may be used to study Islam is to explore the dynamic relationship between religious ideas, artistic expression, and literary contexts in Muslim cultures. My thinking is inspired in part by the prolific cross-disciplinary scholarship of my own teacher, Professor Annemarie Schimmel (1922–2002), Harvard Professor of Indo-Muslim Culture emerita, who fervently believed in the study of world literature, particularly poetry, as a medium of global reconciliation. Many Muslims have enthusiastically embraced the arts and literature as vehicles to express their ideas on a variety of topics, including religion. Thus, poems, short stories, novels, folk songs, rap, miniature paintings, calligraphies, films, architecture, and gardens can provide us glimpses into Muslim worldviews by representing understandings of Islam that often go unrecognized by students of religion. In this regard, studying literature and the arts can "humanize" Muslim countries and cultures that have been "dehumanized" by discourses of nationalism and patriotism, premised as they are on the notion of the Muslim as "the other."

I consider the study of Islam through this framework to be particularly crucial, since literary and artistic genres have played a pivotal role in shaping the development of the Islamic tradition. Let us reflect on the significant ways in which the Qur'an, the scripture at the heart of the tradition, is intimately connected with various arts in Muslim societies. Long before the Qur'an was compiled into a book, it functioned as an aural/oral text meant to be memorized and recited aloud. In Arabic, its name literally means "The Recitation." In form and structure, the Qur'an shows sensitivity to a culture that prized the poetic arts and beauty of oral expression. In pre-Islamic Arabian society, poets enjoyed a special status, for they were believed to be inspired in their utterances by their relationship with spirits, or *jinns*. As a result, their words were conceived to have a powerful spiritual potency. When the Prophet Muhammad began to recite the beautiful verses that eventually came to comprise the Qur'an, his opponents accused him of being a poet. In response to such accusations, he declared that he was a prophet inspired by the one Almighty God. Although the Islamic scripture criticizes egotistical poets who compete with the

Divine Word, it nevertheless displays acute sensibility to the rhythm of speech. With its rhyme schemes and sound patterns, the Qur'an bears all the hallmarks of a text meant to be publicly performed. Reciting it or listening to it was perceived as a way of communing with the Divine. Not surprisingly, Muslims consider the unparalleled beauty and aesthetics of the recited Qur'an as proof of its divine origin, for (according to their thinking) no human could have composed such a perfect text in classical Arabic.

Over the centuries, the Qur'an became the heart of an Islamic soundscape that permeates traditions of spirituality and the arts of poetry, music, and dance as vehicles to transcend the material and the physical and access the realm of the spiritual. Quranic recitation has become such a highly developed art form that every year thousands of Muslims from around the world gather to participate in national and international Qur'an recitation competitions. Just as the Qur'an needs to be melodiously recited so that it moves the heart, it has also to be beautifully written so as to please the eye. Calligraphy in the Arabic script developed into an important religious art form practiced by Muslims all over the world, with distinctive styles emerging in certain regions. For example, among Chinese Muslims, Arabic calligraphy is strongly influenced by the local Chinese traditions. And the art of Quranic calligraphy is not confined to paper. As visual texts, Quranic words and phrases adorn and lend meaning to all kinds of objects: walls of mosques, palaces, and hospitals; ceramic plates and glass lamps; and jewelry and other kinds of ornaments. Since the sacred word is vested with a special power, calligraphic formulas in Arabic can be used to create amulets and talismans to protect against evil. Verses from the Qur'an written in ink on paper may also be dissolved in water and drunk by those seeking to cure a variety of illnesses. The Qur'an has served as an important source of metaphors and symbols, concepts and themes, for Muslim poets and writers as they engage in creating their literary works (similar to the way the Bible permeated works of the so-called Western canon). As a result, it is quite usual to come across subtle and not-so-subtle references to Quranic texts in a wide range of genres—a West African praise poem *(madih)* in the Hausa language, a *qawwali* (a genre of South Asian Muslim devotional music akin to gospel singing), or a rap composed by an African American Muslim artist.

Conclusion

Based on what they have seen or read in the popular media, many people have stereotypical notions about Islam. Contemporary political and military tensions and confrontations, including the Israeli-Palestinian dispute, the conflicts in Iraq, Afghanistan, and Pakistan, and 9/11 and the war on terror, have all contributed to exacerbating misconceptions about the religion. Particularly after 9/11, Islam is perceived in some circles in the United States as an anti-American and anti-Western ideology. As a result of widespread illiteracy about the nature of religion in general, many people have also tended to regard Islam as the root cause of instability and violence in these regions. Unfortunately, this obsession with "religion" as an exclusive factor of explanation, ignoring the complex ways it is embedded in and influenced by its sociopolitical, economic, and cultural contexts, dehumanizes not only people in the region but also adherents of the religion around the world. Ultimately it fails to explain the real causes underlying global tensions and polarizations, perpetuating more misunderstanding and conflict.

In this chapter we have discussed how the contextual approach to the study of Islam, with its insistence that expressions of religion must always be related to a complex web of nontheological factors, is one way in which we can effectively foster literacy about religion and deconstruct the stereotypes and mistaken notions that result in Islamophobia. It is an approach that pays close attention to the dynamic nature of religion as it responds to the ever-changing cultural matrixes in which it is located. Asking crucial questions such as "Which Islam? Whose Islam? In which context?" dissuades us from conceiving of religion as a fixed "thing" or an "object." When notions of religion become reified, people personify them or give them agency by declaring, for instance, that "Islam says . . ." or "according to Islam . . ." As Ernst (2003, 51) correctly observes, "No one, however, has seen Christianity or Islam do anything. They are abstractions, not actors comparable to human beings." A contextual/cultural studies approach reminds us that religions do not have agency; people do. The ways in which people understand and interact with their religious traditions are influenced by the realities of their daily lives and factors such as poverty, feelings of powerlessness and marginalization, sense of humiliation, pride, and arrogance.

Muslim societies, like other societies around the world, are currently searching for a satisfying and legitimate interpretation of religion in relation to a host of issues: nationalism, modernity, globalization, industrialization, and inter- and intrareligious and cultural pluralism. It is crucial to remind ourselves that this search takes place against a particular historical backdrop. In the last 200 years, most Muslims were colonized, directly or indirectly, by various non-Muslim powers who sought, as part of the colonial project, to radically transform these societies in the colonial image. In a postcolonial world, Muslim societies are now seeking to recover and/or discover an identity that is based on values they consider authentically their own, not simply those that are based on foreign ideals and norms. In the process a variety of solutions and interpretations of faith are being proposed, ranging from reactionary to progressive. We should be cautious not to generalize about the entire Islamic tradition on the basis of a single interpretation simply because it manages to capture the attention of the media. If today there are certain interpretations of Islam that are considered "radical" or "extremist" (by Muslims and non-Muslims alike), rather than attributing their origins to an essence located within an imaginary monolithic "Islam," we need to examine carefully the contexts and circumstances in which these interpretations evolved. Many contemporary interpretations of Islam are clearly products of the radical transformation of Muslim societies by forces such as globalization and nationalism. Emphasizing the need to contextualize representations of religion, Carl Ernst (2003, 30) reminds us: "Religion never exists in a vacuum. It is always interwoven with multiple strands of culture and history that link it to particular locations. The rhetoric of religion must be put into a context, so that we know both the objectives and the opponents of particular spokespeople."

The contextual approach also promotes the use of cross-disciplinary and interdisciplinary resources, such as literature and the arts, to study religion. In the case of Islam, this has the advantage of "humanizing" the study of Muslim cultures. It helps us weave the voices of poets, novelists, short story writers, folk musicians, and rock stars alongside those of clerics, theologians, mystics, scholars, and politicians to create a nuanced picture of the rich and multicolored tapestry that we call Islam.

Further Reading

Topics in this chapter are covered in two courses I offer about Islam and contemporary Muslim societies for the Harvard General Education program. "Culture and Belief 12: For the Love of God and His Prophet: Religion, Culture and the Arts in Muslim Societies" employs a literary-artistic perspective, while "Culture and Belief 19: Understanding Islam and Contemporary Muslim Societies" adopts a sociopolitical focus. This chapter draws on material from the introductory chapters of my forthcoming book, *An Infidel of Love: Exploring Muslim Understandings of Islam* (Harvard University Press).

General Bibliography

Bulliet, Richard. 2004. *The Case for Islamo-Christian Civilization*. New York: Columbia University Press.

A brilliant critique of the "clash of civilizations" theory, arguing that the Muslim and Christian worlds have, for most of their history, had much more in common than is popularly assumed. They have experienced the same stages of development and confronted the same challenges; it is only with modernity that the two have followed distinctly separate trajectories on account of differences in economic and sociopolitical contexts.

Ernst, Carl. 2003. *Following Muhammad: Rethinking Islam in the Contemporary World*. Chapel Hill: University of North Carolina Press.
A highly accessible introduction to Islam for the nonspecialist, broad in scope yet careful in not making sweeping generalizations; successfully integrates historical, theological, and cultural contexts in discussing the role of Islam in contemporary Muslim societies.

Gottschalk, Peter, and Gabriel Greenberg. 2008. *Islamophobia: Making Muslims the Enemy*. Lanham, MD: Rowman & Littlefield.
This book explores the demonization of Islam and demeaning of Muslims among Americans, including many liberals who regard themselves as unbiased and broad-minded. It also examines the roots of fear and suspicion about Islam in contemporary America founded on the projection of the Muslim as the "other."

Moore, Diane. 2007. *Overcoming Religious Illiteracy: A Cultural Studies Approach to the Study of Religion in Secondary Education*. New York: Palgrave Macmillan.
Moore makes a strong case for the incorporation of the study of religion into the curriculum of high schools, advocating the use of pedagogic methods that enhance not only religious literacy but also democratic discourse within the classroom and in the public sphere.

Prothero, Stephen. 2007. *Religious Literacy: What Every American Needs to Know—and Doesn't*. San Francisco: Harper.
Arguing that Americans are the most religiously ignorant people in the Western world, Prothero sees America's religious illiteracy as even more dangerous than cultural illiteracy "because religion is the most volatile constituent of culture, because religion has been, in addition to one of the greatest forces for good in world history, one of the greatest forces for evil." He is particularly concerned about widespread public ignorance about the role of religion in America's political and cultural history. Tracing the historical decline of religious literacy in America, the author proposes several remedies with the hope that "the Fall into religious ignorance is reversible."

Renard, John. 1996. *Seven Doors to Islam: Spirituality and the Religious Life of Muslims.* Berkeley: University of California Press.
An introduction to Islam and traditions of Islamic spirituality through the literary and visual arts of Muslim cultures; provides a vivid and colorful portrayal of the devotional lives of Muslims in different parts of the world; a wonderful antidote to the many books on Islam that provide only a narrow one-dimensional depiction of a monolithic religion of empire and conquest, devoid of any artistic and humanistic traditions.

Sachedina, Abdulaziz. 2001. *The Islamic Roots of Democratic Pluralism.* New York: Oxford University Press.
Discusses the pluralist ethos of the Qur'an and the interpretive strategies used by exclusivists to counter it. (For more on this topic, see also my own 2002 article, "Pluralism, Intolerance and the Quran," *American Scholar* 71: 52–60.)

Sells, Michael. 1999. *Approaching the Qur'an: The Early Revelations.* Ashland, OR: White Cloud Press.
An exemplary study of the Qur'an as an aural/oral scripture.

Smith, Wilfred Cantwell. 1964. *The Meaning and End of Religion: A New Approach to the Religious Traditions of Mankind.* New York: Mentor Books.
A provocative examination of the concept of religion, arguing that the ideological way we think about religion today is a product of the European Enlightenment and was disseminated globally through European colonialism; the so-called founders of the world's religions, including the Prophet Muhammad, would be highly disturbed to think that they had founded a religion. See also Smith's chapter "The Historical Development in Islam of the Concept of Islam as an Historical Development," in B. Lewis and P. Holt, eds., *Historians of the Middle East* (London: Oxford University Press, 1962).

Works Cited

Abington Township, Pennsylvania, School District et al. v. Schempp et al. 374 U.S. 203 (1963).

Annan, Kofi. 2004. Address to United Nations Seminar on "Confronting Islamophobia: Education for Tolerance and Understanding," New York, December 7.

Corn, D. 2008. "McCain's Spiritual Guide: Destroy Islam." *Mother Jones,* March 12.

Donner, Fred. 2009. *Muhammad and the Believers: At the Origins of Islam.* Cambridge, MA: Belknap Press of Harvard University Press.

His Highness the Aga Khan. 2006. Remarks on the occasion of the signing of the Funding Agreement for the Global Centre for Pluralism, Ottawa, Canada, October 25.

Karamustafa, Ahmet. 2003. "Islam: A Civilizational Project in Progress." In O. Safi, ed., *Progressive Muslims.* Oxford: Oneworld.

Marks, Alexandra. 2007. "After 'Hatecrime' Melee, Calm Eludes Quaker School." *Christian Science Monitor,* January 29.

Noor, Farish. 2002. *New Voices of Islam.* Leiden: ISIM.

Report of the Task Force on General Education. 2007. Cambridge, MA: President and Fellows of Harvard College. http://www.generaleducation.fas.harvard.edu/icb/icb.do?keyword=k37826&tabgroupid=icb.tabgroup116510.

Wensinck, A. J. (1932) 2007. *The Muslim Creed: Its Genesis and Historical Development.* Routledge Library Editions: Islam, volume 7. London: Routledge.

American Literature and the American Environment: There Never Was an "Is" without a "Where"

Lawrence Buell

This essay arises from a long-held conviction that the arts and humanities have potentially crucial contributions to make toward full understanding of the multiple, accelerating environmental challenges facing the world today. Those contributions include all of the following and more: the qualitative disciplines' sensitivity to the importance of subjective convictions and aesthetic preference in affecting personal choice and public action; their attention to the power of rhetoric, narrative, and image to rivet attention and sometimes also galvanize action; and their grasp of particular cultural heritages both as potential resource and as potential hindrance in shaping individual and public horizons of perception.

To take a simple example from one of modern environmentalism's comparative success stories: How does one transform a "swamp"—a boggy impenetrable tract of no seeming use except when drained for tillage or building sites—into a "wetland" considered worthy of preservation, intrinsically valuable, and even beautiful in its own way? Obviously, such a shift, which has taken place only during the past half century, requires a fundamental transformation of taste and values as well as scrupulous scientific research, protracted advocacy and litigation, careful legislation, and administrative implementation. A mere glance at guidebooks like the National Audubon Society's *Wetlands* that line the shelves of the nature section of a typical American bookstore confirms the importance of narrative and image in helping to bring about and to solidify that transformation of values. These two approaches each have distinctive, though often overlapping, contributions to make. Narrative can both define and underscore the gravity of actual or possible events by means of plotlines involving characters the reader or viewer is made to care about intensely. For example, the sport-hunting industry used to complain that the worst thing that ever happened to it was *Bambi*—an anti-war novel of the 1920s made into a more famous Disney film on the verge of World War II in which many of the appealing forest creatures are killed by ruthless hunters. Free-standing images or sequences of images, often used in combination with narrative, can capture and preserve—in such a way as to make the viewer also want to preserve—endangered landscapes and regions. If restrictions on oil drilling in northern Alaska should continue, much of the credit will need to go to the power of film, photography, and TV nature specials to instill in the American public, few of whom will ever visit the region personally, indelible images of this region's importance as the last unspoiled national wilderness. How a place gets imaged, what stories about it get told, how they are remembered— all this can clearly make a difference not just aesthetically but historically, for public values and behavior.

These convictions have been formed by more than a quarter century of personal research and life experience and, no less importantly, by my teaching of environmentally oriented literature, starting with the introductory course for undergraduates that bears the title of this essay. The first version was launched in the early 1980s at my previous institution (Oberlin College) upon request from the directors of the new environmental studies major for a course in arts and letters. It was exciting to work closely with this new group of colleagues and with a student clientele more eclectic but no less high powered than I had known before, most of them with primary interests outside the humanities. I found myself challenged to think about my home discipline, literature, in new ways, in ways that the discipline itself had never seriously engaged. Apart from one or two figures like Henry

David Thoreau, the whole field of literary environmental nonfiction—"nature writing" as it is more commonly (but somewhat inadequately) called—was still an almost untouched subject. Since 1990—the year I came to Harvard—a scholarly subfield known today as "ecocriticism" has sprung up to the point that it now extends almost worldwide, but back then no such movement was on the radar screen; and this, combined with the acuity and motivation of the students with whom I have always been blessed, prompted me to redirect my research and help develop the emerging inquiry in a more concerted, systematic way. My three critical books on this subject during the past fifteen years owe a great deal to my encounters with generations of undergraduate students during the fifteen or so times I have taught American Literature and the American Environment, at Oberlin, Harvard, and elsewhere. At Harvard, the course aims to serve several purposes. It is a first course in American literature, an introduction to college-level study of literature, and a gateway to further work in American environmental history and other branches of environmental humanities. As such, it attracts an extremely heterogeneous group of students in disciplines from engineering to music. The most predictable common denominator is a keen, often deeply informed, prior interest in environmental issues that goes beyond the merely academic. After graduation, a number of these students embark on careers related to environmental concerns: in law, university and secondary education, public health, early childhood education, and in the corporate world as well—one, after completing a senior honors thesis on the legacy of Rachel Carson, was assigned by a leading investment bank to devise the protocols for its new green investment strategy. This essay pays homage to that course by closely following its account of the evolution of American literature's engagement with environmental issues over the past several centuries.

The swamp-to-wetlands story—and also the continuing struggle between competing narratives and images—is one of a number of preliminary examples I like to use to state the case for environmental imagination as historically important in ways that standard textbook accounts tend to minimize or omit. But my foremost concern is not to pontificate or evangelize but to inquire and to understand: to model a complexity of critical thinking that matches that of the literature itself, also recognizing in the process that authors—like most human beings—never display anything like complete self-consistency or 360-degree vision but more often than not are torn between competing allegiances. In that spirit, this essay ranges through a score of American literary works ranging from early colonial times to the present day, with brief mention of numerous others along the way.

Before getting under way, it is well to review a few basics of literary-critical analysis. First, the world of words is never identical to the actual world. Artistic renderings of the environment are always selective rather than exhaustive, always filtered or mediated by human observation, and always also mediated by the culture(s) within which artistic expression is embedded. Yet these divergences of stylized artwork from replica of an object or scene are potentially sources of enriched perception rather than deception or distortion.

An excerpt from Kentucky poet and regionalist Wendell Berry's "On the Hill Late at Night" (1970) makes a good demonstration case, weaving an evocative sense of place from a very sparse inventory of environmental detail (stars, waving grasses, distant valley below, etc.), in the spirit of Emily Dickinson's late nineteenth-century minipoem:

> To make a prairie it takes a clover and one bee,
> One clover, and a bee,
> And revery.
> The revery alone will do,
> If bees are few.

Landscape in "On the Hill Late at Night" ("I am wholly willing to be here / between the bright silent thousands of stars / and the life of the grass pouring out of the ground") is filtered not only by extreme selectivity of detail but also by the subjective consciousness of a soulful meditative

observer who speaks in a voice reminiscent of much Western nature poetry in the romantic tradition from Wordsworth on down. That makes
for a very different kind of I-figure from that of, say, this Zuni shaman's
prayer for snow to ensure a good spring growing season: "That our
earth mother may wrap herself / In a fourfold robe of white meal / . . . I
have made my prayer sticks into living beings."

In the Zuni poem, the "I" is more a collective than an individual
voice. This contrast in the very meaning of first-personhood across
cultures leads to the further recognition that Berry—like most creative writers—has fashioned his poem from a sizable repertoire of
cultural tropes or devices of much longer history, such as the device of
the intrusion of machine into natural landscape ("Cars travel the valley roads below me"), which dates back to the early industrial era, and
the decision to picture the speaker surveying a broad landscape from
a raised point like the hilltop, a favorite device in English landscape
poetry from the seventeenth century. (Good writers, like good environmentalists, are good recyclers.)

The fundamental reason for calling attention to such artifices is,
again, to combat the common student assumption that environmental
writing does, or should, render faithfully realistic representations of
the external world. For clearly, even attempts to do just that bump up
against an asymptotic limit. Even a "realistic" photograph is selective in
the matter of lighting, coloration, angle of vision, framing and crop-
ping, and so on. It is crucial, then, to recognize from the start how
literature and the other arts regularly offer competing versions of the
same landscape, how art can rewrite or swerve from historical fact,
and how it can invent scenarios for alternative environmental futures
and even planets or ecosystems entirely different from our own, as in
the science fiction we will be examining later on. Geographer D. W.
Meinig's "The Beholding Eye" (1976), a pithy and pungent essay on ten
different ways of sizing up a landscape (landscape as wealth, landscape
as problem, landscape as system, etc.), is an eye-opening mind-jogger
to get one started thinking in this vein.

As I have already hinted, to unsettle the common assumption that literary description is supposed to render landscape detail realistically does not require going to the opposite extreme of defining literature as language games or artifice pure and simple. To appreciate that acts of artistic imagination will—and should—vary according to the context within which the artist writes can also help readers identify when art presses against conventional constraints. The deeper justification of insisting on the distinction between word and world is rather to call attention to art's capacity to engage in as-if experiments that offer up intensified, subtilized visions of the physical world even—and indeed sometimes especially—when taking liberties with literal fact. In Thoreau's *Walden* ([1854] 1971), for instance, the elongation of the Concord summer and, later on, of winter's chilly whiteness bends meteorological fact to dramatize the pleasures and the challenges of the author's two-year experiment in (relatively) self-sufficient homesteading in his local outback at the level of lived experience. So art's creative "distortions" must be approached both with skepticism and with receptivity as to their power to extend the frontiers of environmental perception.

When reading literature for its environmental dimensions, two particularly telling forms of stylization to notice are the art of the persona or narrative voice and the role of metaphor. Attentiveness to the first is perhaps the best single way of reminding oneself that literature is a translucent rather than transparent window onto the objective world, and also to make oneself more self-conscious about one's own role as a subjective perceiver of environments; the narrative voice also connects the art of environmental nonfiction from Thoreau to Rachel Carson with prose fiction's most characteristic strategy for giving its imagined worlds a subjective cast, even novels like Flaubert's *Madame Bovary* or Tolstoy's *Anna Karenina* that employ impersonal omniscient narrators. Critical appreciation of the work of metaphor in literary texts is no less important, for at least three reasons. First, it is that aspect of language use which most visibly differentiates literary from nonliterary writing. Second, it is significant how frequently public talk about the environment, and indeed every other controversial issue, is inflected by metaphor, often recycled unthinkingly: "balance" of nature, "web" of life, "spaceship earth," and for that matter even "global warming"—which overstates the uniform effects of the process and may also subliminally convey a seductive sense of coziness, at least for frost belt types. Realizing this, one becomes a more wary and dexterous consumer and producer of language in general. Third, one specific form of metaphor, personification, is a particularly important resource for environmental literature, not only as a potentially powerful stylistic device but also as a barometer of a literary text's implicit environmental ethics or commitment, and finally as a point of vulnerability for environmental imagination that can cause it to dissipate into wish-fulfilling fantasy. Depending on one's point of view, all three might be said, for instance, of *Bambi* (both Felix Salten's novel and the Disney film) and many other modern animal stories besides.

Literary renditions of the environment cannot be understood only by means of their stylistic elements, crucial as these are. They must also be put in broader cultural and historical context. This means coming to terms with such fundamental concepts and terms as "environment," "nature," "landscape," "place," and "wilderness," and how their meanings vary across cultures and also over time. In every case one faces the tricky challenge of arriving at usable working definitions of these master terms that build in recognition of their slipperiness, including their contestedness at any given point in history.

Obviously a complete account of the meaning and history of these concepts is impossible in a short essay, but here are a few broad brush-strokes. "Wilderness," for instance, needs to be understood as an idea generated by settler cultures' imagination of unknown outbacks, not by aborigines, for whom settler culture itself usually meant "bewilderment." Wilderness is therefore a powerful "fact" of Western environmental imagination as well as an extremely useful concept for environmentalists seeking to protect large tracts of relatively pristine territory from exploitation. But when it is taken to be an absolute rather than a relative term, it can all too easily, as environmental historian William Cronon (1995) warns, get us back to "the wrong nature." By this he means a myth of North America before European settlement as a natural primordium that, at worst, can induce exaggerated fantasies that deny the history—and often also the rights—of the native peoples whom the early settlers tended to discount as they displaced, and their successors tended to romanticize via the stereotype of "the ecological Indian," in anthropologist Shepard Krech III's (1999) phrase.

The shifting senses of the term "environment" itself are even more crucial to bear in mind. "Environment" first entered the English language in the Middle Ages as a verb, "to environ." The modern sense dates back less than 200 years, from the early years of the Industrial Revolution. "Environment" came into being as an omnibus term in English usage when anxieties were just starting to become widespread that humans are no longer intimately part of a cyclically predictable natural order or life rhythm, and that the natural is becoming transformed by the built at an unprecedentedly rapid pace. In principle, then, "environment" in the modern sense encompassed from the start both natural and built aspects, implicitly acknowledging their interpenetration. Yet traditionally and to a large extent even now, "environmentalism" has chiefly been associated with conservation or preservation of nonhuman nature, even though public health-and-safety-oriented forms of environmental concern have at least as long a history, and even though the two forms of environmental concern are historically intertwined, especially since Rachel Carson's *Silent Spring* (1962).

Contrary to widespread popular assumption, then, literary works focused on cityscapes deserve to be considered examples of environmental imagination as legitimate and potentially revealing as a Wordsworthian nature poem or the wilderness writings of John Muir. Walt Whitman's great sundown poem "Crossing Brooklyn Ferry," novelist Charles Dickens's evocations of London (as well as country) landscapes in *Bleak House* and *Our Mutual Friend,* Upton Sinclair's landmark novelistic exposé in *The Jungle* of Lithuanian immigrants exposed to immiserating living and working conditions at the hands of the Chicago meatpacking industry, and the neo-Whitmanian American poet William Carlos Williams's modernist epic *Paterson* are but a few of the memorable works of urban environmental imagination written during the first century of accelerating industrial urbanization. Particularly in my own teaching of twentieth-century literature, I try to make a point of dramatizing this broader reach of literature's environmental imagination by juxtaposing texts that cut across different landscapes, from wild to urban. African American writer John Edgar Wideman's *Hiding Place* (1981), a gritty novel focused on the Pittsburgh ghetto where the author grew up, sits next to nature writer Barry Lopez's *Arctic Dreams* (1986), a panoramic lyrical meditation on boreal ecology and on comparative native and outlander ways of coping with an environment at once exceptionally resistant and exceptionally unstable. Indeed one might validly argue that no work of art in any genre ever crafted since the beginning of time can be fully understood without reference to environmental considerations. For there never was an "is" without a "where."

For a stronger, more calibrated grasp of the relation between artistic practice and its various environmental contexts, "place" is a particularly important concept—equally significant for literary criticism and for environmental(ist) thought, and thus an especially fruitful basis for relating the two domains. Place also happens to be one of the most elusive, elastic words in the English language, "a suitcase so overfilled one can never shut the lid," as architectural historian Dolores Hayden (1995) puts it. Place has both an objective and a subjective aspect. It points outward at what is palpably there and inward to the perceptions we bring to it. It can be thought of in personal, subjective terms, or as a construct defined collectively, or as a physical site—or, most fruitfully of all, in all three ways at once. As artists are well aware, place also admits of enormous flexibility of scale. It can apply to tracts of enormously different size. A place can be as small as a sofa or the particular spot on the sofa where your dog sits, or, at the opposite extreme, it can feel as huge as a planet: earth seen from the moon by the Apollo astronauts or on the cover of the old *Whole Earth Catalog,* and felt as a comfortingly holistic blue-green nurturing presence: our home, our habitat, Gaia. Place can have boundaries relatively distinct or fuzzy, can be felt more or less intensely as force and as value, and it may be thought of both as stable—at a particular moment in time—and unstable, behaving over time more like a verb than a noun. At all events, the exploration of place or emplacement—and its opposite numbers, displacement, diaspora, migration—is a fundamental priority for art with a self-consciously environmental focus.

Readers interested in environmental literature either as an artistic construct or as a carrier of environmental values therefore do well to spend time trying to fathom the construction of place in every text, questioning the degree to which the text ranges about in space versus staying within a single setting or limited range; the value, or lack thereof, set on place centeredness and place commitment; the stability versus mutability with which place is pictured; the tendency to represent the place(s) under view as idyllic, pedestrian, endangered; the degree to which the text seems to invent its place(s) as everyday or familiar versus remote, exotic, surreal; and the degree to which the vision of place is defined through the eyes of the community of inhabitants (sometimes nonhuman rather than human!) or subjectively, as for example through the eyes of a particular character; and the degree to which place is seen as contested ground, between stakeholders or interest groups. All these questions one must ask not only with reference to the "what" but also to the "why" of the literary logic involved and the underlying environmental(ist) commitments that seem to be at stake.

Another way of ensuring that place remains central to your thinking as reader is to try some literary place-making experiments of your own. One means of accomplishing this within the compass of an introductory course that is also easy to replicate on your own is what I call an "environmental imagination project" (EIP). All my students select an outdoor place of their own choosing in which built and natural elements occur in combination or collision, and return to it weekly for a half hour at different times of day, composing nine short (one- to two-page) weekly reflections on stipulated topics that loosely correlate with the reading assignments. The specific assignments change somewhat from year to year, but some of my standby topics include the following:

* Reflect on how your attraction to this particular place might have led you to construct it selectively, to notice certain things at the expense of others.
* Imagine your place from the standpoint of one of the nonvisual senses: hearing, smell, touch, taste. (This in connection with lecture and discussion of the "sight bias" [dominance of appeals to the visual over the other senses] that tends to mark literary renditions of physical environments.)
* Imagine how your place might look and feel from the standpoint of some animal or another nonhuman—as a number of the writers on our syllabus occasionally do.
* Take another person to your place and write about how the experience of place is altered—enhanced or compromised or both—by the change from solitude to companionship. Reflect on some changes, including, but not merely, changes in the season, that you have already begun to notice happening at your place over time.

My students perennially single the EIP out as one of their favorite parts of the course even though it adds to an already heavier-than-average course load. I can well understand why. It provides a kind of practicum enabling forms of creative writing that parallel the readings as well as an alternate form of reflection on the craft of environmental art, and with this a more multidimensional grasp of what place making and place attachment entail, including a more seasoned sense of the value of it all—the pros and cons of place making as an aspect of environmental citizenship in our increasingly migratory age. The point of all this is not to insinuate that a good environmental writer or citizen must be, for example, a "bioregionalist"—a Wendell Berry or a Gary Snyder. Clearly place attachment is not an unmixed good—it can have such negative consequences as turfiness, provincialism, xenophobia. The point is rather to pose the value of place attachment as an open question—a question, incidentally, that I have found is apt to be of special interest to young adults who themselves have recently experienced some degree of displacement as a result of attending a residential college or university.

To dwell so long on the subject of place risks giving a too limited view of the richness and variety of American environmental writing over the past several centuries. Let's now turn to that history, stage by stage. Because the history of printed books dates back to European colonization—although Native Americans had already been making art out of words for millennia—it makes sense to start with early settler culture imagination of the New World as wilderness. From there we proceed to the literary fruits of its transformation over the next two centuries from the initial Eurocentric perception of wilderness as a fearsome, adversarial, though also potentially lucrative, arena to a valued resource of nationally iconic status—a process ushered in by industrial urbanization, the advance of continental conquest, and rising concern in its wake about loss of wildlands and such formerly abundant species as the bison and the passenger pigeon. A good point of departure is Massachusetts Puritan Mary Rowlandson's *Narrative* (1682) of her short but traumatic period of wintertime captivity in 1676 at the hands of Native American insurgents during the most serious threat to the infant colony's survival. A Puritan-era best seller, this text became the foremother of an immensely popular genre that flourished until the end of the nineteenth century. For Rowlandson, wilderness is unequivocally terrifying and unfathomable; she can only explain her experience by means of the tribal vocabulary with which the Puritan colony conceived the meaning of King Philip's War: as a divinely ordained ordeal of spiritual testing and redemption. Yet peeking out through the prison house of this self-protective formula are a series of fascinating glimpses of the author as an increasingly competent survivalist, adapting to her captors' meager diet and learning the ABCs of Native-style foraging and forest lore.

Such were the flickering origins of the much greater ecological literacy and sympathetic receptiveness to the intricacy, variegation, and vastness of the American environment that transfused colonial and national literature after the consolidation of agricultural settlement in the eighteenth century. That receptivity then accelerated with the revaluation of nature by the international romantic movement at the turn of the nineteenth century, and with it the rise of nature poetry and the environmental or nature essay as serious artistic genres. These trend lines can be discerned and traced through the sequence of early national poet William Cullen Bryant, nicknamed "the American Wordsworth"; Thoreau's *Walden* ([1854] 1971); and the sketches and tales of California regionalist Mary Austin's *Land of Little Rain* ([1903] 1988), one of the first and best early attempts to define "the West" as a region starkly different from what earlier American environmental writing had conditioned audiences to expect. The stresses of community building on the Allegheny frontier are dramatized with special discernment by America's first novelist of international renown, James Fenimore Cooper, especially in *The Pioneers* (1823), a semiautobiographical fictionalization of his father's founding of Cooperstown, New York, that introduces one of national literature's most influential figures, the idealized frontiersman Natty Bumppo, later the hero of Cooper's *The Last of the Mohicans* and three other "Leatherstocking" novels. Caroline Kirkland's fictionalized memoir *A New Home—Who'll Follow?* (1839) takes a perceptive, satiric-affectionate look at the tribulations of early Michigan homesteading. For a fuller sense of the early stirrings of environmentalist consciousness among American writers, I recommend especially the Quaker botanist William

Bartram's *Travels in Florida* during the Revolutionary era and after; Susan Cooper's *Rural Hours,* an account of the seasonal cycle and folkways of the Cooperstown region that complements (and in some ways offsets) the work of her more famous father; and the Vermont polymath-diplomat George Perkins Marsh's unevenly written but monumental *Man and Nature; or, the Earth as Modified by Human Action* (1864), the first conservationist manifesto of truly global scope in any Western language.

Some noteworthy themes that emerge from this group of writings include, first, the complex symbiosis and tension between agrarian and pastoral orientations toward landscape ("agrarian" values expressed allegiance to a traditional but perpetually changing steady state of small-scale farming communities, "pastoral" to the dream of returning to a "simpler" state of existence than now prevails); second, the beginnings of settler culture awareness and respect for divergent Native, Hispanic, and other non-Anglo views of place attachment, environmental heritage, and landownership; third, the fascinatingly diverse reservations expressed in American writing from an early date toward the mainstream assumption of land as economic asset that the property holder has a right to exploit at will; and fourth, the paradoxical rise, in environmental nonfiction from Thoreau onward, of scientific literacy in combination with continuous questioning of the adequacy of empirical and quantitative approaches to environmental perception.

Early twentieth-century writers bring to culmination stories of the passing of the frontier, the rise of urban industrialization, and rising concern for a strengthened environmental ethics that would protect against resource depletion, species loss, and the human costs of displacement and the gap between landowner and landless. For example, Willa Cather's novel *O Pioneers!* ([1913] 1992) and William Faulkner's novella "The Bear" ([1942] 1991) are two historical fictions that envisage in divergent ways the process of large-scale transformation of wilderness into productive acreage in the late 1800s, just before the frontier era was thought to have ended and continental settlement completed.

O Pioneers! is an essentially sympathetic, pro-agrarian account of two generations of dramatic growth of an immigrant Nebraska community from hardscrabble origins to farm belt prosperity, but with undertones of regret at the difficulty of maintaining a disinterested ethic of land stewardship and the sacrifice to communal self-sufficiency and family solidarity demanded by agricultural industrialization, as the whole prairie hinterland becomes an interlinked network of production with Chicago and other midwestern cities as the hubs that increasingly control local lives and economies. "The Bear" unfolds a more somber tale of wilderness initiation of an impressionable southern white youth at the moment of wilderness loss, with the Mississippi Delta wildlands on the verge of being decimated by timber interests, against the background of several generations of dynastic history beginning with the grand designs of a ruthless antebellum planter-patriarch, a legacy of exploitation of land and people the idealistic young Ike seeks vainly to escape.

O Pioneers! and "The Bear" both anticipate Aldo Leopold's *A Sand County Almanac* ([1949] 2001), a(nother) classic of American environmental writing, by the conservationist often called the father of modern American environmental ethics. It begins as a neo-Thoreauvian round-the-year series of essays about the author's experiences of trying to rehabilitate an abandoned farm on a tract of abused Wisconsin land but leads from there to a plea for a new "land ethic" that would—he hopes—promote better land stewardship by expanding the idea of the land community to include nonhuman inhabitants and by accepting the right of every species to exist as a matter of "biotic right." (The fact that Leopold makes no distinction here between "good" and "bad" species or "pests" reflects his desire to prevent needless extinction, rather than extreme biological egalitarianism.) More trenchantly even than Faulkner, Leopold conceives the frontier era as a stage of immature or arrested cultural development whose habits of wasteful resource use and unnecessary destruction of animal life and biodiversity linger on into the present. This diagnosis is cast in the form of a series of narrative and essayistic short meditations on cross-species, human-nonhuman relations that oscillate between anthropocentric and ecocentric frames of reference in ways that make *Sand County Almanac* an illuminating companion text for virtually every other book mentioned so far.

Between Leopold and the late twentieth-century environmental writers of the postnuclear era concerned with degradation of the natural world a sharp break seems to occur. Rachel Carson's landmark *Silent Spring* (1962), a densely argued but also hauntingly lyrical brief against chemical pesticides by a professional science writer whose first fame and deepest lifelong commitment was to a more traditional kind of Thoreauvian romanticism, raised the possibility Leopold had not considered a mere dozen years before, that humankind might have brought about dangerous alterations in planetary ecology that could never be reversed. It fearfully envisions the prospect of a planet with no refuge from the effects of toxification. Carson-style toxic discourse continues to this day to serve as an impetus both for environmentalists and for creative writers and other artists. Al Gore, for instance, has claimed that hearing *Silent Spring* read to him as a child by his mother prompted him years later to write *Earth in the Balance*. In literature, the book has inspired a whole genre of environmental cancer memoirs, mostly by women writers, such as Terry Tempest Williams's *Refuge: An Unnatural History of Time and Place* (1991), focused on several generations of a Utah Mormon family who, the author supposes though she cannot be sure, may have suffered the effects of downwind nuclear testing in Nevada during the 1950s; Jane Smiley's novel *A Thousand Acres* (1991), an adaptation of the plot of Shakespeare's *King Lear* to an Iowa farm that tracks the biological effects of years of agrochemical use on the patriarch's daughters; and biologist Sandra Steingraeber's *Living Downstream: An Ecologist Looks at Cancer and the Environment* (1997).

Chemical pesticide use is by no means the only environmental issue with which contemporary American writers and artists have wrestled since Carson. The historic importance of *Silent Spring* for more recent environmental literature lies in two broader factors. First, it brings together the two historic strands of environmentalist thinking mentioned earlier: concern for nature and concern for public health. From this point on, artists, historians, and critical theorists in every field have increasingly come to see them as intertwined. The demography of American environmentalism itself gradually began to diversify in accordance, with increasingly greater participation by women and people of color in the 1980s and after to offset the traditional dominance of middle-class white males. Likewise for the practice of environmental imagination: national literary history itself began to be rewritten, not immediately but in a slow process still ongoing. Earlier urban-focused texts by Whitman, Sinclair, Williams, and many others have belatedly come to seem as important to the understanding of American environmental imagination as those of the laureates of countryside and outback. So too have a number of works by earlier writers on the social margins especially, for whom environmental deprivation appears as a telling mark of the social or racial stigmatization that concerns them preeminently; for example, the narratives of ex-slaves Frederick Douglass and Solomon Northup, the intricate "conjure tales" of the late nineteenth-century African American novelist Charles Chesnutt, and the documentary prose and poetry about the Chicago ghetto by Richard Wright and Gwendolyn Brooks, two of the most gifted African American writers of the mid-twentieth century. During the past two decades, for both environmentalists and creative writers, not only in the United States but worldwide, "environmental justice"—active concern for environmental inequalities between social groups: rich and poor, white and nonwhite—has become a salient concern as never before, as seen on the American literary side in such works as Chicana novelist Ana Castillo's *So Far from God* (1994) and Chickasaw writer Linda Hogan's novel *Solar Storms* (1995). Carson hardly deserves sole credit here, for she herself wrote chiefly to and about the threat to middle-class America. But her redirection of environmental imagination and concern toward public health and welfare concerns was a crucial stage setter.

Silent Spring's greatest achievement, however, may turn out to be its status as the first influential work of environmental imagination to warn that earth may have moved into an entirely new epoch of planetary history, in which anthropogenic influence on the planetary future has irreversibly become the primary shaping force: that we may have moved from the Holocene Age of approximately the past 12,000 years to what today is increasingly being called the Anthropocene Age. This theory, or notion, of the Anthropocene as a distinct geologic era, strictly speaking, is doubly anachronistic when applied to Carson, since it postdates her by several decades and arises rather from the accumulating evidence of anthropogenically accelerated climate change, not of environmental toxification. And it may eventually prove a bogus category, if humankind should manage to reverse the environmental changes it has set in motion. Yet it remains that the most distinctive shared preoccupation for serious environmental writers of the last half century has been the fear of looming ecocatastrophe: fear for the survival of nonhuman life and/or humanity itself in the face of anthropogenically induced disruption—survivability at all levels: ecosystem, community, tribe, planet. Predictably, and properly, these writers offer sharply different assessments and prognostics at different geographic scales from neighborhood to community to region to planet, and direct their gaze toward locations as discrepant as the Arctic and Amazonia—in keeping with the increasingly global reach of American literary imagination as it tracks the working of American economic and cultural influence.

As we get closer and closer to the present moment, it is difficult to be certain whether a given book is likely to endure, so I confine mention here to just three texts to which I find myself returning frequently. Laguna Pueblo novelist Leslie Silko's *Ceremony* (1977), one of the first major achievements of the so-called Native American literary renaissance under way since the late 1960s, develops a return-of-the-native

plot in which a World War II–damaged veteran reaches psychic reintegration through a latter-day version of a traditional Native vision
quest that involves an interweave of retribalization and reconnection
with the physical landscape of his home ground. Central to the larger
stakes of this redemption plot in ways too complex to detail here are
the resources of Laguna storytelling and legend on the one hand and,
on the other, the sad historical fact that uranium ore for the atomic
bombs dropped on Hiroshima and Nagasaki was extracted partly from
Laguna land. As a counterpoint to this book's inspiring but somewhat
wishful fable of communal reintegration, one might turn to the mor-
dant *Do Androids Dream of Electric Sheep?* ([1968] 1996) by science
fiction novelist Philip K. Dick, better known through its (quite different) film adaptation, Ridley Scott's *Blade Runner* (1982), which, when
teaching, I screen for comparison's sake. *Androids* is a postwar fiction
of a very different sort: twenty-first-century San Francisco in the wake
of apocalyptic "World War Terminus," which has made earth almost
uninhabitable, such that the eugenically fit have largely taken off for
Mars and the animal, bird, and insect kingdoms are so devastated that
any living creature is considered precious. Yet technology has continued to advance to the point of producing a race of almost-human
"replicants," as the film calls them, to serve the humans as virtual
slaves. The melodramatic plot (bounty hunter in police employ hunts
down rogue androids) delivers a surprisingly complex meditation on
what culture critic Donna Haraway (1990) calls the three characteristic postmodern boundary breakdowns, between human and machine,
human and animal, and physical reality and virtual reality. In all
three ways, this novel provides a fruitful opportunity for reflecting
back on preoccupations that haunt many earlier authors as to the distinction between nature and culture or fabrication, the proper relation
between humans and other species, and the relation between the actual and the virtual (which in principle might mean any act of artistic
representation).

As such, *Androids* is a good point for a study of the history, nature, and mysteries of American environmental imagination to begin to come to closure. For one of the great benefits of encountering a series of semicomparable works of loosely shared concerns is the sense of accumulated insight—the sense of an increasingly multisided, animated conversation that, above and beyond the virtue of sheer liveliness, makes you want mentally to revisit the ground you have previously covered as you digest each new work in turn. That said, it does not seem true to the vitality either of the natural world or of the human spirit to let a course of study end in an *Androids*-like state of doleful entrapment. Far better a book like Karen Tei Yamashita's *Arc of the Rain Forest* (1990), a rompishly extravagant novel of boom-and-bust entrepreneuring in Brazilian Amazonia in a magical realist vein—a hybrid of graphic description and fairy-tale improbability that underscores the rapid pace and strange profusion of ecological metamorphosis in the tropics from a temperate-zone standpoint. The plot is built on the fantastic but mind-jogging premise that the mysterious plasticoid substance discovered in the deforested outback and then exploited for spectacular profits by a U.S.-based transnational corporation is actually the combined accretion of the world's garbage dumps. The profit engine abruptly implodes when an equally mysterious plastic-devouring bacterium reduces the whole product line to rubble almost overnight, including the new city in the jungle and an adjacent Disneylandish theme park. So the novel becomes an allegory of the folly of hyperexploitation of "pristine" nature and third-world dumping rolled into one. But Yamashita partly relieves this ecocatastrophic determinism through her playfully counterintuitive fantasy elements and by treating the human actors more as foolish innocents than as nefarious agents. This creates a mood of question-posing rather than of doomsday-pronouncing closure, a bit like that of Barry Lopez (1986), musing one night in his sleeping bag in the Canadian far north on the great achievements of Western civilization, from the library of Alexandria to the music of Bach and the humanitarianism of Albert Schweitzer: "Have we come all this way, I wonder, only to be dismantled by our own technologies?" In these perilous times, Western environmental imagination surely does well to keep thrusting forward again and again versions of this same question, particularly for the artists of the nation that, at least for now, remains the world's leading superpower. Yet surely it is right to frame ecocatastrophic anxiety as a question, not as an open-and-shut pronouncement; for environmental imagination itself remains an open field, and so too the human prospect.

Further Reading

Selected American Literary Works

Austin, Mary. (1903) 1988. *Land of Little Rain*. New York: Penguin.
An interlinked collection of descriptive tales and sketches about the desert region along the California-Nevada border, by a major figure in American Western literary history.

Berry, Wendell. 1970. "On the Hill Late at Night." In *Farming: A Hand Book*, 113. New York: Harcourt, Brace, Jovanovich.
A deceptively simple lyric that serves as a gateway to understanding many of the complexities and rewards of environmental imagination.

Carson, Rachel. 1962. *Silent Spring*. Boston: Houghton Mifflin.
A painstakingly argued polemic against the hazards of chemical pesticides for humans and nonhumans alike, made eloquent by the author's exceptional gifts as an award-winning nature writer, highly influential in intensifying and broadening contemporary environmentalism.

Cather, Willa. (1913) 1992. *O Pioneers!* New York: Vintage.
A novelistic epic in miniature of immigrant homesteading in rural Nebraska, featuring one of this author's strongest heroines.

Dick, Philip K. (1968) 1996. *Do Androids Dream of Electric Sheep?* New York: Del Rey.
A postapocalyptic vision of an American city in the wake of "World War Terminus" by one of the masters of modern science fiction, embedding an

intricate, provocative reflection on the relation between human and machine, human and animal.

Dickinson, Emily. (1896) 1998. "To Make a Prairie." In Ralph Franklin, ed., *The Poems of Emily Dickinson,* Variorum edition, 1521. Cambridge, MA: Belknap Press of Harvard University Press.

Faulkner, William. (1942) 1991. "The Bear." In *Go Down, Moses,* 183–315. New York: Vintage.
The greatest short novel by one of the greatest of American novelists. Classic narrative of a young man's initiation into wilderness against the background of a tragic-satiric history of the South from the era of plantation slavery through Reconstruction and beyond.

Leopold, Aldo. (1949) 2001. *A Sand County Almanac.* New York: Oxford University Press.
A diverse collection of essays by a forestry professional-turned-author that builds from quasi-Thoreauvian glimpses of life around the year at the author's Wisconsin "shack" to a visionary statement of a new land ethic in the book's final section.

Lopez, Barry. 1986. *Arctic Dreams.* New York: Scribner's.
A wide-ranging descriptive account of boreal ecology and the challenges of Arctic survival for Eskimo and outlander alike that is at once poetic and scientifically informed. A monumental work of contemporary nature writing.

Rowlandson, Mary. 1682. *The Soveraignty [sic] and Goodness of God, Together with the Faithfulness of His Promises Displayed.* [Widely anthologized.]
The foremother of the hugely popular genre of "Indian captivities" that lasted more than 200 years. Commonly known as Rowlandson's *Narrative.*

Silko, Leslie. 1977. *Ceremony.* New York: Penguin.
The war-damaged Native American protagonist achieves psychic reintegration after returning home through an updated version of the traditional vision quest, whose world-historical stakes are powerfully spelled out in the process. A landmark work of contemporary local/global consciousness.

Thoreau, Henry David. (1854) 1971. *Walden; or, Life in the Woods.* Princeton: Princeton University Press.
The most influential work of American environmental nonfiction or nature writing and one of the foremost American literary classics. A memoir of the author's two-year experiment in voluntary simplicity designed, in part, to demonstrate the possibility of discovering wild places in your own backyard.

Wideman, John Edgar. 1981. *Hiding Place*. Boston: Houghton Mifflin.
The second in a trilogy of semiautobiographical novels that follow seven generations of an African American district of Pittsburgh, Pennsylvania, as the neighborhood cascades from modest prosperity to Rust Belt immiseration.

Yamashita, Karen Tei. 1990. *Through the Arc of the Rainforest*. Minneapolis: Coffee House Books.
A futurist magical realist novel, by turns lighthearted and devastating, of cataclysmic environmental change in Amazonia by a leading Asian American writer who spent years in Brazil researching immigrant Japanese communities.

Selected Secondary Works

Andrews, Richard N. L. 1979. "Land in America: A Brief History." In Andrews, ed., *Land in America: Commodity or Natural Resource?* 27–40. Lanham, MD: Lexington Books.
A concise, excellent account of mainstream conceptions of land use through the centuries.

Basso, Keith. 1996. *Wisdom Sits in Places: Landscape and Language among the Western Apache*. Albuquerque: University of New Mexico Press.
How place-based stories enable cultural coherence and survival for an embattled people.

Buell, Lawrence. 1998. "Toxic Discourse." *Critical Inquiry* 24: 639–665.
Places the literary-rhetorical and argumentative strategies of Carson's *Silent Spring* in a broader historical context of anxiety about environmental degradation.

———. 2005. *The Future of Environmental Criticism*. Cambridge: Blackwell.
A short historical-analytical survey of the "ecocritical" movement. See also Garrard, *Ecocriticism,* below.

Cronon, William. 1995. "The Trouble with Wilderness; or, Getting Back to the Wrong Nature." In Cronon, ed., *Uncommon Ground: Toward Reinventing Nature,* 69–90. New York: Norton.
Trenchant, controversial critique of mainstream stereotypes of wilderness.

Garrard, Greg. 2004. *Ecocriticism*. London: Routledge.
An accessible short introduction to environmental-literary studies, organized topically rather than historically.

Haraway, Donna J. 1990. "A Cyborg Manifesto." In *Simians, Cyborgs, and Women*, 149–181. New York: Routledge.
Influential statement of three characteristically postmodern "boundary breakdowns": between human and machine, human and animal, physical reality and virtual reality.

Hayden, Dolores. 1995. *The Power of Place: Urban Landscapes as Public History*. Cambridge, MA: MIT Press.
Recounts the author's and her students' resourceful attempts to encourage community-based history at the grassroots level in Los Angeles neighborhoods.

Krech, Shepard, III. 1999. *The Ecological Indian: Myth and History*. New York: Norton.
Argues against the stereotypical romantic image of Native Americans as inherently attuned to living in harmony with nature.

Lopez, Barry. 1988. "Landscape and Narrative." In *Crossing Open Ground*, 61–72. New York: Scribner's.
Reflects on the challenge and significance of bringing "inner" and "outer" landscapes into relation, based on analysis of storytelling practices of place-based Native American communities.

Massey, Doreen. 1994. "A Global Sense of Place." In *Space, Place and Gender*, 146–156. Minneapolis: University of Minnesota Press.
Argues for a more expansive sense of place based on analysis of a London neighborhood that sustains a sense of itself amid great demographic diversity and instability.

Meinig, Donald W. 1976. "The Beholding Eye." *Landscape Architecture* 66: 47–54.
Ten different ways of looking at or evaluating a landscape.

Morrison, Toni. 1981. "City Limits, Village Values: Concepts of the Neighborhood in Black Fiction." In Michael C. Jaye and Ann Chalmers Watts, eds., *Literature and the Urban Experience: Essays on the City and Literature*, 35–43. Piscataway, NJ: Rutgers University Press.
Argues that African American urban migration in modern times has thinned out place sense because "the ancestor" is inevitably absent.

Ortner, Sherry B. 1974. "Is Female to Male as Nature Is to Culture?" In Michelle Zimbalist Rosaldo and Louise Lamphere, eds., *Woman, Culture, and Society*, 67–87. Palo Alto, CA: Stanford University Press.

An anthropologist argues for the global ubiquity of this equation as a cultural stereotype and for the need to counteract its systematic disempowerment of women.

Snyder, Gary. 1995. "Language Goes Two Ways." In *A Place in Space: Ethics, Aesthetics, and Watersheds,* 173–180. Berkeley, CA: Counterpoint.
Argues that language both lays a grid on nature and that nature shapes language.

Tuan, Yi-Fu. 1970. "Our Treatment of the Environment in Ideal and Actuality." *American Scientist* 58: 244, 247–249.
The yawning gap between notional belief and actual practice in both Western and Asian history.

The Internet and Hieronymus Bosch: Fear, Protection, and Liberty in Cyberspace

Harry R. Lewis

It is trite but true: We are in the middle of an information revolution. News, gossip, entertainment, lies, and propaganda move over huge distances in the blink of an eye. All of it, from the newspapers of record to juvenile cell phone photos, to what you bought at the supermarket last Thursday, is archived for parties unknown to retrieve, who knows when in the future. Electronic communication already reaches the majority of the world's population, and no technological obstacle prevents virtually everyone from having constant access to everything. In parts of the world where connectivity is lagging because cables are few and electricity is scarce, mobile communication is growing exponentially (see, for example, the statistics of the International Telecommunication Union [2010]). If the world is not fully connected in twenty-five years, it will not be for want of technology or money, but because of politics.

The question before this human generation is how the power of information ubiquity will be used and how it will be controlled. The societies of the world are struggling with the social dilemmas posed by the rapidly evolving technologies. Conveniences that teenagers take for granted—for example, taking photographs anywhere and sending them instantaneously to anyone on earth—neither science fiction writers nor engineers quite foresaw. Nor are such innovations socially inevitable, even when widely disseminated, as Iranians discovered in the summer of 2009 when they tried to send images of postelection uprisings out of the country. Such citizen journalism was simply banned, with heavy penalties imposed on transgressors. With every communications invention comes questions of both exploitation and control.

The Cycle of Invention and Control

The revolution is enlightening, empowering, and alarming. Technologically, it is easier to speak and it is easier to listen than ever before; easier to share knowledge and to gain knowledge; and easier to find and communicate with others who share the same interests. But potentiality is not the same as reality. And the same technologies are as easily used to spread misinformation, defamation, and terror.

Societies respond to what they consider threats. They may try to prevent production of information, to throttle its source, to block its receipt, or to filter it out of the communications network in transit. Any response may regulate much more than the original threat. Overreactions have unintended consequences and are sometimes scaled back; malefactors bypass the regulations, creating incentives to expand them further. By the time a measure of social stability has evolved, other new technologies give birth to unanticipated problems.

This schema of invention and control plays out in widely disparate domains. It frames the story of political censorship in totalitarian countries, the story of uncensored blogging in the United States, the story of age restrictions on Myspace, and the story of music downloading in college dormitory rooms. It is even the story of U.S. government censorship of broadcast television, an old American story given new life by changes in broadcast technology. In fact, as we shall see, it is as old as the most ancient myths of human origin.

The cycle of invention, opportunity, threat, alarm, response, and reaction plays out differently in different societies, but the societies interact with each other, creating more uncertainty and confusion. And so we have anonymous Internet routing that enables Iranian dissidents to view the Internet as it looks in free societies, and so we have self-censorship by U.S. publishers whose Web sites are visible in countries with less forgiving defamation laws.

Politics, Person, and Property

However information is produced and communicated, societies take an interest in exploiting and controlling it in three domains: politics, personhood, and property. For example, the political domain includes democratic participation using mobile phones and the Internet on the one hand, and cyberterrorism and the arrest of dissident bloggers on the other. The personal domain includes the vast opportunities of social networking on the one hand, and the threats to the safety of networked children on the other. Property exploitation and control involve, most famously, the complex relation between the music industry and music fans, whose intercourse as producers, consumers, and "pirates" of recorded music is now entirely digital.

These three domains share digital tools and techniques. The power to detect and censor political dissidents can as easily be exploited to detect and prosecute those improperly distributing copyrighted movies. Once a form of technological control has been invented and deployed, it can be redirected, exported, or adapted.

Claims to the effect that the Internet is making us dumber, or is causing unheard-of levels of sex crimes, should be greeted skeptically. Digital technologies are tools, intrinsically no more dangerous than a book with blank pages. And yet something is different and consequential about the social impact of digital technologies. They are at once the most effective methods of disseminating information ever invented and the best technologies for restricting and monitoring its flow. The digital world is all about control.

The social dilemma at the core of the information revolution is whether it will prove to be liberating or limiting. As we experience it in midstream today, it is to some degree both, for most of us. We can look up baseball statistics at the ballpark and connect to old friends in ways never before possible. We can read Supreme Court decisions day and night without going to the library, and millions of people can hear today an amazing vocal performance that was recorded only yesterday. Yet we fear that casual disclosure of a few digits of information about ourselves will result in our life savings disappearing to Eastern Europe, or that bad people loitering on the information superhighway will take advantage of our elderly or juvenile relatives. We fear that corporations and governments alike will mindlessly aggregate data about the most important and the most trivial activities of our lives—and will then misuse that information or let it slip into hands we wish did not have it.

Information and Power

Humankind has long experience coping with information flows. For as long as people have been telling things to one another, other people have been trying to control who hears what. Some twenty-five centuries ago, Socrates argued that young people are particularly impressionable and should be shielded from corrupting influences. "The first thing," says Socrates in Plato's *Republic* (1888), "will be to establish a censorship of the writers of fiction, and let the censors receive any tale of fiction which is good, and reject the bad." Suppressing fiction was not enough, he opined—sometimes you have to suppress the truth too. "The doings of Cronus, and the sufferings which in turn his son inflicted upon him, even if they were true, ought certainly not to be lightly told to young and thoughtless persons; if possible, they had better be buried in silence." (The Golden-Age god Cronus ate his infant children, knowing one was destined to overthrow him—but the youngest child, Zeus, was hidden away by his mother and survived to gain dominion over his father. Not a family dynamic, apparently, for Greek boys to use as a model.)

Today's revolution is also about the spreading of stories—and not just stories but anything expressible. The revolution is astonishing when we notice it, but often we do not see it happening, because it manifests in mundane things like shopping and gossiping, not headline events such as wars, flu epidemics, and space flights. (And infanticides.)

Commercial interests tend to highlight our convenience and downplay our vulnerability. Cell phone companies do not advertise that they keep copies of our address books and our family photos, which can be subpoenaed when we are hauled into court. We do not think about that even when we lose our phone and are thrilled to find all our data magically restored on the replacement unit.

What drives the revolution is not politics or ideas. The information revolution has its gurus, but no inspirational spokesman could have led this revolution. Inventions caused the explosion: the cell phone, the Internet, the digital camera, the personal computer—and behind them all, semiconductors and integrated circuits and fiber optic cables. It is a disruptive and even destructive technological revolution in the commerce of ideas, knowledge, and thought. Nothing could be more defining of this age of human civilization than how we utilize our new power over those insubstantial products of the human mind—words and images, fantasies and facts. Our descendants will judge us on what decisions we made, and what we allowed others to make for us, about how these technologies would be put to use.

Like many other technological histories, this one is a tale of power shifts: technology empowers those who control it and weakens others. Military technologies, such as the saddle, the gun, and the atomic bomb, were decisive in wars waged before these inventions escaped the exclusive control of their possessors and, for better or worse, leveled the global playing field. Technologies of building construction, locomotion, and food production have all for a time given nations economic advantages over their competitors and control over the welfare of their people. Can the new technologies of insubstantial zeroes and ones really have such dramatic impact on society?

In fact, technologies of information have always precipitated power grabs. Gutenberg started printing books using movable type shortly after 1450—at first just the Bible and perhaps a few grammars. But within fifty years the Catholic Church was burning heretical printed works that were falling into the hands of the faithful. After a century the problem of disapproved books became so serious that the technology was put to work against itself. In 1559 the Church printed the *Index Librorum Prohibitorum*, a book listing all the prohibited books—including the works of Kepler and other scientific tracts that ultimately would dislodge man from the center of the universe and the Church itself from its authority over human minds. The lists of books that should not exist were reissued periodically until 1966, when Pope Paul VI decided that the list itself should no longer exist—a nicely recursive end to five centuries of technologically enabled suppression of technologically enabled information flows.

Liberty, Protection, and Control

So today's struggles over the spread of information are not new in kind, only in degree. As in the past, the key dialectic in the struggle for control of information is between fear and liberty, between protection and control. The spread of information is dangerous, so the technology that spreads it must be regulated. The regulations require human judgment to administer, and those judgments may be colored by incentives to control thought, not merely to protect the vulnerable.

Information regulation requires that someone decide for other people what information they should have. To the extent we believe that human beings can and should decide for themselves what to do with the information that is available to them, any regulation of information is a threat to human liberty. To the extent that information liberty is a precondition to human empowerment, any regulation of information is inimical to social progress.

Plato's censors and the Church's imprimaturs were ultimately ineffective controls over ideas. But with everything reduced to bits, the digital controls are at once more universal and more varied. We see examples every day:

* The Chinese government fears that its citizens will get "wrong" information about Tibet and the Uighurs, so it controls what Web sites are accessible inside China, even attempting to enforce installation of "Green Dam" censoring and tracking software on every computer sold in China. Many other countries have their own Web censorship practices. Little sexual content is available in Saudi Arabia. (For detailed information on Internet censorship worldwide, see the site of the OpenNet Initiative, http://opennet .net/.) The new Iraqi democracy is planning to impose some of the censorship that was lifted after the fall of the regime of Saddam Hussein and to force Internet cafés to register and be monitored. A government minister explains, "We are living in such a dangerous time that we need to control things" (Williams 2009).

* Though politics and sex are the usual reasons for government censorship, once the technology is available it can be retargeted in an instant for other purposes. During the summer of 2009 the Chinese government, embarrassed by a scandal involving dealings of a Chinese company with the government of the African nation of Namibia, ordered that Chinese search engines return no results in response to searches for "Namibia." For those in China who rely on the Web for information about the world, Namibia simply ceased to exist (Heacock 2009).

* Parents, fearing that their children will use the Internet to talk to pedophiles, install monitoring software that enables them to monitor their children's activities and even be notified if their children wander into prohibited regions of cyberspace. The states' attorneys general have instructed the industry to come up with better child protection tools, threatening legal requirements in the absence of voluntary action (Medina 2007).

∗ The recording and movie industries fear that the Internet's capacity to make and distribute copies of digital audio and video files will hurt their profits, and have induced Congress to enact copyright statutes with strict rules and severe sanctions, of which the industries themselves are the enforcers. The policing tools are digital, of course; when teenagers persist in music sharing, the industries lobby for stronger regulations, requiring large-scale monitoring of data flows through the heart of the Internet. For example, in 2010 France passed a "three strikes" law that denies Internet access to users who repeatedly download copyrighted works. "When you violate driving laws, your car is taken away," a French official analogized (Lankarani 2009). This analogy is seductive—why shouldn't transporting bits be regulated like transporting atoms?—but disingenuous. Driving is a public activity that poses an immediate threat of physical harm. Drivers expect to be monitored, not only by the police but by other drivers, whose safety is jeopardized by reckless driving.

∗ Accessing the Internet, at least from one's own home, is a private transport of words and ideas, akin to talking on the telephone rather than driving. Monitoring Internet communications is like wiretapping. In the early days of telephony, warrantless wiretapping was legal. The U.S. Supreme Court ruled in 1928 that if someone installs a telephone, "The reasonable view is that . . . the wires beyond his house and messages while passing over them are not within the protection of the Fourth Amendment" (*Olmstead v. U.S.* 1928). By 1967, the telephone was recognized as an essential vehicle for private speech and the Court (in its decision in *Katz v. U.S.*) reversed the default—the government cannot listen in without a warrant. The practice of Internet monitoring, along the lines desired by the music and movie industries and codified by the French "three strikes" law, resembles the presumptions of early telephony. Internet service providers are allowed, and even expected, to monitor all network activity on the chance that someone is violating some law—even a civil statute such as that prohibiting downloads of copyrighted music. It is as though Federal Express were required to check all packages it delivers for unauthorized music CDs. Monitoring the Internet is monitoring the world of thoughts and ideas and words—some may be illegal, but in an enlightened democracy, the government should show specific grounds for suspicion before monitoring any individual's communications.

* Apple, fearing that Google will gain a competitive head start in the market for consumer control of telephone calls, removed the digital imprimatur it had previously granted to the Google Voice application for the Apple iPhone. Because iPhone apps are "tethered," Apple can unilaterally remove them, without the cooperation of the iPhone owner.

* Apple also uses its control over iPhone software to censor a dictionary. Citing its policy against obscene or pornographic material, Apple refused to allow the Ninjawords dictionary app onto the iPhone until words such as "shit" and "fuck," which appear in virtually every dictionary of the English language, were removed (Gruber 2009).

* Amazon, upon discovering that it sold certain books to Kindle owners without proper authority from the copyright holder, removed the books from the Kindles, issuing refunds. Surprised owners discovered that they never really owned the books in the first place; their Kindles are tethered to Amazon (Stone 2009a). The precedent having been established, Kindle owners wonder whether Amazon might reach into their homes to remove books for other reasons—say a claim that the book is unlawfully obscene or perhaps merely unkind to Amazon founder Jeff Bezos.

Bits Reductionism

The prospect of books mysteriously disappearing from Kindles has a nightmarish resemblance to Savanarola's bonfires of the vanities. But the new information control mechanisms are distinguished from the old by bits reductionism, the simple idea that "it's all just bits"— anything that can be expressed, can be expressed as a series of zeroes and ones. Once content is reduced to bits, there are no more photographs and recipes, pornographic movies and Skype telephone calls, novels and accounts payable. There are just sequences of bits. Any possibility of moving or storing or making a million copies of one sequence of bits is a possibility for any other sequence of bits. And any control that can be exerted over one sequence could be exerted over any other.

The technological revolution in the commerce of ideas is merely a special case in the commerce of bits. Technologically, all distinctions between ideas and any other kind of expression have been obliterated. Bits reductionism has given birth to media convergence. The engineering of radio, telephone, and computer communications is now the same. Movies flow over the Internet, the Internet flows over the cellular telephone network, and Grandma's telephone calls flow into the home through the same digital pipes that bring *American Idol* television shows.

The dual forces of bits reductionism and media convergence make it possible to collapse all forms of regulation. To regulate the flow of ideas one must regulate the flow of bits, and while regulating the flow of bits the flow of other forms of expression can be regulated as a side effect. The antipiracy filters being deployed in France are functionally similar to antipornography filters being deployed in Australia; once deployed for one purpose, the filtering technology can readily be expanded to serve another.

So where the flow of ideas is free, the flow of every form of expression is free. Where the flow of verbal or pictorial trash is regulated, the flow of ideas can also be regulated collaterally.

These convergent and overlapping and collapsing effects of bits reductionism explain why the digital revolution defies analysis into the classical social categories. For Plato a story was a story; perhaps true and perhaps false, but it was not his medical history or grocery list or lute music. There was no way for a medieval pope to put offending private mail on the *Index Librorum Prohibitorum*. With all forms of communication now flowing through the same network, it takes only a software tweak to retarget censorship or monitoring technologies. The old dilemmas about censorship, about mind protection versus mind control, are now convoluted with issues of privacy, creativity, expressiveness, entertainment, business management, education, socialization, reputation, and the very essence of personal identity. Interference with the flow of bits to fix a problem in one area is likely to have an effect in another.

Consider the story of the infamous Lori Drew, the Missouri woman who used a Myspace account to impersonate a nonexistent teenage boy named Josh. Megan Meier, a teenage girl, was distressed by Josh's taunts and committed suicide. No Missouri statute was applicable, but a federal prosecutor successfully brought charges against Drew under a statute enacted to criminalize cyberattacks on the computers of banks and credit card companies. The judge set the verdict aside, reasoning correctly that the prosecutor's legal theory would make almost everyone a criminal; even fibbing about one's age on a Web site (as Megan Meier herself had done) would become a federal crime.

The Lori Drew tale illustrates at least three forms of convergence: an Internet invention created to enhance social connectivity becomes a tool of identity fraud, exciting a demand for regulation (a new Missouri law might have been applicable in the Drew case if it had been enacted earlier); the Computer Fraud and Abuse Act (CFAA), originally enacted to fight interstate monetary fraud, is applied to a social communication between neighbors because the computer they were using was in another state; and the CFAA itself was necessary because the Internet, never designed for secure communication, rapidly became a critical tool of world finance.

Or consider the curiously important question of whether, the First Amendment notwithstanding, the U.S. government can prohibit Nicole Richie from saying "shit" on television. The Supreme Court decided yes, in a 5–4 vote along conservative-liberal lines (*FCC v. Fox Television* 2009). The matter was narrowly decided on a question of administrative process; on its face, the issue had nothing to do with the digital revolution. But Justice Thomas, who voted with the majority and is surely among the most socially conservative members of the court, wrote his own opinion. He noted that communications technology was so much more abundant than it had been in the 1930s, when the Court affirmed the FCC's authority to censor broadcasting, that the old rationale for this exception to the First Amendment—that the electromagnetic spectrum was a scarce resource that Congress had the right to nationalize—might have to be revisited. Thomas signaled that, if a similar case came back on free speech grounds, he might flip his vote.

Internet Universalism

The Internet was designed to be ubiquitous and placeless, both hard to control and highly resilient. Though the scale of the network is vastly greater than its designers conceived, their design goals have largely been achieved. Governments have a hard time keeping disapproved material away from their citizens, and natural catastrophes such as Hurricane Katrina and the December 26, 2006 earthquake in the South China Sea leave the network as a whole running fine. Even more importantly, the Internet was not designed to carry phone calls, MP3s, or e-mail. It was just designed to carry bits and, by extension, anything that could be expressed in bits, which means anything that can be expressed. As Internet standards state,

> The internet protocol is specifically limited in scope to provide the functions necessary to deliver a package of bits (an internet datagram) from a source to a destination over an interconnected system

of networks. There are no mechanisms to augment end-to-end data reliability, flow control, sequencing, or other services commonly found in host-to-host protocols. (Information Sciences Institute 1981)

That passage comes from an Internet design document. It says, essentially, that you can make this network do lots of things; we have not even bothered to think what they might be. What we are giving you is a set of basic tools and raw materials for communications between computers; go use your imagination. If reliable or smooth or secret communication is important to you, those things may be possible, but it is your job to figure out how to achieve them. All we can tell you is that anybody, anywhere in the world, using any kind of computer, who follows these rules and gets connected to another computer on the Internet will inherit all those unforeseen inventions that you build on top.

The Internet was born in a spirit of innocent—perhaps naive—fearlessness. And that is how the Internet, whose earliest uses were dull things such as sharing printers among mainframe computers and sharing software between engineering groups, came to be the engine of Wikipedia and Facebook and Skype and online banking, and also amateur pornography and international money laundering.

So the Internet facilitates the dissemination of dangerous information, because of its inherent lack of moral direction. It is, like a knife, simply a tool, which can be used for good or evil.

Dangerous and Enlightening Knowledge

How do we cope with dangerous knowledge, with knowledge that can be harmful? That is an old question, but not merely an old question. It is perhaps still the ultimate question about the human condition. It is the question we have been asking ourselves since the fateful day the serpent told Eve about the tree in the middle of the garden, and told her that God had a particular reason for warning her about that particular tree: "When you eat of it your eyes will be opened, and you will be like God." Eve reckoned that "the tree was to be desired to make one wise," ate the fruit, and shared it with Adam—at which point God threw them both out of the garden, pausing only to clothe them and to issue a few curses.

Full knowledge is, in many religious traditions, dangerous.

Of course it is also what makes us joyful, and thoughtful, and wise, and inventive. Our capacity to build new and more advanced cultures on top of the accumulated knowledge of the past is distinctively human (notwithstanding the limited forms of cultural transmission that have been observed in animal societies).

The progressive force of knowledge has, as a long tradition in human self-understanding, an association with evil and sin. In fact, our human burden lies in our freedom to master the use of what we know. In Greek mythology, Prometheus, like Adam and Eve, endured a severe punishment for seeking divine knowledge. Prometheus stole fire from Zeus, and with it all the other useful arts of civilization. The price Prometheus paid was to be chained to a rock and to have his liver gnawed at by an eagle, but humankind got its own punishment: Zeus sent Pandora (the first woman) to tempt Prometheus's brother, and when she succumbed to her curiosity and opened her famous box, ills and ailments escaped, afflicting us to this day. (Only Hope remained behind.) Still, Prometheus is remembered not only as the original dangerous technologist but also as the progenitor of the human race; to the Greeks we are actually defined by our curiosity and noble creativity.

To an idealist about the future of humanity, progress is measured by capacity to use knowledge to improve human life. The optimistic view of the effect of universal learning was articulated and revered in the eighteenth-century Enlightenment as never before. Confidence in the power of learning, if only individuals could have access to it, nourished the antiauthoritarian political morality that justified the American Revolution. It is no accident that Benjamin Franklin was both inventor and diplomat, or that Thomas Jefferson was both a visionary polymath and an inspired political revolutionary.

Political freedom has been, from the founding of the American republic, of a piece with information freedom. Self-determination requires the freedom to speak and the freedom to learn, which are characteristic of the natural state of human existence.

Jefferson in particular was prescient on the peculiarities of ideas and information and knowledge, how hard they are to control. He wrote, in an 1813 letter to Isaac McPherson,

> If nature has made any one thing less susceptible than all others of exclusive property, it is the action of the thinking power called an idea, which an individual may exclusively possess as long as he keeps it to himself; but the moment it is divulged, it forces itself into the possession of every one, and the receiver cannot dispossess himself of it. Its peculiar character, too, is that no one possesses the less, because every other possesses the whole of it. He who receives an idea from me, receives instruction himself without lessening mine; as he who lights his taper at mine, receives light without darkening me. That ideas should freely spread from one to another over the globe, for the moral and mutual instruction of man, and improvement of his condition, seems to have been peculiarly and benevolently designed by nature, when she made them, like fire, expansible over all space, without lessening their density in any point, and like the air in which we breathe, move, and have our physical being, incapable of confinement or exclusive appropriation.

If Jefferson saw a downside to the explosive spread of ideas across the globe, he did not mention it here. The conflagration would contribute to the "moral and mutual instruction of man," period. The more people know, the better. Ideas spread naturally and cannot be fenced in. And nature has benevolently provided that you do not lose your ideas when others get them; enlightenment simply spreads without cost to you.

Until recently, the economics of information transfer kept Jefferson's dream in the realm of imagination. To paraphrase John Perry Barlow (1993), you could not get the wine without paying for the bottle—to learn something you had to buy a physical object, a book or a newspaper or a magazine, and publishing cost money. The economics have been radically changed by Moore's law—the exponential growth in computing and storage capacity of silicon chips—and by corresponding improvements in rotating storage. Digital technologies have made possible previously unimaginable decreases in the cost of information storage and communication. The Internet is the realization of Jefferson's dream: the marginal cost of reproduction and transmission are plummeting toward nil.

Yet universal enlightenment hardly seems to be at hand. What stands in the way? Broadband access is far from universal, but that is not the problem—the rule of reason seems not to have triumphed even in zip codes with good Internet service. What has gone wrong?

A technology of liberation has evolved into a technology of control for two related reasons.

The first reason is commercial. Because information (for example, in the form of digital songs and movies) is valuable, the network and the laws that govern it are structured so that information can be monetized. Advertising pays for Internet services we too readily consider free, such as search engines and news services, so the network and the laws that govern it are designed to make advertising effective. With the emergence of commercial information monopolies, or near-monopolies, comes the possibility that the new information universe will become more limited rather than more open.

Amazon's withdrawal of Orwell's *1984* from customers' Kindles (see Fowler 2009) was a creepy event but not a dangerous one, given the continued existence of print copies. But suppose that readers become dependent on Google's vast digital book library and Google, under some future corporate leadership, were to selectively prune its collection for reasons of politics or religion or taste. Or suppose, after the merger of an information carrier such as Comcast with a content provider such as NBC Universal (see Kahn 2010), that competing media no longer flow readily to the carrier's customers. There is no more reason to expect information corporations to act as public servants than there would be to expect an unregulated supplier of oil or electricity always to act in the public interest.

There is a remarkable historical precedent for concern over "network neutrality," as the principle of separation of content and carrier has come to be known. Here is an excerpt from an article titled "The Telegraph Monopoly" from the February 9, 1884, edition of the *New York Times,* reporting testimony before the U.S. Congress in 1884, describing what happened because of the Western Union monopoly on telegraphy:

> A few years ago a man started a news bureau in Cincinnati. A correspondent in New-York [*sic*] filed the market reports each morning and the Cincinnati gentleman sold the information to customers. The Western Union asked him to sell out to them and he refused; thereupon his messages were taken away from the "through" wire and sent by a "way" wire. The difference in time was an hour, and the man was ruined. . . . The Western Union . . . controlled the market prices, all the political and general news sent over its wires—every single important personal communication sent in the country.

The second justification for control of information technologies is the protection of personal security—of individuals and of nations. From the desire to catch the bad guys before they do anything comes the inclination to control any technology used to do ill, and information technologies in particular. Examples include the United Arab Emirates' demand that BlackBerry communications be open for government inspection since antigovernment forces might conspire using encrypted communications (Meier and Worth 2010) and India's proposal to ban Google Earth because the Mumbai terrorists had used it to plan their attack (Blakely 2008). In both these cases, as in many others, fear of the novel clouds the issue. Bad guys use not only BlackBerry phones and Google Earth, but cars and boats, which no one would consider banning. The cost of banning or heavily controlling the new technologies is not as apparent, but every premature restriction on technology leaves many inventive uses stillborn.

The information technologies for protecting commerce and protecting people have a lot in common. In both cases the crucial tools are automatic monitors that watch for patterns of bits in information flows. The result is an unholy alliance between governments and content companies (owners and distributors of copyrighted works). After all, if Internet service providers (ISPs) were required to watch for pirated movies to protect the nation's intellectual property industry, how could any reasonable person argue against using the same monitoring tools to prevent another 9/11?

Internet Fear

The possibility of artificial scarcity for commercial advantage should not blind us to a deeper and more primitive risk to information freedom. Fears, some old and some new, have arisen along with the hopes for the new information technologies; and the reactions to the fears are smothering the liberating forces. Let's look at a few of these fears.

* Jefferson's image of ideas expanding like fire over all space sounds very much like the recording industry's nightmare of a single digital copy of a song going to the laptops of a million teenagers by means of an Internet file-sharing service. The passing into consumer hands of the means of digital reproduction has sparked a remarkable escalation in negative imagery: "theft," "piracy," and so on. And not just imagery but legislation, and even regulation of the manufacture of equipment—attempts to make copying of copyrighted material not just illegal but impossible, no matter what the collateral damage.

* Ancient fears that the morals of youth will be corrupted by what they hear or read have come back to life with new vigor in the Internet era. The U.S. Congress tried to outlaw the display of

"indecent" (though not legally obscene) material to children over the Internet. The law was overturned on constitutional grounds, but similar censorship occurs routinely in other countries, even enlightened democracies acting to protect the morals of adults. Australia is currently testing a national blacklist of sites to be blocked to protect the public morality ("Australia to Implement" 2008).

* Fear that children will associate online with bad people has led to tracking and monitoring requirements and to a market in "nanny software" to make parents aware of their children's wanderings through cyberspace. Of course, the same technologies that can control personal computer use by American children can be directed at monitoring the activities of citizens of totalitarian regimes—or even in the United States, where the Defense Department's Total Information Awareness program was killed only when Congress became aware of its potential as a program of civilian surveillance.

* Even as Google, Amazon, and Facebook accumulate vast amounts of personal information about their users, badly aimed privacy protection legislation threatens to undercut the Web's usefulness. Requirements that children be at least thirteen years old to get accounts on social networking sites have done little to protect children's privacy but have done much, often with parental support, to teach them to lie about their age (boyd et al. 2010).

The Internet was conceived in the defense world, designed by academic and industrial research engineers, and transported into the commercial world only after its core design had been widely deployed. Engineers are naturally libertarian. Whether they are designing cars or computer networks, their ideals are utility, speed, and flexibility. Software engineers are spared the ethical issues that confront the designers of munitions; engineering in the world of zeroes and ones inherits the nonnormative, amoral quality of mathematics. Even cost, safety, and secrecy are imposed by market forces and governments, which had little force in the Internet's gestation period. So there was a Garden of Eden quality to the Internet in its preconsumer days: a combination of fecundity and innocence. The network fostered experimentation and innovation, and little worry about the potential for mischief or evil.

The Garden of Earthly Delights

So we are back to the story of human creation and how we handle the knowledge of our own undiscovered capabilities. The biblical story is usually reduced to its simple outlines: a rather chaste paradise at first, then temptation and knowledge of good and evil, then shame and expulsion, followed by redemptive suffering and labor. But there is one artistic rendering of the biblical myth that interpolates a remarkable middle period. It is called *Garden of Earthly Delights*, and it was painted in the Netherlands by Hieronymus Bosch around 1503—as it happens, just about the time the Church started taking action against heretical books (see Plate 1).

The *Garden of Earthly Delights* is a triptych, a central panel flanked by two smaller ones, the sort of painting that was often used as a church altarpiece. But it is hard to imagine this set of paintings in a church, despite its biblical theme. On the left is the Garden of Eden, complete with peaceful, happy animals, and a rather insignificant-looking God introducing Eve to a slightly leering Adam. On the right, under a burning cityscape and a blackened sky, is hell, full of people undergoing various forms of torture at the hands of demonic animals. The conception of hell is bizarre, but at least we can recognize what it is. But the central panel corresponds to nothing in the Bible and earns the triptych its name. It shows a frenzy of people engaged in all sorts of naughty things, none requiring clothing. Some of the groups are multiracial, and quite a few animals and fruits are enjoying the fun too. Nobody seems to have the slightest hesitation about their cavorting or their nakedness.

This scene is a wonderful mystery—extravagantly detailed and amenable to hours or decades of study. If it were painted today, the art critics would investigate the painter's recreational drug use. There is no tradition of similar scenes by other artists, so its symbolism cannot readily be connected to better-understood analogues.

And so we are left with two possible explanations, without any middle ground. Perhaps it is a depiction of sin relating directly to the third panel's punishments: "If you do that, here is what is going to happen to you." Or else it shows some long-ago, libertine earthly paradise. The didactic interpretation, that the whole is intended as a warning, is more historically plausible; there are plenty of wages-of-sin themes in Christian narratives. And yet . . . if the objective is to warn people off from sinful activities, the artist seems to be going to extremes to document in pornographic detail the fun that will get people in trouble. And if the participants themselves are supposed to be aware that this orgy is not going to end well for them, the warnings are very muted. Based on the evidence from the panel itself, they could reasonably claim that they had no idea that what they were doing was wrong. It all looks fine—nobody is getting hurt and everybody is having a good time.

The lost-paradise interpretation has its own problems—mainly that there is no such biblical story. (Unless it is a wild extrapolation of what the Bible says about earth on the eve of the flood, when God decided to pretty much start over from scratch.) Yet, to my inexpert eye, the "earthly delights" interpretation is more plausible. The central panel simply seems more in the spirit of the paradise panel on the left than of the hell panel on the right.

Internet Liberty and Libertinism

The Internet became a garden of earthly delights when it was opened to consumer-oriented, commercial uses. It is now transitioning out of its earthly delights period, as society decides how to adjust to its potential use for sins and evils, as various cultures define them—not just pornography, of course (though that to be sure), but anonymous hate speech, privacy intrusions, political insurrection, and simple theft and character assassination.

We have seen technologically induced liberation movements before— or to be precise, I have seen one before. The sexual revolution of the 1960s was in no small measure the result of birth control technology. Reproductive control was not a new concept, any more than free speech was a new concept when the Internet engineers sat down to work. But the very sudden, widespread availability of birth control pills in particular was enormously empowering; the development of a class of professional women would have been much harder without it. This revolution was also accompanied by a period of chaotic experimentation—musical, social, pharmacological, and political as well as sexual. When I look at the *Garden of Earthly Delights,* I think of Woodstock.

We are today being overtaken by the Internet fear, fear of consequences. We are past the point of Bosch's middle panel, but just barely; even young adults remember when the Internet was not scary. Nonetheless, we are now threatened with the horrors depicted in Bosch's third panel, and in fact the alarms over personal debasement and the public shaming echo the humiliations of Bosch's hell.

We are past the point of innocence, and moralists and governments and law enforcement urge us to expect information nightmares if we do not get the communications revolution under control. Ironically, Bosch depicts the horrors of hell as effected by technological instruments of pleasure—musical instruments, to be precise. One man is strung up on a harp, another is sucked into a horn, a third is bound to a lute. Only in the third panel does civilization appear, and only to be destroyed by its own devices. In the same way, the forces of fear are threatening us with torture by Facebook, character assassination by RateMyProfessors.com, terrorism by Google Earth, pillage by Kazaa.

We must, we are told, protect ourselves, our children, and our society from technologically enabled evils. And thus we have a variety of laws and regulations, proposed and enacted, fed by fear and aimed at restraining evils—be they political, personal, or commercial.

* Censorship: It is hard to censor the Internet, because of its diffuse, decentralized architecture. But it is easier to censor content from an entire nation than, for example, to allow content to reach adults but not children. China, where Internet use is very widespread, has a robust censorship regime, aimed at controlling access to both sexual and political content (Deibert et al. 2008, 2010). But the United States has its own censorship forces at work: The Communications Decency Act and the Child Online Protection Act both limited speech among adults—in ways the Supreme Court ultimately found unconstitutional—as a by-product of their efforts to protect children.

* Piracy: In just a few years the Internet has radically altered many business models that functioned well for decades. Travel agencies and newspapers are both casualties of the electronic decentralization of information. But no industry has been protected by legislation the way the recording industry has been—not that the protections have been very effective. Armed with effective lobbying, the Recording Industry Association of America (RIAA) effected the passage of the Digital Millennium Copyright Act, which imposes severe financial penalties for copying digital music files. The act is unprecedented in the size of the fines, the use of a strict liability standard, and the assignment to the RIAA itself of responsibility for policing its violations. As a result, cases almost never come to trial—instead, defendants pay up without a fight,

fearing larger penalties if the cases are tried. The strictness of the standard is not only frustrating to the consuming public but injurious to creativity—the very thing that copyright is intended to enhance. The U.S. Constitution says nothing about protecting profits or business models—only about the intent "to promote the progress of science and the useful arts."

* The preferred solution for the recording industry is cooperation from ISPs—cooperation in the form of surveillance of what is flowing through the network, with violations punishable by denial of Internet service to the guilty party. Pressure for such practices is being put on universities, which have captive audiences—students do not get to choose who supplies the bits to their dormitory rooms. This makes as much sense as asking universities to open all packages coming through the postal mail to students in search of pirated CDs. In the United States, about as basic a principle as we have is that there should be specific reasons to believe that individuals are involved in illegal activities before monitoring their communications. And yet the Motion Picture Association of America wants Congress to encourage ISPs to filter Internet content (Kravets 2009) and to sign a treaty that would establish such filtering as a matter of international obligation (Glickman 2009).

* Child safety: The difficulty of reliable identity verification on the Internet has combined with a handful of *Dateline*-style child abduction horror stories to give rise to legislative proposals in the United States for measures to limit adult-child contact. The most developed of these proposals is the Deleting Online Predators Act, originally introduced in 2006 but never enacted into law. It would require school libraries receiving federal funds to disable social networking sites unless an adult was monitoring and supervising their use. Though very popular when voted on in the House during a midterm election campaign, it would have been largely ineffective, since children have so many other points of access to

Myspace and Facebook, including their cell phones as well as computers at Starbucks and at home.

* As in the case of copyright law, the U.S. government has delegated to a nongovernmental entity the job of enforcing certain child safety laws. The official list of "child pornography" Web sites is the province of the National Center for Missing and Exploited Children, a private organization whose practices are beyond the reach of Freedom of Information Act disclosures. Questioning the tactics of those trying to protect children from sexual slavery is unpopular—but overreactions do happen. For example, the cover of the heavy metal album *Virgin Killer* was classified as child pornography in the United Kingdom years after the album was released—temporarily causing the album's Wikipedia page to be blocked in England.

* Defamation and bullying: Web 2.0, the participatory Web, promises public engagement and discussion, a step away from the "broadcast" model of journalism. Alas, the power of anonymous commentary is abused destructively. Measures proposed to fight defamation and bullying include limiting anonymity, in spite of its strong history in the United States going back to the pamphleteering of the Founding Fathers of the American democracy. No less a person than Jefferson himself was the object of an anonymous caricature as a cock strutting with a hen representing his slave, Sally Hemmings. While the cartoon was shocking, it did not lose him the election—but it turns out to have been on the mark.

* Cyberterrorism and cyber war: In June 2010 a bipartisan bill sponsored by senators Lieberman and Collins (S. 3480, Protecting Cyberspace as a National Asset Act of 2010) was introduced into the U.S. Senate to give the president emergency power over the Internet—in essence, the authority to declare cyber war and to marshal the power of the U.S. government to fight it on private cyber territory as a matter of homeland security. The announcement drew skeptical reaction from advocates for privacy and other civil liberties.

The Fight against Fear

In a campaign for public opinion, fear is an easier sell than freedom. We overestimate the probability of unlikely events. Many of us prefer driving to flying for our travels, especially if a horrific plane crash has been in the news. We do not stop to ask ourselves how many people have died in ones and twos in automobile accidents. The answer is that we are safer flying—it just sounds worse to die in a plane crash because so many people die all at once. In the same way, well-publicized Internet horrors create public outcries for regulatory interventions, with little statistical analysis of the incidence of the alleged problem behaviors or the cost to the public, over time, of incursions on freedom of speech and action.

A common argument for "making the Internet safe" is that preventing even one horrible crime is worth any price. Connecticut Attorney General Richard Blumenthal, for example, arguing for age verification on Myspace and Facebook to prevent predators from luring children into unsavory liaisons, said, "This is a basic issue of safety. These kinds of Web sites have created this complete delusion that this is a private world that an outsider does not get into, but it is a total misnomer. Anyone can get in." When confronted with practical arguments against Web site age verification—that it is awfully hard to tell whether someone without any form of government-issued identification is an adult or a child—Blumenthal would snort, "if we can put a man on the moon, we can verify someone's age" (Medina 2007).

Fearmongering is politically popular. One of the basic reasons we have a government is to keep us safe, so when a government official assures us that something, be it the bombing of Baghdad or registration to use Web sites, is necessary to protect us, we are inclined to sympathize. But sometimes the truth does not comport with the alarms. For example, the Internet Safety Technical Task Force (2008) established that the Internet was not a significant cause of child sexual abuse. Child sex abuse cases actually decreased 50 percent between 1990 and

2005, and most sexual propositions to youth come from peers, not adult strangers. Child sexual abuse has gone down while child Internet use has gone up—as a consequence of more vigilant policing and greater public awareness of the problem. But it is politically more profitable to attack a technology than to focus on an awkward social problem. Attorney General Blumenthal, promoting Internet fear in anticipation of his campaign for U.S. Senate, dismissed the report's finding that online social networks "do not appear to have increased the overall risk of solicitation" with an anti-intellectual punch to the public gut: "Children are solicited every day online. . . . That harsh reality defies the statistical academic research of the report" (Stone 2009b).

Indeed, this example demonstrates another unhappy fact about human fear: we much prefer to look for dangerous, mysterious demons and find magic technologies with which to strike at them than to confront problems closer to home. There is a thriving business in tools to prevent children from wandering off to pornographic Web sites or from being seduced by forty-year-old strangers from out of state. But while those things do happen, they account for a small minority of juvenile sexual misadventures. Childhood sexual exploitation is almost always at the hands of people the victims know, often relatives— uncles and cousins, for example. The age difference is often small, not large. And the children are generally on the older edge of childhood and already sexually aware. They enter relationships inappropriately but not innocently. The problem of fifteen-year-old girls having sex with eighteen-year-old cousins is uncomfortable to discuss; many who are alarmed about the *Dateline* scenarios would deny that the cousin scenario ever happens, when in fact it predominates. We prefer to search under the streetlight rather than explore the dark zone where the real crimes occur.

Internet fear has three legs. The first leg is our desire to protect ourselves, our families, our employees, and anyone else for whom we have legal or moral responsibility. The second leg is corporate interest in protecting profits, market sector, and intellectual assets. The third leg is government interest in protecting individuals, institutions, and society from harm. Sometimes the three interact in complex ways. When the RIAA warns teenagers, "You can click but you can't hide," it is protecting its business interests by creating fear in the minds of individuals about prosecution under a federal statute they persuaded Congress to enact and for which they are the enforcers.

All three of these fear engines deserve dispassionate analysis and a reflection on the larger context in which they are visible. It may be possible to monitor constantly what children are doing online and to prevent them, as Socrates hoped, from contact with bad people and corrupting information. Yet for every child caught talking to a pedophile online, hundreds would be discouraged from searching the Internet's vast electronic library for truths their parents will not tell them. Controlling every word children are saying and hearing* isn't child protection or social conservatism. It is the perfect preservation of human prejudice and ignorance.

Education

The antidote to fear is knowledge. Education, in the long run, wins against terror. In the final analysis, the right responses to words are more words; the right response to bad information is good information; the right response to falsehoods is the truth.

Looking at cyberspace from 50,000 feet, we are going to be choosing between two alternative worldviews. In one view of the world, information ubiquity is the natural state; the bits will always leak. There are digital tools, such as encryption and anonymous routing, to make the flows of bits less dangerous to us and less conducive to surveillance and commercial exploitation. But fundamentally, in this worldview, people must be responsible for themselves. They need to learn home-

---

* According to its Web site (as of August 3, 2010), one software product, PC Tattletale (http://www.pctat tletale.com/), "records *everything* your child does when they go online."

spun safety lessons: Don't give away data about yourself if you don't want it abused. Don't believe what you read on a Web site if it's anonymous and can't be traced. Don't believe that anyone, even the government, can collect vast amounts of information and keep it all secret forever.

In spite of the costs of bullying and defamation, we need to remember the difference between words and images on the one hand and sticks and stones on the other. In this worldview the most important thing society can do is to teach people how to take care of themselves, how not to overreact to misfortunes, how to capitalize on the potential of the revolution without assuming its risks.

In the alternative view, information, for all its usefulness, is a fundamentally dangerous substance. It must be bottled up, dammed, diverted, and origin labeled, or packaged and sold for money, even if it is a century old. This is the world of *1984*, except that the information sources are in private hands, not just government hands, and the information users are commercial as well as governmental. This is the world in which the response to every problem is a regulation, or an agency, or perhaps a hardware feature. This is the world of Green Dam spyware and censorship software—China's modern *Index Librorum Prohibitorum* (Mooney 2009). It is also the world of central Internet monitoring in Australia (for obscenity) and France (for copyright infringement, in spite of the provision in Article 19 of the UN General Assembly's 1948 "Universal Declaration of Human Rights" to "receive and impart information and ideas through any media and regardless of frontiers"). It is the world in which the most open societies use the tools of the most repressive, and citizens of democracies are grateful for the safety and prosperity they are promised.

⟅

An ancient technological cycle is being repeated today. One generation creates a technology, responding to an immediate problem and vaguely foreseeing a better future. To the next generation, the world looks very different; the solved problems are forgotten or are eclipsed by the technology's downsides. Commercial and governmental forces make it easy to forget how much power we have over how technologies will shape our future. All of us who live in free societies share that power, and especially the young, who can decide what kind of world they want to inhabit.

We can help make that choice through the political process, by watching what laws are enacted by state and national governments. We can help make it by our choices as consumers, by what we say about the features present in, and missing from, the devices and technologies we buy. We can make it by what we have to say about the workings of the institutions and businesses of which we are a part. We can resist those expurgated dictionaries and those Web sites that want to know things you do not want to tell them. We can speak up. We can leave the box on the shelf. We can click "I don't agree."

Whatever we choose, we should not let one world or the other evolve because others—especially governments and corporations—have made the choice for us. The revolution has its delights, but we need to think beyond them—think how they work, who has the data, and what they can do with it. We need to use our rationality, our knowledge, and our education to shape the world in which we and our children and our children's children will live.

Further Reading

This chapter is based on the final lecture in spring 2009 of my Harvard course "Quantitative Reasoning 48: Bits." My book with Hal Abelson and Ken Ledeen, *Blown to Bits: Your Life, Liberty, and Happiness after the Digital Explosion* (Reading, MA: Addison-Wesley Professional, 2008), is based on the course material and can be downloaded at http://www.bitsbook.com/thebook/. It includes many of the particulars of the course not elaborated in this essay.

General Bibliography

John Perry Barlow's 1993 essay, "The Economy of Ideas," *Wired* 2.0, retrieved August 3, 2010, from http://www.wired.com/wired/archive/2.03/economy .ideas_pr.html, is worth reading in its entirety; this is an early manifesto on the collapse of the copyright and patent system due to digital reproduction by the former lyricist for the Grateful Dead.

John Perry Barlow's utopian manifesto, "Declaration of Independence of Cyberspace," http://w2.eff.org/Censorship/Internet_censorship_bills/barlow _0296.declaration, was written with dramatic flourish in 1996 in response to the censorship provisions of the Telecommunications Act of 1996. Invoking the spirit of the American Revolution, Barlow declares cyberspace ungovernable without the consent of the governed.

Carr, Nicholas. 2009. *The Big Switch: Rewiring the World, from Edison to Google.* New York: Norton.
A light, journalistic history of centralization and decentralization of computing services, and the effect of system architecture on information control.

Lessig, Lawrence. 2006. *Code v2.* New York: Basic Books. (See also http:// codev2.cc/.)
The updated edition of Lessig's classic analysis of the way "East Coast Code" (law) and "West Coast Code" (computer programs) have intertwined and evolved to control the world of information.

Post, David G. 2009. *In Search of Jefferson's Moose: Notes on the State of Cyberspace.* New York: Oxford University Press.
A wonderful analysis of the state of governance of the Internet, with deep parallels to the spirit of the early American state. (While he was ambassador to France, Jefferson had a stuffed moose erected in the lobby of his residence as a symbol of the weird and largely unexplored possibilities of the new world.)

Zittrain, Jonathan. 2009. *The Future of the Internet and How to Stop It.* New Haven, CT: Yale University Press.
The definitive argument on whether the Internet will evolve into a safe but relatively sterile technology or can continue to be "generative," as the book calls it—a seedbed of unanticipated, but not always welcome, inventions and adaptations.

Works Cited

"Australia to Implement Mandatory Internet Censorship." 2008. *Herald Sun* (Australia), October 29. Retrieved August 3, 2010, from http://www.dsl reports.com/forum/r21341775-Australia-To-Implement-Mandatory-Internet -Censorship.

Blakely, Rhys. 2008. "Google Earth Accused of Aiding Terrorists." *London Sunday Times Online,* December 9. Retrieved August 3, 2010, from http:// technology.timesonline.co.uk/tol/news/tech_and_web/the_web/arti cle5311241.ece.

boyd, danah, Urs Gasser, and John Palfrey. 2010. "How the COPPA, as Implemented, Is Misinterpreted by the Public: A Research Perspective." Statement to the U.S. Senate Subcommittee on Consumer Protection, Product Safety, and Insurance of the Committee on Commerce, Science, and Transportation, April 29. Retrieved August 3, 2010, from http://cyber.law.harvard .edu/publications/2010/COPPA_Implemented_Is_Misinterpreted_by_ Public.

Deibert, J., John G. Palfrey, Rafal Rohozinski, and Jonathan Zittrain. 2008. *Access Denied: The Practice and Policy of Global Internet Filtering.* Cambridge, MA: MIT Press.

―――. 2010. *Access Controlled: The Practice and Policy of Global Internet Filtering.* Cambridge, MA: MIT Press.

Federal Communications Commission et al. v. Fox Television Stations, Inc., et al., 07 U.S. 582 (2009). Retrieved August 3, 2010, from http://caselaw.lp .findlaw.com/scripts/getcase.pl?court=US&vol=000&invol=07–582.

Fowler, Geoffrey A. 2009. "Kindle's Orwellian Moment." *Wall Street Journal,* July 17.

Glickman, Dan. 2009. Testimony before the Subcommittee on Government Management, Organization, and Procurement, Committee on Oversight Reform, December 9. Retrieved August 3, 2010, from http://oversight.house .gov/images/stories/Hearings/Government_Management/Intellectual _Property_Rights/DGlickman_Dec_2009_final.pdf.

Gruber, John. 2009. "Ninjawords: iPhone Dictionary, Censored by Apple." *Daring Fireball,* August 4. Retrieved August 3, 2010, from http://daring fireball.net/2009/08/ninjawords.

Heacock, Rebekah. 2009. "No More Namibia: China Blocks Search Results for Entire Country." *OpenNet Initiative,* July 22. Retrieved August 3, 2010, from http://opennet.net/blog/2009/07/no-more-namibia-china-blocks-search-results-entire-country.

Information Sciences Institute. 1981. "Internet Protocol: DARPA Internet Program Protocol Specifications." Retrieved August 3, 2010, from http://www.ietf.org/rfc/rfc791.txt.

International Telecommunication Union. 2010. "ICT Data and Statistics." Retrieved August 3, 2010, from http://www.itu.int/ITU-D/ict/statistics/ict/.

Internet Safety Technical Task Force. 2008. *Enhancing Child Safety and Online Technologies: Final Report of the Internet Safety Technical Task Force to the Multi-State Working Group on Social Networking of State Attorneys General of the United States.* Cambridge, MA: Berkman Center for Internet and Society at Harvard University. December 31. Retrieved August 3, 2010, from http://cyber.law.harvard.edu/pubrelease/isttf/.

Jefferson, Thomas. 1813. [Letter to Isaac McPherson, August 13.] Reprinted in *The Founders' Constitution, Volume 3, Article 1, Section 8, Clause 8, Document 12.* Chicago: University of Chicago Press. Retrieved August 3, 2010, from http://press-pubs.uchicago.edu/founders/documents/a1_8_8s12.html.

Kahn, Gabriel. 2010. "Comcast Official Touts Logic of Marrying Content, Distribution." *Wall Street Journal,* June 2.

Katz v. United States, 389 U.S. 347 (1967). Retrieved August 3, 2010, from http://scholar.google.com/scholar_case?case=9210492700696416594.

Kravets, David. 2009. "MPAA Wants Congress to 'Encourage' 3 Strikes, Filtering." *Wired,* November 4. Retrieved August 3, 2010, from http://www.wired.com/threatlevel/2009/11/mpaa-filtering/.

Lankarani, Nazanin. 2009. "A Push in Law Schools to Reform Copyright." *New York Times,* December 1.

Medina, Jennifer. 2007. "States Ponder Laws to Keep Web Predators from Children." *New York Times,* May 6.

Meier, Barry, and Robert F. Worth. 2010. "UAE to Bar BlackBerry Data Services, Citing Security." *New York Times,* August 2, A1.

Mooney, Paul. 2009. "Beijing's Abortive Censorship Push." *Far Eastern Economic Review* 172: 50–52.

Olmstead et al. v. United States; Green et al. v. same; Mcinnis v. same, 277 U.S. 438 (1928). Retrieved August 3, 2010, from http://scholar.google.com/scholar_case?case=5577544660194763070.

Plato. 1888. *The Republic,* Book II, trans. Benjamin Jowett. Oxford: Clarendon Press.

Protecting Cyberspace as a National Asset Act of 2010, S. 3480, 111th Congress, 2nd Session. June 10, 2010.

Stone, Brad. 2009a. "Amazon Erases Orwell Books from Kindle." *New York Times,* July 17.

———. 2009b. "Report Calls Online Threats to Children Overblown." *New York Times,* January 13.

"The Telegraph Monopoly; What the People Pay for and What They Get. Mr. Gardiner G. Hubbard Describes the Methods of the Western Union to the Senate Postal Committee." 1884. *New York Times,* February 9, 3.

UN General Assembly. 1948. "Universal Declaration of Human Rights." December 10, 1948, 217 A (III). Retrieved August 3, 2010, from http://www.un.org/en/documents/udhr/index.shtml.

Williams, Timothy. 2009. "Iraq Censorship Laws Move Ahead." *New York Times,* August 3.

Nothing in Biology Makes Sense Except in the Light of Evolution: Pattern, Process, and the Evidence

Jonathan B. Losos

Evolutionary biology is unusual: unlike any other science, evolutionary biologists study a phenomenon that some people do not think exists. Consider chemistry, for example; it is unlikely that anyone does not believe in the existence of chemical reactions. Ditto for the laws of physics. Even within biology, no one believes that cells do not exist nor that DNA is a fraud. But public opinion polls consistently show that a majority of the American public is either unsure about or does not believe that life has evolved through time. For example, a Gallup poll taken repeatedly over the past twenty years indicates that as much as 40 percent of the population believes that the Bible is literally correct.

When I teach evolutionary biology, I focus on the ideas about how evolution works, rather than on the empirical record of how species have changed through time. However, for one lecture period I make an exception, and in some respects I consider this the most important lecture of the semester. Sad as I find it to be, most of my students will not go on to become evolutionary biologists. Rather, they will become leaders in many diverse aspects of society: doctors, lawyers, businesspeople, clergy, and artists; people to whom others will look for guidance on matters of knowledge and science. For this reason, although I devote my course to a detailed understanding of the evolutionary process, I consider it vitally important that my students understand why it is that almost all biologists find the evidence that evolution has occurred—and continues to occur—to be overwhelming. If students take nothing else from my course, I want them to understand the evidentiary basis underlying the field of evolutionary biology. And that is what I want you, the reader, to take from this chapter. Of course, that is not to say that each student personally must find the evidence convincing. But, as I tell my students, if they decide not to be convinced by the evidence, not to believe that evolution has occurred, they need to be prepared to address the evidence for evolution and explain why it is not compelling.

The evidence for evolution can be broken into three categories, which I address in separate sections below:

* Demonstrations that natural selection, which is the presumed main mechanism of evolutionary change, operates today.
* Fossil evidence that evolution has occurred.
* Data from fields as disparate as molecular biology, biogeography, and anatomy that make no sense except in an evolutionary context.

Evidence That Natural Selection Leads to Evolutionary Change

So what is "natural selection"? Basically, natural selection occurs when individuals within a population differ in some attribute and, as a result of this attribute, some individuals are more successful at producing more fertile and healthy offspring in the next generation. This enhanced reproductive success can occur in many ways: individuals can live longer and thus have more opportunities to reproduce; they can be more successful in getting to mate more frequently (particularly important for males of many species); they can produce more offspring per reproductive event; or they can produce offspring that are of higher "quality," better adapted to their environment.

For natural selection to produce evolutionary change, one more condition must be met: differences among individuals must be genetically based so that the trait in question tends to be passed on from parent to offspring. If these conditions are met, natural selection will lead to evolutionary change. If the trait is not genetically based, then natural selection will not lead to evolutionary change.

Darwin was not the first to propose that evolution occurs. Indeed, his grandfather, Erasmus Darwin, had proposed a theory of evolution (called "Zoonomia") at the end of the eighteenth century. In the middle of the nineteenth century, ideas about evolution were in the air—Robert Chambers's *Vestiges of the Natural History of Creation* had been a best seller in 1844. Darwin's important advance (independently proposed by the great naturalist Alfred Russel Wallace) was providing a mechanism for evolutionary change to occur. That mechanism was natural selection.

Evolution by natural selection occurs when the genes for traits that cause an organism to produce greater numbers of viable offspring become more common in each succeeding generation (by "viable" we mean "able to reproduce"; it is not enough to produce many offspring if the offspring themselves do not live long enough to reproduce). Natural selection is sometimes referred to as "survival of the fittest," but this is a poor aphorism in two respects: First, the term "fittest" is sometimes misinterpreted to mean "best possible," when, in fact, it just means "better adapted to producing more viable offspring in the current environment than the alternative traits existing in the population." Second, traits that lead to high numbers of viable offspring often have little do with the long-term survival of an individual organism and sometimes can even be detrimental. The long tail of male peacocks, for example, certainly makes these birds more vulnerable to predators. But because females for some reason prefer long tails, males bearing elongated trains tend to father more offspring.*

---

* Mate choice—technically, a form of sexual selection, which is one type of natural selection—is one of the most controversial topics in evolutionary biology today and could easily be the subject of an essay all its own. In many cases, members of one sex—usually females—choose to mate with members of the other sex that can provide either direct benefits, such as a food-rich territory or help in raising the young, or indirect benefits by providing high-quality genes to the offspring. In other cases, it is not clear why a particular mating preference has evolved. With regard to the peacock, all kinds of outlandish ideas have been proposed. One idea, for example, is that females mate with males that have a handicap, such as a long tail that makes them

I want to emphasize that natural selection and evolution are not the same thing. Natural selection is one mechanism that can cause evolutionary change. Other mechanisms include persistent reoccurrence of a particular mutation, immigration of individuals with different genetic makeup, nonrandom mating, and genetic change resulting randomly as a statistical accident, which usually occurs only in small populations.

Nonetheless, natural selection is in most cases the most powerful mechanism of evolutionary change. Darwin's theory was that natural selection is the cause of evolutionary change, and four lines of evidence around us today indicate the efficacy of natural selection in causing evolutionary change.

Laboratory Experiments

Since the early part of the twentieth century, scientists have conducted experiments in which very strong selection is imposed on a population to see whether evolutionary change results. I present just two of a great number of such studies. The first involves selection on the number of bristles on fruit flies. Fruit flies in the genus *Drosophila* have been the workhorse of genetics research for nearly a century because they can be easily raised in the lab and because they have many traits, such as differences in eye color, that are amenable to genetic study by mating individuals with different traits and seeing what their offspring are like. Fruit flies have hairlike bristles on many parts of their bodies, and in one experiment selection was imposed on the number of bristles on their abdomen. In one condition of this experiment, only the flies with the greatest number of bristles were allowed to breed, whereas in the other condition, only those flies with the fewest bristles were bred. In every generation the

---

clumsy fliers, because if a male can survive with such an impediment, then the rest of his genetic makeup must be really stellar to compensate for this disadvantage. Hence, because the female mates with such a male, her offspring will get these high-quality genes. Unfortunately, they will also get the gene for the long tail. Although this idea is still debated, most evolutionary biologists are dubious.

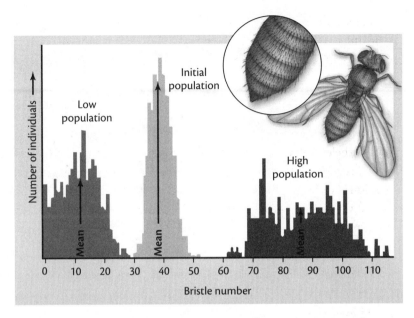

Figure 1. Bristle number in *Drosophila*. *Drosophila* populations selected for high and low numbers of bristles have evolved large differences. (Image adapted from P. Raven, G. B. Johnson, K. A. Mason, J. B. Losos, and S. S. Singer, *Biology*, 9th ed., © 2011 by The McGraw-Hill Companies, Inc.)

scientists would examine the individuals in the population and segregate out those few flies with the greatest or smallest number of bristles (depending on which experiment). Within fifteen generations, the high-selected and low-selected populations were so different that there was no overlap in the number of bristles—the individual with the smallest number in the high-selected population was more hirsute than the most bristly member of the low population (see Figure 1).

Another experiment involved the ability of rats to run through a maze. In this study, how long rats took to learn the correct path through a maze was recorded, and then selection was imposed, as in the previous experiment; the best performers were bred with other quick studies, while the most error prone were similarly paired with

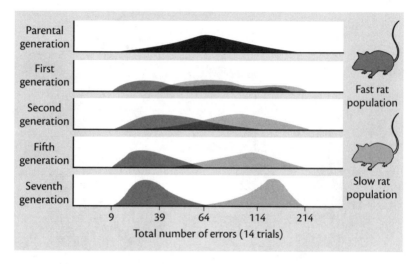

Figure 2. Selection on maze learning in laboratory rats. (Image adapted from P. Raven et al., *Biology*, 9th ed., © 2011 by The McGraw-Hill Companies, Inc.)

each other. This procedure was repeated for seven generations, by which time the population of rodent dummkopfs made, on average, five times more mistakes than the murine Einsteins (see Figure 2).

Artificial Selection outside of the Laboratory

The term "artificial selection" refers to selection imposed intentionally by humans. Besides in the laboratory, such selection has been imposed in a number of ways throughout the history of modern humans. Ranchers, for example, use selection procedures similar to those used by laboratory scientists to increase productivity of livestock. The result is modern livestock, which in many cases bear little resemblance to their wild ancestors, but which are much more productive for the traits for which they have been bred. Consider the milk production of cows, the egg production of chickens, and the amount of fat on the backs of pigs: in all cases, modern breeds are substantially different not only from their wild relatives, but even from the breeds that existed a century ago.

The success of such artificial selection is demonstrated by a long-running selection experiment on oil and protein content in corn, originally begun in 1896 and still being maintained today by scientists at the University of Illinois. At the beginning of the experiment, the average oil content of a corn kernel was approximately 4.5 percent. Throughout the experiment, each year the next high-oil generation was started by choosing the oiliest 20 percent of the corn crop, and the low line was created with the corn in the bottom twentieth percentile of oil content. This experiment has gone on for more than a hundred generations. The results are clear: oil content has increased approximately 450 percent in the high line, and the low-oil line has decreased to about 0.5 percent, a level at which it is difficult to accurately measure corn kernel oil content.

These studies of artificial selection are just a few from a large number. As a gross generalization, we can conclude that artificial selection in domesticated animals and in the laboratory yields essentially the same result. Basically, one can select on just about any trait and increase or decrease its average value; in fact, people have tried to select on an amazing variety of characteristics, almost always successfully. I emphasize that this is a generality and that there are exceptions, but not many; most exceptions occur when variation among individuals in the trait is not the result of genetic differences.

This trend is taken to the extreme in the domestication process. Consider, for example, the vast diversity in breeds of dogs that has resulted from artificial selection. In earlier times, different breeds were produced for particular reasons: greyhounds for their speed, dachshunds for the ability to enter rabbit burrows, and so on. If one looks at various dog breeds, say chihuahuas, dachshunds, and mastiffs, the differences in body size, relative limb length, and face proportions are enormous. By contrast, the differences among wild species of canids—such as foxes, wolves, and coyotes—are substantially less. In

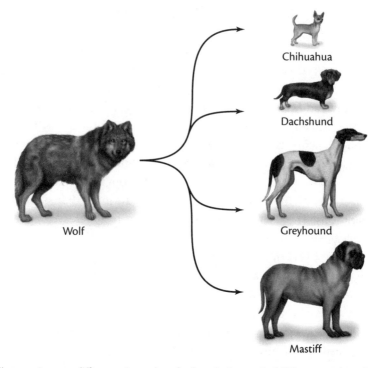

Figure 3. Extreme differences in modern dog breeds. Anatomical differences among these breeds are substantially greater than differences among wild species of canids, such as wolves, jackals, foxes, and coyotes. (Image adapted from P. Raven et al., *Biology*, 9th ed., © 2011 by The McGraw-Hill Companies, Inc.)

other words, in a few hundreds to thousands of years, humans have created substantially greater variation among breeds of dogs than natural selection has created over the greater than 10 million-year span in which modern members of the Canidae have been evolving (see Figure 3).

The same is true in the domestication of agricultural crops. For example, a remarkably diverse group of dinner table vegetables—including cabbage, cauliflower, broccoli, brussel sprouts, kale, and others—were all derived in the last few thousand years from the same ancestral species of cauliflower, which still occurs in the Mediterra-

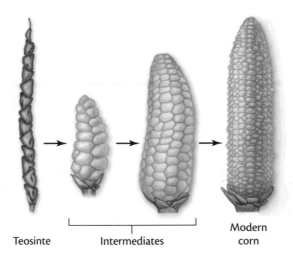

Teosinte   Intermediates   Modern corn

Figure 4. Modern corn compared with its ancestor, teosinte. (Image adapted from P. Raven et al., *Biology*, 9th ed., © 2011 by The McGraw-Hill Companies, Inc.)

nean region of Europe and northern Africa. Similarly, the ancestral species from which corn was developed still occurs in Central America (although it is endangered). Diminutive and bearing only five to ten irregularly shaped kernel-like seeds, teosinte bears little resemblance to our familiar source of niblets and corn on the cob (Figure 4).

Artificial selection is not a perfect analogy to natural selection—it is usually substantially stronger than natural selection, as well as unidirectional (always favoring the same variants, such as the largest or most long-legged individuals) and usually focused on only one or a few traits, whereas natural selection may simultaneously operate on many different traits and may change directionally over short periods of time, sometimes favoring one trait in one year and the exact opposite in the next. Nonetheless, the biological diversity we see around us is the result of hundreds of millions of years of evolutionary diversification. Surely, if selection caused by humans can lead to such substantial evolutionary change in relatively short periods of time, it would seem reasonable to conclude that natural selection, operating over considerably longer intervals, is capable of producing the variety of species extant today.

Natural Selection in Modern Society

Humans have changed the environment in many ways; these changes could be expected to lead to natural selection for new traits. For example, disease-causing organisms have evolved resistance to drugs such as malarial prophylactics and many antibiotics. The way the resistant strains of these microbes evolve is easy to envision. A new drug, such as chloroquine, which is used to protect against malaria, kills almost all of the target microorganisms. However, if a few are, just by chance, less susceptible, or if a mutation causes resistance, then individuals with resistant genes will be able to survive and reproduce. Relatively quickly, such genes will sweep through the microbe population and before long, the drug will be rendered useless.*

The cost in human lives of the evolution of drug resistance is staggering. The Centers for Disease Control and Prevention (CDC) esti-

---

* One of the earliest criticisms of the theory of evolution by natural selection was that it could not create new traits but could only favor one variant already present in a population—such as a gene for antibiotic resistance in a population of bacteria—over another (e.g., the previously common gene that did not provide resistance). To these critics, mutation was the key to understanding evolution; when and how mutations occurred was seen as the crucial factor that determined how evolution occurred, and natural selection was just the arbiter that caused a new mutation to replace a previously widespread one. However, it turns out that for many traits, mutations occur at a high enough rate that new genetic variation is constantly being replenished, and thus variation is often available upon which natural selection can work. For example, when bristle number is selected in fruit flies, within relatively few generations the range of variation exhibited in the experimental population is completely outside that seen at the beginning of the experiment (see Figure 4). This phenomenon is particularly true for traits affected by many genes, which includes all complex traits, such as eyes, as well as continuously distributed traits, such as body height, leg length, and bristle number, which are affected by many genes, with each having only a small effect.

One other important consideration to keep in mind about mutations is that favorable mutations do not arise when they are needed. Rather, mutations occur randomly with respect to the environment and natural selection; indeed, the vast majority of mutations are detrimental. Nonetheless, this does not mean that mutations occur randomly throughout the genome. Rather, modern molecular genetic studies have revealed that mutations occur much more commonly in some parts of the genome than in others. So mutations themselves do not occur randomly; however, their occurrence with respect to whether or not they are beneficial is random.

mates that more than 45,000 deaths annually in the United States are caused by infections by bacteria resistant to at least one commonly used antibiotic. The most recent problem is with a strain of bacteria known as methicillin-resistant *Staphylococcus aureus* (MRSA). Methicillin is the drug that was developed when penicillin resistance evolved. In 2007 the CDC reported that 100,000 serious infections a year in the United States are caused by MRSA, including 19,000 fatalities. Particularly worrisome is that this problem is no longer found only among people confined to hospitals, where risks of staph infection from *S. aureus* are particularly high. Now MRSA infections are increasingly being reported from people without any hospital exposure; for instance, there have been reports of infections spread through skin contact in high school football players who developed infections in skin abrasions received while playing on Astroturf.

An even bigger concern is that we are running out of antibiotics to use. For example, the drug that is now considered to be the last resort for treating staph infections is vancomycin, but recently some strains of MRSA were found to have evolved vancomycin resistance. Fortunately, these bacterial strains have not yet become widespread.

Resistance has evolved repeatedly to other products, such as pesticides and herbicides. It is a continually escalating evolutionary war, and, for all intents and purposes, it seems that we are losing. For example, resistance has evolved in more than 500 pest species, and one recent study put the economic cost in the United States, in terms of lost agricultural crops, at $3–$8 billion per year.

Natural Selection in Wild Populations

Darwin built his theory entirely by thought exercises and analogy to artificial selection. The reason is simple: there were no data from wild populations; no one at that time was studying whether natural selection actually occurred in nature. In recent years, however, many researchers have gone to the field to measure natural selection, and they have found that its action can frequently be detected. We now know that natural selection is a very powerful force. Nonetheless, it is not ubiquitous and it is not all-powerful, and the way it operates on particular traits varies; for example, in some circumstances, natural selection does not favor larger individuals, whereas in other cases, it does. In fact, sometimes this changes from one year to the next.

In addition, natural selection sometimes is not strong enough to outbalance other evolutionary processes, such as the immigration of individuals importing genetic variation from genetically different populations. For example, on isolated lava flows in the American Southwest, black mice blend in better than normal, light-colored mice, and thus are less vulnerable to predators. However, because small lava flows are surrounded by light-colored sand, where light-colored mice are favored, the continual influx of genes for light color, brought in by mice that wander in and live long enough to reproduce, prevents the population on the lava flows from becoming composed of only black individuals. Nonetheless, on the whole, natural selection is surely the most powerful force driving evolutionary change, and it is often detected when researchers look for it.

Evolutionary biology is an unusual science in that we still look to Darwin's writings for inspiration and ideas. In other fields of science, foundational works are usually of little more than historical interest, but Darwin's writings still contain much of substance, in part because he was an excellent naturalist, adept at observing and interpreting the world around him, and in part because he was remarkably correct in many of his ideas about how evolution proceeds.

Nonetheless, Darwin was wrong in two major respects. The first is that his ideas about inheritance were muddled and completely mistaken. Of course, that is not surprising. Mendel's famous studies on peas, though conducted just after *On the Origin of Species* was published, received little attention and were not rediscovered until 1900; DNA itself was not discovered for a further half century.

With regard to natural selection, however, Darwin was wrong in a second respect, as field studies have now made clear. Darwin predicted that natural selection would not be very strong and that, as a result, evolutionary change would occur only slowly, taking many thousands, if not millions, of years to produce detectable change ("We see nothing of these slow changes in progress, until the hand of time has marked the long lapse of ages" [Darwin 1859]). He had, of course, no actual data to inform this prediction; rather, it sprang from Victorian sensibilities about the pace of change in general, in accord with the prevailing wisdom of the time about the slow and gradual manner in which change occurs in both geology and human civilization. Darwin's views in this matter influenced evolutionary biologists for more than a century—well into the 1970s, most thought that evolution usually occurred at a snail's pace. Spurred by data from long-term studies of natural selection that began in earnest around that time, as well as by ideas promulgated by Harvard evolutionary biologist Stephen Jay Gould and others, we now know that Darwin was far off the mark. Many studies now clearly indicate that selection in nature is often quite strong and that, as a result, evolutionary change can occur quite rapidly. I provide two examples.

Darwin's finches. Among the most renowned organisms in all of evolutionary biology are the finches that occur on the Galápagos Islands. They are famous because Darwin saw them and realized that they were a perfect example of an ancestral species evolving into a variety of species adapted to different parts of the environment. The common version of this story gives Darwin a bit too much credit, invoking a Eureka-like moment when Darwin was making his observations during the voyage of the *Beagle*. Actually, during his visit to the Galápagos, Darwin misinterpreted what he was seeing, believing that the various species of finches were actually members of a number of different bird families. It was only when Darwin returned with his specimens to

London that the noted ornithologist John Gould set him straight, explaining that the birds were all members of a single, newly discovered family. It was at this point that Darwin (1845) realized what they represented, remarking in *The Voyage of the Beagle:* "Seeing this gradation and diversity of structure in one small, intimately related group of birds, one might really fancy that from an original paucity of birds in this archipelago, one species has been taken and modified for different ends."

In recent years, researchers from Princeton University have carefully studied a population of one species, the medium ground finch. What they found is that variation exists in the size of the beak. Moreover, this variation has important consequences: birds with bigger beaks can crack larger seeds, but birds with smaller beaks are more adept at manipulating small seeds. Following this population for over thirty-five years, the researchers found that in times of heavy rains, plants grew luxuriantly and seeds, most of them small, were abundant. As a result, birds with small bills were particularly successful at exploiting this cornucopia, and the population evolved to have a smaller beak size. However, when droughts occurred, all of the small seeds were quickly eaten, leaving only the larger, tougher-to-crack seeds. In these times, only the birds with the largest beaks survived, and as a result of this episode of natural selection, average beak size increased. These results clearly indicate that natural selection can be a powerful force and that it can produce rapid evolutionary change. They also demonstrate, however, that natural selection can be inconsistent and can actually counter itself over the course of many years, producing no net change, even if changes from one year to the next can be quite large.

Guppies. Everyone is probably familiar with the guppy, an extremely colorful fish popular in the pet trade. Guppies are native to northern South America and nearby islands. A few years ago, researchers studying guppies on the island of Trinidad discovered that populations varied along the length of streams that cascaded down from the mountains. At high elevations, the fish were extremely colorful, but lower down, they were much blander. Why might this be? It turns out that a major predator of these fish, the pike cichlid, is limited to lower stretches of these streams. Where it is present, the guppies need to be able to blend into their background as much as possible to avoid standing out and being preyed upon by the larger predators. By contrast, high in the mountains, the pike cichlid is absent. In these circumstances, males are extremely colorful. Why? Laboratory studies indicate the females greatly prefer more colorful males for reasons that are still obscure. In the absence of predators, there is no penalty to being colorful, and so selection has favored those males that are the most vibrant, whereas in lower parts of the stream, the more colorful males might have an advantage with the ladies, but this does them little good, as they are not likely to survive long enough for it to matter.

A nice story, but how could it be tested? The first test of this hypothesis was conducted in large pools set up in greenhouses at Princeton University. Ten pools emulating mountain guppy habitats were established, and a group of guppies was randomly split up and placed in the pools. The fish were allowed to breed for several generations to reach a large population size, at which point pike cichlids were introduced into some of the pools, while the other pools remained as predator-free controls. After fourteen generations, scientists examined all the guppies and discovered that populations in the two types of pools had diverged. Guppies in the pools without the pike cichlids were all brightly colored. In contrast, the surviving guppies in the pike cichlid pools were drab in coloration. These results support the hypothesis that it is selection resulting from the presence of the predator that leads to evolutionary differences in color in guppies. But these experiments were still artificial, in the laboratory.

To further test the hypothesis, several experimenters went into the field in Trinidad and transferred guppies from pools containing pike cichlids to nearby pools above a waterfall that contained neither guppies nor their predators. Coming from pools originally inhabited by cichlids, the guppy populations were initially drab. However, two years (about fifteen guppy generations) after the transfer into a predator-free environment, the bland color patterns of the guppy population had shifted toward the more complex and colorful pattern typical of guppy populations living where there are no predators. This study not only clinched the predator selection hypothesis for the evolution of guppy color but also demonstrated that, at least in some cases, the study of evolution can be conducted in an experimental fashion in natural conditions.

Note that one limitation on the ability to conduct evolutionary experiments in the wild is that scientists do not want to move species to localities where they do not occur naturally. In this particular study, the fish were only moved a few yards upstream to the immediately adjacent pool, so little disruption of natural ecosystems occurred, but more substantial introductions are frowned upon. However, evolutionary biologists are increasingly focusing on what happens to species unintentionally introduced to areas in which they are not native, studying how these introduced species adapt to their new circumstances and, in turn, how the native fauna and flora respond evolutionarily. Although such invasive species can be a huge ecological and economic problem, they do provide quasi-experimental studies in which evolutionary change can be studied.

These lines of evidence make clear that selection, whether natural or artificial, can quickly lead to substantial evolutionary change. Some people who do not believe in evolution do not dispute these findings but claim that the observed evolutionary changes are relatively minor fine-tuning, rather than the substantial changes that would be required to understand the evolution of the vast biological diversity in the world around us. That is, these are changes that allow a species to adapt to different conditions. What these people contend, however, is that one species cannot evolve into another. A guppy is still a guppy, they say, or a dog still a dog.

This argument is not compelling for several reasons. First, the amount of evolutionary divergence produced by human-caused selection can be substantial. If paleontologists discovered fossils of the various breeds of dogs, they would be classified not only as different species but even as different genera—dog breeds are that different in comparison to extant species and genera of canids. The differences between many other domesticated species of plants and animals and their ancestors are also greater than the differences between different closely related species in nature. Second, many scientists contend that what makes one species distinct from another is the inability to interbreed—two individuals are members of the same species if they would mate and produce fertile offspring, whereas they are members of different species if they are unable or unwilling to do so. By this criterion, too, scientists have been able to document the evolutionary process, both observing the evolution of new species in nature, as members of two populations evolved to no longer interbreed, and conducting selection experiments in the laboratory that have produced populations of fruit flies and other organisms that do not interbreed, usually because their mating behavior has changed so that members of the two nascent species will no longer mate, even if given the opportunity. In sum, the critics' claims are without foundation. Selection clearly has the power to produce substantial evolutionary change, rather than just fine-tuning, and it can lead to the production of new, noninterbreeding species.

Evidence from the Fossil Record

Darwin noted the imperfections in the fossil record. Although many more fossil species have been discovered in the 150 years following the publication of *Origin,* it is still correct to say that for most types of organisms, we have only a sketchy fossil record. Opponents of evolution make much of these missing fossils. They claim that there is no evidence of "missing links" and hence no evidence for evolution. Although it is true that we cannot show how every extant species has evolved from its primordial ancestors, many very well-documented fossil sequences show the evolution of modern forms. I briefly provide a few examples.

Horses

The ancestor of all horses was a fox-sized animal looking somewhat like a deer, named *Hyracotherium*. Although modern horses only have one toe, the hoof, *Hyracotherium* had four toes on the forefeet and three on the hindfeet. How did these evolutionary reductions in toe number occur? Horses are actually quite common in the fossil record, and we can clearly trace the evolutionary reduction in toe number from four to one through a series of intermediate forms. At the same time, horses were also evolving larger molars and overall body size, and again, the fossil record documents in exquisite detail these increases in size through time.* These changes were coincident with the widespread occurrence of open grasslands in North America approximately 20–25 million years ago. *Hyracotherium* was likely a forest dweller, adapted to move nimbly through dense underbrush and nibble on tender ferns and shoots. By contrast, the changes documented in horse evolution likely represent adaptations to living in wide-open expanses. In such a setting, concealment from predators would be difficult, and speed—enhanced by long limbs capped by a single supporting toe—would be at a premium. Moreover, the food of choice in grasslands is, not surprisingly, grasses, which contain large quantities of grit, requiring sturdy teeth to withstand the continual abrasion.

---

* Horse evolution used to be portrayed as a linear progression from a small, many-toed, small-toothed ancestor to the modern equids of today. However, detailed examination of the fossil record reveals that horse history is much more complex, with many side branches in the horse evolutionary tree. Moreover, although the general trend in horse evolution has been as described, not all evolutionary change has occurred in the same direction. For example, at some points, some species evolved to be smaller than their ancestors.

Birds

From what did birds evolve? At first glance, this would seem to be a difficult question, because birds appear to be so distinct from all other animals alive today. The oldest known fossil bird is a famous species named *Archaeopteryx* from the Jurassic Period in the middle of the age of dinosaurs, 165 million years ago. Fossils of this species come from particularly fine geological deposits in Germany in which details of the specimen are unusually well preserved, including soft parts that usually do not fossilize. Some fossil specimens of *Archaeopteryx* include structures that very clearly are feathers, indicating without a doubt that this species was a bird. Nonetheless, examination of *Archaeopteryx* reveals a number of reptilian traits, including teeth, clawed fingers, abdominal ribs, and a long, bony tail. Based on these characteristics, scientists believe that *Archaeopteryx* evolved from a particular type of dinosaur, which was fairly closely related to *Velociraptor*, the star of *Jurassic Park*. In fact, a few years ago, a paleontologist discovered a fossil specimen of *Archaeopteryx* in a museum cabinet. In this specimen, the feathers had not been preserved, and it was misclassified as a dinosaur. Thus, in many respects, *Archaeopteryx* was no more than a feathered dinosaur—take away the feathers, and it would be mistaken for a dinosaur. Many of the other skeletal features characteristic of birds must have evolved later.

Whales

Scientists have long suspected that whales evolved from four-legged mammals related to today's ungulates (hoofed mammals such as cows). However, this idea was based on similarities in certain features of the skeleton and in DNA; no direct fossil links were known. In recent years, however, a series of transitional fossils has been discovered, documenting the evolutionary move from land to sea. Most impressive was the finding of a four-legged animal whose skeletal anatomy revealed that it was the earliest ancestor of the lineage that gave rise to whales.

Snakes

In a similar fashion, scientists long had recognized the many similarities between snakes and certain types of lizards and had hypothesized that snakes evolved from lizards. As with whales, however, until recently the early stages in snake evolution were not documented in the fossil record. However, several recent discoveries in Israel revealed fossils that, while clearly snake ancestors due to the structure of the skull and elongate body form, nevertheless possess small, but well-developed, limbs.

～

In summary, the fossil record provides many well-documented cases in which we can trace, step by step, the evolution of modern species from their very different ancestors. Paleontology currently is experiencing a golden age, with expeditions occurring throughout the world and important discoveries occurring routinely. Recent years, for example, have seen the discovery of *Ardipithecus,* the common ancestor of humans and chimps, as well as *Tiktaalik,* a primitive fish exhibiting the first hints of the transition from fins to legs (Figure 5).

More generally, the combination of studies of natural selection in present-day populations with the fossil record makes a compelling case for the theory of evolution by natural selection. Natural selection clearly has the ability to produce large-scale change, and the fossil record indicates that such change, has, indeed, occurred.

Data That Make No Sense, Except in an Evolutionary Context

Evolutionary biologists are fond of quoting a statement by the noted evolutionary biologist Theodosius Dobzhansky, who said that nothing makes sense in biology, except in the light of evolution. Although

Figure 5. *Tiktaalik*, a fossil fish that lived nearly 400 million years ago and was a transitional form between fish and land-dwelling amphibians, was discovered on an expedition led by Harvard paleontologist Farish Jenkins, curator of vertebrate paleontology at Harvard's Museum of Comparative Zoology, and Neil Shubin, a Harvard-trained PhD now at the University of Chicago. (Photo: The Shubin Lab/University of Chicago.)

perhaps a slight overstatement, this comment has a lot of truth to it. Consider the following sorts of evidence.

Homologous Structures

Homologous structures are features in different species built from the same elements. For example, the forelimbs of all mammals are made from the same skeletal elements: one long element, two paired elements (sometimes fused), a bunch of little bones (the wrist), and a set of long bones arranged in lines (fingers). Vertebrates use their forelimbs for many different purposes: birds and bats, for example, use their forelimbs to fly, whales and seals to swim, primates to grasp, and horses to run. Nonetheless, the structure of the forelimb of all of these species is fundamentally the same (see Figure 6). This makes perfect sense if they are all descended from a common ancestor and their limbs have been modified by natural selection for different ends; in the absence of evolution, however, such similarity, with no functional explanation, would not be expected.

Vestigial Structures

Related to the concept of homology are vestigial structures (i.e., structures that have no current use and are presumably holdovers from useful structures in ancestors). These are my favorite examples of evidence of evolution and I will quickly provide a number of examples of vestigial structures:

* Each year, I ask my students how many of them can wiggle their ears, and invariably one or two can do so. Many mammals move their ears around as social signals or to facilitate hearing. This ability is retained in some humans, although it aids neither hearing nor social communication.

* Similarly, humans retain some of the muscles used to move tails, even though the most recent ancestor of humans that bore a tail lived more than 20 million years ago.

* Whales have no hind limbs, yet they have skeletal remains of a pelvis (see Plates 2 and 3). Some snakes also have slight remnants of their hind limbs. As already discussed, both whales and snakes evolved from four-legged ancestors, and their rudimentary pelvises are vestiges of their quadrupedal past.

* Many animals that spend their entire lives in lightless caves still have eyes, although they often are not functional because some elements are missing. Why a troglodyte would have eyes would be a mystery, were it not known that they have evolved from surface-dwelling ancestors.

* Most beetles (such as fireflies) can fly, but beetles on many islands have lost this ability. Beetles have a hard outer shell, called a

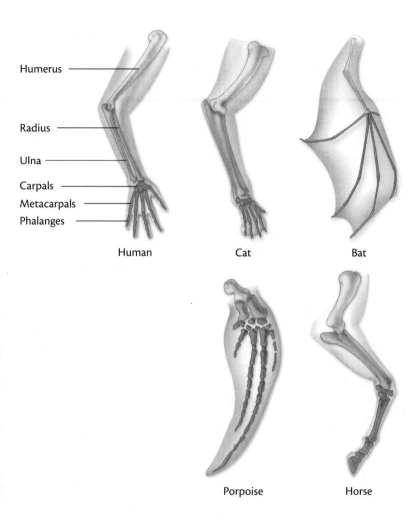

Figure 6. Homologous vertebrate forelimbs. Note that the limbs of these animals, though very different in structure, are composed of the same series of bones. (Image adapted from P. Raven et al., *Biology*, 9th ed., © 2011 by The McGraw-Hill Companies, Inc.)

carapace. When a flying beetle takes off, it elevates the carapace, exposing the wings that lie underneath. In flightless beetles, the carapace has fused shut and cannot be opened. Nonetheless, if you dissect away the carapace in such species, underneath it you find the structures of the wing.

Vestigial traits can also be seen in the genomes of many organisms. For example, the icefish is a bizarre-looking, nearly see-through fish that occurs in the frigid waters of the Antarctic. The icefish's transparency results not only from a lack of pigment in its body structures but also from the near invisibility of its blood. What makes our blood red is the presence of red blood cells, which contain hemoglobin, the molecule that transports oxygen from the lungs to the tissues. However, oxygen concentration in water increases as temperature decreases. In the waters of the Antarctic, which are about 0° Centigrade (32° Fahrenheit), there is so much oxygen that the fish do not need special molecules to carry oxygen. The result is that these fish do not have hemoglobin, and consequently their blood is colorless. Nonetheless, when the DNA of icefish was examined, scientists discovered that they have the same gene that produces hemoglobin in other vertebrates. However, the icefish hemoglobin gene has a variety of mutations that render it nonfunctional, and thus the icefish does not produce hemoglobin. The presence of this inoperative version of the hemoglobin gene in icefish means that its ancestors had hemoglobin; however, once the icefish's progenitors occupied the cold waters of the Antarctic and lost the need for hemoglobin, mutations that would be harmful and thus would be filtered out by natural selection in other species were able to persist in the population. Just by chance, some of these mutations increased in frequency in the population through time, eventually becoming established in all individuals and knocking out the fish's ability to produce hemoglobin.*

---

* This process, by which a mutation may randomly increase or decrease in frequency in a population through time in the absence of natural selection, is termed "genetic drift." A new mutation will initially begin

"Fossil genes" or "pseudogenes," such as the hemoglobin gene in the icefish, are actually quite common in the genomes of most organisms: when a trait disappears, the gene does not just vanish from the genome; rather, some mutation renders it inactive, and once that occurs, other mutations can accumulate.

I could provide many more examples of vestigial structures; modern genome sequencing is a particularly rich vein that continually discovers new, vestigial pseudogenes. These examples only make sense when one considers that these structures were probably of use in ancestral forms and have not yet been entirely lost.

Geographical Differences

One of the observations that most struck Darwin was that many of the species in the Galápagos are endemic and are found nowhere else in the world. Yet these species are almost always similar to species in South America. Darwin wondered: Why was this? If each species was created independently, there would be no reason that they should be particularly like species in nearby regions. Moreover, the climate and structure of these islands is not like that of South America, so there is no reason that species in the two localities should be similar. Indeed, Darwin pointed out, the Cape Verde Islands off the western coast of Africa are similar to the Galápagos in topography and climate. Nonetheless, species on the two island archipelagoes are not notably similar to each other. Rather, the Galápagos species have affinities to South America and the Cape Verde species to Africa. Darwin ultimately realized that this is evidence of evolution—islands tend to be colonized by plants and animals from the most proximate continent, thus explaining the similarities of island inhabitants to those of nearby landmasses.

---

with a very low frequency in the population because it is found in only one individual. Most such mutations, which start at very low frequency, would eventually disappear just by random fluctuations through time; some, however, may become widespread in the population and replace the formerly common genetic form.

Geographical evidence of a different sort comes from Down Under. In Australia, almost all of the mammals are marsupials (i.e., they have pouches, like kangaroos, where their offspring—born in an embryonic state—spend most of their developmental period attached to a teat). Many Australian mammals exhibit great similarities to their placental counterparts in the rest of the world (most mammals are "placentals," so named because the embryo develops for an extensive period within the mother's body, nourished through the placenta). There are, or were until recently, marsupial "cats," "wolves," "moles," "mice," "gliding squirrels," "badgers," and "anteaters." Why should such "duplicate" forms exist in Australia, but as marsupials, whereas everywhere else they are placental mammals? In evolutionary terms, it makes perfect sense. When Australia broke off from the rest of the ancient landmass of Gondwanaland more than 70 million years ago, placental mammals did not occur in that part of the world. After the dinosaurs disappeared, mammals everywhere experienced an evolutionary flowering, diversifying to occupy many of the ecological niches previously inhabited by dinosaurs. However, this adaptive radiation—as it is called—was undertaken by marsupials in Australia, and primarily by placental mammals elsewhere. In many cases, similar ecological niches were occupied evolutionarily in similar ways, a phenomenon termed "convergent evolution," resulting in marsupial and placental counterparts in different parts of the world.

Embryology

Some of the strongest anatomical evidence supporting evolution comes from comparisons of how organisms develop. Embryos of different types of vertebrates, for example, often are similar early on, but become more different as development proceeds. Early in their development, human and fish embryos both possess pharyngeal pouches, which in humans develop into various glands and ducts and in fish turn into gill slits. At a later stage, every human embryo has a long bony tail, the vestige of which we carry to adulthood as the coccyx at the end of our spine. Human fetuses even possess a fine fur (called lanugo) during the fifth month of development. Similar evolutionary holdovers are seen in other animals: baleen whale embryos have teeth; horse embryos have three toes; embryos of frogs that have lost the tadpole stage still produce—and then lose—a tail. These vestigial developmental forms suggest strongly that our development has evolved, with new genetic instructions modifying ancestral developmental patterns.

Conclusion

I would like to conclude with one thought of a more philosophical nature. What I want to discuss is what we mean by the term "fact." In common terms, people think of things as facts if they can be directly demonstrated: apples are red, water is liquid at room temperature, and so on. But these statements are completely mundane. What about atoms? We cannot see them. How do we know they exist? Or gravity? We know that something keeps us from floating off into space, but how can we know that it is the mass of our planet that is responsible?

I would argue that something should be considered a fact when the available evidence compellingly supports that conclusion. With regard to evolution, I would argue that the evidence is so overwhelming that it should be considered a fact, rather than a theory. In this context, there are many theories about how evolution occurs, one of which is that it is driven by natural selection.

Not everyone takes this perspective. Some people—both scientists and nonscientists—draw a distinction between the terms "theory" and "hypothesis," at least as used in a scientific context. They use "hypothesis" for speculative ideas, and theory only for those ideas that are strongly supported by many lines of evidence, like the theories of gravity and evolution. In this sense, it is important to recognize that evolution is not just "another theory"—the term "theory" is not the equivalent of a hunch or a notion, or even an idea spouted by a scientist. Rather, it is a well-tested phenomenon, so well supported by data that it is hard to envision what sort of data might be found to disprove it.

So this has been a quick survey of the types of evidence that persuade most scientists that evolution is a very well-established scientific idea. Data from so many disparate fields of biology all are explicable in an evolutionary framework that it is hard to envision any other plausible explanation amenable to scientific investigation. Moreover, the power of the evolutionary perspective is continually demonstrating itself. For example, an important new approach to computer software writing was invented a few years ago. Called "genetic algorithms," this approach uses a process modeled after natural selection to devise solutions to programming problems that otherwise were not evident. Essentially, from a simple starting program, random changes in computer code are introduced, and those programs which perform best are selected, followed by more random changes. This procedure is repeated many times until a program is produced that solves the problem at hand.

Scarcely a decade ago, most molecular biologists had little use for evolutionary biology, as it generally was of little practical importance in their investigations about the workings of the molecular machinery underlying life. However, when the human genome was first sequenced in 2001, molecular biologists realized that to understand the structure and functioning of the human genome, it was critical to understand how it was constructed. And to do that required sequencing the genome of other species, allowing comparisons that helped identify which parts of the genome are uniquely human and which we have inherited from our ancestors, both recent and distant. For example, comparison with the genome of the platypus has shed light on the evolution of milk production and the origin of the mammalian sex chromosomes, whereas comparison to the genome of the chimpanzee has identified many genes potentially involved in the evolution of the human brain and the development of speech. Today, one of the most vibrant areas in evolutionary biology is the study of genome evolution, a subdiscipline that has united molecular and evolutionary biologists and proven that, indeed, nothing in biology does make sense except in the light of evolution.

Appendix

As I mentioned at the outset of my essay, evolutionary biology is unusual, if not unique, among the sciences in that many people (at least in the United States) do not believe in its basic tenet, that evolution has occurred. Of course, one of the great virtues of American society is that people are free to believe whatever they want, especially for topics that may have religious implications. However, this freedom runs into other cherished principles when we consider whether alternatives to evolution should be taught in our public schools. The key question concerns whether there are scientific alternative theories that should be taught in science classes, or, to put it in recent parlance, should we "teach the controversy"?

The history of what has—or has not—been taught in the public schools spans most of a century and goes back to the famous Scopes Monkey Trial (*State v. Scopes*, 152 Tenn. 424, 278 S.W. 57 1925). I will only briefly review this history here, but a number of books and Web sites are available that treat the subject in great detail.

In the 1960s opponents of evolution, "creationists," invented what they called "scientific creationism," which began with the claim that geological formations were the result of the Great Flood that inundated the world for forty days and forty nights. Proponents of this view argued that the reason that we see different fossils in different rock strata is that animals were trying to escape the rising water, and some were able to get higher than others. Thus, rocks, and the fossils they contained, were said to be several thousands of years old, rather than millions.

When the U.S. Sixth Circuit Court of Appeals struck down the teaching of creationism in *Daniel v. Waters* (515 F.2d 485 6th Cir. 1975), creationists retooled their approach by removing all reference to biblical quotations. Several states subsequently passed laws mandating the teaching of this new "creation science" alongside evolution. However, there was not much science in this creation science. There were no testable hypotheses; rather, the approach was to try to find evidence supporting the literal wording in the Bible. In addition, a primary point was to poke holes in evolutionary science—"Where are the missing fossils?" and so on—and then conclude that if evolution could not explain diversity, creationism must be the answer. In other words, instead of laying out testable hypotheses that supported creation science, the approach was to argue that perceived inadequacies in evolutionary science were the same as positive evidence in favor of creationism. The Supreme Court was not fooled by this and recognized in *Edwards v. Aguillard* (482 U.S. 578 1987) that this "science" was just religion masquerading in a pseudo-scientific coat, striking down laws mandating the teaching of creationism. Harvard's Stephen Jay Gould was one of the key experts for the plaintiffs in this case.

When creation science was ruled to be nothing more than religion, the creationists took a new tack. They eliminated the word "creationism" and instead came up with the term "intelligent design." The idea is that the complexity in life is too well designed to have arisen by a process like natural selection. Hence, some designer must be responsible. The proponents of ID, as it is called, are very careful not to say who or what this designer is: "Sure, it could be God, but maybe it's some extraterrestrials or who knows what else? But certainly, this is a scientific idea, with no religious overtones."

This is actually an old idea, going back to William Paley in 1804. Paley stated that the existence of a watch implies the existence of a watchmaker. Darwin, of course, knew of this argument and made great efforts to oppose it, concluding late in life: "We can no longer argue that, for instance, the beautiful hinge of a bivalve shell must have been made by an intelligent being, like the hinge of a door by man. There seems to be no more design in the variability of organic beings and in the action of natural selection, than in the course which the wind blows. Everything in nature is the result of fixed laws" (Barlow 1958, 87).

In considering ID, there are three key considerations:

1. Are organisms too well designed to have resulted from the process of natural selection?
2. Are organisms, in fact, so well designed? (What about the eye of backboned animals such as ourselves, with the visual nerve exiting in front of the photoreceptors and causing a blind spot? What about the human back, which seems more like a disaster waiting to happen than an optimally, intelligently designed structure?)
3. Is ID a scientific theory? If so, how is it tested? In theory, ID is a theory. But in reality, to make it a testable theory—that is, an idea that potentially could be refuted—we would have to be able to specify what constitutes a design too good to result from natural selection (point 1 above). No one has come up with a successful means of doing this.

In response to this point, ID proponents have a reasonable response. Is evolutionary biology truly a testable theory? What sort of evidence could disprove that evolution has occurred? In fact, they argue that whenever evolutionary biologists disprove a hypothesis, they erect explanations that can account for the discrepancy, rather than simply concluding that evolution does not occur. For example, suppose you did an experiment in which you selected on a trait in fruit flies, say, bristle number, and you did not get an evolutionary response. Would you conclude that, in fact, the theory of evolution was incorrect? Probably not. Rather, you would ask why the trait had not evolved. In this case, my first inclination would be to suggest that in fact the variation upon which selection occurred was not genetically based, and thus evolution could not occur. IDers say that this is what goes on all the time, and that as a result evolution is no more a scientific theory than ID.

Evolutionary biologists have two rejoinders. First, they argue that evolution has passed so many tests so many times that any single failure to find evidence for evolution is more parsimoniously explained by looking at the circumstances of that particular instance rather than rejecting evolution wholesale. Certainly, if we never got a response to selection, we would have real doubts about the theory of evolution by natural selection. But, in fact, most of the time tests such as this—as well as many other types of evidence—support the theory that evolution has occurred.

Second, one evolutionary biologist suggested that evolution could be falsified in this way: if we found a fossil rabbit in rocks that were a billion years old. Because everything we know about evolution says that mammals evolved through a process that began with unicellular organisms and did not produce mammals until about 125 million years ago, a billion-year-old rabbit would be utterly incompatible with our theories of evolution. So, in some sense, the fossil record is a potential means of disproving evolution. Discovery of fossils completely discordant with our understanding of how life has diversified through time could cast serious doubt on our conclusion that the history of life documents the existence of "descent with modification" (Darwin's original term for what we now call evolution).

The intelligent design argument has led to the development of one new idea, the theory of irreducible complexity. The idea here is that natural selection cannot build up a structure part by part unless each added part is favored by natural selection. Thus, if you have an object with, say, ten parts, and all ten are necessary for the object to function, then it is not possible for natural selection to have built that structure, because it could not have put together the first nine parts, given that at that point, lacking the tenth part, the structure would have had no functional advantage, and thus would not have provided any increased fitness. Such structures are termed "irreducibly complex," and their existence is said to be evidence of the existence of a designer. One purported example of an irreducibly complex structure is the rotary motor of a bacterial flagellum (the little tail-like structure that some bacteria use to propel themselves), which is said to be nonfunctional if any of the parts are not present, although this is disputed.

The basis of this argument is that natural selection can only operate by building an adaptation for the same function throughout the structure's existence. If this were so, then, of course, every incremental improvement would have to be advantageous and lead to increased fitness (eyes may have evolved in just this way, as every increase in the ability to detect and focus light provides an advantage over the previous condition). But this is not always the case. Rather, many traits initially evolved for one purpose and then were subsequently modified for another. In this way, it is possible to see how a so-called irreducibly complex trait could evolve. It might not be able to function at all for its current task if one component were removed, but it still might be useful for some other purpose. It has been argued that this can explain the rotary motor of the flagellum, as well as many other structures. For example, the first feathers that evolved in dinosaurs did not have the aerodynamic properties that allow modern birds to fly. Rather, they probably evolved to provide insulation—like a goose's down—or as ornaments used in courtship behavior. Only after the initial protofeather evolved did subsequent changes occur that permitted feathers to provide flying capability.

There is another way in which irreducibly complex structures are compatible with the action of natural selection. It may well be that a perfectly functioning structure adds a component that, though not essential, makes it function even better. At this point, the structure is not irreducibly complex, because that last part can be removed without rendering the structure functionless. However, subsequent adaptive evolution may build on this new part, so that at a later date, it does become integral to function, and thus the structure becomes irreducibly complex, but as a result of natural selection–driven evolution. Here's an analogy. Consider the GPS unit, now standard in many cars. Certainly a nice addition, but by no means essential—if the GPS unit breaks, the car still is fine. But it is not difficult to imagine that fifty years from now, cars may be driven by their GPS units: just type in (or shout out) the address and the car does the rest. At that point, the car would be irreducibly complex with respect to the GPS.

In summary, there really are no tenable, alternative scientific theories to explain the diversity of life we see around us, and hence no other ideas are appropriate to be taught in science classes, a view once again affirmed in 2005 by a U.S. federal court when it considered and rejected the teaching of ID in *Kitzmiller v. Dover Area School District* (400 F. Supp. 2d 707 M.D. Pa. 2005). In other words, there is no scientific controversy to teach.

Further Reading

Darwin, C. 1845. *The Voyage of the Beagle*, 2nd ed. London: John Murray.
This travelogue, a best seller in its time, tells of the natural history wonders Darwin recorded in his epic, five-year circumnavigation of the world. Fascinating today as it was to his contemporaries, in it the reader can see the early stages of Darwin's formulation of the theory of evolution by natural selection, as well as many fascinating tidbits of the biology, natural history, and sociology of far-flung corners of the world. This book is a particular must-read for anyone traveling to the Galápagos, as one can see today the exact geological formations and life forms that Darwin detailed in his journey.

———. 1859. *On the Origin of Species by Means of Natural Selection, or the Preservation of Favoured Races in the Struggle for Life*. London: John Murray.
Although a bit dense, it is all here, the overwhelming mass of evidence from so many different areas of scientific inquiry that convinced the educated world that evolution had occurred, even if support for his proposed mechanism for evolutionary change, natural selection, did not solidify for another fifty years.

Barlow, Nora, ed. 1958. *The Autobiography of Charles Darwin 1809–1882: With the Original Omissions Restored. Edited and with Appendix and Notes by His Grand-daughter Nora Barlow*. London: Collins.
This and the other Darwin publications can be found online at http://darwin-online.org.uk/.

Weiner, J. 1994. *Beak of the Finch.* New York: Vintage Press.

Weiner follows the work of Princeton biologists Peter and Rosemary Grant as they conduct their pathbreaking studies on Darwin's finches in the Galápagos. Although now a bit out of date (the Grants have made many important new discoveries in the past seventeen years), the book is still an exceptionally well-written discourse on how biologists study evolution, branching out from its focus on the Grants to cover the field as a whole. I continue to assign this book to my class, and the students still love it. For a more up-to-date account of the finch work, written for a slightly more advanced audience, try the Grants' *How and Why Species Multiply: The Radiation of Darwin's Finches* (Princeton, NJ: Princeton University Press, 2007).

Quammen, D. 1996. *Song of the Dodo: Island Biogeography in the Age of Extinction.* New York: Scribner.

Possibly the best book on the evolution of biological diversity written for a popular audience. Quammen seamlessly intertwines three themes: the diversity of life on islands, the development of scientific theories to understand how such diversity arose and how it is maintained in modern environments, and how diversity is studied, starting with the parallel stories of Darwin and Alfred Russel Wallace up to the present-day research of Harvard's Edward O. Wilson and other scientists. This book is about my area of research, so I already knew much of what he wrote, yet I could not put it down and still enjoy rereading it. Quammen understands the science at a very deep level and portrays it in completely accurate, yet lyrical, terms.

Carroll, S. 2006. *The Making of the Fittest: DNA and the Ultimate Forensic Record of Evolution.* New York: Norton.

Carroll, a leader in the field of evolutionary biology, reviews the evidence for evolution by natural selection with special emphasis on recent findings from studies of DNA.

Shubin, N. 2007. *Your Inner Fish: A Journey into the 3.5-Billion-Year History of the Human Body.* New York: Pantheon Books.

Shubin, a remarkable scientist who conducts paleontological research in remote parts of the Arctic and DNA studies in the laboratory, illustrates how the oddities of the human body make sense when understood in an evolutionary context. Along the way, he describes the rigors of fieldwork and the excitement of discovery of a truly remarkable fossil, *Tiktaalik,* a fish caught, in an evolutionary sense, halfway along the road to the conquest of land.

Coyne, J. 2009. *Why Evolution Is True.* New York: Viking Press.

Dawkins, R. 2009. *The Greatest Show on Earth: The Evidence for Evolution.* New York: Free Press.

Reznick, D. 2009. *The* Origin *Then and Now: An Interpretive Guide to the* Origin of Species. Princeton, NJ: Princeton University Press.

These are three of the best books written to capitalize on the celebrations of 2009, the 200th anniversary of the birth of Charles Darwin (born on the exact same day as Abraham Lincoln) and the 150th anniversary of the publication of the *Origin*. Coyne and Dawkins cover similar ground, making the same case, in much extended form, that is the subject of this essay. Reznick reviews the *Origin* and explains it in light of modern ideas about evolution and biological diversity.

Global History for an Era of Globalization: An Introduction

Charles S. Maier

How better to start a course in world or global history than by recall-
ing one of the great icons of our age: the beautiful image of the earth
transmitted from the first manned spaceflight to orbit the moon,
Apollo 8, on Christmas Eve 1968. It shows "earthrise" from close to the
surface of the moon (see Plate 4). Half of our planet reflects sunlight to
the astronauts; half remains unilluminated. With the blue ocean and
swirling white cloud cover, it was delicate and evocative. It plucked at
the growing ecological awareness of the 1960s and became a reminder
of the environmental fragility of our species' homeland. It can also
serve as a summons to understanding the history of our world as a
whole. If we see the planet as a whole, as a common home, is there not
a global history—a record of the past—for the humans who inhabit it?

"Earthrise"—Who Lives beneath the Cloud Cover?

We live as a species on that sphere in space and we have lived there for
thousands of generations, constantly interacting with the physical
constraints earth originally set us, but which we continually modify.
These include climate and weather systems; large bodies of water that
separate our communities but also facilitate transportation between
them; vegetation and forests that we can renew or deplete, and earlier
vegetation buried and compressed for millions of years that provides
vast deposits of carbon-based fuel; ores that furnish the metals for
strong rigid structures and others scarce and durable enough to be
endowed with high exchangeable value. In addition, there are other
animal species that we have utilized for fabrics, food, transportation,

and even companionship, or perhaps heedlessly extinguished. And there are microorganisms that have periodically devastated human populations, but which we can also contain and combat.

So there is a global history, a story of changes over time created by the species as a whole. At the same time, however, the people on that distant planet have until relatively recently lived their lives in separate communities, many of which have developed their own art and technology, religions and political systems, ideas of property and systems of labor and exchange, and institutions for raising and acculturating continuing generations. Each of these communities has its own history, often profoundly influenced from outside, but continually generated from within. In what respects these multiple collective experiences can be understood as constituting a unified world history remains a fundamental issue for the historian who wants to grasp them as a whole.

This chapter is written as a preface to the study of a history that at some level thus remains a wager on a global community. What follows is not a summary of world history but an effort to define the field and outline its contributions to a general education. It begins with a brief discussion of why history itself has seemed important at least since written texts appeared in ancient Europe, the Middle East, and Asia, and probably even earlier and universally in oral narrative forms. Then it asks what special challenges world history presents. Is there, to begin with, a cohesive subject of study under the cloud cover rather than just a collection of peoples, each with its own history? How does the subject hang together? After citing some early philosophical responses, I explain three promising approaches: first, the story of humanity as a species in dealing with problems that impact us all, deriving, say, from environmental changes or technological advances; second, the history of encounters, conflicts, and connections among the world's different cultures or states; and, third, the comparative analysis of social and political institutions or behavior within different societies.

Finally, I take up the question of the possible starting points for a course in global history that these respective approaches imply, likewise the content that each would suggest was relevant. Thinking in terms of a course focuses the inquiry.

Why History?

Before these subjects are broached, think for a moment about historical study in general. Why should we bother with history when it is all about what's over? This is a basic question about all historical research, not just global history. What use might it have, or is it just an idle indulgence? As the old song goes, "Don't know much about history"— and it does not suggest that the lack is regrettable. And yet, situating our species in time, between past and future, has been a widespread impulse since antiquity. Historians aspire both to represent or depict the past and to analyze it, to learn what happened and why. Thus history shares the objectives and methods of both the humanities and the social sciences. Insofar as it functions as a social science, historical study presents peculiar characteristics. Other social sciences focus their study on aspects of behavior that human beings may share; psychology and economics, for example, seek to generalize about cognition or material motivation. Some historians share this aspiration and seek to emulate it by systematic comparison of features among different communities. But most historians have generally felt the commitment to emphasize what differentiates societies, their uniqueness as countries or villages or their particular events such as wars or elections. In the dialectical tension between whole and part that has characterized social studies since Aristotle, historians have always felt the pull of the particular or the local. Even in the case of world history, historians will not want to lose sight of differing senses of identity and experience. They are similar to anthropologists in that regard—but with an emphasis on the past.

Historians share the conviction, usually left implicit, that sequence in time best accounts for how and why events take place. This might seem obvious, but other social sciences make do without chronology. The fact that only earlier events can account for later ones is virtually tautological, but its banality should not diminish its importance for understanding the social as well as the natural world. Historians were practitioners of path dependency long before other social scientists decided to formalize it. Narrative reconstruction tends therefore to be essential to their reconstruction of causal chains, although occasionally historians attempt the depiction of past societies, in effect, as snapshots without development.

Narration in turn rests upon the interpretive interaction with data—a practice sometimes called "hermeneutics." This is the point at which history becomes akin to the humanities. Except at the most basic level, such as a date, historians do not believe "facts" have much importance shorn of their interpretation, that is, their significance or meaning. Think about the photo of earthrise a bit longer. Philosophers could argue for a long time over what we actually see. Much of what is visible is an electronically transmitted image of the reflection of sunlight from cloud cover, not the earth beneath it. So, too, in history what we discover is not the past as such or human beings acting in the past—but data they leave behind. Sometimes it consists of documents they wrote, whether to explain to others what had to be done or to rationalize what they were doing. Sometimes they also leave "artifacts," household furnishings or buildings, or items for personal display, from which we try to discern what they might have been thinking, and of course they leave works of art created to satisfy aesthetic impulses. For nineteenth- and many twentieth-century historians, the archive (i.e., the written documentary collection), often assembled in the service of one governmental department or another, was the sanctuary for data. Even when they exercise the most imagination about context, historians feel bound to that data. On that basis they attempt three interwoven tasks: first to narrate what happened, second to explain or account for why it happened, and finally, to interpret or assign some measure of significance, that is, to answer the question "So what?" or "What difference did it make?"

Historians tend to answer this last question in light of subsequent developments. What is important about the past is what shaped the future of that past, including the ideas and values that became persuasive in the interim between then and now. Historians thus constitute a profession licensed to practice hindsight. Given the crowd of social scientists who believe themselves licensed for prediction, it is probably valuable that societies have also tolerated the contribution of historians. Any decision maker who attempts prediction (including policy making) must resort to some guidance from the past. But the past never teaches unambiguous lessons; what it suggests, via the historian, is the immensely textured complexity of events and the importance of unanticipated developments.

What Distinguishes World History?

The range of problems sketched above attends all history, not just world history. The problem of global or world history as a subfield is a different one. If there had been an astronaut with a camera thousands of years ago, he might well have taken an image close to earthrise (just as one might see a similar image a thousand years from now—assuming that global warming has not thickened earth's cloud cover). But we know that the peoples under the cloud cover who are now in continuous contact often remained ignorant of each other in the past. They had perhaps heard of faraway kingdoms or tribes or even of mythical monstrous beings, but had no real sense of how these remote peoples lived as organized communities or of the languages they spoke. Can there be a "global history" when global communities go their separate and unsuspecting ways over centuries? The Muslim conquests of the Middle East and North Africa were occurring in the same decades that Mayan civilization was flowering in today's Guatemala and southern Mexico—each group oblivious of the other. Do they form a subject for world history in the same way that there is a subject, say, for American history or European history? Is there some sense of shared community, or is there just a species? And do we require some sense of shared community to claim we have a global history? Or is it enough to research and write what amounts to side-by-side histories of the different peoples who inhabit the globe?

This introduction addresses these issues, first by examining how historians and philosophers have made the argument for an overarching historical unity of human development. A global perspective that originally derived in the West from a Christian notion of human redemption and then became a secular moral commitment to shared humanity motivated early ideas of world history. When the German poet, dramatist, and historian Friedrich Schiller gave his first university lecture as a twenty-one-year-old in 1789, he asked, "What is the meaning and the purpose of universal history?" Then he answered that "universal history"—the closest equivalent then to world or global history—could not just be an aggregate in which national particles were suspended like gravel in tar. He believed that universal history had to presuppose some cultural unity that had gradually emerged with the ancient Greeks. Understanding it required philosophical contemplation as well as historical research.

No global historian today would so privilege the European sources of a world cultural heritage, but the idea of finding a shared culture of humanity was a powerful one in the eighteenth century. Schiller's older contemporary, the philosopher Immanuel Kant, likewise sketched a universal history with "cosmopolitan intent," which he, too, believed could demonstrate the shared values of humanity. The same impulse has informed the massive UNESCO *History of Humanity* (1994–2008), to which many authors (including this one) have contributed. Intellectuals in emerging nations have often encouraged national histories of their culture and their politics to claim long-term legitimacy. It is not surprising that those who aspire to a sense of global community would turn to world history for the same objectives.

Nevertheless, most academically trained historians today feel uncomfortable presupposing that a moral purpose or "cosmopolitan intent" should motivate their study of world history. What they might like to find is not necessarily what they do find. But there are broad behavioral patterns—sociopolitical and cultural—that also offer a starting point. Four hundred years before Schiller, the great Islamic theorist of history, Ibn-Khaldūn, who traveled from the fringes of Muslim Spain though North Africa and had to negotiate the surrender of Damascus to the Central Asian conqueror Tamerlane, speculated on the great movements of ascent and decline of world civilizations. In his *Introduction (Muqaddimah)* to history he traced the cyclic movement of vigorous tribally organized rural states, as they conquered and then yielded to the blandishments of wealthy sedentary urban civilizations and tended in turn toward decay until the cycle was renewed.

Khaldūn's *Introduction* suggests that great speculations on world history are likely to arise when a new or reenergized set of actors seems to be claiming or reclaiming a role on the global stage that had long been denied them: Arabs in the seventh and eighth centuries, Turkic and Mongol conquerors in the fourteenth century, West Europeans and North Americans from the sixteenth through the twentieth centuries, East and South Asians today. A similar motivation for writing global history derived from the intensity of interactions, hostile or peaceful, among once-separate civilizations since the age of "discoveries," or more accurately "encounters." Most recently the intense economic, cultural, and social interchange we call "globalization" testifies to the condition that none of our national communities really can determine its own fate without a constant barrage of influences from outside its own boundaries.

Sixty years ago, American universities stressed the legacy of Greek, Roman, and medieval Christian thought for understanding what we then termed the "Western" values that had been at stake in World

War II and then the Cold War. Twenty years after the Cold War, and confronted by other challenging developments that are not easily placed into a framework of ideological competition, an updated search for orientation mandates broader historical perspectives, focused less on defining exclusive Western legacies (itself a shaky assumption) and more on elements manifested in different cultures, whether—to name just a sample—the public role of religious commitments, forms of economic organization such as family capitalism, or political patterns (e.g., clientelism). This is not to argue that our cultures are now or will in the near future melt into one world culture. Many elements of diversity will probably persist even as consumption and work patterns converge. Nor am I claiming that the study of individual nations is not a demanding task that can take up a whole scholarly lifetime. Most historians in Europe and the United States remain national historians. But they can no longer follow their own national society as just the product of events and developments that originated within its own borders. Each individual society's history is the product of influences— migrations of people and ideas and commodities, ongoing conflicts, rivalries, and dialogues—that emanate from the global space that incorporates them all.

Historians in every era have tried to write world history. But as a scholarly topic—that is, a common effort in which scholars recognize common problems, build cumulatively on each other's work, read and contribute to common journals and Web sites, and form a community— world history is really a new discipline. Those studying it are participating in an exciting new effort to figure out the connections between peoples and societies who have often been widely separated in space. These researchers and writers share the belief that some deeper relationship existed even when peoples were not in direct contact. But the emerging community of global history scholars do not all pursue the same approaches to the subject, and it is important to understand what alternatives they follow.

Three Approaches to Global History

Three different approaches, in fact, seem promising.

⁓

1. The first explores the developments that societies underwent in common, as experiences of the species taken as a whole, even if some communities remained outside the overall trajectory. For early times (15,000–3000 BCE), this research agenda examines the transition from hunter-gatherer societies to sedentary settlements based on varieties of agriculture, a long transformation that advanced social hierarchies and differentiation of gender and vocational roles, ideas of territory, the domain of the sacred, aesthetic expression, and competition for goods. But this effort to understand human development as a whole is just as relevant for the modern age. A course in recent global history since 1700 will emphasize how major changes in the human experience interact with each other. Focus first perhaps on demography—the growth of world populations and the reasons that rates of increase have changed profoundly, and sometimes unexpectedly, and for reasons hard to discern. The British parson Thomas Malthus around 1810 claimed that population growth would always press upon available food resources and confront societies with recurring subsistence crises. But the clearing of new lands (and their periodic exhaustion) and the development of better agricultural technologies made such a process of increase and limitations anything but automatic. For those largely rural societies that increased in the eighteenth and nineteenth centuries—China's population rose from 300 million in 1700 to perhaps 450 million by 1850; Ireland's jumped from 4 million to 8 million and then collapsed disastrously in the famine of the 1840s—the answer may originate with better nutrition. Crops from the New World—including the potato, the sweet potato, the yam (this last actually of African origin), corn, and the peanut—account for much of the increase. Famine, though, remains a recurrent topic in my own world history course, although as economist Amartya Sen has stressed, the

reasons are often rooted as much in political decision making removed from democratic controls as in natural (environmental) causes. British officials allowed disaster to overtake the vulnerable dependent population in Ireland and then in Bengal a century later (during World War II, when local crop failures and skyrocketing food prices led quickly to starvation for perhaps 2 million to 3 million people); Mao Zedong's ideological convictions helped plunge China into perhaps the greatest episode of mass starvation in modern times. Explaining the waves of growth and then stabilization of populations is more difficult. For industrializing societies, such as Great Britain, whose population increased from 12 million to 40 million between 1800 and 1900, the answer may lie in better public health in the growing cities. Medical advances, such as vaccination, play a role but tend to lengthen the life of adults, which may not have as powerful an effect on cumulative population growth. Clean water supplies will eliminate typhoid and cholera epidemics; antiseptics and just washing up will make childbirth and surgery safer. Still, progress spreads unevenly: infant mortality rates in rural Europe (and not its poorest regions) often remained above 20 percent until about 1914. Modern pharmaceuticals arrived only in the 1940s.

In any case, global population, which perhaps hovered around half a billion at the beginning of the great ancient empires (c. 200 BCE), took until about 1800 to reach 2 billion, then vaulted to 6 billion by 2000 and is likely to stabilize at about 9 or 10 billion by 2050. Having attempted to account for the growth in population, the historian must explain why the rise of populations slowed after 1960 in Europe, and more recently in the developing world. This is the most recent development in a long and surprising history: medical advances and the successful assault on infant mortality came to less developed countries a generation or two before the adoption of family planning, which meant two generations of massive population increase in Latin America, Africa, and South and Southeast Asia. Yet that surge has now slowed, in some places to rates that barely promise steady-state maintenance (usually set at 2.1 children per adult female). Populations and particularly women have become able—and motivated—to choose family limitation; contraception has become a fundamental and accessible technology in the last fifty years. Recognizing this, the historian faces the issue of what prospects motivated women to adopt available possibilities—the availability of industrial work? The desire not to be caught in cycles of repetitive pregnancies and risks? Perhaps the loosening hold of male domination within families? Or just the expectation for men and women that more of their infants would live until adulthood?

The question of population growth unavoidably opens up issues of industrial development. Economic historians debate the issues continuously. Population growth depended on improved agricultural production but also interacted with the shift into industrial and urban employment. Looking at the increases of nineteenth-century Britain and Europe, global historians must ponder the early development of industrial production in Britain, then Belgium, France, and Germany—that is, above all, they must examine the Industrial Revolution, which can be defined in many ways (the rise of factory labor, attendant urban growth, new production methods), but whose single best index may consist of the energy sources available to the individual worker in the manufacturing sector. The mobilization of mechanical power under the factory roof distinguishes industrial production per se from the large-scale adaptation of so-called protoindustrial production—the term used for spinning and weaving carried on in multiple households—in the textile regions of Flanders or Germany or, similarly, the silkworm cultivation of Japanese provinces.

The Industrial Revolution, like the European settlements in the Americas that began three centuries earlier, clearly had an epochal impact on global history—although one that separated regional, national, and continental levels of development and wealth. Although overall national rates of growth did not increase dramatically in the early years of the Industrial Revolution, productivity in the industrial sector grew significantly. Britain found it profitable to specialize in its mechanized sector and rely on imports for food and raw material. The rising population of industrial countries found employment in factory production. But population increases in countries that remained agricultural either brought stagnation of income or had to be supported by opening new tracts of land, whether in the grasslands, as in the Americas or Russia, or by extensive deforestation, above all in China since its medieval era, and Brazil more recently, but also in India and Europe. In China deforestation brought widespread soil erosion, flooding, changes in the great waterways of the country, and often vast misery and political weakening of the central state. In the Americas, whose pampas, forests, and prairies supported relatively few inhabitants in the sixteenth to the nineteenth centuries, the surging migration of Europeans brought great changes in property relations as settlers drove the earlier indigenous inhabitants off the lands the newcomers felt should be theirs for the taking.

2. This sad but widespread pattern of intercontinental ethnic exploitation introduces the second great focus of a world history course or research program, which focuses less on the common human interface with the constraints and opportunities of the physical world than on the interactions among peoples. This is the approach historians have taken to calling "entangled histories" (or in French, *histoires croisées*). Any course in global history must take account of the arrival of the Europeans in the New World, and the demographic havoc that weakened and eliminated many of the indigenous inhabitants even before they were conquered. Some American Indians referred to this epoch as "the great dying," as they were exposed to diseases for which they had no antibodies—smallpox (even more fatal for the Indians than Europeans) and perhaps measles. But this approach also follows the patterns of cultural diffusion, whether through war or peaceful interactions, coerced religious conversion, or the trading of artifacts and of foodstuffs and plants. The historian Alfred Crosley gave the term "Co-

lumbian Exchange" to the results of the European encounters with the New World, as the Europeans brought lethal pathogens but also the horse, while the peoples of the Western Hemisphere introduced Europeans (and via the Europeans, Ottomans and Asians) to chocolate and chili—they went from Mexico to India as well as Europe—tobacco, tea, coffee, and cane sugar (which soon was processed into molasses and rum and sold for high profits in Europe, and used in turn to buy the slaves in Africa whose labor kept the sugarcane plantations running).

The global historian understands that the development of commodities that created new mass consumption patterns also transformed the organization of labor systems needed to produce them. In the case of coffee, tobacco, sugar, and cotton—crops that thrived in tropical and semitropical conditions—that meant reviving a method of exploiting labor last prevalent in Mediterranean antiquity: the "latifundia," extensive plantations with slave populations. Slaves, often taken in war, then sold, remained a major feature of world history deep into the nineteenth century; and human trafficking and gang labor still persist even after the institution has supposedly been legally eliminated in most societies. But the mass capture of black slaves from African homelands and shipment (via horrendous sea voyages, which killed many en route) to Brazil, the West Indies and Cuba, and the North American colonies to raise sugar, coffee, tobacco, and eventually cotton under coercive gang labor was unique in its scale, scope, and combination of racial and plantation servitude. Sometimes theorized as a stage of production that preceded modern capitalism, African American slavery in fact was deeply integrated into a global merchant capitalist system. The plantations of the American South kept the mechanized factories of New England and British Lancashire in business. Only the mines of Latin America and conquered Africa operated with similar brutality. Not every profitable product had to rest on such an infrastructure of coerced labor, although the profits from these commodities helped to support more genteel trades, whether the important circulation of arms that every organized population wanted to possess or of artifacts prized on a global scale, in particular furniture, fine textiles, and porcelain.

We are left with one of the great questions of modern global history: why it was Europeans who took greatest advantage of constructing these highly profitable chains of chattel labor, ferrying irresistible commodities (sugar, tobacco, cotton) between the continents to the immense profit of those who could organize the links in the chain; shipping black prisoners from the West African coast to the semitropical areas of the New World; taking the sugar and its derivatives including rum, and later cotton, to the factories of the Atlantic temperate zone; and investing the profits in a new cycle of voyages. In contrast, the slave trade of the Black Sea area usually involved smaller numbers of men and women assigned as servants or sexual partners. And trade of commodities from South and Southeast Asia to China (including opium) and to Europe (textiles and, in the twentieth century, rubber) involved mass migration of labor in Southeast Asia and often plantation cultivation—but generally under some form of contract and not in chains. The innovations in long-distance navigation and sailing can be traced to many different cultures, but they were harnessed for private profit and state revenue increasingly for Western entrepreneurs. Many answers have been proposed: the particularly restless religions of the Europeans, aggravated perhaps by the rivalry between the recently fractured branches of Christendom; or perhaps it was the goad of state competition in Europe, as the weakening ideal of Christian empire yielded to the reality of ambitious dynastic states.

One of the abiding challenges of historical research arises from the very number of possibly valid explanations: political scientists tend to search for parsimonious explanations, but historians accept that outcomes may in fact not merely require many causes, but may be fundamentally overdetermined. On the other hand, in their eagerness to explain economic development, say, or political stability, or the approach of war, historians too often cite all relevant preexisting conditions—

habits, values, technologies, stratification, and so on—as causal, producing in effect thinly disguised just-so stories.

Lest it be thought that historical influences involve only economic connections or technologies, let me emphasize that any global history narrative recognizes that artistic styles and works, along with religious currents, have long constituted important intercivilizational links. From the third-century-BCE statues of the Buddha in northwestern India, Pakistan, and today's Afghanistan, whose draped robes evoke the Hellenistic styles that Alexander the Great's armies spread into the East, to the impact of Japanese woodcuts on late nineteenth-century French painting, artistic influences spread far and fast. While the western Chinese of the post-Han dynasties (c. 200–600) developed a taste for Roman sculpture, by the seventeenth century Europeans became fans of the fine white decorated porcelain that would be called china and for which they had not yet discovered the secrets of manufacturing. Chinese and Japanese artisans in the eighteenth century responded by producing the designs that Europeans favored. In a later era, sports reflected these exchanges: the British carried cricket to India, the Americans took baseball to Japan and Cuba. Music traveled as well. For instance, the Western orchestra and marching band adopted many of its instruments from Turkish military instruments during 300 years of warfare on the Balkan frontiers. And no one can go to a concert without noting that Asians have taken up Western music with skill and enthusiasm, just as many of the rhythms of reggae and other beats migrated to the West from Africa via the Caribbean.

~

3. The third major approach for global history is comparative or institutional. It uses history to investigate similarities in social and political organization among global societies, revealing what they share even as it allows for their unique features. Its narrative is generated not by, say, an overarching environmental or technological impact,

but by the social differentiation that all communities of a certain size seem to generate. Once human settlements adopted farming and cultivation—perhaps 7,000–8,000 years ago—they developed class distinctions. Military leadership, religious observance and/or aesthetic production, and agriculture became assigned to different individuals or families. Differing privileges came with these roles and produced remarkably similar hierarchies of prestige. Further differentiation generated ruling groups, which left written records. A global history concerned with the ancient world at, say, the turn of the "Common" or "Christian" era (a designation that is itself profoundly centered on Europe) will likely focus more on the commonality of institutional development—especially the extensive empires of China and Rome that emerged so powerfully in these centuries—than on the interactions between these systems so distant from each other. Jane Burbank and Frederick Cooper's massive history, *Empires in World History* (2010), starts with these huge societies, emerging in the same centuries, widely separated in space but both addressing issues of large-scale rule and governance over multiple peoples.

Major historical developments, naturally enough, shape institutions within individual societies even as they integrate them into international systems of exchange and interdependence, such as slave trading from the ancient world to the mid-nineteenth century. When elites derive their income and status from the extraction of income from agricultural producers by virtue of political control rather than market relations, the system is often designated as "feudal." Until the nineteenth or even twentieth century most states and empires had to rely on this system to ensure local administration and military recruitment. Consider, too, the economic arrangements we call capitalism— reliance on private entrepreneurs and investors to produce goods in return for their right to control technology, hire and fire employees, and retain profits. The historian can recount the emergence and subsequent modifications of this system in terms of comparative national institutions or as a transnational network that entails trade, international finance, and migration of labor. Of course variants of this system have emerged over time, and a global approach must explain why. American capitalism has sought to minimize the intervention of public authorities so long as profits are robust, whereas European mixed economies have tended to accept greater government redistribution and control.

But then the reader may ask: Do subjects such as these mean that world history is merely comparative history on a broad scale? The distinction is not absolute, indeed blurs at the margins, but the objectives, I believe, are different. Comparative historical research can focus on selected activities in two or three cases. Forty years ago, this author aspired to write comparative history and did a dissertation on political stabilization in post–World War I France, Germany, and Italy. World or global history, however, has to step outside a given region and usually involves a longer time period and sometimes a more encompassing theme. Alternatively, the reader can ask how the focus on social and political institutions or "structures" differs from the discipline of sociology. Major sociologists from the nineteenth century on have sought to understand how in given eras diverse societies organized their marriage and kinship patterns and their systems of production and distribution of goods; how, too, they controlled scarce water resources for irrigation, raised armies, provided for religious rites, and so forth. What then distinguishes the two intellectual enterprises? Is it just the department that votes the PhD? Again, the inquiries overlap; nonetheless the sociologist usually aspires to reveal underlying societal mechanisms or structures abstracted from their time and place, whereas the historian hopes to account for events immersed in a temporal context. Many sociologists have sought to explain the French Revolution as an instance of revolution in general, whereas the historian seeks to account for the specific French crisis of the late eighteenth century. Put simply, the historian has to explain not merely why, say, the Bolshevik revolution or the Nazi seizure of power occurred, but why they happened when they did, in 1917 and 1933, respectively. For the historian, no explanation of why is adequate without a consideration of when.

This implies further that historical explanation treats events as open ended. Some historians may describe events as inevitable, but only in the context of highly specified circumstances. For all the pre-conditions that might be present, they need not occur; and for all the times they seem unlikely, they can still take place: consider the abrupt collapse of European communist regimes in 1989. Historians have to analyze counterfactuals even when protesting that they do no such thing. Still, history and what is labeled historical sociology can overlap a good deal in analyzing macro-outcomes, as the analysis of premodern regimes illustrates. Both historians and sociologists, for example, have converged in the study of state development in the premodern world of 1500–1800 CE. This was an era in which monarchs and aristocracies often squared off over taxes and the costs of warfare. Some bureaucratic states succeeded in repressing popular protest and co-opting elite opposition, as did the capable rulers of seventeenth-century Prussia and France. A century later, however, the French monarchs had lost this capacity, first to an aristocratic defense of class privilege and then to a broad coalition of revolutionaries demanding human rights. In Britain during the same period, the elite subordinated the monarchy to its own oligarchical control, averting both absolutism and mass revolution. Elsewhere rulers sought the cooperation of regional elites with lucrative offices, as in Mughal India, but at the price of increasing sacrifices of central control. Successful Chinese dynasties won the service of administrative elites with a system of meritocratic honors, but over cycles of several centuries were unable to prevent landlord exploitation, peasant immiseration, foreign invasion, and the emperor's loss of legitimacy.

Global history becomes more demanding but narratively rich when the many constellations among supposedly sovereign units are taken into account. One constant of global history has been the failure of any single state to achieve a world-encompassing empire. There has

always been a multiplicity of units—today close to 200 in the UN—
that claim the quality of sovereignty or independence even if they accept entering alliances or even paying tribute to another power. All
these relationships, as well as their breakdown in times of war, comprise a good part of what we term international history. As it is used
today, the term international history tends to include many of the
themes described in the first two of the research agendas described
above, namely developments that confront the human community in
general and the interactions among different societies. Still, international history as a field tends to take the multiple units of sovereignty
as a baseline for research in a way that global history does not. That
said, scholars of global and international history alike have found a
common interest in the study of empire—until recently one of the
most recurrent efforts at global organization, even if its formal historical role may have ended or at least transformed into informal influence or regional organizations, such as the European Union.

Empires have certainly been with us since the beginning of settled
and differentiated political communities, and the prevalence of this
institution makes it a central thread of global history. Empires are
usually defined as large structures in which the elite of one people, defining itself by language, descent, or a shared history, rules other peoples, often after conquest. Empires, like other states, tend to emphasize
the need for military and executive power; they often are fighting at
their frontiers; they often propagate a universal value—whether religion (Christianity, Islam), or the idea of law, or economic development. Much of global history can be studied as the history of empires.
But they are not all alike. The most durable of empires, the Chinese,
rested on a great awareness of its ethnic cohesion and religious values;
but this did not prevent foreign peoples—Mongols in the twelfth and
thirteenth centuries, Manchus in the seventeenth through nineteenth—
from taking over the empire and fusing their sense of particularity
with the rich civilization they decided to manage. Some empires were
land based; they expanded by conquering neighboring territory: for

instance, the Roman, the Turkish or Ottoman Empire, the various empires in the Indian subcontinent before the British ruled, and the Aztec and Inca imperial federations. Others were seaborne—developing from oceanic networks of trade and commerce, and then often expanding into the hinterlands of their coastal enclaves: the Dutch, the British, and the Portuguese. The Spanish and the French developed overseas conquests from the beginning, and so did the United States (if only fitfully and for a brief period) and the Japanese.

On the other hand, world history asks us to take account of institutions that develop autonomously in many places. From one perspective, warfare is one of the true universals of the global community. It claims, justifiably, a large measure of attention. Still, in each of the three approaches that have been outlined here, we study the development of states and societies not primarily as contending units per se, but as communities responsive to common and underlying developments—the rise of religious teachings and organizations that enthuse millions of adherents across political borders; decisive transformations of technology, whether the stirrup and the plow, instruments of navigation, gunpowder, steam power, or recently the transistor and computer; the large migrations of ethnically related groups into territories already settled by others; the transmission of music and art and games.

When to Begin?

These considerations lead in turn to the issue that every historian must face: where to begin and where to end. What constitutes a historical era or epoch? Historians debate when historical eras can be said to begin and end because the dates follow from the developments they believe were fundamental in shaping any given interval of time. If we think it important to understand the development of the great world religions, then the long millennium and a half from 1000 BCE onward repays systematic scrutiny. This period was distinguished by Judeo-Christian development in the West and Hinduism, Buddhism, and Confucianism in Asia, and, by the seventh and eighth centuries CE, the rapid spread of Islam from the Middle East.

If the contact between East and West—between Asia, Europe, and the northern half of Africa—is of interest, then the period from about 400 BCE to 1200 CE might seem crucial. We know that the Mediterranean basin was an area of interchange and migration from the Phoenicians onward (c. 1100 BCE). Minoan civilization, with its Aegean and Greek settlements, predated 1000 BCE, as did the arrival of the Hebrews in today's Israel. Hellenistic and Roman expansion linked Asia and Europe for a thousand years from about 350 BCE to 750 CE. Sustained contacts around the Indian Ocean can be followed from the same era and continue into the twentieth century. Mayan civilization reached its classical period around 600–900 CE, but the development of empires and confederations in the Americas at that time was separate from European impact except in the far north, where the Scandinavians (Norsemen, Vikings) pushed to Greenland and the coasts of Newfoundland, having already established trading routes deep into Russia and conquering some of the rich provinces of Europe, including eastern England, Normandy, and Sicily. By this time there had long been trade across the Indian Ocean and around Southeast Asia; the Arabs had conquered North Africa and most of Spain between the death of Muhammad in 632 and their furthest incursion into today's France (up to the Loire) a century later. By 800 CE or so, three significant empires—the Carolingian, Byzantine, and Islamic—were all very aware of each other's presence; they traded and their rulers exchanged gifts. The Chinese had reestablished a powerful unitary empire under the Tang Dynasty. Organized African states and their focal sites, such as Timbuktu in the Mali Empire or the remnants of Great Zimbabwe, came to the attention of Europeans from the beginning of the sixteenth century, as did the sustained and devastating contacts of Europeans with Mesoamerican and Andean empires.

Hence, the fifteenth and sixteenth centuries offer another plausible beginning point for a treatment of global history, the era of transition in which political societies in different continents entered into continuing cumulative contact. This portal would include the great "discoveries" of Columbus and the "conquests" by Cortez, Pizarro, and other soldier-explorers. They also include the first circumnavigation of the world by Magellan, the growing recognition that the Americas form a vast continental landmass, and the realization by students of astronomy that the whole globe itself orbits the sun. Jesuit missionaries and scholars became active at the Ming court, while Portuguese and Dutch traders and religious orders established influential outposts at the edge of the Japanese islands. If a global history is to devote attention to the connections and intertwining of the world's major political units and civilizations, it must logically begin here. From the fifteenth and sixteenth centuries onward, the density of interactions, whether trade, warfare, or migration, will become an ever more compelling theme.

Nonetheless, the theme of encounters and interconnections is just one of the narrative threads that influence my own choice of a starting era. The seventeenth century also brought remarkable transitions within widely separated societies. The great empires created at the end of the Middle Ages—Ming and Mughal, Hapsburg, Muscovite, and Ottoman—all underwent transformative crises in the seventeenth and eighteenth centuries. Within their institutional carapaces, new principles of ethnic loyalty and revised religious legitimation emerged, as did powerful new political units outside their imperial frontiers—preeminently the nation-states of the modern era, including our own. Experimental science and reflections on the role of national political economy, bold philosophies that cast loose from conventional religious justifications, all opened up the mental frameworks that we identify with Western modernity. We know how inconsistent these attainments were. Still, they suggest the appropriateness of a later starting point and a focus on comparative institutions and economic development as much as "exchanges." Indeed, global historians now set the Western developments into a framework of "multiple modernities."

For pedagogic purposes, I try for a compromise framework—first a brief introduction to the conquests and exchanges among the world empires in 1500 to convey a sense of interconnectedness in terms of commodity exchange and intellectual influences; then a more intense scrutiny of institutional development, focusing on the political conflicts (exacerbated by climatological adversity) that gripped so much of Europe and China, for instance, in the mid-seventeenth century; and thereafter an examination of the recovery and stabilization of aristocratic cultures by the mid-1700s and their revolutionary transformation another 50–100 years later. Underlying much of the changes were profound alterations of landownership and agrarian hierarchies as commercial rents, tax burdens, and the advent of market relations (and indebtedness) undermined traditional elites and hierarchies in Europe, South Asia, and Latin America—a development sometimes downplayed by historians—and spanning the mid-eighteenth to mid-nineteenth centuries.

Other teachers and scholars might postpone their entry into global history until the Industrial Revolution and the renewed impact of Europeans or Americans in the Pacific, but the contours of technology, new liberal and revolutionary ideologies, and of capitalism seem already well in place by then. It seems to me that the great encounters between widely separated peoples, the shock of recognition and the temptations of exploitation these encounters produced, the rivalries created in a newly explored globe, the patterns of long-distance commodity and labor transfer, and the explosive progressive growth of science and technology offer the most appropriate points at which we can feasibly plunge into the ongoing stream of events.

A case, too, can be made for beginning as late as the twentieth century and returning to a historical agenda that again treats humanity as a whole. Contemporary issues, above all the destructiveness of war and mass violence; the intensity of investment, trade, and the internationalization of economic institutions that once remained largely within borders, such as the modern corporation; and the accumulating impacts of large-scale environmental change, today militate for historical programs that once again take the species as a whole, indeed as one species in a fragile ecosystem. A new sense of shared vulnerability thus sends today's historians back to the idea of global unity that eighteenth-century writers derived from abstract philosophical commitments. They do so knowing that economic crises, say, or the spread of violence within states, or the mutations of pathogens, will not merely tug at their sympathies but can ravage their own local communities. Nonetheless, we find ourselves, as does every era, in the middle of our own modernity.

The "Uses" of Global History

When Schiller lectured on universal history, it was possible for the West to seem "universal." It embodied values that appeared to Europeans and Euro-Americans self-evidently valid for the species as a whole. Other cultural experiences were intriguing and picturesque but for those very reasons less crucial. When Hegel a generation later delivered his lectures on the philosophy of history, his attitude was perhaps even more confident. He understood there were great civilizations in Asia, but to him they lacked dimensions of freedom and cultural attainment that Western, and in particular Christian and Protestant Christian, societies developed. When historians at the beginning of the twentieth century discussed development, they assigned a hierarchy as well, but based on race and evolution, not on religion. And indeed when Harvard University began a General Education program after World War II, its designers assumed that the values that the United States and Great Britain had fought for claimed a certain moral and political preeminence. During the Cold War this conviction was extended to economic and political organization.

But in the age of the global, in a century by whose end China and India may well be as wealthy and powerful as the European Union and the United States, such a teleological view cannot serve as the basis for historical understanding. This does not mean one cannot appreciate the values—civic, religious, moral, and economic—of the society within which one has come of age. Neither does the study of global history require teacher or student to accept a slush of moral relativism. Values can be maintained—but as scholars and as teachers we cannot claim that historical processes somehow validate or credential the values we cherish. General Education in a new age makes no presuppositions of higher and lower levels of civilization. And in fact, there has been a robust tradition represented by European thinkers such as Montaigne and Montesquieu that insists on understanding the multiple claims of truth. Montaigne looked around at the massacres carried out in the wars of religion and asked why his countrymen held cannibals in such contempt. Montesquieu wrote one of the great texts, *The Persian Letters,* in which visitors from Iran asked whether the treatment of women was any less degraded in Paris than in the bondage of the seraglio. This universalist tradition continued to inform the great anthropologists, including most eminently the late Claude Lévi-Strauss, whose work emphasized the complex attainments of so-called primitive art and thought. I assign texts such as theirs as my own ideological starting point for any inquiry into a genuine global history.

No single scholar can claim expertise in global history. All that he or she can do is suggest what a lively and curious intellect might find worthwhile to ask in light of the state of today's knowledge and today's public concerns. For history, local and global, is indeed entitled, and expected, to provide a mode of orientation. For some readers, history might satisfy as a source of the picturesque and the interesting, or as the study of "real people," supposedly just like us—or alternatively as a catalog of horrors to be avoided. It remains the conviction of this teacher that history instructs best not by simplifying, but by revealing how complex institutions are and how surprisingly events can develop or run awry. Policymakers look to history for a storehouse of analogies and case studies. They are entitled to seek some useful guidelines, but the analogies will always remain imperfect, useful to illustrate at best one plausible outcome among many. In what sense if any, then, can history be said to have a use? Well, even if we cannot rely on similarities to predict outcomes, we can use them to understand multiple possibilities. Historians love to cite the quote: "The past is another country." But the past is just as truly our country, revealing to us motivations, ambitions and conflicts, hierarchies and utopias that are our own. Otherwise they would remain profoundly unknowable to a degree that would frustrate all efforts at historical recovery.

Perhaps a personal note is an appropriate way to conclude an introduction that endeavors to set out a personal vision of what I hope to achieve. I have come to global history late in my career, after investigating modern Germany and Europe, international relations, the United States' role in the world, and the impacts of war, the Holocaust, and economic catastrophe. It has been a new venture—and from the viewpoint of teaching, the most difficult to date because of the sheer volume of new information students confront. Teaching a course like this is not the same as doing the focused historical investigations that occupy whatever little research time the modern university allows. Still, introducing global history strikes me as imperative for historical teaching today given the developments we as citizens, as well as students, must experience—the readjustment of American power and wealth, the migrations of new citizens, the clamorous challenges of inequality and environmental fragility. A generation ago, scholars, teachers, and activists called for history to provide us with a usable past, by which they meant, in effect, a version of our own past and our own traditions designed to sustain satisfaction with our gender or racial identity or political commitment. In today's world, this self-regarding objective, no matter how compelling it might earlier have seemed, no longer suffices, and understanding other pasts—which are not always so alien—is just as urgent and inviting. Recall an older traveler, Tennyson's aging Ulysses:

> Much have I seen and known; cities of men
> And manners, climates, councils, governments . . .
> How dull it is to pause, to make an end,
> To rust unburnish'd, not to shine in use . . .
> Come my friends, 'Tis not too late to seek a newer world . . .

Sometimes the newer world is an older one too.

Further Reading

The reader who wants to pursue further study of global history can take several different routes. General syntheses are relatively few, but there are many studies of particular aspects, often comparisons of economic development or such widespread phenomena as imperialism. For a fine overall survey of diverse approaches, resources, and the history of the field in its own right as of almost a decade ago, see Patrick Manning, *Navigating World History: Historians Create a Global Past* (New York: Palgrave Macmillan, 2003). Manning, who began his career as a historian of Africa, is one of the major American practitioners.

The field's major English-language scholarly periodicals include the *Journal of World History,* published semiannually from 1990 and then quarterly since 2003 by the University of Hawaii Press, and the *Journal of Global History,* published three times a year since 2006 by Cambridge University Press for the London School of Economics. These publications include general theoretical articles as well as specific studies in comparative history.

Earlier approaches to world history reflected particular methods and approaches. I cite in the text the reflections of Ibn Khaldūn (1332–1406), whose *The Muqaddimah: An Introduction to History* has been most recently published by Princeton University Press in 2005 (translated and introduced by Franz Rosenthal, abridged and edited by N. J. Dawood, and with a new introduction by Bruce B. Lawrence). Arnold Toynbee's twelve-volume *A Study of*

History (New York: Oxford University Press, 1934–1961), with several subsequent abridgments, tracked the rise and decline of individual regions by applying a causal model of challenge and response. But it did not attempt a synoptic history of global regions simultaneously. Marxist-derived critiques of imperialism offered an implicit view of unequal global development and helped prompt Immanuel Wallerstein's three-volume history *The Modern World System* (New York: Academic Press, 1974–1989), covering the period from 1600 to the mid-1840s. If interested in economic approaches to world history, the reader can also tackle the monumental three-volume study by the late, great French historian Fernand Braudel: *Civilization and Capitalism, 15th–18th Century,* trans. Siân Reynolds (New York: Harper & Row, 1982–1984; Berkeley: University of California Press, 1992).

Focusing on politics, exemplary recent syntheses include Jane Burbank and Frederick Cooper's vast work, *Empires in World History* (Princeton, NJ: Princeton University Press, 2010), and Christopher Alan Bayly's *The Birth of the Modern World: 1780–1914: Global Connections and Comparisons* (Malden, MA: Blackwell, 2004), a large-scale pioneering effort with a full Asian focus as befits a notable historian of the British empire in India. Jürgen Osterhamel, a German historian of China's interactions with Europe, has written an epic synthesis of global history in the nineteenth century—still in German only—*Die Verwandlung der Welt* [The Transformation of the World] (Munich: Beck Verlag, 2010) but currently being translated by Princeton University Press. Kenneth Pomeranz, another historian of China, has written a notable and provocative effort to compare British and Chinese economies at the dawn of industrialization, *The Great Divergence: China, Europe and the Making of the Modern World Economy* (Princeton, NJ: Princeton University Press, 2000), and along with Edmund Burke III, a historian of North Africa, has edited *The Environment and World History* (Berkeley: University of California Press, 2009). It is noteworthy that these recent major contributions are the works of specialists in non-Western history who perhaps have responded to the impulse to establish their regions on a par of historical importance and interest for a readership often content to remain enclosed in their more familiar fields.

For a narrative of individual regions in the contemporary era, see J. A. S. Grenville, *A History of the World in the 20th Century,* rev. ed. (Cambridge, MA: Harvard University Press, 2000).

John R. McNeill, an environmental historian, and his father, William H. McNeill, have coauthored *The Human Web: A Bird's-Eye View of World History* (New York: W. W. Norton & Co., 2003).

The UNESCO *History of Humanity: Scientific and Cultural Development*, 7 vols. (New York: Routledge, 1994–2008) enlisted a large number of researchers to cover world cultural and political developments from prehistory through the twentieth century (my own contributions include chapters 1–3 of volume 7, on the twentieth century).

For the examples of European but non-Eurocentric social theory cited in the essay, there are convenient new editions of Charles de Secondat, Baron de Montesquieu's *Persian Letters*, trans. Margaret Mauldon, ed. Andrew Kahn (New York: Oxford University Press, 2008); Michel de Montaigne's *The Essays: A Selection*, trans. M. A. Screech (London: Penguin, 2004) and *The Complete Works*, trans. Donald M. Frame (New York: A. A. Knopf, 2003); and Claude Lévi-Strauss's autobiographical *Tristes Tropiques*, trans. John Weightman and Doreen Weightman (New York: Penguin, 1992).

Medical Detectives

Karin B. Michels

Public health has been relevant since ancient times and remains very much so today. Concerns about deadly flu epidemics, about the consequences of the worldwide rise in obesity, and about the presence of environmental toxins and pollutants in the air we breathe, the food we eat, and the products we use are omnipresent. Moreover, ubiquitous travel has made the world a smaller place and has profoundly influenced the rapidity with which disease can spread, substantially increasing the danger that epidemics may become pandemics. In the current epoch, however, we know more about the causes, vectors, and treatments of diseases than were known, for instance, in the times of the Great Plagues such as the Black Death in the fourteenth century, which killed millions of people especially in Europe, so public health can be a science, rather than just a "concern."

The mission of public health professionals is to keep the world a healthy place: to curb epidemics, to prevent human illnesses, and to maintain human health. At the heart of public health, epidemiology uses frequencies and distributions of data to understand possible threats of disease outbreaks and to find determinants of diseases in humans. The ultimate goal of epidemiologic research is the prevention or effective control of human disease. The aims of this chapter are to convey appreciation for the challenges of public health; to provide an introduction to the basic concepts of risk factors, risk prediction, and risk prevention in public health; to discuss how epidemiologists work like medical detectives to uncover the causes of acute disease outbreaks and chronic diseases; and to delineate how studies in epidemiologic research are conducted, what possible study designs can be used, and what biases may threaten the validity of such studies.

A Cholera Outbreak in London:
Detective Work of the First Epidemiologist

In 1854 Queen Victoria's anesthesiologist, Dr. John Snow, set out to solve the mystery of a very severe cholera outbreak in London (Snow 1855, 1936). Within ten days it had claimed the lives of 500 people in the inner city of London (Figure 7), the most populous city in the world at that time. The etiology of cholera was not known, nor was its mode of transmission. For instance, in New York City the Board of Health advised "sleep and clothe warm, do not sleep or sit in a draught of air, be temperate in eating and drinking, avoid raw vegetables and unripe fruit, and avoid getting wet" (Woodhull 1849). Respected physician Dr. William Farr believed that cholera was carried by polluted air. One of the first medical statisticians of his time, he compiled statistical evidence to prove his theory by demonstrating that the likelihood of dying from cholera was linked to the height at which one lived above the River Thames (Eyler 2001; Bingham et al. 2004). He interpreted this as support for the "miasmic" theory, suggesting that the air at lower altitudes was polluted.

In the meantime, Dr. John Snow used a different approach to solve the mystery of transmission. In meticulous detective work, Snow went from house to house, recording the number of deaths and date of death from cholera and collecting information about one factor he suspected might give valuable clues about the origins of the outbreak: the drinking water sources. Snow had soon compiled a map that revealed some interesting distributions, and for his pioneer work he is now considered to have been one of the first epidemiologists (Tufte 1997). The area of the highest mortality rates encircled Broad Street and its water pump. Snow reported, "nearly all the deaths had taken place within a short distance of the pump" (Snow 1855). For each person who died in that area, Snow tried to ascertain from relatives whether the victim had consumed water from the Broad Street pump. But what about deaths in more distant locations, near other pumps? Snow traveled to

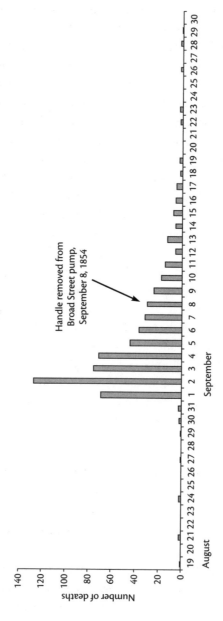

Figure 7. Daily deaths from cholera in the city of London during the 1854 epidemic.

those places to collect more information. A widow in the West End had come to like the taste of the water from the well on Broad Street so much that she sent her maid every day to fetch a big bottle. Several children drank water from the Broad Street pump on their way to school. But why did only five people die at a workhouse that employed 535 people at the epicenter of the epidemic? Based on Snow's observations, if the mortality in the workhouse had been similar to that in the surrounding area, at least 100 people would have died. Snow found that the building had its own well. And why did none of the workers from the brewery on Broad Street die? Snow discovered that beer was free in the brewery, so why would the employees drink water?

Dr. Snow's suggestions that cholera was spread through water and that the Broad Street pump was contaminated were met with great skepticism by the Board of Health. However, he was eventually permitted to remove the handle of the Broad Street pump. It has never been resolved whether the subsequent decline in cholera deaths was indeed due to the closing of the contaminated well, or whether the epidemic simply subsided as Londoners fled the city. At the very least, however, Dr. Snow correctly concluded that cholera was transmitted through water, not air. Removing the handle from the Broad Street pump is an example of a public health intervention implemented without knowledge of the cause of the disease. The bacterium *Vibrio cholerae* was discovered a few years later.

Modern Epidemics: Who Is Going to Catch the Bug?

Epidemics are cyclic. Like cholera, which returned as outbreaks and pandemics in irregular intervals throughout the nineteenth and twentieth centuries, influenza pandemics occur with a certain frequency (Morse 2007; Fauci 2006). Typically, 500,000 lives are claimed worldwide every year by the flu. Influenza pandemics occur when a new strain of the influenza virus is transmitted to humans from another animal species. These novel strains are unaffected by any immunity people may have to older strains of human influenza and can therefore spread extremely rapidly and infect very large numbers of people. The Spanish flu in 1918 was the most serious pandemic in recent history and claimed the lives of an estimated 50 million people worldwide. Flu pandemics have emerged at regular intervals. Based on past patterns, a new influenza pandemic may strike within the next few years. While the avian influenza (H5N1) and subsequently the swine flu (H1N1) were tapped as candidates for the new influenza pandemic, fortunately neither rose to this dimension.

How do infectious disease epidemiologists predict how dangerous a new type of influenza is? Besides the virus subtype (classified by two large glycoproteins on the outside of the viral particles, H and N) and severity of the illness it causes (how life threatening it is), the most important characteristics of a new type of flu are the "basic reproduction number" and the relation between the "incubation" and "latency" periods. The basic reproduction number indicates the average number of secondary infectious cases directly infected by a single infectious case during the entire infectious period—in other words, how many people become sick (and infectious themselves) due to exposure to a single infected person (Mills et al. 2004). Only if this number is greater than 1 can the disease spread. The incubation period is the time between infection and clinical onset (appearance of symptoms) of the disease, and the latent period is the time between infection and infectiousness. If the latent period is shorter than the incubation period (i.e., infectiousness precedes symptoms), the infection is likely to spread. Infectious diseases that do not spread prior to symptoms have a much better prognosis for control and generally do not develop into epidemics or pandemics because people who feel ill tend to voluntarily reduce contact with others (or can be convinced to do so), and healthy people tend to practice better hygiene and other preventative measures when around noticeably sick (symptomatic) individuals. Influenza and HIV infections are examples of diseases that are infectious before symptoms appear, making them prone to become epidemics (Mills et al. 2004; Anderson and May 1979). Conversely, severe acute respiratory syndrome (SARS) was not infectious before symptoms appeared, explaining at least in part why preventive efforts were successful in averting a pandemic (Wallinga and Teunis 2004).

In the meantime, everybody is concerned about catching the bug that causes serious illness. Preventive measures such as regular hand washing (the cornerstone of public health) and asking infected individuals to stay home reduce the spread of many infectious diseases.

Virus in the Limelight: The Human Papillomavirus

Some cancers are also spread via infection. The human papillomavirus (HPV) is a necessary cause of cervical cancer and has recently received a great deal of attention. Cervical cancer is the second leading cause of death from cancer among women worldwide. Mortality from cervical cancer has declined over 70 percent in developed countries since the introduction of Papanicolaou smear-based screening in the 1950s. The screening test developed by Greek physician Dr. Georgios Papanikolaou aims to detect and allow the treatment of potentially premalignant changes in cervical tissue. Despite its poor sensitivity (about 50 percent), it is a highly successful screening program because it is repeated annually or biennially (Koss 1989). The Pap smear is a classic example of a public health intervention that was highly effective without the identification of the actual cause of the disease. HPV was identified as the causal agent of cervical cancer only thirty years later by German physician Dr. Harald zur Hausen, who in 2008 was awarded the Nobel Prize for his discovery (Dürst et al. 1983).

One reason HPV is receiving a lot of attention is its high prevalence, 25 to 30 percent in women and men between fourteen and sixty years of age, which results in a high opportunity for infection with this sexually transmitted virus (Dunne et al. 2007). The lifetime cumulative incidence of HPV infection in the sexually active population is 80 to 90 percent. While the virus is eliminated from the body within less than two years in 80 percent of infections, persistent infections are fostered in older individuals and those with compromised immune function

Prevalence and incidence of infections with the human papillomavirus

	HPV infections (%)	Reference
Prevalence (ages 14 to 60 years)	25–30	Dunne et al. 2007
Lifetime cumulative incidence	80–90	Michels and zur Hausen 2009
Clearance rate within 2 years	80	Stanley 2006

(Stanley 2006); see table. HPV is an example of a necessary but not sufficient cause: an HPV infection is necessary to develop cervical cancer, but many women with HPV infections do not develop cervical cancer. While a persistent infection fosters the development of cancer, researchers are trying to identify other factors that make an HPV infection more likely to cause cervical cancer.

An efficient way to curb an epidemic is to develop a vaccine. The discovery of HPV allowed the development of the HPV vaccine. Before a vaccine can be applied for population prevention strategies, its safety and efficacy have to be tested. Large randomized trials were conducted to determine whether vaccinated individuals were less likely to become infected with HPV than those who were not vaccinated. Only girls and young women from the ages of eleven to twenty-six (the target group for the vaccine) have been included in these studies, and whether women who were vaccinated were actually less likely to develop cervical cancer has not been tested. Trials to date have suggested that the two available HPV vaccines substantially reduce the incidence of new infections with the HPV types that are most frequently found in cervical cancer and in genital warts, and also reduce premalignant lesions (Ault and the Future II Study Group 2007; Paavonen et al. 2009). At least in the short term, the vaccine seems safe. Will the HPV vaccine reduce the incidence of cervical cancer? A large reduction in cervical cancer mortality in the developed world is unlikely, because Pap smear screening (and possibly HPV testing) will continue to pick up a large proportion of early-stage cervical lesions and therefore continue to prevent invasive cervical cancer in most patients. However, much painful preventive treatment can be avoided by getting the vaccine. Moreover, in the developing world, HPV vaccines could reduce cervical cancer incidence and mortality substantially, though these populations have insufficient resources to afford the vaccine on a large scale.

If our ultimate goal is to eliminate the HPV virus altogether, it is not sufficient to vaccinate girls and young women. The age range would have to be expanded to all sexually active women, and boys and men would have to be included in the vaccine program (Michels and zur Hausen 2009). Other vaccine programs, such as those for polio or smallpox, were applied on a population basis with the goal to eradicate the virus. Population-wide public health programs (e.g., public water supply fluoridation to prevent tooth decay and folic acid fortification of staple foods to prevent neural tube defects in unborn children) need to weigh benefits and risks for the population and often cannot account for the needs and wants of the individual, which opens complex moral, political, and religious morasses. Conversely, public health programs targeting individuals generally have little effect on the health of the population as a whole.

Why the Finns Do Not Drink but Die and the French Drink but Do Not Die: Lessons from Different Study Designs

A successful public health prevention program requires knowledge of factors that may increase the likelihood of maintaining health or developing disease. Several different study types can be employed to gain a better understanding of such risk factors. Which study type is most appropriate depends on the question at hand; each study type has its own set of strengths and weaknesses.

Initial explorations of the relation between a suspected risk factor and a disease may include examining their correlations across several countries (Armstrong and Doll 1975). For example, plotting estimated alcohol consumption per capita and death rates from coronary heart disease (CHD) against each other reveals that the population of Finland has low alcohol consumption but very high mortality from CHD. Conversely, the French have a high consumption of alcoholic beverages but one of the lowest death rates from CHD (LaPorte et al. 1980). What can we learn from these observations? Such ecological studies suggest that alcohol consumption may reduce the risk of dying from heart disease. But this picture could be distorted by other lifestyle factors correlated with alcohol consumption and also with CHD mortality. The Finns have a high consumption of saturated fat, which is associated with a high risk of heart disease, and the French have a diet rich in vegetable oil and fresh fruits and vegetables, which are associated with a low risk of heart disease—although the French do like their butter, too. So are these other dietary factors, rather than alcohol consumption, truly responsible for the differences in heart disease mortality? If so, they would confound the association between alcohol and CHD mortality. And then there is Japan: the Japanese do not drink much alcohol and they do not die from CHD! This observation confirms that the story is not straightforward and that other factors may play important roles in influencing or confounding the association of interest. A confounder is a third variable that is associated with the risk factor or exposure of interest and is itself a risk factor for the disease. We can think of many factors that fulfill these conditions and can therefore distort the association of interest. Our goal is, therefore, to exclude the influence of confounders. To do this we would need data on the individual level. And we need to be able to measure the potential confounders. We can then eliminate their influence statistically by holding their level constant in so-called regression models (which allow for the simultaneous adjustment of many confounding variables).

International correlation studies can only provide interesting leads for potential associations, which subsequently need to be examined more carefully using other study types that allow linkage of individual data. Correlation studies are based on aggregated data, which do not, by their nature, contain any information about whether it is the particular individuals who do not consume alcohol who have CHD. This is because the researchers have to use indirect measures, such as data on the production, import, and export of alcohol in each country, to estimate national per capita alcohol consumption, irrespective of age or individual preference; similarly, they have only the overall number of individuals who died in that country from CHD, but no data on their individual diets or other behaviors. Potential confounding factors (those that may be associated with both alcohol consumption and CHD mortality) may distort the association and may have created a spurious correlation (Gordis 2009, 251–256).

Similarly, there is an ecological correlation between per capita dietary fat intake and breast cancer mortality (Carroll 1975). Fat disappearance data—which are based on production, import, and export but which do not account for waste, animal feed, and other uses—are used to estimate per capita fat intake, and these numbers are high in industrialized countries such as the United States and much of Europe, as is breast cancer mortality. Fat disappearance is low in developing countries in Southeast Asia and some South American countries, and breast cancer mortality is also low. However, confounding factors such as the gross national product (the value of all goods and services produced in a country), which is correlated with both fat disappearance and breast cancer mortality, may have created a spurious association. Indeed, when the association between total dietary fat intake and the risk of breast cancer was followed up in more detailed studies with specific information based on individuals (instead of indirectly estimated on a per capita basis), and a clear time sequence (measuring fat intake of participants prior to a diagnosis of breast cancer), no association was found (Hunter et al. 1996). The correlation between alcohol consumption and a reduced risk for CHD, when studied at the individual level, however, turned out to be robust (Stampfer et al. 1988).

Other study types that could be used to address the question of whether alcohol consumption affects the risk of CHD and whether fat intake affects breast cancer mortality are the case-control study and the cohort study. In a retrospective case-control study, individuals with the disease (the cases, e.g., those with CHD) and without the disease (the controls) are identified. All participants are then asked about their exposure to the risk factor (e.g., to recall their alcohol consumption during the past year). There are two main difficulties with this design. First, it is very difficult to select controls in an unbiased way. The purpose of the controls is merely to provide information on the exposure distribution (e.g., alcohol consumption) that the cases (those with CHD) would have had if they had not contracted the disease. Therefore we must select controls who would also have been selected as cases had they contracted the disease. If the selection of controls is inadvertently influenced by any factor related to the presence of the exposure, the study results are biased; we call this selection bias. The other tricky issue with retrospective studies is that many cases may be influenced by their awareness of their disease in what they report, that is, they may over- or underreport their exposure to the risk factor (in this case, alcohol consumption). This bias is termed recall bias (more about this below).

In a prospective cohort study, a population of disease-free individuals is identified, their exposure status is assessed, and they are followed until a certain number of them develop the disease of interest. This allows us to draw some conclusions; however, since the exposed and the unexposed may differ in other factors, confounding may again threaten the validity of our study. In a well-controlled study, as many confounders as possible are also measured and their influence is statistically eliminated.

Do You Have to Throw Out That Plastic Bottle?
How to Design a Study for a Specific Question of Interest

It has been all over the media: some data from animal studies and from a cross-sectional study in humans have suggested that a chemical called bisphenol A (BPA), which is found in hard plastics such as water bottles, may negatively affect health. BPA belongs to a class of chemicals called endocrine disruptors that interfere with the body's hormone system. Possible health effects of BPA range from developmental and reproductive problems to cardiovascular disease and diabetes. BPA is released from polycarbonate plastic bottles, which are so convenient to take everywhere and use during sports because they are light and difficult to break. How can we find out whether the BPA in the plastic actually gets into our bodies? We design an intervention study: we line up Harvard College students, provide them with stainless steel bottles, and ask them to drink all cold liquids from these bottles and avoid hard plastic bottles. After one week we ask them to provide a urine sample, and we measure the BPA concentration in their urine. Then we provide the students with polycarbonate plastic bottles and ask them to drink all their cold liquids from these bottles for one week. At the end of that week we take another urine sample. Indeed, the BPA concentrations in the urine have increased by two-thirds (Carwile et al. 2009). Concerned about that plastic bottle?

In intervention studies, individuals are assigned to a particular exposure of interest. One factor is changed in the study participants' lives. An intervention study can include a control group, or it can be conducted as a crossover study like the bottle study, in which participants are first assigned to one intervention and then cross over to the other intervention, one of which is the control, or comparison, intervention. The most common type of intervention study is the randomized clinical trial, in which two groups of participants are randomized to either an active intervention or a control intervention (Gordis 2009, 131–146). Since people are allocated to the intervention and the control group in a random fashion, the two groups are—if the sample is sufficiently large—equal in all characteristics other than the intervention, avoiding the problem of confounding. The randomized clinical trial is particularly useful to determine the effectiveness of treatments such as therapeutic drugs. Many drug trials in the United States are placebo controlled, because the Food and Drug Administration requires placebo comparisons for market approval of a new medication. This requirement is in conflict with the Declaration of Helsinki, the ethical code developed by the World Medical Association that governs the conduct of human research and proscribes the use of placebo if another effective treatment is already available (Rothman and Michels 1994).

Is Margarine or Butter Worse for Your Health?
How Confusing Scientific Evidence Gets Generated

Why is there confusion about whether margarine or butter is worse for your health? One day researchers say margarine is less bad. The next, it seems, butter is the lesser of the evils. How do we know what constitutes a healthy diet? Evidence comes from large population-based studies, with the most valid data derived from prospective cohort studies (Willett 2008). It is not sufficient to evaluate a food's or nutrient's contribution to health solely on the basis of its constituents or biochemical properties. How a food or nutrient affects health has to be evaluated in the context of its interactions with other dietary components and the metabolic complexities of the human body. A good epidemiologic study of diet and disease will look for associations between the incidence of disease and dietary patterns (e.g., high or low consumption of foods or food groups such as vegetables, or nutrients such as saturated fat), while also controlling for other biological factors (e.g., age, sex, other health conditions) and other behavioral factors (e.g., exercise and smoking); genetics and environmental exposures (exposure to air pollution, for instance) may also influence the association between diet and health, so optimally these types of data would also be collected.

For the study of diet and disease, retrospective case-control studies are not appropriate, because study participants who have the disease under study (cases) and study participants who do not have the disease (controls) are asked to report their past dietary habits. The recall or reporting by cases is likely influenced by their awareness of their disease: a woman with breast cancer may associate her disease with having consumed too much fat; a man with hypertension attributes his high blood pressure to having consumed too much salt—both are likely to overreport the frequency of consumption of foods considered less healthy. Conversely, foods considered healthy, such as fruits and vegetables or whole-grain products, are likely to be underreported by the cases. Controls may report their diet more accurately than the cases do—or they may overreport dietary habits considered to be healthy in what is called "social desirability bias" (they want to look good to the interviewer). These differences in reporting result in differential misclassification: the cases are incorrectly classified as having consumed more fat or more salt than they actually have (and possibly the controls as having consumed less)—and a spurious association can emerge. Randomized clinical trials are similarly inappropriate to study the effects of diet on health—unless the study is short and all meals are provided. In most studies, however, the long-term effect of diet is of interest. Randomizing humans to a particular diet is difficult. Although participants may initially agree to maintain whatever diet is allocated to them, over an extended time period (possibly years, depending on the study) most find it hard to change their habits and personal preferences. In the recent Women's Health Initiative study, postmenopausal women who initially consumed 38 percent of calories from fat were randomly assigned to either continue their diet unchanged or to adopt a diet containing about 20 percent of calories from fat—a drastic change (Prentice et al. 2006). This dietary regimen was to be followed for eight years to evaluate the effect of total fat intake on breast cancer risk. Participants received counseling from dieticians on how to prepare their meals. However, neither group adhered to their assigned diet: individuals randomized to continue their usual diet started consuming less fat because they were participating in a research study and were aware of its goals; women assigned to the low-fat arm of the trial could not keep up the dramatically altered diet and fell back into their previous habits. Thus the contrast diminished, and it remained unclear whether a meaningful difference in total fat intake persisted in the two groups at the end of follow-up. At the conclusion of the trial, breast cancer incidence rates did not differ in the two groups, rendering the results uninterpretable (Michels and Willett 2009). The prospective cohort study (where dietary habits in healthy individuals are simply measured, rather than assigned) remains the gold standard for the study of diet and disease.

What Is Your Risk of Developing Diabetes?
Using Results from Large Population-Based Studies
for Inferences about the Risk to the Individual

Mostly, we are interested in our own risk of developing a certain disease. Large observational studies, however, ask whether a risk factor increases or decreases the risk for a specific disease in the population studied. This question is answered based on the distribution of the data. Population means are compared: is the mean homocysteine level in the blood significantly higher among men who subsequently suffer a myocardial infarction than among men who do not? Categories of risk factors are compared: Do women with a birth weight of 4 kg or above have a significantly higher risk of developing breast cancer later in life than women with a birth weight of 2.5 kg or below? Do college students who listen to iPods five hours a day have a significantly higher risk of hearing loss than college students who never listen to iPods? Distributions seen in data sets enable us to make predictions and develop probabilistic associations for populations, but they allow only limited inferences regarding the individual. While the probability of developing breast cancer is higher among women with high birth weights, not every woman with a birth weight above 4 kg will develop breast cancer. Nevertheless, we can use the results from observational studies that control for confounding variables and minimize other biases to construct models to predict an individual's risk of developing a disease over a certain period of time, for example the next five years.

So, what is your risk of developing diabetes? A risk prediction model takes into account your age, gender, history of high blood sugar, height and weight, consumption of whole grains, refined carbohydrates, and vegetable oils, your alcohol intake, cigarette smoking, physical activity, family history of diabetes, and ethnicity ("Your Disease Risk" 2007–2010). For each of these variables the model integrates the information obtained from the population-based studies: individuals at the high end of the physical activity distribution were at the low end of the diabetes-risk distribution, and so on. Based on your values for these factors, the model will tell you whether your risk of developing diabetes is very high, high, average, low, very low, and so forth. Often a risk prediction is made compared to a person with the same gender and age: "Compared to a typical woman your age, your risk for diabetes is very much below average" ("Your Disease Risk" 2007–2010).

How Many Lives Could Be Saved by Banning French Fries? The Promise of Population-Based Intervention Programs

Public health intervention programs may be implemented on a population basis or may target subgroups of the population at particularly high risk. Water fluoridation to prevent dental decay, folate fortification of flour, rice, and grain products to prevent neural tube defects in newborns, and vitamin A and D fortification of milk are population-based prevention programs. When weighing the risks and benefits of an intervention program, one relevant question is the number of lives that can be saved or illnesses that can be prevented. The number of lives saved or illnesses prevented must be large enough to justify the intervention, especially if it is to be implemented on a population-wide basis and does not specifically target high-risk groups. The "attributable risk" helps public health professionals decide which intervention programs will be most successful. The population-attributable risk estimates how many cases of disease or death can be avoided by eliminating a particular risk factor or by adding a protective factor (Hennekens and Buring 1987).

A recent population-based public health intervention program has targeted trans-fatty acids. Trans fats are generated when normally liquid vegetable oils are artificially hardened. This hardening process is used to manufacture margarine, to make French fries and cookies crisp, and to extend the shelf life of many bakery and other products. The resulting artificial trans-fatty acids substantially increase the risk for cardiovascular disease and CHD death, because they increase the bad cholesterol (LDL) and decrease the good cholesterol (HDL) in the blood (Ascherio and Willett 1997). The New York City Department of Health (2005) has been exemplary, making New York the first city in the United States to ban artificial trans fats from restaurants. This drastic program intervenes on the level of the food provider, thus protecting the consumer, who cannot know the fat content of restaurant meals. This proactive initiative in New York City is likely to save many lives. Similar intervention programs have been announced in other cities in the United States. One country has already managed to become entirely trans-fat free: Denmark is free of trans-fatty acids, and introducing trans fat into food is considered a criminal act (Denmark Executive Order 160 2003). These population-based prevention strategies will contribute significantly to the health of the population.

"A New Study Conducted at the Harvard School of Public Health Has Found . . .": How to Critically Evaluate and Use Health and Science News

You wake up in the morning and hear on the radio about a new study conducted by researchers at Harvard School of Public Health, suggesting that skipping breakfast increases the risk of obesity. Should you immediately change your lifestyle and adopt that big breakfast, which you have dreaded so much? Well, not so fast. Think back to some of the concepts that were covered above. These should now help you to critically evaluate such reports (see list below). You may want to ask: How was the study conducted? Which study design was used? Was a retrospective case-control study design chosen? If so, recall bias may have led to the results, and you dismiss the study (Gordis 2009, 177–200). Were the controls selected in a way that makes selection bias likely? Or was it a prospective cohort study (Grimes and Schulz 2002)? In this case, you become more interested. How did the investigators assess whether people eat breakfast; was it a valid and reliable assessment? Or is there reason to believe that there was bias or measurement error in the way it was recorded? How did they assess obesity among their study population? Again, you are concerned about the validity and the reliability of this assessment. How big was their study? If the study was small, you know better than to force yourself to eat breakfast. But if it was large, you may think twice. Were there possible confounders that may have created a spurious association (Gordis 2009)?

Then you hear about another study while brushing your teeth. Researchers at another institution reported that frequent cell phone use may increase the risk of brain cancer (Figure 8). Panic! Clearly, this is the end of your omni-connectedness. But just as you are ready to drop

Study types used in epidemiology

International correlations (ecological studies)

Migrant studies

Cross-sectional studies

Case-control studies

Cohort studies

Crossover studies

Randomized clinical trials

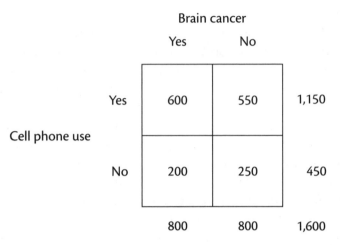

Figure 8. Hypothetical example of a study on cell phone use and brain cancer. The 2×2 table is an essential instrument used by epidemiologists to evaluate distributions and calculate associations between a risk factor and a disease.

that cell phone in the trash, you pause to consider whether those researchers might have made some crucial mistakes in their study. You note that they asked people newly diagnosed with brain cancer about their cell phone use only in the preceding year. Furthermore, their only comparison was with cell phone use among residents of a nursing home. Since the development of brain cancer takes many years, cell phone usage rates in just the prior year are clearly not sufficient data to conclude there is a link; nor was the control group matched in age (and potentially many other factors) to the test group (brain cancer patients), potentially introducing confounds. Not to worry then—that cell phone is safe (at least for today).

Summary

Public health professionals, specifically epidemiologists, use different study types to investigate the causes, origins, and risk factors for diseases—for disease outbreaks and chronic diseases alike. Depending on the research question, one study design or another will be preferable and may minimize bias. Once the cause or mode of transmission for a disease has been discovered, appropriate prevention programs can be implemented. A successful prevention program may not require knowledge of the causative agent: by understanding the mode of transmission and the source of the contaminated water, Snow was able to stop the spread of the cholera in London years before the bacterium *Vibrio cholerae* was discovered. Similarly, Pap smear screening programs substantially reduced the mortality from cervical cancer for several decades before the cause of cervical cancer, the HPV virus, was identified. Whether a public health prevention program is implemented on a population-wide basis, such as fortification of foods with several nutrients in the United States or mandatory vaccination or screening, or on an individual basis, such as the recommendation to consume five servings of fruits and vegetables every day, depends on benefits and risks to the population. Decisions made by governments differ (e.g., there is no water fluoridation and little food fortification in Europe). Individuals can benefit from the results of large observational studies and randomized trials that provide valuable insights into the health risks and benefits of certain lifestyle factors.

Further Reading

General Bibliography

Aschengrau, Ann, and George R. Seage III. 2008. *Essentials of Epidemiology in Public Health,* 2nd ed. Sudbury, MA: Jones and Bartlett.
An introductory textbook in epidemiology.

Dworkin, Mark S. 2009. *Outbreak Investigations around the World.* Sudbury, MA: Jones and Bartlett.
A collection of case studies in infectious disease field epidemiology.

Gordis, Leon. 2009. *Epidemiology,* 4th ed. Philadelphia: Elsevier Saunders.
An introductory textbook in epidemiology.

Hulley, Stephen B., S. R. Cummings, W. S. Browner, D. G. Grady, and T. B.
Newman. 2006. *Designing Clinical Research,* 3rd ed. Philadelphia: Lippincott.
An introduction to designing medical research studies.

Roueche, Berton. 1991. *The Medical Detectives.* New York: Plume.
A collection of real-life public health cases.

Willett, Walter C. 1998. *Nutritional Epidemiology,* 2nd ed. New York: Oxford
University Press.
The standard text in nutritional epidemiology.

Works Cited

Anderson, R. M., and R. M. May. 1979. "Population Biology of Infectious
Diseases: Part I." *Nature* 280: 361–367.

Armstrong, B., and R. Doll. 1975. "Environmental Factors and Cancer Incidence and Mortality in Different Countries, with Special Reference to
Dietary Practices." *International Journal of Cancer* 15: 617–631.

Ascherio, A., and W. C. Willett. 1997. "Health Effects of *Trans* Fatty Acids."
American Journal of Clinical Nutrition 66(4, suppl): 1006S–1010S.

Ault, K. A., and the Future II Study Group. 2007. "Effect of Prophylactic Human Papillomavirus L1 Virus-like-Particle Vaccine on Risk of Cervical
Intraepithelial Neoplasia Grade 2, Grade 3, and Adenocarcinoma in Situ:
A Combined Analysis of Four Randomised Clinical Trials." *Lancet* 369:
1861–1868.

Bingham, P., N. Q. Verlander, and M. J. Cheal. 2004. "John Snow, William
Farr and the 1849 Outbreak of Cholera That Affected London: A Reworking of the Data Highlights the Importance of the Water Supply." *Public
Health* 118: 387–394.

Carroll, K. K. 1975. "Experimental Evidence of Dietary Factors and Hormone-
Dependent Cancers." *Cancer Research* 35: 3374–3383.

Carwile, J. L., H. T. Luu, L. S. Bassett, D. A. Driscoll, C. Yuan, J. Y. Chang, X.
Ye, A. M. Calafat, and K. B. Michels. 2009. "Polycarbonate Bottle Use and
Urinary Bisphenol A Concentrations." *Environmental Health Perspectives*
117: 1368–1372.

Denmark Executive Order No. 160 of 11 March 2003 on the Content of *Trans*
Fatty Acids in Oils and Fats etc. Retrieved April 11, 2011, from http://www
.uk.foedevarestyrelsen.dk/Food_Safety/Trans+fatty+acids/forside.htm.

Dunne, E. F., E. R. Unger, M. Sternberg, G. McQuillan, D. C. Swan, S. S. Patel, and L. E. Markowitz. 2007. "Prevalence of HPV Infection among Females in the United States." *JAMA* 297: 813–819.

Dürst, M., L. Gissmann, H. Ikenberg, and H. zur Hausen. 1983. "A Papillomavirus DNA from a Cervical Carcinoma and Its Prevalence in Cancer Biopsy Samples from Different Geographic Regions." *Proceedings of the National Academy of Sciences, USA* 80: 3812–3815.

Eyler, J. M. 2001. "The Changing Assessments of John Snow's and William Farr's Cholera Studies." *Soz Präventivmed* 46: 225–232.

Fauci, A. S. 2006. "Pandemic Influenza Threat and Preparedness." *Emerging Infectious Diseases* 12: 73–77.

Gordis, L. 2009. *Epidemiology,* 4th ed. Philadelphia: Elsevier Saunders.

Grimes, D. A., and K. F. Schulz. 2002. "Cohort Studies: Marching towards Outcomes." *Lancet* 359: 341–345.

Hennekens, C. H., and J. E. Buring. 1987. *Epidemiology in Medicine,* 87–93. Philadelphia: Lippincott Williams & Wilkins.

Hunter, D. J., D. Spiegelman, H. O. Adami, et al. 1996. "Cohort Studies of Fat Intake and the Risk of Breast Cancer—a Pooled Analysis." *New England Journal of Medicine* 334: 356–361.

Koss, L. G. 1989. "The Papanicolaou Test for Cervical Cancer Detection: A Triumph and a Tragedy." *JAMA* 261: 737–743.

LaPorte, R. E., J. L. Cresanta, and L. H. Kuller. 1980. "The Relation of Alcohol to CHD and Mortality: Implications for Public Health Policy." *Journal of Public Health Policy* 1: 198.

Michels, K. B., and W. C. Willett. 2009. "The Women's Health Initiative Randomized Controlled Dietary Modification Trial: A Post-mortem." *Breast Cancer Research and Treatment* 114: 1–6.

Michels, K. B., and H. zur Hausen. 2009. "HPV Vaccine for All." *Lancet* 374: 268–270.

Mills, C. E., J. M. Robins, and M. Lipsitch. 2004. "Transmissibility of 1981 Pandemic Influenza." *Nature* 432: 904–906.

Morse, S. S. 2007. "Pandemic Influenza: Studying the Lessons of History." *Proceedings of the National Academy of Sciences, USA* 104: 7313–7314.

New York City Department of Health and Mental Hygiene. 2005. "Health Department Asks Restaurateurs and Food Suppliers to Voluntarily Make an Oil Change and Eliminate Artificial Trans Fat." Press release, August 10.

Paavonen, J., P. Naud, J. Salmerón, C. M. Wheeler, S. N. Chow, D. Apter, H. Kitchener, et al., for the HPV PATRICIA Study Group. 2009. "High Efficacy of the HPV-16/18 AS04-Adjuvanted Vaccine against Cervical

Infection and Pre-cancer Caused by Vaccine and Non-vaccine Types: Final Event-Driven Analysis in Young Women (The PATRICIA Trial)." *Lancet* 374: 301–314.

Prentice, R. L., B. Caan, R. T. Chlebowski, et al. 2006. "Low-Fat Dietary Pattern and Risk of Invasive Breast Cancer: The Women's Health Initiative Randomized Controlled Dietary Modification Trial." *JAMA* 295: 629–642.

Rothman, K. J., and K. B. Michels. 1994. "The Continuing Unethical Use of Placebo Controls." *New England Journal of Medicine* 331: 394–398.

Snow, John. 1855. *On the Mode of Communication of Cholera*, 2nd ed. London: John Churchill.

———. 1936. *Snow on Cholera: Being a Reprint of Two Papers*. New York: Commonwealth Fund.

Stampfer, M. J., G. A. Colditz, W. C. Willett, F. E. Speizer, and C. H. Hennekens. 1988. "A Prospective Study of Moderate Alcohol Consumption and the Risk of Coronary Disease and Stroke in Women." *New England Journal of Medicine* 319: 267–273.

Stanley, M. 2006. "Immune Response to Human Papillomavirus." *Vaccine* 24(suppl 1): S16–S22.

Tufte, E. R. 1997. "Visual and Statistical Thinking: Displays of Evidence for Making Decisions." In *Visual Explanations: Images and Quantities, Evidence and Narrative.* Cheshire, CT: Graphics Press.

Wallinga, J., and P. Teunis. 2004. "Different Epidemic Curves for Severe Acute Respiratory Syndrome Reveal Similar Impacts of Control Measures." *American Journal of Epidemiology* 160: 509–516.

Willett, W. C. 2008. "Nutritional Epidemiology." In K. J. Rothman and S. Greenland, eds., *Modern Epidemiology*, 3rd ed. Philadelphia: Lippincott-Raven.

Woodhull, C. S. 1849. "Notice: Preventives of Cholera!" New York Board of Health broadside. Retrieved April 11, 2011, from http://resource.nlm.nih.gov/64730880R.

"Your Disease Risk." 2007–2010. An educational Web site of the Siteman Cancer Center at Barnes-Jewish Hospital and Washington University School of Medicine. http://www.yourdiseaserisk.wustl.edu.

The Human Mind

Steven Pinker

> What a piece of work is a man!
> How noble in reason!
> How infinite in faculty!
> In form, in moving, how express and admirable!
> In action, how like an angel!
> In apprehension, how like a god!
>
> *Hamlet*, act 2, scene 2

Of all the ways of appreciating Hamlet's ode to the human being, the scientific study of the mind is perhaps the most enlightening. Ordinarily, we take for granted our capacities for reason, moving, action, and apprehension. We open our eyes, and a world of objects and people displays itself; we feel a desire, and a plan to attain it materializes in our consciousness; we will our limbs to move, and objects and bodies fall into place. Our mental processes work so well we tend to be oblivious to their fantastic complexity, to the awe-inspiring design of our own mundane faculties. It is only when we look at them from the vantage point of science and try to explain their workings that we truly appreciate the nobility, the admirability, the infinite capacity of human faculties.

People often think of psychology as the study of the weird, the abnormal, the striking—of prodigies and psychotics, saints and serial killers. But the heart of psychology is the study of pedestrian processes like vision, motor control, memory, language, emotions, concepts, and knowledge of the social world. And the starting point I recommend for appreciating these processes is not the study of extraordinary people; it is not the study of people at all. It is robots. If you had to build a robot that does the kinds of things we do as we make it through the day, what would have to go into it? How would you get it to see, move, remember, reason, deal with other people, deal with its own needs? Today you cannot buy a household robot that will put away the dishes or run simple errands. That is because the feats that go into understanding a sentence or grasping a glass, though they are literally child's play, are beyond the limits of current technology. The challenge of designing a robot with simple human skills is one way to emerge from the "anesthetic of familiarity," as the biologist Richard Dawkins has called it, and to become sensitive to the complexity of the human mind.

Here is just a sample of the feats a human accomplishes without reflection, but which represent formidable engineering challenges in the design of a humanlike robot.

The visual world, as it presents itself to the brain, begins as two massive spreadsheets of pixels, one from each eye, with each pixel representing the intensity and wavelength of the light bouncing off a bit of matter in the world. Each pixel combines information from the intensity of the illumination (how bright the sun or the sky or the lamp happens to be) and information about the nature of the surface (whether it is lightly or darkly pigmented). A white shirt seen indoors reflects the same amount of light to the retina as a lump of coal seen outdoors. Yet as the illumination changes, say when we go from indoors to outdoors, or turn on another lamp, the lightness of surfaces remains unchanged to our minds—a phenomenon called lightness constancy.

Psychologists like to awaken people to their own perceptual processes by concocting illusions, cases that unmistakably confront us with the errors of our minds. Edward Adelson's "checkershadow" illusion is one of my favorites (see Plate 5).

Incredibly, the squares labeled A and B are the same shade of gray. It is impossible to see them that way, because the process of lightness constancy tries to compensate for the shadow cast by the cylinder to render the B square as a pale gray in our consciousness. It is an "error" in perceiving the actual physical input to our senses, but it is the desired outcome from the standpoint of designing a well-functioning perception

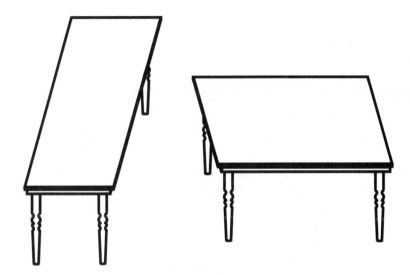

Figure 9. An illusion first demonstrated by Roger Shepard. (From *Mind Sights*, W. H. Freeman, 1990; illustration drafted by J. M. Shephard.)

system, because in the actual world a pale square in a shadow really does project a dark patch onto the retinas of our eyes. No existing robot or camera can undo the effects of shading and perspective to recover the actual properties of the world in the way the human brain can.

The perception of an object's size and shape is also a feat we take for granted. The image of an object on the retina expands as it approaches and contracts as it recedes. It bends and twists as the object is rotated, or as you walk around it. Nonetheless you perceive its shape accurately and unchangingly. It often takes an illusion to remind you of this feat, and here is one devised by the psychologist Roger Shepard (see Figure 9). He called it "Turning the Tables," because if you were to turn one table to the orientation of the other, you would see that the two parallelograms are identical. Your brain ordinarily compensates for the foreshortening caused by projective geometry, so you see a long table on the left, because a table in the world that projected such an image really would be long.

Figure 10. Examples of the letter A.

⑈211371120⑈ 567552615‴ 1050

Figure 11. Check numbers.

To negotiate your world, not only do you have to perceive the shapes in it, but you have to assign each one to a category, like a particular tool or a face or an animal. One only has to look at the different shapes that we categorize as an example of the letter A (see Figure 10) or imagine different chairs (dining room, office, wheelchair, recliner, director's, beanbag) to appreciate the feats of abstraction that go into shape recognition.

Once again, you have to think like an engineer to appreciate the complexity in the natural. The oddly shaped numbers at the bottom of your checks (Figure 11) were designed many decades ago so that their contours would overlap as little as possible and they would be readable by electronic circuitry, because even the best computers would have been flummoxed by the ordinary printed numbers that any child can read.

Of course, today shape recognition by computer is far more sophisticated, but it is still no match for a human. That is why, when you

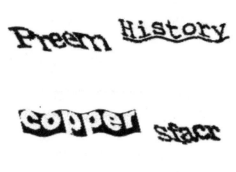

Figure 12. CAPTCHAs from http://www.captcha.net/ and the reCAPTCHA project (http://www.google.com/recaptcha).

open a Yahoo! account (or visit other protected Web sites), you have to read and type in the letters in a distorted "CAPTCHA" display to prove you are not a spambot (Figure 12). A human can read the distorted text; at least for the time being, no computer algorithm can.

"In form, in moving, how express and admirable!" The process of motor control, by which we control the muscles in our hands, arms, and bodies, is also an engineering wonder. The human hand is not like a Swiss army knife, with a separate tool for each job. Instead, our brains control the tensions and positionings of our ten fingers so that they can accomplish the feats of dozens of different hooks, clamps, chucks, and grips. Our legs, too, are remarkable appendages. We may consider the invention of the wheel to be a milestone in the progress of civilization, but legs are far more impressive. Wheels require roads or rails, but legs can also traverse steep or uneven terrain strewn with rocks and gullies. But to enjoy the advantage of legs, we need brains that control them—that dynamically switch between propelling the body forward, shifting its weight from one leg to another, keeping the precarious body from toppling, and, in the case of running, propelling us into little leaps of flight. We can appreciate these feats when comparing our bodies to even the best consumer robots, like a Roomba vacuum cleaner—itself an amazing piece of engineering, but unable to climb over a ridge, or extricate itself from the fringe of a carpet. We can also appreciate the design of our motor control system by thinking about how one would design prosthetics that duplicate its feats—an artificial arm that could grasp a milk carton without crushing it or dropping it, or artificial legs that could maneuver up stairs.

The challenges only multiply when we go from a person's peripherals to the central processors. What are the units of thought that get manipulated as we reason? It is notoriously hard to capture the concepts that underlie the words in our language. When Louis Armstrong was asked to define "jazz," he replied, "When you got to ask what it is, you never get to know." This is true not just for subtle and emotion-laden concepts, but even for seemingly straightforward ones. Logic teachers sometime use the word "bachelor" as an example of an easily defined concept: "An adult human male who has never been married." But as the computer scientist Terry Winograd has shown (see Dreyfus 1979), in reality even this simple concept depends on a vast knowledge base of human relationships. Say you were to consult the definition to help a friend invite a set of bachelors to a party. How would you classify Arthur, who has been living happily with Alice and their two-year-old daughter, but has never gotten the piece of paper that would make them officially married? What about Bob, who needed a green card, so arranged with his lesbian friend Barbara to have a justice of the peace marry them, allowing him to apply for citizenship? Or Faisal, who is allowed by the law of his native Abu Dhabi to have three wives, currently has two, and is interested in meeting another potential fiancée? Or Father Gregory, the bishop of the Catholic cathedral at Groton upon Thames? In every case the definition would fall well short of the way we in fact reason about the concept.

This is all "common sense," but common sense is a staggeringly complex system of inference that no one knows how to duplicate. (If they did, we would not get so infuriated when we telephone a company and get stuck in "voice-mail jail," longing for a human being to answer a simple question.) Consider these "stupid questions":

* Irving put his dog in the car. Is his dog in the house?
* Sheila went to church. Did her head go with her?
* Bruce is in the house. Did he enter the house through an opening?
* Mabel is alive at 9:00 a.m. and alive at 5:00 p.m. Was she alive at noon?
* Jack bought a new goldfish. Was it wearing underwear?

Consider what it would take to get a computer to answer them. The computer would have to know, or be able to deduce, thousands of facts we take for granted: that objects can only be in one place at one time; that the parts of objects move together; that solid objects cannot pass through barriers; that when people die, they stay dead—and millions of others, such as that water is wet; that everyone has a mother; that when you let go of things they usually fall; and on and on and on. Human common sense, then, is a profound scientific puzzle. Do we accumulate hundreds of thousands of facts through everyday experience? By being instructed in them when we were children? Or do we have a smaller number of core beliefs about the basic constituents of reality—objects, minds, living things, artifacts, quantities, places— and a set of inferential rules that generate new facts from old ones?

I have been speaking about our cognitive skills, but our motivational and emotional faculties are no less impressive as feats of engineering. We keep our fragile bodies from being broken, cut, frozen, cooked, poisoned, or eaten by all the entropic and malevolent forces in the world (not least other people). This constant self-defense requires a suite of dynamic emotions that register the dangers around us, such as fear, disgust, and anger. We exchange complex ideas and negotiate clever agreements just by making noises with our mouths and interpreting the sounds with our ears—the gift of language, which itself is embedded in a system of understanding other people's intentions.

Figure 13. Image courtesy of Victor Johnston.

And we manage to find a person who is willing to merge his or her DNA with ours and do what it takes to create and raise a new human being. At least, every single one of our ancestors successfully did so, bequeathing us tools for charming others and discriminating among those attempting to charm us. To pick just one instance of the complexity of those faculties, consider the two individuals in Figure 13.

Most people find these people to be attractive, indeed, riveting. But they exist only as pixels. These images were created by the psychologist Victor Johnston with the help of thousands of volunteers who simulated the process of evolution on a computer. The computer generated a set of variations of a face at random, and the respondents picked the one they found most attractive. The computer used the winner to generate another set of random variations, which were rated, allowed to "reproduce," and so on. After several hundred generations of simulated evolution, these images emerged.

The psychological puzzle is why these collections of pixels should be so compelling. We know nothing about these people—they aren't even people—yet if we were in search of a romantic partner, then, all things being equal, they would be top candidates. The humorist Fran Lebowitz captured the challenge of explaining romantic attraction when an interviewer asked her why she had never been married (in

Winokur 1992): "People who marry someone they're attracted to are making a terrible mistake. You really should marry your best friend. You *like* your best friend more than you're apt to like anyone you happen to find attractive. You don't pick your friend because he has a cute nose, but that's all you're doing when you get married. You're saying, 'I'm going to spend the rest of my life with you because of your lower lip.'" Why should the shape of a lower lip affect the most important decision in our lives? Research in the psychology of attractiveness has provided an answer: the "engineering requirements," if you will, in picking a mate consist in judging the health, fertility, and genetic quality of the different candidates, and the anatomical features that go into physical attractiveness are those that, on average, predict health, fertility, and genetic quality. The virtual people in these images, which were shaped by the tastes of the users who helped evolve them, have extreme versions of each of these features. By finding some faces and bodies more attractive than others, our brain is doing a quick and approximate assay of the biological fitness of a possible mate.

✧

How does one even begin to make sense of something as intricate as the human mind? There have been many schools of psychology, such as Sigmund Freud's psychoanalysis, which equipped the mind with a large inventory of unobservable agents and mechanisms (id, ego, superego, psychic energy, etc.), and B. F. Skinner's behaviorism, which outlawed any appeal to mental entities whatsoever: beliefs, desires, emotions, motives, images, memories, and consciousness were all deemed unobservable and hence unfit for scientific investigation. Only the stimuli in an organism's physical environment and its history of learning were deemed appropriate subjects for a scientific psychology.

The approach that dominates the scientific study of mind today can loosely be called the cognitive biological approach. As articulated by big thinkers such as the ethologist Niko Tinbergen, the computational neuroscientist David Marr, and the linguist Noam Chomsky, it maintains that the mind cannot be understood at a single level of explanation. Multiple levels of explanation are necessary: to understand a feature of the mind, one has to characterize its brain physiology; the computations it carries out; how it developed in the individual; how it evolved from earlier species; and what adaptive pressures selected for it. Let's consider them in turn.

The cognitive part of the cognitive-biological approach begins with the observation that contra behaviorism, beliefs and desires are indispensable explanations of behavior. Why did Lisa just get on the bus? The answer that best predicts her behavior is that she wanted to visit her grandmother and knew the bus would take her there. If we knew that she had no desire to visit her grandmother, or that she had learned that the route had changed, we could accurately predict that her body would not be on that bus.

So the first challenge for a science of mind is explaining what beliefs and desires are and how they can mesh with the physical world and control the body. For millennia, the standard answer was mind-body dualism: the idea that beliefs and desires reside in an immaterial soul. This theory, though, has fatal problems. One is the puzzle of how this ethereal soul can react to the physical objects and events in the world, and how it can pull the levers of behavior. Another is that we now have an enormous amount of evidence that mental life depends exclusively on the physiological activity of the brain.

For example, using techniques such as functional magnetic resonance imaging, cognitive neuroscientists can almost read people's thoughts from the blood flow in their brains. They can tell, for instance, whether a person is thinking about a face, or a sentence, even whether a picture the person is looking at is of a bottle or a shoe. And the contents of our consciousness can be pushed around by physical manipulations. Electrical stimulation of the brain during surgery can cause a person to have hallucinations that are indistinguishable from reality, such as a song playing in the room or a childhood birthday party. Chemicals that affect the brain, from caffeine and alcohol to Prozac and LSD, can profoundly alter how people think, feel, and see. Surgery that severs the corpus callosum joining the two hemispheres (a treatment for epilepsy) spawns two consciousnesses within the same skull, as if the soul could be bisected with a knife. And when the physiological activity of the brain ceases, as far as anyone can tell, the person's mind ceases to exist—attempts to contact the souls of the dead (a pursuit of serious scientists a century ago) turned up only cheap magic tricks. Finally, the staggering complexity of the brain—a hundred billion neurons connected by a hundred trillion synapses—is fully commensurate with the complexity of thoughts and feelings.

~

We know not only that the brain is the place to look for mental processes; we know where to find many of them. It is not that the brain is neatly divided into squares devoted to particular psychological traits, like the maps from the nineteenth-century pseudoscience of phrenology. Nor is it true that the brain is a meatloaf, in which every kind of mental activity is distributed over the whole. From a bird's-eye view, one can link major anatomical regions of the brain with coarse psychological functions like vision, motor control, language, memory, and planning. We know this from studies of people who have suffered damage to the brain from strokes or head injuries, which sometimes reveal surprising dissociations, in which a person has lost one psychological skill but retains others.

For example, damage to the ventral (lower) surface of the temporal lobes of the brain can lead to agnosia, a difficulty in recognizing objects and, in some cases, a specific difficulty in recognizing faces. Damage to the dorsal (upper) parts of the parietal lobes can lead to a syndrome called neglect, which consists of a difficulty in paying attention to half of one's visual space: a patient may fail to name everything on the left side of the room, forget to shave the left side of his face, and forget to eat from the left half of his plate. The complementary patterns of impairment suggest that the visual system is divided into a "what" system and a "where" system, and that the unitary nature of our visual experience—in which a scene appears like a single picture—is an illusion.

Memory, too, is not a unitary brain system. We all sense the difference between a word or image reverberating in our consciousness as we think about a problem, and our vast long-term knowledge base of facts and personal memories. This difference between "working memory" and "long-term memory" has anatomical correlates, the former corresponding to a reverberating pattern of neural activity and the latter to permanent changes in the strengths of synapses. The storage of a long-term memory depends on a seahorse-shaped structure called the hippocampus, which is embedded in the inner surface of the temporal lobe in each hemisphere. If a person loses the hippocampus in both hemispheres, he will be able to hold things in mind over the short term and will retain his autobiography before the accident or surgery, but will be unable to learn anything new. He can hear a joke repeatedly and laugh every time, or be introduced to a person repeatedly and have no memory of having met her.

In some cases a person with amnesia will lose all conscious knowledge of an entity but retain his emotional reaction to it—for example, greeting his wife with a warm smile and a hug but having no idea who she is. This suggests that the brain system for investing memories with emotion is separate from the system for connecting them to verbal and conceptual knowledge. The amygdala, an almond-shaped organ next to the hippocampus, is thought to be the seat of many of our emotional reactions to experiences.

Even the highest-level psychological processes—planning for the future, empathizing with others, making moral choices, controlling our urges—can be linked to a part of the brain, specifically, the prefrontal cortex, the part of our frontal lobes in front of the strip that controls our muscles. People with frontal lobe damage may become impulsive or obsessional (e.g., locking the door repeatedly or being unable to get out of the shower) or may be unable to engage in even the simplest kinds of moral reasoning, such as suggesting what two people should do if they disagreed on which TV channel to watch.

The study of dissociations following brain damage surprises us by showing that the flow of thought and behavior is actually a composite of many streams of information processing. Functional neuroimaging confirms that any particular thought, act, or feeling always involves complex networks scattered all over the brain, which work together to produce coherence of behavior and thought.

∼

The fact that our skulls are packed with complex tissue does not explain how that tissue makes us smart. To explain how intelligence can emerge from a physical object like the brain, and to bridge the gap between the matter of the brain and the abstract entities called beliefs and desires, psychologists must invoke a level of explanation that is more abstract than brain tissue. That level is information processing or computation.

Information may be defined as a pattern in matter or energy that correlates with the state of the world. A simple example is that the number of rings in a tree carries information about the age of the tree, because the number of rings is proportional to the number of years the tree has been growing. One can equate a "belief" with an information representation in the brain: a pattern of activity or connections that correlates with some state of the world: when a person knows it is raining, his brain is in a different state of activity than when he knows it is sunny. "Thinking" can be thought of as the transformation of one representation into another in a way that reflects laws of logic, statistics, or cause and effect in the world. And "desires" (emotions, motives, moods) can be understood as cybernetic feedback systems, a bit like a thermostat. A feedback system represents a goal state, such as a desired room temperature; the current state (e.g., 65 degrees); and connections to a physical device that can reduce the difference—a heater when the temperature is lower than the desired one, an air conditioner when it is higher. Similarly, human motives and emotions register some discrepancy between a goal state (various comforts and satisfactions) and the current state and trigger plans of behavior that are known to reduce the difference (finding food in the case of hunger, getting away from the edge of a cliff in the case of fear, finding a friend in the case of loneliness, etc.).

The idea that mental life can be explained in information-processing terms is not the same as the idea that the brain is a computer. The differences are legion: computers are digital, making all-or-none distinctions; brains are mostly analog, registering continuous quantities. Computers are serial (doing one thing at a time); brains are largely parallel (doing millions of things at once). Computers are built of reliable components; brains are built of noisy components, that is, neurons. (However, while a computer with a single bad bit on its disk, a smidgen of corrosion in one of its sockets, or a brief dip in its supply of power can lock up and crash, a human being who is tired, hungover, or brain damaged may be slower and less accurate but still can muster an intelligible response.) Computers are good at calculation and data retrieval, and bad at seeing, moving, and common sense; brains have the opposite distribution of strengths and weaknesses. The use of information-processing constructs in psychology and neuroscience is not a claim that the brain is a computer but that the brain and the computer are both examples of computational systems—arrangements of matter that achieve intelligence by processing information. An analogy is that some of the same principles of optics and image formation allow us to understand the eye and the camera, without claiming that the eye actually is a camera.

Not only do we have reason to believe that the brain engages in information processing, but we have an inkling of how it does so. The field of neural network modeling has shown that simple circuits made of neurons connected by synapses can compute elementary logical functions such as AND, OR, and NOT, together with the kinds of probabilistic and fuzzy computation that seem to characterize human commonsense reasoning. There are also neural network models of more complex operations, like recognizing a printed word or associating one fact with another. In many cases, perceptual illusions and aftereffects, of the kinds that have appeared on cereal boxes and in psychology textbooks alike, can be directly explained by the wiring diagram of circuits found in the visual systems of simple organisms.

We also know something about the basic computational properties of the brain—answers to the questions one would ask about any computational device, such as which functions are computed serially or in parallel, and what formats of data representation it uses (the equivalent of graphic files, text files, programs, etc.).

For example, we know that certain visual features pop out from their surroundings, such as a red flower in a green field, whereas others require a slow and conscious search, such as a tool in a cluttered toolbox. This suggests that the visual system begins with an effortless parallel analysis of simple features like color and angle everywhere in the visual field. This is followed by a slower, effortful, serial search for combinations of these simple features. In other words, the brain does parallel processing at one stage and serial processing at another.

Another body of research suggests that the brain has separate memory formats for verbal material, for visual images, and for the abstract gist or meaning of a sentence or scene. For example, in answering the question, "What shape are a German shepherd's ears?" most people report that they visualize the shape of the dog's ears in a mental image, since they never had that fact encoded as an explicit proposition; many experiments have confirmed that visual representations of space and contour are active in the brain when people answer such questions.

In contrast, when people have read a long passage of text, they will retain little memory of its exact wording and may even have a false memory of having seen a composite sentence that captures part of its meaning. (For example, having been shown "The ants ate the jelly" and "The jelly was sweet," they may falsely remember having read

"The ants ate the sweet jelly.") This is one kind of evidence that the brain stores abstract, semantic memories, of the kind that underlie the meaning of a sentence. As in computer systems that use pointers in which a single symbol can stand for a complex data structure, human semantic memory is hierarchically "chunked." We package a thought into a single conceptual unit, embed that unit in a more complex thought, package that thought and embed it in turn, and so on. Many mnemonic devices take advantage of this feature of memory. So does efficient writing and studying, which organizes material into nested chunks of no more than four or five concepts apiece.

The study of cognitive information processing has given rise to the experimental study of consciousness. Philosophers sometimes distinguish the so-called easy and hard problems of consciousness. The easy problem is the difference between conscious and unconscious processing. Some kinds of information, like the surfaces in front of you, your plans for the day, your pleasures and pains, are conscious: you can ponder them, discuss them, and let them guide your behavior. Other kinds, like the control of your heart rate, the rules that order the words as you speak, and the sequence of muscle contractions that allow you to hold a pencil, are unconscious. Many of the distinctions in information processing psychology shed light on the easy problem: for example, keeping information in working memory and examining the contents of a busy visual scene one object at a time are both examples of conscious processing, whereas the computations affecting lightness and shape constancy (as in the illusions with the checkerboard and two tables) and motor control are unconscious. More generally, consciousness (in the easy problem sense) functions as a kind of information blackboard, on which the various brain processes that work in parallel can post their intermediate results, making them available to a wide range of other brain processes.

The hard problem of consciousness is why it feels like something to have a conscious process going on in one's head—why there is first-person, subjective experience. The problem is "hard" because no one knows what a solution might look like or even whether it is a genuine scientific problem in the first place. Some philosophers and scientists maintain that it is a pseudoproblem. Others say that it will eventually be solved by research into the easy problem. Still others believe that it is mysterious to a human brain because of quirks in the way that it functions: just as we find certain facts of quantum mechanics to be paradoxical and strange, we may find the fact that brain activity feels like something from the inside to be paradoxical and strange. (Perhaps a superintelligent alien scientist would not find it paradoxical at all.) In any case, our inability to solve the hard problem at present makes no scientific difference to ongoing research on the easy problem.

⁓

The study of cognitive information processing leaves open the question of why the brain is so different from a computer in what it can and cannot do. The answer to that question comes from the other major levels of explanation that make up the cognitive-biological approach.

One of them is development: what kind of brain can you grow out of neural tissue following the kind of instructions that are coded in the genome, under the guidance of sensory and biochemical input? Another is phylogenetic history: what did evolution have to work with as it tinkered with the brains of the primate species that were our ancestors? And the third is adaptive design: what was the system "designed" (by natural selection) to do?

Ever since William James wrote his classic *Principles of Psychology* in 1890, evolution has been an indispensable level of explanation. I began this chapter trying to impress you with the complex engineering design of our mental faculties. This is an example of the central problem in biology, explaining signs of complex design in the living world, such as the eye or the heart. The traditional explanation invoked a cosmic designer, God, but we now have overwhelming evidence that complex design in the living world, including humans, is a product of evolution. More to the point, we have evidence that the processes of evolution have produced not just our bodies but also our brains. The arrangement of human brain systems for vision, memory, motor control, motivation, and emotion is very close to that of other mammals. And many of our emotional responses make sense only in the light of the functions that they played in our ancestors. One example is the facial expression of anger, in which we raise the upper corners of the lips as if to unsheathe our canine teeth in preparation for attack, even though our canines have shrunk into line with the rest of our teeth. Another is the goosebumps we get when in a state of fear, as if to fluff up our fur to appear more formidable, even though we have become naked apes.

The mechanism of adaptive evolutionary change is natural selection. It begins with a replicator—a system with the ability to make a copy of itself. The copies make copies, and each of those copies make copies, leading to an exponential increase in the number of replicators in the environment. In any finite environment, they will inevitably compete for energy and materials, and not all of them can continue making copies. Since no copying process is perfect, the replicators will come to differ from one another. If any copying error fortuitously leads to more effective replication, its descendants will start to crowd out the others and will take over the population. After many generations of copying, we will be presented with an illusion that the replicators we see have been engineered for effective replication, whereas in fact we are just seeing the result of a process of differential reproduction among variant replicators.

Evolution by natural selection should not be confused with "evolution" in the vernacular sense of progress, advancement, or enlightenment. The theory of natural selection predicts only the emergence of gadgets for solving problems, not a general advance in intelligence, culminating in humans. Intelligence is a gadget that worked for our ancestors. Some species evolved to be larger or faster or fiercer or more poisonous; ours evolved to be smarter. The intelligence of our ancestors allowed them to occupy the "cognitive niche" in natural ecosystems, outsmarting other plants and animals by building models of the environment and anticipating what would happen, in service of trapping, ambushing, poisoning, and so on. It also allowed our ancestors to cooperate, achieving outcomes that could not be achieved by a solitary individual.

Evolution does not make people adapted to life in the abstract. It only adapts them to effective reproduction in the kind of environment in which our ancestors spent most of their evolutionary history, namely the hunter-gatherer or foraging lifestyle, which prevailed until the appearance of agriculture, civilization, government, written language, and cities less than 10,000 years ago. This has testable predictions for what kinds of subsystems could have evolved in the brain. It is possible, for example, that humans have an innate ability to acquire spoken language in childhood without needing formal lessons, since complex language has been documented in every human society, including all hunter-gatherer societies. But written language was invented just 5,000 years ago in a handful of civilizations and slowly spread to others, so it is unlikely that humans would have an innate capacity to learn to read and write. Other aspects of human psychology are also explicable in terms of the discrepancy between the world in which we evolved and the world in which we now find ourselves. Visual illusions are displays that have been carefully crafted to violate the properties of ecologically natural displays. Fears and phobias generally respond to ancestral dangers, like snakes and spiders, rather than to present-day dangers, such as driving without a seat belt or using hair dryers near bathtubs. Sexual desire was shaped to maximize surviving offspring in the past, even though modern contraception and fertility treatments have disconnected reproduction from sex.

Any evolutionary analysis has to distinguish adaptations, that is, useful innate features that were products of natural selection, from by-products of adaptations. The eye, for example, is surely an adaptation, having been shaped by many generations of mutation and selection, because it has too many finely meshing parts, all uncannily contributing to image formation, to have arisen by chance from a single mutation. The redness of our blood, in contrast, is surely a by-product (not, say, a contributor to camouflage or beauty), because it is a physical consequence of the chemical properties of hemoglobin, which evolved to carry oxygen to our tissues. Among possible psychological adaptations, some obvious candidates include perceptual constancies and motor control, which allow us to respond to the world and manipulate it. Some less obvious candidates include the moral sense (which allowed us to enjoy the advantages of trading favors in groups without being exploited by cheaters), beauty (which, as mentioned, may help us seek out the most fertile potential mates), sexual jealousy (which may protect men against cuckoldry and women against desertion), and disgust (which may be a defense against infectious microorganisms). And some traits may not be adaptations in the biologist's sense at all, even though they play a large role in our lives. Dreams, music, and religious beliefs might be examples.

In psychology, like the rest of biology, one must determine whether a given trait is an adaptation or a by-product empirically. Adaptationist hypotheses are neither after-the-fact just-so stories, nor can they be accepted uncritically. The relevant data pertain to the goodness of fit between the engineering specs of a putative adaptation and actual facts of the human being revealed in the lab or the field.

One example of an adaptationist hypothesis that has received empirical support is Margie Profet's (1992) theory that pregnancy sickness is an adaptation to prevent women from ingesting naturally occurring chemicals that induce birth defects. For example, it correctly predicted that

1. plant toxins in dosages that adults tolerate can cause birth defects when ingested by pregnant women;
2. pregnancy sickness begins at the point when the embryo's organ systems are being laid down and the embryo is most vulnerable to

chemicals that induce birth defects, but is growing slowly and has only a modest need for nutrients;

3. pregnancy sickness wanes at the stage when the embryo's organ systems are nearly complete and its biggest need is for nutrients to allow it to grow;

4. women with pregnancy sickness selectively avoid bitter, highly flavored, and novel foods, which are in fact the ones most likely to contain toxins;

5. women's sense of smell becomes hypersensitive during the window of pregnancy sickness and less sensitive than usual thereafter;

6. foraging peoples (whose environments resemble the ones in which we evolved) are at even higher risk of ingesting plant toxins, because they eat wild plants rather than domesticated crops bred for palatability;

7. pregnancy sickness is universal across human cultures;

8. women with more severe pregnancy sickness are less likely to miscarry;

9. women with more severe pregnancy sickness are less likely to bear babies with birth defects.

An example of an adaptationist hypothesis that has, in contrast, been falsified is the proposal that homosexuality is an adaptation to investing in nieces and nephews, who share a quarter of one's genes. It was scuppered by studies showing that in fact gay men do not spend more time with their nieces and nephews than do straight men.

Many debates in psychology hinge on nature and nurture, and it is critical to realize that they are not alternatives. We know, for many reasons, that learning is crucial in all aspects of behavior. The genome does not have nearly enough information to wire up the entire brain. There are differences in human cultures that certainly cannot be attributed to genetic differences, as we see in the effects of immigration: children of immigrants who are immersed in the culture of a new country do not retain the language or lifestyle of their ancestors in the old country. We also know that the brain can change as a result of experience, a phenomenon called neural plasticity.

On the other hand, we also know that no explanation of the mind can do without an understanding of what is innate. Learning cannot take place in the first place unless there are innate mechanisms to do the learning. There are differences between species that cannot be attributed to their environments (such as the contrast between common chimpanzees, who display lethal aggression between coalitions of males, and pygmy chimpanzees or bonobos, in which females dominate males and sexuality is an important social signal). We have reason to believe that many of our behaviors today were adaptive in the environment in which we evolved, but are not particularly adaptive in the world where we find ourselves today, such as our taste for sugar, salt, and fat. And though cultures differ dramatically in many ways, anthropologists have documented hundreds of human universals: emotions, motives, and behaviors that are found in all human cultures, from aesthetics and anthropomorphization to weapon use, a worldview, and a word for the color white. Finally, the field of behavioral genetics, using studies of twins and adoptees, has shown that virtually all psychological traits are heritable: variation among individuals within a population is correlated with variation in their genes.

Any explanation of a psychological trait, then, must show how our innate learning mechanisms interact with physical and social input from the world to shape our capacities. This may seem obvious, but nature and nurture continues to be a politically incendiary topic. Many observers are concerned about any explanation that appeals to heredity because they fear that inequality between classes, races, genders, or individuals might be attributed to genetic differences and hence take our attention away from discrimination and other sources of inequality. But it is essential to distinguish political issues from scientific ones. Even when there is evidence for quantitative average differences between men and women in certain psychological traits (such as risk taking, a desire for sexual promiscuity, or mental rotation of 3-D objects), they always consist of overlapping distributions, not discrete traits that all men have and women lack, or vice versa. The core of our commitment to equality is that individuals have to be treated as individuals, not prejudged by the average traits of their race, sex, ethnic group, or class. This is a political and moral principle that is not threatened by any empirical discovery that averages of groups do or do not differ.

∾

With this general background in place on how the mind works, let's now consider three surprising facts of human psychology, taken from the hundreds that you would find in an introductory psychology course or textbook—one involving reasoning, one involving the emotions, and one involving social relationships.

Reasoning researchers begin with a distinction between normative models, which specify the nature of rationality (how we ought to reason) and descriptive or psychological models, which specify how humans do reason. A normative model for deductive reasoning (which is logically certain and goes from generic to specific) would be logic; a normative model for inductive reasoning (which is probabilistic and goes from a set of individuals to a generalization) is probability theory.

Many experiments have shown that when people reason, they systematically depart from the applicable normative theory. For example, people are shown a set of cards, each with a letter on one side and a number on the other (D, F, 3, 7), and asked to turn over the fewest cards that will allow them to verify whether the following rule holds: "If a card has a D on one side, then it has a 3 on the other." Most people choose the D, or the D and the 3. The correct answer is D and 7. The standard explanation is that people have a "confirmation bias"—they seek information that is consistent with a hypothesis and neglect to seek information that would falsify it. Interestingly, people do far better at the task when abstract symbols are replaced by concrete content, especially if it has to do with social obligations, and falsifying the rule is tantamount to detecting cheaters. Thus people have no trouble with this logically identical problem: "You are a bouncer in a bar and have to enforce the rule, 'If a patron is drinking beer, he must be over twenty-one.' Consider a person drinking beer, a person drinking Coke, a sixteen-year-old drinking something, and a thirty-year-old drinking something. Which of the four do you have to examine more closely?" In that case people correctly select the beer drinker and the sixteen-year-old patron, the equivalent of the D and the 7. This suggests that our reasoning abilities may have originated in more specific kinds of social or physical cognition, rather than working as abstract symbol manipulators.

Psychologists have documented fallacies of probabilistic reasoning as well. One of them is the gambler's fallacy: if a coin lands heads seven times in a row, what are the chances it will land tails the next time? Many people feel it is "due" to land tails (the correct answer, of course, is that the odds are still exactly fifty–fifty), as if the coin had a memory and a desire to appear fair. People misunderstand the "law of averages" as a process of balancing or feedback (as if the coin tries to land tails to make up for the previous times that it landed heads), whereas in fact it is a process of dilution (lots of heads and tails eventually swamp the earlier run of heads).

Another fallacy is the availability bias. People judge, for example, that airplanes are more dangerous than cars (it is the other way around), because everyone can remember a gory plane crash with its horrific number of people all killed at once, whereas the far more frequent car crashes seldom make page 1 of the newspapers. The explanation is that the brain uses ease of retrievability from memory as a shortcut to estimating probability. The heuristic often works, because more frequent events do tend to stick in memory, but sometimes it does not, because an event may stick in memory owing to its being emotionally evocative.

A third flaw in unaided human statistical inference is a difficulty in using evidence to judge the probability of a hypothesis. The poster girl for this quirk of our psychology is Linda, a hypothetical character in a famous reasoning experiment, who is "thirty-one years old, single, outspoken, and very smart. She majored in philosophy. As a student, she was deeply concerned with diversity and social justice, and also participated in antiglobalization demonstrations. Which is more probable: that Linda is a bank teller, or that Linda is a bank teller and is active in the feminist movement?" Many people pick the second alternative, even though it is mathematically impossible; a conjunction can never be more probable than either of its terms. People reason from how stereotypical an exemplar is of a category to the probability that it belongs to that category, ignoring the base rate of how plentiful the examples of the category are. A skilled polemicist can exploit this vulnerability by embroidering a scenario with plausible details that ought to make the scenario less likely but psychologically make it more likely. What is the probability that John Doe killed his wife? What is the probability that John Doe killed his wife to get the proceeds of her life insurance policy and move away with his mistress? The latter has to be less likely (he could have killed her for other reasons), but unless one explicitly recalls the laws of probability theory, it intuitively seems more compelling.

∼

Now let's take an example from the study of emotion. An old problem in evolutionary biology is how to explain the existence of altruism in the narrow sense of conferring a benefit on someone at a cost to oneself. At first glace, it might seem as if any altruistic tendency should be selected out in competition with tendencies for more selfish motives. The major solution to this problem (other than for favors bestowed on kin, which can be readily explained by the genetic overlap) is that altruism can evolve among organisms who reciprocate. If one organism confers a benefit to another at one time, and takes a compensating benefit at another, both of them win. A hypothetical example is a species of birds that have to pick parasites off their bodies but cannot reach the top of their heads. If one expends a trivial amount of time grooming the head of another, and gets groomed in return, each benefits.

But any strategy of delayed reciprocation is vulnerable to cheaters, who might take a benefit (getting groomed) without paying a cost (grooming another). The biologist Robert Trivers showed that reciprocity can, nonetheless, evolve, if it is implemented by cognitive faculties that allow organisms to remember who conferred a benefit and who stinted, and emotional faculties that impel the organism to respond to each individual in kind. These would include sympathy for someone who might need a favor, gratitude toward someone who has extended one, guilt when one has accepted a benefit without returning it, and anger at cheaters who have taken a benefit without paying the cost. Many experiments have shown that the triggers for these emotions are exactly what is called for by a theoretical analysis of the strategies that would allow cooperation to evolve.

In the case of humans, there is an additional twist: we have language. A person does not need to interact with another person to determine that he or she is a cheater but can hear about it from a third party. Gossip becomes a significant factor in human cooperation, as does reputation, the commodity distributed by gossip. The motive to maintain one's reputation may explain the otherwise puzzling behavior of people in experiments on the "ultimatum game." One person proposes a division of a pot of money supplied by the experimenter, and a second person can take it or leave it; if he leaves it, neither party gets anything. The optimal strategy for the proposer is to keep the lion's share for himself. The optimum strategy for the responder is to accept any crumb he is offered. In reality, proposers offer almost half the pot, and responders refuse anything less than half, as if to spite an ungenerous proposal. This makes no sense from the standpoint of a narrow rational-actor model of the kind favored in economics and political science. But it can be explained by the hypothesis that people are concerned about their reputation for cooperation. A responder does not want to seem as if he can be easily exploited and, driven by a sense of righteous anger, punishes a selfish proposer accordingly. The proposer anticipates this and makes an offer that is just generous enough to be accepted. We know that the proposer's generosity is driven by the fear of a spiteful response because of a variant called the "dictator game," in which the proposer simply divides the sum between the two players and there is nothing the respondent can do about it. With no fear of spite, the proposer makes a far stingier offer.

Behavior in the ultimatum game supports a hypothesis about human passion first proposed by the political scientist Thomas Schelling: that many seemingly irrational emotions may actually be "paradoxical tactics" that strengthen one's bargaining position in life. For example, someone who issues a threat is always in danger of having his bluff called, because it may be costly to carry out the threat. But if he is such a hothead that he would carry it out regardless of the cost to him, the threat is that much more credible. In the other direction, a suitor has to persuade a skeptical romantic partner that he will not dump her as soon as someone better comes along, even though it may be in his interests to do so (or vice versa, for a woman courting a man). If he shows signs of being head over heels in love with her, rather than simply assessing her coolly as the best partner, it may implicitly guarantee his promise to stay with her, making it more credible. In both cases, a credible display that an emotion is heartfelt, fervent, and involuntary confers a strategic advantage: the anger makes the threat credible; the romantic passion makes the promise credible. The seemingly irrational behavior in the ultimatum game—and perhaps in human passion in general—seems less strange when one considers the value of paradoxical tactics in implicit negotiations.

❧

Finally, let's turn to our interactions with people—including our interactions with ourselves. Contrary to the commonsense idea that each of us has access to a pure self behind the masks we present to others, research in social psychology suggests that we all tend to believe our own PR campaigns. This "impression management" is designed to convey an aura of "beneffectence": the sense that we are beneficent (generous and kind) and that we are effective (competent and influential).

The problem with trying to convey an exaggerated impression of kindness and skill is that other people are bound to develop the ability to see through it (via contradictions, physiological giveaways such as twitches and sweating, etc.), setting in motion a psychological arms race between more effective liars and more effective abilities to detect lies. In his theory of self-deception, Robert Trivers proposed that the mind keeps double books of its own abilities: we lie to ourselves, so that we are more convincing when lying to others. At the same time, an unconscious part of the mind registers the truth about our own abilities, so that we do not get too far out of touch with reality.

Many experiments have shown that people do indeed burnish their estimation of their own talent, autonomy, and rationality. One example is the Lake Wobegon effect, named after the mythical town in which all the children are above average: a majority of people rate themselves above average in any trait that matters to them. Another is what social psychologists call the actor-observer discrepancy: People overinterpret the degree to which someone's behavior is determined by stable personality traits (as opposed to the exigencies of the situation), except when it comes to themselves. Why did Joe work so slowly? Because he is not ambitious. Why did you work so slowly? Because the job is boring.

Probably the most famous set of demonstrations of self-serving biases falls under the umbrella of "cognitive dissonance." According to its original formulator, Leon Festinger (1957), people have a drive to resolve contradictory beliefs by altering one to conform to the other. For example, a person will delude himself into thinking that he enjoyed a boring task if he had been pressured to recommend it to others and was given a paltry sum for doing so. (If the person had been pressured to recommend the task and was paid generously to do so, he will accurately recall that the task was boring.) We see the phenomenon in everyday life when people rationalize patently irrational choices such as smoking and risk taking or seek positive reviews of products after they have bought them. Subsequent analyses have shown that such rationalization is not just a drive to maintain logical consistency: there is no logical contradiction between the proposition "The task is boring" and the proposition "I was pressured into lying that the task was fun." The dissonance arises only from the fact that people do not like to think of themselves as being easily pressured into lying. A better explanation of cognitive dissonance is that people doctor their beliefs to preserve a positive image of themselves—to eliminate any contradiction with the proposition "I am a generous, decent person, and I am in control of my life."

⟿

What should one do with an understanding of the human mind? The ways that human nature bears on our public and personal lives are too many to mention, but here are a few obvious ones.

The study of perception and cognition is tremendously relevant to the design of our surroundings. The infamous "butterfly ballot" that confused so many voters in Florida during the closely contested 2000 U.S. presidential election is an example of a visual display that works against every principle of visual organization. Had a psychology graduate designed the ballot, we might have had a different president between 2001 and 2009, and the world would be in a very different state today.

Not only is psychology relevant to solving practical problems, but with the increasing interconnectedness of knowledge it is becoming woven into other fields of science and scholarship. A prominent example is one of the major frontiers of biology today, neuroscience. Why do people find the brain, of all organs, so fascinating? Why has there been a Decade of the Brain, but no Decade of the Liver? It is because the brain is the seat of the mind; the sciences of mind tell us what to look for when we study the brain. The study and practice of law, too, will increasingly have to look toward the human mind as advances in neuroimaging and genetics begin to challenge the simple conceptions of responsibility and voluntariness on which many laws are based. Many bridges can be built between the arts and the study of mind—how music taps into auditory perception, or painting into visual perception; how poets use linguistics, and novelists tap into readers' intuitive psychology. Perhaps most of all, economics stands to profit from a psychologically more plausible model of economic decision making. Some economists believe that the economic crisis of the past few years was triggered by misunderstandings in how people intuitively perceive risk.

The sciences of mind can inform our handling of other issues in the headlines. It is impossible to make sense of policies relating to discrimination, profiling, and affirmative action without knowing both the distribution of traits across human populations and the patterns of prejudice and moralization with which people react to them. As the preamble to the UNESCO charter reads, "Since wars begin in the minds of men, it is in the minds of men that the defenses of peace must be constructed." Perhaps if leaders had a better appreciation of the research on self-deception and overconfidence, they would be less likely to embroil their countries in disastrous wars.

A knowledge of the mind can, I believe, also be applied to self-improvement. Instead of taking our own passions at face value, we can step back and ask ourselves whether we may not be in the throes of an emotion that has a self-serving function but may be out of touch with reality (perhaps a personal enemy is not as unspeakably loathsome as he seems, and our rage against him is just a feature of our brains designed to make our threats more credible). At other times, we may second-guess our attraction to an inappropriate partner and ask ourselves whether we are putting too much of our fate in the service of an evolutionary response to a lower lip that does not neces-

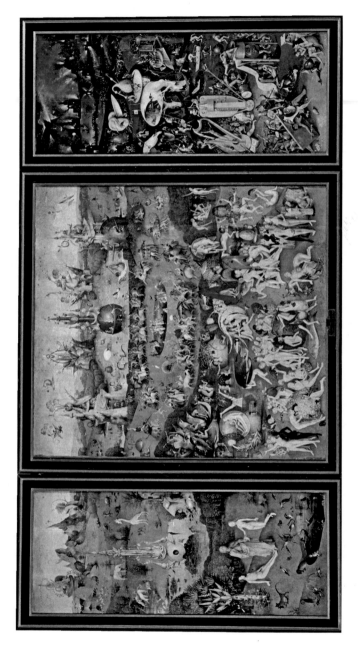

Plate 1. *Garden of Earthly Delights*, ca. 1503. Oil painting on wood by Hieronymus Bosch (ca. 1450–1516). Left wing: Paradise (Garden of Eden); central panel: Garden of Earthly Delights; right wing: Hell (Inferno). (Triptych with shutters; wood; central panel 220 × 195 cm, wings 220 × 97 cm. Cat. 2823 Museo del Prado, Madrid, Spain. Photo: Erich Lessing/Art Resource, New York.)

Plate 6. The PS20 solar power tower located near Seville, Spain. The system became operational in 2009 and produces about 20 megawatts of power. Heliostats (mirrored surfaces) reflect sunlight to a central tower, and the heat is used to generate steam that drives turbines and generates electricity. (Photograph courtesy of Abengoa Solar.)

Plate 5. *Checkershadow Illusion.* (Image © 1995 by Edward H. Adelson. Reprinted with permission.)

Plate 4. *Earthrise.* Apollo 8 lunar mission, December 24, 1968. (Image credit: NASA.)

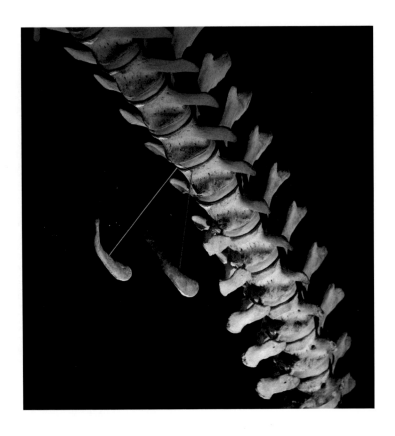

Plates 2 and 3. Whale pelvises can be seen easily in the whale skeletons hanging from the ceiling in the Great Mammal Hall at Harvard's Museum of Comparative Zoology (MCZ). These photographs show one of the two MCZ whales that have been mounted in Harvard's Northwest Laboratory Building; a close-up of the pelvis is shown here. The Museum of Comparative Zoology is one of Harvard's treasures and a place where students can see firsthand examples of evolutionary diversity. (Museum of Comparative Zoology, Harvard University; D. Luke Mahler, photographer.)

hie zerbrach Parzifal sin schwert
vnd wolt d' heiden mit mer linn
Im forhtten vnd erkunneren doo

em andern von frart vnd name
vnd sprungen vff vnd hielsent
ein andren vnd warent fro·

Plate 7.   Feirefîz and Parzivâl. (Burgerbibliothek Bern, Cod. AA91, f. 158v, ca. 1467.)

Plate 8. *View of Boston Common*, ca. 1750. Embroidery by Hannah Otis, 1732–1801. (Wool, silk, metallic threads, and beads on linen ground; predominantly tent stitch; original frame and glass 61.59 × 133.98 cm. Museum of Fine Arts, Boston. Museum purchase with funds donated by a Friend of the Department of American Decorative Arts and Sculpture, a Supporter of the Department of American Decorative Arts and Sculpture, Barbara L. and Theodore B. Alfond, and Samuel A. Otis, and William Francis Warden Fund, Harriet Otis Cruft Fund, Otis Norcross Fund, Susan Cornelia Warren Fund, Arthur Tracy Cabot Fund, Seth K. Sweetser Fund, Edwin E. Jack Fund, Helen B. Sweeney Fund, William E. Nickerson Fund, Arthur Mason Knapp Fund, Samuel Putnam Avery Fund, Benjamin Pierce Cheney Fund, and Mary L. Smith Fund, 1996.26. Photograph © 2011 Museum of Fine Arts, Boston.)

sarily bode well for our long-term happiness. We may stop ourselves in the midst of a dogmatic argument, or a moralistic outburst, and ask whether our self-serving circuitry has made us blind to our own shortcomings.

But even if our knowledge of the mind were to lack these applications, I believe that it would deepen our experience of ourselves and our lives. It would be another case in which science has revealed a world of wonders beneath the mundane particulars of everyday experience, in this case, the hidden complexities in the faculties of seeing, moving, reasoning, and apprehending. As such, the science of mind can truly allow us to appreciate what a piece of work is a human being.

Further Reading

General Bibliography

Darwin, Charles. (1872) 1998. *The Expression of the Emotions in Man and Animals: Definitive Edition.* London: HarperCollins.
Darwin's most psychological work, with countless insightful observations, and the first use of photography in science. Edited with an extensive introduction and afterword by Paul Ekman, one of the foremost researchers in emotion today.

Dawkins, Richard. (1976) 1989. *The Selfish Gene,* new ed. New York: Oxford University Press.
A classic of science writing, and a lucid explanation of the evolution of social behavior.

Etcoff, Nancy L. 1999. *Survival of the Prettiest.* New York: Doubleday.
The science of beauty: why we find faces and bodies attractive.

Gazzaniga, Michael S. 2008. *Human: The Science behind What Makes Us Unique.* New York: Ecco.
A recent integrative and informal overview of findings from neuroscience and psychology.

Gilbert, Daniel. 2006. *Stumbling on Happiness.* New York: Knopf.
The science of happiness, from the Harvard social psychologist.

Gray, Peter. 2010. *Psychology*, 6th ed. New York: Worth.
Who says you cannot read a textbook for enjoyment? An engaging and comprehensive introduction to the vast field called psychology, presented with more of a biological orientation than most of its rivals.

Harris, Judith R. 1998. *The Nurture Assumption: Why Children Turn Out the Way They Do*. New York: Free Press.
In one of the great stories of a scientific outsider challenging an entrenched dogma, an independent writer from New Jersey uses behavioral genetics, ethnography, and studies of child development to refute the doctrine that parents shape their children's intelligence and personality.

James, William. (1890) 1950. *The Principles of Psychology*. New York: Dover.
William James was said to be the psychologist who wrote like a novelist (his brother Henry was the novelist who wrote like a psychologist). This 1890 textbook has stood the test of time—it anticipated many themes in cognitive science and evolutionary psychology—and is great fun to read.

Marr, David. 1982. *Vision*. San Francisco: W. H. Freeman.
An elegant (though sometimes technical) presentation of a unified theory of vision by a computational neuroscientist who is often considered one of the most brilliant theoreticians in the history of cognitive science.

Pinker, Steven. 1997. *How the Mind Works*. New York: Norton.
My own synthesis, written for a wide audience.

———. 2002. *The Blank Slate: The Modern Denial of Human Nature*. New York: Viking.
The political, emotional, and moral dimensions of the nature-nurture debate, and how they enter into our understanding of politics, violence, gender, children, and the arts.

———. 2007. *The Stuff of Thought: Language as a Window into Human Nature*. New York: Viking.
What language reveals about cognition, emotion, and social relationships, including analysis of why semantics makes a difference in our lives, why we swear, and why we use innuendo rather than blurting out what we mean.

Schacter, Daniel L. 2001. *The Seven Sins of Memory: How the Mind Forgets and Remembers*. Boston: Houghton Mifflin.
The science of memory.

Schelling, Thomas C. 1960. *The Strategy of Conflict*. Cambridge, MA: Harvard University Press.

Thomas Schelling is a humane Dr. Strangelove and a recent winner of the Nobel Prize in economics. This 1960 classic is not so much about the human mind itself as it is about the rules of engagement that govern any rational social creatures. But it introduced dozens of profound ideas on culture, emotion, conflict, and communication, whose implications we are only beginning to explore.

Simon, Herbert A. 1969. *The Sciences of the Artificial*. Cambridge, MA: MIT Press.

A collection of essays on information processing (human and artificial) by the Nobel Prize–winning economist, cognitive psychologist, and cofounder of artificial intelligence. Intermittently technical.

Steckel, Al. 2009. *Optical Illusions: The Science of Visual Perception*. Buffalo, NY: Firefly Books.

An exploration of vision through mind-blowing illusions.

Tavris, Carol, and Elliot Aronson. 2007. *Mistakes Were Made (but Not by Me): Why We Justify Foolish Beliefs, Bad Decisions, and Hurtful Acts*. Orlando, FL: Harcourt.

An eminent psychologist and a science writer review the social and cognitive psychology of self-serving biases and self-deception.

Works Cited

Dreyfus, Hubert L. 1979. *What Computers Can't Do: The Limits of Artificial Intelligence*, rev. ed. New York: Harper & Row.

Festinger, Leon. 1957. *A Theory of Cognitive Dissonance*. Stanford, CA: Stanford University Press.

Profet, Margie. 1992. "Pregnancy Sickness as Adaptation: A Deterrent to Maternal Ingestion of Teratogens." In Jerome H. Barkow, Leda Cosmides, and John Tooby, eds., *The Adapted Mind*. New York: Oxford University Press.

Winokur, Jon. 1992. "Fran Lebowitz." In Jon Winokur, ed., *The Portable Curmudgeon*. New York: Penguin.

Securing Human Rights Intellectually: Philosophical Inquiries about the Universal Declaration

Mathias Risse

The Universal Declaration of Human Rights (UDHR) was passed by the General Assembly of the United Nations on December 10, 1948. The evening before, Charles Malik, a Lebanese philosopher and diplomat, one of its drafters, introduced the document:

> [He] pointed each country to places in the Declaration where it could either find its own contributions or the influence of the culture to which it belonged. The Latin American countries had brought to the process the ideas and experiences gained in preparing the Bogotá Declaration on the Rights and Duties of Man. India had played a key role in advancing the nondiscrimination principle, especially with regard to women. France was responsible for many elegancies in drafting. The United Kingdom and the United States had shared the wisdom acquired in their long experience with traditional political and civil liberties. The Soviet Union, with broad support from many quarters, had championed the newer social and economic rights in the interest of "improving the living conditions of the broad masses of mankind." The importance of remembering that rights entail duties had been emphasized by participants from China, Greece, Latin America, the Soviet Union, and France. Many countries had contributed to the article of freedom of religion and rights of the family. Due to the immense variety of its sources, the Declaration had been constructed on a "firm international basis where no regional philosophy or way of life was permitted to prevail." (Glendon 2001, 164)

Malik's insistence that "no regional philosophy or way of life was permitted to prevail" received a striking confirmation in Eleanor Roosevelt's speech that stressed that, had the United States gotten its way, certain aspects of the UDHR would look different (which presumably meant that social and economic rights would have been emphasized less).

The language of human rights has become the most common language of emancipation. When organized power is criticized for harming those whom it ought to benefit, appeals to human rights tend to be used, rather than the language of Marxism, critical theory, modernization theory, dependency theory, or other moral languages, such as the language of justice or plainly of rights and duties as opposed to "human" rights.* Politicians and political activists (even academics in their research) frame their goals in the language of human rights, aligning themselves with the UDHR or other major human rights documents. Especially since the end of the Cold War, the human rights movement—earlier often confined to candlelight vigils—has established a major presence in international politics. Organizations such as Amnesty International, Human Rights Watch, Doctors without Borders, Human Rights First, and many more have become very visible.

Social scientists have recently started to explore whether the use of human rights language correlates with improvements in people's lives. For instance, they have asked whether a country's signing of human rights conventions is linked to improvements in the conditions of the population (fewer civil rights violations, improved abilities to make a

---

* By critical theory I mean approaches, inspired by Marxist ideas about society, that focus less than Marx did on theorizing the exploitation of the working class, but instead seek to explain how capitalism manages to secure the actual allegiance of human beings although their true interests cannot be realized under capitalism. A crucial task for any such approach is to account for the use of the term "true interest." Emancipation is then liberation of individuals from influences that keep them from unfolding these true interests. Modernization theory attempts to identify the social parameters that contribute to social and economic development of societies and seeks to apply insights thus gained to societies that such approaches classify as underdeveloped. Emancipation then amounts to the adoption of factors that will bring progress to the society in question. Dependency theory argues that poor countries at the "periphery" of the world economy cannot develop as long as they are enthralled to rich nations at its "center," because (as one version has it) prices of primary commodities (their main exports) are bound to fall relative to those of manufactured goods. Other versions identify different mechanisms for the dependency relationship. Emancipation of countries at the periphery then amounts to terminating this disadvantageous relationship.

living, etc.). So far the results are mixed. Qualitative, case-study-based inquiries have generated a fair amount of optimism in this regard, whereas more quantitative, statistically oriented inquiries have nourished pessimism. Case-study-based inquiries have identified mechanisms through which human rights documents and organizations could readily make a difference in domestic politics. For example, to improve its reputation abroad and perhaps obtain better access to foreign aid, a country ruled by an oppressive regime may ratify treaties incorporating human rights standards. Domestic opposition might then challenge the government to abide by rules it has ostensibly accepted. International organizations may contribute to this process of "naming and shaming" or provide logistic support or training. Eventually the government can no longer ignore these pressures, and first has to engage the human rights activists politically (a victory for the latter), and eventually make changes for the better.

Social scientists have reported success stories of this sort, for instance in some countries in Eastern Europe and Central America. However, more quantitatively oriented researchers—conducting statistical analyses on cross-country data sets—have failed to confirm this optimism. This is a peculiar state of affairs, but this area of study is still emerging, and much more work needs to be done (for case studies that inspire optimism, see Thomas Risse et al. 1999; for the statistical pessimism, see, e.g., Hathaway 2002). In any event, one should not confuse the recent ubiquity of human rights language with actual impact. Inquiries into the effects of human rights language are only one example of the newly burgeoning field of human rights studies. Other developments include the study of the history of intellectual and political changes in various nations that led to the human rights movement, as well as anthropological research on the impact of the human rights movement on the ways indigenous people articulate complaints about mistreatment.

But it is not a social-scientific evaluation of the human rights movement that is the topic of this chapter. My concerns are with the philosophical foundations of the concept of human rights. The idea behind "human" rights is that individuals have rights simply by virtue of being human, and therefore the realization of those rights is not merely of concern to the states in which the individuals happen to live but is a global responsibility. To assess the intellectual credibility of human rights we must ask: Why would human beings have such rights, and what are these rights precisely? These are the guiding questions of this chapter, and they take us into foundational questions about morality that are becoming increasingly important in a politically, economically, and culturally interconnected world. Related topics we must explore include the relativism-universalism debate and the place of social and economic rights, rights whose standing as "human rights" has often been criticized, on both philosophical and political grounds. How valid is the criticism that human rights are simply nineteenth-century standards of civilization in disguise—standards that determine the conditions under which people elsewhere get to enjoy the benefits of interaction with Europeans and their descendants?

It is by virtue of asking such questions that the course on which this chapter is based, "Ethical Reasoning 11: A Philosophical Introduction to Human Rights," is part of the ethical reasoning segment of Harvard's General Education curriculum. Still, practicing ethical reasoning in the domain of human rights discourse presupposes some familiarity with the history and politics of the human rights movement. So I must also provide the reader with some background to that movement. The next section, then, introduces some of the history and the political reality of human rights. The third section discusses the UDHR itself. The fourth, fifth, and sixth sections address the central question of why individuals would have human rights in the first place. By way of concluding, I make a few remarks on the universalism-relativism debate. In a short chapter I cannot address all the topics that I would cover in a course, but this discussion offers an introduction to its major themes.

The Human Rights Movement: History and Political Reality

Most cultures whose intellectual endeavors have reached a certain degree of complexity have developed ideas of universal morality. There have been earlier declarations specifically of rights, including the American Declaration of Independence of 1776 and the French Declaration on the Rights of Man and the Citizen of 1789. However, until the late eighteenth century, at the earliest, logistic possibilities for any kind of international movement were lacking. And until the twentieth century there were no institutions with realistic global aspirations through which such moral standards could be implemented. Connected to those two points, until the twentieth century individuals had no standing in international law, which operated entirely at the level of states. Documents such as the 1648 Treaty of Westphalia (which ended the Thirty Years' War and paradigmatically incorporated basic principles for the interactions of states with each other) guaranteed protection to minorities, but could not be said to give individuals standing in international law. A world order based on national sovereignty had limited use for the idea that individuals deserved to be protected from their own governments. The human rights movement—loosely speaking, the set of international and domestic (governmental and nongovernmental) organizations and documents devoted to the realization of rights individuals have in virtue of being human—is in many ways a phenomenon of the twentieth century (for the history of the human rights movement, see Lauren 2003; Morsink 1999).

The human rights movement arose from a range of campaigns concerned with more specific issues. The first large-scale humanitarian effort of international proportions was the antislavery movement that began in the late eighteenth century and saw its first major victory with the passing of the British Slavery Abolition Act in 1833. The labor movement of the nineteenth century—which responded to the dismal living conditions of the working class following the Industrial Revolution—also counts as predecessor to the human rights movement.

The International Committee of the Red Cross should be mentioned too. That organization was founded by Henry Dunant after his devastating experience at the Battle of Solferino in 1859. Dunant was shocked by the terrible aftermath of the battle (which left 40,000 on the battlefield), especially the near-total lack of medical attendance. Thus inspired, he founded an institution (with standing under international law) charged with protecting the life and dignity of victims of armed conflicts. Finally, I should mention the women's emancipation movement. In 1879 the performance of Ibsen's play *A Doll's House* caused an international scandal by questioning the nineteenth-century understanding of marriage. The heroine, Nora Helmer, famously exclaims: "I believe that before anything else I'm a human being—just as much as you are." This quotation illustrates why the women's emancipation movement should indeed be considered a predecessor to the human rights movement.

At the 1919 Paris Peace Conference, yet another issue surfaced that would become central to the human rights movement: equality among "races." But while "self-determination of peoples" became an important goal of the conference, racial equality was sidelined. Among the results of the conference was the founding of the League of Nations (the predecessor to the UN); peace became an international priority (and the connection between peace and justice was acknowledged); and the International Labor Organization was founded to address the concerns of the labor movement. However, alongside the reluctance to acknowledge racial equality came a reluctance to question the colonial system that defined world politics. And as the economist John Maynard Keynes (a British delegate) illustrated in *The Economic Consequences of the Peace* (1988), moral language was often used in a disingenuous way (making a case for certain measures as morally required although the reason why these measures were taken was self-interest of the victorious countries) to accommodate Woodrow Wilson, the American president, whose prejudices played a major role in excluding racial equality from further consideration.

An important step toward the UDHR was the Atlantic Charter of August 1941. Arising from a meeting between Churchill and Roosevelt on a ship on the Atlantic, the charter stated goals for a peaceful world: self-determination, self-government, improved labor standards, economic advancement, social security, and "freedom from want and fear." The charter became a rallying point for those who fought in the Second World War against Nazi Germany and its allies, and it was followed, on January 1, 1942, by the Declaration by United Nations (which founded the UN). The Charter of the United Nations (adopted in 1945) gave a prominent role to human rights, but without explicating them in detail. That function fell to a separate declaration. The charter included commitments to three ideas: self-determination of peoples; territorial integrity of states; and human rights of individuals. Any two of them can stand, and frequently have stood, in conflict.

Charged with drafting a declaration on human rights acceptable to members of the United Nations of rather diverse cultural backgrounds, the Commission on Human Rights started deliberating in January 1947. Since, for the first time ever, individuals were given an explicit standing in international politics, this project triggered plenty of debate, reactions, and correspondence. The work of the commission was a long-winded process of struggling with formulations designed to be widely acceptable. This involved political struggles as well as philosophical debate (including an opinion poll of leading thinkers across the world). The commission was remarkably diverse by the standards of the time. It was chaired by Eleanor Roosevelt, who was not only Franklin D. Roosevelt's widow but a formidable public persona in her own right, and also included the aforementioned Charles Malik, the Chinese playwright, philosopher, and diplomat Peng-Chun Chang, the Canadian legal scholar John Humphrey, the French judge René Cassin, the Indian educational reformer Hansa Mehta, and others from around the world. (Keep in mind, though, that when the UN was founded, it had only slightly more than fifty members because large parts of the world were still colonized. Now there are more than 190 states.) The UDHR took the legal form of a declaration and was not binding at the time. Work then began to formulate binding treaties on human rights, which eventually (with much delay) led to the International Covenants on Civil and Political Rights, and on Economic, Social, and Cultural Rights. Both were adopted by the United Nations only in 1966 and went into effect in 1976. The momentum the Second World War had created was difficult to maintain during the Cold War.

Even as news about extermination camps became confirmed, the Holocaust had little impact on the immediate war aims of the Allies. However, Nazi atrocities were very much in mind during the commission's deliberations. One human rights document is older (by one day) than the UDHR: the Convention on the Prevention and Punishment of Genocide. Its passing—on December 9, 1948—was the result of remarkable efforts by one man, Raphael Lemkin, a Polish-Jewish lawyer who had studied genocide before the Second World War and then barely escaped it himself. Not only did he spend years advocating for a convention concerned with this crime, but he also invented the term "genocide." There had previously been no word for deliberate and systematic killing of ethnic or national groups.

Reading the Universal Declaration of Human Rights

The UDHR is a reaction to many of the evils humankind has experienced in history, not merely the Second World War and the Holocaust, but also, for instance, the concerns expressed by the predecessor movements mentioned above. The document also reflects an eagerness to have a broadly acceptable international bill of rights. The preamble talks about "inherent dignity" and "worth" of human beings as well as of "equal and inalienable rights," but that is as far as its philosophical or religious commitments go. The preamble reiterates the link between justice and peace that had been acknowledged in 1919 but insufficiently implemented. The preamble ends by referring to the list of human rights as a "common standard of achievement for all peoples and all nations" and makes clear that responsibility for their realization lies with "every individual and every organ of society." Mentioned especially is a charge to promote respect of human rights "by teaching and education."

Whereas a concern with nondiscrimination was brushed aside in 1919, the insistence in Article 1 that all human beings are "born free and equal in dignity and rights" is immediately interpreted, in Article 2, to mean that "everyone is entitled to all the rights and freedoms set forth in this Declaration, without distinction of any kind, such as race, color, sex, language, religion, political or other opinion, national or social origin, property, birth or other status." It is only after nondiscrimination has been introduced that Article 3 declares that "everyone has the right to life, liberty and security of person." Article 4 revisits the concerns of the original humanitarian movement, the antislavery campaign, insisting that "no one shall be held in slavery or servitude." Article 5 adds that "no one shall be subjected to torture." To avoid limited interpretations of what counts as torture, this prohibition is also extended to "cruel, inhuman or degrading treatment or punishment." The UDHR does not explicitly prohibit the death penalty, nor does the International Covenant on Civil and Political Rights. Whereas some human rights organizations, such as Amnesty International, regard the death penalty as "cruel, inhuman or degrading," it is only the second optional protocol to that covenant (of 1989) that prohibits executions.

Articles 6–12 are devoted to judicial matters, insisting on every individual's right to recognition as a person before the law; on equality before the law; on the availability of remedies of rights violations; on prohibition of arbitrary arrests; on equal access to a fair and public hearing; on a presumption of innocence; and on protection against arbitrary interference with privacy. All of these matters had been ignored by Nazi judges. Article 13 guarantees freedom of movement within one's country as well as the right to leave any country and to return to one's country, but includes no right to enter other countries. Article 14, however, guarantees a right to asylum from persecution. The presence of this article is a response to the widespread unwillingness to help those persecuted during the Holocaust. Article 13 is often referred to by Palestinians insisting on their right to return to the areas they left during the animosities between Israel and several Arab countries in 1947–1948. Article 15 states that "everyone has the right to a nationality," whereas Article 16 ensures the "right to marry and found a family." This too was a right the Nazis had trampled, restricting marriage on racial grounds. Article 17 guarantees a right to own property, which, alongside the right to asylum, was omitted in the subsequent covenants. It turned out to be politically infeasible to include these rights in legally binding documents.

Article 18 guarantees the "right to freedom of thought, conscience, and religion," Article 19 the "right to freedom of opinion and expression," and Article 20 the "right to freedom of peaceful assembly and association." Article 21 provides for a right to "take part in the government" of one's country, "directly or through freely chosen representatives." The UDHR does not state a right to democracy per se. Whether there is such a right has been the subject of some debate. Article 21 does, however, talk about the will of the people as the basis of governmental authority, which "shall be expressed in periodic and genuine elections which shall be by universal and equal suffrage and shall be held by secret vote or by equivalent free voting procedures."

The following articles address social and economic rights. Article 22 states a "right to social security" and does so in the context of mentioning "national effort and international co-operation." Articles 23 and 24 have attracted criticism for stating rights many think do not have the necessary urgency to be human rights, or should not be considered rights at all because it is not always practically up to states to realize them. Article 23 guarantees a "right to work, to free choice of employment, to just and favorable conditions of work and to protection against unemployment," as well as a number of other labor rights.

In addition, Article 24 recognizes the need for recuperation from labor, stating a "right to rest and leisure, including reasonable limitation of working hours and periodic holidays with pay." These rights are the legacy of the labor movement. One of the most comprehensive articles, Article 25, declares a person's "right to a standard of living adequate for the health and well-being of himself and of his family, including food, clothing, housing and medical care and necessary social services, and the right to security in the event of unemployment, sickness, disability, widowhood, old age or other lack of livelihood in circumstances beyond his control." Article 26 provides for a right to education as well as a right of parents "to choose the kind of education that shall be given to their children" (as opposed to being ideologically prescribed by the state, as, say, in the Hitler Youth).

The UDHR also contains cultural and community rights. Article 27 states a right "freely to participate in the cultural life of the community, to enjoy the arts and to share in scientific advancement and its benefits." Article 28 even states an entitlement to "a social and international order in which the rights and freedoms set forth in this Declaration can be fully realized." Only Article 29 mentions duties, namely, "duties to the community in which alone the free and full development of his personality is possible." Article 30, finally, insists that "nothing in this Declaration may be interpreted as implying for any State, group or person any right to engage in any activity or to perform any act aimed at the destruction of any of the rights and freedoms set forth herein."

Why Would People Have Human Rights: The Natural Rights Approach

But why would people have such rights? How is it that humans stand in the kind of relationship where they can make such demands upon each other? This question concerns us for the remainder of this essay. I discuss three different responses. But let us begin with the question of what it means for people to have a "right." We are interested in moral rather than legal rights. What it means to have a legal right is determined through the entitlements that a given legal system generates. But what does it mean to have a moral right? We are not yet asking why people would have moral rights, but simply what it means to have them.

This question is surprisingly difficult. In one view, to have a right means to have an interest whose protection is important enough to require a certain behavior of others and to put the rights holder in a position to demand such behavior. This is the "interest theory" of rights. This view is intuitive to such a degree that one may wonder whether it says anything nontrivial. But consider: if this is what it means to have rights, it would be peculiar to say God has a right to X, since it would be peculiar to say that God's having a right would depend on his having an interest. Perhaps we do not want to say that God has rights, but it would be odd for this to be excluded on conceptual grounds regarding the notion of rights. Rights of officeholders would also become elusive. For instance, judges have rights ex officio, but their exercise is not necessarily connected to an interest. Those sorts of rights, to be sure, are in the first instance legal rights, but to account for any moral force they may have, we have to show that they are also backed by moral rights.

Partly in response to such concerns, others have proposed a different view of what it means to have a right, the "will theory." According to this view, to have a right means to be allowed to control whether others must act in particular ways. This theory makes sense of the rights of God and of officeholders. But this account too has problems. There could now be no "inalienable rights," which are rights that one cannot surrender. But there could be no such rights in this view because one way of controlling behavior of others in a certain domain is to get them to ignore one's wishes with regard to that domain—and for that reason, the will theory implies that one must be able to surrender all of one's rights. Moreover, on this account, nobody could have rights who cannot exercise control (animals, infants, the comatose).

Some hybrid theory between these approaches is most likely to be correct, one according to which rights may be either interests or exercises of choice (exercise of the will). We need not pursue this matter further, but it is worth noting that even this seemingly straightforward matter raises tricky issues (for more on these topics, see Edmundson 2004).

So why would people have "human rights"? Why do people stand in the kind of relationship with each other that renders rights talk applicable? One traditional answer is "by nature." Natural rights are rights that are not contingent upon the laws, customs, or beliefs of particular societies. For example, the American Declaration of Independence offers one way of thinking about this matter: "We hold these truths to be self-evident, that all men are created equal, that they are endowed by their Creator with certain unalienable Rights, that among these are Life, Liberty and the pursuit of Happiness." Saying something is self-evident means that no further justification is possible or needed. But the thesis that there are equal natural rights for all is easy to doubt. Historically, many sophisticated people have taken for granted that people have differential rights, and that some have none, and they often had arguments in defense of this position. So it has not historically been self-evident that all humans have human rights. "Self-evidence" is not a good guide to truth. Self-evident to us is often merely what we have gotten used to. This approach to thinking about natural rights is not helpful.

A common way of making sense of natural rights is through theology. Being "natural" means something like "being part of the divine creation." This approach permeates the reasoning of one of the major thinkers in this tradition, John Locke (1632–1704). Locke's *Second Treatise of Government* is among the most important writings in the canon of Western political thought. "To understand political power right, and derive it from its original," says Locke, "we must consider, what state all men are *naturally* in" ([1689] 1988, section 4). Locke envisages a "state of nature," a scenario without political arrangements. Rights are "natural" as opposed to "conventional" if people have them in this state. Why would people have rights in this state of nature, and how would we know?

Locke characterizes the state of nature as follows:

> A state also of equality, wherein all the power and jurisdiction is reciprocal, no one having more than another; there being nothing more evident, than that creatures of the same species and rank, promiscuously born to all the same advantages of nature, and the use of the same faculties, should also be equal one amongst another without subordination or subjection, unless the lord and master of them all should, by any manifest declaration of his will, set one above another, and confer on him, by an evident and clear appointment, an undoubted right to dominion and sovereignty. ([1689] 1988, section 4)

God did not create us in such a way that one group is superior, so Locke says. But why should we agree with him? After all, one may say (and many have insisted) that if God did not want one group superior to another, why did he create them differently? A little later, Locke points out that the "state of nature has a law of nature to govern it, which obliges every one: and reason, which is that law, teaches all mankind, who will but consult it, that being all equal and independent, no one ought to harm another in his life, health, liberty, or possessions" (ibid., section 6). We also learn that with regard to life, health, liberty, and possessions, persons have both duties and rights (ibid., section 7). Where possible without harming themselves, individuals must help others in preserving their life, liberty, health, limbs, or goods.

Unlike Jefferson, Locke does not think rights themselves are plainly self-evident, but actually derives them from more foundational ideas about the equality and independence of human beings. But why do "equality" and "independence" lead to rights and duties, and in what relevant ways are we equal? We could continue to read this text, but would not find explicit answers. Locke tells us that we are the "workmanship" (ibid., section 6) of God, but that is consistent with a hierarchy among human beings. The best way of making sense of Locke's text is to interpret "equality" to mean not just that we are all God's creatures, but that we are all created in the image of God. Hence, because as human beings we have enough of a likeness to God, a basic moral equality among us is generated. This does not mean people are equal in every way, or even in every morally important way. But enough equality is created thereby. Unfortunately, if God is the source of rights, our theory of natural rights will intellectually be only as secure as our theology.

Others have tried to derive natural rights from human nature, famously Jacques Maritain (1882–1973), a French-Catholic theologian who was nevertheless committed to natural law that does not presuppose God.

> I am taking it for granted that you admit that there is a human nature, and that this human nature is the same in all men. . . . [M]an is a being gifted with intelligence, and who, as such, acts with an understanding of what he is doing, and therefore with the power to determine for himself the ends which he pursues. On the other hand, possessed of a nature, being constituted in a given, determinate fashion, man obviously possesses ends which correspond to his natural constitution and which are the same for all—as all pianos, for instance, whatever their particular type and in whatever spot they may be, have as their end the production of certain attuned sounds. If they don't produce these sounds they must be tuned, or discarded as worthless. But since man is endowed with intelligence, and determines his own ends, it is up to him to put himself in tune with the ends necessarily demanded by his nature. This means that there is, by very virtue of human nature, *an order or a disposition which human reason can discover and according to which the human will must act in order to attune itself to the necessary ends of the human being. The unwritten law, or natural law, is nothing more than that.* (Maritain 1943, 60–61)

But we must wonder, once we have set aside theology: Do human beings really have a function in the same way in which pianos do, and a corresponding excellence? More importantly, even if there were such an excellence, why must we act in accordance with it? It is hard to accept such reasoning once we have removed God from the picture. What Maritain says we might just as well deny, and then wonder how to make progress on the matter. In response to such difficulties, some have argued that—for better or worse—the idea of human rights, or the idea of equality, is untenable without theology. In any event, we cannot use theology to provide a philosophical account of human rights. We need to solve the problem of parochialism for such rights. That is, we must find some way of arguing that people have them that does not turn on philosophical and theological presuppositions that dissenting individuals cannot be reasonably expected to share. Theology does not meet this test. Yet moving to a natural rights approach of the sort Maritain proposed—deriving rights from views about human excellence—is even less promising for this task.

Why Would People Have Human Rights: The Kantian Approach

Let us turn to a different approach, that of the German philosopher Immanuel Kant (1724–1804). Natural rights theorists of the sort we just encountered tried to locate rights "out in the world," in the sense that they were entailed by human nature, or else in the sense that God endowed human beings with rights in much the same way in which he endowed trees with leaves. In contrast, Kant derives morality, including rights and duties, from the sheer fact that we are beings endowed with reason. A being endowed with reason falls into a contradiction in her own mind when failing to abide by certain principles of morality. Kant is also the philosopher who has done most to theorize the notion of dignity that we also find in the UDHR.

The work of Kant that is most commonly read in introductory classes is *Groundwork for the Metaphysics of Morals* ([1785] 2002). In this he argues that being "agents with reason" means that we can see our inclinations as possible grounds for action and can decide whether to adopt such inclinations as guidelines for action, that is, as principles or maxims. It is the will that decides which inclinations to endorse by making them such maxims. Being an agent is not just feeling motivated by a sequence of desires, the strongest of which becomes action guiding. Instead, it means to let the will make a decision on that matter. The will decides whether I become the kind of person who under certain circumstances performs a certain kind of action. In an analogy that is sometimes used, the will is like the captain of a ship who looks down from the bridge on the whole group of seamen and decides which one of them gets to do what. (This is a philosophical model of rational agency, not empirical psychology: of course, not all human behavior will unfold in such a way.) The will is not entirely free in deciding which inclinations become principles of action. Some principles rationally constrain the will of a being with reason, principles Kant calls "objective" or "imperatives." Imperatives may be "hypothetical" or "categorical." Hypothetical imperatives presuppose an end and recommend an action in its pursuit: "You need to do X if you want Y." The will is constrained because X does need to be done if the will wants Y. By way of contrast, categorical imperatives constrain the will not relative to any end, but unconditionally. Categorical imperatives are guidelines of action whose worth we recognize by reason alone and recognize as greater than the worth of any object of inclination. In other words, in certain cases, a rational being cannot help but will to do certain things. Actions may or may not actually be implemented then, depending on whether the agent in question is actually motivated, and thus psychologically capable, of following his will. This by itself might be a matter of education and positive reinforcements from the agent's environment.

As Kant argues, there is only one categorical imperative, which he calls the "practical law," the "imperative of morality," or the "supreme moral principle." The categorical imperative is what morality is "all about." Kant offers various equivalent formulations of the categorical imperative. One of them is: "Act so that you use humanity in your person, as well as in the person of every other, always at the same time as an end, never merely as a means" ([1785] 2002, 4:429). The term "humanity" here is used to connote the quality of "being endowed with reason." The categorical imperative prescribes that each person must always treat all others with the kind of respect that beings endowed with reason deserve. The point is not that we should never treat each other as means to ends. If I buy some bagels, I use the shop attendant as a means to getting my bagels. There is nothing problematic about such behavior. But I would treat her merely as a means if I just walked away without even calling for help if she collapsed with a heart attack right after finishing up with me. Paradigmatic violations are acts of coercion or deception: nobody would reasonably consent to such treatment, and thus treating people in such ways means not treating them "as an end," that is, as an agent whose perspective matters. Rational agents may not ever be coerced or deceived even if general welfare requires such treatment for particular agents. According to the perspective taken by the categorical imperative, actions are acceptable only if they take into account the viewpoint of each rational agent: nobody is supposed to be treated merely as a means even if this greatly helps all others. (Think of a case where sacrificing one innocent person would calm down rioters who otherwise would wreak havoc.)

The categorical imperative also prescribes that one should treat oneself in a respectful way. For instance, according to Kant, one treats oneself merely as a means and not as an end if one commits suicide and thus uses one's capacity to reason for the purposes of ending an existence endowed with that capacity. The categorical imperative is not the same as the Golden Rule, according to which one should always act as one would have others act toward oneself. The Golden Rule leaves much more to individual discretion than the categorical imperative. The categorical imperative asks about what could be justified to each rational being as a rational being. The Golden Rule asks individuals not to inflict on others the sort of behavior that they themselves happen to dislike. However, a masochist, for instance, would not thereby be precluded from inflicting pain on others.

So far I have merely given a rough sense of the contents of the categorical imperative. How does Kant derive the categorical imperative? Why does this principle constrain any act of willing, simply in virtue of its being an act of willing? That is, why does this principle constrain the manner in which a rational agent can select some of his inclinations and adopt them into principles that guide his action (which is what, according to Kant, the will does)? Generations of scholars have built their professional lives around throwing light on Kant's work. It would be a striking success of philosophical reasoning to derive foundations of morality from considerations that a rational will cannot help but accept. Roughly, here is what Kant says. Being endowed with reason implies that one sets ends or goals. That is, the will chooses to do certain things rather than others. By setting ends, the rational will thinks of those ends as having value. For the will to adopt an inclination into a principle guiding action, it must endorse the end. In that sense, the rational will thus thinks of itself as conferring value. But we have reason to regard ends we set for ourselves as good, as having value, only to the extent that we esteem our capacity to set ends as something good. By assuming anything matters to us as an end, we must assume we matter ourselves. Setting ends or goals means not merely seeing something as valuable somehow, but seeing it as valuable because it contributes to one's own life. We can see something as valuable in this way only if we think of ourselves as valuable. In a second step Kant asks us to see that every other being with reason also represents his existence in this way on the same grounds. That is, Kant says that if an agent views herself as having a value-conferring status, and as valuable, by virtue of her power of rational choice—as she must—she must also understand that anyone else with that power must have this same view of himself.

Why would this reasoning take us to the categorical imperative? Suppose I am treating somebody merely as a means to an end. (For instance, suppose I did nothing to help the person who just sold me some bagels and then collapsed with a heart attack.) The reasoning above implies that this person whom I am so treating must, rationally, see herself as a source of value. However, the capacity by virtue of which she must do so is the same capacity by virtue of which I must view myself as valuable. Disregarding her capacity means disregarding a capacity I (necessarily) value. So, indeed, each rational nature must be taken seriously as an end in itself, as a source of value, and hence as a being whose perspective matters and whom I cannot merely treat in terms of his or her usefulness for my purposes. To disregard another person is to draw a distinction between myself and that person that on rational grounds is unacceptable. Doing so would mean that I fall into a contradiction with myself. That is why, according to Kant, we can derive the supreme moral principle in this way. Examples Kant gives to illustrate the categorical imperative in addition to those I already mentioned above include duties not to lie, not to steal, not to let one's talents rust, to refrain from excessive pride, and not to engage in mockery or gossip. Ruled out are also drunkenness, snobbery, servility, and excessive humility. Kant discusses other cases as well, but, of course, disagreement might remain between Kant and his readers as to precisely what is entailed by the categorical imperative.

"Dignity," according to Kant, characterizes the kind of worth rational beings have by virtue of the properties discussed above: they set goals, and thus choose principles of action. This choosing, as an act of a rational being, is subject to the categorical imperative. Thereby, rational beings are the source of all other value. Dignity is an absolute worth grounded in the rational capacities for morality, and not conditional on how well these capacities are exercised. Dignity is not diminished through vice or bad action, nor is it increased through virtue or morally correct action. Instead, in the case of vice or bad action, the agent fails to live up to what her own dignity demands, whereas in the case of virtue and morally correct action, the agent does live up to what dignity demands. Wrongdoing may call for punishment (including death) and may be grounds for forfeiting certain rights, but not for regarding the wrongdoer as worthless. Respect based on dignity is not something anybody has to earn. In the Anglo-American context, talk about respect is more common than talk about dignity. Dignity, however, in addition to appearing in the UDHR, features prominently elsewhere, especially in the German legal tradition. The German Basic Law (http://www.bundestag.de/htdocs_e/documents/legal/index.html) begins with a reference to dignity in Article 1, paragraph 1: "Human dignity shall be inviolable. To respect and protect it shall be the duty of all state authority." Dignity appears before the right to life, which is a striking expression of the Kantian legacy. Life imprisonment without parole is unconstitutional because it violates dignity. Recently, a law to shoot down planes used as weapons was declared unconstitutional in Germany on grounds of dignity. The first law legalizing abortion in 1975 was unconstitutional because the Constitutional Court held that embryos had dignity. (Abortion continues to be illegal, but the state declines to prosecute.) Peep shows were once ruled to violate the performers' dignity, regardless of their own attitudes. According to Kant, one cannot relinquish one's dignity. Shows where performers cannot see the viewers remain outlawed. Here too disagreement might remain about the particular implications of dignity and thus of Kant's understanding of morality. But these are some prominent examples of how Kant's thought has influenced the constitution and the laws in the country where his impact on these matters is greatest.

Let us apply Kant's ideas about dignity to the question of the acceptability of torture. Article 5 of the UDHR states that "no one shall be subjected to torture or to cruel, inhuman or degrading treatment or punishment." Nevertheless, the debate about torture continues. At its heart we find references to "ticking-bomb cases." Suppose we know for sure that X planted a bomb that is about to explode and would kill many. X confesses but refuses to reveal the location of the bomb. Suppose there are no other ways of extracting this information. Surely, the argument concludes, we should be allowed to apply torture (for this argument, see Shue 1978). One cannot simply respond that "torture does not work anyway." Whether torture "works" depends on the circumstances. If the question is "Did Saddam Hussein collaborate with Osama bin Laden?" confessions under torture might well be useless. Yet if statements are readily verifiable, one would make a mistake in excluding torture based on the assumption that it could not possibly work. Another bad response is to say that using torture is unwise because it will only make the "enemy" even angrier. That response might leave us with cases of torture that could be carried out in secret.

Better pragmatic responses are these two: first, the assumptions of the "ticking bomb" argument are strong. Rarely do we know for sure that a person is guilty as charged. Rarely is torture the only remaining possibility for ascertaining the information. Other tactics include incentivized cooperation; the good cop/bad cop strategy; the pushing of emotional buttons (say, making the perpetrators see the victims as persons, or making them think about the pain they would inflict on their own families); and a pumping-up of the ego ("unlike those people, you are not the kind of person who would do such things"). A second pragmatic point is that if torture were permitted, there would have to be torturers, and they would have to receive instruction and supervision. Torture would have to be institutionalized. It is unrealistic that this could be done without torture being applied more widely than intended. To put the point bluntly, in a manner ascribed to Mark Twain: "To a man with a hammer, everything looks like a nail." An exacerbating factor is that people often have limited capacities to relate to another's pain, to understand "what torture is like."

So the ticking-bomb argument can be resisted in a pragmatic fashion, to the extent that the possibility of such extreme scenarios is supposed to have any implications for the regulation of torture. However, we need to resort to other, moral, considerations to articulate the idea that "there are certain things we must never do to people." The notion of dignity does this work. Consider the following account of what is troublesome about torture, and how this involves the notion of dignity:

> The torture victim finds herself to be not only physically and morally defenseless, but exposed to a will that appears largely if not completely arbitrary. The victim's greatest interests are completely subject to the caprice of her torturers. . . . Insofar as she is able to form any estimates of their motives and intentions, the victim must trust in the sincerity of people who have already shown that they have no scruples about how they treat her. (Sussman 2005, 7)

> Torture fails to respect the dignity of its victim as a rationally self-governing agent. . . . [T]orture . . . *involves a deliberate perversion of that very value, turning our dignity against itself.* . . . It is perhaps not accidental that many of the most common forms of torture involve somehow pitting the victim against himself, making him an active participant in his own abuse. In Abu Ghraib, captives were made to masturbate in front of jeering captors. Here the captive was forced into the position of having to put his most intimate desires, memories, and fantasies into the service of his torturers, in a desperate attempt to arouse himself for their amusement. The US soldiers could beat and kill their prisoners, but only the prisoner himself could offer up his own erotic life to be used against himself in this way. (Sussman 2005, 19–22; emphasis added)

This account of the wrongness of torture—emphasizing the perversion of dignity—proceeds differently from the two considerations against the ticking-bomb argument I offered above. It makes the notion of dignity central to what could be extended into an argument against any application of torture, as stated by Article 5 of the UDHR.

Why Would People Have Human Rights: A Contemporary Approach

Recall our guiding question: what would the nature of the relationship among human beings have to be like for us to claim moral rights vis-à-vis each other? Kant offers one rather prominent response to this question, one based on consistency of reason: that we have certain rights because beings with reason cannot with logical consistency treat others in ways that do not grant them rights. The centrality of reason to this account also allows for the articulation of the notion of dignity that has become so important to the human rights movement.

Alas, there are problems with the derivation of the categorical imperative. The derivation aims to pinpoint a contradiction that arises if I am treating somebody merely as a means. However, that I value certain things only permits the inference that I must value my having the capacity to value, or my partaking of humanity. By the same reasoning, you must value your having the capacity to value, or your partaking of humanity. I must value the capacity to value, or to set ends, insofar as it is a capacity that I possess. You must value that capacity insofar as it is a capacity you possess. I do not need to value your capacity to value, and vice versa. Neither you nor I must value the capacity to value per se. No contradiction arises if I am using you as a means to ends that have value because I have conferred it upon them. What the argument demonstrates is how you become intelligible to me as an agent, how I come to see your actions as more than mere chance events—by coming to realize that, in a fundamental way, we are alike. It might imply more, but not that I am inconsistent when not treating you as an end (i.e., when merely treating you as a means to an end). A Kantian might object that we are now drawing an arbitrary distinction between your capacity to value and mine. But if it is arbitrary to do so, that move will be unreasonable, but not introduce an inconsistency. The goal of the Kantian enterprise has been to offer an inconsistency argument, and that goal seems out of reach.

Kantians set the standards high. If indeed rights can be established only by showing that their violation leads to a contradiction in the mind, perhaps we are asking for too much. What we should seek to establish is the unreasonableness of treating people merely as means or even of treating them as moral unequals, rather than the inconsistency in doing so. Consider the following statement by the philosopher Joel Feinberg (1973, 93):

> The real point of the maxim that all men are equal may be simply that all men equally have a point of view of their own, a unique angle from which they view the world. They are all equally centers of experience, foci of subjectivity. This implies that they are all capable of being viewed by others imaginatively from their own point of view. They "have shoes" into which we can always try to put ourselves; this is not true of mere things. It may follow (causally, not logically) from this way of so regarding them that we come to respect them in the sense tied to the idea of "human worth." . . . In attributing human worth to everyone we may be ascribing no property or set of qualities, but rather expressing an attitude—the attitude of respect—towards the humanity in each man's person. That attitude follows naturally from regarding everyone from the "human point of view," but it is not grounded on anything more ultimate than itself, and it is not demonstrably justifiable.

In the spirit of this statement, we should seek to show that it would be unreasonable to disregard human rights, rather than inconsistent (and to do so without getting into the problems we encountered with the natural rights approaches to human rights). Being immoral, that is, does not mean to fall into a contradiction with oneself in this view. This move would give up on a major ambition of moral thought, to offer an actual derivation, an unassailable demonstration of morality. But we have found some indication that this is asking too much.

A number of philosophers have recently made attempts to provide accounts of human rights along the lines just sketched. One such account is James Griffin's 2008 book *On Human Rights*. Griffin views human rights as protections of "normative agency," the agency involved in choosing a worthwhile life. According to Griffin, "what we attach value to, what we regard as giving dignity to human life, is our capacity to choose and to pursue our conception of a worthwhile life" (p. 44), and "it is the mere possession of this common capacity to identify the good that guarantees persons the protection of human rights" (p. 46). Throughout, Griffin argues for the enormous normative significance of certain aspects of our shared humanity by way of comparison to other goods, and insists on the unreasonableness of disregarding these aspects—without, however, insisting that somebody who fails to respect these aspects falls into a contradiction with himself.

Central is the idea of a distinctively human life:

> Human life is different from the life of other animals. We human beings have a conception of ourselves and of our past and future. We reflect and assess. We form pictures of what a good life would be—often, it is true, only on a small scale, but occasionally also on a large scale. And we try to realize these pictures. This is what we mean by a distinctively *human* existence—distinctive so far as we know. . . . And we value our status as human beings especially highly, even more highly than even our happiness. This status centers on our being agents—deliberating, assessing, choosing, and acting to make what we see as a good life for ourselves. (Griffin 2008, 32)

To be an agent, in the fullest sense, one must choose one's path through life (that is, not be dominated or controlled by someone else); one's choice must be real (that is, one must have at least a minimum of education and information, be able to act, and have at least a minimum of resources and capabilities); and others must also not forcibly stop one from pursuing what one sees as a worthwhile life. Therefore what human rights ought to protect is a certain amount of autonomy, liberty, and the availability of at least minimal provisions. At this level, Griffin thinks, the approach holds universally and applies across societies. This does not mean that the concept of human rights has independently arisen in different cultures. Nevertheless, notions of human rights have developed in reaction to abuses, especially religious intolerance, government oppression, and discrimination. These abuses occur everywhere, and the substantive values human rights protect are appreciated everywhere.

What are protected, following this reasoning, are a right to life and security of the person (otherwise personhood is impossible); a voice in political decision (a key exercise of autonomy); free expression, assembly, and press (for the exercise of autonomy not to be hollow); the right to worship (a key exercise of what many take to be the point of life); the right to basic education and minimum provisions needed to be functioning as a person (which is more than what is needed for mere physical survival); the right not to be tortured (since, among its several evils, torture destroys one's capacity to decide and to stick to the decision). What would be hard to obtain under this account, as far as the rights in the UDHR are concerned, are a right to freedom of residence (included in Article 13), a right to protection against attacks on one's honor and reputation (included in Article 12), a right to equal pay for equal work (in Article 23), and a right to holidays with pay (Article 24).

Recall that for Kant, dignity is inviolable. (Kant himself had a very rigid view on this matter: dignity is indeed inviolable under all circumstances.) Applied to torture, this means torture is arguably never justified. According to Griffin, dignity is not categorically inviolable, though the standards for violations are high. If we apply this reasoning to torture, we find that it is not categorically impossible to justify torture in particular cases (such as ticking-bomb cases), though plausibly this reasoning would nevertheless support a general prohibition of torture, based on the considerations that ticking-bomb cases will be rare, and that regulation of torture entails its own problems. Empirical information about human nature and human societies, as well as about the limits of human understanding and motivation, enters into Griffin's account and is needed to determine the contents of human rights. "Practicalities," as Griffin says, help determine how much is expected, and who is expected to do it. As an example, consider the right to life. This right implies a claim to health support necessary for maintaining "human status" but not that life be extended as long as possible, given the enormous costs of end-of-life care. Other people could not reasonably be expected to bear such costs.

Conclusion: Moral Relativism and Human Rights

An account like Griffin's, by and large, strikes me as the most sensible way of grounding human rights, understood as rights we have "simply in virtue of being human." I say an account "like" Griffin's because other philosophers have offered accounts of human rights not built on the idea of normative agency, but on ideas such as basic human needs or capabilities. But for each of these accounts it is true that it does not make good on the ambitions of natural rights thinkers who located the basis for such rights "in the world," nor does any of them make good on the Kantian ambition to base rights on the consistency of reason alone. Instead, each develops ideas about the normative significance of the distinctively human life and the unreasonableness of acting in ways that threaten such life. That much is all we can do to secure human rights intellectually, but that much is also all we need to do to that end.

I conclude with a few remarks on moral relativism. Moral relativism is the thesis that fundamental values and ethical beliefs are culture bound in a sense that does not allow for any critical engagement with people who do not belong to that culture, and makes the case that there is no right and wrong, but merely a "right for" and "wrong for." The emphasis on "fundamental" differences is crucial. Often differences in moral codes are due to differences in living conditions rather than to fundamentally diverging commitments. In contrast, universalism of the sort that motivates the human rights movement holds that there are values that apply across cultures, even if the cultures themselves do not accept them. To the extent that the arguments for an approach like Griffin's succeed, we ipso facto have a rebuttal of relativism, but let me nevertheless make a few additional remarks on this subject on account of its importance for the enterprise of grounding human rights.

To begin with, we live in an interconnected world, and the question of what we ought to do for each other arises in numerous ways: we have to confront it. Human beings have irreversibly encountered each other. Second, persons across cultures share vulnerabilities: they suffer from physical pain, require food and water to survive, and are susceptible to disease and malnutrition. People across cultures also aspire to common goods: bodily health, bodily integrity, and a desire to be treated with some respect in their affiliations. The idea of a distinctively human existence, if we understand it narrowly, is not culture bound. Common vulnerabilities and goods make intercultural exchange intelligible. The human rights movement answers the question of how we ought to live together at the global level, by taking seriously common vulnerabilities and goods, by considering how, historically, these have been assaulted and ignored, and by then formulating a language specifically of rights in response.

Third, views that categorically restrict the scope of fundamental moral values to particular cultures or circles within cultures inevitably draw on reasoning that is hard to defend and force upon others. History abounds in failed attempts to do so, fascism, sexism, and racism being egregious examples of recent and to some extent ongoing prevalence. And finally, those who speak in support of relativism are often those in power, whereas those who reject it generally focus on the standpoint of the victims. To the extent that representatives of certain cultures reject human rights by saying something like "around here we do things differently," their argument often rests on an attribution of unanimity in their own culture that does not exist, and is especially implausible for egregious human rights violations. As Scanlon (2003, 119) put it, we must then wonder: "Which is the more objectionable form of cultural superiority, to refuse to aid a victim on the grounds that 'they live like that—they don't recognize rights as we know them,' or to attempt to protect the defenseless even when they themselves feel that suffering is their lot and they have no basis to complain of it?" In specific cases this actually is a genuinely open (and very difficult) question. But often enough, I think, the correct answer is the second one.

Further Reading

Edmundson, Williams. 2004. *An Introduction to Rights*. Cambridge: Cambridge University Press.
A comprehensive introduction to philosophical issues that arise about rights.

Feinberg, Joel. 1973. *Social Philosophy*. Englewood Cliffs, NJ: Prentice Hall.
A classic introduction to philosophical questions about society.

Glendon, Marie Ann. 2001. *A World Made New: Eleanor Roosevelt and the Universal Declaration of Human Rights*. New York: Random House.
A fascinating account of the process that led to the Universal Declaration, focusing on the role of Eleanor Roosevelt.

Griffin, James. 2008. *On Human Rights*. Oxford: Oxford University Press.
A contemporary philosophical approach to human rights.

Hathaway, Oona. 2002. "Do Human Rights Treaties Make a Difference?" *Yale Law Journal* 111: 1935–2042.

Ibsen, Henrik. (1879) 2008. *A Doll's House,* trans. Michael Meyer. London: Methuen Drama.

Kant, Immanuel. (1785) 2002. *Groundwork for the Metaphysics of Morals,* trans. Allen Wood. New Haven, CT: Yale University Press.
One of the central works in the canon of Western philosophy.

Keynes, John Maynard. 1988. *The Economic Consequences of the Peace*. New York: Penguin.

Lauren, Paul Gordon. 2003. *The Evolution of International Human Rights*. Philadelphia: University of Pennsylvania Press.

Locke, John. (1689) 1988. *Two Treatises of Government,* 3rd ed., ed. Peter Laslett. Cambridge: Cambridge University Press.
A classic in political philosophy, and one of the founding documents of modern liberalism.

Maritain, Jacques. 1943. *The Rights of Man and Natural Law,* trans. Doris C. Anson. New York: Charles Scribner's Sons.

Morsink, Johannes. 1999. *The Universal Declaration of Human Rights*. Philadelphia: University of Pennsylvania Press.
A detailed account of the process that led to the text contained in the Universal Declaration.

Risse, Thomas, Stephen Ropp, and Kathryn Sikkink, eds. 1999. *The Power of Human Rights: International Norms and Domestic Change.* Cambridge: Cambridge University Press.

Scanlon, T. M. 2003. "Human Rights as a Neutral Concern." In *The Difficulty of Tolerance.* Cambridge: Cambridge University Press.

Shue, Henry. 1978. "Torture." *Philosophy and Public Affairs* 7: 124–143.

Sussman, David. 2005. "What's Wrong with Torture?" *Philosophy and Public Affairs* 33: 1–33.

What Is Morality?

T. M. Scanlon

Terms such as "moral," "morality," and "morally wrong" occur frequently in personal discourse and political argument. But it is often unclear what the people using these familiar terms have in mind, and unclear whether they are all even referring to the same thing. For example, many people seem to believe that sexual conduct is a central element in morality. When you read in the newspaper that there is a question about some politician's morals, you know right away that it has to do with sex. But others believe that, although some moral wrongs, such as rape or infidelity, involve sex, these things are wrong because they are instances of more generic wrongs that are not essentially concerned with sex, such as coercion or promise breaking. When no other form or harm or wrong is involved, sex itself is not a moral issue, according to this view. Differences such as this, which are not so much about the content of morality as about its scope—the range of actions it applies to—suggest that people disagree not just about which things are morally wrong but also about what it is to be morally wrong.

A common element in these different views of morality is that moral standards are ones that we all have good reason to accept as a normally conclusive basis for deciding what to do and for assessing our claims against others. Some people may have specific ideas about the reasons why moral standards are authoritative. They may believe, for example, that these standards are commands of God. But different people may have different ideas about this, and I believe that many people, even though they take moral standards seriously, are quite unclear about exactly why one should do so.

Explaining why one should care about morality has been one of the central aims of moral philosophy since its beginning. Plato's dialogue

Gorgias, for example, is devoted to the question of whether there are correct answers to basic questions of morality and politics, or whether, as some participants in the dialogue maintain, these are matters of opinion rather than knowledge, and mere persuasion rather than argument. Callicles, the toughest of these participants, holds that the best life, if one could attain it, would be a life in which one was able to persuade other people to do whatever one wanted them to, without regard to considerations of justice or morality. Socrates' response to this challenge illustrates several important features of this central question of moral philosophy.

The first is that any attempt to answer the question "Why be moral?" faces a dilemma. On the one hand, a satisfactory answer to this question cannot be based on any avowedly moral claim. It would be obviously circular to argue that one should obey moral requirements because it would be morally wrong not to do so, or because one would be morally bad if one did not. On the other hand, a response to this question that appealed to some consideration that was obviously unconnected to morality—such as that being moral would make one rich—would offer the wrong kind of answer, one that would fail to give morality the kind of significance that it is generally thought to have. It would be more like a bribe, making what had been thought of as noble behavior in fact self-interested.

Socrates' answer responds to this dilemma. He maintains that immoral or unjust action is only possible if one has a disordered soul, and that the health of one's soul is the most important thing in life. Because of this, he says, acting unjustly is worse than suffering even the most severe injustice at the hands of others. This answer may not be very convincing, but it has the form required to avoid the dilemma I just described. Socrates' conception of the health of one's soul is not simply a circular appeal to morality; it offers an independent reason for being moral that does not seem like a bribe.

When Socrates offers this answer, Polus, another participant in the dialogue, says that it is ridiculous. He adds that if Socrates were to go into the assembly and say that committing an injustice is worse for a person than suffering an injustice, people would laugh at him, and no one would agree. Socrates responds that the kind of inquiry he is engaged in is not settled by taking a vote. The only relevant way to show him to be wrong, he says, would be to offer an argument refuting what he has claimed.

This illustrates a second important point about philosophical inquiry into morality (or into any other philosophical issue). However plausible or implausible Socrates' thesis may be, any answer to the question he is addressing is bound to be controversial. Given any account of the reasons for taking moral requirements seriously, there are bound to be some people who reject this account and are not convinced by the arguments we offer (like the opponents in Plato's dialogue, who seem in the end not to be really convinced by the argument Socrates has offered).

This would be discouraging if the aim of philosophical inquiry were to find an argument that would force any imagined opponent to accept one's conclusion. But this is not the aim of philosophy, not only because it is unrealistic to think we could attain it, but also because it is not the main thing we have reason to aim at. Philosophical inquiry is a process of making up one's own mind what to think. It is not, primarily, about convincing others. After all, as Socrates argues in this dialogue, one does not know what one wants to convince others of until one figures out what to think oneself. The dialogue format of Plato's writings can be confusing on this point. It is natural to read dialogues as debates, in which Socrates is trying to "defeat" his "opponents." But this is not the way Socrates himself sees it. He emphasizes that being shown to be wrong is not defeat, but something to be welcomed, because one will have benefited by learning something. He sees his interlocutors not as opponents but as co-investigators. This is why he insists that he is only interested in talking with people who will say only things that they themselves believe, and will submit to questioning about what they say.

The fact that philosophical inquiry aims at deciding what to believe oneself rather than at convincing real or imagined opponents does not mean that one is free to ignore what others think. It just alters the relevance of conflicting opinions. The question raised by disagreement is not "How could I convince them?" "They" may be unreasonable and refuse to accept even good arguments. The relevant questions, rather, are "Why do they think that?" and "Do their reasons provide good grounds for me to accept their view?" If one can resolve these questions satisfactorily, then one need not change one's mind, even if others continue to disagree.

Before taking up the question of the basis of morality, we need to consider the broader question of what makes a life a good life for the person who lives it. This is relevant to an account of morality in two ways. First, an answer to the question "Why be moral?" must consider how morality is related to the kind of life that is desirable for the person whose life it is. Second, the content of morality depends in part on the answer to this question, since one thing morality requires of us is that we help others in various ways, and at least not harm them. So to know what morality requires, we need to know what is good for people—what makes their lives better and what makes them worse.

In his argument with Callicles, Socrates considers and rejects two accounts of what makes a person's life better that still have appeal for many people today. These are "hedonism," which is the view that the quality of a life for the person who lives it is measured by the amount of pleasure that it contains, and a "desire theory," according to which the quality of a life for a person depends on the degree to which it fulfills his or her desires. Although each of these views has considerable appeal, neither is in fact a satisfactory account, for reasons that Plato recognized.

Consider hedonism. There is, of course, the difficult question of exactly what pleasure is, and which kinds of pleasure are most worth having. Advocates of hedonism may underestimate this problem, but there is a further objection to hedonism, which can be seen by noting that it is a form of "experientialism"—that is, it makes the quality of a life for the person living it depend entirely on the experience of living that life. Robert Nozick (1974, 42–44) provided a famous argument against experientialism with his thought experiment of the "experience machine." Suppose, he said, that it were possible to have oneself connected to a very powerful computer, which would stimulate your brain in a way that would make it seem to you exactly as if you were living whatever kind of life you take to be best. Would a life connected to such a machine actually be as good as a life could be? Nozick claimed, very convincingly I think, that it would not be. The quality of a life depends on what one actually does, and what actually happens to one, not just on what it seems like. The same point can be made without the science fiction involved in Nozick's example. Consider the possibility that the people whom I think of as my good friends are in fact not friends at all. Perhaps, just to make the point graphic, they are alumni of the *Harvard Lampoon* who have a project of deceiving me and who meet every week to plot their strategy and laugh at how gullible I am. It seems clear that I have good reason to want this not to be the case. It matters whether I have friends or not. Similarly, it matters whether the arguments in my articles are really valid, rather than containing subtle errors. And these things are so even if I never discover the errors or the falseness of my supposed friends.

So even though the experience of living a life—whether it is enjoyable, exciting, satisfying, and so on—matters to how good a life it is, and is perhaps one of the most important factors, it is not the only thing that matters. This weakness of experientialism also brings out how hedonism, as a form of experientialism, differs from a desire-fulfillment theory. The two may sound the same because "fulfillment" may be taken to refer to the experience of having one's desires fulfilled. But this is not the way a desire theory should be understood. The relevant idea of a desire being fulfilled is like the idea of a belief being true: a desire is fulfilled, in the relevant sense, if the world is in fact (not just seems to be) the way the person desires it to be, whether or not the person is aware that this is so. So according to a desire theory, the things that make a person's life go better include factors that lie outside that person's experience, as Nozick's experience machine example and the other examples I mentioned suggest. Indeed, these examples might be taken to support a desire theory, that is, to call our attention to the fact that if a person cares about whether he or she has true friends or whether his or her arguments are valid, then that person's life is going better if these things are in fact the case.

But we should not be too quick here. The correctness of a desire theory depends on whether the "if clause" in the previous sentence is really necessary. A desire theory maintains that things such as friendship make a person's life go better only if he or she desires these things. Contrary to what a desire theory maintains, however, it may be the case that friendship would make a person's life better even if she or he does not desire friendship, and that, therefore, the person *should* desire to have friends.

This brings us to another famous argument of Plato's, from his dialogue *Euthyphro*. In this dialogue, the title character tells Socrates that he is going to the assembly to denounce his father because this is the pious thing to do. Socrates asks Euthyphro what piety is, and he replies that piety is doing what is pleasing to the gods. Socrates then asks Euthyphro whether actions are pious because they are pleasing to the gods or whether these actions please the gods because they are pious. This is one of the most famous questions in all of philosophy because it has application to any attempt to explain a property in terms of the reaction that some person or persons would have under certain conditions. So, for example, if it is said that an object is red if it would look a certain way to a normal human observer in good light, then it may be asked whether things are red because they look that way, or whether they look that way because they are red.

In the case just considered, the proposal was that certain things make a person's life better if that person desires them. The "Euthyphro question" is then whether these things make a person's life better because he or she desires them or whether the person desires them because they make his or her life better. And the answer seems to be that in most cases the latter is closer to the truth. That is to say, we do not generally think that we have reason to pursue things because we desire them, but, rather, we desire them because we see something about them that seems to us to make them worth pursuing.

These reflections strongly suggest that neither a hedonistic theory nor a desire fulfillment theory gives the full explanation of what makes someone's life better, although each contains an element of the truth. A plausible account of what makes someone's life better needs to recognize that the quality of a life depends at least on the following:

1. The quality of the experience of living it; the extent to which it includes more of desirable states such as pleasure, excitement, and challenge, and less of undesirable ones such as pain, sorrow, and frustration.
2. The person's success in achieving his or her main aims, provided that these are ones that there is reason to pursue.
3. The degree to which it includes other valuable things, including personal relations such as friendship and the development and exercise of valuable talents.

The first of these points gives hedonism its due: pleasure (or more broadly the quality of one's experience) is a good and important one, even though it is not the only good. The second point recognizes the truth in desire theory: the things that make a person's life better or worse depend on the aims that person actually has. But aims or desires do not, by themselves, make things valuable: they do so only if they are aims worth having. Achieving a foolish aim, such as getting up every day at exactly the same time, does not make one's life better. Finally, the third point recognizes that some ingredients in a life other than success in one's aims are worth desiring for their own sake, rather than being good only if one desires them.

These three points are just a list, not an overall theory of what makes a life better. It is not at all clear that there could be such a theory. But the foregoing reflections seem to me to strongly suggest that, whether it is an overall theory or a list, a plausible account of what makes someone's life better will be a "substantive good" account: a claim or set of claims about what things are good in themselves, not good because they are desired. Hedonism is one such an account; it is just an implausibly narrow one, a list that includes only one element. Socrates' claim about the health of the soul is also a substantive good account, although not to my mind a very plausible one.

Any account of what makes someone's life go better, especially one that rests on claims about what is substantively good, is bound to be controversial. So one might ask (as some student in my course always does), "Who's to decide what makes a life better?" It is important to see that this is a facile debating move, not a serious question. To say of some person that he is "the one to decide" whether A is the case or not suggests that this person has the authority to settle this question: that his deciding that A is the case would make it so. Sometimes, in some institutional settings, for example, there is authority of this kind. The Supreme Court, for example, has the authority to decide whether something is the law of the United States. But with respect to the questions we are considering there obviously is no authority of this kind. So the answer to the question "Who's to decide?" is "No one." That is to say, no one has the authority to settle the question.

But in another, more relevant, sense the answer to "Who's to decide?" is "Each of us." That is to say, it is up to each of us to make up his or her own mind about such questions as what makes a life better for the person who lives it. This is not to say that each of us has any authority to settle this question. It is up to each of us to assess the merits of competing answers and arrive at our own conclusion as to which one is correct. But whether this conclusion is correct depends on its merits, not on our decision.

It may seem that each person has special authority to settle the question of what life is the best life for him or her. This may be true in a sense, but not in the sense relevant to our present discussion. It is up to each person to decide how to live, and each person has authority over this question in the sense that (within limits, at least) his or her decision has a claim not to be interfered with. But authority of this kind should not be confused with authority to settle the question of what makes a life worth living—to determine, by one's decision, what the right answer to this question is. We do not have this authority. We can be mistaken about what life would be best for us, although it is also true in many cases that our choices about how to live, even if misguided, ought not to be interfered with.

There is now a growing body of empirical investigations, by psychologists and economists, of what makes people happy, and it might be thought that these findings could provide an answer to the question we are considering. At the most fundamental level, this is not so, for a reason that goes back to our discussion of Socrates' philosophical method. Philosophical questions, such as whether the quality of a life for the person who lives it depends only on the person's experience, or only on what he or she desires, or also on something else, cannot be settled by taking a poll. The correctness of an answer depends on the merits of the argument supporting it, not on how many people believe it to be correct.

Our present discussion is, however, relevant to these empirical findings in two ways. The distinctions we have been making are important in deciding how to interpret these data and in deciding what kind of importance they have. Consider, for example, a study reported by Betsey Stevenson and Justin Wolfers (2009) in their article "The Paradox of Declining Female Happiness." Stevenson and Wolfers considered the results of surveys in which women were asked how happy they were with their lives. These surveys were conducted over a period of more than thirty years, from the early 1970s to 2006, and Stevenson and Wolfers report that over this period women's happiness declined both in absolute terms and relative to the reported happiness of men.

The first question to which the present discussion is relevant is how to understand what the women in these surveys were reporting. They were sometimes asked to say how happy they were. In other cases they were asked how satisfied they were with their lives, or with how their lives were going in certain respects: as far as their family life was concerned or their careers. The former wording suggests that in answering this question they were assessing their lives on the basis of a hedonistic standard. The latter suggests they were reporting how fully they thought their desires about their lives (or about some part of their lives) were fulfilled. This makes a difference to the significance of the results. If the subjects are assessing the quality of their experience, then, presuming they know how they feel and are being truthful, these results indicate a decline in at least this particular aspect of well-being (the first component on my list above). On the other hand, if the subjects are assessing how fully their desires are fulfilled, this is something they can be mistaken about, and what the data may indicate is not that the women in 2006 are worse off by a desire fulfillment standard but rather that they have a different view about the degree to which their desires are fulfilled, or a different idea of the level of fulfillment it is reasonable for them to hope for.

It is also quite possible that the women in the later period had different, perhaps more ambitious, desires than women interviewed in 1972. If so, then in order to decide whether the reported "decline in happiness" was a bad thing or not, we would need to decide whether it was better or worse to have lives that led them to have these new desires if this involved having a lower level of desire fulfillment. That is to say, to assess the significance of this study we need to distinguish between the different aspects of well-being that we have been discussing and make judgments about their relative importance.

I return now to questions of moral right and wrong, which are our main topic. I will consider two theories that aim to give a general characterization of morality that, on the one hand, explains the authority and importance of conclusions about right and wrong and, on the other, provides an account of the kind of reasoning that leads to these conclusions. The two theories I consider are John Stuart Mill's version of utilitarianism and my own version of contractualism. Both of these theories characterize morality in entirely secular terms. Before considering them, however, I want to consider why it might seem that morality must have a religious basis and that there can be no morality if there is no God. Many people seem to believe that this is so, including both some believers in God, who understand morality as his commands, and some people who do not believe in God and conclude that morality is a sham. Without taking either of these positions, I want to consider why the premise that they have in common, that there can be no morality if there is no God, should seem plausible.

A crude answer, which I mention only to set it aside, would appeal to God's role in rewarding those who obey moral requirements and punishing those who do not. Morality, as I have said, purports to be a set of standards that everyone has good reason to follow, and the idea is that only Divine sanctions could ensure that everyone has such reasons. I refer to this as a crude answer because it does not provide the right kind of reason for being moral. Someone who avoids morally wrong actions—who does not kill his neighbors and steal their possessions, for example—only out of fear of punishment and hope for future reward is not a moral person. As I said earlier, a satisfactory answer to the question "Why be moral?" cannot appeal to morality itself, but it also cannot appeal to purely extrinsic factors, as this account seems to do. This is not, however, the only way to understand the idea that moral requirements have a religious basis.

A much more plausible interpretation would see moral requirements, or some specific set of such requirements, as the commands of a loving God, a God that is concerned for all of us and gives these commands out of his concern for us. We should follow moral requirements, it would be said, out of respect for God's wisdom and in response to his love. This account of our reasons for being moral avoids the dilemma I mentioned above: it is not circular, nor does it appeal to considerations that are implausibly extrinsic to morality.

This account also avoids one standard objection to a Divine command theory of morality, which is an application of the Euthyphro question. If morally right actions are those which accord with God's commands, are these actions right because God commands them, or does God command them because they are right? If the former, then, it might be objected, these commands are arbitrary: God could just as well have commanded the opposite, and then those things would be right. On the other hand, if God commands things because (antecedent to his commands) they are right, then what is morally right does not, after all, depend on what God commands. The present account avoids this objection. It holds that actions are right because God commands them, but his commandments are not arbitrary. They are based on his knowledge of what is (antecedent to these commands) conducive to our well-being.

So understood, a Divine command theory seems coherent, and plausible if there is reason to believe in God. But such an account does not seem to be the only plausible basis for morality. According to such an account, moral requirements are the rules of behavior that God commands because following them is conducive to our well-being. But these things are conducive to our well-being whether God commands them or not. So the authority and importance of morality can be seen as resting simply on its relation to our well-being. This is what secular moral philosophies do, in various ways. Secular accounts differ in how they interpret the way in which the good of each person is understood (corresponding to what a loving God would be concerned about) and in how they get from this kind of concern for each person to principles of action (corresponding, in particular, to how a loving God would decide between principles that benefit some and principles that benefit others).

Utilitarianism is a moral theory formulated by Jeremy Bentham at the very end of the eighteenth century and given a more subtle and sophisticated form by John Stuart Mill in the middle of the nineteenth century, in his famous short book *Utilitarianism*. Utilitarianism identifies individual well-being with happiness, and in its simplest form holds that an action or policy is right if it would produce a greater sum of happiness than any alternative, taking into account the happiness of everyone affected and giving the happiness of every person (or every sentient being) equal weight.

Bentham was primarily a legal reformer, interested in particular in the reform of the British penal system. He believed that pleasure was the only thing good in itself and the only form of human motivation. The aim of legal reform and social policy, in his view, was to establish rewards and penalties that would (making use of pleasure and pain as motivators) induce people to behave in ways that would lead to the greatest sum of pleasure for all. Although legal reform and social policy were his main aims, he also stated utilitarianism as a general account of what we ought, morally, to do. When they are interpreted in the way that utilitarianism prescribes, he wrote, "the words *ought*, and *right* and *wrong*, and others of that stamp, have a meaning: when considered otherwise, they have none" (*Introduction to the Principles of Morals and Legislation;* see Ryan 1987, 67). One thing he may have meant by this is that the general happiness is the only value sufficient to give moral requirements the authority and importance they are generally assumed to have. If they are understood as having any other basis, he thought, the supposed authority of these requirements is mere pretense.

Bentham understood pleasures as specific psychological states that could be compared and evaluated in terms of their duration, their "intensity," and what he called their "fecundity": their tendency to produce other pleasurable states. Mill came to believe that this represented a narrow and impoverished conception of what made human lives better. Although he continued to speak of "happiness" as the only thing desirable in itself, his conception of what it involved was much richer and more complex than Bentham's. His conception gave special place to "higher pleasures" such as the enjoyment of poetry, and he even allowed that virtue could be valued for its own sake, but said that when a person valued it, then being virtuous had become "a part of his happiness" (*Utilitarianism*, chapter IV; see Ryan 1987).

Mill's account of the relation between moral wrongness and the promotion of general happiness is more complex than the simple version of utilitarianism that I stated a few paragraphs back, according to which an action is wrong if it would lead to less total happiness than some alternative available to the agent. Mill calls an action, policy, or state of character "expeditious" if it tends to promote the general happiness. But the fact that an action is not expeditious does not, in his view, mean that it is morally wrong. "We do not call anything wrong," he writes, "unless we mean to imply that a person ought to be punished in some way or other for doing it; if not by law, by the opinion of his fellow creatures; if not by opinion, by the reproaches of his own conscience" (see Ryan 1987, 321). As a utilitarian, Mill takes the general happiness as the basis for determining what "ought" to be the case. So, in his view, to say that an action is morally wrong is to say that it would be *expeditious* (that is, productive of the greatest total happiness) for such actions to be punished in one of the three ways he lists.

In understanding morality in this way, as a system of institutionalized norms backed by formal or informal punishments that are justified by their tendency to promote the greatest happiness, Mill is in one way just following Bentham—applying Bentham's view of law to morality, as Bentham himself would have done. But Mill also criticizes Bentham for the way in which he understands the "expeditiousness" of a policy, and hence the rightness or wrongness of an action. Bentham's greatest error, Mill said, was to assume that in assessing the rightness or wrongness of an action (in asking whether it would be "expeditious" to punish such actions) we should consider only the consequences of that action, or of similar actions if performed generally. We need also to consider, he said, the kind of character that these punishments would lead people to form. The character of people around us (the kinds of things that they are likely to do if a suitable occasion arises) can affect general happiness in ways other than through the actions that these people actually perform. Their character affects happiness by determining the kinds of relations (of trust, for example) that others can have with them, the kinds of cooperation that are possible, and the kinds of precautions that we need to take in dealing with them. For example, if others are not generally disposed to help us when we need help, then we need to be prepared to help ourselves should the circumstances arise, and this imposes a cost whether or not an occasion ever arises on which we need their help, and they refuse to give it.

The account of morality offered by utilitarianism is appealing in many ways. First, the general happiness seems to be a sufficiently important value to explain the authority of moral requirements, and it offers an explanation of the right kind: neither circular nor implausibly unrelated to morality. Second, this standard has an appealingly egalitarian character: "each to count for one, none for more than one," as Bentham wrote. Third, it offers an appealingly clear and simple account of the basis of all of morality, giving reason to believe that all moral questions have, in principle, determinate answers—although it may in practice be difficult to ascertain what these answers are because of the difficulty of predicting which actions and policies will have the best consequences.

Mill's utilitarianism is a version of the common idea that morality is a system of social control—an informal version of law. In his view, it is a system aimed at and justified by the general good. In determining what is right, it takes everyone equally into account, but one may question whether it does this in the right way. In utilitarian moral thinking, everyone is taken into account in two ways: as someone whose happiness is a part of the overall goal that is to be promoted and as an agent who is to be motivated by sanctions (one might say manipulated) to act in ways that promote this goal.

Although this mode of thinking is formally egalitarian—it gives each person's happiness equal weight—there is no guarantee that it will require that everyone be treated equally. Whether this is so depends on whether equal treatment would yield the largest sum of happiness, and there is no limit, in principle, to the degree to which the interests of a few might be sacrificed to produce greater happiness for many. Given the fact that it is the sum of happiness that is to be maximized, there is even no limit to the degree to which very small increases in happiness for a great many people could justify great losses to a few. It appears that we could, for example, be justified on utilitarian grounds in letting someone die in order to prevent a sufficiently large number of brief headaches.

Mill attempts to forestall such objections by pointing out that what he calls "security," by which he seems to mean assurance that one's life will not be interfered with in certain ways, is the most important precondition for happiness. But this still leaves the question of whether small increases in the security of a sufficiently large number of people would not, on his view, justify serious invasions of the security of a very few. The larger question that this raises is whether people are "taken into account" in the right way simply by having their happiness counted as contributing to the sum that is to be promoted.

A second question concerns the way in which agents are supposed to be motivated by utilitarian morality. Responding to the idea that there can be no morality without God, Mill observes that, through proper education, people can become motivated to follow utilitarian moral standards just as they can be led to internalize any other standards. But, he observes, if this is merely a process of indoctrination, then when people reflect on this motivation it will come to seem arbitrary to them, and its effects will "yield by degrees to the dissolving force of analysis" unless it is linked with some powerful class of natural sentiments.

Another way to approach the same question is to ask what the content of guilt feelings is supposed to be according to Mill. He says that an action is wrong if it would promote overall happiness to have people feel the reproaches of conscience if they do such things. But what is it, according to Mill, to feel these "reproaches"? It cannot be just to feel that it would promote the greatest happiness if people felt that it was wrong to do such things, since this still leaves the content of the feeling "it would be wrong" unexplained. Mill's answer, in chapter III of *Utilitarianism*, is that the "natural basis of sentiment for utilitarian morality" lies in "the social feelings of mankind, the desire to be in unity with our fellow creatures."

The idea that we have such a desire is an attractive thought, but it figures in Mill's theory simply as a psychological propensity that can be drawn upon to provide a motivational basis for utilitarian morality. The moral theory called "contractualism" interprets "being in unity with one's fellow creatures" in another way, as being able to justify one's actions to them. It also draws on this idea in a different way than Mill does, by treating the desire to be in unity with one's fellow creatures not just as a psychological state (such as empathy) that motivates us to comply with morality, but also as a desire whose content helps us to see what morality is about, and why we should care about it.

According to contractualism, moral standards are not primarily instruments of social control. Rather, they arise out of our interest in acting in ways that we can justify to others. An action is wrong, in this view, if a principle that permitted it would be one that others could reasonably reject, even if they, too, were concerned with the justifiability of their actions. This account of the content of morality is directly linked with an account of its motivational basis: we are motivated to do what is right, according to contractualism, because we care about whether our actions are justifiable to others, and we have good reason to care about this.

This seems to me to capture very well the experience of believing that one has done the wrong thing. To take a familiar example, Peter

Singer (1972), in his famous article "Famine, Affluence, and Morality," argued forcefully that we are morally required to do much more than is commonly recognized to help starving people in other parts of the world. He defends this demand, in part, on utilitarian grounds: greater happiness would be produced by a starving person's having the food he or she could buy with five dollars than would be lost by my giving up the coffee and pastry that I would buy if I kept this money. But the sense that it is wrong not to do more to help people in starving lands does not seem to me to be well captured by the thought that this would produce greater happiness. Much more relevant is the thought that, given how much the money would mean for them, and how little I would lose, I could not justify to them a policy of keeping it for myself.

More needs to be said about the relevant notions of justifiability and reasonableness than I can undertake in this chapter (for fuller discussion see chapters 4 and 5 of my book, *What We Owe to Each Other* [Scanlon 1998]). Here I have to confine myself to a few important points. The first is that to decide whether it would be reasonable for a person who would be affected by a principle in a certain way to reject that principle, one needs to compare that person's reasons for objecting with the reasons that others have for insisting on such a principle (that is, for objecting to the way they would fare under alternative principles.) To "take a person into account" in the way that morality requires is, according to contractualism, simply to recognize him or her as someone to whom justification is owed, someone whose reasons for objecting to a principle need to be considered and answered.

Second, I should make a few points about the kind of reasons that can be grounds for rejecting a principle. These cannot include objecting to a principle on the grounds that the conduct it would allow would be wrong. This would make the contractualist account of morality circular. In addition, although this is more controversial, according to the version of contractualism I favor, a principle cannot be rejected on the grounds that it would permit actions that would lead to states of the world that are bad in an impersonal sense, even though they are not bad for any person (for example, bad because some object of great beauty would be destroyed, even though no one would otherwise have enjoyed seeing that object).

Although the reasons for rejecting a principle must have to do with how some person is affected, they need not be concerned narrowly with a person's happiness or welfare in the hedonistic sense. They can also include, for example, the reasons that people have to want to be in control of their own lives and not be controlled by others (even if others could manipulate them in such a way as to make them happy).

The question that contractualism tells us to address in deciding whether an action is right or wrong is not whether a principle that allowed it is one that someone would reject. People can be unreasonable and reject any principle that does not favor them, no matter how this would affect others. But this does not mean that it would be wrong to ever treat such people in a way that they would not accept. Conversely, people who have low self-esteem and are accustomed to being treated very badly might not object to a principle that gives them less than equal status, because they believe that this is all that someone like them (someone of their race or gender, for example) could expect. But this does not make it permissible to treat such people as inferior. What the rightness or wrongness of an action turns on, according to contractualism, is not whether a principle permitting it is one that others would accept, but on whether a principle permitting it is one that anyone *could reasonably* reject. Deciding whether a rejection is reasonable involves a judgment about the relative strength of the reasons on both sides—those that a person would have to object to the way he or she would be affected by the principle and those that others have for insisting on it.

This requires substantive normative judgment. Contractualism provides no general method for deciding whether it is reasonable to reject a principle on certain grounds, just as utilitarianism provides no general method for deciding which quantity of happiness is greater. Similarly, applying a Divine command theory requires judgment about what a loving God would command. (As we saw, it cannot itself answer this question without making God's will arbitrary.) What each of these views does is just to identify, or claim to identify, the question that we should be asking when we are trying to decide whether an action would be right or wrong. According to all three views, answering this question requires a further normative judgment.

I mentioned above that one problem for utilitarianism is that it seems to support implausible forms of aggregative reasoning: preventing a sufficiently large number of very minor headaches might produce a greater sum of happiness than saving a life. Contractualism has the opposite problem. Insofar as it considers only individuals' objections to various principles, it seems unable to explain why, if one were faced with a choice between saving a larger group of people and saving a smaller group, it would be wrong to save the smaller group. One way of dealing with this problem would be to drop the restriction to personal values. We could then say that it would be reasonable to reject a principle permitting one to save the smaller number rather than the larger because it is worse, impersonally, for the larger number to die, even though this is not worse for any individual. An alternative response would be to say that what contractualism describes is only that part of morality that concerns obligations to specific individuals. If an agent who is faced with a choice between saving two groups of people saves the smaller group, no one individual is wronged. Nonetheless, there is a moral objection to such an action, since the agent could, without wronging anyone, have done much more good and, absent some special reason, is open to criticism for doing less good rather than more. This allows for the kind of consideration that utilitarianism is based on to play some role in determining what we should do, even though this role is limited to cases in which producing more good does not involve wronging any individual.

Whether this suggestion is accepted or not, it is clear that contractualism covers only a part of "morality" as that term is commonly employed. For example, as I have said earlier, various forms of sexual conduct between consenting adults, such as homosexual sex, are seen by some people as morally objectionable. Such actions are not wrong according to contractualism, since no one has reason to reject principles allowing people to engage in them. This does not strike me as an objection to contractualism, since I do not believe that there is any moral objection to these practices.

This is not, however, the only way in which what contractualism (or utilitarianism) covers is narrower than "morality" as it is generally understood. Being extremely lazy and putting no effort into developing one's abilities is a serious fault, plausibly called moral, even when it does not involve violating any obligation to others. Failing to show the kind of special concern for one's friends, children, and parents that these relationships call for is also plausibly called a moral fault. But these special obligations are not well accounted for by contractualism, which deals rather with what we owe to people in general. (The same is true, I believe, of utilitarianism.)

It seems to me an advantage of contractualism that it calls attention to this diversity within what is generally called "morality." The objection to laziness is not that it violates some imperative but that it involves a failure to appreciate the fact that developing and exercising one's talents is something worth doing, and one of the things that makes a life better for the person whose life it is. And a person who treats his friends or family badly is failing to understand and respond to the value of these special relationships which, among other things, are some of the greatest goods in life. So, although faults of these kinds may be called moral, they consist in failures to appreciate and respond to important values, and failures to understand what makes a life better for the person who lives it. If hedonism or a desire theory were the correct account of what makes a life better, then there would be no room for criticism of this kind. But as we have seen, these accounts have serious flaws.

Recognizing this diversity within what is generally called morality also helps to make better sense of the idea of sexual morality. As I have said, I do not believe that homosexual sex, sex between unmarried adults, and masturbation are morally wrong. But this does not mean that, aside from general duties not to harm, coerce, or deceive others, there is no objection, plausibly called moral, to any sexual practice. It is a serious problem in our society that people are encouraged to give sex and sexual attractiveness an exaggerated and mistaken importance in their lives. Living in this way is open to moral criticism not because it violates prohibitions against particular forms of sexual conduct but because it represents a mistaken view about what makes a life better for the person whose life it is. The proper objection to excessive concern with sex is like the objection to being excessively ambitious, or a workaholic: it represents a misunderstanding of one of life's important goods, a misunderstanding that also undermines one's relations with others, by leading one to try to manipulate and dominate them.

These objections are grounded in a conception of what makes a life better for the person who lives it. They would therefore be undermined if hedonism, or a desire theory, were the correct account of what makes a person's life better. The suspicion that one of these views is correct may be what leads people to think that if there is a "nonsubjective" basis for assessing attitudes toward sex, it must lie in a set of moral prohibitions against specific forms of sexual conduct, on a par with prohibitions against lying, stealing, and harming others. Since the idea that there are such sexual prohibitions is implausible, this may lead many to conclude that there is no such thing as sexual morality, beyond the requirements that no one be harmed or coerced.

Recognizing that an adequate account of what makes a life better for the person who lives it will be what I called above a substantive good theory thus allows room for a fuller account of what is generally called morality. There is, first, the core morality of obligations to each other, supported by the value of justifiability. Going beyond this, there are the attitudes, accomplishments, and relationships that contribute to the quality of a life, from the point of view of the person whose life it is. Failing to recognize and respond appropriately to any of these counts as a moral fault. But these faults have different bases.

I began by suggesting that people have differing ideas about what morality is and why it is important, and I have ended by suggesting that morality as we commonly speak of it is best understood as incorporating a variety of different values, which are important for different reasons. The claims I am making are not, however, sociological or psychological observations about what most people think, or descriptions of what I myself think. Rather, like Socrates, I have been reporting my attempt to decide what to think. What I ask of you, the reader, is to consider the reasons I have offered and to consider whether, on reflection, you think this too.

Further Reading

Nozick, Robert. 1974. *Anarchy, State and Utopia*. New York: Basic Books.
A famous statement of libertarian political philosophy, which includes, as asides, many sharp observations about other matters, including the "experience machine" argument against hedonism.

Parfit, Derek. 1984. *Reasons and Persons*. Oxford: Oxford University Press.
A classic work in twentieth-century moral philosophy, known for its defense of a novel view of personal identity and of a form of utilitarianism. Appendix I offers, in condensed form, an instructive assessment of possible answers to the question, "What makes someone's life go best?"

Plato. 1987. *Gorgias,* trans. D. J. Zeyl. Indianapolis: Hackett.
A Platonic dialogue dealing with the questions of why one should care about what is right and just, and what kind of life we have reason to want.

———. 2000. *The Trial and Death of Socrates,* 3rd ed., trans. G. M. A. Grube, rev. J. M. Cooper. Indianapolis: Hackett.
Includes *Euthyphro* and other dialogues.

Ryan, Alan, ed. 1987. *Utilitarianism and Other Essays*. London: Penguin.
Includes the classic statements of the utilitarian view by Jeremy Bentham and John Stuart Mill.

Scanlon, T. M. 1998. *What We Owe to Each Other.* Cambridge, MA: Harvard University Press.

An elaboration and defense of a contractualist account of moral right and wrong, along with discussions of well-being, moral responsibility, and moral relativism.

Singer, Peter. 1972. "Famine, Affluence, and Morality." *Philosophy and Public Affairs* 1: 229–243.

A trenchant argument that we should be doing much more than is commonly recognized to aid people in poverty-stricken lands.

Stevenson, Betsey, and Justin Wolfers. 2009. "The Paradox of Declining Female Happiness." *American Economic Journal: Economic Policy* 1(2): 190–225.

Energy Resources and the Environment: A Chapter on Applied Science

John H. Shaw

Modern industrialized societies depend on tremendous supplies of energy and material resources to fuel their economies and satisfy the needs of their people. These demands have grown rapidly as global population has expanded—indeed, our population has doubled in the past half century, a growth rate unprecedented in our history. As this burgeoning population seeks to modernize, to improve its standards of living, it increasingly depends on a large and steady supply of energy.

Let's consider the energy budget of our species, and how it is impacted by industrialization. Hundreds of thousands of years ago, as primitive hunters and gatherers, our ancestors' energy budget essentially represented their daily intake of food—on the order of perhaps 2,000 kilocalories (kcal) or 8.3 megajoules (MJ) per day. This was the energy that kept us warm and fueled our muscles to avoid predators and gather the food that was needed to survive. Today, in an industrialized society like the United States, we of course still rely on this daily caloric intake. However, to achieve it, with the rich diversity of foodstuffs available in a modern grocery store and the desire to drive a car to the store, to prepare the food in a modern kitchen, and enjoy all of the other comforts of life, we obviously consume a much greater amount of energy (Aubrecht 2006). Considering the total amount of energy used in the United States to fuel its residential, transportation, and industrial sectors, each inhabitant "consumes" an average of about 237,000 kcal (990 MJ) per day (U.S. Department of Energy 2009a)—about a 120-fold increase over our modest days as hunter-gatherers. Moreover, if we consider a similar calculation for a developing nation such as India, we see that the per capita energy consumption under this

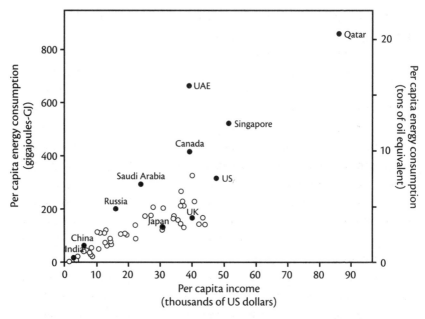

Figure 14. Annual per capita primary energy consumption related to average per capita annual income levels in U.S. dollars for various nations in 2008. All nations are plotted for which data were available from the following data sources: IMF (2009) and BP (2009). Select nations are labeled. (Compiled by Renyi Ang and J. H. Shaw.)

metric lies at about 13,000 kcal per day (54 MJ)—substantially more than our hunter-gatherer ancestors, but only about 6 percent of that consumed in the United States. Indeed, energy consumption generally correlates directly with standards of living, reflected by average income levels, for nations across the globe (Figure 14).

Herein lies one of the major challenges facing humanity in the twenty-first century—as developing nations strive to improve the standards of living for their citizens, will they follow the same course of energy consumption as the United States and other industrialized nations? Will our planet be able to provide the raw materials needed for this growth? If so, can our environment withstand the impacts of this consumption—including air and water pollution, and climate changes induced by greenhouse gas emissions—and support a healthy global population?

The answers to these questions are not yet known. Indeed, they cannot be, because choices that we make as individuals, communities, nations, and a global society over the next several decades will determine these outcomes. Will we continue to use fossil fuels—coal, oil, and natural gas—as our primary energy source? If so, will we invest in clean fossil energy technology and carbon sequestration to mitigate the environmental impacts of this consumption? Alternatively, will we replace significant amounts of the current fossil energy budget with alternatives: nuclear, wind, solar, geothermal, biomass, or other options? If so, what mix of these alternative energy technologies will we choose? The goals of this chapter are to examine the ways that we currently meet the energy demands of our societies and to assess the impact these activities have on our environment, such that we can gauge the sustainability of these practices. In addition, I explore the wide range of alternative energy options and briefly consider the factors that will likely determine their future roles in our energy economy.

Fossil Energy

Fossil fuels include coal, oil, and natural gas, which together comprise the backbone of our energy economy. About 85 percent of global energy demand is met by these fuels (Figure 15) (U.S. Department of Energy 2009a). Most of our electricity is generated by burning coal or natural gas, and refined products of petroleum—gasoline, diesel, and jet fuel—largely drive our transportation sectors. While fossil fuels are often maligned today for their adverse impacts on our environment, they are nevertheless remarkable substances. Power packed—common forms of coal offer three times the energy of a similar mass of wood (ICCOP 1963)—they are available in abundance, readily transportable, and easily milled or refined into usable products. Indeed, we owe much of the growth in our global economy and standards of

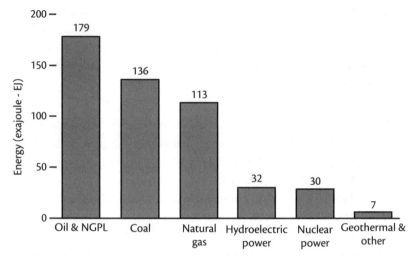

Figure 15. World primary energy production by source (U.S. Department of Energy 2009a). NGPL = Natural gas plant liquids. "Other" refers to net electricity generation from wood, solar, waste, and wind.

living over the nineteenth and twentieth centuries to these remarkable fuels. Yet they pollute our water and air and are the primary source of carbon dioxide (CO_2) emissions to our atmosphere, which are inducing significant climate changes.

As the name implies, fossil fuels represent the remains of ancient plants that have converted the sun's energy through photosynthesis, and animals that have consumed plants that do so. This energy is stored in sugars and a wide array of other organic compounds in their tissues. To yield a viable fossil fuel deposit, the remains of these organisms must be deposited in abundance in an environment with little available oxygen and buried in sediments at great depths in the earth, where they are exposed to high temperatures and pressures that convert them into combustible fuel sources. Oxygen-poor environments are required to ensure that the organic materials are not simply consumed by other organisms and thus returned to the living carbon cycle.

Given this complicated path, it is clear that most organic deposits do not become fossil fuels. Only a small percentage of organic material in the biosphere is deposited in sediments, and most of this is scattered in low concentrations through common sedimentary rocks, such as shales and mudstones. Of the carbon present in these sediments, perhaps only a few percent occurs in sufficient abundance and follows the necessary path to form fossil fuels (Barnes et al. 1984; Craig et al. 2001). Costs of development, political boundaries, and environmental concerns dictate that not all of these deposits can be accessed. Thus, only a very small fraction of the carbon entrained in rocks resides in commercially viable deposits of fossil fuels. Nevertheless, these deposits are sufficiently abundant, and geologists are good enough at finding them, that they remain our primary sources of energy.

To explore the nature of these fossil fuel deposits, we can start with the requirement of an abundant source of organic material. If we consider the organic productivity of different environments on the Earth (see table on page 272), we see that coastal, forested wetlands and off-shore continental shelves are the two hot spots. These regions form the primary environments for the deposition of coal and petroleum precursors, respectively. In the following sections, I explore both of these types of fuels, examining the environments in which they form and the paths they follow to yield economically viable deposits. I also introduce the methods used to explore for and exploit these resources, discuss how these resources are currently used in our societies, and address the environmental impacts of these activities.

Energy from Coal

Dark, dirty, and dusty—all terms we might use to describe coal. Accurate, to be sure. However, these descriptions of coal often lead to misapprehensions—that coal is an ancient fuel, relegated to the industrial revolutions of the late nineteenth and early twentieth centuries, with no place in our future. Why would anyone use "dirty" coal when

Organic productivity by region (see Brown and Skipsey 1986)

Environment	Global area (10^6 km^2)	Organic carbon (10^{10} ton/yr)
Desert	68	0.2
Grassland	26	0.65
Forest	41	3.25
Agricultural land	14	0.9
Near-shore seas	2	0.4
Continental shelf	84	2.325
Open ocean	276	2.275

cleaner, more environmentally friendly options exist? Yet today, we produce about 6.5 billion tons of coal annually around the globe, more than at any time in our history (U.S. Department of Energy 2009a). Moreover, many estimates place global coal reserves at nearly 1 trillion tons. Given such massive reserves, the United States appears capable of maintaining its current rate of production (about 1.1 billion tons) for several hundred years. Thus, coal is likely to be a major part of our energy future throughout the twenty-first century.

Most coal represents the remains of ancient land plants—specifically plants with abundant cellulose, or woody tissues. Based on the types of sedimentary rocks in which coal is found, as well as trace fossils of the plants themselves, we know that ancient coastal forests, mangrove swamps, and delta floodplains were common environments where coal precursors were deposited. These environments foster abundant plant growth, and the stagnant waters are generally low in dissolved oxygen because much of it is consumed by organic decomposition. The plant life is so abundant, however, that all of the organic materials cannot be fully decomposed, and much becomes entrained in the sediments. Subsequent burial of these deposits protects them from further decay and exposes them to temperatures and pressures that convert them to coal.

The maturation process of coal starts with the formation of peat, a complex mixture of partially decayed plant remains. Peat is very abundant today, forming the substrate of bogs and swamps around the world. In its own right, peat represents a viable energy source, as it can be burned. However, peat is bulky, with relatively low energy density (3,000 kcal/kg), and typically needs to be dried, a process that consumes energy—often from burning wood or fossil fuels—before it can be used as a fuel. Thus peat sees modest use as a fuel source and is generally only suitable for local consumption. True coal is formed by the further burial and chemical alteration of peat. In general, the organic composition of peat and coal are so complex and varied that they are usually not described by specific chemical formulas. Rather, proportions of carbon, oxygen, and hydrogen are used to establish the rank of coal. In the initial stages of coal formation, oxygen is removed from coal, followed at higher stages of maturation by reduction of hydrogen (Brown and Skipsey 1986). At various stages, this process yields different grades of coal, each of which has unique properties—the most important of which being its energy value (see the table below).

Peat is first transformed into brown coals, called lignites, then into subbituminous and bituminous coals. These latter coals represent the common form of coal that most of us would conjure up—black, shiny coals often filled with fractures, known as cleat. Further maturation of these coals yields anthracites, shiny metallic coals that are packed

Average heat content for coals (see ICCOP 1963)

Coal grade	Heat content (kcal/lb)	Heat content (MJ/kg)
Peat	3,000	12.6
Lignite	4,000–5,500	16.7–23.0
Bituminous	7,000	29.3
Anthracite	8,650	36.2

with energy, and then eventually graphite—essentially pure carbon, with all of the oxygen and hydrogen removed. With increasing coal grades come greater amounts of energy per unit of mass burned. In the early days of the Industrial Revolution, coal miners in the Appalachians targeted anthracite coals, given that they were less bulky and thus easier to mine and transport. Today, most of the accessible anthracites in the Appalachians have been mined out, and production has turned largely to bituminous coals. In the western United States, both bituminous and lignite coals are produced in abundance. The lignites do not pack the same energy as their higher-grade counterparts, but their relative abundance in easily accessible deposits has led to their development. Use of these bulky coals has also led to the trend of building coal-burning power plants in the vicinity of mines, in part to lower the costs of coal transport.

Coal deposits occur in seams, from centimeters to as much as ten meters thick, which alternate with sandstones and other sedimentary rocks. These alternating sequences of coal seams and sediments reflect the variable nature of the depositional environments in which the coal precursors formed. Coal seams only occur in rocks that are about 396 million years of age (called the Devonian period) or younger, given that prior to this time there were no land plants to form coal precursors. Indeed, the first widespread occurrence of coal deposits is found in rocks that are about 300 million years old, a period aptly termed the Carboniferous (Craig et al. 2001). Moreover, most accessible large coal deposits occur in areas where sediments have been buried, then uplifted, bringing mature coals to the surface or shallow subsurface where they can be mined efficiently. Thus, many large coal mines are found in mountainous terrains.

Coal has traditionally been excavated in subsurface mines that follow along coal seams. Coal is simply broken into small pieces and moved by conveyor to the surface. In the United States, the productivity of subsurface coal mining has essentially remained constant over the last fifty years. However, the development of large earth-moving equipment, combined with the rapid growth in coal mining west of the Mississippi River, has spurred the growth of surface or "strip" mining operations. In the 1950s surface mining accounted for about 25 percent of U.S. coal production, and today it represents about 75 percent (U.S. Department of Energy 2009a). Strip mining does not get its name because it "strips the land bare," although this well may be the case in its careless implementation. Rather, the name reflects that the mining is usually conducted in strips of land, where soils and sedimentary rocks above the targeted seams are removed, the coal is mined, and the sediments and soils are replaced (Brown and Skipsey 1986). The stripping ratio, or the ratio of overburden to reserves, is often a key factor in determining the economic viability of a coal deposit. The relatively modern practice of mountaintop removal mining takes this approach of surface mining to an extreme, where the overburden, essentially the mountaintop, is removed by blasting and shed into adjacent valleys. As we will consider, such forms of surface mining have the potential for significant environmental impacts due to their disruption of the land surface and tendency to acidify groundwaters. Nevertheless, production trends show that, left unchecked, surface mining will continue to grow as the preferred method of accessing coal reserves in the United States and around the world.

Once coal is mined, it is further milled, and noncoal components—pieces of sandstone and shale—are mechanically separated and removed. Otherwise, the coal is ready for transport to market, typically by rail or barge. As we have seen, the energy potential of coal is influenced significantly by its grade. Nevertheless, it remains a bulky resource when compared to other fossil fuels such as oil and natural gas, and coal transport usually accounts for a significant percentage of the total cost of production. Thus, most of the top coal-producing nations—including China, the United States, Russia, Germany, and India—are also top coal consumers (U.S. Department of Energy 2009a).

A traditional coal-burning power station consists of a few basic components: a railhead or harbor to bring the coal to the station, a conveyor system that brings the coal into the station, and a set of pulverizers that convert the coal to a dust that has the consistency of wheat flour, helping ensure that it is fully combusted when placed in the furnace. The burning coal heats water that is converted to steam, which is used to drive turbine blades that spin a generator, producing electricity. The steam is then condensed back into water, with cold water from a nearby river or ocean, or cooling towers, providing the chill. Hot gases and particulates are produced by the furnace and released through smokestacks. These emissions typically include CO_2, which is linked to global warming, and sulfur dioxide (SO_2), which can cause acid rain. In addition, flue emissions typically include fine ash and trace amounts of mercury, which are thought to have adverse human health effects. I discuss the impacts of these emissions, and ways to address these challenges, in the following section.

Environmental Impacts of Coal

When a laptop is plugged in, a cell phone is charged, or a light is turned on, most people are simply unaware that coal is often the primary source of the electricity they use. Electricity is clean, has no emissions, no pollution, and essentially no adverse environmental impacts. Yet the same cannot be said of the way most of it is produced. Using coal as an energy resource has two major types of environmental impacts—the first involves effects to local environments due to mining coal, and the second relates to by-products of its combustion that can pollute the atmosphere and hydrosphere. As discussed, coal is excavated in both subsurface and surface mining operations. Coal mining is a relatively dangerous occupation, leading on average to tens of deaths per year in the United States (U.S. Department of Energy 2009d) and hundreds, if not thousands, of fatalities worldwide. Mines also affect the land surface in many ways, including some degree of aesthetic impact, with surface strip mining and mountaintop removal practices offering the greatest eyesores.

As significant as these local impacts might be, the greatest hazards posed by coal mining operations relate to acidification of the environment. About 2 to 6 percent of coal's weight is sulfur, derived from the organic materials that formed the coal precursors (Craig et al. 2001). In mature coal, the sulfur is present in the form of pyrite—FeS_2 (also known as fool's gold)—or in a myriad of complex organic compounds. When exposed to water, much of this sulfur is oxidized and converted to sulfuric acid (H_2SO_4); pulverization of the rocks in the mining process accelerates the oxidation process. This strong acid can substantially lower the pH of surface and groundwaters, harming vegetation, fish, amphibians, and a host of other marine organisms (e.g., Turco 2002). Acidic groundwaters also tend to leach metals from rocks and soils, such as aluminum, lead, and arsenic, that are known to have toxic effects in humans and other organisms. Acid runoff is often most severe in abandoned mine shafts and in coal mining operations where waste rock, known as talus, is exposed to rain and groundwater by being kept at the surface or, in the case of mountaintop removal, is dumped into adjacent valleys and stream beds. Acid runoff can be addressed by buffering the systems with lime or other compounds to raise the pH and by using carbon filters and other systems to leach metals and other toxic compounds from the water. These mitigation approaches, however, are not universally applied today to address acid drainage problems from coal mines due to the large scale of these operations and the resulting costs of the mitigation efforts.

The second major environmental impact of using coal relates to emissions. Burning coal emits ash, SO_2, nitrogen compounds, mercury and other metals, and CO_2. Indeed, in 1872 Robert Smith coined the term "smog" to describe an acidic mix of smoke and fog that plagued London. London smog was caused when atmospheric conditions "trapped" the emissions from coal burned in factories and residences at low elevations, preventing the ash and other chemicals from dispersing. Several incidents of intense smog over the late nineteenth and twentieth centuries led to hundreds of deaths in London (Turco 2002), generally impacting elderly populations and those with respiratory diseases.

Smith also recognized that emissions of SO_2 from combusting sulfur-bearing compounds in the coal were causing an increase in the acidity levels of rain and bodies of water around London. The SO_2 is readily transformed in the atmosphere to sulfuric acid, similar to the process that occurs in mine runoff. However, the sulfur compounds produced by combusting coal can be dispersed over wide areas by winds, and thus can adversely affect large regions. The sulfuric acid is precipitated as acid rain, which increases the acidity of groundwater, lakes, and streams, with a number of harmful effects. Many types of plants are intolerant of low pH levels, and thus acid rain can cause widespread deforestation and declines in agricultural productivity. Indeed, forests in parts of northern Europe and eastern North America experienced major declines due to acid rain in the 1970s and 1980s. Many aquatic species are also intolerant of low pH levels, as well as the toxic metals—such as mercury, aluminum, lead, and arsenic—that are mobilized in acidic waters. These effects can be dramatic. For example, many of the lakes in the Adirondack Mountains of upstate New York became sterile in the last few decades. These lakes lie downwind of major coal-burning power stations and industries in the midwestern United States.

There are several strategies for reducing the emissions of coal-burning power stations. Ash and other particulates can be effectively removed by electrostatic systems or filtration units, known as "bag houses." The best of these systems are capable of removing the vast majority of this ash. Moreover, some of the mercury can also be removed by adding activated carbon to the flue stream. However, systems in operation today cost about $60,000 USD per pound of mercury recovered (U.S. Department of Energy 2009c). Given that mercury emissions from coal-fired plants in the United States exceeded 45 tons in 2005, the cost of reducing mercury emissions is substantial. Nevertheless, the Environmental Protection Agency has established standards for mercury emissions from new and older coal-burning power plants, and targets a 70 percent emissions reduction relative to 2005 levels by 2020 (U.S. Environmental Protection Agency 2010).

Attempts to reduce sulfur emissions from coal burning often start at the source. Certain coals naturally contain lower amounts of sulfur and thus produce less SO_2 when burned. Indeed, many coal-burning power facilities choose to meet targeted reductions in SO_2 emissions by burning lower-sulfur coals. This generally increases fuel costs and has led to an expansion of the international trade in coal. Plants in the northeastern United States, for example, import low-sulfur coals from South America or Indonesia, which they combine with higher-sulfur domestic coals to meet emissions targets. Perhaps the most effective strategies for reducing sulfur emissions involve "scrubbing" the SO_2 from the flue gas. Dry and wet lime systems remove the SO_2 by mixing it with lime solutions, forming various compounds that precipitate out of the flue steam and are collected. Wet lime systems are generally the most efficient, reducing SO_2 emissions by up to 90 percent. This is done by converting the SO_2 to gypsum—$CaSO_4(H_2O)_2$—by the following reaction:

$$SO_2 + CaCO_3 + 2H_2O + \tfrac{1}{2}O_2 = CaSO_4(H_2O)_2 + CO_2$$

Although installing these systems involves significant expense, and they require large amounts of water, the by-product—gypsum—can be sold to manufacturers of drywall and other building products. Revenues from these sales often go a long way toward reducing the costs of these wet lime systems. While this seems like an attractive solution to reducing sulfur emissions, many coal plants in operation around the globe today do not have such wet lime systems in place, given the substantial costs of retrofitting these systems in older power plants.

Finally, combusting coal generates large amounts of CO_2, an important greenhouse gas. Greenhouse gases in the atmosphere allow sunlight to pass through but absorb a large amount of the heat that is radiated back from the earth, thus warming the atmosphere. The production of CO_2 is the simple result of burning—or oxidizing—the carbon in coal, petroleum, wood, or any other carbon-based fuel. However, combusting coal generates proportionately more CO_2 per unit energy than most of these other fuels. The amount of CO_2 produced per unit energy depends somewhat on the coal grade, but estimates for an average bituminous coal are about 1 pound of CO_2 per 5 million joules of generated power (U.S. Department of Energy 2009b). That is about 30 percent more than the amount generated to produce the same amount of power from gasoline, and 50 percent more than from natural gas. Thus coal-burning power stations account for a large percentage of our global CO_2 emissions, and any future progress we might hope to make in significantly reducing these emissions will involve changes in the amount of coal burned, or the way it is used, to generate electricity. Given that this problem also applies to oil and natural gas, I will discuss various options for reducing CO_2 emissions after I have discussed these other fossil fuels.

Oil and Natural Gas

If coal is a fuel of the past and future, oil is the energy of today. No energy source is produced in such abundance (see Figure 15), at such expense, from such depth, and in so many inhospitable locations. Oil and its counterpart, natural gas, are produced, refined, transported around the globe, and bought and sold in global markets, all to meet our demands for a portable, power-packed energy source. Oil is primarily used today to fuel our transportation systems—cars, trucks, planes, and just about everything that runs on an internal combustion or jet engine. Natural gas is used largely to generate electricity, heat our homes and businesses, and generate nitrogen fertilizers. Oil and natural gas are derived from the remains of aquatic organisms, mostly plankton, deposited in oxygen-poor sediments on continental shelves in the ocean or in deep lakes. These organically rich sediments must then be buried and exposed to temperatures that alter their chemistry, converting them to oils and natural gases. The first step in this process involves the formation of kerogen, a jellylike substance composed of fossilized organic matter. With further increases in temperature, this kerogen matures into oil and natural gas. For typical kerogens, oils are generated at temperatures of 50 to 200°C, corresponding to typical burial depths of 2 to 6 km, a region known as the oil window. Greater temperatures yield large amounts of gases, culminating in production of essentially pure methane—CH_4—at the greatest depths and temperatures (Hunt 1995). Methane can also be produced at shallow depths by biogenic processes and at great pressures and temperatures by inorganic processes. Biogenic gas contributes to many large gas fields in Russia and other areas. Inorganic production of gas has been reproduced in the laboratory but has not yet been shown to contribute in any substantial way to economic oil and natural gas deposits.

Composition of Oil and Gas

Oil and natural gas are hydrocarbons, comprised of various molecular structures that bind hydrogen and carbon atoms in chains and rings. These hydrocarbon building blocks include chains (paraffins), pentagonal rings (napthenes), and hexagonal rings (aromatics). Each of these molecular structures includes a variety of specific compounds with different numbers of hydrogen and carbon atoms present, and thus with different molecular weights. The relative proportions of these compounds dictate the characteristics of the oil, including its density and viscosity (Hunt 1995). Refinement of crude oil, a process first discovered by Arab cultures in 1000 CE, is essentially a process of separating these different molecular weight compounds by distillation (Craig et al. 2001). As the crude is heated, the components vaporize at temperatures in proportion to their molecular weights. At the lowest temperatures, distillation separates low molecular weight molecules, mostly paraffins and napthenes, forming gasoline and kerosene. Intermediate weight paraffins, napthenes, and aromatics yield diesel fuel and heating oils, and the highest molecular weight compounds, rich in aromatics, are used for lubricants.

Oil and Gas Reserves

What does it take to form an economically viable deposit of oil and natural gas? Clearly, this requires an organically rich deposit of ocean or lake sediments, known as a source rock, that can be buried to depth and undergo the maturation process that I have described. Most oil source rocks are shales or limestones. However, the oils and gases generated by this process are generally too widely distributed in the source rock to be extracted efficiently. Thus, viable hydrocarbon deposits generally consist of oils and gases that have been expelled from the source rock and accumulated in porous and permeable rocks, known as reservoirs (Figure 16). Good petroleum reservoir rocks generally contain about 10–25 percent pore space and have sufficiently high permeability to allow the fluids to be extracted at high rates. Most hydrocarbon reservoirs are sandstones or limestones in which porosity and permeability are often enhanced by natural fractures.

Hydrocarbons migrate from the source to reservoir and accumulate in a trap, often formed by a fault or fold of the strata (known as a structural trap), or by a pinch-out of the reservoir rock (known as a stratigraphic trap). Finally, the reservoir and trap must be overlain by an impermeable rock, known as a seal, that prohibits the hydrocarbons from migrating toward the land surface and dispersing. Hydrocarbon seals, commonly made up of shales or evaporate deposits, are everything that reservoir rocks are not—having low porosity and permeability. The evaporates, consisting of salt and other minerals deposited during the evaporation of ancient oceans, often form the best seals,

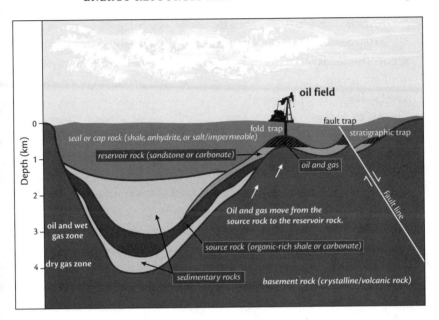

oil field

fold trap

fault trap

stratigraphic trap

seal or cap rock (shale, anhydrite, or salt/impermeable)

reservoir rock (sandstone or carbonate)

oil and gas

fault line

Oil and gas move from the source rock to the reservoir rock.

oil and wet gas zone

source rock (organic-rich shale or carbonate)

dry gas zone

sedimentary rocks

basement rock (crystalline/volcanic rock)

Depth (km)

0

1

2

3

4

Figure 16. Elements of a basic petroleum system. (Shaw and Holdren 2007; drafted by Michelle Hardy.)

given their low permeability and ductility, which lessens the likelihood that they will be breached by fractures and faults. All of these components—source, reservoir, trap, and seal—are required to form a traditional petroleum accumulation, and together comprise a hydrocarbon system (Magoon and Dow 1994) (Figure 16). The scarcity of large oil and gas deposits results not from the lack of any one of these components but from the requirement that all are in place at the appropriate times.

The geologic history of a region dictates the extent to which the various hydrocarbon system elements are in place, and hence the amount of oil and gas resources that is present. These resources are not distributed evenly among sedimentary basins, continents, or nations of the world. About 60 percent of the world's petroleum reserves reside in the Middle East (U.S. Department of Energy 2009a; BP 2009). In contrast, only about 3 percent of the world's petroleum reserves occur in the larger and more heavily populated Asia Pacific region (BP 2009). This leads us to the international system of petroleum exploration, production, sale, transport, refining, and marketing that dominates today's energy economy.

Oil and natural gas are discovered and produced today largely by studying the geologic history of a basin, using a variety of geochemical methods to establish the presence of mature hydrocarbons and geophysical methods to image traps and characterize reservoirs and seals. Prospects are tested by drilling wells using mud rotary rigs and running a series of tools down the borehole to detect the presence of hydrocarbons and assess reservoir properties, including porosity and fluid pressures. If initial assessments are positive, wells are tested to assess fluid flow rates and resulting pressure changes, which can be used to infer the size of an accumulation and the prospects for developing the field. Data are then assimilated into a computerized model of the reservoir, which is used to simulate oil and gas production using a range of development strategies. Based on this assessment, fields are subsequently developed by drilling a series of wells to optimize production rates and the total amount of oil and gas that can be recovered. Primary production simply involves developing fields by pumping or allowing the natural pressures to push the oil and gas to the surface. Secondary or enhanced oil recovery practices involve pumping fluids such as natural gas, steam, or CO_2 into the reservoir to help maintain pressures and enhance production. A number of other techniques are used today to help maximize well performance. These include drilling deviated or horizontal boreholes, which substantially increase the thickness of the reservoir section in contact with the borehole. In addition, by increasing fluid pressures within boreholes, fractures can be generated in low-permeability reservoirs to enhance the flow of oil and gas.

In 2008 about 82 million barrels of oil were produced each day around the world (BP 2009), and the rate of oil production has been

climbing over the past few decades. Given that oil and gas are nonre-
newable resources, many have forecast an imminent peak to world oil
production, with the subsequent decline having dire impacts on an
unprepared economy. Yet rates of oil production, to this point in time,
have been able to meet global demands. This ability to keep pace reflects a number of factors. First, new technologies of geophysical
imaging and reservoir characterization are enabling more effective
exploration for new fields and development of existing ones. Drilling
technologies are also allowing for exploration in deep water and other
geologically complex areas that were previously inaccessible. The application of advanced drilling and well completion practices, such as
horizontal drilling and reservoir fracturing, are also enabling the development of reserves that were previously not viable. Some of today's
most active developments involve applying these practices to recover
shale gas, essentially gas reserves that reside within source rocks. Shale
gas deposits now account for about one-third of natural gas resources
in the United States (Potential Gas Committee 2008). Finally, the proven
practice of liquefying natural gas by compression and cooling allows it
to be transported great distances by oceangoing tankers. Production of
liquefied natural gas (LNG) has enabled many "stranded" gas deposits
in areas far from their markets to be developed. In 2008 the United
States received about 13 percent of its imported gas as LNG and had
about twenty new facilities for receiving LNG tankers under construction (U.S. Federal Energy Regulatory Commission 2009). More recently, U.S. LNG imports have slowed due to emergence of shale gas
supplies, but LNG will likely continue to play a major role in nations
that lack their own domestic gas reserves.

In a similar vein, much of the world's remaining oil deposits lie
in tar sands and oil shales. The former contain heavy oils trapped in
reservoirs and exposed at or near the surface. The oils are produced
largely by mining the sands and using hot water, other reagents, and
centrifuges to extract the lighter weight fraction of the oil. Deeper tar
sands are also being developed in the subsurface by drilling and steam

injection. Finally, huge resources of oil reside in shales—essentially in the source rocks from which they were produced. Several technologies are currently being explored to extract the oil from these rocks, employing processes that are generally similar to those used to produce oil from tar sands. However, developing all of these nontraditional supplies of petroleum is costly, requiring energy—usually in the form of diesel fuel and natural gas—to mine the reserves and to generate heat and steam. As a result, these nonconventional methods of oil production deliver less energy for every barrel of oil. In the case of tar sand production, mining delivers only about 70 percent of the energy for each barrel of oil produced when compared with conventional oil and gas production. Subsurface tar sand production delivers only about 50 percent (Canada PRA 2009). So why are these resources being so aggressively developed today? Well, conventional oil is getting more difficult to find and more costly to produce. Moreover, the remaining reserves of these nontraditional deposits are tremendous. While it is estimated that we have about 1.2 trillion barrels of conventional oil reserves today (BP 2009), we may have more than 5 trillion barrels of oil resources in such nonconventional heavy oil deposits that could reasonably be exploited with future technology and prices (EMD 2009). While there are essentially no shale oil reserves today, the size of this potential resource—over 300 trillion barrels (Craig et al. 2001)—is even more staggering. If technology is developed to extract even a modest fraction of this resource, we might find ourselves with plenty of oil on hand, albeit expensive. Thus, it seems likely that the future of petroleum in our energy economy is not likely to be dictated by a sheer lack of availability of this resource, but rather by how much we are willing to pay for it and how we judge the impacts of its use on our environment.

Environmental Impacts of Producing and Using Petroleum

Almost every aspect of the petroleum cycle—from frontier exploration to burning gasoline in your car—has some form of direct impact on our environment. Exploration in remote areas can provide access, by building roads or clearing areas of jungle, to sensitive environments that are exploited by others. Oil drilling and production can also yield hydrocarbon-bearing saline waters, as well as toxic (H_2S, hydrogen sulfide) and greenhouse (CO_2) gases, and fluids that are contaminated with toxic metals (mercury, lead) and radioactive (e.g., radium) compounds. If these drilling activities and by-products are not properly managed, they can have very negative impacts on local environments. The 2010 BP oil spill in the Gulf of Mexico is a clear example of what can go wrong when adequate safety measures are not in place. While the investigation into the Deepwater Horizon drilling rig explosion and well blowout is still under way, the Committee on Energy and Commerce of the U.S. Congress has indicated that BP failed to ensure that an adequate casing system was in place to prevent such a disaster. Casing is a series of steel pipes that are lowered into a borehole and cemented in place to maintain the integrity of the well and prevent the uncontrolled flow of oil, gas, and other fluids. BP and its contractors made several key decisions related to the well's casing program that were inconsistent with conventional practices and that compromised the well, apparently to save time and money (U.S. House CEC 2010). The faulty casing system, the failure to recognize it in well pressure tests, and the failure of the blow-out preventer—a device designed to shut off the well as a last line of defense—caused the disaster.

Large oil spills like the recent BP blowout, as well as tanker accidents such as the 1989 *Exxon Valdez* incident, pose clear threats to marine ecosystems. Aside from the eyesore of oil washing up on scenic coastlines, large oil spills can cause extensive damage to populations of marine birds, mammals, fish, crustaceans, and a range of other organisms. The heavier molecular weight compounds in crude oils tend to coat and smother animals, reducing the buoyancy and heat retention abilities of birds and mammals, and coating the filtering devices of intratidal organisms such as shellfish and barnacles. The lower molecular weight compounds in oils tend to be more soluble in water and thus are ingested by marine organisms and work their way up the food chain. These hydrocarbon compounds are generally stored in lipids and other animal tissues and can cause lysis—rupture of cell membranes—and have a range of other toxic effects (Laws 2000).

Many different methods have been proposed to address oil spills once they occur, such as sinking slicks by adding sand or chalk, or dispersing oils using hot water or detergents. Most of these techniques are out of favor, as they are feared to do more harm than good. Natural processes of evaporation and degradation of oils by bacteria are known to be the most effective. Thus, aside from efforts to offload, burn, or physically contain spills, most current responses are aimed at promoting natural processes, such as adding fertilizers to promote biodegradation. Another controversial approach is using chemical agents to disperse oils. These dispersants turn slicks into smaller droplets and spread oils over larger areas, which, proponents argue, enhances biodegradation and negates many of the hazards posed by the slicks. Others argue that the dispersants themselves are harmful, and that the smaller oil droplets are more toxic to various marine organisms. Ultimately, the best approach seems to be preventing these accidents from happening in the first place. Establishing and enforcing adequate guidelines for drilling and shipping procedures perhaps offers the greatest promise to avoid future catastrophes. For example, the 1990 U.S. Oil Pollution Act will phase out large, single-hulled tankers completely by 2015, and replace them with double-hulled tankers that are far less prone to cause spills.

The adverse environmental impacts of refining and burning petroleum are in many ways harder to address. The process of refining oil is energy intensive, and the products are consumed largely by our transportation sector—cars, planes, trains, tractors, and boats—that effectively distribute the combustion products across the globe. These primary pollutants—compounds essentially emitted out the tailpipe—include carbon monoxide (CO), nitric oxide (NO), and a range of partially combusted hydrocarbon compounds and other particulates.

NO and the hydrocarbon compounds react with ultraviolet radiation from the sun to form nitrogen dioxide (NO_2), ozone (O_3), and a variety of other organic compounds such as peroxyacetyl nitrate that contribute to urban air pollution (Turco 2002). This pollution covers many of the world's cities in a thick haze and is accentuated by certain atmospheric conditions that hold this polluted air in place. Urban smog is known to have direct human health effects, primarily impacting the respiratory system, and high levels regularly trigger pollution advisories that recommend restricting outdoor physical activities.

Much has and can be done to limit this source of air pollution. Better-tuned engines, catalytic conversion, and oxygenated gasolines can contribute to reducing the amounts of CO and hydrocarbons that are produced. Diesel engines also yield less nitrogen compounds and are generally more fuel efficient. These and other measures to limit pollution from industry and at power plants have led to reductions in ozone and nitrogen compound emissions in many parts of Europe and North America (U.S. Environmental Protection Agency 2007). Furthermore, burning various natural gas compounds in lieu of oil also can substantially reduce emissions. Burning pure natural gas (methane), for example, yields only water vapor and CO_2.

Greenhouse Gas Emissions and Climate Change

All of the gaseous products of combusting coal and petroleum that we have discussed, including sulfur, nitrogen, and hydrocarbon-bearing compounds, are important because of their potentially hazardous impacts to local and regional environments. However, in sum they represent a relatively small fraction of what comes out of the tailpipe or smokestack. Aside from water vapor, most of what is produced is CO_2, a simple oxidized form of the many complex carbon compounds that make up our fossil fuels. CO_2 naturally occurs in our atmosphere, and by the process of photosynthesis in plants is used to generate the carbon building blocks of life. How could such a compound be of concern? Indeed, no one was concerned in the late nineteenth and early twentieth centuries when we were building our energy economy based on fossil fuels. However, today we clearly know that CO_2 acts as a greenhouse gas, allowing visible and similar wavelengths of light from the sun to pass through, but absorbing infrared radiation that is emitted back from the earth. This causes a heating of the atmosphere and thus contributes to global warming. Although CO_2 has only modest capacity as a greenhouse gas, indeed tens to thousands of times less effective than methane, nitrous oxide, and chlorofluorocarbons, it is responsible for about 80 percent of the greenhouse emissions to our atmosphere (U.S. Environmental Protection Agency 2006), given the vast amount that we produce as we generate energy. Based on records of atmospheric CO_2 levels and temperatures from ice cores, we know that atmospheric CO_2 concentrations have closely tracked average temperatures over the past several hundreds of thousands of years (Petit et al. 1999). Thus, a link between these concentrations, given the known greenhouse effect, leads most to believe that CO_2 is largely responsible for, or at least is rapidly accelerating, global warming. The effects of global warming—melting of polar ice caps, rising of sea levels, changes in precipitation patterns, increased frequency of damaging storms, changes to local ecosystems—are well documented, and a fuller treatment would simply be beyond the scope of this essay. In any case, we know that burning fossil fuels for energy is responsible for more than 95 percent of the CO_2 released into our atmosphere (U.S. Environmental Protection Agency 2006). Thus, any attempt to curb greenhouse gas emissions and to combat accelerated global warming must deal with energy production.

All of the fossil fuels that we use to generate energy are not the same in terms of their carbon footprint. As we discussed, combusting coal generates about 1 pound of CO_2 per 5 million joules of generated power. Producing the same amount of energy by burning gasoline or natural gas produces about 25 percent and 50 percent less CO_2, respectively (U.S. Department of Energy 2009b). Thus, choices we make about the types of fossil fuels we use, for example, using more natural gas and less oil and coal to generate electricity, heat our homes, and fuel our transportation systems, have an impact on our greenhouse gas emissions. Indeed, cheaper gas prices led to reductions in U.S. greenhouse gas emissions in 2008 and 2009, as natural gas has been used to generate more electricity in lieu of coal (U.S. Environmental Protection Agency 2011). However, the abundance of coal and the existing infrastructure for using oil as our primary transportation fuel work in opposition to this path. Thus, we must likely consider incentives to make such changes, as well as investing in other alternatives to substantially reduce greenhouse gas emissions and the effects they have on our environment.

Energy Options

To mitigate the adverse environmental impacts of our energy consumption, we have several options. The first is simply to be more efficient in our energy production and use. Wasting less energy, insulating our homes and businesses, implementing higher fuel efficiency standards in our cars and trucks, and building more modern, thermodynamically efficient power plants have the straightforward effect of reducing fuel consumption and emissions. Conservation and efficiency have few downsides. However, these steps alone are unlikely to address fully such far-ranging problems as climate change, given the way most of our power is currently produced, and the desires of developing nations to seek inexpensive forms of energy to enhance the standards of living for their people. We also have the option to mitigate the harmful impacts of energy consumption by cleansing our emissions. In the case of sulfur emissions from coal-burning power plants, we have seen that using low-sulfur coals and lime scrubbing systems has proven very effective at reducing our sulfur emissions in Europe and North America. Notably, these reductions were largely facilitated in the United States by Title IV of the Clean Air Act, which was first implemented in 1995 and targeted a reduction of SO_2, NO_2, and NO emissions below 1980 levels. The act set up a cap-and-trade system, whereby the right to generate emissions was awarded based on historic production at a rate of $1,500 USD (adjusted for inflation) for each ton of SO_2 per year. This established a trading system and thus put in place a clear financial incentive to reduce emissions. The effect seems clear, in that the United States has substantially reduced its SO_2 emissions over the past few decades, despite the growth in its economy.

The European Union has such an emissions reduction cap-and-trade system in place for CO_2. However, the United States and most other nations do not regulate carbon emissions, perhaps given fears that it would adversely impact their economies by increasing energy costs. Indeed, the best methods of reducing carbon emissions from fossil fuel combustion are also uncertain. One strategy is to prevent carbon emissions from reaching the atmosphere by sequestering the CO_2 into geologic reservoirs (e.g., Schrag 2007a, 2007b). Several options for CO_2 sequestration are currently in development, including pumping CO_2 into saline aquifers or oil. Indeed, the elements of an ideal petroleum system, less the hydrocarbon source, also make for good carbon sequestration sites. In fact, oil companies are the largest "sequesterers" of CO_2 today, pumping the gas into their reservoirs to maintain pressures and enhance production—a process called enhanced oil recovery. Other strategies include injecting pressurized CO_2 deep into the ocean, where it would be more dense than seawater and thus remain entrained in seafloor sediments (House et al. 2006). Alternatively, enhancing forest growth or the natural productivity of oceans, by adding iron, urea, and other fertilizers, would help promote natural sequestration. We could also inject CO_2 into certain types of rock formations, where it would precipitate as calcium and magnesium carbonates. Finally, technology is under development that may allow CO_2 to be converted back into usable hydrocarbon fuels with the use of sunlight and nanotubes. While not formally sequestering the CO_2, this approach could help substantially reduce emissions by effectively recycling the carbon. While saline aquifer injection, largely in oil and gas reservoirs, is the only sequestering method in significant practice today, several of these approaches may become important strategies for reducing atmospheric levels of CO_2 in the future. If we continue to burn large amounts of fossil fuels, we will have to do something with the CO_2 if we are to avoid increasing atmospheric concentrations of this gas.

Another approach to reducing emissions is to transition our energy economy away from fossil fuels to cleaner alternatives. These alternative energies all tap a specific part of the earth's natural energy flux—power from the sun, from tides, and the atom. In the following sections I discuss alternative energy options in these three categories and conclude with an assessment of future energy trends.

Harnessing the Power of the Sun

Most of the earth's accessible energy comes in the form of sunlight. Some of this energy heats our atmosphere, causing pressure changes that drive winds, which can be harnessed by turbines to generate electricity. Wind power generated from a standard turbine can be described by the following simple equation:

$$P = \tfrac{1}{2}\rho v^3 \pi r^2 C$$

where P equals wind power in watts, ρ is the density of dry air (1.225 kg/ m^3 at 15°C), v is the wind velocity in meters per second (m/s), r is the rotor radius in meters, and C is an efficiency factor based on turbine and generator designs that is generally less than 0.25 (after AWEA 2009).

Thus, size and velocity do matter. Power production is scaled to the square of the turbine size and to the third power of the wind velocity. A standard turbine design with a rotor diameter of about 50 meters in 9.4 m/s (21 mph) winds would produce about 1 megawatt of power, or about 1/1,500 of that produced by a large coal-burning power station.

Sites suitable for large-scale wind production must have adequate average wind speed, generally above about 6.4 m/s (referred to as class 3 winds). Adequate wind resources are abundant around the world but not evenly distributed. In the United States, for example, class 3 or higher wind resources are concentrated in the western plains states, from the Dakotas to northern Texas, in the mountainous regions of the western and eastern parts of the country, and along much of the coastline (U.S. Department of Energy 2009e). Given advances in wind turbine technology over the past few decades, combined with increases in the costs of fossil fuels, wind power is approaching cost competitiveness in many areas with adequate wind resources. The challenges of wind power are that it is intermittent—only producing electricity when the wind blows—is often available far from areas of peak demand, and requires large turbines that some view as aesthetically unpleasant. Nevertheless, wind power is one of our most important and fastest-growing renewable energy sources.

Sunlight also drives evaporation of water from our oceans. Water vapor subsequently precipitated on our continents stores potential energy that is released as the water flows through rivers back to the sea. Hydropower captures a portion of this energy by using falling water to spin turbines and generate electricity. Today, most hydropower is produced using impoundment dams and large water reservoirs, allowing the water falling through the dam to generate power. Alternatively, hydropower can be generated at natural waterfalls by diverting a portion of the river flow to spin the turbines. Hydropower can be produced very efficiently and is cost effective, and aside from the efforts to build the dam it produces essentially no emissions. Power production is also very steady and reliable, and when excess power is produced it can be used to pump water back into the reservoir, storing it for use at a later time. These benefits explain why hydropower is an important source of electricity production in the United States, where hydropower accounts for about 6 percent of electricity production and about 34 percent of total renewable energy production (Figure 17). To

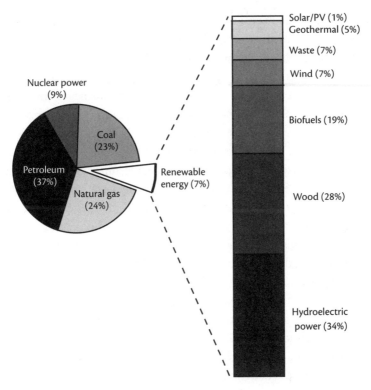

Figure 17. Renewable energies as shares of primary energy consumption in the United States in 2008 (U.S. Department of Energy 2009a).

accomplish this, most of the nation's conventional hydropower re-sources are developed (Holland and Petersen 1995; Graf 1993). Canada and nations in Europe, South America, and Southeast Asia also pro-duce significant amounts of hydropower. Hydropower does, however, have its detractors. River dams drastically change local ecosystems by flooding above the dam and restricting water flow below. Dams also pose challenges for migrating fish species, a problem that can be par-tially addressed by installing fish ladders. Dams have a limited life-time, principally due to the process of siltation. As water slows upon entering the reservoir behind the dam, the mud and silt that it carries falls out of suspension and is deposited. Over time, these sediments fill the reservoir, displacing the water that is necessary to generate power. Due to this problem, many dams have life expectancies of only about fifty years.

Some of the energy in sunlight reaches the land surface and is available for use by plants in photosynthesis, converting the energy to sugars and other compounds in their tissues. This biomass can be used directly (e.g., by burning or fermentation to generate combustible fuels) as a source of energy (and over geological time scales this biomass is, of course, the ultimate source of our fossil fuels). Sunlight can also be captured and converted to electricity by photovoltaic cells, a type of semiconductor that induces a flow of electrons when exposed to sunlight. Photovoltaic cells have many advantages, in that once manufactured they produce clean electricity without any moving parts and thus are largely maintenance free. However, they obviously require a source of light to produce power, and the sun does not always shine. Moreover, they are costly to produce and require large surface areas to generate significant amounts of power. A standard photovoltaic design, for example, might generate about 0.4 watts per $7\,cm^2$ of area. To equal the power production of a large fossil fuel–burning power plant, an area of $40\,km^2$ would have to be covered with photovoltaic panels (U.S. Department of Energy 2001). As a result, photovoltaic cells prove to be useful only in certain applications, such as rooftop panels that generate electricity for residential use or powering light posts and communication systems in remote locations that are not connected to a power grid. However, we generate only a very minor amount of electricity with these devices in the United States (Figure 17) and around the globe, when compared with the scale of our total energy demand. Ongoing research on the design of photovoltaic cells, however, offers promise for making these devices more efficient and at lower cost, thereby expanding their prospects for becoming a larger part of our energy portfolio.

Alternatively, sunlight can be captured by devices called solar power towers (Plate 6), which reflect and concentrate this light onto reservoirs of molten salt or other compounds. The light-reflecting devices, called heliostats, must be capable of tracking the sun's movement over the day to ensure that the light is properly collected at the top of the towers. The superheated materials in the tower are then used to generate steam, which spins turbines and generates power in the conventional manner. In areas of intense sunlight, solar power towers are relatively efficient at producing power. The largest solar power tower in the world today is in Spain, and yields about 20 megawatts of electricity (compared to a large coal-burning plant, which yields about 1,500 megawatts). Like all solar energy, power towers require the sun to shine in order to generate power. However, current and pending designs offer the means to store the heat over several hours—and into the evening—allowing for more regular power production.

Power from the Earth's Tides

The gravitational pull of the moon and sun, and the control it exerts over tides, also represents a part of the earth's energy flux that can be used to generate electricity. Tidal power can be captured in restricted basins and used to generate power in the same manner as a hydroelectric dam. A dam placed at the mouth of a bay or cove delays the flow of water out to sea during the ebbing tide. Once a sufficient difference between the water level on either side of the dam is achieved, water is allowed to flow through the dam, spinning turbines and generating electricity. Some systems are able to reverse this process on the incoming tide. Nevertheless, power production is intermittent and controlled by the tidal cycle, which is not always in sync with electricity demand.

A tidal power station operates today in the La Rance River estuary in northern France. The station became operational in 1966 and has the capacity to generate about 240 megawatts of power. Thus, tidal impoundment dams are a proven technology but have yet to see widespread application. This is largely due to a lack of suitable sites—impoundment systems require a large tidal flux, often in excess of 7 meters—and the dams also pose hazards to coastal ecosystems by impacting migrations, changing water levels, and causing siltation behind the dams (Craig et al. 2001). Thus, the future of tidal power probably lies with turbines placed in open oceans on estuaries with strong tidal currents. These large turbines would be fixed or tethered to the seafloor and would use the flow of water currents to generate electricity. Ocean tidal power obviates many of the environmental concerns related to impoundment systems, but like all ocean-placed energy technologies it faces challenges in development and maintenance costs, and reservations of coastal communities. Nevertheless, recent deployment in Northern Ireland of the SeaGen system—an underwater tower with two large rotary blades that generates about 1.2 megawatts of power—demonstrates the feasibility of such systems (Figure 18).

Power from the Atom

The third component of the earth's energy flux is its internal heat, captured during the formation of the planet and produced by radioactive elements in the crust, such as uranium and thorium. Geothermal power captures this energy directly. Most geothermal power today is produced by pumping hot steam, or hot water that is converted to steam, from the earth, and using this energy to spin turbines and generate electricity. Today, significant amounts of geothermal power are produced in Italy, Japan, Mexico, the Philippines, Indonesia, New Zealand, and the United States. One of the largest plants, the Geysers station in Northern California, has a generating capacity of about 2,000 megawatts. Moreover, Iceland—a nation that resides directly on a mid-ocean ridge and hot spot—meets about 50 percent of its modest power needs through geothermal systems. However, sites that are

Figure 18. Illustration of the SeaGen system, located in Strangford Lough, Northern Ireland. The system generates electricity with turbines that rotate due to tidal currents. This system is being evaluated to assess the technical feasibility and environmental impacts of installations in open oceans. (Courtesy of Marine Current Turbines Ltd.)

suitable for this type of geothermal power production are limited, mostly occurring in active volcanic environments such as Japan, the Philippines, Indonesia, and Central America. Thus, an alternative geothermal power system—known as dry rock or enhanced geothermal power—may have the greatest potential for expansion. Dry rock systems pump water into the ground—rather than relying on natural groundwater or steam—to capture some of the heat in the rocks. This water is then pumped to the surface and used to produce steam that spins turbines generating electricity in the conventional manner. This method requires large amounts of water, as some is lost after injection, and a relatively high geothermal gradient (generally above about 60°C/km) to ensure that sufficiently elevated rock temperatures (>150°C) can be accessed by drilling (Tester et al. 2006). These high geothermal gradients are often produced by bodies of crystalline rock that contain high levels of naturally radioactive elements. These geologic deposits are common in many parts of the world, present in every major continent, and thus offer opportunities for significant expansion of geothermal power production. The main challenges of enhanced geothermal systems are locating areas that are suitable for deployment and designing sustainable fluid flow systems.

Finally, nuclear power essentially accelerates the natural process of radioactive decay and is a widely established means of generating electricity. This is generally accomplished by bombarding naturally fissile uranium 235 atoms with neutrons, which causes them to split into a range of daughter products, expelling neutrons and energy in the process. The expelled neutrons are available to cause fission of other uranium 235 atoms, causing a chain reaction that produces heat, which can be used to generate electricity. Uranium is found in a variety of geologic deposits and other materials. Most uranium ore today is in the form of uranium oxides, specifically uraninite (UO_2) and triuranium octoxide (U_3O_8), in a dark black rock known as pitchblende. Pitchblende is found in hydrothermal deposits that formed during the last stages of cooling of a magma body and can be concentrated in sedimentary rocks by a variety of chemical and biological processes (Craig et al. 2001). These ores are mined by traditional methods, crushed and milled, and the uranium is leached from them with the use of acids. Ultimately, this process leads to the formation of yellowcake, a powdered form of uranium oxides that is used to generate nuclear fuels.

Most nuclear reactors in operation today, however, require about 4 percent uranium 235 in their fuel, whereas naturally occurring uranium has only about 1 percent uranium 235 and 99 percent uranium 238. Thus, a process of enrichment is required to generate nuclear fuel. This process is difficult, because uranium 235 and the more abundant uranium 238 have very similar properties and only a slight difference in mass. Most uranium is enriched by forming uranium hexafluoride gas (UF_6), which is passed through filters and spun in centrifuges to concentrate the lighter uranium 235. Uranium enrichment is also an important step in developing weapons-grade materials, and thus facilities that perform this task—especially in nations with perceived aspirations for nuclear weapons—are always under scrutiny.

Most nuclear reactors consist of a few basic components (Figure 19). Enriched uranium fuel, in the form of pellets, is placed in metal tubes separated by control rods, made of materials such as boron, that can effectively absorb excess neutrons. These rods are raised and lowered between the fuel elements to control the reaction rate. The fuel is also generally submerged in a moderator. The role of the moderator, which may include compounds such as graphite, gas, water, salt, and liquid metals, is to slow the neutrons sufficiently to increase their efficiency in causing fission when they strike a uranium 235 atom. Neutrons moving too quickly simply deflect off of the uranium 235 atoms. Moderators such as water also tend to control the reaction rate because when heated they become less dense and, therefore, less efficient at slowing neutrons. Moderators also are used to transfer heat away from the reactor core, where it can be used to generate steam, drive turbines, and generate electricity. Most commercial nuclear plants in operation today use boiled or pressurized water reactors, where water and steam are used as moderators and to extract heat from the reactor core. In pressurized water systems, the heated water in the reactor is transferred through heat exchangers to generate steam from clean water, ensuring that the turbines and other parts of the plant are not contaminated with radioactive particles.

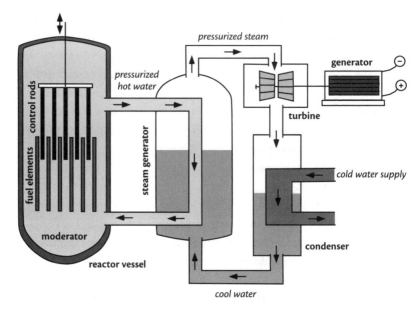

Figure 19. Basic design of a pressurized water nuclear reactor. Nuclear fission occurs in fuel elements submerged in a moderator, with the raising and lowering of control rods influencing the reaction rate. The nuclear reaction creates pressurized hot water within the reactor vessel, which is converted to steam and used to spin turbines and generators to produce electricity. Steam is then condensed to water using an external cold water supply, such as from a cooling tower, river, or ocean. The cool water is then recycled into the steam generator. (Design after the Nuclear Regulatory Commission.)

A variety of other types of reactor designs are in use or development today. Fast-breeder reactors rely on a small core of highly enriched uranium surrounded by a blanket of the more abundant uranium 238. The core undergoes fission, without requiring a moderator, and produces excess neutrons that are absorbed by the uranium 238, producing plutonium, which can be used as fuel. The advantage of these fast breeder systems is that they do not rely on a moderator to control the reaction rate, and they breed their own fuels, thereby requiring a smaller amount of enriched uranium than do traditional pressurized water reactors. One of the downsides to these systems, however, is that they produce plutonium, a fuel for nuclear bombs. Thus, many nations have taken steps to reduce the proliferations of these fast breeder reactors, and many other reactor designs are being developed today that may reduce such risks with enhanced efficiency.

Given relatively abundant sources of nuclear fuels, an array of nuclear reactor designs, and the ability to produce large amounts of electricity without any direct production of atmospheric pollutants (including CO_2), we might imagine that nuclear power is an energy supply of choice. Indeed, many nations, including the United States, France, and Japan, now produce considerable amounts of nuclear power. However, growth of nuclear power in most nations has been limited over the past few decades due largely to the perceived risks of catastrophic accidents and the challenges of managing the high-level nuclear waste that is produced by nuclear fission. Although nuclear power plants have had generally good safety records, three incidents—at the Three Mile Island, Chernobyl, and Fukushima Dai-ichi nuclear plants—have indelibly marked the public consciousness about nuclear power. On March 27, 1979, the Three Mile Island nuclear facility, located near Harrisburg, Pennsylvania, had a cooling system malfunction, causing a loss of water flow to the reactor. This caused the water in the reactor to heat up and a portion to convert to steam. By design, a pressure valve opened, releasing some of the steam. However, unbeknownst to the operators, the valve failed to close once the pressure was released. This caused the pressure in the reactor to become low, which operators tried to remedy by further slowing water flow into the reactor. Ultimately, the water level became low enough to expose a portion of the reactor core, causing it to melt and releasing radioactive gases to the atmosphere over a period of about seven hours. Seven years later, the Chernobyl nuclear station, located in Ukraine, had a planned test to assess whether, in the event of a loss of external electric power being supplied to the plant, the facility could produce enough power in the process of slowing down the reactor to continue running the water pumps. Due to an inexplicable series of events, including an unplanned pause to the reactor shutdown given demands in the electric grid, the test went bad. At a critical stage, the operators chose to fully raise the control rods in the reactor—to temporarily increase the reactor's energy production. A series of other events led to a spike in power production, which the operators tried to control by lowering the control rods. This happened too slowly, however, and part of the fuel assembly burst, thereby preventing the control rods from fully engaging. The result was a catastrophic meltdown of the reactor core, which emitted hazardous radiation into the atmosphere for about ten days (IAEC 2006).

Most recently, the Fukushima Dai-ichi plant in northeastern Japan, which houses six nuclear reactors, was struck by a massive (M 9.0) earthquake and tsunami. While earthquake early warning systems triggered a shutdown of the plant's three operating reactors, it remained necessary to circulate cooling waters to keep the reactors from overheating. The tsunami inundated the facility, however, cutting off electric power to the plant and swamping the backup generators that were to supply power for the water circulation pumps. As a result, water and steam in the reactor units overheated, generating hydrogen gas that caused explosions in reactor units 1, 2, and 3. Moreover, failure of circulating pumps in other units caused spent fuel storage pools to overheat, exposing some of the fuel elements and causing radiation leakage.

While the Three Mile Island accident arguably did little if any physical harm to the people who worked at the plant or lived nearby, the same cannot be said of Chernobyl. Thirty-one people died directly from the accident, mostly those involved in the many attempts to contain the reactor core, and radioactive materials were distributed in a wide area across Ukraine and northern Europe. It is estimated that the released radioactivity will lead to a few percentage points' increase in the cancer death rate for the roughly 600,000 persons receiving significant exposure (IAEC 2006). If this comes to pass, it will undeniably be a tragic impact on the lives of thousands of people. While the full impact of the Fukushima Dai-ichi disaster is yet to be known, high levels of radiation have been recorded in water leaking from the plant, leading to elevated radiation levels in soils, seawater, and agricultural products. Moreover, it seems clear that the cleanup of these reactor units will take several years, if not a decade. Like Three Mile Island and Chernobyl, this cleanup effort will serve as an ongoing reminder that catastrophic accidents at nuclear power plants can occur, and these incidents will influence the opinions of many around the globe about nuclear power.

Another main challenge for nuclear power is what to do with the nuclear waste, including spent fuel assemblies and other irradiated parts of the plants' reactor and plumbing systems. Standard nuclear fission produces a wide array of radioactive elements, whose production of radiation decays with time. The products of a standard light water reactor, the most common type of system in use today, remain hazardous to humans for about 10,000 years (Brookins 1984). When spent fuel is removed from the reactor, it is typically placed in a water pool within the plant for temporary storage. This allows many of the radioactive compounds with short half-lives to decay, thereby reducing the overall radioactivity of the waste. For long-term storage (tens of thousands of years), most nations have opted to target subsurface, geologic repositories for the waste. Ideal storage sites protect the air and groundwater from becoming contaminated and have low risks of natural disasters, such as earthquakes and volcanic eruptions, that could cause a catastrophic release of radiation. Moreover, some nations choose to reprocess nuclear waste, extracting usable nuclear materials and reducing the amount of material that needs to be stored. While some nations, such as France, have made clear decisions on how to handle their waste and place it in storage, the United States—the largest producer of nuclear energy—has not. In the United States, prospects for long-term storage over the past few decades have focused on Yucca Mountain in Nevada. The waste would be placed underground in steel containers within dense volcanic rock, and the site is sparsely populated and very arid—having a low water table, thereby reducing the risks of groundwater contamination. However, for a variety of reasons, mostly political, plans to bring Yucca Mountain online as a national waste repository have stalled. This poses a major problem because many U.S. nuclear plants, built in the 1970s and 1980s, no longer have adequate space in their pools to store the spent waste. The U.S. Nuclear Regulatory Commission now grants permits to plants for onsite dry storage of spent waste, often in retasked parking lots or other areas around the plant site. Thus, while there are risks associated with transporting and storing large amounts of waste in a single national repository, the lack of such a facility creates risks associated with distributed local storage of spent fuel in places that were originally not designed to hold it. In any event, it is clear that the future of nuclear power in the United States and many other nations relies on choices we make about how to deal with the radioactive waste.

Energy Futures

Why do we use the energy sources that we do, and what will impact the future of these energy options? In the case of fossil fuels, we rely on them today because they are remarkable sources of energy—power packed, flexible, and relatively abundant. Given the known reserves of coal, this fuel is very likely to continue playing a large role in our energy future. While conventional deposits of oil and gas may wane over the coming decades, alternative sources of these conventional energies, such as tar sands and shale gas, may provide a path toward continuing our fossil fuel economy. Is this a future that we seek? Will we be able to tolerate the continued pollution of our air and water, and the effects of global warming? If not, are we willing to invest in cleaner fossil power plants and cars, and in carbon sequestration? If we prefer to move toward a future more dependent on alternative energies, which of the various types— solar, wind, geothermal, nuclear, or others—will prove most viable? Based on the current picture, it seems unlikely that one horse will win this race. The alternative energy systems that are most viable today—nuclear, wind, hydro, and geothermal—are clearly the ones that can produce electricity at costs that are increasingly competitive with conventional fossil fuel plants. Nuclear power offers a nearly limitless potential; however, we must learn to minimize and/or decide to tolerate the risks associated with these plants and the hazardous waste they produce. Wind power is currently cost competitive in many regions and markets, and that is why it has experienced rapid growth. However, the wind does not always blow, and where it does so often, many prefer not to look at a field of turbines. To address the intermittent nature of wind power, as well as other alternative energies, we likely need to develop better ways of storing energy, or plan to rely on a hub of more reliable energy sources to meet continuous demand. Thus, our energy future seems inevitably to be a patchwork. Our task is to decide upon the makeup and sizes of these patches. Hopefully in doing so, we will also fulfill our obligations as stewards of the environment for future generations.

Further Reading

General Bibliography

Aubrecht, G. J. 2006. *Energy, Physical, Environmental, and Social Impact,* 3rd ed. San Francisco: Pearson Addison Wesley.
A comprehensive text that addresses energy from a physical perspective.

Harvard-Smithsonian Center for Astrophysics. 2007. *The Habitable Planet: A Systems Approach to Environmental Science.* Washington, DC: Annenberg Learner. http://www.learner.org/courses/envsci/.
An online course for students and adult learners about the earth and human impacts on the environment.

Schrag, D. P. 2007a. "Confronting the Climate-Energy Challenge." *Elements* 3: 171–178.
A concise summary of strategies for addressing climate change.

Turco, R. P. 2002. *Earth under Siege, from Air Pollution to Global Climate,* 2nd ed. New York: Oxford University Press.
A comprehensive text on pollution and its impact on our environment.

U.S. Energy Information Administration. Annual Energy Review. http://www
.eia.doe.gov/aer/.
A comprehensive assessment of U.S. energy production and use, issued each
year by the Energy Information Administration of the U.S. Department of
Energy.

Works Cited

AWEA. 2009. *Wind Energy FAQ.* Washington, DC: American Wind Energy
Association.

Barnes, M. A., W. C. Barnes, and R. M. Bustin. 1984. "Chemistry and Evolution of Organic Matter." *Canada Geosciences* 11.

BP. 2009. *BP Statistical Review of World Energy June 2009.* London: British
Petroleum.

Brookins, D. G. 1984. *Geochemical Aspects of Radioactive Waste Disposal.*
New York: Springer Verlag.

Brown, G. C., and E. Skipsey. 1986. *Energy Resources: Geology, Supply, and
Demand.* Berkshire, UK: Open University Press.

Canada PRA. 2009. *Energy Facts and Statistics, 2009.* Calgary, Canada: Petroleum Registry of Alberta.

Craig, J. R., D. J. Vaughan, and B. J. Skinner. 2001. *Resources of the Earth:
Origin, Use, and Environmental Impact,* 3rd ed. Upper Saddle River, NJ:
Prentice Hall.

EMD. 2009. *Oil Sands.* Houston, TX: American Association of Petroleum
Geologists, Energy Minerals Division. Retrieved January 11, 2011, from
http://emd.aapg.org/technical_areas/oil_sands.cfm.

Graf, W. L. 1993. "Landscapes, Commodities, and Ecosystems: The Relation-
ship between Policy and Science of America's Rivers." In *Sustaining Our
Water Resources,* a report of the Water Science and Technology Board,
National Research Council. Washington, DC: National Academy Press.

Holland, H. D., and U. Petersen. 1995. *Living Dangerously: The Earth, Its
Resources, and the Environment.* Princeton, NJ: Princeton University
Press.

House, K. Z., D. P. Schrag, C. F. Harvey, and K. S. Lackner. 2006. "Permanent
Carbon Dioxide Storage in Deep-Sea Sediments." *Proceedings of the National Academy of Sciences* 103: 12291–12295.

Hunt, J. M. 1995. *Petroleum Geochemistry.* San Francisco: W. H. Freeman.

IAEC. 2006. *The Chernobyl Forum: 2003–2005*, 2nd rev. ed. Vienna, Austria: International Atomic Energy Commission.

ICCOP. 1963. *International Handbook of Coal Petrography*, 2nd ed. Oviedo, Spain: International Committee for Coal and Organic Petrology.

IMF. 2009. *World Economic Outlook Database (September 2009)*. Washington, DC: International Monetary Fund.

Laws, E. A. 2000. *Aquatic Pollution, an Introductory Text*. Hoboken, NJ: Wiley.

Magoon, L. B., and W. G. Dow, eds. 1994. *M60: The Petroleum System—from Source to Trap*. Tulsa, OK: American Association of Petroleum Geologists.

Petit, J. R., J. Jouzel, D. Raynaud, N. I. Barkov, J.-M. Barnola, I. Basile, M. Benders, J. Chappellaz, M. Davis, G. Delaygue, M. Delmotte, V. M. Kotlyakov, M. Legrand, V. Y. Lipenkov, C. Lorius, L. Pépin, C. Ritz, E. Saltzman, and M. Stievenard. 1999. "Climate and Atmospheric History of the Past 420,000 Years from the Vostok Ice Core, Antarctica." *Nature* 399: 429–436.

Potential Gas Committee. 2008. *Potential Supply of Natural Gas in the United States*. Golden, CO: Potential Gas Agency, Colorado School of Mines.

Schrag, D. P. 2007b. "Preparing to Capture Carbon." *Science* 315: 812–813.

Shaw, J. H., and J. P. Holdren. 2007. "Energy Challenges." In Daniel P. Schrag, ed., *The Habitable Planet: A Systems Approach to Environmental Science*. Online textbook. Washington, DC: Annenberg Learner. http://www.learner.org/courses/envsci/unit/index.php.

Tester, J. W., B. J. Andersen, A. S. Batchelor, D. D. Blackwell, R. DiPippo, E. M. Drake, J. Garnish, B. Livesay, M. C. Moore, K. Nichols, S. Petty, M. N. Toksoz, and R. W. Veatch Jr. 2006. *The Future of Geothermal Energy: Impact of Enhanced Geothermal Systems (EGS) on the United States in the 21st Century*. Cambridge, MA: MIT Press.

U.S. Department of Energy. 2001. *Photovoltaic Cells*. Washington, DC: Department of Energy, Solar Energy Technologies Program.

———. 2009a. *Annual Energy Review 2008*. Report DOE/EIA-0384. Washington, DC: Department of Energy, Energy Information Administration.

———. 2009b. "Fuel and Energy Emission Factors: Tables." Washington, DC: Department of Energy, Energy Information Administration, Voluntary Reporting of Greenhouse Gases Program. Retrieved January 11, 2011, from http://www.eia.doe.gov/oiaf/1605/emission_factors.html.

———. 2009c. *Mercury Emission Control R&D*. Washington, DC: Department of Energy, Fossil Energy Office of Communications.

————. 2009d. *Mine Injury Statistics*. Washington, DC: Department of Energy, Mine Safety and Health Administration.

————. 2009e. *Wind Resources Maps*. Washington, DC: Department of Energy, Wind and Hydropower Technologies Program.

U.S. Environmental Protection Agency. 2006. *Inventory of US Greenhouse Gas Emissions and Sinks: 1990–2004, ES-1*. Washington, DC: Environmental Protection Agency.

————. 2007. *Clean Air Status and Trends Network (CASTNET) Annual Report*. Washington, DC: Environmental Protection Agency.

————. 2010. *Clean Air Mercury Rule*. Washington, DC: Environmental Protection Agency. Retrieved January 11, 2011, from http://www.epa.gov/mercuryrule/basic.htm.

————. 2011. *Inventory of US Greenhouse Gas Emissions and Sinks: 1990–2009, USEPA #430-R-11-005*. Washington, DC: Environmental Protection Agency.

U.S. Federal Energy Regulatory Commission. 2009. "LNG Projects Summary." Washington, DC: Federal Energy Regulatory Commission, Office of Energy Projects.

U.S. House CEC. 2010. [Letter to BP executive Tony Hayward.] Washington, DC: House of Representatives Committee on Energy and Commerce. Retrieved January 11, 2011, from http://online.wsj.com/public/resources/documents/WSJ-20100614-LetterToHayward.pdf.

Interracial Literature

Werner Sollors

The United States now has a president whose mother was a white American from Kansas and whose father was a black African from Kenya. There may be nothing unusual in that for today's student generations, but not so long ago a person like Barack Obama would have been called a mulatto and generated worries that his "miscegenous body" unites different races—races that, like species, should not have been, and should never be, united. For example, a mixed-race couple in Anna E. Dickinson's novel *What Answer?* (1869) encounters this bias in America, where doors were shut and extended hands withdrawn when the man's dark face was seen: "we were outlawed, ostracized, sacrificed on the altar of this devilish American prejudice, . . . I for my color, she for connecting her fate with mine." When William Dean Howells (1869) reviewed the novel for the *Atlantic Monthly,* he proposed returning to the intractable question of interracial marriage a full thousand years after the publication of the novel: "We should not, we hope, be saying in this answer that a mixture of the races is desirable. We reserve our opinion on this point for publication in the January 'Atlantic' of 2869, when the question will be, perhaps, practically presented." (At least he had faith in the longevity of the *Atlantic.*)

Racial difference, especially the black-white divide, has always mattered in the United States, a democracy that started out with African slavery, a major obstacle to the promise that "all men are created equal." Race affected not only political rights and social mobility but also marital choices and family belonging, making interracial marriage and the public and legal recognition of kinship across the American color line difficult if not completely impossible. Everett C. Hughes (1965) used the formula "Negroes who would be kin if they were not

Negro" to describe this cultural trait. According to Gunnar Myrdal's massive study *An American Dilemma* (1944), white American attitudes in the mid-1940s rested on the concern for "race purity" and on the rejection of "social equality" in any form of interracial mingling. Interracial marriage was especially targeted, and prohibited in thirty of the forty-eight states, among them all Southern states—where the majority of black Americans resided. What Myrdal called the "anti-amalgamation maxim" was "the keystone in the white man's structure of race prejudice" and "the end for which the other restrictions are arranged as means." It was this very core maxim of race relations—overturned by the Supreme Court only in the 1967 *Loving v. Virginia* decision—that Obama's parents violated, and it is this violation of which Obama himself would, not so long ago, have served as a worrisome reminder. The American choice to call all black-white mixed-race people "black" (on the basis of fractional ancestry rather than skin color) may have been, and may still be, one way to avoid the confrontation with race mixing itself. It is also apparent in the logic by which white American women can give birth to black children, while black American women cannot give birth to white children—a strange logic once you start thinking about it. ("Quadroon, mulatto, or negro, it is all one," a white character announces in *What Answer?* "I have no desire to split hairs on definition.")

It was unthinkable that an African American or mixed-race person would ever be in any position of leadership over whites, let alone represent the whole country. It is telling that Irving Wallace's (1964) *The Man,* the only American novel I know that represents a black American president, could not imagine his accession to power as the outcome of an electoral mandate but only as the result of the deaths of a white president and vice president.

This state of affairs raises the question whether race in the primary American sense of color differentiation is a human universal or a more local and time-bound distinction. Living in the optimistic age of Obama may already suggest an answer to this question, in the sense that if race thinking has become somewhat attenuated in the United States today and may become weaker yet in the years ahead, this can only be so because race thinking is a time-bound matter. *Time* magazine's special issue on race mixing with a computerized mixed "New Face of America" on the cover (November 18, 1993) may indicate the growing acceptance of what was once one of America's most powerful taboos. The growing black-white intermarriage rate in the United States (though still lower than those of all other interracial unions) would be another sign that a time-bound racial distinction is declining in significance today.

Yet this essay is not about the future but about the past. And it is probably no exaggeration to say that from the time the word "race" was coined until well into the twentieth century it has been a concept whose significance has generally increased. Perhaps derived from a medieval French word for horse breeding *(haraz)* that entered into Italian *(razza),* or from Latin *radix* or a contamination of Latin *ratio* and *generatio,* the word entered Castilian and Spanish *(raza)* where it was used to name the succession of generations *(de raza en raza)* (see, for instance, Contini 1959; Prospero 1992; Sabatini 1962; Spitzer 1933; and the 1970 Real Academia Española's *Diccionario de la Lengua Española*), but it also took on the double meaning of both "nobility of blood" and "defectiveness" or "taint" (Stolcke 1994). Hence the word could convey a positive sense in connection with the doctrine of purity of blood *(limpieza de sangre),* and a negative meaning of "admixture of the races of Moors, Jews, heretics, or *penitenciados* (those condemned by the Inquisition)"; it was used to expel from Spain people "tainted" by Jewish and Moorish blood. Yet the list of people to whom the doctrine of purity of blood was applied included descendants of heretics and of "those condemned by the Inquisition." Thus, from its terrible beginning, "race" was based on a religiously and politically, hence culturally, defined distinction that was legislated and believed to be hereditary, innate, immutable—in short, as natural as the distinction between different species. Equivalents of the word *raza* soon circulated in many Western languages

(Portuguese *raça*, French *race*, English *race*, German *Rasse*, and so forth). A new word had emerged and received further conceptual support in later centuries from studies of heredity and genetics.

The term "interracial" has been around at least since the 1880s and has been used in connection with conflict, cordiality, dating, and marriage. I was inspired to adopt the term by Georgia Douglas Johnson, a Harlem Renaissance poet based in Washington, D.C., who gave the title "Interracial" to a poem she sent to Carl Van Vechten, a novelist, critic, and photographer in New York, on October 25, 1943. The poem ends with the wish: "Oh, let's build bridges everywhere / And span the gulf of challenge there." For my purposes, interracial literature consists of works originating in many different countries and time periods, but which represent a certain repertoire of interracial themes: love and marriage across the black-white color divide, the role of children born from such unions and adult biracial figures as heroes and victims, as well as more extended and multigenerational interracial family plots, including the motifs of crossing the racial line in the form that is called "passing," the detection of racial ancestry through secondary signs, and more generally, conflicts between belonging to a family and to a race.

Interracial themes have been widespread in Western literature, but unlike such themes as "autumn" or "the voyage," they have at times been enmeshed in urgent and explosive social and political meanings. I have chosen to focus here on a medieval romance (Wolfram von Eschenbach's *Parzival*) and a modern drama (Eugene O'Neill's *All God's Chillun Got Wings*). These two works, one from before the word and concept of race had emerged and one from the twentieth century, stand for many others.

Wolfram von Eschenbach, *Parzival* (1197–1210)

Eight hundred years ago, there seemed to be no urgent or explosive meaning palpable in a medieval romance that gives us a very full account of an interracial love-and-marriage story. In Wolfram von Eschenbach's Middle High German *Parzival*, the French knight Gahmuret goes to the kingdom of Zazamanc where he saves and marries the black Queen Belacâne, who gives birth to their "piebald" son Feirefîz. Gahmuret leaves her on a knightly errand, later marries Queen Herzeloide, and fathers Parzivâl, and near the end of the romance the half brothers Feirefîz and Parzivâl encounter each other in battle. Consisting of 25,000 rhymed verses that were originally meant for recitation rather than for quiet reading (its units of thirty lines are relatively easily remembered with such mnemonic devices as epic epithets and catalogs), *Parzival* is primarily a romance of the Grail, based on French sources. (Wolfram's Grail is, incidentally, imagined not to be a chalice, but a slab of stone.) Though Wolfram mentions an Arabic source (a certain Kîôt, unidentified by scholars) and his sorceress Cundrîê offers an astronomy survey, giving the names of the planets in Arabic, the unusually rich frame narrative of Gahmuret, Belacâne, and Feirefîz is apparently originally by Wolfram. This frame gives the reader a lively sense of these characters' human emotions. Furthermore, it offers some nuanced descriptions of various perceptions of color difference. *Parzival* is popular and has been adapted many times, including by Richard Wagner in his opera *Parsifal* (which, however, omits the frame narrative), and translated into various modern languages: Jessie Weston, the author of *From Ritual to Romance* (a book that meant much to American modernists like T. S. Eliot) dedicated her 1894 English verse translation of *Parzival* to Wagner.

When Gahmuret, who is not the firstborn but the second son of Gandîn, the king of Anjou in France, goes on a quest for knightly adventures and serves the "bâruc" (Baruch) in Baldac (Baghdad), he chooses not his hereditary heraldic sign but a white anchor. He fights victoriously in many places from Damascus to Morocco and Persia; and he also makes his way to the kingdom of Zazamanc in Africa, which is under siege by the relatives of the Moor Îsenhart, who had lost his life in his pursuit of Queen Belacâne's love. Belacâne's name may have been derived from the biblical Queen of Sheba (Hebrew Pilegesh, Greek Ballakis, and Arabic Bilqis), which places Gahmuret in the position of Solomon. The narrator describes the inhabitants as "dark as the night" and reiterates a bit later that the whole town was populated by male and female Moors (*mœre und mœrinne;* 19: 18). When Queen Belacâne wants to speak with Gahmuret, she notices that he is colored differently than she and her people are, but she is also a strong and worldly-wise cosmopolitan ruler and "knew how to judge a fair face, since fair heathens she often had seen." The poet's description of Belacâne is an explicit departure from European love poetry conventions: "unlike to the dew-dipped roses was her colour," and although she is not baptized, Gahmuret responds strongly to her, for "her purity was her baptism." They sit and talk, she explains to him the story of Îsenhart, and they are quite smitten with each other. Soon they cannot take their eyes off each other, "and the root of true love and longing it sprang up the twain between." Gahmuret cannot sleep at night after their meeting because he keeps thinking of Belacâne, emphatically referred to as "the Queen of the land, the black mooress" (*diu swarze mœrinne, / des landes küneginne;* 35: 21–22) who had "vanquished his heart."

On their wedding night the queen's black hand removes the hero's armor, and Wolfram comments: "So the queen in the arms of her true love found guerdon of sweet delight, / Tho' unlike were the twain in their colour, / Moorish princess and Christian knight!" Translated as "delight" in English, the Middle High German word *minne* signifies the high medieval ideal of courtly love that reflects divine love and may (as it is in the case of Gahmuret and Belacâne) or may not be physically consummated. Their love is indeed high and pure, and Gahmuret values his black wife more than his own life.

Yet just as Aeneas had to leave Dido (Wolfram mentions them later, 399: 11–14), so Gahmuret has to return to knightly adventures and deeds. He leaves Belacâne secretly for Spain but puts a letter (written in French) in her bag, assuring her of his continuing love; it also conveys his Angevin genealogy in case she should give birth to a boy and twice expresses regret that she is a heathen. She reads the letter and wishes only that he would return; then she could quickly become a Christian. Gahmuret never goes back to Zazamanc but continues to yearn for Belacâne. He particularly resents the notion that he supposedly left her because she was black: "Now many a fool would say / That I, for her colour, fled her, to my eyes was she light as day! / For her womanhood true I sorrow; o'er all others her worth stood high / as the boss from the shield outstandeth." In Kanvoleis he wins in a tournament the hand of the virgin queen Herzeloide, and though he is still sad about having left his beloved wife Belacâne he is compelled by a judge's verdict to honor Herzeloide's claim on him, for he has won the prize of her, and his marriage to a heathen is not considered an obstacle to the new union. Soon after the wedding night he is summoned again by the bâruc in Baldac, who is now under attack from the kings of Babylon; Gahmuret leaves Herzeloide and soon dies in battle near Baghdad before their son Parzivâl is born.

Meanwhile Belacâne has given birth to a boy whom his father, Gahmuret, will also never see. The description of the black-white couple's child is striking:

> Then the queen at the time appointed bare a son,
>   who was dark and light,
> For in him had God wrought a wonder, at one while was
>   he black and white.
> And a thousand times she kissed him where white as his sire's skin.
> And she named the babe of her sorrows Feirefîz Anschevîn.
> And he was a woodland-waster, many spears did he shatter fair,
> And shields did he pierce—as a magpie [*agelster*] the hue of
>   his face and hair.

Feirefîz, his name, is probably of French origin and may mean either proud (*fier*) or checkered (*vair*) son (*fils*). While he is one of the first fully drawn children of a black-white couple in Western literature,

Wolfram's startling description of him as "piebald" raises questions. How are we to read the analogy between Feirefîz and a magpie in a poem in which there is more bird imagery—for example, in the description of the women of Zazamanc as "raven-black" (*nâch rabens varwe was ir schîn;* 20: 6)? And how does skin color relate to the Christian tradition of associating lightness with goodness and heaven and blackness with sinfulness and hell?

Parzival opens with a prologue in which the image of the magpie is central:

> If [doubt] [*zwîvel*] in the heart find dwelling, then the soul it
>   shall reap but woe;
> And shaming alike and honour are his who such doubt shall show,
> For it standeth in evil contrast with a true man's dauntless might,
> As one seeth the magpie's plumage, which at one while is
>   black and white [*agelstern varwe*].
> And yet he may win to blessing; since I wot well that in his heart,
> Hell's darkness, and light of Heaven, alike have their lot and part.
> But he who is false and unsteadfast, he is black as the darkest night,
> And the soul that hath never wavered stainless its hue and
>   white! (1: 1–14)

Given this description, should we consider Gahmuret, Belacâne, and Feirefîz figures who illustrate black and white as a moral dichotomy? Is the meeting of the Zazamanc queen and the French Christian knight an allegory of an encounter between "Hell's darkness, and light of Heaven" that results in the birth of "doubt" in the figure of the checkered son Feirefîz? Or is *Parzival* a poem that suggests that external appearance, skin color, has little to do with purity of heart? Is it possible for a Christian poet in the Middle Ages to write both within the black-white symbolic realm and yet to represent specific characters whose black, white, or piebald color ignores a moral charge and is quite independent of it?

Wolfram offers descriptions of color difference in the love story that appear, indeed, to have nothing to do with his general image of black and white in the Christian moral and metaphoric sense. He emphasizes that the raven-colored, non-Christian queen has the purest of hearts, that Belacâne's blackness is merely external, for "Is there aught that than day is lighter? Then it likeneth not the queen!" (The paradoxical description of a black-skinned character as being "lighter than day" or being "white inside" may nowadays sound awkward or seem to be reinstating a color hierarchy, but for Wolfram the point may simply be that skin color is an accidental, not an essential, quality.) Furthermore, color difference can be attractive. This is already apparent in Gahmuret's and Belacâne's enamoration, and it is a theme that continues in the later adventures of Feirefîz, when Wolfram comments that Feirefîz is particularly attractive to the ladies because of his unusual coloring: "Yet some in such favour held him, they had been of his service fain— / Methinks the unwonted colour of his face [*sîniu vremdiu mâl*] did their fancy gain!" (774: 7).

The central drama upon Feirefîz's return near the end of the romance comes in his encounter, in battle, with his half brother Parzivâl. Though Belacâne's and Herzeloide's sons do not know of their relationship, Wolfram reveals early on that both were the sons of one father, Gahmuret, and that Feirefîz is fighting his own brother:

Then on high flashed the sword of the heathen, and many such
  blow had slain,
To his knee Parzivâl was beaten—Now see how they fought, the twain,
If twain ye will still account them, yet in sooth shall they be but one,
For my brother and I are one body, e'en as husband and wife are one!

The phrase "one body" *(ein lîp)* summons a strong image of unity of the different-colored siblings. It is also remarkable that in a Christian romance from the time of the Crusades the poet prays for both of Gahmuret's sons, the Christian as well as the heathen brother: "God have Gahmuret's son in His keeping! And the prayer it shall stand for both, / For the twain shall be one nor, I think me, to own it were either loth." Chivalry is presented as a universal value, and Feirefîz is a true model of chivalry, for he does not take advantage of the fact that Parzivâl's sword breaks; instead, he stops fighting and offers to identify himself first. When Feirifîz describes himself as coming from the line of Anjou, the epithet "Anschevîn" triggers the recognition scene, and the proof of their siblinghood is in Feirefîz's appearance, which Parzivâl has heard described like "written parchment, both black and white" (*als ein geschriben permint / swarz und blanc her und dâ;* 747: 26–27). Then he is that brother, Feirefîz declaims as the gallant knights remove their helmets and Parzivâl recognizes his opponent as his brother: "For straightway he knew the other, (as a magpie, I ween, his face,) / And hatred and wrath were slain here in a brotherly embrace."

For Wolfram, writing around 1200, someone's skin color may resemble that of a magpie—but that does not have to be the magpie of doubt that his prologue describes. The brotherly kiss (*kusse;* 748: 9)—beautifully illustrated in the 1467 Bern codex—shows the literally half-black Feirefîz kissing Parzivâl (see Plate 7). Comparing it with the illustration of the battle scene, one notices that the black half of Feirefîz's face has moved from one side of his face to the other, rendering the simultaneous presence of black and white more important than its precise representation. After the recognition scene and the kiss, Parzivâl tells Feirefîz of their father's death, and the memory of their father only strengthens the relationship as well as the indivisible oneness of the brothers:

> In this self-same hour have I lost my great joy, and yet joy have found,
> For myself, and thou, and my father, we three in one bond are bound;
> For tho' men as three may hold us, yet I wot well we are but one,
> And no wise man he counts that kinship 'twixt father, methinks,
>   and son.

What seem to be three different people are truly just one (*wir wâren gar al ein;* 752: 9). As heathen and Christian children of one father they suggest the universal value of brotherhood, of uniting by a fraternal kiss. The sorceress Cundrîê pronounces Parzivâl's destiny to become Grail King, and Parzivâl and Feirefîz ride toward King Arthur's court, where they are honored. Then they move on to the Castle of the Grail, where Parzivâl reunites with his wife Kondwîrâmûrs and their sons Kardeiz and Loherangrîn, and where Feirefîz converts in order to marry Repanse de Schoie.

A hero goes to a faraway land where he marries a black woman; he leaves her; and she raises their child while he founds a new family. Later the son of the first marriage encounters and battles his white half brother. This outline of the frame story of *Parzival* sounds very much like the story Quentin Compson and Shreve McCannon imaginatively reconstruct, in William Faulkner's novel *Absalom, Absalom!* (1936), from the various versions Quentin has heard of Thomas Sutpen's Haitian marriage to Eulalia Bon and his firstborn child Charles, Sutpen's second marriage to Ellen Coldfield, and the encounter of their son Henry Sutpen with his half brother Charles Bon, whom he ultimately kills. (Absalom is also mentioned in *Parzival* [796: 8], and the biblical story of incest and fratricide among King David's children, Amnon, Tamar, and Absalom [2 Samuel: 13–29] is of central significance for Faulkner.) But whereas Gahmuret explicitly does not leave Belacâne because of her skin color and deliberately gives her his genealogy to confer to their son, Sutpen abandons Eulalia when he finds out about her racial background and never recognizes his offspring— so that the two brothers, Henry and Charles, cannot unite in the name of their shared paternal lineage but are, despite their consanguinity, their oneness, tragically divided on a path that ultimately leads Henry to fratricide. For Wolfram, skin color was merely an external feature, but by the time Faulkner was writing, race had taken on a powerful plot-shaping reality, and the color line was of greater importance than family relationship.

Eugene O'Neill, *All God's Chillun Got Wings* (1924)

The color line was also very prominent in a little-known play by the most important playwright to modernize American drama, Eugene

O'Neill; it also affected that play's reception. The breakthrough of the serious modern stage was initiated by the Provincetown Players, a small avant-garde theater group that produced almost 100 plays between 1915 and 1929 at the Wharf Theater in Provincetown and at the Playwright's Theater (later Provincetown Playhouse) at 133 MacDougal Street in New York City. Their starting point was the drama of marital strife, often presented in a new one-act form of unresolved short plays that might be classified as tragedies, comedies, or tragicomedies, and that were increasingly influenced by Freudian psychology. Some of the play-wrights had come out of a workshop by Harvard professor George Pierce Baker, who had opened his "47 workshop" in 1905 so that young playwrights could work on their writing skills and see their plays pro-duced. Eugene O'Neill's career took off while he was involved with the Provincetown Players, a career that led him from a point of deep de-pression in 1912—when he tried to commit suicide—to being awarded the Nobel Prize in 1936. He wrote his first play, *The Web*, in 1913–1914; in 1914 he participated in Baker's Harvard workshop; and in 1916 *Bound East for Cardiff*, his first play to be performed, was produced by the Provincetown Players. (The critic Eric Mottram [1971] called this moment "the beginning of serious American theatre.") O'Neill's tal-ent was soon recognized: he won the Pulitzer Prize for both *Beyond the Horizon* and *Anna Christie* (1920 and 1921). He may be best known now for such experimental plays as *The Emperor Jones* (1920), his fam-ily drama *Long Day's Journey into Night* (1956), or his Greek-inspired modern tragedies *Desire under the Elms* (1924), *Strange Interlude* (1928), and *Mourning Becomes Electra* (1931).

In the play *All God's Chillun Got Wings*, originally defined as "A Comedy of Manners in Two Parts with Incidental Music," O'Neill rep-resents a black-white couple on stage and insisted upon casting a black actor (the young Paul Robeson) to play the part of Jim Harris, who mar-ries the lower-class Ella Downey (played by Mary Blair). The manu-script was finished in December 1923, published in *American Mercury* in February 1924, and first performed at the Provincetown Playhouse in

New York on May 15 of the same year. With its "incidental music" of popular tunes and spirituals, the play follows the story of Jim and Ella from childhood through their deeply problematic marriage. Ella thinks she is superior to Jim, while Jim tries desperately to move up and succeed in the world. In these aspects, O'Neill drew on the way he regarded his own parents—his potato-famine Irish father, Jim, and his lace-curtain Irish mother, Ella—as terribly mismatched: O'Neill even used his own parents' first names for his characters, thus interracializing their story. (Several other American writers in the period also used this interracializing strategy of dealing with troubling autobiographical materials, Gertrude Stein, for example, and Langston Hughes.) The critic Louis Sheaffer (1968) suggested that O'Neill's "father's fondness for quoting *Othello* may have been among the unconscious factors behind the writing of *All God's Chillun Got Wings.*" The first notebook entry for what became the play also links it to Joe Smith, a black man whom O'Neill had befriended in Greenwich Village: "Play of Johnny T.—negro who married white woman—base play on his experience as I have seen it intimately—but no reproduction, see it only as man's" (Floyd 1981).

The stark stage directions suggest mechanically arranged scenes at the crossroads between white and black America. Here are examples from the first scene:

> *In the street leading left, the faces are all white; in the street leading right, all are black. . . . On the sidewalk are eight children, four boys and four girls. Two of each sex are white, two black. . . . From the street of the whites a high-pitched, nasal tenor sings the chorus of "Only a Bird in a Gilded Cage." On the street of the blacks a Negro strikes up the chorus of: "I Guess I'll Have to Telegraph My Baby." (505)*

The symmetrically arranged stage is sharply divided by the color line, but Jim and Ella are not yet part of that division, though they are nicknamed Jim Crow and Painty Face by the other children. Ella says to Jim, "I wish I was black like you" (506), and Jim confesses to her that he has been drinking chalk and water three times a day in the hope that it would make him whiter. Each wants to be like the other ("Let's you and me swap," Ella says), and when she asks him whether he wants to be her "feller" and Jim agrees, she says, "Then I'm your girl." At the end of the scene Ella throws a kiss at Jim and *"runs off in frantic embarrassment"* (507).

This state of childhood innocence soon ends as Ella enters a white (and racist) adolescent and adult world and becomes a fallen woman— first she is the girl of no-good Mickey, who deserts her when she gets pregnant (her child dies), then Shorty offers to make her part of his "stable." Jim is her only anchor in this sordid world, and she tells him, "You've been white to me, Jim" (515). Their relationship takes on a sado-masochistic tone, with Jim literally wishing to be Ella's "slave." When they get married, the actual marriage ceremony is not shown; one only hears a Negro tenor sing the spiritual "Sometimes I Feel Like a Motherless Child" (with the ominously tragic line "Sometimes I wish that I'd never been born") and a church bell ringing. Again, the stage directions map a starkly black-white world:

> As if it [the church bell] were a signal, people . . . pour from the two tenements, whites from the tenement to the left, blacks from the one to the right. They hurry to form into two racial lines on each side of the gate, rigid and unyielding, staring across at each other with bitter hostile eyes. The halves of the big church door swing open and JIM and ELLA step out from the darkness within into the sunlight. The doors slam behind them like the wooden lips of an idol that has spat them out. JIM is dressed in black, ELLA in white, both with extreme plainness. (516; see Figure 20)

Facing this hostile crowd, Jim asks Ella to look heavenward and says, with hysterical ecstasy, "We're all the same—equally just—under the sky—under God" (517). An escape from America by steamer to France, to the side of the world "where Christ was born," leads nowhere, however, and the color line remains drawn between them. Two years later, Jim and Ella are back in America. "We'd run away from the thing—

Figure 20. Scene from 1924 stage production of *All God's Chillun Got Wings*. (J. W. Debenham, photographer. Photograph courtesy of the Billy Rose Theatre Division, The New York Public Library for the Performing Arts, Astor, Lenox and Tilden Foundations.)

and taken it with us" (520), Jim explains to his sister, Hattie, who wishes to strengthen Jim's individual and collective pride: "We don't deserve happiness till we've fought the fight of our race and won it!" (518), she says, whereas Ella treats her sister- and mother-in-law so condescendingly and with such an indifferent superiority that they leave.

The dominating stage prop in the second act is a *"Negro primitive mask from Congo"* that seems to grow unnaturally large and acquire a *"diabolical quality"* (517) while the walls of the room in which Jim and Ella live at first *"appear shrunken in, the ceiling lowered"* (523), until in the last scene the *"ceiling barely clears the people's heads"* (527). Ella feels threatened by that mask as well as by Jim's studying. She does not want Jim to pass the Law Board, and she begins to wield a large carving knife: *"Her eyes fasten on* JIM *with a murderous mania"* (526). At the end Ella has gone mad, and when she learns that Jim has not "passed" (and the word now refers not just to the bar examination but to crossing the racial line), she plunges the knife (the audience fears the worst now)—not into Jim but into the mask. She thinks that the devil she had feared is now dead: "If you'd passed it would have lived in you. Then I'd have had to kill you, Jim, don't you see—or it would have killed me. But now I've killed it" (528). The play ends as they resume their childhood play: "Pretend you're Painty Face and I'm Jim Crow. Come and play!" (529). The play's title is taken from a black spiritual that O'Neill originally had Ella singing at the very end of the play. After what are her last words in the published version of the play—"Come and play!"—the following stage directions appeared in the manuscript: *"(She begins to sing in negro dialect)* 'Oh I got wings. And you got wings. And all God's chil[lun] Got Wings!' What's the rest of it, Jim? let's sing? I'm so happy. Come on and play!" Jim's response and the final lines of the play originally were:

> I'll sing with happiness, too, Honey. I'll play right up to the gates of Heaven with you! *(He sings with excited, truly negro fervor)* All de people talk about Heaven ain't a-going there! Heaven! Heaven! Heaven! *(Her childish voice joins in on the "heavens" at the end.)*

All God's Chillun Got Wings is not a realistic but a highly stylized play. The black and white worlds contrast starkly in stage sets with expressionistic features that are important for the action: the *"Negro primitive mask from the Congo"* visualizes how the racially generalized "black man" overwhelms and destroys Ella's specific relationship with Jim—just as it annihilates their shared space (Murphy 1987, 126–127). The set denotes dramatic function, not realistic verisimilitude. Language is generally understated, dialect is only suggested, and there is a lack of resolution. It is a serious play, yet O'Neill's original characterization of it as a comedy of manners also seems weirdly appropriate. Artificially superimposing a marital psychodrama onto racial antagonism (on the streets of modernity with modern black and white music, tenements, and elevated trains in the background), O'Neill gives a willfully mechanical account of the physical, territorial, and mental barriers between human beings—that he here finds best exemplified by race in America—even though the autobiographical investment must have been highly emotional for him, too. The world that emerges is one of inevitable doom, failure, and madness, and the viewer ponders the question of where the human race is left in a place where there is only white and black. All God's children may have wings in heaven, all may be "the same—equally just . . . under God," but not in the here and now of America. (No wonder Jim's Judgment Day prophecy in the manuscript version was that people who talk about heaven "ain't a-going there.")

O'Neill's artistic efforts did not fail to elicit praise from prominent intellectuals, black and white. W. E. B. Du Bois wrote supportive program notes for the original Provincetown Playhouse production (Du Bois 1923–1924). Paul Robeson, who would—as late as 1942—become the first African American to play Othello on an American stage (the Brattle Theatre in Cambridge, Massachusetts [Wilson 2005])—was proud to star in a play he genuinely liked, "a play of great strength and beautiful spirit, mocking all petty prejudice, emphasizing the humanness, and in Mr. O'Neill's words, 'the oneness' of mankind" (Robeson

1924). He continued with a very strong claim for O'Neill's powers as a playwright: "I honestly believe that perhaps never will I portray a nobler type than 'Jim Harris' or a more heroically tragic figure than 'Brutus Jones, Emperor,' not excepting 'Othello.'" The then-well-known literary critic Ludwig Lewisohn (1924) and the play's director James Light (1924) noted the play's affinities with Greek tragedy. Fannie Hurst (1924), who had not yet written *Imitation of Life,* found O'Neill's play "fiercely and relentlessly true" and the performance "a rare treat." Among the laudatory reviews of *All God's Chillun Got Wings,* two were particularly striking: Edmund Wilson (1924) considered it "one of the best things yet written about the race problem and among the best of O'Neill's plays" and particularly liked that it showed "two equally solid characters in collision instead of only one character wrestling with himself." And T. S. Eliot (1926) compared *All God's Chillun Got Wings* favorably to *Othello* (as had Robeson), since O'Neill succeeded in "implying something more universal than the problem of race—in implying, in fact, the universal problem of differences which create a mixture of admiration, love, and contempt, with the consequent tension. At the same time, he has never deviated from exact portrayal of a possible negro, and the close is magnificent."

Much of the public reception of O'Neill's play was of a different order than these critics' responses and was indicative of the nervousness that the theatrical representation of interracial marriage could generate at a time when miscegenation was still criminalized in many states. Before the play's opening, the *Boston Daily Globe* ("White Actress for Negro Leading Man" 1924) and the *Washington Post* expressed, in nearly identical language, a not-so-subtle worry that Ella's role included the requirement that the actress kiss a black man's hand:

> A young woman whose name is being withheld has agreed, after one leading actress and many near stars refused, to play opposite a negro leading man in an inter-racial play, "All God's Chillun Got Wings," soon to be staged by Eugene O'Neill, it was revealed today. The white woman is required in the closing scene of the play, to kiss

the hand of the negro, whose wife she has become. ("White Actress to Play Opposite Negro 'Lead'" 1924)

In the *Chicago Defender,* an African American weekly, Tony Langston (1924) reported the "tremendous howl from the white press" with some irony, but added that there was also black indignation at the story of an educated and refined black man eloping with "the tossed-aside, degenerate concubine of a plug-ugly" and at the report that a leading white actress supposedly had refused to play opposite Paul Robeson, "a man of breeding and education." Because Mary Blair's illness delayed the opening night for at least a month, journals had ample opportunity to heat up the discussion. When E. A. Carter (1924) published a largely laudatory review of *All God's Chillun Got Wings* (before its first production) in *Opportunity,* he ended it with the statement: "I venture to assert that this play will not be popular. Colored people will feel that it is 'punk propaganda' and white America does not relish any such assaults on its 'Credo' concerning the Negro." This turned out to be an understatement at best. As the writer Eric Walrond (1925) noted in his review, the Harlem-based Reverend Dr. Cleveland G. Allen strongly objected to the play; and Paul Robeson (1924) and George Jean Nathan (1924) alluded to more black criticism of the play as racial libel since it portrayed an educated Negro marrying a white woman of the streets. There were also objections to the casting of Robeson in what was seen as a racially demeaning part. The *World* reported on March 3 that "newspapers, public officials, and the playhouse were inundated by protest mail" (Frank 2000). According to the New York *American,* there were widespread protests against the play, "based on the fact that in it a white woman kisses the hand of her negro husband. . . . The protests come from both whites and negroes, in about equal numbers" (Gelb and Gelb 1973). Still, if there was some black disappointment that Robeson's Jim was neither a race man nor a role model, the nature of some white responses was of a completely different level of intensity, for the mere presence on stage of a black-white married couple was explosive—even though *All God's Chillun Got Wings* could hardly be considered an advertisement for interracial marriage. On March 16 the *American* wrote of "the advisability of substituting an octoroon for Miss Blair," suggesting the light-skinned African American actress Evelyn Preer for the part (so as to blunt the issue of miscegenation), and on March 18 a leading member of the New York Bar, the New York Board of Education, and a founder of the United Daughters of the Confederacy stated "that the play should not be produced" (Macgowan 1924; Gelb and Gelb 1973).

Political reactions from white racist American organizations were more vocal and forceful. A Georgian chapter of the Ku Klux Klan wrote to O'Neill: "You have a son. . . . If your play goes on, don't expect to see him again." The Klan's Grand Kleagle also threatened: "The theatre will be bombed and you will be responsible for all the people killed." O'Neill's answer was as short as it was brave: "Go fuck yourself" (Gelb and Gelb 1973; Frank 2000). In an editorial in the Klan's *Fiery Cross*, Billy Mayfield took the Catholic O'Neill to task for fomenting race riots; the American Legion sensed that there was German propaganda hidden in the play and suspected that the producers of the play must be German or German American. The Texas chapter of the Ku Klux Klan thought that they had to be Jews—whereupon George Jean Nathan (who had initially invited O'Neill to contribute the play to the opening issue of the *American Mercury* and published it there over H. L. Mencken's objections) pointed out that their names were "clearly of a German-Yiddish flavor, to wit, Macgowan, O'Neill, and Jones" (Nathan 1924; Gelb and Gelb 1973). James Light was accused of being a Jew hiding under an English Christian name, and O'Neill was called a "dirty Irish mick." In a 1924 letter O'Neill remembered anonymous letters ranging "from those of infuriated Irish Catholics who threatened to pull my ears off as a disgrace to their race and religion, to those of equally infuriated Nordic Kluxers who knew that I had Negro blood, or else was a Jewish pervert masquerading under a Christian name in order to do subversive propaganda for the

Pope!" (Gelb and Gelb 1973). Mary Blair and Paul Robeson also received hate mail.

On March 4, 1924, the *New York World,* a Hearst paper, demanded that the Board of Aldermen suppress the play for the reason that, in *All God's Chillun Got Wings,* "an act which is illegal in more than half the country and is viewed with disapproval in the other half is to be represented in a manner indicating approval in a public theatre" (Rogers 1952). (Any representation of miscegenation could be considered advocacy.) In a satirical rejoinder to the "theory that a playwright must be limited to law-abiding drama," Heywood Broun (1924) pointed out that "Tristan violated the Mann Act," that "Camille transgresses fundamental social statutes," and that "Hamlet suffered from the heresy of the Ku Klux Klan and undertook to take the law in his own hand." The objections to the performance of the play expressed in the press and in many letters of protest to city officials were shared by New York City Mayor John F. Hylan, who "looked with extreme disfavor on the production of the play, but there was no advance action that city officials could take to prevent the production of the play." Hence the mayor's office—on the afternoon before the opening night—resorted to the strategy of refusing, without citing grounds, to give routine licenses (which "must be issued before child actors can play in New York") to the eight children who were to act in the first scene, in which Ella throws a kiss at Jim and says, "I'm your girl." Later statements from the mayor's office explained that the decision was due to "the tender ages of the children"—ten to thirteen—and "not to any protests that may have been received regarding the racial issue raised by the drama" ("Mayor Still Bars Children in Play" 1924). On May 15, opening night, because of the mayor's action, the director, James Light, "read the first scene to the opening night audience partially made up of armed policemen ready to stop the play in case of a disturbance" ("Hylan Bars Scene in O'Neill's Play" 1924). According to O'Neill, however, "the opening night was anti-climactic . . . to the critics who seemed to feel cheated that there hadn't been at least one murder" (Gelb and Gelb 1973). The *New York Times* reported that the "sole indication of the presence of a possible discordant element was a yellow volume entitled 'The Ku Klux Klan,' which was found in the theatre after the audience had left" ("Hylan Bars Scene in O'Neill's Play" 1924). In later performances in 1924, it was explained that the children "were playing in the first scene through permission of the Mayor, their permanent appearance or disappearance to be decided . . . upon the basis of a report from the commission of investigation to be appointed by the Mayor."

The first-night audience in the small theater reportedly gave the play a warm reception, and *All God's Chillun Got Wings* ran for about 100 additional performances. The reviews of the play, the actors, and the whole production were overwhelmingly positive yet also gave much room to discussing the controversial nature of intermarriage and the underlying issue of racial equality. The *Wall Street Journal,* for example, seconded the notion that it would have been better to have cast a colored actress in the role of Ella, and for an oddly contorted reason: "Contacts hinted at in the text and unpleasantly present in the minds of the spectators might have been made excusable if based on physical manifestations of tenderness not possible to be shown in scenes between a negro actor and a white actress" ("Stage Miscegenation" 1924). John Corbin (1924), who sounded a more moderate note against the campaign of race hatred and bigotry that had accompanied the production, still found it necessary to write in the *New York Times:* "let me say with all possible emphasis that I do not believe in mixed marriages, especially between races as different as the white and the black. Common observation tells us that in many respects, both mental and moral, the average negro is inferior to the average white, and the army mental tests have strongly confirmed it."

All God's Chillun Got Wings remained controversial enough that, although a British production with Robeson was staged in 1933, and there were successful runs also in Moscow and Paris, the first major U.S. revival was not staged until 1975, when George C. Scott directed it at the Circle in the Square, with Robert Christian as Jim Harris and Trish Van Devere in the part of Ella Downey. Reviewing it in the *New York Times*, Clive Barnes (1975) found that the play's original impact and implications "are almost impossible for us to comprehend half a century later." But Walter Kerr (1975) wrote: "A queasy question hovers, really unanswered: Is there a genetic barrier that can never be crossed?" He concluded that the play "comes from a time, and a set of inbred dispositions, that are part of our own history, perhaps of our lingering history."

The half century that divided the play's original production from its revival, and especially the decades after World War II, witnessed a sea change in racial attitudes. It is telling that a *New York Times* editorial endorsed the 1954 *Brown v. Board of Education* school integration decision by the Warren Court under the headline "All God's Chillun"—an explicit reference to O'Neill's play. ("What the court is saying, in its formal but not complicated style, is a part of what Eugene O'Neill said in a play called 'All God's Chillun Got Wings,'" the *Times* editorialized.) Representations of interracial relations had become common enough for a journalist to ask, "Are Interracial Love Affairs the Coming Trend on Broadway?" contrasting 1964 plays like *The Owl and the Pussycat* (with Diane Sands and Alan Alda) and *Golden Boy* (starring Sammy Davis Jr. and Paula Wayne) as well as films like *One Potato, Two Potato* (with Bernie Hamilton and Barbara Barrie) with the turbulent reception of *All God's Chillun Got Wings* in 1924 (Funke 1964a, 1964b).

"Mutts Like Me"

Four score and four years after Eugene O'Neill's play proved so amazingly controversial, Barack Obama was elected president of the United States, and soon after the election he referred to himself jokingly as a "mutt" (Fram 2008). He had already offered his story more seriously as an American allegory:

I am the son of a black man from Kenya and a white woman from Kansas. I was raised with the help of a white grandfather who survived a Depression to serve in Patton's Army during World War II and a white grandmother who worked on a bomber assembly line at Fort Leavenworth while he was overseas. I've gone to some of the best schools in America and lived in one of the world's poorest nations. I am married to a black American who carries within her the blood of slaves and slaveowners—an inheritance we pass on to our two precious daughters. I have brothers, sisters, nieces, nephews, uncles and cousins, of every race and every hue, scattered across three continents, and for as long as I live, I will never forget that in no other country on Earth is my story even possible. It's a story that hasn't made me the most conventional candidate. But it is a story that has seared into my genetic makeup the idea that this nation is more than the sum of its parts—that out of many, we are truly one. (Obama 2008)

The symbolic weight of this story and of the 2008 election for American interracialism is enormous. Yet it is also worth remembering that not that long ago, Obama's story, and the story of his parents' marriage, would not have been possible in America, would in fact have been considered "unthinkable." Whether his story will usher in a new flourishing of interracial literature or a return to the "queasy questions" lingering from the past remains to be seen, though probably we will not have to wait a thousand years for the answer. Whatever that answer may turn out to be, works of interracial literature written elsewhere and in different eras have imagined tales of black and white love and marriage, of a mixed-race hero and knight of the Grail, and of different-looking family members who "are but *one*."

Further Reading

This essay is based on a course that started in 1999 as "Afro-American Studies 138" and was then reshaped when it became part of the new General Education program in 2008. My study *Neither Black nor White yet Both: Thematic Explorations of Interracial Literature* (New York: Oxford University Press, 1997) addresses general issues of the field in close readings and broader thematic surveys. Many of the recommended readings, including the two discussed in detail in this essay, are included in my books, *An Anthology of Interracial Literature: Black-White Contacts in the Old World and the New* (New York: New York University Press, 2004) and *Interracialism: Black-White Intermarriage in American History, Literature, and Law* (New York: Oxford University Press, 2000), two collections that grew out of source materials for the original course. I am grateful to Stephen Kosslyn and Jennifer Shephard for inviting me to write this essay and for comments on a first draft, and to Jennifer Kurdyla for research assistance and additional suggestions for revision. I am also indebted to my colleague Eckehard Simon, who came to my Interracial Literature class on several different occasions and lectured on *Parzival*.

Recommended Readings

Andersen, Hans Christian. 1840. *Mulatten.*
Danish romantic comedy of an ideal mixed-race hero who marries a noble-born heiress.

Cable, George Washington. *Old Creole Days* (1879); *The Grandissimes* (1880); *Madame Delphine* (1881).
Works by an American romance writer that are set in New Orleans and explore interracial family stories.

Chesnutt, Charles W. *The Wife of His Youth and Other Stories of the Color-Line* (1899); *The House behind the Cedars* (1900); *The Marrow of Tradition* (1901).
Short stories and novels by an American writer with a deep interest in interracial family plots and the theme of passing.

Chopin, Kate. 1893. "The Father of Désirée's Baby."
Short story set in Louisiana about secret racial origins.

Cinzio, Giambattista Giraldi. 1565. *Hecatommithi.*
Italian Renaissance novella cycle. One novella served as the source for Shakespeare's *Othello*.

Dickinson, Anna E. 1869. *What Answer?*
Novel about prejudice against interracial marriage in America.

Dumas, Alexandre. 1843. *Georges.*
French novel featuring an ideal romantic mixed-race protagonist on the island of Mauritius.

Duras, Claire Lechat. 1823. *Ourika.*
French novella in which an African adopted by a French aristocrat tells her story.

Faulkner, William. 1936. *Absalom, Absalom!*
One of Faulkner's many novels and short stories about race and family relations in Mississippi.

Hampton, Orville, and Raphael Hayes. 1964. *One Potato, Two Potato.*
Film script about interracial couple in custody dispute about children from an earlier marriage; film starring Barbara Barrie and Bernie Hamilton was directed by Larry Peerce.

Howells, William Dean. "The Pilot's Story" (1860); *An Imperative Duty* (1891).
A poem and a novel about mixed-race protagonists and interracial family relations by a champion of the realist movement.

Hughes, Langston. "Cross" (1925); "Mulatto" (1927); *Mulatto: A Tragedy of the Deep South* (1935).
Harlem Renaissance writer's poems and play about interracial families.

Johnson, Georgia Douglas. "The Octoroon" (1922); "Cosmopolite" (1924); "The Riddle" (1925); "Interracial" (1943).
Poems on interracial themes by a Harlem Renaissance writer.

Kleist, Heinrich von. 1811. *The Engagement in Santo Domingo.*
German novella about the tragic love between the mixed-race Toni and the Swiss Gustav, set during the 1803 Haitian revolution.

Larsen, Nella. *Quicksand* (1928); *Passing* (1929).
Novels by an American about passing and interracialism set during the Harlem Renaissance.

Manhoff, Bill. 1964. *The Owl and the Pussycat.*
Broadway play about an interracial affair starring Diana Sands and Alan Alda. (Film version removed interracial plotline.)

Masuccio Salernitano. 1475. *Il novellino.*
Italian Renaissance novella cycle containing stories about interracial affairs.

Maupassant, Guy de. 1889. "Boitelle."
Ironic short story about a provincial Frenchman who falls in love with an African woman.

Neville, Henry. 1668. *The Isle of Pines.*
Tale of the shipwrecked George Pine, who has sexual affairs with four women, one of whom is a black slave girl, and founds a whole island population.

Odets, Clifford, with Charles Strouse and Lee Adams. 1964. *Golden Boy.*
Musical starring Sammy Davis Jr. and Paula Wayne (who kiss), based on 1937 play that did not have an interracial plotline.

O'Neill, Eugene. 1924. *All God's Chillun Got Wings.*
American drama about interracial marriage.

One Thousand and One Nights.
Arabic short story cycle, with frame story and several other stories about interracial themes.

Pushkin, Alexander Sergeyevich. 1827–1828. "The Blackamoor of Peter the
   Great."
Russian historical novel fragment based on story of Pushkin's African ancestor.

Schuyler, George. 1931. *Black No More.*
Raucous satirical novel about scientist who can make black pigmentation disappear and throws America into complete disarray.

Séjour, Victor. 1837. "Le mulâtre."
French short story by an African American expatriate about a mixed-race slave rebel.

Shakespeare, William. c. 1604. *Othello.*
English Renaissance tragedy.

Steele, Richard, and Joseph Addison. 1711. "Inkle and Yarico."
British *Spectator* essay about an island romance and its horrific ending.

Stein, Gertrude. 1909. "Melanctha."
Experimental novella about a working-class mixed-race heroine.

Storm, Theodor. 1863. *From beyond the Seas.*
German regionalist novella about the love and marriage of a German architect and the mixed-race Jenni.

Toomer, Jean. *Cane* (1923); "Withered Skin of Berries" (1923).
Experimental multigenre book and short story by an American modernist writer of the Harlem Renaissance with a deep interest in interracial themes and utopian hopes for a world without racial labels.

Wallace, Irving. 1964. *The Man.*
Novel about a black pro tempore Senate leader who ascends to the presidency.

Wolfram von Eschenbach. 1197–1210. *Parzival.*
A Middle High German medieval romance featuring a black-white marriage and a mixed-race knight of the Grail.

Works Cited

"All God's Chillun." 1954. *New York Times,* May 18, p. 28. [Editorial on *Brown v. Board of Education.*] ProQuest Historical Newspapers.

Barnes, Clive. 1975. "'All God's Chillun' at Circle in the Square." *New York Times,* March 21, p. 30. ProQuest Historical Newspapers.

Broun, Heywood. 1924. "New York Editor Praises O'Neill's Drama." *Chicago Defender,* March 15, p. 1. ProQuest Historical Newspapers.

Carter, E. A. 1924. "All God's Chillun Got Wings." *Opportunity,* April, p. 113.

Contini, Gianfranco. 1959. "I piú antichi esempi di 'Razza.'" *Studi di Filologia Italiana* 17: 319–327.

Corbin, John. 1924. "Among the New Plays." *New York Times,* May 18, p. X1. ProQuest Historical Newspapers.

Du Bois, W. E. B. 1923–1924. "The Negro and Our Stage." *Provincetown Playbill* 4: 2.

Eliot, T. S. 1926. Review of *All God's Chillun Got Wings,* by Eugene O'Neill. *New Criterion* 4: 395–396.

Floyd, Virginia, ed. 1981. *Eugene O'Neill at Work: Newly Released Ideas for Plays.* New York: Ungar.

Fram, Alan. 2008. "'Mutts Like Me' Shows Obama's Racial Comfort." MSNBC, November 8. Retrieved April 11, 2011, from http://www.msnbc.msn.com/id/27606637/ns/politics-decision_08/.

Frank, Glenda. 2000. "Tempest in Black and White: The 1924 Premiere of Eugene O'Neill's *All God's Chillun Got Wings.*" *Resources for American Literary Study* 26: 75–89.

Funke, Lewis. 1964a. "Are Interracial Love Affairs the Coming Trend on Broadway?" *Philadelphia Tribune,* November 24, p. 9. ProQuest Historical Newspapers.

———. 1964b. "Are Interracial Stage Romances on the Rise?" *New York Times,* November 8, p. X1. ProQuest Historical Newspapers.

Gelb, Arthur, and Barbara Gelb. 1973. *O'Neill.* New York: Harper.

Howells, William Dean. 1869. Review of *What Answer?* by Anna E. Dickinson. *Atlantic Monthly,* January, pp. 134–135.

Hughes, Everett C. 1965. "Anomalies and Projections." *Daedalus* 94: 1133–1147.

Hurst, Fannie. 1924. Letter to the editor. *New York Times,* June 8, p. X1. ProQuest Historical Newspapers.

"Hylan Bars Scene in O'Neill's Play." 1924. *New York Times,* May 16, p. 1. ProQuest Historical Newspapers.

Johnson, Georgia Douglas. 1943. "Interracial," ms. in James Weldon Johnson Collection, JWJ, Shelf ZAN, Johnson, Georgia Douglas, folder 5, Beinecke Library, Yale University.

Kerr, Walter. 1975. "O'Neill's Uneasy Study in Black and White." *New York Times,* March 30, p. 79. ProQuest Historical Newspapers.

Langston, Tony. 1924. "White Actress Co-star with Robeson in O'Neill Drama." *Chicago Defender,* March 1, p. 1. ProQuest Historical Newspapers.

Leitzmann, Albert, ed. 1961–1965. *Wolfram von Eschenbach,* 7th ed. Rev. Wilhelm Deinert. 3 vols. Altdeutsche Texbibliothek 12–14. Tübingen: Max Niemeyer Verlag. [Source of the Middle High German text of *Parzival* cited in this chapter.]

Lewisohn, Ludwig. 1924. "All God's Chillun." *Nation* 118: 664.

Light, James. 1924. "On Producing O'Neill's Play." *Opportunity,* April, p. 113.

Macgowan, Kenneth. 1924. "O'Neill's Play Again." *New York Times,* August 31, p. X2. ProQuest Historical Newspapers.

"Mayor Still Bars Children in Play." 1924. *New York Times,* May 17, p. 18. ProQuest Historical Newspapers.

Mottram, Eric. 1971. "O'Neill, Eugene." In Malcolm Bradbury, Eric Mottram, and Jean Franco, eds., *The Penguin Companion to American Literature.* New York: McGraw-Hill.

Murphy, Brenda. 1987. *American Realism and American Drama, 1880–1940.* New York: Cambridge University Press.

Myrdal, Gunnar. 1944. *An American Dilemma: The Negro Problem and Modern Democracy.* New York: Harper and Brothers.

Nathan, George Jean. 1924. "The Theatre." *American Mercury,* May, pp. 113–114.

Obama, Barack. 2008. "Speech on Race." NPR, March 18. Retrieved April 11, 2011, from http://www.npr.org/templates/story/story.php?storyId=88478467.

Prospero, Adriano. 1992. "Tra natura e cultura: dall'intolleranza religiosa alla discriminazione per sangue." In Girolamo Imbruglia, ed., *Il razzismo e le sue storie,* 113–129. Naples: Edizioni Scientifiche Italiane.

Robeson, Paul. 1924. "Reflections on O'Neill's Plays." *Opportunity,* December, p. 369.

Rogers, J. A. 1952. *Sex and Race,* vol. 1, p. 15. New York: Helga M. Rogers.

Sabatini, Francesco. 1962. "Conferme per l'etimologia di *razza* dal francese antico *haraz.*" *Studi di Filologia Italiana* 20: 365–382.

Sheaffer, Louis. 1968. *O'Neill: Son and Playwright.* Boston: Little, Brown.

Spitzer, Leo. 1933. "Wortgeschichtliches." *Zeitschrift für romanische Philologie* 53: 300–301.

"Stage Miscegenation." 1924. *Wall Street Journal,* May 17, p. 3. ProQuest Historical Newspapers.

Stolcke, Verena. 1994. "Invaded Women: Gender, Race, and Class in the Formation of Colonial Society." In Margo Hendricks and Patricia Parker, eds., *Women, "Race," and Writing in the Early Modern Period,* 272–286. New York: Routledge.

Walrond, Eric D. 1925. "All God's Chillun Got Wings." *Opportunity,* July, pp. 220–221.

Weston, Jessie, trans. (1894) 2004. "*Parzival* by Wolfram von Eschenbach." In Werner Sollors, ed., *An Anthology of Interracial Literature: Black-White Contacts in the Old World and the New,* 8–53. New York: New York University Press.

"White Actress for Negro Leading Man." 1924. *Boston Daily Globe,* February 22, p. 4. ProQuest Historical Newspapers.

"White Actress to Play Opposite Negro 'Lead.'" 1924. *Washington Post,* February 22, p. 3. ProQuest Historical Newspapers.

Wilson, Edmund. 1924. "All God's Chillun and Others." *New Republic,* May 28, p. 22.

Wilson, Fredric Woodbridge. 2005. *Paul Robeson as Othello: The 1942–1945 Margaret Webster–Paul Robeson production of Shakespeare's Othello.* Cambridge, MA: Harvard Theatre Collection.

"Pursuits of Happiness": Dark Threads in the History of the American Revolution

Laurel Thatcher Ulrich

According to a recent survey by the Pew Forum on Religion and Public Life, 74 percent of Americans think there is a heaven, but only 59 percent believe there is a hell. Americans like to look on the bright side. Perhaps our optimism is grounded in the stories we tell about our nation's founding. We want to believe with Jefferson that "the pursuit of happiness" is one of the "inalienable rights" of humankind.

Today, happiness is a growth industry in the United States. While researchers attempt to measure it, marketers offer formulas for its pursuit. On colleges campuses across the United States, students crowd into courses in "positive psychology," while in print and in cyberspace, historians, filmmakers, theologians, novelists, philosophers, and a whole host of bloggers offer their own glosses on Jefferson's words. Experts tell us that wealth does not make us happy, but what does? Is the secret in our natures, our circumstances, or our choices?

The questions are not new. Americans have been obsessed with happiness for at least three centuries, perhaps at no time more so than in the years surrounding the American Revolution. Despite wars, economic upheaval, and wave after wave of epidemics, Americans still held out hope for a better life. Even those who placed their ultimate hopes in an afterlife believed they had a right to a little bit of heaven on earth. Among serious thinkers the pursuit of happiness was a given. As John Adams wrote, "Upon this point all speculative politicians will agree, that the happiness of society is the end of government, as all divines [clergymen] and moral philosophers will agree that the happiness of the individual is the end of man."

By the middle of the eighteenth century, women's embroidery also reflected commonplace assumptions about happiness. In 1996 the Boston Museum of Fine Arts paid more than $1 million for a needle-point tapestry completed in about 1750 by Hannah Otis, the little-known sister of Revolutionary orator James Otis and poet and historian Mercy Otis Warren. Hannah filled her canvas with classic pastoral motifs—leafy hillocks, soaring birds, oversized strawberries, and grazing cattle (see Plate 8). But within this idealized landscape she placed identifiable Boston landmarks—the steeple of West Church, the flag on Beacon Hill, and Thomas Hancock's grand mansion on the corner of the Common. On the left of the canvas, a happy couple purported to be Hancock and his wife overlook a pond. In the foreground, a young man said to be John Hancock, the future signer of the Declaration of Independence, rides a prancing white horse. To his right, a boy plays with a bow and arrow.

Every detail in Hannah's embroidery speaks to eighteenth-century notions of happiness. The house with its neat white fence signifies the central theme of most political writing—property. As the British pamphleteers Thomas Gordon and John Trenchard put it, "Happiness is the Effect of Independency, and Independency is the Effect of Property." Only those with the ability to sustain themselves could be truly free. Just as telling is the boy with the bow and arrow. He is not dressed like an Indian and he does not appear to be Cupid. He looks like an ordinary boy aiming at a bird or squirrel. Yet the image presages a theme in a famous speech by Hannah's older brother. In his 1761 attack on the "Writs of Assistance" that allowed customs officers to search for smuggled goods, James Otis invoked the old proverb "a man's house is his castle." Barring any suspicion of wrongdoing, he argued, a man had an incontestable right to his own property. "The club that he had snapped from a tree, for a staff or for defense, was his own. His bow and arrow were his own; if by a pebble he had killed a partridge or a squirrel, it was his own. No creature, man or beast, had a right to take it from him."

The happy couple holding hands beside the pond reflects another dominant theme in eighteenth-century literature—"domestic affection." When an eighteenth-century wife addressed her husband as "Dearest Friend," she acknowledged a cultural shift reflected in political philosophy, poetry, advice literature, and especially in the sentimental novels that were the newest addition to the literary scene. Conventional concepts of the family—husband and wife, parent and child, master and servant—emphasized a hierarchy of authority and dependency. In contrast, friendship was reciprocal. It was chosen. Most important, friendship reflected a capacity to identify with the feelings of others, a quality eighteenth-century writers called "sensibility."

The ripe strawberries, flowering branches, and spotted cow in Hannah's picture reflect themes from neoclassical literature as well as politics. Following Virgil, eighteenth-century poets frequently contrasted the tranquility of rural life with the venality and corruption of the city. Hannah's sister Mercy adopted such a theme in a poem addressed to her husband James, who was serving in the General Court in Boston:

> Come leave the noisy smoky town,
> Where vice and folly reign,
> The vain pursuits of busy men
> We wisely will disdain.

Hannah's embroidery makes the same argument, though, naively perhaps, she located her rural paradise in that supposedly vice-filled city. For Hannah and her sister Mercy, the contrast was not geographical but conceptual. It was not the countryside but the private household that was the seat of political virtue. Hannah's imagery also reflects the millennial dream expressed by the Hebrew prophet Micah and invoked often in political literature, that every man might sit under his own vine and fig tree.

But stitched into its happy landscape are darker themes. When aligned, the spire of West Church and the flag on Beacon Hill guided ships into Boston harbor, ships that carried not only Hannah's embroidery thread from England but slaves from Africa and the West Indies, a reality acknowledged by the presence in Hannah's picture of a diminutive slave doffing his hat. Hancock's ships were deeply implicated in both the profits and the horrors of the Atlantic economy. Shipping contracts secured during England's wars with New France and its Indian allies paid for Hancock's impressive mansion. And of course for men less prosperous than Hancock the only hope of securing what Gordon and Trenchard called "independency" was moving onto so-called unimproved land, such as the Maine lumber lands that the Abenaki Indians called home.

Hannah's embroidery raises another issue as well. Although a man might have an incontestable right to his possessions, a woman did not. If she married, any property she brought to the union passed into her husband's control. If she remained single and somehow acquired her own property, she was excluded by virtue of her sex from political decision making. In another of his famous pamphlets, Hannah's brother questioned that exclusion. In the event of the abdication of a king, "had not apple women and orange girls as good a right to give their respectable suffrages for a new King as the philosopher, courtier, *petite-maître,* and politician?" He was making a theoretical point about who belonged to the political community that, in John Locke's theory, created government. But within less than a decade, American independence gave his questions practical importance. What was the place of women in the new American polity? Unfortunately, James succumbed to mental illness before he could offer an answer.

Lurking around the frame of eighteenth-century visions of happiness are troubling questions about war, race, and gender. The problem is not just that revolutionary Americans left some people out of their political compact. It is that the compact itself was built upon those exclusions. That may be why it is so difficult for us to acknowledge the dark threads in our national tapestry.

Happiness, Property, and American Indians

The poet Robert Lowell's grim couplet, "Our fathers wrung their bread from stocks and stones / And fenced their gardens with the Redman's bones," captures an aspect of the American story that twenty-first-century Americans would like to forget. Phrases like "virgin land" or "uninhabited wilderness" still creep into our histories even though we know there were several million people in North America when Europeans arrived. By the eve of the Revolution, Indians, though much diminished, were still a compelling presence not only on the borders of settlement but in diplomatic councils and in enclaves not far from colonial capitols. Yet until recently, their stories have been ignored in accounts of the Revolution, which has been seen as primarily a matter of thirteen British colonies rejecting their "mother country."

This omission is really rather astonishing since Indians were integral to the story. Where did George Washington begin his military career? In the French and Indian War. Why did Parliament need to tax the American colonies? To pay for that war. What was that strange "Proclamation Line" marked on textbook maps? A British boundary designed to prevent colonists from moving across the Appalachians onto Indian lands. Colonial resentment of that constraint is right there in the Declaration of Independence, which accuses King George of preventing "new appropriation of lands" and, worse yet, of trying "to bring on the inhabitants of our frontiers the merciless Indian savages, whose known rule of warfare is an undistinguished destruction of all ages, sexes and conditions."

Memories of prior wars reverberated through official rhetoric and public oratory during the early years of the Revolution. A congressional declaration of 1775 insisted that English colonists "at the expense of their blood effected settlements in the distant and inhospitable wilds of America, then filled with numerous warlike nations of barbarians." When rumors flew through the colonies that British agents were negotiating with Indian allies and promising to free slaves, Thomas Paine exclaimed that there were "thousands, and tens of thousands, who would think it glorious to expel from the continent that barbarous and hellish power, which hath stirred up the Indians and Negroes to destroy us."

Yet even as the colonists fought the native inhabitants of North America, they idealized their courage, stoicism, and apparent freedom. The men who dumped tea into Boston harbor were neither the first nor the last to adopt Indian garb when engaged in extralegal protest. And in every war that they fought, including the Revolution, colonists were joined by Indian allies. For "red" men as well as white men, the American Revolution was a civil war, pitting brother against brother. Within and across the color line the prize was control of the American landscape.

John Locke's famous statement that "in the beginning all the world was America" explained the struggle. Locke argued that when God "gave the world in common to all mankind," he also commanded them to labor. A man who "subdued, tilled and sowed" some part of the earth consequently attached to the land "something that was his property, which another had no title to, nor could without injury take from him." He said that although American Indians were rich in land, they remained "poor in all the comforts of life" because they had failed to create property through their labor. They had "not one hundredth part of the conveniences we enjoy; and a king of a large and fruitful territory there, feeds, lodges, and is clad worse than a day-laborer in England." Hence it seemed inevitable, at least to those who followed this line of argument, that white settlers would supplant them. That Indians fought back only reinforced the point. These men were "savages."

Popular images of the American Revolution focus on colonial cities or farms—crowds in the narrow streets of Boston or Philadelphia, minutemen firing from behind rock walls. But in its bloodiest moments, the Revolution was a frontier war that continued a cycle of revenge and retaliation that on the edges of European settlement ended hopes for peaceful coexistence. The evidence of a hardening divide was there as early as 1751, when a Presbyterian missionary spoke to a council of Indians in the Wyoming Valley of Pennsylvania. When he tried to offer his Christian message, one speaker responded with disdain, telling him that God had created white men last and never intended that they should control others. "And furthermore, they understood that the White people were contriving a method to deprive them of their country in those parts, as they had done by the sea-side, and to make slaves of them and their children as they did of the Negroes."

Ten years later, when white squatters burned a village occupied by Delawares friendly to the government of Pennsylvania, Indians retaliated by torturing and then killing settlers who had the audacity to occupy Delaware land. In retaliation, white vigilantes who called themselves "Hickory Boys" wiped out a village of Moravian Indians who had nothing to do with the original conflict and who had rejected the call for war. In a defense of their action, they said, "We have long been convinced from sufficient evidence that the Indians that lived as independent commonwealths among us or near our borders were our most dangerous enemies." Resenting the dismissal of their concerns by leaders living in the safety of Philadelphia, the Hickory Boys insisted that "no nation could be safe especially in a time of war, if another state or part of a state be allowed to live among them." The Hickory Boys got away with this atrocity in part because Americans had so much difficulty distinguishing one Indian from another.

During war with French Canada and her Indian allies in 1755, Hannah Otis's father employed much the same logic. When the Penobscots of Maine refused either to take sides or to submit to the colonists' protection, Otis and three other members of the Massachusetts Council warned "that it will not be Possible for the forces in the Service of this Province to distinguish between that Tribe and any other Tribes with whom we are at War, and that if any of their People are killed by our Forces when in pursuit of the Enemy, they must attribute it to their refusal to comply with the proposals made by this Government out of regard to their Safety." But as New England Indians had already discovered, "protection" meant being removed from their homes and forced to live in detention camps. And as southern New England tribes had already learned to their sorrow, even those who retained their own lands were often subject to "Guardians" who, like Hannah's father, leased supposedly "unused" Indian lands to whites.

Not surprisingly, the Revolution, too, became a war for control of native land. When part of the Iroquois confederation sided with the British, supporting attacks on frontier settlements, including those in the Wyoming Valley, George Washington ordered his troops "to carry the war into the Heart of the Country of the six nations; to cut off their settlements, destroy their next Year's crops, and do them every other mischief of which time and circumstances will permit." Soldiers entrusted with this mission were confused when they found frame houses and neat fields rather than the wigwams they had imagined, but they carried out Washington's orders. Some of them returned after the war to claim land once occupied by native farmers.

As historian Daniel Richter (2001) has written, "If the crown's protection of Indian land had been a major grievance before the Revolution, the victims now redressed that grievance with a vengeance," putting native leaders on notice that if they resisted expanding settlement into the Ohio Valley, the new government would "extirpate them from the land where they were born and now live." Without question, the biggest losers in the War for Independence were not the British but the native groups who sided with them. As Colin Calloway (2006) has observed, "Indian people had been virtually everywhere in colonial America, building new worlds on the ruins of old worlds. . . . The United States looked forward to a future without Indians."

Most Americans did not like to imagine themselves as Indian haters. In backcountry settlements, Euro-Americans wore moccasins and traveled in canoes, and during the Revolution some of Washington's soldiers wore a fringed shirt supposedly adapted from "Indian dress." During and after the war, cartoonists continued to imagine America as an Indian maiden. But there was no question about where the future was heading. The purpose of the war was to make America safe not only from British taxation but from the demands of Britain's Indian allies. Having chosen the losing side, some native tribes relocated in Canada; others moved beyond the edge of white settlement—only to face new incursions later. Land speculators as well as land-hungry white settlers rushed onto newly cleared land. The new nation's dream of happiness required the continuing transformation of the American landscape.

In *The Discovery, Settlement, and Present State of Kentucke,* published in 1784, a former Pennsylvania schoolmaster named John Filson wrote, "Thus we behold Kentucke, lately an howling wilderness, the habitation of savages and wild beasts, become a fruitful field." Filson's was the first book to celebrate the life of Daniel Boone, whom he portrayed as a man of nature attuned to the ways of the Indians he fought. Although Filson's Boone finds happiness in the wilderness, his ultimate dream is to bring his family across the Appalachians to Kentucky, which he "esteemed a second paradise." John Mack Faragher (1992), Boone's modern biographer, summarized the myth and the man in this way:

> I was a woodsman, says Boone, a man who loved nature and sought a place to hunt and live at ease, but who opened the way for thousands to follow and crowd me out. I was a husband and father devoted to my family, but who craved solitude. I was a man who loved the Indians and hated violence, but who rose to fame as the leader of a war of dispossession. I was a man of contradictions.

So, we might add, were his fellow Americans. Boone's cabin was a far cry from Hancock's elegant mansion, but both men believed that white men would ultimately claim the American landscape.

Happiness, Liberty, and Slavery

The slave in Hannah Otis's embroidery signifies the ability of some men to turn other men into property. Curiously, in the years leading up to the American Revolution, powerful white men claimed that they too were slaves. The idea was not as far-fetched as it seems. The English common law defined liberty as a right to the undisturbed possession of property. Revolutionaries believed that Parliament was depriving them of both liberty and property by taxing them without their consent. In the words of Thomas Paine, "If being bound in that manner, is not slavery, then is there not such a thing as slavery upon earth." That real slaves were toiling in American fields did not undercut the argument. For some, it may have enhanced it. Slave owners like George Washington knew exactly what it meant to be a slave. So did Benjamin Franklin, who owned slaves most of his life, and whose newspaper, *The Pennsylvania Gazette*, published frequent advertisements for the return of runaways. Only late in life did Franklin join the antislavery movement. John Adams did not own slaves, but as a lawyer he sometimes defended men who did.

Some writers argue that an emphasis on slaveholding by our Founding Fathers has more to do with "political correctness" than history, that slavery was so much a given in the eighteenth century that contemporaries actually did not see the contradictions between liberty and slavery that to us seem so glaring. That argument ignores a mass of historical evidence to the contrary. At different moments and in different ways, American patriots, their British antagonists, and thousands of runaway slaves noted the inconsistency of fighting for liberty while denying it to others.

No one was more eloquent on this issue than Thomas Jefferson, who in a famous passage from *Notes on the State of Virginia* admitted the evil of a system that allowed one half of a people "to trample on the rights of the other." Slavery, he argued, turned owners into despots and slaves into enemies, destroying the morals of one and denying the other the ability to love his country. "For if a slave can have a country in this world, it must be any other in preference to that in which he is born to live and labour for another." Although Jefferson deplored slavery, he also feared emancipation, believing that Africans and whites were so different that they could not coexist as free men. In the first draft of the Declaration of Independence, he had actually tried to blame England for the slave trade, adding to the list of grievances against the king the charge that he had promised runaways their freedom. Congress wisely excised that clause.

There is no mention of slavery in the Declaration. But it was there in the society for all to see. Shortly after arriving in New York in July 1776, a low-level British official denounced the "Impudent, false and atrocious Proclamation" recently issued in Philadelphia. In America, he reported, "there is nothing to be heard but the Sound of Liberty, and nothing to be felt but the most detestable Slavery." He did not understand how British colonists living under a constitutional monarchy—that in his view was the freest government on earth—could treat other men "as a better kind of Cattle," buying and selling them to suit their interest. In a prize-winning recent book, Christopher Leslie Brown (2006) has argued that the Revolution helped to create a full-fledged and effective antislavery movement in England by giving imperial officers reasons for embracing the cause once promoted only by visionaries.

When news swept North America in 1772 that a British court had freed James Somerset, a slave who had come to England with his master, Americans feared for their property. Even though the Somerset decision was ambiguous at best, designed as much to protect the racial purity of the mother country as to liberate the enslaved, many Americans thought that slavery had been banished from English shores. In June 1774 a Virginia planter advertised the disappearance of his slave Bacchus, claiming that the man would "probably endeavour to pass for a Freeman by the Name of John Christian, and attempt to get on Board some Vessel bound for Great Britain, from the Knowledge he has of the late Determination of Somerset's Case." Bacchus may or may not have known about the Somerset case, but his master certainly believed that he did.

Slaves began to offer their services to Governor Dunmore of Virginia even before he issued his famous proclamation of 1775 offering liberty to any slave willing to join him in putting down the American rebellion. One master complained that a slave named Charles had run away "from no cause of complaint, or dread of a whipping (for he has always been remarkably indulged, indeed too much so) but from a determined resolution to get liberty, as he conceived, by flying to lord Dunmore." Thousands of slaves ran to the British lines during the war, including Jefferson's "Black Sall" and Washington's "Harry." Had the British been more aggressive in recruiting runaways, the war might have taken a different turn, but fear of upsetting slaveholding loyalists or, worse, of inciting rebellion in England's West Indian colonies held them back.

In the North, arguments about liberty opened legal opportunities for emancipation. In Massachusetts, so-called freedom suits began even before the war. One of the earliest was instituted by a woman named Jenny Slew. Although one court said she could not sue because she was a slave and another because she was a wife, she persisted and in 1766 won her freedom. Over the next few years, efforts to win freedom moved from individual to collective protests. Three times in 1773, twice in 1774, and again in 1777, slave petitioners addressed the governor and legislature highlighting the contrast between patriot claims to liberty and their own abject condition. A 1773 petition from "many Slaves, living in the Town of Boston" echoed patriot ideals of happiness: "We have no Property! We have no Wives! No Children! We have no City! No Country!"

A June 1773 petition insisted that Africans "have in common with other men a naturel right to be free and without molestation to injoy such property as they may acuire by their industry." The next year, a similar document begged the Commonwealth of Massachusetts to "give and grant to us some part of the unimproved land, belonging to the province, for a settlement, that each of us may there quietly sit down under his own fig tree." The image of the fig tree echoed the biblical passage frequently used by white patriots. The land they alluded to (in what is now Maine) was of course the homeland of the Penobscots and others among the Wabanaki.

In southern New England, blacks and Indians worked together to assert their rights. In a 1773 letter to the Mohegan Christian leader Samson Occum, the black poet Phillis Wheatley wrote, "in every human Breast, God has implanted a Principle, which we call Love of Freedom." She did not think it would take a philosopher to discover that the American "Cry for Liberty" did not fit very well with "the exercise of oppressive Power over others." Wheatley's letter was published in a Connecticut newspaper and widely distributed. Wheatley's poetry had caused a sensation in England when Protestant supporters arranged for its publication. Thomas Jefferson was not impressed. "Religion, indeed, has produced a Phyllis Whately," he wrote, "but it could not produce a poet. The compositions published under her name are below the dignity of criticism." (Today's critics disagree.)

By the end of the war, the nature of slavery in mainland North America had been dramatically altered. Most northern states had either ended slavery or taken steps to do so. There were even abolitionist societies in Virginia, where a number of prominent men, including Jefferson's mentor George Wythe, freed their slaves. But most planters were simply too dependent on their slaves or too fearful of the consequences of emancipation to join the movement. When Thaddeus Kosciuszko, a Polish commander who served in the Continental Army, left Jefferson money to free as many as eighty of his 130 slaves, Jefferson let the will go into probate rather than accept the bequest.

In the wake of the Haitian Revolution, fears of slave rebellion hardened racial codes, and new methods of processing cotton increased the profitability of plantation slavery. A constitutional provision establishing a date for ending the slave trade actually accelerated the pace of imports. Between 1783 and 1807 an estimated 100,000 Africans were brought into Savannah and Charleston. By 1790, Georgia's slave population was nearly double the prewar figure. But the biggest boost to slavery came from the opening of new lands. White men pursued their dreams of property by rushing across the Appalachian barrier onto former Indian lands, eventually spreading slavery into the Mississippi Valley.

For most slaves, the revolutionary opening had ended. Ona Judge was one of the lucky ones. Taken from Virginia to Philadelphia to serve as a parlor maid to Martha Washington, she escaped in 1796, fleeing north on a friendly vessel. The president was horrified. Ona had been treated well. Surely she had been seduced by some scoundrel. When an agent located her in New Hampshire, Ona explained that though she loved the president and his lady, she loved freedom more. Warned that any attempt to carry her away by force would cause a scandal, Washington gave up his efforts to retrieve her. Ona's response to Washington's appeal to family feeling marks a larger conflict in eighteenth-century America between the claims to property and the promise of "friendship," a theme most apparent in discussions over the status of women.

Happiness, Citizenship, and Marriage

Building on long-standing European tradition, colonial Americans imagined "the family" as something close to what we would consider "the household," which typically included workers of all kinds, including indentured servants, apprentices, and slaves, as well as a wife and children. Although the status of these persons obviously varied, they had in common the inability to act independently of the household head. Despite the new emphasis on friendship and family feeling, these ideas persisted. Thus, when men talked about liberty, they usually meant the liberty of households rather than individuals, and households were represented on tax lists, censuses, and in store accounts by their heads. Although a few women, usually widows, were heads of households, only men participated in town meetings, parish vestries, or other governmental bodies.

The political philosophers on whom the Founding Fathers relied tinkered with the idea of less than total subservience for wives. Locke framed marriage as a contract rather than a sacrament. "Conjugal Society is made by a voluntary Compact between Man and Woman," he wrote, though he did not challenge the ultimate authority of the husband in case of conflict. Since it was necessary "that the last Determination, i.e. the Rule, should be placed somewhere, it naturally falls to the Man's share as the abler and the stronger." The Scottish philosopher Francis Hutcheson emphasized the mutuality of decisions in marriage: "Nature has designed the conjugal state to be a constant reciprocal friendship of two." For him reciprocity meant complementarity, not equality. Nature, he argued, had divided domestic matters "into two provinces, one fitted for the management of each sex, to which the other should seldom interfere except by advising." If each honored this division of labor, there would be harmony. But what if one partner violated the compact? Hutcheson offered no solution.

Since husbands had the upper hand by virtue of their economic and legal power, truly desperate wives were left with the only option open to other dependent persons—to leave. First-time readers of colonial newspapers are usually shocked to see side by side on the back pages advertisements for runaway horses, runaway slaves, runaway servants, and runaway wives. These advertisements existed in a legal system that linked support with cohabitation. As a judicial opinion in a famous English case put it:

> The husband is the head of the wife as fully as the King is the head of the commonwealth. . . . When the wife departs from her husband against his will, she forsakes and deserts his Government: erects and sets up a new jurisdiction; and assumes to govern herself, besides at least, if not against, the law of God and the law of the land.

A husband could not execute his wife for treason, but he could declare her dead to his household and could therefore withhold support. He did that by advertising her departure from his "bed and board."

In an important study, historian Kirsten Sword (2011) found more than a thousand "elopement" or "runaway wife" advertisements in Pennsylvania, New Hampshire, Massachusetts, and Virginia newspapers between 1745 and 1789. In only ninety cases did wives respond, but when they did the competing visions of marriage were often stark. When a mariner named Patrick Markham advertised in the *New Hampshire Gazette* that his wife had carried off his goods while he was at sea, she countered that he only wanted to besmirch her good name because his own reputation was in question. She said that a certain girl in the town was about to complain on oath that he was "the Father of the Child with which she is now pregnant," forcing him to pay child support. His answer amounted to "So what?" Surely the pregnant lover was lying. Why, she had even admitted to sleeping with a married man—himself! Newspaper readers may have been more entertained than shocked by this blatant expression of male privilege.

Interestingly, some women began to employ a language already familiar from revolutionary protests. Their husbands were trying to reduce them to the status of slaves. Eunice Davis, in answering her husband's newspaper ad, said, "If I am your Wife, I am not your Slave, and little thought when I acknowledg'd you as my Husband, that you would pretend to assume an unreasonable POWER to tyrannize and insult over me; and that without any just Cause." Elizabeth Markham went further, associating her husband's mistreatment of her with slave masters' abuse of their female slaves. He had treated her, she said, "in the same way some Gentlemen I have heard of, do some of their young Negro Wenches,—lodge with them by Night, and give them the Strappado by Day."

In most advertisements, though, wives were silent, though their absence spoke volumes. In Massachusetts and Connecticut divorce was possible, though on limited grounds. For most couples, however, an extralegal separation was the only option. A public advertisement alerted creditors that the spouses had parted, as in the case of a Philadelphia man who advertised that his wife had "eloped from [him], and gone off with the British army." For women, of course, the limiting factor was the ability to secure alternative support—from another man, from kin, or from whatever low-paid work might be available. Town fathers looked askance at unattached women and were likely to send them packing if they sought public support.

For women like these, idealized notions of marital "friendship" were of little help. Even in otherwise stable families, the expectation of enduring affection may have added to the disappointment of those who found their spouses wanting. "I have had my house work to do and worse than all my hard work to bear frowns (from one who Calls him Self my friend)," wrote midwife Martha Moore Ballard on a day when her husband disappointed her. Although Ballard operated confidently within the local exchange economy, she too was subject to patriarchal authority. When her husband was jailed for debt, her son moved his family into her house, relegating her to a single room, as had been the custom for generations when a woman was widowed.

The contradiction between revolutionary political ideas and conservative notions of household governance is apparent in a famous exchange between Abigail Adams and her husband John. In a 1776 letter she urged him to "Remember the Ladies" in the new code of laws that she supposed Congress was about to make. "Do not put such unlimited power into the hands of the husbands," she wrote, applying to marriage the same critique of absolute power that her husband had used to justify resistance to Britain. "Remember, all Men would be tyrants if they could. If perticuliar care and attention is not paid to the Laidies we are determined to foment a Rebelion, and will not hold ourselves bound by any Laws in which we have no voice, or Representation." She was teasing about the rebellion, but not about the need for new laws. She knew that under the strictures of common law a wife could be subject to the arbitrary will of a tyrannical or incompetent husband.

John's response betrayed his own and his critics' concerns about maintaining social order. "As to your extraordinary Code of Laws, I cannot but laugh," he wrote. "We have been told that our Struggle has loosened the bands of Government everywhere. That children and Apprentices were disobedient—that schools and Colleges were grown turbulent—that Indians slighted their Guardians and Negroes grew insolent to their Masters. But your Letter was the first Intimation that another Tribe more numerous and powerful than all the rest were grown discontented." By grouping women with children, apprentices, Negroes, and subjugated Indians, he implied that wives too were mere dependents.

Then he abruptly shifted ground, teasing Abigail with the notion that her sex was actually more powerful than his. "Depend upon, it, We know better than to repeal our Masculine systems," he teased. "We have only the Name of Masters, and rather than give up this, which would completely subject Us to the Despotism of the Petticoat, I hope General Washington, and all our brave Heroes would fight." His quip reflected a general sentiment among political thinkers. As the French philosopher Montesquieu expressed it, "women have never been wont to lay claim to equality, for they have so many other unusual advantages that for them equality of power is always a situation for the worse." Men ruled by right of law, women through the power of personal—and sexual—attraction.

Abigail might have pushed back. Her original letter contained a perfectly logical answer to John's argument. In the face of a true tyrant, female influence was of little value. "Men of Sense in all Ages abhor those customs which treat us only as the vassals of your Sex," she wrote. "Why then, not put it out of the power of the vicious and the Lawless to use us with cruelty and indignity with impunity?" That was, of course, the argument John and his fellow Whigs were using against supposed British tyranny. But instead of reiterating her point, Abigail demurred. She and John had both been shaped by the new sentimental culture that imagined relations between husbands and wives as a kind of exalted friendship. It was difficult to make war with one's "Dearest Friend."

The argument ended in a draw because the two spouses employed competing ideas about power. Abigail argued by analogy to politics. She was interested in legal authority. John appealed to influence, the informal power that women supposedly exercised in face-to-face relations. In Abigail's view, the logic of formal politics had some relevance for the household. In his, the two domains operated by different rules. In the end, Abigail fell back upon influence, closing her second letter with a borrowed couplet that advised women to get their own way in an argument by pretending to give in: "Charm by accepting, by submitting sway / Yet have our Humour most when we obey." In a letter to Mercy Otis Warren, she was more candid: "I have tried him and found him not disinterested." That is, John's self-interest as a man prevented him from giving a fair hearing to her case.

Abigail was an intelligent and articulate woman, but in the midst of a revolution she was in no position to challenge the existing gender order. Her friend Mercy Warren was a more visible supporter of the Revolution. Her satirical dramas assailing Governor Thomas Hutchinson helped to fuel the patriot movement in Boston in the 1770s, and after the war she published a three-volume *History of the Rise, Progress, and Termination of the American Revolution.* But she, too, failed to challenge the exclusion of women from the body politic. She believed that ideas themselves were powerful. "I think it very immaterial if they flow from a female lip in the soft whispers of private friendship or are thundered in the Senate in the bolder language of the other sex." This contrast between softness and boldness in women and men was also a contrast between the household and the state. Although the state of New Jersey briefly experimented with giving single women the vote, this division of labor, what later generations called "separate spheres," won out.

Happiness and the Constitution

In lectures given in Philadelphia in 1790–1791, James Wilson, one of the framers of the newly ratified Constitution, assured women in his audience that they were included in the new political compact. "You have indeed heard much of publick government and publick law, but these things were not made for themselves; they were made for something better, and of that something better, you form the better part—I mean society—I mean particularly domestick society." In Wilson's view, "domestick society," the realm portrayed so evocatively in Hannah Otis's embroidery, was the seat of human happiness and government only a prop to sustain it. "By some politicians," he continued, "society has been considered as only the scaffolding of government, very improperly, in my judgment. In the just order of things, government is the scaffolding of society; and if society could be built and kept entire without government, the scaffolding might be thrown down, with the least inconvenience of regret."

According to constitutional provisions that Wilson himself had drafted, domestic society also included slaves. One of the most difficult issues for delegates at the convention had been whether to apportion representation according to a state's population or its wealth. Because slaves were property, representation by wealth would have given the South an advantage. But to exclude slaves, while basing representation on the number of inhabitants, would have tipped the balance toward the North in ways that might have threatened ratification. The compromise was the infamous "three-fifths clause" found in Article 1, Section 2, which used population as the basis for allotting representatives and, after "excluding Indians not taxed," added "to the whole Number of free Persons . . . three fifths of all other Persons."

By rejecting the inclusion of slaves as property, the convention acknowledged some part of their personhood, however discounted. But Article 1 also wrote into the Constitution a vision of domestic society that included slavery. Slaves and women were bound together as persons represented in the new government but who most assuredly would not be allowed to represent themselves. It is no surprise then that the antislavery movement that developed in the 1830s also nurtured a women's rights movement. In 1837 Angelina Grimké, southerner turned abolitionist, argued that without political rights women were "mere slaves known only through their masters." Nor is it surprising that slavery's proponents struck back by claiming that both the abolitionist movement and the women's rights movement were an assault on the American family.

The seemingly offhanded reference in the three-fifths clause to "Indians not taxed" also foreshadowed an ongoing struggle over Indian sovereignty. In the nineteenth century, the United States offered American Indians only two choices—they could give up their wasteful reliance on hunting and join white society or they could move beyond the ever-receding bounds of white settlement. As Daniel Richter (2001) has observed, it was no accident that among the most popular politicians of the 1830s were men responsible for completing "the revolutionary work of ethnic cleansing." In his message to Congress in 1830, President Andrew Jackson, known to contemporaries for his participation in the Indian wars, exclaimed, "Toward the aborigines of the country no one can indulge a more friendly feeling than myself, or would go further in attempting to reclaim them from their wandering habits and make them a happy prosperous people." Unfortunately, Jackson continued, their race was destined to disappear.

> Nor is there anything in this which, upon a comprehensive view of the general interests of the human race, is to be regretted. Philanthropy could not wish to see this continent restored to the condition in which it was found by our forefathers. What good man would prefer a country covered with forests and ranged by a few thousand savages to our extensive Republic, studded with cities, towns, and prosperous farms, embellished with all the improvements which art can devise or industry execute, occupied by more than 12,000,000 happy people, and filled with all the blessings of liberty, civilization, and religion.

For Jackson, as for many of his predecessors, happiness required the removal of American Indians from their land.

Historians tell such stories not to induce guilt among present-day Americans but to enlarge our sense of who we are and where we came from. In the Gettysburg Address, Abraham Lincoln described a nation "conceived in Liberty and dedicated to the proposition that all men are created equal." One hundred and forty-four years later, Barack Obama alluded to a Constitution tainted by the "original sin" of slavery. The metaphors of birth in the two speeches form an intriguing contrast, one an upbeat allusion to the promise of revolution, the other a sober recognition of its fateful compromises. Both speakers emphasized the responsibility of later generations for fulfilling the Revolution's promise, and both attached the dream of equality to an unfulfilled hope for unity, a theme invoked in Obama's reading of the phrase "a more perfect union" from the preamble to the Constitution.

The United States had neither an immaculate conception nor a virgin birth, to borrow Lincoln's and Obama's metaphor. Nor has ours been a heaven without a hell. Acknowledging the dark strands in our nation's history is a step toward maturity. The historian Carl Becker once suggested that the purpose of studying history, like the value of the humanities more generally, was in enlarging our vision of the world. "By liberalizing the mind, by deepening the sympathies, by fortifying the will, history enables us to control, not society, but ourselves, a much more important thing; it prepares us to live more humanely in the present and to meet rather than to foretell the future." May that be so.

Further Reading

Some of the material in this essay is adapted from my own previous work. In *The Age of Homespun: Objects and Stories in the Creation of an American Myth* (New York: Knopf, 2001), I explored the relationship between European pastoralism and ideas about household self-sufficiency in early American life. In *A Midwife's Tale: The Life of Martha Ballard Based on Her Diary, 1785–1812* (New York: Knopf, 1990), I examined the aftermath of the Revolution in one frontier community with particular attention to the place of women in the local economy. In chapter 4 of *Well-Behaved Women Seldom Make History* (New York: Knopf, 2007), I traced links between race and gender from the Revolutionary period into the nineteenth century.

My interpretation has also been shaped by the work of my former students, Sarah M. S. Pearsall, whose *Atlantic Families: Lives and Letters in the Later Eighteenth Century* (Oxford: Oxford University Press, 2008) explicates the transatlantic spread of ideas about marriage, and Kirsten Sword, whose *Wives Not Slaves* (forthcoming from the University of Chicago Press, 2011) explores relationships in law and popular culture between marriage and other forms of household dependency. Margot Minardi's *Making Slavery History: Abolitionism and the Politics of Memory in Massachusetts* (forthcoming from Oxford University Press) shows how later generations of African Americans redefined the interpretation of Revolutionary-era figures like Phillis Wheatley and Crispus Attucks. Others who helped in the development of the course on which this essay is based include Mark Hanna, Eliza Clark, Sharon Sundue, Michelle Morris, Linzy Brekke-Aloise, Phil Mead, and Judith Kertesz.

In the section of this essay on American Indians I have relied on Daniel Richter's *Facing East from Indian Country* (Cambridge, MA: Harvard University Press, 2001), a clearly written and insightful history that ends with the American Revolution but provides an essential framework for understanding it. Readers interested in learning more about the prelude to the American Revolution might also consult Fred Anderson's *Crucible of War: The Seven Years War and the Fate of Empire in British North America, 1754–1766* (New York: Knopf, 2000), an expansive and compelling narrative that links conflicts in the interior of North America with imperial contests in Europe and even suggests that what happened before 1766 may be as important as what happened later. Colin Calloway's *Scratch of the Pen: 1763 and the Transformation of North America* (Oxford: Oxford University Press, 2006) offers a vivid sketch of the state of North America at the end of what textbooks used to call the French and Indian War and is an excellent place to begin a study of the Revolution.

Gordon S. Wood's landmark works on American political culture include *The Creation of the American Republic, 1776–1787* (Chapel Hill: University of North Carolina Press, 1969) and *The Radicalism of the American Revolution* (New York: Knopf, 1991). His brief *The American Revolution: A History* (New York: Modern Library, 2002) offers an accessible overview of major events for those who have forgotten or never had a basic course on early American history. Gary B. Nash's survey *The Unknown American Revolution* (New York: Viking, 2005) integrates much of recent social history into the classic narrative. The published version of his 2004 Huggins Lectures at Harvard, *The Forgotten Fifth: African Americans in the Age of Revolution* (Cambridge, MA: Harvard University Press, 2006) lays out his own answer to the provocative question "Could slavery have been abolished?"

Ira Berlin's *Many Thousands Gone: The First Two Centuries of Slavery in North America* (Cambridge, MA: Harvard University Press, 1998) is a powerful survey of the history of slave systems in the Americas including the impact of the Revolution. Woody Holton's *Forced Founders: Indians, Debtors, Slaves, and the Making of the American Revolution in Virginia* (Chapel Hill: University of North Carolina Press, 1999) and J. William Harris's *The Hanging of Thomas Jeremiah: A Free Black Man's Encounter with Liberty* (New Haven, CT: Yale University Press, 2009) demonstrate how fear of slave revolt shaped Southern commitment to independence. David Waldstreicher's *Runaway America: Benjamin Franklin, Slavery, and the American Revolution* (New York: Hill and Wang, 2004) complicates popular notions about Franklin nurtured by his own self-portrait as a "runaway." Christopher Leslie Brown's *Moral Capital: Foundations of British Abolitionism* (Chapel Hill: University of North Carolina Press, 2006) offers an essential Atlantic perspective on slavery and the Revolution.

The pioneering works on women in the age of the Revolution are Mary Beth Norton's *Liberty's Daughters: The Revolutionary Experience of American Women, 1750–1800* (Boston: Little, Brown, 1980) and Linda K. Kerber's *Women of the Republic* (Chapel Hill: University of North Carolina Press, 1980). The hundreds of books and articles written since then are indebted to their work. Carol Berkin's *Revolutionary Mothers: Women in the Struggle for America's Independence* (New York: Knopf, 2005) is a brief, highly accessible survey that integrates the new scholarship while reassessing nineteenth-century popular histories and memoirs. Kerber's *No Constitutional Right to Be Ladies: Women and the Obligations of Citizenship* (New York: Hill and Wang, 1998) has important new material on the legal position of American women during and after the Revolution. Jan Lewis's arguments about the position of women in the Constitution are most accessible to general readers in an online essay, "Why the Constitution Includes Women," in the online journal *Commonplace* (vol. 2, July 2002). Those interested in the intersection of race and gender in early America will also want to consult Annette Gordon-Reed, *Thomas*

Jefferson and Sally Hemings: An American Controversy (Charlottesville: University Press of Virginia, 1997) and *The Hemingses of Monticello: An American Family* (New York: W. W. Norton, 2008), as well as an important anthology edited by Jan Ellen Lewis and Peter Onuf, *Sally Hemings and Thomas Jefferson* (Charlottesville: University Press of Virginia, 1999).

There are many other themes worth pursuing. In *A Revolutionary People at War: The Continental Army and American Character, 1775–1783* (Chapel Hill: University of North Carolina Press, 1980), Charles Royster pulls together passages from hundreds of soldiers' diaries, letters, and memoirs to expose the double bind in which many soldiers found themselves as they forfeited their own liberty to sustain the war. Alfred Young's *The Shoemaker and the Tea Party* (Boston: Beacon Press, 1999) and *Masquerade: The Life and Times of Deborah Sampson, Continental Soldier* (New York: Knopf, 2004) offer powerful interpretations of the lives of ordinary New Englanders, one male, one female, both of whom became soldiers. Young's books are especially noteworthy for their sophisticated use of early nineteenth-century memoirs to recover otherwise obscure stories. In *Daniel Boone: The Life and Legend of an American Pioneer* (New York: Henry Holt, 1992), John Mack Faragher also makes effective use of legendary material, as does David Hackett Fischer in *Paul Revere's Ride* (Oxford: Oxford University Press, 1994) and *Washington's Crossing* (Oxford: Oxford University Press, 2004), which offer richly detailed accounts of iconic moments in the War for Independence.

Two very different works explore the role of consumer goods in the era of the American Revolution. In *The Refinement of America: Persons, Houses, Cities* (New York: Knopf, 1992), Richard Bushman traces the spread of gentility from the middle of the eighteenth century and beyond. In *The Marketplace of Revolution* (Oxford: Oxford University Press, 2004), T. H. Breen considers the impact of consumer demand and consumer debt in uniting the mainland colonies in their struggle against taxation. Books and catalogs by museum curators provide an even richer context for interpreting these arguments. To take just one example, Linda Baumgarten, in *What Clothes Reveal: The Language of Clothing in Colonial and Federal America* (Williamsburg, VA: Colonial Williamsburg and Yale University Press, 2002), considers soldier's garb and slave and servant clothing as well as lavish waistcoats and gowns.

There are of course dozens of helpful online sources including digital collections of diaries and memoirs. For general audiences it is also worth visiting the many national parks devoted to the history of the Revolution, paying close attention to what is and is not included in these nationally sponsored histories of our nation's founding. Public television has also offered several memorable series, including the Middlemarch Production *Liberty,* which brings period voices to life by matching current-day actors with likely eighteenth-century characters including common soldiers, women, and slaves.